STRIVERS ROW

STRIVERS ROW

A Novel

KEVIN BAKER

HarperCollinsPublishers

HarperCollins books may be purchased for educational, business, or sales promotional use. For information, please write: Special Markets Department, HarperCollins Publishers, 10 East 53rd Street, New York, NY 10022.

FIRST EDITION

Designed by Laura Lindgren

Printed on acid-free paper

Library of Congress Cataloging-in-Publication Data is available upon request.

ISBN 10: 0-06-0195835
ISBN 13: 978-0-06-0195830

06 07 08 09 10   /RRD   10 9 8 7 6 5 4 3 2 1

To my mother, Claire Slade Baker,
with all my love,
for all that she has given me throughout my life,
and as always
to Ellen—
Je t'adore

DRAMATIS PERSONAE

Jonah Dove, minister of the Church of the New Jerusalem, in
Harlem.
Amanda Robb Dove, his wife.
Milton Dove, Jonah's father, and the founder of the New Jerusalem.
Sophia "Sophie" Dove, Jonah's sister and Milton's daughter.
Malcolm Little, a hustler.
Louisa "Louise" Little, his mother.
Earl "Early" Little, his father.
Reginald Little
Philbert Little } his brothers
Wilfred Little
Wesley Little

"Butch" Little
Earl Little, Jr., a.k.a., "Jimmy Carlton," } his half-brothers
Yvonne Little, his sister

Ella Little } his half-sisters
Mary Little

Miranda Dolan, a cabaret singer
West Indian Archie, proprietor of a policy "bank"
Sammy McKnight, a pimp
Adam Clayton Powell, Jr., minister of the Abyssinian Baptist Church,
and Harlem's first black city councilman
Isabel Washington Powell, his wife, and a former dance hall performer
Charlie and Ed Small, proprietors, Small's Paradise

Alton "Pappy" Cousins, steward of the Yankee Clipper
Lionel Beane
Willard Chandler } the kitchen crew of the Yankee Clipper
Sandy Thorne

Malcolm Jarvis, a friend of Malcolm Little's, from Roxbury
Laura, another friend from Roxbury

Jakey Mendelssohn, owner of a small department store in Harlem
Sadie Mendelssohn, his mother
Lazar Mendelssohn, his cousin, and a refugee from Europe

PROLOGUE

Harlem waits.

Patched and tarred. Hawked and bitten in the winter, smothered and melted in the heat.

Harlem waits...

Under its broad skies, pincered between two rivers. Within sight of salvation, the city's lights, the jeweled bridges. Battered and besieged, on its knees but unbowed. With blood in its mouth—

Harlem waits, and listens for its savior.

CHAPTER ONE

MALCOLM

He thought about the rabbits sometimes, lying awake at night in the little room in Ella's house, under the eaves.

It had been back in West Lansing, when he was twelve years old, just after his mother had taken ill and they had all been split up. A Sunday afternoon in the late fall, nearly winter. The smell of something burning off in the distance. The men and boys walking through the yellowed grass, holding the straining dogs tight on their leashes. Malcolm was walking with Mr. Gohannas and Big Boy, dangling the .22 off his hip, trying to whip it all about like he'd seen the gunfighters do in the Western serials. He held it to his eye and aimed it here, there, even at the backs of the men around him, until one of them turned and caught him.

"You watch that gun, boy," he scolded. "Don't you be pointing it at nobody!"

Malcolm had blushed and put his head down, holding the gun steadier, glancing up furtively now at the other men to see if they had noticed his shame. All of them darker than he was, their skin the color of burnt coffee or railroad coal, faces lined and creased like worn car seats. Wearing their field overalls and work boots, redolent with the scent of men's sweat and dirt. Some of them with their boys next to them—wearing their handed-down overalls; faces exactly the same only smoother, as if all the creases had been ironed out. Their ragged hair knotted up in burrs and tangles, like the farmers they were and would always be.

"Get ready now," Mr. Gohannas told them, his voice urgent though still kindly.

"Right 'bout *here*—"

The men stopped at the edge of an open field. At its far end Malcolm could make out a tangled clump of bent scrub trees, and thorn bushes. The men looked at each other, a few of them nodding solemnly, then they let the dogs go and began to fan out, kneeling in the high grass.

"Here they come now!"

The loosed dogs had run straight toward the thicket, baying and scuffling their way in past the lowered tree branches. There was silence for a few, long moments—then the renewed sound of pounding feet, as the first rabbits flew out from the bushes. Lean, gray, winter hares, leaping ahead with their eyes wide and their long ears back, the dogs scrambling after them.

"Easy now," the man nearest to Malcolm whispered tenderly to his son, a boy younger than Malcolm was, toting a shotgun.

"Let them come back—"

Leaving the hounds still immersed in the brambles, the hares made a wide, panicked bolt around the perimeter of the field. Running so fast and hard that Malcolm thought they must surely escape—the only sound their powerful, widened winter feet thumping softly over the grass. He could not understand why the men hadn't fired, all these old, slow, black men still staring out from the bushes, and he rose as if to run after the rabbits. But then he felt Mr. Gohannas's hand on his arm, pulling him back down—and sure enough, the hares turned and headed back, toward their hidey-holes in the thicket.

"Now!" the man next to him exclaimed, and the boy fired the crude old shotgun. The blast knocked him flat on his back but the birdshot picked off one of the galloping hares in midair, flipping his thin gray rabbit body head over heels, leaving him to twitch and heave on the ground.

The rest of the men and boys fired at nearly the same time— a fusillade from all their battered, ancient guns that stunned and nearly deafened Malcolm. He shut his eyes, and lowered his head against the noise. When he looked up again he could see five or six more hares on the ground. The younger boys already running out to claim theirs, picking them up by their long ears and smashing their heads with lengths of lead pipe if they were still moving, an act that made Malcolm look away, and his stomach turn.

"Here now," Mr. Gohannas told him, placing a gentle hand on his chest and turning him around.

The dogs were already flushing the thicket again, and a few minutes later out came more hares. Running slower and a little raggedly this time, if just as frightened. For all of their fear they ran in the exact same direction, around the edge of the field. Making the same long loop back to their homes, the men firing and yelling exultantly as they turned.

Malcolm fired wildly himself, his shot rustling the branches in some nearby trees, the men nearest to him snorting in surprise and indignation—

"Where you *shootin'*, boy?"

—but he had an idea now. The dogs went in to flush the hares a third time—both dogs and hares moving noticeably slower now—and after he reloaded Malcolm scrambled out of the blind before Mr. Gohannas could stop him, Big Boy calling plaintively after him.

"Hey, where you *goin'*, Malcolm?"

He was already running up along the border of the field, his cracked, patent leather city shoes slipping along the dead winter grass. He ran to a spot that was halfway along the hares' trajectory, as best he could figure it, just before the point where they were bound to turn and head back to their thicket. He heard the alarmed shouts of the men behind him, but he ignored them. Kneeling and aiming carefully this time, taking down one hare, then another, before they ever got back within range of the rest of the hunters. The exhausted creatures always flipping over the same way, their long back feet catapulting them over in one final, cinematic somersault.

When the shooting stopped it was Malcolm who ran out after them this time, plucking his hares up by their big ears. Ignoring the continuing, angry shouts of the older, blacker men—smiling to himself, to think how he had been able to figure it out when the rest of them had not. They broke cover and ran up to him, Mr. Gohannas among them, his wide, brown face looking uncomfortable behind his spectacles.

"Tha's not right!"

"*Ev'rybody's* supposed to get a fair shot! Movin' up like that!"

They scowled at him, outraged, until one of them nudged the shoulder of the man beside him.

"That's *Earl's* boy. You know. Early Little."

"Oh. Oh, *him.*"

They stayed where they were, looking down at him, but with their faces changed now into something softer, even sorrowful.

"Wit' the mother. *You* know—"

"Oh. Well. Tha's good shootin', son."

"You know how to handle a rifle. Reg'lar Dead-Eye Dick."

"Yessir."

Malcolm basked in their compliments, no longer trying to keep from grinning. Mr. Gohannas looked relieved.

"That's all right, then."

He stayed out ahead of them for the rest of the day, making sure to move up whenever they came to a new thicket, to where the hares made their turn. Sometimes he even allowed Big Boy to come with him, and bag a hare or two himself with the old beebee gun Mr. Gohannas had entrusted to him. He hauled along his growing brace until his arms ached under their weight. There were at least a dozen of them, the rabbit blood streaking his worn-out corduroys and its smell making him feel dizzy again, but he would not give them up.

"This's enough to feed all of them," he told his foster father, his voice brimming with excitement and triumph. "Once I get 'em skinned an' cut up, it's enough to feed 'em all! An' maybe we can take some over to Mama on Sunday—"

And Mr. Gohannas had smiled down at him, and touched his cheek, and told him, "Yes, son, I believe we could do that."

All the rest of that day he had stayed out in front of them, until it got too cold and too dark to see the hares in the gray, winter evening. What he could never understand—not even to this day, lying in the upstairs room under the eaves of Ella's immaculate house— was how they had failed to figure it out. Glancing back at the others, through the gloom of the winter evening, their faces brown blurs in the underbrush. Wondering at how it was that all of these grown men, some of them with gray in their burred hair, could not figure out what he had—that when the hares turned back, all you had to do was move up a little to get to them first. The thought growing in him like something dirty, dark, and forbidden and only half-acknowledged at first. Then becoming conscious, causing him to smirk despite himself as he put it into words, spreading all through his being as he looked down at the somewhat lighter, red-dish skin on his arms, by the light of his little lamp under the eaves:

The niggers. The stupid old niggers.

CHAPTER TWO

MALCOLM

He would lead the train, waiting until it was almost gone before he grabbed on. It was a little move he had perfected, just for the rest of the kitchen crew. Slowing to a walk beside the beautiful silver cars. Matching his stride to the revolution of their wheels as they slowly picked up speed—turning over one, two, three beats every ten seconds. Letting the marvelously streamlined, green-and-gold-striped electric engine go by. Then the stainless-steel kitchen, and the club car with the big blue, stretched-out letters spelling *THE YANKEE CLIPPER*. The rest of the crew grinning and hollering at him from the door of the kitchen car, Lionel Beane and Sandy Thorne and Willard Chandler, all in their working whites, as gleaming and spotless as the club-car china.

"You gonna have to saunter all the way to New York, you don't stop that!"

"Oh, one a these days that niggah's gonna tear off a arm. Then he won't look so good in his killer-diller!"

He only grinned back at them. Their faces all as black as raisins, these older men who had already put in a good sixty years between them on the Dope, or the Pennsy. Always half-laughing and sniggering behind his back, even after they had become his friends.

The train was picking up speed but he let it go. Running a hand disdainfully down the wide lapels of the new sharkskin zoot he had picked out expressly for the occasion. Its narrowed waist and broad shoulders making the upper half of his body look like one big inverted triangle; the cuffs of the Punjab pants so tapered he had to take off his knob-toed, sweet-potato-colored shoes before he could pull them on.

This was the trip, today was the day—

The sleek, bullet-nosed GG-1 engine was about to reach critical acceleration now. He could feel its heat on his face, the big silver cars deceptive in their speed. Once he had watched as a signalman in the Dover Street Yards, a veteran trainman, had absentmindedly stuck out a leg to stop a sleeper that was ambling slowly backward along a siding, only to see his foot sheered off effortlessly at the ankle.

Still, he waited. Adjusting his beat to the train, trying to think of it as a number, like listening to Jimmie Lunceford's band bang out the "Yard Dog Mazurka" in the Roseland ballroom the week before, just trying to let his feet get the feel of it. Picking up his tempo but still refusing to run. Still waiting, counting off the cars, letting it come to him—beat, beat, beat-beat-beat. Waiting until the last car was already passing, the train going too fast now, hurtling by him—and only then taking one, two more quick strides. Throwing his trainman's bag up through the open door with an easy, overhanded motion. Snapping the gray hat with its four-inch brim and matching gray feather off his head so it did not get caught in the backdraft and—at the same time—sticking out his other hand to *just* grab hold of the railing on the very last doorway before it passed. Letting the momentum of the entire train, throttling along at full power now, pull him up. Pivoting casually on the balls of his feet as it did, so that he swung up easily into the coach instead of pulling out his shoulder, or plastering his face against the side of the moving car, or falling under the last, flashing set of wheels.

The face of his father rising suddenly before him. All but cut in half. That was what she had said at the time, all but cut in half but still alive. Still able to talk and groan out his last breaths, even after he had fallen under the slashing metal wheels—

Then he was inside, rushing up the aisles to the kitchen car. Laughing out loud as the passengers turned to stare at him—big, lunatic, zoot-suited Negro, running up through their train. Changing, too, even as he ran. Shrugging out of the long gray coat of his zoot suit, tugging the spotless white linen jacket on over his undershirt. Undoing the narrow belt with its gold-plated "L" for "Little" on the buckle even as he tumbled into the kitchen—grinning like a wolf at the rest of them, Lionel and Sandy and Willard staring back at him in amazement despite themselves.

"What say, Cholly Hoss? Thought I was back in the Bunker Hill Apple?"

"Oh, Sandwich Red, makin' a flash. Pappy gonna conk you up *good* for this one!"

"I swear it, he was made this time! Gonna skin yo' marin-y little ass for you."

The other men tsking and and shaking their heads as they went about their tasks—bent over the stove, stuffing the sandwiches into their dozens of little plastic bags and boiling up the endless pots of coffee. But still impressed, Malcolm could tell.

"Ah, I ain't comin' on that tab," he snorted back at them as he shucked off his pants and shoes. "You know Pappy *love* me. I'm light an' bright an' damn near white with the man."

He pulled on the rest of his sandwich man uniform, the dark blue pants with a red crease down the legs, matching blue hat with its brass badge. Pretending to himself as always he did that it was a military uniform, like the dozens of uniforms they saw on the train every day now. *Navy dress whites, maybe. Like a commander, or a rear admiral.* He stuffed his small leather train bag with its razor and toothbrush, a change of underwear, and his Amazing Man and Sub-Mariner comics into the bottom of the little pantry closet. The gray zoot he mounted carefully on a wooden hanger, praying that somehow nothing would spill on it, or that the rest of the crew wouldn't play him some awful practical joke, the suit still out on credit from the Jew store.

"Ooh, dig Mr. High Pockets," Lionel cooed at him. "He's lookin' fine as thine for the big night."

"You know it," Malcolm winked back at him. "Got to be togged to the bricks, you gonna make time with those Harlem chicks."

"Listen to him knockin' his gums," Sandy Thorne scoffed, pouring out streams of coffee into the five-gallon silver thermos that would be Malcolm's constant burden for the next six hours.

"Boy don't know any more about Harlem than a pig knows about Sunday or napkins!"

"I will tonight!"

Tonight. He would be in Harlem tonight.

This was finally it—a layover in New York after two and one-half months working straight down to D.C. Spending his nights in streets with names like Pig Alley and Goat Alley, full of craps-shooters and wandering stumblebums, and half-naked children still running around at midnight, begging for pennies. Most nights he preferred to sleep sitting up in Union Station, between all the uniformed soldiers and sailors there. Pretending to himself that, like them, he was on his way to ship out to Algiers, or Tahiti, or Salerno—

But tonight was going to be something else. *Harlem.* He remembered the photographs of it, in his father's copies of the Pittsburgh *Courier* or the Chicago *Defender.* A vast crowd of smiling, confident, well-dressed black men and women. All of them cheering and pointing up at Joe Louis where he stood on the balcony of the Theresa Hotel, the day after he'd won the heavyweight championship of the world. And Louis himself waving back at them, looking as poised and self-assured as an emperor.

"You gonna take me out," Malcolm said, alarmed—uncomfortably aware that his voice sounded suddenly high and childlike, but unable to help himself.

"If we got the time—" Sandy started to say, teasing him.

"You *said* you was. You said you'd take me everywhere!"

"Listen to the Home from Rome. Yeah, we'll boot you to the play, all right. I just don't know you can *handle* all the action we'll get you—"

"I'll let you know what I can *handle!*"

"Ah, boy, this ain't none a that down-home Michigan mess we're talkin' 'bout."

"We ain't talkin' no faust, only a fine dinner—"

"Hey, I'm dracula when it comes to the ladies!"

"Is anybody plannin' to feed the passengers today?"

Pappy Cousins stood in the doorway, with his arms crossed sternly over his chest, but his steward's cap slightly askew and his blue eyes shining. He looked at Malcolm first, as usual.

"Jesus Christ, but you ah gonna miss one a these days!" he sputtered, his words slurring. "We're gonna pull into Grand Central with nothin' but a black arm hangin' off the back a the train, like a Chinaman's cue!"

"Ah, that ain't nothin'. You should seen me last Sat'd'y night, Pappy," Malcolm told him lightly, but he hurried to grab up the heavy, shoulder-strap sandwich box and the coffeepot that would push him up and down the aisles, bending his back and making his neck ache all the way to New York. He tried to dodge past Pappy and out to the train, but the steward stopped him.

"Hang on theah. Let's have a look at you now."

He inspected Malcolm with open, fatherly affection, brushing down his sleeves with his whisk broom, straightening his hat. Usually the stewards lorded it over the colored kitchen crews, but not Pappy. He liked to joke with them, turned a blind eye to their lesser hustles, even took their part in disputes with passengers or the railroad. He was a small, fragile-looking man; an old Maine Yankee with leathery skin and large, mournful eyes and a protruding Adam's apple that made him look more than a little ridiculous, but they would do anything for him. At night in the room in Ella's house, Malcolm liked to dream of coming on the *Yankee Clipper* with his own band someday, togged out to the nines. Walking up to an astonished but proud Pappy and stuffing a thick roll of bills into his pocket, telling him, *See, Pappy? See what I made of myself?*

"You watch yourself out theah today," he told Malcolm now, gripping his arm hard, to impress the seriousness of what he was saying upon him.

"There's some soldjah boys in the parlor car, goin' down to ship out, an' they're some mean little peckahs. They're workin' on a fifth, too, I seen it."

"You *seen* it? You sure that all you done, Pappy?" Malcolm teased him, the smell of cheap scotch wafting off the little steward through the peppermint he was perennially sucking on. He heard Willard and Lionel chuckle and Pappy's merry blue eyes spun for a moment, but then he was serious again, crooking a finger at Malcolm.

"Nevah you mind what they give *me*. You're different to them. Nevah forget that with those fellas."

"I won't," Malcolm said, feeling suddenly hurt, though he knew the older man was only trying to warn him.

"All right then."

Pappy stood back a step, looking him over with obvious pride, and Malcolm instinctively straightened his long body under his gaze. Drawing his back up under the weight of the sandwich box even as he wondered: *How could any man like you so much? Any stranger? And why wouldn't a father?*

"So tonight's the big night, eh?"

"Yeah, it is." Malcolm grinned despite himself, thinking about it.

"Ah, geez, I remembah my first night down in Scollay Square." Pappy smiled, shaking his head. Before Malcolm could react he slipped a bill into the pocket of his white linen coat, just below the sandwich box.

"Buy a round on me."

"Thanks, Pappy."

"Go on now. An' remembah what I told you."

Then he was out in the coaches, flying back down the aisles between the high, green, upholstered seats with his box. The voice in his head already going. *Tom it up, Tom it up—*

"Sandwiches! Sandwiches for sale! Eat 'em now, before they gets stale! I got some ham an' cheese, make you weak in the knees!"

He sold them slices of chocolate layer and coconut cake, and the sandwiches in their individual plastic bags, and boxes of Cracker Jack and bags of potato chips. Coffee from the five-gallon thermos balanced in one corner of his box, and ice cream wrapped in wax paper and kept as far from it as possible. Hershey bars and jujubes, Chicken Dinners and Three Musketeers; tar babies and licorice sticks; and Life Savers and sealed packs of cards and packs of chewing gum and cigarettes, and ten-cent cigars, and little pillows for those who wished to rest their heads and try to sleep on the sweltering, oversold train.

The box was heavy even when it was empty, but once he worked himself into a rhythm he could make it dance. Letting the momentum of the train carry him. Letting his legs roll with the rocking of the car, and sway with the weight of the box until, after six hours on the aisles, he would feel his knees buckle when they hit concrete again, and for the rest of the night would walk as bowlegged as a sailor.

"I got chicken salad an' egg salad, I got turkey an' that's no baloney!" he sang out. "I got no fried fish, but I got whatever else you wish—"

Tom it up, Tom it up now!

—the sardonic little chant he sang to himself *underneath* all the bright patter. The way they all did, every black man on the train crew, from the porters to the dining car waiters to the baggage smashers, knowing that the more elaborate their performance, the better their tips would be. Propping the box on his knee and swinging open the door to the next car where he would, inevitably, watch the twin rows of white faces look up distractedly and suddenly brighten, just to see him standing there.

Oh, but how they like to see us work!

Business was good, with the war on. Every seat was filled, with more bodies jammed into the parlor cars and the diners, standing up the whole trip around the bar car. The coaches full of smooth-faced young soldiers and sailors, looking hungover and frightened. Workingmen on their way to the shipyards, and men in sharp gray business suits, and pregnant young mothers, and card sharps, and aging whores, and whole families. All of them going *somewhere*—to see off a loved one, or make some money, or cut a deal, and *why not me?* He was on his way to *Harlem* after showing up in Boston six months ago still smelling of the country, with his red hair and a green suit so short his arms and legs stuck out—

I'm in it now. I'm on my way.

Tom it up!

He was almost at the end of his second run down the train when he came upon the soldiers Pappy had warned him about. They had just stopped in New Bedford, and the *Clipper* was idling on a siding right next to the ocean, waiting while some troop trains rattled slowly by. Malcolm had finally worked his way down to the last day coach, when he wrenched open the door and spotted them immediately.

They were standing in the narrow aisle or sprawled carelessly over the seat backs. Laughing and talking as loudly as they could, ignoring the discomfort of the other passengers around them. Drinking openly from a bottle of rusty liquid with a rose on it. There were five of them altogether, and they looked drunk and mean, and like they were spoiling for a fight.

Moving closer, he caught a glimpse of what it was the soldiers had chosen to amuse themselves with. There, sitting very erect in one of the last aisle seats, was a young white minister—with a black woman. He blinked at the sight, but there was no mistaking it: The white minister, wearing a clerical collar and a palpable air of studious martyrdom. The woman truly black, her skin as dark and smooth as the skin of a plum, the two of them sitting side by side, holding hands as if they were man and wife.

The soldiers were all over them—two in the seat just behind them, two leaning over the seat just in front, a fifth propped up against the seat across the aisle. The soldiers in front were leaning right into the couple's faces, laughing belligerently while the two behind them were doing the sort of irritating, schoolboy things that could be relied upon to drive anyone to murder—pushing the straw Panama the man was wearing forward on his head, flicking his ears with their fingers; picking at the white, plastic curl of flower on the woman's hat.

The woman was staring straight ahead into nothingness, with a blankness that Malcolm recognized at once. The minister was looking slightly upward, as if toward Heaven—though at the same time, ludicrously enough, he was still trying to make small talk with the woman. She only continued to stare straight ahead, into the middle distance, so that they made a kind of perfect triangle—the soldiers baiting the minister, the minister trying to ignore the soldiers, the woman trying to ignore her husband. He might have laughed at the ridiculousness of it all—except that as he came still closer down the aisle he could see how tightly the couple's hands were clenched together, the man's knuckles almost white with the effort.

But he wasn't, Malcolm realized then. He could see it when he got up close—the man's hair just a little too curly above his clerical collar, and his good, seersucker suit. His irritatingly smooth, plump cheeks just the lightest shade of olive. So light that without the black woman along, Malcolm might never have suspected.

The minister was colored, too.

The soldiers had realized it as well, Malcolm understood now. Abusing him for his propriety, his haughtiness—for being so light-skinned. He felt the palms of his hands itch as he came toward them, a reckless urge washing over him again, just as it had when he was waiting to gauge the train and jump onboard. Unsure of just what it was he wanted more, to smash the soldiers' faces in or to poke at the nearly white preacher with them.

"Howzat again?" brayed the drunken soldier who was poised over the minister's face. "Don' go tellin' me yer *black!*"

His back was turned but Malcolm could tell he was a bruiser all the same, almost as tall as Malcolm was himself and much more solidly built, with a shock of black hair and a sergeant's stripes on his arm. He was obviously in charge—the rest of them laughing when he laughed, and picking right up on whatever he said.

"Don' tell me yer a *minister,* neither! No nigger preacher ever looked like *that.* You just wear that getup to get the *ladies,* don'tcha? Particul'y the *dark* ladies!"

The sergeant was so close to him now that Malcolm could see little flecks of his spittle landing on the preacher's face. But the man sat where he was, somehow not flinching, his chin still turned imploringly toward Heaven. Only his grip on the dark hand of the woman beside him betrayed his fear. His face still impossibly refined and serene, so much so that Malcolm could not help but want to smash it in for him.

Goddamn high-yaller Episcopal bastard. Like all the others out strolling around the Hill on Sunday, thinking they were whiter than God—

At that moment, though, he caught the woman's eye. She was plain-looking, except for her skin, which was flawless and almost blue-black. She wasn't even dressed like a preacher's wife, wearing only that hat with its plastic flowers and an ordinary print dress with more flowers on it, faded from purple to deep lavender. Malcolm wondered for a moment if she wasn't really his wife at all, but she looked too ordinary to be something on the side. The only exceptional things about her were her fine black skin, and her eyes, which were large and brown and fierce.

They appealed to him now. Breaking that stare into the middle distance that she had been holding, that he had seen so many times before on the faces of colored people. Here on the train—on his mother, near the end, in the presence of the social workers or the neighborhood ladies when they came by to try to reason with her. She broke it off and stared right at him, her eyes still hard but entreating. Begging him to do something to help them, to help her husband with the soldiers.

He realized only then what he usually saw the moment he walked into any coach. They were the only colored people in the car. The trains weren't segregated, at least not north of Maryland, but the colored passengers would usually sit together if they could. Some would even ask, very quietly, where the *black* car was today. Malcolm always knew it, too. He would never put on much of a show when there were others in the car. His performance on such occasions as stilted as a deacon's taking around the offering plate even though he knew they were the only ones who were copped to it, who could hear the sarcasm and the barely veiled insults, just beneath the bowing and the scraping.

But how much of an insult is it, when they don't even get it?

Now he realized they were all alone—himself, and the minister and his wife. The white faces all carefully diverted. The men, especially, staring out the windows as if fascinated by the sprawling summer marshes of the South Shore.

All right then, it's all me, Malcolm thought, the recklessness growing inside him as he hovered just behind the soldiers.

"C'mon, what's your secret?" the one across the aisle was saying, picking up his sergeant's cue. "We wanna get to know some colored ladies, too!"

"C'mon, be a *sport!* We wanna get some hot-blooded gals!"

For a long moment the minister's eyes stayed fixed on God, somewhere in the suitcase rack above his head. Then, without any warning, he lowered his gaze and spoke directly to the sergeant.

"I am a Negro," he said, in a dull, flat voice.

There it was, out in the open. Spoken so suddenly and strangely that it amazed Malcolm, and even the soldiers were flabbergasted into silence for a moment. *I am a Negro*—the words seeming to burn in the close air around them, so strange and utterly ridiculous.

The sergeant laughed unpleasantly.

"Yer a Negro? Then what the hell're you doin' takin' up a seat when ther're white men fighting for their country on this train?"

The preacher said nothing, but the sergeant pressed in still more closely on him, moving his face to within a couple of inches of his. The soldiers closed in around him on cue, smirking at him and at each other—all save for the sergeant, who Malcolm could see was truly angry.

"Huh? Whattaya got to say to that? You black bastard. I been up since five this morning. Where the hell'd *you* come from? Huh?"

How long would they let it go on? Malcolm wondered, looking at all the white faces still peering out their windows. *Until they cut the preacher, or beat him? Or well after that?*

"I think it's time you stood for your betters!"

The sergeant grabbed hold of the minister then, the rest of the soldiers right behind him. Before the man could even get his hands up, they had pulled him up and out of his seat like a bag of potatoes. Standing him up in the aisle, deliberately crumpling up his seersucker in their hands—

"Here, pal-ly, have a drink, show there's no hard feelin's," one of the soldiers said, trying to thrust what was left of the whiskey bottle in his face. But the sergeant already had his hand back out, reaching for the minister's wife. She bristled at him, and shrank back in her seat, her eyes like two blades. The preacher moved to help her—accidentally slapping the whiskey bottle away. It fell out of the soldier's hand and broke on the car floor. They all stood there for a moment, the minister looking pained, the soldiers grinning gleefully—looking to their sergeant, who cursed again and cocked a fist.

"Hey, you black son of a bitch!"

That was when Malcolm stepped forward, pushing the big sandwich box ahead of him. He rammed it into the sergeant's kidney, sending him falling forward with a small *Oomph!* Banging into his men, all of them going down like ninepins, one of them falling into the glass from the whiskey bottle.

"Jesus Christ!"

The soldier held up his bleeding hand. The rest of them staring up drunkenly, not quite comprehending how they had arrived on the floor.

"Sorry, gennelmens, sorry!" Malcolm sang out. "Aw, was that your whiskey I knocked over? I do got some ice creams here, though, some candy fo' your sweet tooth, ain't that the reet truth. Cake for the snake, smokes for the yolk—"

"What the hell!"

The sergeant was scrambling to pull himself up, glaring murderously. Everyone in the car was looking at him now, Malcolm knew. The minister staring at him in bewilderment, his wife's face suffused with gratitude. The other white passengers in the car stealing glances away from the windows and their *Life* magazines now.

Tom it up!

"Oh, sorry, sorry, gennelmens," he said, leaning forward and picking the last, dripping ice cream bar in its wax paper out of the sandwich box.

"Here, let me make it up to you. On me."

He shot out his hand and pressed the rapidly melting ice cream hard against the sergeant's short green Eisenhower jacket before the man could stop him. He looked down, incredulous, at the white and chocolate-specked stain spreading rapidly across his front.

"You li'l coon bastard—"

The sergeant started for him, but Malcolm was already dancing backward up the aisle, keeping the box between them. As he did he saw that the soldier still had the penumbra of a shiner on his rugged red face; a big broken nose. *A fighter all right,* he thought excitedly, almost giddy with anticipation.

He kept retreating up the aisle—waiting until the sergeant started to pull off his jacket with the ice cream still oozing slowly down the front. When he did Malcolm leaped forward, tugging the jacket down around the sergeant's arms to immobilize them, then sucker-punching him in the jaw and the gut. The sergeant wobbled, struggling desperately with his uniform, and Malcolm hit him with the sandwich box, driving it up under his chin with enough force to knock him to the floor again.

"Son of a bitch!"

The other white people in the car were all watching now, distracted at last from the pretty New England scenery. The soldiers were helping their sergeant to his feet—two of them taking off their belts, wrapping them around their fists with the buckles facing out. Malcolm stood his ground, the adrenaline surging crazily through him now, waving them on.

"Oh, you got it comin' now, pal-ly. You *earned* it!"

They had the sergeant back on his feet, a little wobbly still but with his jacket finally off, a grim eagerness in his eyes. Malcolm backed up again, grinning at him, still taunting him, but without any good idea what he was going to do. Not knowing how he could get away from the rest of the soldiers even if he somehow managed to fight off their sergeant, but not caring—

"That'll be enough a that! That's enough a that on my train!"

Malcolm felt a hand on his elbow, knew who it was before he turned around. Good old Pappy, come to look for him. The little Yankee moved fearlessly between Malcolm and the sergeant, certain in the authority of his steward's uniform.

"You stop this right now! I got the MPs comin'—"

The sergeant swatted Pappy away with the back of his hand—the steward sputtering to the floor, his arms and legs waving wildly—

"You little pissah—"

Malcolm had already laid the sandwich box down, going toward the sergeant. He hit him with a left and a right to the head before he could get his hands up, then with three more combinations, cutting open his lips and his eyes. The sergeant was hitting back by then but Malcolm kept moving forward, oblivious to how often he was hit, or the blood oozing from his own face. He grabbed up the sandwich box and knocked him over with it again. When he had him on the floor, he hit him with the coffee thermos, then he kicked him in the kidneys until he rolled over, and then he jumped on top of him and hit him in the face again.

He was still on top of the man by the time Willard and Sandy came running down the car, Lionel hopping after them as he pulled the straight razor out of his shoe. Pappy, his face beet red, back on his feet now, and waving in the MPs.

"Whoa, there, Cholly Hoss!"

"Get this mothah*fuckah* off my train!"

The MPs pulled him off—but Malcolm managed to reach back in and yank the sergeant up by the arm and one ear, bum-rushing him up the coach. All of the white passengers' eyes glued to him as he passed, gaping openly now.

"Don't you *never* lay a hand on Pappy Cousins!" Malcolm shouted at the sergeant. "You hear me? Don't you *never* mess with that man!"

He threw the half-conscious sergeant off the idled train, sending him rolling down the few feet of sand toward the gently lapping waters of the bay. The MPs followed, dragging the other soldiers— glowering at Malcolm. But Pappy was in between them again, keeping up a steady chatter.

"Them fellas attacked me like I was Tojo. Like I was Hitler! Thank God one a my boys was here to help me! Remember, those were the drunks I warned ya about before!"

Then they were gone, hauling the soldiers off. Malcolm watched them, standing out on the sand with Pappy and the rest of the kitchen crew, and a couple of colored porters who had come up to see if they could help. The others grinning at him, teasing him, but gazing at him with a new respect, he could see. Lionel still holding his razor up in the excitement. Pappy pulled out his handkerchief and dabbing mutely at the cuts the sergeant had opened along the side of Malcolm's face, and one corner of his mouth.

"Didn't I tell ya to be careful," he finally said, his voice so soft it was barely audible. Then he handed the handkerchief over to Malcolm without another word, patting him once on the shoulder before he headed back into the train with the rest of the kitchen crew.

Malcolm held the handkerchief in place, on his lip—but looking down he was both pleased and a little nauseated to see several splotches of blood on his white uniform jacket. He knelt and wet the cloth in the ocean water and tried to clean them off with little success. Then he put the handkerchief back on his lip, letting the saltwater sting his open cut.

When he stood and looked back at the train, he saw their faces. Staring out through the streaked, mottled window glass—all the white faces there, and the preacher and his plain, dark wife, too. All of them staring at *him*, now.

The *Clipper* gave a warning whistle, the last of the troop trains finally pulling past, but he didn't want it to end just *yet*. To go back to peddling sandwiches and cigarettes, collecting his nickels and dimes.

Tom it up—

Just down the spit of beach they were on there was a little platform, some rickety wooden structure built to convey mail or water or something in the old days. Malcolm ran the few yards down the beach and swung himself up on it. Still in full view of all the watching, wondering faces on the train.

He gave them his widest grin, then flung out his arms. Then he bowed, and turned his backside to them, and flung himself out into the waters of Buzzards Bay.

CHAPTER THREE

JONAH

He couldn't understand why the boy had jumped into the water. Until then he had taken it almost as a visitation—that sandwich boy, looking so young and innocent one moment and literally Satanic the next. That ridiculous red conk sticking out from under his trainman's cap, his mouth turned up in a sardonic, V-shaped leer. Coming upon them just as the whole situation was out of hand and he was about to be shamed in front of Amanda.

He had tried to ignore the soldiers, then he had tried to stand up to them. He had attempted to overawe them with his authority, his solemn Christian dignity. But that hadn't happened. They were about to work him over—when that boy had shown up. Seemingly fearless, taking them all on, hauling the drunken sergeant off the train as if endowed with the strength of ten men.

But then there had been that dive, right into the bay. The other passengers gawking, thinking he had drowned himself for some reason. Instead he had surfaced quickly, and climbed back up on the platform, his white trainman's uniform dripping wet. Bowing again and again for all of them in the car, strutting and grinning before all the white faces that turned away from the spectacle as abruptly as they had from Jonah's own humiliation. The Nigger Triumphant, something no more to be looked upon than a lynching—

He tried to banish that last thought from his head. It was unworthy, he thought—even uncivilized. *How uncivilized everything had become, as soon as they had gotten off the island.*

"He cut off her head!" Adam Powell's voice boomed out through the summer evening.

"Adam!"

There had been the sound of laughter, the tinkling of ice in a glass. Adam held his hands out wide, in self-absolution.

"He did! I didn't make it up! It's right there in the book!"

Only the night before, they had been sitting out on Adam's front porch in Oak Bluffs, watching the sun set over the trees and the Ink Well down below. Sipping highballs with Adam and his wife, Isabel, and their show business friend, Hycie. Amanda and he both still a little dazed, although they had been there for two weeks. In part it was the drinks themselves: gins-and-tonics served in tall, sweating glasses with a slice of lime. Amanda came from a temperance family, and neither of them were much used to drinking. In part it was everything else—the sheer, casual opulence of their surroundings; the risque, irreverent talk, right down to the offhanded sophistication of referring to the strip of colored beach by the steamship landing as "the Ink Well."

All evening Amanda had shot him wide-eyed, incredulous, slightly delighted looks over the lip of her glass. As if to ask, just as she had for the past two weeks—*What are we doing here?* They had never gone anywhere more adventurous before than the Shinnecock Arms or Wright's Cottage, or maybe The Notch. They had heard about Oak Bluffs, of course, living on Strivers Row as they did, but Amanda's conservative, newly middle-class family was thoroughly intimidated by anything to do with Harlem society, and Jonah's father had never paid any mind to such pretensions. The immaculately dressed couples promenading, or cruising their big cars down the Circuit. The green, rolled tennis courts filled with men and women in their tennis whites; the art shows and the yachting regattas; the cocktail parties served under huge, striped tents down by the water.

But above all, there was Adam. Dressed in an outlandish, bright yellow suit, now complete with matching socks and shoes. Throwing back his big handsome head to laugh at his own jokes and stories, dancing down the porch like some sort of bacchanate to wave the gin bottle over their drinks—

That last evening Amanda had brought up the Wright book, *Native Son*, which she had finally convinced her Ladies' Self-Improvement Class at the New Jerusalem to read that spring. Jonah had been wary but he hadn't tried to warn her off it, figuring it was her business—and, as he had suspected, she had been more outraged by the book than the ladies of the congregation. When she decided to give voice to that outrage on Adam Clayton Powell's front porch, Jonah had cringed inside but said nothing—wanting, he had to admit, to see his wife hold her own against Adam.

"I thought it demeaned the race," she had insisted. "That boy, that Bigger Thomas, is an animal, hardly human at all! He is every-thing that a Rankin or a Bilbo would have white people believe about the modern Negro—"

To Jonah's surprise, Adam had nodded, and knocked out his pipe against the bottom of his loafer.

"I didn't like it very much, either," he said, starting to fill the pipe again. "I thought it was much too optimistic."

"*Optimistic?*" Amanda stared at him.

"Sure, it's downright Pollyannaish. Much too easy on the white man!" he said calmly, puffing the pipe to life—winking at Jonah as he did.

"How in the *world* could you possibly find that depraved book *optimistic?*"

"Consider it," Adam told her. "Here you have that white boy— what's his name? The communist? Bigger takes his girlfriend and *kills* her. Strangles her like a chicken, in her own bedroom. Then he *cuts off her head* and stuffs the body into a furnace. He does! My apologies, ladies—"

He grinned over at his wife, and at Hycie, who only giggled back at him. Amanda was listening furiously, her brow furrowed in con-centration that way Jonah had always loved. Realizing some kind of fun was being had at her expense, but still trying to decipher exactly what it meant.

"But that's what he does!" Adam appealed. "He kills her, stuffs her body into the furnace. And nevertheless, by the end the white boy—because he's a good little Communist—*forgives* him!"

"But—"

"I mean, *he cut off her head!*" Adam had roared again, pulling his pipe from his mouth and grinning from ear to ear.

"He cuts off his girl's head, stuffs her in the furnace, and the white man *forgives* him. *There's* your racial propaganda! What kind of tinhorn saint is that white boy? I swear, we got nothing on these communists when it comes to the religion business!"

All of them were laughing now, swept along by Adam's sheer ebullience. Even Jonah—even Amanda, though he could see that her laughter was halting, and more frustrated than anything else, but trying to be a good sport. Adam could sense it, too—and gently steered the conversation off in another direction.

"Say, did I ever tell you about the summer I met Robert Todd Lincoln, up in Vermont?"

"Oh, Adam!"

He had, many times. But Isabel and Hycie knew that Amanda had never heard it before, and so they clamored obligingly for an encore.

"Tell it! Oh, tell it anyway, Adam!"

"All right then."

He sat back down in his hurricane chair and leaned in confidentially toward Jonah and Amanda, a small grin working its way across his face. Drawing them back in, including them all again, especially Amanda, in that inimitable way he had.

"It was when I was working summers as a bellboy up at the Equinox House, in Manchester, Vermont, and Robert—Todd—Lincoln himself was a guest there all season," he began, sonorously sounding out all three names of the Great Emancipator's son, almost as if to imply they were a cheap imitation of his own.

"He was an old man by then, and mean as a snake. Above all, he haaated Negroes! Haaated 'em! He would leave his cottage and come over to have supper in the dining room every night. Have himself driven over in his big old touring car. But whenever one of the colored valets put his hand out to open the car door for him— bang! He would bring his cane down hard, right on the knuckles!"

He paused to demonstrate this with the gin bottle, banging it down on imaginary knuckles so vividly that all of them winced, and pulled back their hands, smiling and laughing. Adam looked back up at them, grinning wider.

"Now, this was a bit of a predicament, since every valet they had at the Equinox House was a Negro! I don't know why, exactly."

He pretended to look thoughtful.

"They used to dress us up in little vests and caps. Maybe they thought we looked like colored lawn jockeys, all standing out there. This was the enlightened North after all, where most white folks don't even mind having a black boy step and fetchit to open a car door for them. But not Robert—Todd—Lincoln!"

He leaned forward even more now, and they leaned in toward him, drawn as if by a magnet, though save for Amanda they had all heard the story.

"So then the manager asked me—since I have on occasion been, uh, shall we say, mistaken for white—he asked me if I would open the door of Mr. Lincoln's car every night. Of course, he didn't know if it would actually work, you see. It's hard for a white man, once they know you're a nigger—"

—Adam went on, and out of the corner of his eye, Jonah saw his wife's back stiffen at the word—

"—once they know you're a nigger, to know if you really can pass. It was going to have to be trial and error, the scientific method. And if it failed—"

He gestured with the gin bottle again, swinging it down hard—

"Then bang! another rap on the knuckles!"

They nearly convulsed with laughter, even Amanda breaking down and chuckling despite herself.

"So—that night, along comes Mr. Robert—Todd—Lincoln's big old chauffered touring car," he went on. "It pulls up to the Equinox House, and there he was, waiting in the backseat. The only surviving son of Abraham Lincoln, the Great White Father himself! Former cabinet member, president of railroads. And he's got the cane ready, he's all set to bring it down on any black hand that dares to open the door of his car! I step forward—a little nervous, I must tell you, all set to pull my hand back the second I see him start to bring that cane down—and he looks down, directly at me, this big, tall, scary old white man...and he smiles.

"He smiles! He was satisfied my hand was white—or white enough, anyway. And for the whole rest of the summer, only I could be trusted to open Mr. Lincoln's door. The manager paid me an extra ten dollars a week and Mr. Lincoln himself gave me a dollar every night, just to open that door. I tell you, I was so glad to have that money I even kept my right hand in my trouser pocket the whole rest of that summer, just so it wouldn't get too dark."

"Oh, Adam, now that's too much!"

"No, no, it's the gospel truth. To this day my right hand is lighter than my left. Look, I'll show you!"

He held out both hands before him, the right one palm up, the left one palm down—and roared with laughter again to see that he had made them look. Even in the fading summer light, Jonah thought how light both of them looked, palm or back. But still not as light as mine—

He glanced back at Amanda, to see if she was all right, or if she had been further offended. It was usually just the sort of thing she wouldn't like, what she considered a mintrelsy "l.c."—lower class—sort of story.

Yet he was relieved to see that she was truly laughing. He had wondered about bringing her to Oak Bluffs at all, knowing the sort of crowd Adam moved in, but it had been too much of a temptation to turn down. He had known Adam all his life but they had rarely socialized outside the usual church picnics, and prayer breakfasts, and ministerial convocations. Adam and Isabel were the very pinnacle of Harlem society. Together, they were the most stunning couple anyone had ever laid eyes on, like something off a movie screen. Jonah had thought that Adam must want something from him to be graced with a sudden invitation to their sanctum sanctorum, the summer house on Martha's Vineyard.

But Adam had made them feel right at home from the moment they stepped off the Woods Hole ferry. His booming, irrepressible laugh, his teasing jibes and stories making it seem as if they were all in on one great big joke together. He had never been one to hide his light under a bushel back in Harlem, but here Jonah thought he seemed positively outsize. He had even grown a rakish beard for the summer, romping about the island like a big happy satyr. Driving out along its narrow, winding woods roads at frightening speeds with Wingee, his remarkable one-armed chauffeur. Taking them riding along the beach in the mornings, galloping his horse through the shallows as if he were to the saddle born, while they struggled just to stay upright. Plying them with seafood and alcohol, lively talk and music every evening around the porch.

"Oh, Adam, you haven't changed a bit!" Hycie had exclaimed, clapping her hands. "Why, I remember when he would walk into my apartment and just start swigging gin, right from the bottle. 'Adam,' I'd say, 'at least pull the shades down before somebody sees you!'"

Amanda looked away again, at the mention of Adam blithely walking into the apartment of a woman who was not his wife. But Isabel seemed unperturbed, chuckling along with her friend. She sat curled up in her chair, wearing a flowery print dress that showed off her dancer's legs, and a flamboyant, wide-brimmed hat. In Harlem she dressed more modestly for the sake of his parishioners, but here on the island she let it out a little, too. When they went sailing Adam would insist that both she and Hycie—who was nearly as beautiful, and as light-skinned—go up and pose near the bow in their bathing suits, so that it would look as if he were cruising through Nantucket Sound with two rich, long-legged white girls on the front of his boat, their hair blowing in the wind.

Their marriage had been a shock. She a chorus girl from Connie's Inn and the Cotton Club, already divorced and the mother of a little boy—and a Catholic at that. Adam, meanwhile, was church royalty, heir to his father's pulpit at the Abyssinian Baptist, the biggest church north of 110th Street. The women of his congregation called him "Mr. Jesus," Jonah knew, and they all but fainted when he walked up to the altar in his robes, or his gorgeous tweed suits. Before the wedding, so many death threats had been received against Isabel that detectives had been hired to sit in the aisle seats. Isabel herself had been more worried about Adam Senior, when he put his hands on her shoulders, and pressed her firmly down into the baptismal font for the ritual that officially freed her from the clutches of the Church of Rome.

"Oh, my goodness," she had confided to Amanda with a giggle, "I thought, 'This old man is going to get rid of me now!'"

Three different ministers had presided over the ceremony, including Jonah's father. The mobs of people spilling out of the church and onto the sidewalk, more still renting out apartments across 138th Street for the day, just to get a glimpse of the handsome couple. Isabel's mother had made a gigantic seven-layer wedding cake, and at the reception Isabel had personally handed out over two thousand pieces of it, each one in its own box and tied with its own individual ribbon, and shaken hands until her knuckles were bleeding through her long, white wedding gloves.

From that day on, over ten years ago now, she had been the perfect minister's wife. She had lowered her dress hems, and relegated herself to singing spirituals in the Abyssinian's choir. She took part in the women's Bible classes, and the reading and sewing and cooking classes, and all the dozens of other ambitious programs the Abyssinian ran, and that Jonah could only look upon with envy. She had even won over Adam's mother, and his father, the abdicating king, to the point where Jonah thought that sometimes they seemed more enamored of Isabel than Adam did himself.

It was nothing very definite. It was just that at times, during their two weeks on the island, he thought he detected a certain detachment beneath all the clowning. The way Adam's face looked strangely hard, and remote, sometimes when he thought there was no one watching—

Most likely he was only weighing his options, Jonah had told himself. For Adam, everyone knew, was a man on the verge. Over the last two years alone, he had become the first Negro ever elected to the New York City Council, and started his own newspaper, The People's Voice. Fearlessly flaying everyone in his "Soap Box" column, even taking time out from the beach to peck out the latest one in the cottage living room. He was considering a run for the new Harlem seat in Congress that would be created next year, and neither Jonah nor anyone else he knew doubted that it was his for the taking. All he had to do was decide what it was he wanted. Jonah had never seen a more charismatic man, or a more natural leader. He looked at him leaning back in his wicker chair now, his eyes spinning, obviously considering some new mischief.

"Did I tell you I got my draft form from the army, wondering if I was claiming conscientious objector status?" Adam asked them.

"No, you didn't."

Jonah shifted uncomfortably in his seat, thinking of his own form. It was basically an automatic waiver for established clergymen, but he had wrestled with it anyway. Taking great pains with his argument for why, as a Christian minister, he objected to killing anyone—and all the while thinking, But why not? They won't stop unless they are killed. And wouldn't I be better off there—anywhere—doing some good?

"I haven't fully made up my mind yet," Adam announced.

"Adam!"

"I haven't!" he told them, chuckling, having achieved just the affect he wanted.

"Why do I have to explain why I shouldn't have to fight for this country? They should have to explain to me why I should. Maybe I should make them throw me in jail, as a protest!"

There were more peals of protest and laughter from Isabel and Hycie—all of them knowing full well that the congregation of the Abyssinian would never permit its minister to go either into the armed forces or to jail. But Amanda pursued the subject, her lovely dark eyes serious again—still hurting a little over how Adam had teased her before, Jonah knew.

"But why wouldn't you fight? Theoretically, I mean? Are you a pacifist?"

"No, madam, I can't say that I am."

He gave her a little, playful bow of his head.

"So why not, then?"

"Fight whom? For what?"

"Why, for democracy."

"What democracy? Where? Not here! I can't say truthfully say that the black man has done any better in this country than he would have under Stalin, or Hitler."

"Oh, Adam, you know that's not true!" Isabel objected. "You're just leading Amanda along!"

"I am not. America keeps talking about the creation of a new world, but her own conscience is still full of guilt—"

"For Christianity, then," Amanda interjected. "Would you fight for that? At least America is a Christian country."

"Oh, America is not a Christian country!" Powell told her, waving her declaration away good-naturedly. "It is a country of churchianity, full of anti-Christian doctrines of pure, Jim Crow racism. The only truly Christian churches in this country are those that welcome all the sons of man."

"Like the ones in Harlem?"

Adam snorted.

"You can count on your fingers all of those worth keeping open. Bunch of spiritual sissies. Theological twisters. Pulpit pounders and clerical clowns," he said, working himself up. "All of these high-and-mighty Negroes, holding themselves above the masses because their skins are a little bit lighter, or they can trace their family trees back a few generations!"

He shook his head ruefully.

"Hell, most of the time you move any of our family trees six inches, we're right back in a cotton patch, or among the mangrove trees. All this big mystical talk of heaven from the pulpit, pouring it on for the poor grandmothers in the pews! What the masses want is men who'll teach them how to lead a just life, right now."

"Don't you believe in the afterlife then, Reverend Powell?" Amanda persisted, her voice icy.

"No, sister, I don't," he told her more soberly now. "There is no afterlife. At least, I don't believe that there is any heaven or hell. No other place that we're going to go to after we die."

"So the Holy Bible is a lie, then?"

"Oh, the Bible's a great book. But, outside of the Gospels, maybe, it's too filled with contradictions to possibly be the revealed word of any coherent god."

"Adam!"

"How about the New Jerusalem, Adam?" Jonah interrupted, before he could shock his wife any more—and because he could not stop himself. "Is that worth keeping open?"

Adam smiled and reached over to him, squeezing his shoulder.

"Of course, Jonah. You do a real good job over there," he said, his voice sincere—and despite himself Jonah felt suffused with relief.

"I always thought so," Adam went on. "You and your father before you. How's the Reverend doing these days?"

"Oh, you know, he doesn't get out much anymore," Jonah told him, picturing his father in the little apartment behind the church where he insisted on living. His church, right to the end—

"But his mind is still good. He still remembers you, I know."

Adam looked very pleased—and Jonah suddenly understood what he was doing in Oak Bluffs.

"Well, that's great. That's just great, Jonah!" Powell was booming again, slapping his knee. "Please give him my best."

Jonah nodded and turned away, looking down to the beach. Watching as the last few bathers toweled off and made their way up from the Ink Well. They were little more than silhouettes now, blackness merging into blackness.

What a splendid place this is, he thought, regretting fiercely that they would have to leave it the next day—even if he did know the real reason, now, why they had been invited. He was suddenly, deeply moved by the beauty of everything around him—the long-legged women on their hurricane chairs, the shimmering glass in his hand. The lace curtains of Adam's cottage blowing gently in the breeze. The elegant piano music from the phonograph, drifting out from the front parlor.

"Say, what's that you got on there?" he asked Adam, trying to change the conversation again. "I've never heard anything quite like it."

The music really was extraordinary—what sounded like very complicated jazz riffs, played on classical themes.

"That's Hazel Scott, she's terrific," Adam said casually, bouncing up off his chair and going inside. "Here, let me turn it up for you!"

"Oh, now don't be doing that, sugar, I believe Preston went to sleep already!" Isabel called after him, but it was too late—the music flaring up, drawing the smoky blare of a Village nightclub suddenly out onto the porch with them. Making Jonah think of what Sophia was doing these days. His lost sister—

"She's down at Café Society," Adam told them as he sat back down. "You and Amanda ever been? It's about the only place out-side of Harlem where people of all colors can sit down together and enjoy a little music! We'll have to take you some night, after we get back to the City."

"Well, I don't know," Jonah said too quickly. Afraid that he would discover Sophie there, and what that would mean.

"I hear the place is a front for the Communists—"

"So what if it is?" Adam scoffed, snapping his fingers. "Political party days are coming to a close. It's not going to matter anymore whether you're Democrat, Republican, Communist—just so long as you're marching black."

"Well, perhaps, perhaps," Jonah mumbled, wanting to drop the whole subject as quickly as he had brought it up.

He was saved by the appearance of Preston in the doorway, rub-bing his eyes. Jonah had been surprised to see how big he'd got-ten—nearly a teenager now, though still a boy, his thick mop of hair turned almost blond by the summer sun. He was wearing a pair of Adam's old fishing trunks, one of his T-shirts hanging baggily down over his waist, and when he stretched his arms and yawned all the adults on the porch smiled. Jonah knew without looking that Amanda's eyes were on him again. Wondering the same old ques-tion, when they were going to have theirs—

And what would be the purpose of that? To bring them into this world?

"Somethin' woke me up," Preston mumbled.

"Mmm, that would be your daddy," Isabel said, pretending to cast a stern look at Adam. "Him and Hazel Scott."

"I had bad dreams," Preston said, a small frown crossing his smooth, innocent face.

"Aw, that's too bad," Adam said gently, getting up and taking him by the hand. "C'mon, let's get you back to bed so you can have some good ones and wipe 'em out."

They all followed Adam and the boy back into the cottage, the mosquitoes and the blackflies beginning to bit now. Isabel turned off the record, the rest of them resettling themselves around the living room while Adam took Preston up to bed.

His acceptance of the boy had been the crowning grace of their marriage, Jonah knew. There had been much speculation about what would happen if he and Isabel had their own child—another heir to the throne!—but they never had, and Adam had formally adopted Preston as his own son.

It was more than just an adoption, though—Adam truly seemed to love the boy. Here on the island he was always teaching him things. In the afternoons he would take him out on the sailboat, schooling him in how to tack and to jibe, and to clam and crab and fish. They would tromp back along South Circuit Avenue together, grinning like a couple of maniacs in their shorts and sandals, Adam insisting on showing off their catch to everyone they passed.

Back at the Abyssinian he let Preston run the camera that captured Adam's every sermon, and the sound system that projected his voice out on the street, to all the faithful who couldn't get a seat inside. The boy would go dashing back and forth down the block, making sure everything was working—watching as the windows went up, and men and women leaned outside to hear the voice of his adopted father rolling up and down West 138th Street. Sometimes, in one of his more histrionic moods, Adam would charge down from the pulpit and right out onto Seventh Avenue. Plunging into the crowds there, Preston grinning and holding on to his hand, just as Jonah knew that Adam had held on to his own father's hand, walking the streets of San Juan Hill years before.

To have a child. A son, to pass something on to. What, exactly?

He didn't want Amanda looking at him just now—knowing what they would both be thinking about. He stood up abruptly, announcing that he would help Adam put Preston back to bed even though he half-expected to hear them whispering about him when he left the room, making his way slowly upstairs and along the second-floor hall of the house.

The cottage was just as stylish and outrageous as everything else about Adam. Most of the other colored homes in Oak Bluffs were austere and understated. Tasteful old houses that looked as if they were trying their best to melt into the background, more Yankee than the Yankees. Adam's house, by contrast, was a loud, green, gingerbread cottage, just like the white folks' houses by the old Methodist Campground. The fishing tackle he used every day hung proudly along the wall, much as—and precisely because—it would have appalled the most proper members of the Abyssinian.

That was Adam, too. Poking fun at the pretensions of white people and his own congregation, all at the same time.

Above the fishing tackle were hung a series of family photographs. Adam with his parents, and his late sister. Adam and Isabel and Preston on the boat. Adam in the Abyssinian pulpit in full robe and regalia—

Jonah stopped when he saw what might have been his own face, cast in a much darker shade. It was a photograph of his father, posing with Adam Senior, and the Rector Hutchens C. Bishop, of St. Philip's. The three men holding up masonry trowels at what must have been the laying of the cornerstone at one of their churches, nearly twenty-five years ago, trying to look as grave and dignified as befitted the occasion. But peering closely at the picture, even in the darkening hall, Jonah could see how they couldn't help smiling from ear to ear, their lips just barely managing to keep their teeth covered.

And why not, after all they had accomplished? Men who had made themselves from nothing, brought their people up from nothing, the founders and the very embodiment of their churches—

They had been "The Three Kings," the ministers who had first made the great exodus uptown. Moving their churches up to Harlem lock, stock, and congregation when it was still a place where goats and pigs wandered through the streets. Powell, Bishop, and his own father—the Reverend Milton Dove, pastor and founder of the Church of the New Jerusalem.

He was the least of The Three Kings, perhaps, the one with no real theological training. The New Jerusalem not as large or as influential as the Abyssinian, nor as Old New York and high hat as Episcopal St. Philip's. But it was, more than either of them, the church of the working people of Harlem—the church of the new people, just up from the fields of Mississippi and Georgia, and South Carolina. Heartsick and lost in the big city, just like the first, ragged band his father had so famously led out of the Wilderness.

To do such a thing—

He stared for a long moment at that face. It really could have been his own, a few years older. Save for the darker coloring, of course, and the scars that still remained from when—eighty years ago, now—he had nearly been beaten to death by a white mob on a City street. He knew that his father had been a good-looking man in his youth and he could see, in the photograph, the same elements that people said made Jonah himself handsome—the gracefully rounded cheeks, the noble brow; a prominent nose and full, sensuous lips. Nearly the same face—save for the color, and the scars.

I am not capable of anything like what he did. So what does he want from me? Even to name me as he did. A Jonah man, I'm a Jonah man—

He was gripped in the old fear then. Knowing that his father was the church, that he could not possibly replace him, and on impulse he walked the rest of the way down the hall into Preston's room, wanting desperately to ask Adam if he had ever felt the same way.

The moment he was through the door, though, he realized it was pointless. It was impossible to believe that Adam Clayton Powell had ever felt incapable of succeeding anyone, right up to God Almighty, should He ever get tired of the job. He sat now in a low rocking chair in a corner of his adopted son's room—the very picture of self-assurance, lighting up a cigarette while he watched over his boy.

"It's so easy to sleep at their age," he said softly when Jonah entered, gesturing to where Preston was sprawled out on the bed, one arm flung heedlessly over his head.

"He gets so tired, just being out on the boat. Swimming all day. They have all the energy in the world, then when it's time to sleep they nod right off. It's natural. It's not till we're adults that we learn to clutter up our minds with so many worries and ambitions."

"Hard not to worry, these days," Jonah said.

"You mean about the world?" Adam shrugged, fanning the smoke away so it wouldn't reach his sleeping son. " 'Let the day's own worries be sufficient for the day.' You just have to see to what's closest to you, to do what you can do."

"Did you really believe what you said out there?" Jonah asked abruptly—a little offended though he told himself he shouldn't be, that it was just Adam, quoting Scripture not five minutes after he had denied the whole divinity of the Bible.

"Hmm? About what?"

"You know. About the afterlife."

He felt like a child even saying the word.

"Sure," Adam said matter-of-factly. "Heaven and hell are both right here, in the span of years that we spend in this body, on this earth. That's all there is, and after it's over we're gone."

Jonah flinched, hating to hear such things—though it was how his father usually talked about God. Jonah himself really believed, much as he hated to admit it before someone as worldly as Adam. He knew how ridiculous so much of it sounded—all those kings slaughtering each other at God's command in the Old Testament, Paul railing about the godliness of chastity. All that mystical nonsense in Revelations—

But he loved the Christ—His words, and the very idea of Him. Jonah had never had some burning revelation, so far as he knew it. No blinding light, or life-changing conversion, like so many of his brother ministers, or his fellow students back at the Angel Factory in Pennsylvania claimed to have experienced—like so many of the men and women in his congregation knew they had experienced. He had had nothing more than a feeling of Christ, which he was intelligent enough and honest enough to admit might be no more than his own inchoate longing. But still he believed.

"Besides, how could there be a God?" Adam was saying, looking up at him. "What God could let what's happening go on now? Why, today it's almost an insult to God to believe in him."

"I know," Jonah nodded grimly. "I've been talking to Jakey Mendelssohn. He has a cousin who got out of Europe somehow, works in his store now. He says it's true. The Nazis have whole camps where they're slaughtering Jews on—on an assembly line."

"Yeah, I've heard the same things from Maury Rosenblatt, over at the Amalgamated," Adam said, shaking his head. "They want to wipe out the whole race. Better God shouldn't exist."

"Wipe out the whole race," Jonah repeated, wondering at the concept.

He turned away, gazing out the bedroom window. It was almost pitch-black now, darker than it ever got in the City with the U-boat blackout here. The blackness merging into the blackness. The lights were going out all up and down Nantucket Sound, the only noise the faint ringing of the marker buoys, far out in the bay. As if to demonstrate how the world will end. He thought then that the island did not seem very special after all, that it offered no refuge. What place did, now?

"Why should it surprise you?" Adam said, not unkindly, standing and giving his shoulder a consoling squeeze. "They've been trying to do it to us for years. Whatever you want to believe, you just have to take what's right in front of you, face that. Your father was always very good at that. He always served the people."

So that was it. The mention of his father confirming Jonah's
earlier suspicions, out on the porch. That was why they had been
invited up to this marvelous place, to nail down his father's endorsement for Adam's next election. He doubted that Adam would need
it, but in Harlem politics you could never be too careful. Jonah's
politico O'Kane "cousins," in with Ed Flynn's machine up in the
Bronx, they'd have understood it right away. Nothing too direct, or
unsubtle. Have Jonah and his wife up for a couple weeks, be sure to
plant some nice words that would get back to his father—

He knew that he ought to be angry, but he was too preoccupied.
Instead, he chose to vent some more of his self-pity.

"But am I worthy of that?"

"Well, of course you are! Worthy as anybody."

Adam's big face looked puzzled.

"Holding up a church in a world without God? In a world without hope, where we're hated on all sides? How can I do that?"

"You can do it. Just like your father did," Adam said in a com-
forting voice, putting his hand on his back and guiding him out of
his son's bedroom.

"Remember, you want to be like the great man, then be the great
man. What's that, Socrates?"

"Aristotle."

"Well, one of those Greeks," Adam laughed, guiding him back
downstairs to the ladies. "You see, my education wasn't completely
wasted!"

Back down in the living room, of course, he had had to act like a
man in front of his wife, and Isabel and Hycie. Going through the
motions, making small talk with the rest of them. That night in bed
Amanda had clung to him, sensing there was something wrong, as
she always did. Asking him if Adam had disturbed him. He had told
her that everything was fine, not even sharing with her his revelation as to why they had been invited. They had made love with
more passion than they had in some time, and afterward they had
lain awake in the narrow, guest room bed, listening to the tinkling
of the buoys out at sea while the delicate subject of a child, and all
that entailed, lay silent between them.

And early the next morning—when Wingee had driven them
down to the ferry in his usual alarming fashion, whipping the steering wheel wildly back and forth with his one, incredibly strong
arm—the sun had been shining, and Jonah had thought that per-

haps he could do it. Putting behind him any remaining hurt over why Adam had invited him in the first place. Accepting his warm handshake and continuing pastoral concern as he left. No wonder he was so good. Isabel had produced a picnic basket for the train, packed to overflowing with exquisite little chicken and cucumber sandwiches, and fine pastries they had acquired somehow, on an island, despite shortages and ration cards.

They had climbed up the ferry gangplank, waving good-bye to Adam and Isabel and their son, and he had thought that, Yes, I can do this, there is no reason to go. We can have a good life, just like other people. Even a life with children.

But when they reached the mainland again, and got back to America, everything changed. Even before they had docked, Jonah had noticed the sharp looks that he and Amanda got from some of the other passengers. Trying to figure out if they really were both colored, he knew, giving them a wide berth in any case. There had been some derisive laughter, some things said—as always, just out of earshot.

He had tried to ignore it, but then they had reached New Bedford and he had bought the newspapers. It was the same thing again, all the news they had been shielded from on their island off the rest of America, plastered across the front page of the Pittsburgh Courier edition he had managed to pick up. A colored private and his mother, both beaten by police and MPs for daring to use a phone in the white waiting room of a Houston train station... a colored officer in Columbus, Georgia, who was told to go to a different window for nigger tickets, then who was knocked to the ground over and over again by fourteen separate white cops armed with nightsticks. His wife struck down, too, when she put out her hand to help him... Eleven Negro shipyard workers hospitalized, two more feared dead in Mobile—

The trouble had started when they had tried to put black welders on a job building Liberty ships—and the white welders had attacked them with iron bars and homemade clubs and bricks. Rioting until the government had been forced to give in, and put all the colored welders on a separate, segregated wharf—

Segregated Liberty ships. His father had always talked about how his grandfather had been a skilled shipbuilder, but they wouldn't let him make warships, not even in New York during the Civil War. Claiming, This is an all-white waterfront—

"Well, that's progress for you. Eighty years, and we get our own Jim Crow wharf," he had murmured.

"What's that, honey?" Amanda had asked, but he had only shaken his head.

The worst, though, was just a small item buried in the back pages of the Boston Globe, a white paper—about a lynching in Vigo County, Indiana. It concerned a thirty-three-year-old colored man, James Edwards Persons, honorably discharged from the army. He had been accused of looking into farmhouse windows, and tracked down and beaten by a mob organized by the local sheriff to hunt him through the fields. But the very worst part of all was that it had happened months before. Somehow, even after his beating—even after the terror that must have suffused his being, turning his legs to nightmare lead weights—even after all that, Persons had escaped the mob, and hidden himself away. Only to be found dead now, not truly escaped from anything—

Jonah was still thinking on the story when the white soldiers came into the car. No doubt he would have noticed them earlier if he hadn't been so preoccupied, might have even discovered some ruse to hustle Amanda away from trouble. He was always alert, wherever he was, for groups of white men like that, though he always tried not to let Amanda see his fear. He had slipped his clerical collar on before they left, an added precaution he thought worthwhile even if it had drawn a quizzical look from Adam, hoping that its authority would help him.

But it hadn't mattered. Nothing had, save for the color of his skin, and his wife's. The soldiers had spotted them at once, the moment they had walked in from the parlor car, half in the bag and looking for a fight. Sticking their faces, with their sour, whiskey-soaked breath, right into their own—

And no one around them had raised a hand to help. None of the white people in the car had said a thing, no one had even gotten up to look for the MPs, or the conductor. He had been left to sit there, in his seat, and pray to Jesus as best he could while his wife was insulted, and he was humiliated in front of her. About to be beaten, or even worse, just as in all the other shameful, mortifying attacks on black men around the country that he had just been reading about but had never had to endure himself—

Then that crazy boy had shown up. Showing no fear at all. Bantering with the soldiers, tricking them. Throwing the sociopath of a sergeant right off the train. Looking like Satan himself when he grinned, that ridiculous boy with his conked hair—but still fearless all the same.

But why, then, the jump into the bay? Why would he do such a thing? Just to show off? To mock them—all the white people in the car? And himself?

That was the thing Jonah couldn't figure out, even though he thought about it all the way back to New York. He might have asked him. The boy had come back to the car several more times, selling his sandwiches and ice cream. It was the hungriest car of white folks Jonah had ever seen, all of them hastening to slide large tips into his jacket pockets, as if their nickels and dimes and even quarters could make up for their own silence in the face of watching another human being humiliated and beaten.

He could have asked him, could have stood up and thanked him, straight out, man to man. But he hadn't. Every time the boy had come near, he had meant to—but each time he saw his own wife's eyes light up, in gratitude. Amanda, too chary of his own feelings, too sensitive to actually buy something. Turning instead to the picnic basket Isabel had provided. But she had given him that grateful smile, and every time he came by, the thought of standing up and thanking in front of his wife some crazy young street Negro for saving him kept him glued in his seat.

What was still worse was how Amanda had silently, solicitously offered him one of the petite chicken sandwiches that Isabel had prepared—her way of acknowledging his ruined pride. And though he knew that she meant well, Jonah could not even get through one of them. To him it tasted of the porch at Oak Bluffs, and highballs and tennis courts, and fine, intellectual conversations, and all those other wonderful amenities of life that he knew did not mean a thing in the face of a few drunken white soldiers on a public train.

CHAPTER FOUR

MALCOLM

He had his bag on before they hit the station. Ripping off the still soggy sandwich uniform, forcing his long legs through the gorgeous reat pleats as they pounded down the tracks along the Hudson. Barely noticing the wide, slow-moving river, the elegant silver bridge shimmering in the late afternoon haze as they flashed by.

"Pe-ennnsylvania Station! Pennsylvania Station!" the conductor was hollering, in words that even he couldn't help make sound like a song.

Then they were bolting up into a world of vast steel spiderwebs, and large black-and-white clocks floating in the sunlight pouring through the roof. Below the towering metal trellises, the platform waiting benches were filled with young men, in uniform or without. Packed around the railing above them were girlfriends and wives and mothers, staring wistfully down, so close to the objects of their affection but separated by the closed train gates, not daring to call out lest they break their men's hearts or their own. The soldiers and soon-to-be soldiers sitting in their own glum silence, avoided their gaze, smoking or pacing around.

Then they were out in the cavernous main hall. The crowds there even thicker, their quietest murmurs echoing off the marble walls, sitting or sleeping on their duffel bags and suitcases. Thousands of people, waiting alone together. They ran past a mother—a large white woman with gray hair, and a simple worn smock of a housedress. Her face was twisted up in undisguised agony, the tears running freely down her face, while her rough, thick hands twisted

violently at the handle of her pocketbook. But Malcolm noticed that
no one stopped to talk or to console her, those men and women
who walked by her looking annoyed, even angry, as they might pass
someone with a contagious cough.

There was the sound of singing then, a beautiful woman's voice
with a light Irish brogue descending from above. So beautiful and
startling that he slid to a stop, his flat sweet-potato shoes skidding
on the smooth marble floor. He peered into the ropes of cigarette
smoke that twisted up to the reaches of the vaulted honeycombed
ceiling far above him, trying to discern where the voice was coming from. Dizzied by the sheer scale and beauty of it, the vertigi-
nous marble columns and the lustrous amber walls—realizing only
dimly that the lovely Irish voice was not singing at all, merely reading out endless lists of departing trains, and their destinations.

"What you gawkin' at, boy? Those Harlem frails ain't gonna
wait forever!"

Sandy Thorne thumped him on the back, pushing him on.

"Oh, man, this is the place!" Malcolm exclaimed. "Just like I
thought!"

"Mr. High Pockets, out on a bat!"

They rushed on, under a huge, blue-and-buff mural of the Western Hemisphere, then down a hall past a long arcade of shops and
offices, their functions skimming by in peeling, gold-leaf paint:
LOST-FOUND*NATION L TICK T RES VATIONS*FAR DES-
TINATIONS—Laughing and shoving each other, weaving in and
around the mobs of people. The rest of them, Lionel and Willard
and Sandy still in their white crew uniforms, but heads turned as he
ran by in his sharkskin zoot—the faces of the soldiers and sailors
smirking or frowning or laughing derisively; Malcolm uncaring,
grinning into their stares.

They ran on out to the taxi portico, where the other three stood
in front of him, trying to hide the zoot from view, but it was no
use. The huge, flying-saucer hat stood out like an electric sign, an
advertisement for social deviance, and they had to wait for a colored
hack before they got a cab up to Harlem. Piling into the cavernous
backseat of his Checker, the others forcing Malcolm to sit facing
them, like a little boy, on the lower, foldable jump seat.

"Ho, ho—stay there, Square! We got to look you over!"

"Got to make sure you're ready for the chippies uptown!"

Their teasing more good-natured now—Malcolm still the hero

from his fight with the sailors back at the New Bedford siding. The whole rest of the run they had hustled to pack up his box for him, and left his drape alone. He would even have sworn, when he put it back on, that the high, rigid shoulders of the coat had been given a careful brushing. His pockets stuffed with the additional bills Pappy Cousins had slipped into them; the outrageous, guilty tips from every one of the passengers riding in the car from which he had so forcibly evicted those soldiers.

Everyone—except for that preacher himself. His wife had looked at him, all right, her fierce brown eyes just as grateful as they had been imploring. But not her husband. Every time Malcolm had returned, singing out his wares, the man had turned his smooth, sensitive, all-but-white face toward the window, as if he could not abide the sight of him. Snotty yaller bastard—

The rest of the crew were giggling like schoolboys, shrugging off their kitchen uniforms in the cab. Struggling into suits that were more conservatively cut than Malcolm's but still sharp—light blues and greens, and creamy whites, with bright, skinny ties that gave him a pang of consternation.

"I thought you said this was a righteous town," he scoffed at them. "How'm I gonna be gunnin' the hens with you three togged like that?"

"Listen to Mr. Samuel D. Home," Paddy scoffed at him. "Son, you should latch on to the fact that this is the Apple."

"You gonna get conked up good, you don't mind us!"

Malcolm grinned back at them, feeling as if he would burst out of the cab.

"Hey, I'm mellow as a cello, rippin' an' rompin', trippin' an' stompin'."

"Uh-huh. This is Harlem, son."

"So where is it?!"

"Well, you watch now. Keep an eye out here, when we reach the Main Stem."

"Huh?"

"One hunnert twenny-fifth street, son."

"What for, what for?"

He peered avidly out the cab window, wondering if it had anything to do with women.

"Keep lookin'."

"For what?"

Then he saw him. A monolith. A fantastic hallucination, a human balloon swaying in the waves of heat floating up from the pavement. But there was no denying him—at least six-three and two hundred seventy-five pounds, standing right out in the middle of the street, directing traffic. A black man in a police uniform.

"That's Lacy!"

"There he is! Hey, Lacy!"

They waved out the window, calling his name, making mocking noises though there remained a note of pride in their voices. Lacy only stared at them balefully, planted inalterably in the middle of the intersection, lugubriously waving the cars on. Malcolm still gawking out the back window of the cab as they passed, unable to get his mind around the sight.

"A cop. A black cop," he marveled.

"Sure, they got 'em up here, you know," Lionel snorted. "You should see Big Ben Wallace. Ol' Mr. Terror make Lacy look like a schoolteacher. Or the Four Horsemen—"

But Malcolm had already stopped listening, staring out at the amazing sidewalk scene emerging all around them. Suddenly there was color everywhere, as if someone had just switched the screen to technicolor, like in The Wizard of Oz, which he had seen six times back in Michigan. Men wearing green, and yellow, and red sports shirts. Men wearing porkpie hats, and Panamas, and fedoras, men in white and lemon-lime and peach ice-cream suits—even men wearing sharper zoots, he had to admit, than what he had on himself.

And women. He was sure that he had never seen so many beautiful women in his entire life. There were women everywhere, at least two for every man, not counting the clusters of soldiers and sailors gaping and gesturing at them on every street corner. Women wearing gold and ruby red glass in their ears, and open-toed platform heels that made them sway with every step. Women in tight violet and red and blue print dresses, held up only by the thinnest of shoulder straps over their smooth brown backs. Women striding up from the subways, stepping regally down from the trolleys and the elevated, and women, everywhere he looked, strolling out of smoking storefronts, as if their smoldering presence had touched them off.

"What—they on fire?" Malcolm asked in bewilderment, squinting at the smoky little shops, the mysterious lettering in their windows that boasted WE OFFER: The Apex—Poro—Nu Life—Hawaiian Beauty Systems—

"Mm-hmm, you bet they are," the cabbie laughed up front. "Those Thursday girls, they always on fire! Even when they ain't gettin' their hair straightened—"

"You in luck, Nome," Lionel told him. "It's Thursday. Kitchen Mechanics' Night. All those maids an' mammies, an' calkeener broads—Friday's they one day off. They be gunnin' for you tonight."

"For real?"

"'Course for real, Samuel D.!"

"Where you think we should take him first?" Willard asked the others. "Up the Savoy, beat out a few hoof riffs? Braddock's? The Elks? Take him to a buffet flat an' have a good laugh?"

"Nah, man. We gotta take him by Small's first."

"Yeah, Small's. That's the place to get him his first drink in Harlem!"

First they had the cab let them off at Mrs. Fisher's boardinghouse, where they dropped off their train bags in the sliver-thin rooms where they would bunk for the layover. They clambered right back out onto the sidewalk—and it was then that Malcolm realized everything was moving even faster than it had looked from inside the taxi; as if the sidewalk itself had been set on some war-speed assembly line, activated the moment they put their feet to it.

It caught them up immediately, rushing them past chicken restaurants and hamburger joints, and closed-up basement dance halls, and heat-dazed winos lying in the doorways. Past barbershops that advertised "Conk It Up! No Burning!" and more of the smoking beauty parlors where Malcolm could now make out the women in pink smocks pressing irons down on other women's hair like it was so much laundry.

They moved past all the squatting curb vendors selling used books, and carved African animals, and jewelry that shone a little too brightly. Past men with carts full of wilted daisies, and roses and violets, and men selling long, red-orange slices of cantaloupe and watermelon, with the glistening cut mouth of the remaining melon set just above their heads, so that they seemed to mimic their own red mouths and wagging tongues. There were men selling halves of oranges, and alligator pears, and rings of coconut slices floating in dishes of water and their own fragrance while they chanted ritually over them, "Yo tengo guineos! Yo tengo cocoas! Yo tengo pinas, tambien!"—and the fish peddlers who made sudden, high-pitched, terrifying noises, shrieking "Wahoo! Wahoo! Wahoo!" before throwing back their heads and singing out their ditties to the sky, or at least to the upper stories of the tenements above them:

"Can't go home till all my fish is gone,
Stormy weather.
Can't keep my fish together
Sellin' 'em all the time—the time!
Don't see why
You folks don't come an' buy—"

There were other people, men and women both, who they could not walk past but who came straight at him, sticking their hands in the pocket of his coat. Grabbing for whatever they could find, or leaving small cards and flyers there before he struck their fingers away. One man coming up right behind his ear, whispering, "All kinds of women, Jack. Want a white woman?" so close and intimate that Malcolm was simultaneously startled, and repulsed, and intrigued.

"I had a white woman, back in Michigan," he announced loudly to the others in the crew. "No hype! Woman named Sally, fine as a ocean gull—"

"Yeah, Nome, tell us about that later!" Lionel said, taking him by the arm and pulling him, despite the potential alteration of luck involved, right through and under a stepladder that was set up on the corner.

Malcolm looked up—and saw a short, beige-colored man standing on the top rung, wearing a small, round skullcap, and what looked like a magician's robe. Both the fez and the robe were full of crescent moons and stars and ringed planets—not unlike the stars and moons the Comet wore on his crime-fighting costume, he thought idly. Most incongruously of all, there was a large freestanding American flag set up on the corner next to the ladder. The man haranguing the passersby in a voice of bottomless, righteous anger:

"Why should the so-called Negro have to shed his blood for Franklin Roosevelt's America, for Cotton Ed Smith and Senator Bilbo. For the whole Jim Crow, so-called Negro-hating South, for the low-paid, dirty jobs for which we have to fight—"

Malcolm stopped and gaped up at the little man, the words and the scornful, defiant certainty with which they were said striking a chord in him. They reminded him so much of something else he had heard, somewhere, even though most of what the little man said was no more than gibberish to him. The assembly-line sidewalk didn't slow down just because he did, the people bumping into him as they passed, cursing and tsking at him. Malcolm paid them no mind—recalling now where it was that he had heard such language before, back in his father's Garvey meetings. So struck by his realization that he didn't even notice at first that his friends had moved on, or the menacing-looking figures in dark suits, and red fezzes, who had quietly ringed themselves around the man on the stepladder.

"Remember—white man's Jesus is a false god!" the little man cried out, holding up some thick, leather-bound book that Malcolm assumed was a Bible. "W. D. Fard is God, and Elijah Muhammad is his Prophet! Elijah Muhammad is God! All others are from the devil!"

"Sacrilege!" one of the men who had surrounded the ladder yelled back. "Blasphemer! Murderer! Elijah Muhammad is a murderer and a false prophet! Brown Eel is the true heir of Fard!"

"No! It is Elijah, who is also One Much, and Ghulam Bogans, and Robert Talcis, and Black Moses—"

But at that moment, the other men in fezzes rushed the stepladder. Shoving past Malcolm, jostling the beige little man in the magician's skullcap off its top step. He flailed away at them with his fist and the holy book in his hands before the whole ladder teetered, and went down, entangling the flag with them. A woman screamed, and there were a few muffled shouts and curses. The whole brawl quickly submerged behind the continuing, fast-paced mobs of people moving along the sidewalks, most of them not pausing to give it a second look.

"C'mon, Nome, we almost there!"

Lionel and Willard, who had doubled back, each grabbed an arm, pulling him onward. Clustered at the next corner there were two separate crowds of servicemen, one black, one white, eyeing each other warily. A cordon of MPs with armbands, and mounted police with hooded eyes and high-crowned hats stood before them—reluctantly letting most of the black soldiers and sailors pass through. Stopping the white servicemen, many of whom tried to double back and get past them anyway, ducking around the legs of the skittish, weaving horses.

"Oh, what I wouldn't give for a black skin right now!" he heard a white sailor exclaim as he sauntered off down the street.

The edges of the crowd kept flaring up, like a fire curling the edge of a page. The colored people in the crowd trying to get through, cursing and throwing up their hands as the cops turned their horses obliviously into them, trying to cut off the white soldiers and sailors. Staring into their angry, contorted faces Malcolm was amazed by how furious they seemed. The cops finally winching their horses grudgingly out of the way to let them by—their haughty, mounted-policeman eyes following Malcolm in his shark-skin zoot.

"He must be vital to the war effort!" one of them said, and spat past his horse's left ear. But by then they were already stepping up to a door with a long, glittering marquee above it that read SMALL'S PARADISE.

"Now don't be actin' the fool in here, boy!" Sandy whispered to him, though the moment Malcolm set eyes on the place there was no need to warn him again.

Inside, everything was instantly cool and dark. A wall of glimmering bottles and glasses rose up before them, with red-and-black-leathered booths and stools surrounding the elegantly curved bar. It was so quiet that Malcolm could hear the panting of the air conditioner, and he thought at first that they must be alone in the place. Only when he had taken a second look around did he realize that the bar was in fact dotted with men—leaning over their drinks, speaking in low, deliberate voices when they spoke at all. Some of them already looking him over, their own faces inscrutable, before turning wordlessly back to their drinks.

"Mmm, more boys just in off the ponies. You want Frank to get you a table?"

Behind the bar stood a pair of stubby stoical-looking men, so much alike they might have been twins.

"No thanks, Charlie. We just gonna cop a squat at the bar," Willard said.

"Suit yourself." Charlie shrugged his thick shoulders, as if he thought that was a bad idea but was not about to bother talking them out of it.

"What's your pleasure?"

"Bourbon!" Malcolm blurted out.

"What brand?"

"Uh," Malcolm said, hurriedly studying the bottles on the shelves behind his head. He had never actually had bourbon, but since they had been in the cab he had been thinking he would have it for his first drink in Harlem, the word had always sounded so elegant and sophisticated to him.

"Umm. J. T. S. Brown. Yeah, that's it."

"Straight up?"

"What's that now?"

He felt Sandy punch him in the back. Charlie looked Malcolm up and down, from his sweet-potato shoes to his broad-brimmed hat, then turned to the rest of the kitchen crew.

"Who your gate here? He of age?"

"Old enough for whatever you got, old man!" Malcolm told him, but the rest of the kitchen crew quickly pulled him around to the one open stool they could find and sat him down there.

"That's Charlie Small! His brother owns the place! What we tell you just now?"

"He all right, Charlie. He's with us, he'll be cool," Lionel called out.

"All right then. Just make sure you school him," Charlie said, shooting them another warning look as he turned away to get their orders—his brother now staring bleakly at them, too.

"It's heavy on all fronts these days, with the MPs an' the police dicks in every hour, on the hour. I can't afford to have no underage boys drinkin' here."

Malcolm noticed that many of the older heads around the bar had turned back his way, looking him over again, and he felt thrilled to have their attention even if the look on their faces was one of disdain.

"You got to forgive him for jumpin' salty, it's his first night in Harlem," Lionel called down the bar again.

"But he a man, all right, don't worry. Ain't never seen no boy throw a couple ofay soldiers off a train!"

"Yeah?" said Charlie, sounding almost intrigued now, coming back with their drinks. "How 'boot that?"

"That's right!" Malcolm couldn't help speaking up again. "They was gettin' playful with a preacher an' his wife. I showed 'em off the train by their ears!"

"Nice, high-yaller preacher an' his wife," Willard chimed in. "The grays come lookin' for trouble—five of 'em! He tells 'em it's the last stop!"

"Well, now, that's a good story, Red," Charlie Small said, his face breaking into what was almost a smile. "This bein' your first night in Harlem, I think it's worth one on the house."

To his utter joy and amazement, the older hustlers around the bar began to move in around Malcolm then, their dark, scarred faces showing real interest. The face of his father flashing through his head again. Reveling in the respect in their eyes—

He told them about it over and over again, adding and altering details as the story, and the bourbon, moved him. Trying to make his voice sound as cold, and his eyes glaze over just like Robert Taylor did it in Johnny Eager, his favorite gangster movie. Feeling lighter each time, as if he were about to finally levitate over the bar, it was so close to the waking daydreams he had every shift, lugging his sandwich box around the train. The older men sending over more drinks, grumbling their approval.

"Damned straight! This ain't Georgia, you know—"

"The young lane showed 'em. Those days are over."

Telling them everything but the last, when he jumped into the bay in his trainman's uniform. Not wanting them to think he was a fool, a boy. Not sure yet himself just why he had done it. Jumped into the water before all those people—

Yet after an hour or so he noticed that more and more of the old hustlers had drifted away, slipping off their stools and out of the barroom as stealthily as cats. They were replaced by a flashier crowd, women as well as men, well-dressed and already smelling heavily of alcohol—none of them interested in hearing his story. A gaggle of white sailors burst in, having somehow avoided the MPs and the police for the moment, arguing and laughing loudly among themselves, and Lionel and Willard hauled him toward the door. Before they left, though, Charlie Small came out through all the commotion around the bar, and shook his hand.

"You come on back, son, sometime when it's quieter," he told him. "You ever get tired of the railroad an' need another slave, I fix you up."

Out on the sidewalk, Lionel and Paddy were pounding his arms with their fists.

"Oh, man, Charlie Small his own self!"

"Hey, quit that!"

"Oh, Nome! Your first time in Harlem! Man, that's enough for a whole night!"

But out on the street it wasn't even dark yet. The sun was just setting, in cinematic striations of purple and orange flung across the broad evening sky. Looking south he could see all the way down to the dimmed, yellow tops of the Empire State Building and the Chrysler Building, peering up like periscopes over the vague blocks of the City.

"Where we goin' now?"

"How 'bout the Savoy? Hamp's band is there, with Dinah Washington—"

"Go to The Track? On Kitchen Mechanics' Night?"

Lionel shrugged.

"Couldn't hurt to try!"

The crowd was backed up half a block from the front door by the time they got to 140th Street. A skinny, drunken whore sat on the curb before them with her dress curled back over her knees and her legs apart, cursing disgustedly.

"Goddammit, but a pro don't have no play tonight, they's so many amateurs out givin' it away!"

He could see what she meant. The crowd around him made up almost entirely of women, wearing next to nothing in the heat, and standing so close to him Malcolm wanted to reach out and touch their cheeks and arms, their bare backs. Their skin so smooth, so brown and sable, and coal black, and mariny red like his own, and even white, at least under the distant light of the Savoy marquee. Giddy and impatient to get on the dance floor, squealing and laughing and swearing lustily with each tremor of movement through the crowd.

"Goddammit, we ain't nevah gonna get in!"

"I ain't goin' back to work fo' I get one dance in—"

After twenty minutes they were about to give it up, the immense dance hall, an entire block long itself, never seeming to draw any closer. But just then the MPs and the police extracted another mob of white soldiers, arguing and throwing punches wildly. The crowd lunged forward as one, Malcolm and the rest of the kitchen crew laughing out loud as they pushed and shoved, and were pushed and shoved right through the front doors.

The lobby looked nearly as huge as the waiting rooms in Pennsylvania Station and even more colorful than the Harlem streets, a

blur of brilliant reds and greens, oranges and blues. Half a dozen of
the most beautiful women Malcolm had ever seen stood amidst the
milling throng with their noses in the air. All of them café au lait,
dressed in long, formal gowns and elbow-length gloves, gesturing
imperiously toward a marble staircase under a cut-glass chandelier.
They climbed on up—and there, momentarily empty, shining in the
middle of the ballroom, was the dance floor.

It was at least two hundred feet long, Malcolm thought. An endless expanse of polished maple and mahogany, undulating faintly in
the reflected, golden light. More than twice the size of the Roseland State Ballroom up in Boston, and far bigger and grander than
anything he had ever seen back in Michigan—with not one but two
bandstands down at the end, and nothing but the vast, shimmering
space of unlimited possibility from here to there.

The music started again, and the floor was instantly filled with
dancers. Every one of them, men and women, better dressed, better
looking, moving faster and looser than any crowd he had ever seen
before. Hampton's band he had seen up in Boston, but he had never
heard them play this fast or this tight. They played as if there were
something they were dying to catch up to before it got away. The
frenzy of the crowd and the band playing off each other, surging
back and forth across the dance floor, as if daring each other to the
edge. Illinois Jacquet stood for his solo, then all the rest of Hampton's incomparable sidemen, Alvin Hayse, and Joe Newman, and
George Jenkins—tenor sax, then trombone, trumpet, and drums,
before Hamp himself raised his sticks, and everything stopped on
a dime. The dancers grinning as they caught their breath, the people seated at the side booths still jumping and dancing in place—
imploring Hamp to play their favorite.

"Oh, play 'Flying Home'! Oh, please, Hamp, play 'Flying Home'!"

"'Flying Home'! 'Flying Home'!"

The band teased them, playing the first few notes of their big
hit—then launching into "Pick a Rib," instead. The dancers gleefully took it up anyway. Their speed all the more remarkable to
Malcolm for how crowded the floor was, every inch of it filled save
for a ten-foot square just to the right of Hamp's bandstand that was
almost empty. There were only six dancers there, moving apart
from all the rest, centered around a tall man with impossibly long
legs and a face that was screwed up into a permanent smirk. He was
dressed all in white, with a white hat that was even broader than

Malcolm's lid, and he moved faster than anyone Malcolm had ever seen—keeping the same disdainful expression on his face.

"Who that?" Malcolm asked, enraptured

"That's Twist Mouth Ganaway, son—the King of The Track," Sandy warned him. "Keep away from him, Nome. You go on Cat's Corner there without his permission, he gonna break your ankles for you, an' that's no joke, son."

"I bet he would, too," Malcolm said, grinning weakly—dying to get out on the floor now but still holding back. Remembering what had happened up in Boston with Laura—

Instead he stayed back with the rest of the kitchen crew, just behind the floor-side booths and tables. Nearly half of these were occupied exclusively by white people. Some of them were just watching the darker-skinned dancers, he saw, but others rushed out on the floor to dance as freely as everyone else—many of them white women lindy-hopping with colored men, allowing themselves to be as freely handled and flung about as anyone else. He had seen black men dancing with white women at the Roseland, of course, but it had never been anything like this—never so free and easy. Up in Boston the mixed dancers had always had a furtive, slightly shamed air about them, the white women hurrying off the dance floor with their heads down when a number ended.

Here, it felt different—as if the ballroom had nothing to do with what was outside, all the shoving MPs and the loud, crude mobs of white soldiers and sailors. The white women on the floor actually laughing out loud, their black partners grinning back. He saw at least two mixed couples kiss on the mouth as they left the floor. Nobody looked at them twice, or said anything. The crowd around the dance floor only working itself up into a lather as they watched the jitterbuggers, still insisting on their favorite:

"'Flying Home'! 'Flying Home'! Play 'Flying Home'!"

At last the band gave in. They swung almost casually into the number, as if it were no big deal, teasing the crowd some more—but the dancers wouldn't let them get away with it. Malcolm could feel the floor bounce under his feet from the first note on Hampton's vibraphone. Couples were running out onto the dance floor, holding hands, throwing themselves into the struggling, wriggling mass out there, the women throwing off their heels and whipping on sneakers in anticipation.

He wanted to go out himself, he wanted to grab the nearest girl

to him—one of those bare-backed, barely dressed cooks and maids
all around him—but he held back. Still thinking of how it had been
with Laura, at Roseland. His embarrassment as he saw how much
better she was. Tripping over his own feet when she let loose—that
demure, light-skinned girl. Who knew—

He felt a hand slip into his own and turned, startled, to find a
woman pulling him out to the floor. She was tall and lithe, with long
legs and long straight hair, combed up with a single orchid in it
that matched the color of her side-cut, lavender skirt. Her palm was
soft and moist against his own, and she had a sensuous face—her
lips and cheeks just slightly swollen. It reminded him overwhelm-
ingly of someone, though he was certain he had never seen her
before, that he could never have forgotten such a face. She was easily the most beautiful woman he had seen all night—and she was
white.

Still he hung back, as much as he wanted to dance, thinking of
the disaster with Laura. The white woman still pulling him out,
laughing at him—

No, not laughing at him, he saw then. Laughing with excitement
at the whole scene, the dancers throwing themselves wildly about
all around them, the sweat spraying through the air like sea foam—

He let her take him. Tripping on out to the floor as the tempo
built, the drum pounding atop the bass line, then the trombones
circling back to the theme again and again in long, dizzying loops,
working the dancers harder and harder—

Flying home,
Flying home—

She pulled him to her, but once he was out there she let him
take control. He had never had a partner, black or white, who was
so responsive. All it took was the slightest touch on her arms, her
back, her high, slim waist and she would go where he wanted her to
go. Spinning her away from him, pulling her back and turning her
around. He felt infinitely powerful, half-afraid that he would throw
her up so high she would hit the ceiling—

Flying home!

Then came the moment they had all been waiting for. Illinois
Jacquet stepped forward again, a slim, scowling boy, barely older
than Malcolm himself but almost regal in his concentration. With-

out any further ceremony he launched into the solo they had all been waiting for. He played it impossibly fast and hard, even faster and tighter than anything that had been played already that night. Breaking always on the same, single note—bop!—over and over again, an incredible twelve times in a row, stunning them into submission. Then doing it again—another twelve times, coming back again and again just when it seemed impossible that he could play it again.

It drove them mad. The crowd chanting and counting out the number of times he hit that note. The noise welling up all around them, one couple after another falling out from sheer exhaustion well before the young man with the saxophone did. The dance floor was thinning out—and now Malcolm was aware of how many people were watching them, him and this mysterious woman, cheering them on. When Jacquet finally finished and turned it back to the band, he could hear their cries of, "Go, Red! Go, Red! Work that white girl!" He was the center of all their attention, it was another daydream come true, and it spurred him on to move even faster, pushing her as fast as she could go.

But she could keep up. He had never seen a dancer like her, moving with him as if she knew what he was going to do before he did it. He circled slowly backward toward the center of the dance floor, his own feet moving more easily and naturally than they ever had. Bringing her with him, swinging her up over his hip, his elbow, his shoulder. Straight up, sideways, backward—all of it as if she were weightless.

When he pulled her to him, he tried to get a good look at her face—but all he saw was that her eyes were watching his. Large and grey and steady, anticipating everything he could do. He reached for her waist—and she was already vaulting up into the air. Whirling around, her loose skirt snapping as he split, stood up, spun her up the other way, split again, stood up and caught her in his arms. Her heels gone now, flung off somewhere along the way, doing it all in her bare feet.

Flying home! Flying home!

Joe Newman's trumpet was swapping riffs with Hampton's vibes now, back and forth, back and forth, the music still building relentlessly. Through a veil of sweat Malcolm made out that he and his partner were now making their way up toward the section Sandy had pointed out as Cat's Corner. He could see the long man with the twisted mouth watching him as he came, and his stomach knotted. He tried to look down, to see where his feet were, save himself from the lightning-fast kick that he was sure would leave lying him on the floor in pain and humiliation—but there was no time for that.

He slid her through his legs, and she came out the other side, whirled around, and caught his tie in one hand. Leading him forward while he followed dumbly for a moment—a little embarrassed, unsure of what she was doing—but then grinning, snapping his fingers, putting a step into it. Letting her lead him until she turned again, slid back through his legs and clung tightly around one pants leg, just waiting for him to pull her up. He boosted her off his left hip, then his right, then back again, over and over—as all the brass jumped in now, the saxes and the trombones and the trumpets, and Hamp's band headed at last to the big finish. Her eyes still following his, mirroring everything he did, and he knew in that instant he had never danced so well in his life. Even the tall man in the white suit grinning at him—at least Malcolm thought he was, through that twisted, sardonic mouth—and backing away, giving him room as they conquered every inch of The Track, and the band made its last, dizzying turn, and came back to earth.

Then the other couples were all around them again, shaking his hand, asking where he came from. Twist Mouth Ganaway himself half-bowing to them, grinning, pretending to wave away smoke from the boards—"Oh, no more dancin' here for a while! No dancin'! He left the floor too hot to follow!" Lionel and Willard and Sandy pounding his back like lunatics—

"Oh, Red, oh, Red, this is your night!"

"Where'd you learn to dance like that, you marin-y son of a bitch!"

Malcolm only looked around frantically for his partner, thinking she had slipped out in the confusion. But no—she was right there in front of him again, as Hamp's band swung into a slower number. Sliding her hand into his again, putting his left one around her waist, he remaining too stunned for the moment to do it himself.

He felt slightly uncomfortable, embarrassed by the sweat sticking his zoot jacket to his back by now. She still looked as cool as lemon ice somehow, even the purple orchid that she wore in her hair to match her dress still in place. That was the one, unhip part about her, even he recognized, the flower like some white girl's

clumsy imitation of Billie Holiday. But he didn't care, it just gave
him confidence, endeared her to him all the more in her unknowing,
white-girl way. Her body was still floating with his, lingering casually against him from time to time as they danced.

"What's your name?" he asked when he could say anything at
all—hating the slight tremble in his voice.

"Oh, never mind about that," she said, her voice throaty and
deep, and somehow familiar, too, just like her face, though he still
could not fathom where he might have seen her before. Thinking
maybe that she reminded him of a Merle Oberon, whom he had
dreamed about for weeks after seeing her in Forever and a Day at
the Loew's on Mass Ave—

"Red, that's what they call you?"

"Oh, yeah, for the conk," he said, suddenly embarrassed, running
a hand up under his wide-brimmed hat. "I prefer Harpy. At least I
used to."

"Nah, you're Red. I like that. This your first time here, Red?"

He wanted to lie but he knew she would see through it, and so
he just nodded his head.

"Mmm, I thought so. You'll do fine," she murmured, then put
her head down on his shoulder. Malcolm moving stiffly again, so
conscious of her beautiful face against his jacket, of the other couples sneaking looks at them. Smelling her perfume, the fragrance of
her skin so close. They swayed about the dance floor for two slow,
lingering numbers like that, his new partner only lifting her head
from his shoulder to smile and kiss him on the cheek.

Then a voluptuous young woman he didn't know strutted onto
the stage like a queen, and proceeded to sing the house down with
"Salty Papa Blues." Her voice as rich and full as a whole brass section, and Malcolm cheered and clapped along, and stomped his feet
with everyone else. But when he looked around for his partner again,
he found that this time she had gone, vanished back into the crowd.

Oh, I got a man
He treats me like a rat
He gets me so worried
Oh, I don't know where I'm at.

The rest of the kitchen crew materialized back at his side.
"Where'd she go?"

"That white hen? Over there someplace—"

Willard waved vaguely toward the side booths.

"Where? I wanted another number with her!"

"Ah, Red, you know these chalk chicks. They come an' go like they please."

"She was a hard-hitting gray, though," Lionel admitted.

"A hurricane blizzard!"

Papa why are you so salty?
Why do you drive me down?
There's no complaints
When my other man comes 'round—

He insisted on staying right where he was, in case she might be coming back. Only when the young girl with the big voice had wrung the last note out of her song, when Hamp's band took its break and the house band, the Savoy Sultans, mounted the number two bandstand and began to swing into "Second Balcony Jump," did Malcolm finally let them drag him out. His crewmates were rubbing their eyes by then, but he still wasn't ready to go back to the boardinghouse.

"I'm dead-beat for shut-eye. Maybe we should cop a trot over Mrs. Fisher's, collar some winks 'fore they give away our softies—"

Malcolm hung back, fidgeting around in his zoot-jacket pocket for a smoke—and pulled out one of the scraps of paper someone on the street had thrust on him earlier. There was an address printed on it, and an invitation:

Many folks wonder why my Baby cries,
His Mama eats Onions and wipes her eyes.
Take this Card as a Gentle Hint,
I'm giving a Party to raise My Rent!
Tonight
From ten o'clock until—

"Let's go!" he said, flashing the card in front of them.

"I dunno, Red. We gotta train to catch tomorrow—"

"Ah, let's take the boy. First night in Harlem, he oughta see a rent party!"

They flagged a cab, just beating out a pair of white soldiers who banged their hands angrily on the trunk, a string of profanities trailing them up Seventh Avenue. By now it was completely dark, the summer night around them hot and close. It was not as dark as Roxbury, where there was a real blackout enforced every night, but the dimmed, soupy light from the streetlamps made everything seem unreal—as if they were in some time between real night and day. It was after midnight but it felt as though nobody was asleep yet, the streets filled with murky figures, still walking quickly somewhere.

"Here it is!" Lionel called out when they arrived in front of the towering redbrick apartment house on St. Nicholas Avenue.

"'Most Sugar Hill. Nome, you're gunning for some high-class action now!"

They looked up for the window with the blue light in it that would indicate the rent party, but it wasn't necessary. They could hear the party the moment they stepped inside the front door. Not just the usual party noises of excited talk and drunken laughter, but the roll of a live piano and horns, and even a drum. The neighbors leaning sleeplessly out over their landings in their robes and pyjamas, listening to the music reverberate down the stairs. The four of them hurried after it, even potbellied Sandy, wheezing with every new half flight of stairs until they came to a partly open door on the fourth floor. They pushed it open—and came face-to-face with a short, dour-faced woman wrapped in a sarong, who immediately thrust a hand out at them.

"It's my party. Seventy-five cents!"

"Seventy-five! It's only fifty cent to get in the Savoy!"

"You never heard a wartime inflation? Seventy-five cents, an' you get a taste a Mr. King Kong."

She held out a coffee cup in her other hand, half-filled with liquid that looked as clear and smooth as tap water. Malcolm reached for it but Lionel stopped him before he could hand over his six bits.

"Hold on, Nome! You got to test that it's real shake-up whiskey, an' not just some Sterno an' Whistle."

"Sterno an' Whistle!" the dour-faced woman snorted. "That's real king kong, made fresh last night in the bathtub!"

Lionel took the cup and gave it a hard shake, perusing the resultant bubbles as carefully as a jeweler looking over a fine diamond before he finally nodded his head in agreement.

"All right. That looks okay."

"What you mean, looks?" the woman said, but Malcolm was already tossing back his mouthful. It tasted surprisingly smooth at first—then something like an electric shock crackled up his spine, making his tongue go dry and his eyes tear up.

"Oh, that's cawn, all right!" he heard Lionel gurgling from what seemed like very far away, and the hostess grunted in grudging acknowledgment of the compliment.

"It's a dollar for a shortie," she informed them. "Plus fifty cent for a plate a pigs' feet, an' seventy-five for chitlins. There's craps in the front bathroom, an' plain coon-can, five-up, Georgia skin, black-jack, chuck-a-luck, three-card monte, an' dirty hearts in the back. Plus it's a quarter for any record you want to put on, long's they ain't cuttin'."

Malcolm didn't reply, his head still pulsating from the corn liquor. He let himself be pushed on down an endless, darkened rail-road hallway, filled with smoke and people. Most of them women again—not only Thursday girls, but laundresses and waitresses and beauticians right from work, still wearing their pink-and-white uni-forms, and smocks. Laughing and gossiping, smoking and elbowing each other—

"I said, 'That's fine, ma'am, how much do you pay?' She say, 'Five dollars a week.'"

"What you say?"

"Well, I had a look all around the room then. She say, 'What you lookin' for?' I told her, 'I'm lookin' for what I can steal. You must expect me to steal somethin', you only gonna pay me five dollars a week.'"

"Oh-oh!"

Looking him over lewdly as he pushed by, making clucking sounds with their tongues—

"Lookit that one, now! He beats them mammy dodgers and dicty niggers in there all to pieces."

"Come here, sugar, and tell me all 'boot it—"

Malcolm grinned shyly and kept moving, going past a bathroom crowded with men kneeling on the tiles as if they were praying, bones rattling in the bathtub. More men were clustered in the other rooms, smoking and throwing cards down exultantly on the bed-spreads.

The hallway led at length to a large living room that was almost as crowded as the Savoy ballroom. The rug and the furniture were stacked back against the sideboards and there was an upright piano in one corner, but no one was playing it. Instead, there were only some couples lazily dancing the bump or the mess around to a record of "Evil Woman Blues" while the musicians took their break. Sitting on the chairs and the couch pushed up against the wall, balancing both cigarettes and bottles in their left hands while they held on to their horns with the right.

From time to time, Malcolm noticed, more men would walk out from a back hallway in the seemingly infinite apartment. A woman would generally emerge soon afterward, wiping her face or fiddling with the hem of her dress. When she did, the dour-looking hostess from the door would go over and hand her a couple of bills, plus a little vanity case or a pair of stockings.

Just then he heard someone say, "Here come the boys!," and then a whole new crowd of workingmen began to push their way down the hall and into the already overcrowded room. Truck drivers and longshoremen, porters and waiters; welders and riveters and mechanics just off from the night shift of the defense plants out in Jersey. Still wearing their uniforms, too, dressed in dungarees and overalls, and with grease-stained faces, swearing and laughing, all the maids and calkeener girls following them in as if they were magnetically attracted. The phonograph record came off, and the musicians got up off the couch. Someone started in on the piano and then they were all playing, the workingmen dancing and whooping with their women in the middle of the floor.

Malcolm felt slightly embarrassed in their presence, and too intimidated to compete with them for the women. Instead he retreated to the kitchen, drawn by a home smell that went back deep in his brain—

How it felt when he walked into the kitchen back in Lansing and there was food. Not just pudding made from day-old bread, or the lungs the men used to throw out the back of the slaughterhouse—

In the kitchen there were three more women who looked not unlike the dour-faced woman at the door, filling up whole platters with pork, and fresh-baked bread, and beans. He got a plate of pigs' feet for himself, along with potato salad and cornbread, and another plate of bacon and cabbage on the side. It tasted just as good as it smelled, and he wolfed it down, pausing only to tap a cup on the kitchen table.

"Knock me a shortie," he called out, and one of them took a small cream pitcher and dipped it deep into the washing vat that sat on the floor behind the icebox. She poured it into his cup, and he drank it down at once. Slamming down his dollar on the table, his head swimming now but feeling sated, and better than he had since he'd moved into Ella's, months before. Through all the lonely nights in his little room under the eaves, then up in Portland on that shipyard job, always worrying the boats would fall on him. The trainmen boardinghouses along those reeking Washington alleyways. Feeling so bad for so long—

He rested for a while in the euphoria of his satiety, but then the smell of the food being prepared all around him made him think again of his mother in her kitchen—standing straight-backed as ever at her stove, haughtily dropping the porgies and hushpuppies into the frying pan, filling the whole house with their aroma. But also near the end, when all she did was rock back and forth, all day in the corner. Or the last time he had seen her, in the state hospital. The bottom dropping out of his momentary, food-stoked happiness as he remembered those once quick gray eyes now clouded over as she stared up at them uncomprehendingly. Repeating her litany over and over—

"All the people have gone now—"

I got a gal in Kalamazoo-zoo-zoo—

Malcolm looked around for his friends from the crew, thinking they should go now. Feeling the edge of this great night, the specialness of it beginning to slip away. But there was a growing commotion in the hall then, and Malcolm looked out from the kitchen, happy to be interrupted in his solitude.

"Miranda's here!" he heard a man's liquored voice cry out exultantly. "Put the twisters to the slammers! Miranda's here!"

"Now there's some fine Carstairs!"

It was her—the woman from the Savoy. He thought so almost before he actually saw her, or rather he hoped against hope it was her, with the blind, childlike faith with which he had hoped for things ever since the night his Daddy had died, and always been disappointed. Not tonight. It was her all right, he knew her at once even though she had changed her dress, her shoes, her hair. She was wearing a tight yellow wrap now, held up by two thin straps, and her hair was combed down and just over one eye, almost like Veronica Lake. She had even changed the silly flower in her hair, now sporting a yellow daisy that matched her dress. But there was no mistaking her.

"Hello, boys! How was work?" She grinned and winked at the riveters and truckers, the burly longshoremen still in their overalls, as they hooted and whistled back at her.

She was the only white person in the apartment, at least the only white person he could see, other than a couple of faces peering timorously into the living room from the hall—a salty-haired man with a pipe clenched between his teeth and a tweed jacket, of all things, despite the summer heat; and a plain-looking woman in a strapless black dress. Miranda walked by them without a glance, striding right across the bared floor, the big men and even the smirking, scowling kitchen-mechanic gals making way for her.

"Now we'll have ourselves some recreation," she called out, and winked at them again.

"What kept you, honey?" another man's voice called out.

"Why, sugar, you know I always like to do an encore!" she grinned at them. "How's the kong?"

"Fine as thine!"

"Mind if I dive right in?" she asked, sashaying over to a man in the front of the ring of men watching her and grinning now. As Malcolm watched, wide-eyed, she lifted the coffee cup of corn liquor out of his hand and drank it off in one quick swig—the workingmen howling in delight, the Thursday girls cursing to see it. She sauntered back across the room and, after a word to the man at the piano, dived right in again, as if the two of them had been playing it together for a whole cross-country tour:

Now listen boys and girls
I got one stick
You give me a match and let me take a whiff quick—
I'm gonna knock myself out
I'm gonna kill myself
Knockin' myself out gradually by degrees—

Her voice was full and soft, and pitch-perfect, almost like someone singing in the movies—like Lena Horne's in Stormy Weather, he thought. A little huskier around the edges, perhaps, from all the smoke in the room, but that only made it all the more appealing. She sang slow and blue, but with that secret, ironic smile that half-mocked the words at the same time. It was a tone that seemed to say to Malcolm that nothing very bad was going to happen, or that it had happened already, and that things couldn't get any worse. So different from how his mother sang. Her voice fine, too—but always with that note of pure, plaintive desperation in it—

I never blow gigs
Didn't drink no wine
My man left me
And it changed my mind!
That's why I'm knockin' myself out
Grad-u-ally by de-grees—

There was a shout of approval as she wound it down, the men surging in around her. But Malcolm stood by himself in all the uproar, afraid to go up to her again. She obviously sang professionally with some band here or downtown, was known to the other musicians, the horn players beside him laughing and digging each other in the ribs as she sang.

"Yeah, Miranda truly there tonight!"

"Ain't no one comin' up to that tab—"

He had still thought to just creep away, to go back down the hall and find his buddies, wherever they were. But then she was coming straight toward him, was almost on top of him before he could move. He didn't know what she would do—terrified that she might pretend not to know him at all, and look right past him. Knowing that if she did there was absolutely no play he could make, that he would just have to stand there and take it.

"Red," she said instead, in a low, soft voice that made him ache with relief. Walking right up to him and, to his utter delight, taking his hand in hers again.

"How'd you find your way up here? I didn't think they would let you out of the Savoy," she asked, her smile playful now, making fun of him—but not, he thought, too much.

"Well, you know…" were the only sounds that he was able to produce. Looking around once more for his friends, hoping they could see this but also hoping they had gone.

He started to tell her more, about where they had gone all night and what they had done, but then he stopped abruptly— realizing that he was talking much too much now, and how unlikely it was to impress her. Thinking, too late, that he should have come up with some snappy line for her, some way to play back. He stopped talking altogether, mortified—but then he saw that she was looking at him closely. Smiling a little bit, to be sure, but not grinning, not mocking him at all. Instead it was a look like only his mother had ever given him sometimes, in her moments of clarity. A look full of unfathomable affection, though still regretful over something—

"Do you know what a beautiful boy you are?" she said all of a sudden, her voice still low and intimate. And he was so startled that he could only answer her truthfully:

"No!"

She raised a hand as if she were going to adjust her hair, but instead she touched his face, his eyebrow, his cheek down to his chin. Very swiftly, her hand darting out just like that, so that no one else in the still crowded room would quite catch it. But he had felt it just the same.

"You are. You're such a beautiful boy. How old are you, Red? Seventeen? Younger?"

He laughed, trying to sound derisive, like he knew how she was funning him—but he was rattled again. He had just turned eighteen the month before, but ever since Jarvis had conked his hair for him back in Roxbury he had looked hard and mean enough to earn his favorite name yet—Satan.

No one else had guessed how young he really was. How had this white girl done it?

A new wave of musicians came down the hall, just freed from their gigs downtown, and the cutting began in earnest. Soon it seemed to Malcolm as if everybody in the room was facing off against each other then—ax against ax, trumpet against trumpet, even piano player against piano player on the same bench, all the empty beer bottles and glasses and cups of corn set atop the upright jangling with each note now. The dancers filling up the floor again, so that they were pressed back against the wall, Malcolm desperate not to let go of her in the crowd and Miranda seeming to understand his confusion.

"Come on. You feel like busting down?" she asked him, and he nodded his head vigorously though he wasn't at all sure what she meant.

She leaned over him then, and said something in that same soft voice to a sax player standing on his other side, waiting his turn to blow; something that sounded like Hey, Mezz, how 'bout a mezzroll?—but he was too overwhelmed by the sudden, sweet smell of her skin like flowers, the sweep of her breasts across his chest, to know what she was talking about. She passed a bill over, got back something long and round that the saxophonist suddenly produced in his hand like an extra digit, and immediately tucked it away down her dress.

"C'mon, Red. Let's go make our own teapad."

She led him down the back hall, where he had seen the women going with men for a vanity case, or a roll of stockings, but she had no trouble finding an empty room now, with everyone out on the floor. She sat him down on the bed there, and produced what the sax player had given her again from the front of her dress—the joint as long as a man's index finger and as thick as a thumb. She sat next to him, and pulled a small engraved silver lighter with a diamond chip in it from her purse. Flicking it once to light the joint, then taking a long, stiff pull before she passed both the lighter and the mezzroll over to him.

Malcolm took them nervously. He had blown gage before, back in Boston with Jarvis, and some of the crew, but he was never sure if he was getting it right. He was more agitated than ever by the idea of doing it in her presence—so close beside her on the bed, thinking of how her breasts had moved over him when she scored the joint. He flicked his thumb repeatedly at the lighter, misfiring—and then when he did get the joint going took such a deep drag that the smoke poured out his nose, making him gag and cough.

He would have run out of the room then if she had laughed. He thought that he would have run all the way back to Boston—but instead she cupped her smooth hand around his, flicking on the little jeweled lighter. She lit the joint again, and moved right up against him. Outside now, back up the hall, he could hear a woman's voice singing slow and dreamy, nearly as good as her own.

> *But soon this dance will be ending,*
> *And you are gonna be missed.*
> *But me, I'm not pretending,*
> *I think that it is fun*
> *I think it's fun to be kissed*
> *In the dark—*

"Here, let me show you," she whispered, and reclaimed the joint, taking another long pull on it. Then she put both her hands on his face and kissed him deeply, openmouthed—sending the sweet smoke drifting slowly back into his throat and up to his brain. He sputtered again, but she only smiled and took another long drag, repeating the process. Going even slower this time, letting her lips run slowly across his teeth, his tongue, before she pulled back, just giving him time to expel the smoke.

We'll just let the rest of the world go by.
They can just dance
We're gonna find romance
In the dark—

She kissed him again and again, until he felt he was breathing the gage along with her, the smell of her skin. A great contentment, unlike anything he had ever fully known before, settling in his chest and head, the constant, racing desire in his head just stopping for the moment. She kept kissing him even after she had handed the joint back to him, and for a long time they had nothing to say—stopping for a drag, then necking again. Malcolm kissing his way down to a small cove where her neck met her white, powdered shoulders. There he just rested his head for a long time, happy enough never to move again, basking in the smell and the touch of her.

He raised his head at last to see that she was looking at him, the whites of her dark eyes shining. All around them the room seemed to pulsate agreeably. It was a small space, furnished only with the bed and a chest of drawers, a single chair, but there was a large, blue window—its color the rich, glowing purple-blue that was the last shade of night.

Malcolm stood up and walked over to it, but by the time he got there it was already changing, just replaced by the tattered gray first light of morning. He looked out, down over the Harlem Valley—the rooftops of the tenements, and the bigger, blocky apartment houses with their cone-shaped water towers squatting on top of them like little party hats. A few milk trucks, and the earliest, horse-drawn vegetable and fish carts making their way through the gray streets. The taxis still swooshing their way around them, people in suits and silk dresses still coming out of bars and up from basement after-hours joints.

It's already going again, Malcolm wondered, or don't it ever stop? He remembered dimly that his train was supposed to be leaving early this morning, but he was not going anywhere.

"What do you see?" Miranda called lightly to him from the bed, and he came back to her. "What you lookin' at, baby?"

Something in her voice seemed different, just for a moment, and he glanced at her sharply before he shrugged and sat back down, taking the joint from her again—still trying to understand what seemed so familiar about her.

"Just all of it," he said. "All of it."

"You up here alone?" she asked him solicitously—her white girl's voice clear and churchy once again. "You have any family? Any friends?"

"Nah. Just those guys from the train."

He sat up a little straighter then, turning to her with his eyes bright.

"I'm gonna be a entertainer, too, you know."

"That so?"

He thought at first that she might be making fun of him, but then she reached out and stroked the side of his head again. He took another big toke and decided to tell her all about it, the words pouring out of him.

"That's right. Just like my half-brother. Earl Little Junior. Maybe you heard of him? He used to sing under the name Jimmy Carlton sometimes?"

"Can't say that I have."

"Well, that's prob'ly 'cause he dead. He died a couple years back, they said it was tuberculosis, but we think he was poisoned," Malcolm told her, lowering his head for a moment, before his eyes lit up again.

"I know these things. We all got the second sight in my family, you know. We ain't just trash. My daddy was a Garvey man, an' my mamma's an educated woman. She could always see things, you know."

"Could she, now?"

"Yeah. She saw my daddy's death, too," he said, and went momentarily quiet—seeing that afternoon, and the rabbit's body still running in the dirt.

Miranda leaned in closer and put an arm around him, and suddenly he was surrounded again by the flowery smell of her skin.

"Go ahead," she said, kissing her way down his cheek to his mouth. "You can tell me anything you want."

He couldn't help talking about it, then. That day when he was six years old, and he had come back from school to find them fighting over the rabbits again. They had kept a hutch full of them behind the house in Lansing, jackrabbits and conies and cottontails. They had kept chickens, too, and raised most of their own food on the three acres they owned before the court took it away from them. His mother would kill the chickens, all right, twisting off their heads without blinking—but she never liked to kill the rabbits. She argued that they made more money selling them out by the road, but Malcolm knew what she really believed, that the Bible held they were unclean for eating—though she didn't dare say that to her husband, who was a jackleg preacher and considered himself the final authority on all things having to do with God's word.

That day when he was six, Earl had ordered her to take one of them from the hutch for his supper, and they had waged another one of their monumental battles, ranting and throwing things at each other all through the house, and out onto the front porch. There Malcolm had waited, trembling, until they both came storming through the screen door. Barely noticing him, intent as they were on fighting each other. His father cursing, his mother weeping and spewing out insults the way she did when she was maddened beyond all reason or fear.

She was still holding the long, gray rabbit by its ears, Malcolm saw, when she stalked out on the porch. It was one of his favorites, a bunny he had named Betty, after a white girl at school he was partial to. The rabbit was still alive, writhing and struggling under his mother's tight grip, though things had a way of smashing when his mother was in this sort of rage and she was already clenching her fist around Betty's ears so tightly that it was making desperate, squeaking rabbit sounds.

She ignored it, running down the porch steps and after her husband as if in a trance. But just as she reached him, Earl had turned and yanked the animal out of her hands. Before they could do anything he had closed one large hand around the animal's head and pulled it right off—dropping both the head and the quivering, blood-gushing body of the rabbit in the bare, packed dirt of their front yard. Then he had turned and walked off again through the yard without another word, heading down the road toward town. His mother stunned into silence for the moment—staring down with Malcolm at the rabbit where it still seemed to be trying to run, its legs twitching. The head lying on one side, the rabbit's single, visible eye fluttering as it stared up blindly into the afternoon sun.

"That was when she saw it," Malcolm told Miranda on the bed. "She saw it right in that rabbit there, an' she grabbed up her apron and she run after him."

"Saw what?" she asked.

"'Early!' she was yellin' after him. 'Early! If you go, you won't come back!'"

"And did he?"

He told her the rest of it right then, feeling warmer and more secure in her arms than he ever had in anyone's, even his mother's. He told her how his father had waved, strangely enough, at the bottom of the hill just down from their house. Turned, despite all his rage, when he heard her voice and waved just like that, as if he were only going on one of his preaching or Garvey trips for the afternoon.

He told her, too, how it had felt, waiting all through the night for his Daddy to return. His mother picking up the rabbit from the ground, skinning it and parsing it with her kitchen knives, and carefully frying up its pieces for supper as she had been told. They had all sobbed and carried on about the idea of eating Betty, and Malcolm had felt sick to his stomach at the prospect. But as the evening wore on and they got hungrier, they had eaten up their rabbit pieces, delicious in the collards and onions and butter she had cooked it in. All of them falling asleep right where they were then, at the kitchen table or in the front parlor, in the unaccustomed luxury of having enough to fill their bellies.

Only his mother had stayed up, pacing about the house, rigorously cleaning up the plates and pans. She was the only one still awake when the police car had come, its headlights shining through their windows, starting Malcolm and the rest of them from their sleep. Usually they would be told to stay low and keep quiet when the prowler came by, a visit from the police meaning courts and liens, and eviction notices. But this night his mother had run to the door in her bathrobe, screaming already when she saw the cop standing there, knowing what it meant even before he could tell her what had happened.

She had gone with him at once, had wrapped her robe tighter around her and gone with the policeman to Sparrow Hospital without another word, leaving the rest of them to sit up and talk through the night, speculating on what had happened. Wilfred and Hilda had thought their Daddy was in jail, and Philbert had thought he might be in the hospital, but Malcolm was sure already he was dead.

"I knew it right then, maybe even before he *was* dead," he told Miranda, very seriously. "When something is about to happen, I can feel it. Nothing in this world ever catches me napping. It's the truth!"

"All right, I believe you," she told him, gently pulling him back down to the bed, smiling sympathetically—but still not laughing at him.

"I could see him lying right out on the trolley tracks there—"

Only when the sky was the same tattered gray it was now had his mother returned, looking numbed. They were all hungry by then, their stomachs aching for some kind of breakfast, but instead they had stood silently around the kitchen listening to her tell them, in her newly numbed voice, how she had found their father— his left arm crushed and his left leg splayed open and almost cut off above the knee, barely alive by the time she arrived. Unable to say a thing, drugged up on morphine as he was—only staring up at her from the hospital bed with his one good eye, his chest heaving.

"They say he tried to step up on the trolley, and he missed his step—but we never believed that!" Malcolm told Miranda, almost shouting now to remember it. "They said he didn't see the trolley 'cause there wasn't any streetlights, an' he had one eye. But we knew who killed him!"

"Who?"

"It was the Black Legion!" Malcolm told her in a low voice now. "They killed him, 'cause he was a race man! Everybody knew that about my daddy. He was a proud black man, an' they left him to die on the trolley tracks."

"Come here," she said to him, but he didn't move on the bed, still thinking that maybe she was laughing at him.

"You don't know 'bout such things, bein' a white girl—"

"I know about a lot of things," she said, and took one more toke and pressed her lips against his. Then she raised the skirt of her dress, and sat on his lap and pushed him slowly down onto the bed. Kissing him again and again as she lay over him. Carefully undoing his drape, unbuttoning his coat. Peeling off the pleats, undoing the big, gold letter "L." She undressed him as she would a child, until he lay all but naked beneath her, and then she began to move on top of him.

He reached his hands up gingerly to feel her breasts, and she let him—but then she grabbed his wrists and made him stop when he began to squeeze too hard and enthusiastically. Still smiling at him as she lowered the strings of her yellow dress, working it slowly down until her breasts were bared to him. They were full and heavy, with aureolas and nipples that were large and dark in the half-light, and he reached for her eagerly again, but she made him go slow. Holding his hands again and running them over her gently, showing him how she liked it. Sliding them on down her sides, where he could just feel the ridges of her ribs, the slope of her fine, wide hips and bottom. When she leaned down and licked and sucked on his fingers, he thought he would not be able to bear it anymore, but she just looked down and chuckled at him.

"Hold up now, Red," she told him, and got up to shuck her tight dress the rest of the way off her body, then her panties and her shoes after it, until she climbed back on the bed altogether naked now, and still chuckling. Leaning down over him again, the gracious slope of her breasts just touching his chest.

She held herself wholly against him for a moment, like a blanket. Her sweet-smelling arms around his neck, her thighs pressed against his, the scratch of her hair against him almost unbearably promising. Then she kissed him on the mouth again, long and hard, and sat up—still teasing him, still not doing anything right away, until in his desperation he finally gave her what she was looking for:

"Put me in you," he whispered frantically, mortified by the words even as they came out, but desperate to say them. "Put me in you!"

She laughed once more—a light, pretty sound—and began to work her hips against him.

It was over fast, but afterward she lay silently with him, stroking his cheek, his hair, his body, and soon they began again. This time it went slower, and he was astonished and gleeful over her reaction, and this time, afterward, they lay grinning together, almost nose to nose, with her arm around his neck and his hand still on her hip.

"Goddamn, goddamn," he said, unable to get over it. "It was never nothin' like this. Goddamn!"

After that they talked for a long time again, and though he had regretted at first saying anything at all about his mother or his father, he told her still more—things he had never thought he would tell anyone. He told her how soon after Earl had died, his mother had walked over to Mrs. Stohrer's, a white neighbor she liked and often confided in about the travails of her husband, and pulled a butcher knife out from under her coat. Dangling it, point down, on her own knee for a while, before she pointed it at Anna Stohrer and explained how white people had killed her husband, and now, she was sorry, but she had to take a white life in return. Mrs. Stohrer had been frightened enough to pick up her chair in self-defense, but just then her husband had come in and his mother had run back out into the still, Michigan night. The Stohrers had not pressed charges, but stories about the incident had begun to circulate throughout Lansing, and then down through the Pleasant Cove school, and that was when Malcolm had first begun hearing from white people that his mother was crazy.

And he told her about how for a long time after his Daddy's death he would not eat—something that would soon be easy enough to do in his mother's house—telling everyone who would listen that those who try to eat disappear, and never return. He had stopped sleeping as well, claiming, Only dead people stretch out. But then he really had gotten out of the habit of it, and terrified by the darkness that seemed to grow blacker and denser around him, every minute of the night, he had tried to literally wiggle beneath his brothers' bodies in the bed. Still half asleep, they had kicked him off, irritated, so that he had to lie back and just watch the dark— able to finally nod off in relief only when he saw that last, purple-blue glow that told him the night was finally about to release its grip.

And then, one more thing he had told her, when it was already well on into the morning, and she had finally tried to shush him and begun to move against his body again—

"You're my first white girlfriend," he had whispered, right into her ear, as if this were the deepest, darkest secret of all. Thinking, First that wasn't holding a hat over her face, anyway. But he had decided she should be the first.

"Don't tell nobody. Particu'ly not those guys on the train. I told 'em I already had one up in Boston, they'd have a helluva laugh if they knew. But you're my first."

She had only chuckled again.

"Oh, sugar," she said. "Your secret's safe with me."

CHAPTER FIVE

MALCOLM

He sat up suddenly in the little room, fully awake. It took him a few seconds to remember where he was—the fantastic, dreamlike night he had had, and the white girl. But Miranda was gone now, and he was all alone in the narrow bed. He slung his long legs over the side, still naked, his head throbbing—not sure if it had all been a dream, or if he was awake even now.

But the big uncovered window was bright yellow and white in the late morning sun. So bright and streaked that he had to shield his eyes from it, so that at first he did not even notice there was another man in the room with him.

He almost jumped in the air when he did—swinging his legs back onto the bed, scrambling to yank the sheet up over his body. He looked around frantically for his drape with his wallet in the inside jacket pocket, remembering everything he had heard on the train about setups like this—

The man only sat where he was, in the room's one chair, staring calmly at the wall in front of him. His back perfectly straight, hands resting on his knees. He appeared at first glance to be very old, even ancient. A small, frail old man, with lined, papery skin the color of almonds, and hooded, knowing eyes—though looking closer Malcolm thought that he might not even be fifty.

But the most unusual thing about him was his clothes. He was wearing a plain black meeting suit with a prim bow tie, and on his head was a little cap—much like the one Malcolm had seen on the man standing on the ladder, haranguing the crowd the night before.

A round black cap, embroidered in gold with all the symbols of the universe, with suns, and comets, and planets, but most prominent of all a single star, embraced by a crescent moon.

"Who are you?! What you doin' here?" Malcolm sputtered. But the man only smiled.

"You might as well ask who you are, what you're doing here," he answered softly, still without looking at Malcolm. His voice sounding like the Deep South—Alabama, or maybe Georgia—and looking more closely at him, Malcolm thought that he could even be the man he had seen on that ladder, next to the big American flag.

"What the hell you talkin' 'bout, old man?"

"Black man, sittin' in a white woman's bed," the old man said. "Black man in a white man's land. How came you here? What are you looking for?"

What's that to you, Malcolm wanted to tell him. But he could not say it—the man's words piercing through him, though he wasn't even sure he knew what they meant.

"Why shouldn't I be here?" he asked instead, truly inquiring despite himself, and looked closely at the man's face again. His eyes didn't seem to move or even blink, much less turn in his direction, so that Malcolm wondered if he might be blind.

"Who are you, anyway?" he asked him.

"Oh, I go by many names," the man said. "I am called One Much and Muk Muhd. I am called Muck Muck and Muck-a-Mud, and Eli Muck Muck and Muck Eli Muck and Elijah Muck Muck. I am One Eli and One Elizah, and Elijah Black, and Elijah Ford, and Elijah Bogans. I am Bulam Bogans, and Gullam Bogans, and Gulam Gogans. And Elijah Poole and Robert Poole, and Robert Takahashi and Robert Takis, and James Dodd and J. Dodd and Mohammed Rassoull, and Black Moses.

"And that's only for starters," he said, and laughed deeply. "I have many more names, almost as many as the names of God—far more than the white man's government down in Washington can keep track of. But each one is my own name, given to me by God and by the Estimable Wallace D. Fard, and not one of them is a slave name, such as your own."

"My Daddy give me my name!" Malcolm told him indignantly, but the little man in the chair only seemed to shrug.

"So you say. So you believe."

"And why shouldn't I be here?"

"No reason. As a so-called Ne-gro, why shouldn't you root around in the muck for slops? Why shouldn't you rut with the white man's dog-fornicatin' woman? Drink his whiskey, listen to his devil's music? No reason a'tall. Not so long as you consider yourself to be a useless, no-'count, so-called Negro."

"What the hell're you talkin' about, old man? 'Course I'm a Negro!" Malcolm shouted at him—but the man only laughed again, and went silent. Slowly, gradually, right before Malcolm's eyes, his papery skin seemed to grow thinner and thinner, his whole body became more and more transparent—until at last he faded away altogether, leaving behind only the chair.

Malcolm stared after him for a long time—then he felt his head pounding again, and lay back in bed, and shut his eyes.

He awoke sometime later and looked over to the chair immediately, only to see that it was still empty. Miranda was still gone, and his head still hurt. The yellow light coming through the dirty, streaked window was more blinding and painful than ever—though he was gratified, now, to see his things all laid out by the chest of drawers with touching care. His zoot was hung up on hangers, and his shirt and even his underwear were carefully folded and placed on top of the bureau—his wallet and watch placed neatly on top of them.

He got dressed quickly, working the Punjab pants over his legs as fast as he dared while still careful not to wreck them in his hungover state. Thinking all the time about the dream he had had—one of those dreams that seemed more real than life. A manifestation of the street preachers he had seen, the kong he'd been drinking, the whole enveloping rush of Harlem, all around him. One of those dreams that stuck in the back of your head, to be worked over, and gnawed at all day long. So vivid, so detailed, even if it didn't make any sense. There was something very familiar about the little man that stuck with him—something he recognized beyond his resemblance to the man on the ladder. It was in the way he spoke, the Deep South in his mouth, how sure he was of himself, and the way he called upon God, and damned the white man—

He slipped back on his jacket and watch, shoved his wallet into his coat pocket after a hurried count of his cash, making sure his trainman's pass was still there. Intent first on just getting out of there, still not certain it wasn't a setup—the white girl, the strange brown man, all of it.

But the rest of the apartment was silent as a funeral parlor, not a living soul in evidence. Only the rolled-back rug and the chairs scattered around the living room, the upright piano with all the bottles and glasses still on top to provide any sign that he had not simply imagined everything that had happened to him in his first eighteen hours in Harlem.

He padded quietly down the long hall, still expecting to meet someone at any moment, but all the doors of the rooms were shut. He thought of knocking on one, still hoping to find Miranda—but it seemed highly unlikely to him that she actually lived in this place.

That was all right. He had a name for her now, at least. There couldn't be too many white women like her in Harlem, or anywhere else. First things first. His train had gone, and he had to recover his bag from Mrs. Fisher's and get a new pad, a job. He had to get breakfast.

He padded noiselessly out of the apartment in his soft-soled, sweet-potato shoes. Shutting the door behind him as quietly as he could, then walking quickly down the hall and swinging himself down the stairs, whistling as he did.

Flying home—

Outside, the full heat of the day had not yet descended, and the air and sunshine felt good after the dark, smoky cave of the apartment. He strode down St. Nicholas Avenue, still whistling, until he reached Broadway. There he found a soda fountain where he bought a doughnut and a Coke through the window, and stood eating them along the sidewalk, just watching all the people on their way to work. The maids, and the calkeener girls already back out on their day off. Some of them obviously in the same clothes they had worn the night before, on their way to see a movie or a show—and looking him over from top to bottom. Colored men carrying lawyers' briefcases, and doctors' bags, strutting self-importantly to their offices in their conservative suits. Giving him the fish-eye, in his zoot, though he didn't care, just thrilled as he was to see them—

Real Negro doctors, and real Negro lawyers! Not like those ridiculous pretenders up on the Hill, the Boston Four Hundred Ella was always trying to join. Strolling off every morning with their newspapers, only to sweep the floors of the firms, or the hospitals they worked in—

He wondered what he could do in such a place, or if he should just go back to the railroad and beg for his old job back. Surely Pappy Cousins would get it for him, if anybody could. He would still be back in Harlem for layovers like this, even whole weekends, if he could swing it. Maybe he could track down Miranda then—

A diminutive brown woman turned the corner and came down the block toward him. She was pushing an old baby carriage with the hood torn off it, and the bed filled with gleaming silver porgies, and sea trout. As he watched she stopped there, crooked her head up at the tenement windows, and began to sing out her own song:

"A tisket, a tasket,
I sell fish by the basket,
And if you folks don't buy some fish
I'm gonna put you in a casket.
I'll carry you on down the avenue,
And not a thing you'll do.
I'll dig, dig, dig, all around,
Then I'll put you in the ground.
A tisket, a tasket,
I sell 'em by the basket—"

Malcolm smiled, then laughed out loud, and finished up his doughnut and the Coke in its little cone-shaped paper cup. Heading on down Broadway, thinking that he might head over to Small's, and ask about that slave—knowing that he was going to stay.

CHAPTER SIX

JONAH

The City hit them in the face like a dirty washcloth. *It was the worst place in the world to come home to,* Jonah always thought—the heat and the dirt and the noise reenveloping them at once, as if they had never been away. It took him days to adjust to it again, to the crowds, and the pace, and the hardness. *Was this what it was like, coming back to a faithless lover? Of course he wouldn't know, he had been spared so many of life's humiliations. Until today.*

Amanda sat in the Checker with her head back against the top of the seat, eyes half closed and fanning herself with her hat. Acting as if she was all but overcome with the heat, though he was sure that she was just trying to spare him from feeling he had to talk about it. They rode in silence up Seventh Avenue, and as they crossed 110th Street and passed into Harlem, he felt both a sense of relief and a whole new weariness wash over him.

Everything he saw appeared to him to be old, and worn, and lacking. Usually he loved to see so much activity on the streets, the sheer human energy there at all hours of the night and day. But now he saw only what was dreary, and pathetic. The sidewalks filled with women, strutting off bravely into the early summer evening, their hair pressed and scoured and primped into some stiff facsimile of what they thought a white woman's hair looked like. Their dresses too tight or too short, the stitching showing where they had been taken in so many times after being passed down from family or friends, or employers.

And right behind them, the men. Many of them in uniform—

Harlem's latest plague. Their faces—black or white—leering and wolfish. Others loping along the sidewalk in their ridiculous new zoot suits, or gang jackets, whistling and calling out to every pretty girl they passed. Most of them obviously looking for a hustle, corn liquor, reefers, cocaine, worse. Not a one of them with a thing on their minds beyond a drink and a dance, a woman—

Even the things he saw that usually gave him solace, the little things that delighted him, felt sour and heavy now. Along the sidewalks the fire hydrants were still open, half-naked children shrieking as they dashed back and forth through the spray. No pools still, and hardly any playgrounds. Old men from the Islands with their potbellies and goiters, spread out on the steps of the stoops or sitting at little folding card tables, slamming down their dominoes. The women leaning over the apartment-house window ledges in short-sleeved housedresses, waiting for the fish man or more likely the policy runner to come by. Screeching out numbers as they threw down their last nickels and dimes wrapped in scraps of paper. Snatched up by the quick, furtive young men on the sidewalk who nodded, and ran off—

Too many people in too little space, with too little to do. Still not enough good jobs, even with the war. No good hospitals, no doctors. Everything needing to be changed, fixed, made better. By whom?

Even the beautiful old buildings that he always loved to look at seemed dismal, and tattered now. He noticed every broken pane of glass, every missing shingle, or cornice. The blocks of fine brownstones with their stained-glass windows, the Victorians with their turrets and rounded brick; the stately redbrick apartment houses— all of them now seemed to him no more than the crumbling ruins of some greater, vanished civilization.

Poisonous thoughts, on a bad day. And yet there was that sense of relief, too. How long does it take to get used to one's ghetto? To cling to it?

The relief was only the comfort provided by familiarity, he told himself. Seeing all the reassuring landmarks, the jeweled, electric towers and marquees of the RKO Alhambra and the Regency, the Apollo and the Renaissance Ballroom. The proud stone-and-brick fronts of the great churches, each of them carefully distinctive. The Greek temple that was Mount Olivet, with its massive Corinthian columns; Metropolitan Baptist with its huge, sloping, black-shingled roof and conical spires; Salem Methodist with its spectacular round stained-glass window out front, and the Abyssinian, and Mother A.M.E. Zion, and Bethel African, and on and on. All of them trying so hard to shine before the Lord. Their ministers and deacons, ushers and elders and church mothers who he all knew so well—the same people staying, doing their duty, year after year.

But it was more than that, he knew. He still felt some of the excitement, the physical joy he used to feel whenever he came back to Harlem, for all the life around him. All of these people, all of these bright and shining and still hopeful souls, making their way as best they could. Despite all the Lord had denied them—

He was at home here. And here, he knew, he might live out his whole life in comfort and prestige, just by virtue of who he had been born. Free from any worry of being beaten in front of his wife.

He tried to tell himself that this was an illusion. That he could, even here, even in his clerical collar, still be picked up off the street at any time for so much as giving lip to a white cop. Taken down to the precinct house, given the third degree just as so many members of his congregation had been, even some of the very deacons who had hired him. But he knew that was a lie, too—that he was one of the very, very few with an exemption. And an escape, if he wanted it.

Their cab turned onto West 139th Street, and they were home. Amanda started to reach for the door handle, but he put a hand on her arm, gently restraining her, just wanting to look at it for another long moment. Entranced as he always was by what a beautiful place they lived in—perhaps the most beautiful block in the entire City. Strivers Row.

The brick front of their home was usually a rusty, burnt color, but through some trick of the late afternoon sunlight it looked almost golden now, floating above the graceful trees. Our golden ghetto. A block and a half of connected townhouses, designed a generation before by the best architects in the City—built for a white upper class that never quite did show up. Their own built in the style of the Florentine Renaissance, rumor had it by Stanford White himself. Fourteen rooms and two baths, with veined marble fireplaces and cut-glass doors, and French hardwood floors. Shaded by rows of slender trees in front, with a separate garage in the alley out back, where their green, streamlined, prewar Lincoln was slumbering now.

They had even been named the Kingscourt Houses, officially. Strivers Row the nickname applied by their fellow Harlemites who affected to mock its residents' pretensions though everyone knew that they, too, would give their eyeteeth to live here. Here, the local beat cops touched their caps with their nightsticks when he passed by, their ruddy Irish faces grinning broadly. Their smiles more than a little patronizing, he knew, full of the guileless joy one might see on the faces of people watching a particularly cunning monkey in the Central Park Zoo: Well, well, look at all the wealthy darkies!

But no more a threat than that. Nothing more ominous than a permanent condescension. Don't make it into that, he told himself. Don't make your running into some kind of protest, some statement against hypocrisy. He was safe here, at least for now. For as long as he chose to stand it.

He helped their cabbie carry their bags up the high front stoop, and then it was just the two of them inside. Standing a little uncertainly in the marble foyer, like guests in their own home, breathing in the dark, faintly musty atmosphere of a house that had been closed up for two weeks. Jonah was acutely aware of the stillness—sure that Amanda sensed it, too. Their footsteps echoed in the hallway, the front parlor, and the connected dining room. The early evening light filtering down on them through the tinted, blue skylight that dominated the house just as the great, stained-glass window behind the altar—the single eye of God—dominated a cathedral. *His father's eye?*

The house was too big for the two of them. Jonah could already feel again how oppressive it was, how they might rattle around in it for years. It was a house in which one felt bound to have children, and he was sure that was no small reason why his father had picked it up for two thousand dollars, twenty years before, when it finally became apparent that the white people weren't coming, and after all the years of moving on, he was sure he had found a place to plant his seed.

Jonah knew the old man would have been indifferent to anything so fancy for himself, having been raised on a waterfront alley. His indulgences had always run to much more immediate, visceral desires, such as food. The excuse was that it was supposed to serve as a rectory, but after Jonah had married Amanda, his father had forced the diaconate to sign it over to him, personally, and gone to live in his two small rooms in the back of his church. Just as his father had forced them to accept his son in the pulpit, his money and his will never truly distinguishable from the church's to begin with, making sure to bind his congregation to him by the ties of New York real estate, as well as the ties of God.

Well, then, they would have children. This silence was intolerable. Unless. Unless there was another way out—

"I should go check on Daddy," he murmured.

"All right," Amanda said, her voice strained, and distant. Still angry at him—no, still embarrassed for him from the train, he knew, and it made him feel ashamed all over again.

"I'll start airing the place out, and see about supper."

"Don't bother yourself about it. Sandwiches will do fine."

"All right. Better go on, then," she said, looking past him, her face still hurt and questioning and puzzled.

He wanted to stay and talk to her then, to take her in his arms and try to explain to her. To tell her all the things that kept moving through his head these days, unceasingly, the way the movie newsreels looped the same, short clips of tanks and marching men over and over again. But he felt the tears welling up in his own eyes, and he moved quickly to retrieve his hat and head for the door. The last thing he wanted, now, was to be comforted by her.

"Don't wait up for me if I'm too late, you know how he likes to talk—" he called as he went out. Thinking: Is this what it will be like that day? Saying I'm just going out to see him?

He padded quickly down the stoop of the golden house, walking to the east. Passing the sets of pillars with their aristocratic admonishment—Walk Your Horses!—leftover from the vanished days when the white sportsmen used to use Lenox Avenue as their track, racing their trotters down from the Polo Grounds to Central Park. The street very quiet this evening, most of their neighbors away still. Many of them probably up at Oak Bluffs themselves, or one of the other carefully restricted Negro resorts. On any other night he might exchange courtly nods with all the varied elite of Harlem who were not up on Sugar Hill. Dining out on the encounters—

"It's better than any upper-class white neighborhood," he liked to say. "They tend to segregate themselves by occupation. Why, anytime I want I can look out the window and see an architect, or a jazz pianist, or a prizefighter go by. I bet they can't do that on Fifth Avenue!"

It was his standard line, whether they were at a dinner party up on the Hill, or having cocktails somewhere out in the little enclave in St. Albans, or some gala at the Hotel St. George, and it never failed to draw a laugh of recognition. The other young couples agreeing righteously—Why, that's so! There's so much more diversity in Negro society. We're the true egalitarians—

But lately he had begun to think about something Jakey Mendelssohn's cousin had said about Poland. They put everyone together, he had told Jonah—or rather Jakey had said it, sitting on a stool in the shoddy back room of his department store, translating grimly out of the young man's pidgin of Yiddish and halting English.

They picked them up, and put them all in the ghetto together— rich Jews and poor Jews, and everybody in between. Violin players and furniture merchants, and street peddlers. It didn't matter who you were, in you went—

Which is how we live already, Jonah had thought. Which is how you live when they round you up. Rich and poor, the talented tenth and all the rest—all thrown in together. Same as in the ghettos of Warsaw and Cracow, and Theriesen. And what then?

He cut over to Lenox Avenue, heading north, and into the Thursday-night crowds. Beginning to feel a little better again among so many people, relieved to walk amidst the raucous goings-on of a City street again after all the carefully orchestrated strolls up on the Vineyard.

So what if all these people, all these young women, were going out to have a good time? he told himself, knowing that was what Adam would say. Weren't they entitled to have a little before going back to the work week? "And never a laugh but the moans come double; And that is life—"

But as he walked on uptown he sensed that even here, out on the avenue, there was something missing from the usual hilarity. Something almost palpable, which he had noticed as well before they had gone to the Vineyard, but which he still could not quite put his finger on.

He could see it in the faces of the police—patrolling the streets in their radio cars, on horseback or on foot or those damned motorcycles. Since the war had started there, were more cops in Harlem than Jonah had ever seen before. Always at least two or three of them together, their eyes wary, even their horses jumpy and skittish. Their policeman's sixth sense picking up something—though he suspected that they, too, did not quite know what it was, the crowds no more or less than what they had been for months.

Then he saw it. What it was that made the cops so jumpy, what was making everyone so uneasy, even if they didn't know it. It was how the people were together, out on the stoops and street corners, outside the bars and barbershops, leaning against lamp posts and parking meters. The people who were gathered everywhere, and who Jonah now realized had been there all along, partly hidden behind the shifting screen of servicemen, and excited Thursday girls hurrying along the sidewalks.

That was no thing, by itself. Harlem lived half its life out on the street, especially in the summer. People hanging out of windows, sleeping on fire escapes, drinking and roistering on the rooftops. Doing anything to escape the suffocating heat of kitchens, and the overstuffed railroad flats.

But this was different, different in a way that Jonah had never seen before and in a way that the cops, never being more than wary visitors to Harlem, could only sense unconsciously but would never put their finger on. He saw it clearly now. The little huddles of hustlers and numbers runners—sitting around in the barbershops with middle-aged workingmen who usually spent all their time complaining about their wives, or jawing over the relative merits of Satchel Paige and Martin Dihigo. Church mothers who could generally be found chatting in beauty parlors—sitting out on the stoops now with chippies and working girls, with their scarred faces and backless, stained satin dresses. There were race men with Holiness disciples, Seventh Day Adventists with Methodists, Garveyites with zoot suiters, Islanders with Southerners. All the impassable divides of Harlem society had been bridged almost overnight, as if by magic in these street-corner congregations, and Jonah felt bewildered and not a little chagrined that he himself, had as their supposed shepherd, not seen it before.

Stranger still, they all seemed to be gathered around some piece of paper, something written, whether it was a telegram, or a scrap of stationery, or a sheet of newsprint. Harlemites were always reading, of course, it was the only way to pass a life spent waiting on line, for the bus, the trolley, half a chance. Poring through paperbacks and library books and newspapers; copies of Life magazine, and racing forms and dream books, and the Bible.

But this was different, too. Now they were reading out loud, instead of silently to themselves. Jonah realized that he had been seeing that all spring and summer, one person reading from a paper while the rest leaned in, listening intently, sometimes taking the paper and reading from it themselves, as if they could not quite believe what they had heard. He sidled over to a stoop when he saw one young woman's lips moving over a leaf of ruled paper, as if from a child's elementary school notebook, and slowed his steps so he could listen to her:

"'...we are fed only on cold cuts if we get that and kept completely cut off from the rest of the camp here. None of us colored soldiers are allowed to go to the hospital even for a social disease but are just given a shot and left to work in the kitchens,'" the girl reading in a halting monotone, while the women on the steps all around her—church women, and laundry girls, and chippies with big gaps in their teeth—grunted and tsked, and shook their heads.

"Tha's not right!"

"They can't do that, not no more!"

"'...our officers have been taken away and we are now under white officers from Southern colleges. So when we are right we are wrong. They tell us niggers from New York are too damned smart and don't know this is a white man's country. If you please can, I want you to bring these conditions to someone's attention and request that we be removed out of Georgia as soon as possible. I'm writing you at great personal risk, so act according'—"

"It's just like we been sold South again!"

"Who knows what can happen to them boys down there—"

The faces of the women twisted with anger, as they leaned forward to look over the paper. He had seen them before—the mothers and wives and girlfriends who had come to his church office with similar letters from their young men down in army camps in Georgia and Mississippi, and Louisiana. Their boys kicked and cursed in the South Pacific, robbed of their boots by white soldiers in London. Fed jam and bread, when they got any supper at all, forced to sleep on the floors, and in the baggage racks of troop trains—

He had sent each one of them on to the adjutant general's office in the War Department, as he had promised, along with a polite note—and with the signatures and any identifying salutation carefully sliced out, so afraid had the mothers been of retribution being visited upon their boys. After more than a year he had received a single, mocking form letter—almost more insulting than if he had heard nothing at all—thanking him for his interest in the welfare of the nation's troops.

But what will it do for us, now that we're all together? What did it do for those Jews in Poland?

He had seen, too, the graffitti on the alley walls: This is a white mans government and a white mans war and its no damn good. Had even heard about the late-night meetings in certain basement rooms, where hard-core race men, and mysterious visitors gathered to celebrate each new Japanese victory. Telling each other that this time the white man was finally finished. Nonsense, to be sure, and most people knew it was. But still—

He pulled himself away from the women on the stoop, and continued on up Lenox Avenue to West 144th Street. There he turned the corner again, and stood across from his father's church in the fading light.

Everything, in that moment, was just as he had remembered it from when he was a boy, which was exactly what he had wanted. Smelling the pungent odor of the river, only a couple of blocks away. Listening to the crackle of somebody frying fish, the blat! of a clarinet warming up in one of the clubs.

And before him, the Invisible Institution. Made flesh by his father—

It was easily the least pretentious of all the great Harlem churches, even more homely than the ostentatiously humble St. Philip's. A massive, humpbacked structure, built completely out of redbrick, without any flourishes like the pearly white baptismal font at the Abyssinian, or the imperial green dome and beveled stained-glass windows of Mount Morris Ascension. Built from no real architectural style, with a simple archway for an entrance and one high steeple and bell tower placed over its west wing.

"It's got to have a steeple on it," was all that his father had insisted on when it was built. "A church has got to have a steeple!"

But his first church hadn't had one. That had been long before his time, but Jonah had seen photographs of it, carefully preserved by the New Jerusalem church historian. It had been only one more storefront church, down in the old colored neighborhood on Minetta Lane—just like the small-fry cults that filled so many of the blocks of Harlem now, and which so many of his fellow ministers liked to mock with that sobriquet but which nearly all of their higher and mightier edifices had sprung from. After Minetta Lane there had been a converted stable in the Tenderloin, then a brownstone on Columbus Hill. Even when the congregation had first moved to Harlem, they had still been too few and too poor to do any more than rent a carriage house on West 135th Street.

It was his father who had willed the church into being. Conjuring it from the ground up, cajoling and browbeating it into existence. They had called it the Penny-a-Day church, after his father's insistence that every member of the congregation, including women and children over the age of five years, had to contribute at least a penny a day. Or their labor, or some thing, a nail, a brick, a two-by-four. No questions asked, in his father's eternally pragmatic way, about whether they had gotten it from one of the City's innumerable construction sites.

He had commanded it, and they had obeyed. Why wouldn't they? Jonah could remember the chill that had run through him when, still in short pants, he had sat in the first pew and listened to his father hammer at his flock from the makeshift pulpit in the old carriage house.

"This church will purify you as you build it!" he had told them, raising his fist high over the Bible. "Each one of you has a sin, a penny's worth of sin you can give up. Or if you do not—if you really are that poor—each one of you has at least an hour's worth of sinning you can give up for the Lord! Building this church will sweat the sin off you!"

—and then shifting just as dramatically. Not simply berating them but firing their imaginations, with not only what the church could be but what they could be as well—

"We can do this thing. There's many things in life that are beyond a man's power. There are things in this world, evil things, that even a mother can do nothing about, and that is the Will of God and why we need the saving grace of Jesus Christ our Lord.

"But this is something we can do, here and now. Something we can take hand to hammer, and brick, and do right here. We will do this thing, we will build this church to the glory of God. And people will look upon it, and they will know that our people can do anything in this world!"

He could feel it, too, only six or seven years old, sitting up in his hard wooden pew. Jonah could feel how he had them. The congregation standing and leaning forward, overflowing the sweaty, overcrowded carriage house that still smelled of horseflesh and dung, and old seat leather. Holding them so enthralled that had his father announced they were going to go forth that very morning, and march up to the weedy, dismal site a block from the Harlem River and erect the entire church before nightfall, Jonah thought that they just might have tried it.

If only he had ever felt a response like that himself—

He tried to dismiss the thought as one more vanity, but he couldn't help himself. Standing across the street from the church his father had built out of words—

What must it be like? That sort of power? And him not even truly a believer!

Jonah crossed over, and pushed open one of the heavy, oaken front doors—the sounds of the street banished instantly. Inside, he was hit at once with the familiar churchy smell of wax and flowers, paper and dust.

The sanctuary was nearly as simple as its exterior. The exposed crossbeams holding up a simple white ceiling and walls, the only color the stained-glass Bible stories in the windows, and the flowers piled up around the altar, tiger lilies and snapdragons, liatris and roses. The rounded, bowl-like nave lit solely by candles, all but obscuring the four or five worshipers scattered around the broad half circle of bare wooden pews, their heads bowed.

He paid no attention to any of that, though, but simply stood, listening, just inside the vestibule. Trying to hear him—the deep, raspy breathing that seemed to Jonah to fill the entire church, as if it really were just one great extension of his body—

"Good evening, Rev'rend Minister. It's good to see you home, sir!"

Henry Thigpen, the church usher in attendance, came walking quickly down the aisle to greet him. Carrying himself with immense dignity in spite of how heavily he was perspiring in his white gloves, and the formal frock coat with a bright purple usher's ribbon pinned to the lapel.

"I trust you and Mrs. Dove had a fine vacation, Rev'rend?" he asked, not taking Jonah's hand but folding his own gloved hands before him. Cocking his head slightly to one side in the solemn, deferential manner he had perfected as a banker's valet on Park Avenue.

"Yes, it was…fine, Brother Thigpen," Jonah told him. His eyes sweeping over the dim church before him. Still listening.

"Not much of a turnout tonight, is there?"

"Well, it's the summer, you know..." Thigpen said, dropping his eyes to the ground.

"Yes."

His father had always insisted on keeping the church open twenty-four hours a day and he had honored the tradition—an usher or a church mother always on duty, day and night, in case anyone might be troubled enough in soul to want him summoned.

Yet no one ever did. In all the time since Jonah had been ordained and pushed through the diaconate by his father to succeed him—nearly ten years now—he had never been called. Not even on a Saturday night, or a Sunday afternoon when, he had been told by his brother ministers, the claims of the Lord lay heaviest on a soul.

When his father had still been active, there had been dozens of worshipers in the sanctuary every night, even on a sweltering mid-week summer evening like this one. The women—and yes, even the men—in the pews often weeping, or moaning aloud, so bestirred and troubled were they by the Spirit. Rarely did a night go by without him being summoned from their house on Strivers Row. An apologetic tap on the etched door glass, his father's solid bulk rumbling along the upstairs floorboards.

"Okay," he would call softly down the stairs to the caller. His voice tired or bleary, but never angry.

"Okay, tell 'em I'll be right there," he would call, already trundling down the stairs, pulling on his preacher's coat and collar. "Tell 'em to hold on, I'm comin'."

Jonah had just turned thirteen when his father had first taken him with him on one of those midnight calls to the soul. Sitting straight up in his bed when he had stumped past his bedroom, knowing he would look in, as he always did, and grin to see his son awake.

"Lookit him, pokin' his head up like a ferret out of his hole. Well, c'mon then!"

His much younger wife, Jonah's mother, protesting, "Oh, no, Milton, the boy ought to be in bed! And you should be, too!"—but his father shrugged her off.

"It'll do him good to see what I do. It's not like I'm takin' him out dicin'!"

They had walked up through the same streets he had traversed just now in the gray, foggy, Harlem morning. Jonah thrilled to be up at this unfamiliar hour—particularly pleased to know that he had left his older sister, Sophie, still sleeping torpidly in her back bedroom, where she was never awakened by these night distur-bances.

At the church his father had flung open the doors and marched straight up the center aisle. A murmur going through the men and women in the pews just to see him—for a self-taught preacher, he had a superb instinct for the dramatic. Jonah had walked up the aisle just behind him, clutching his hand, still wearing his pajamas under his coat, a little chilly in the early spring weather. His eyes wide, staring at all the troubled souls in the pews smelling faintly of the work they did, an intriguing, mixed scent of perspiration and scouring powders, food and cleaning wax and machine oil.

He had seen his father at work many times before, of course—at least every Sunday and during the Wednesday Bible classes, and during the tarry service on Saturday night—but never this close, or this personal. He had strode right up to the altar where Pete Moore, the usher in attendance that night, was standing solicitously over a woman who had thrown herself down on the red carpeting there, and was clutching tight to a leg of the altar table. Mr. Moore, an elderly man with great, round, Coke-bottle glasses, stood helplessly patting her back from time to time with his gloved hand, and from the way they both looked and how hard the woman was breathing, he expected her to be sobbing. But when his father helped Brother Moore pull her up, Jonah saw that she was dry-eyed, and staring off into space with an expression that was more unnerving than any crying could have been.

"You come on now, Lu," his father had said to her, walking her unceremoniously away from the altar—her body all but limp in his big, bearlike arms.

"You come along now, Sister Lulabelle, you have a talk with me in the back where you can unburden yourself, and we don't have to disturb all these fine people before they go back to work."

The woman acknowledged him only with another dull stare. To Jonah, at the time, she had looked old beyond reckoning, though much later he realized that she could not have been forty yet. Her hair was laced with gray, and while her red-brown Trinidadian face was not unpretty, it was weathered and deeply folded, like those of so many women who worked at the dryers and steam presses in the big industrial laundries downtown.

His father had half-carried, half-dragged her back to the vestry rooms, with Jonah and Brother Moore tagging along—a further intrigued murmur rising like the surf behind them as they left. His father had ignored it, though, and back in the vestry he had sat her down amidst all the comfortable, well-aged furniture of his office; the soft, enveloping old stuffed sofa where Jonah and Sophie had all but busted the springs as toddlers, jumping up and down on them for hours while their daddy laughed and laughed behind his cluttered rolltop desk. Now his father carried himself more somberly—but still casually, as if the lifeless, dead-eyed woman in his study were no more than any other routine piece of business to him, a meeting with the church custodian, or the deacons' finance committee.

"Tell me what's on your mind now, Lulabelle," he had begun just as routinely when she was finally seated on the broken couch, still staring out into space.

"C'mon now, you can talk to me. Lulabelle? One step at a time now. You got to tell me what's troubling you, sister. C'mon now."

Slowly, slowly the woman began to move her jaws, as if her mouth had been fastened shut for a long time, and she had to work up to saying something.

"I cahn't go back there," she croaked out at last—in her surprisingly crisp Island diction.

"Go back where, Lulabelle? Where can't you go back to?" his father prodded her—his voice sounding impatient and almost callous, Jonah thought.

"I cahn't go back to the Slave Mahket again," she got out, shaking her head. "I cahn't do it. They layin' us off at the laundry, an' I cahn't face it, goin' back up there again."

Even then, Jonah knew what the Slave Market was. His father had taken him up specifically to see it—the patch of pavement outside the five-and-dime at Gerard Avenue and 167th Street in the Bronx, where the women gathered hoping to get day work cleaning white ladies' homes on the Grand Concourse. They were there every day from eight in the morning until one in the afternoon. Squatting on wooden crates and boxes in the shadows of the elevated, just up the street from the majestic grey walls of Yankee Stadium. Their price dwindling steadily as the day went on, dropping from twenty cents an hour to ten, to even a nickel as it turned noon, and the housewives began to thin out. In the winter they stuffed newspapers up under their coats, and into the crumbling tennis shoes and the cut-out men's shoes they wore on their feet to keep warm. They carried their own tools, in brown paper bags, and broken traveling grips—mops and brushes, sponges and dusters, and used toothbrushes to pry dirt out of the white people's woodwork.

His father had wanted Jonah to see it all—the frowning white housewives stalking back and forth before them, trying to tell them apart and remember who had worked for them before, and what they could get away with. Many of them, Jonah had learned long since, finding an excuse not to pay even the few cents an hour they had promised. Hard as they were, the laundries paid a little better, and there the women could talk and sing together as they worked. But there were always layoffs, and strikes that made the jobs nearly as precarious as those to be found at the Slave Market.

"Now, Lulabelle, you have eight children, don't you?" Jonah's father had said matter-of-factly to the crazy Island woman, looking down and writing at something on his desk.

"Yes, I got eight children," the woman said, as if tortured by the fact.

"Those children I always see sittin' so nice and still in the pews every Sunday, or down in the basement learnin' their lessons? With their faces washed clean, an' their hair combed?"

"Yes—"

"Who takes care a those children, an' provides for 'em, ever since your husband passed?"

She stared up at him then with as frank and despondent a look as Jonah had ever seen on a person's face. Asking him something so odd that he could tell even his father was surprised.

"Tell me, Rev'rend. Is there memory in Hell?"

"In hell?"

"Because you know, more 'n' more, I feel I'd like to just kill all of them. Cut all they throats with the kitchen knife, an' just walk right out the door."

"And then you'd go to hell—"

"But first, I'd have some time, just by myself! They cahn't punish you for you sins if you cahn't remember what they were. I'd remember killing all my babies, I know that would be my punishment. But I would have a memory of a good time, too. And I'd know my babies would be safe. They wouldn't have to suffer growin' up in this world, they be safe in Heaven, 'cause Heaven is forgetting, an' Hell is remembering."

She looked as if she had come back to herself when she had finished. Her eyes dry, her face nearly beatific over how she had figured it out.

"But, Sister, don't you know, if you were to kill your children,
there would be only that evil memory," his father had told her. "There
wouldn't be any good time. You'd walk outta that house like a zombie. Whether you went to Hell or not, there wouldn't be any pleasures. Just the memory of you killing them, always before your eyes."

His father had been lolling back in his swivel chair, the same one
that Jonah and Sophie loved to push and race across the office floor.
But now he lurched up, the chair spring twanging as he stood. Hovering above the woman, running a hand along her grey hank hair—
the kitchen hacked short as so many laundry workers did, in the
hope of receiving just a single cool draft on the back of the neck.

"There is only memory, in heaven and hell," his father was saying now. "Which is why Jesus always remembers you. Don't you
think Jesus is standing beside you at that Slave Market? Don't you
think he's standing there, just as he's beside you every Sunday in
this church? Just as he's beside us right now in this room? Don't
you think he'll remember what you did for your children?"

She looked up and started to speak, but he cut her off.

"Not a woman in this world, not a mother or a father, don't feel
like they could as soon kill their children as look at them some days.
No one! If they tell you that they don't, they're lyin'. There's never
been a human being yet didn't have the worst thoughts there ever
was. Never was a human being who didn't at least contemplate
doing the worst thing you could ever consider, right down to nail-
ing our lord himself up to a tree."

"But—"

"I know. I seen it."

He was down next to her then, kneeling on the floor, moving
with remarkable grace for a man of his size, and age.

"Not just thought about it, even, but did it, right here in the
streets of this City! And you have done nothing like that."

Confronting her with the founding story of the church, Jonah
knew, which was not quite that of the Crucifixion. The story of
what had been done to his mother, and to him.

"Remember—he is with you always, even standing beside you at
the Slave Market. He will be strong with you! And if he is with you,
we—all of us!—are with you as well."

His father had stood back up abruptly, his joints cracking audibly in the small vestry office. He had snatched a slip of paper off his desk, thrusting it at the still waiting usher.

"Here, Brother Moore! Kindly deliver this over to the deacons' welfare committee tomorrow morning, will you, an' let's see if we can't raise the sister's assistance a little."

"Yes, sir!"

"And, Brother Moore!"

"Reverend?"

"If she would be so kind, could you see if Mrs. Moore or one of the other deaconesses might not mind sitting with Lulabelle here for a spell, an' maybe see her through the morning?"

"Yes, sir!"

He went out immediately, and Jonah's father went back to the woman. She was still sitting in the chair but looking reanimated now, her breathing heavier, her hands gripped firmly around the arms. His father had helped her slowly stand up, then kissed her gently on her forehead and slipped a couple of bills into her hand.

"Sister, you go on home now and make your children something nice for breakfast. Sister Moore will be there to help you. You watch them smile, then you go out to that Slave Market for them, and I guarantee that Jesus will be with you there."

"Yes, Brother Rev'rend," she had said, delivering the words in one long sigh, as if she were freeing herself of something, and walked out of the office with her legs stiff but her head held high.

Jonah had watched her go, and staggered back out into the church himself. That was when he had had his first, false conversion—walking out all but blinded by the sudden morning light pouring through the yellowy stained-glass windows up by the pulpit. Once before, in Sunday School, his teacher had told them all to shut their eyes and put their heads down, then asked them to raise their hands if they were ready to accept Christ Jesus into their hearts. And afterward the principal, a kindly older woman, had come up to him and told him how glad she was to hear that he had accepted Christ, but he had only felt that his confidence had been betrayed, and that in any case Christ had not come into his heart.

Yet that morning, stumbling blindly toward the altar, he had felt sure that the Spirit had entered into him. Filled as he was with the miracle of seeing that nearly comatose woman walk proudly out of the church, but even more with the beauty of how his father had achieved it. He hadn't realized, then, that he would have to reach bottom—that he would have to be as much in despair as that woman had been, clutching the altar with both hands, before he could really be saved himself. But seeing his father work had been almost like another calling, to the practical application of his vocation. Stepping back inside to the vestry, after his revelation in front of the blinding windows, he had been about to tell his father what he had just undergone when the old man had looked up at him from his desk, where he once again sat calmly writing.

"Well, what did you think of all that?" he had asked, with a sour expression on his face.

"You saved her!" Jonah told him, breathless.

"No, son. I just told her Jesus was standing beside her in this room."

"And He was!"

"No, he wasn't. He isn't at that Slave Market, neither," his father had shrugged, a small, tired smile on his face. "Sometimes I feel guilty about it, all the things I put down to his name."

"But you saved her!"

"Son, I didn't save anybody—me or Jesus, neither," he said, drumming his fingers thoughtfully on his desk, then jotting down another note. "Who knows but she won't cut those eight babies' throats. We better have somebody keep a eye on her—"

"But Jesus—"

"I give 'em Jesus because that's all I got," his father said, shaking his head irritably, as if ridding himself of some annoyance.

"All that stuff about what it's like in heaven and hell! You come up with an all-forgiving God, the Prince of Peace. An' then you make out he has a place where he keeps his creations for all eternity, punishing them forever an' ever, over an' over again for their wickedness. It's enough to choke a man!"

Yet as much as his father's words had shocked him, Jonah had remained transcended by the moment. Putting down his father's peremptory dismissal of Jesus as just another of the odd things he liked to say about God, usually at home and only among the family.

It was actually another, more practical visitation he had received that day, Jonah knew now. The realization of what it took to be a working minister. Doing things for other people, for his people. Giving them strength, telling them their duty—propping them up, if need be. That was what he had held on to, even when his faith had faded after a few, luminous days. To be recaptured only years later, in the depths of his despair after the college upstate—

And yet what had it availed him? There was no need for his own services, here in his father's church. No calls in the middle of the night—even if he was the one who actually believed. *The founding myth was lost. Buried alive in the back of the church—*

Jonah walked back to the vestry, down the hall filled with photographs that had been up since he was a boy, too; now beginning to brown and fade around the edges. All the social organizations his father had been a member of, representing the elite of Harlem society. Rows and rows of preachers and real estate agents, cooks and undertakers, in boiled shirts and tails, lined up in overstuffed, Victorian drawing rooms. Surrounded by ferns and thick velvet drapes, their faces solemn to the point of melancholy. The Boule and the Alpha Bowling Club. The Comus, and the Society of the Sons of New York, open only to gentlemen who had been born in New York and constituted "the cream of colored society."

How his father had busted a gut laughing over that one. "The cream of colored society!" Sometimes he would just start repeating it, keep laughing until he ended up in a coughing fit on the floor—

He went up to his father's old office door and paused just outside, listening. There it was. The heavy, raspy breathing that seemed to reverberate throughout the church. His church—

He knocked then, and entered the little apartment kitchen. Greeting the elder and the church mother who were on duty, Brother Spottswood and his wife. Someone always there, twenty-four hours a day, a woman and a man, in case they were called upon to deal with anything indelicate. He knew his father was embarrassed and a little irritated by so much attention, and he had tried to get the deacons to let him hire a visiting nurse instead, but they wouldn't hear of such a thing. No doubt mortified by the thought of how it would look to the other churches if their founder were to die alone and unattended in his own sanctuary.

The Spottswoods gushed over Jonah, asking about his vacation. Treating him with the same deference that all the congregation did, forcing him to smile, and lie for a few more minutes, then slipping discreetly away. He waited for a moment, collecting himself, then he cleared his throat loudly and walked on into the same room where he had first thought that he had found Christ.

His father was sitting behind the rolltop desk, dark and still and vast. His great girth swaddled in his black, priestlike shirt and white collar. He was slouched down so that the top of his massive bald head tilted toward Jonah—leaning forward at such an angle that he might have thought he was dead, save for the deep, laborious breathing that now filled the entire room.

His old office was almost barren now. The broken-springed couch gone, along with the most of the chairs. All that remained was the desk, and a metal-frame cot and some of his books, lying in careless piles around the floor. His sole concession to the heat a rickety metal fan that Jonah realized to his embarrassment might have been making the noise he had thought he heard coming from his father's lungs. Only these things were left—and the yellowing skull he kept on the very top of his desk, which had always fascinated Jonah as a child, the one his father had retrieved from Cold Harbor, and which may or may not have belonged to his own father.

Jonah had no idea what he did all day at the desk. He didn't write anything, at least not anything that Jonah saw; seemed barely able to hold a book in his hands. Yet there he was, every day when Jonah came to see him.

"Hello, Father," he said formally, but went forward to kiss him on the top of his bald, rutted head.

His father had been almost beautiful when he was a boy. Jonah had seen him in the ancient mottled daguerreotype that was one of the church's most treasured icons. It sat on his own desk, back on Strivers Row, now—the old man's solitary gift two Christmases ago, wrapped in simple brown butcher's paper and tied with string. He had mutely handed it to Jonah when he had come to see him that Christmas Eve, not three weeks after the war had begun. A family portrait from nearly a hundred years ago, the images in the daguerreotype seeming to shimmer and shift continuously after so much time.

There he was, his father, the oldest child, staring into the camera with boyish sincerity. His brothers and sisters—all gone now—standing or sitting around him. Milton's father—Jonah's grandfather—proud and forbidding, scowling back from the studio chair and the hidden photographer's stand that held his head rigidly in place.

And there she was, the white woman, standing beside her husband. His grandmother's face, faded away almost into nothingness when the daguerreotypist had overexposed the plate in order to capture all those shades of color in black and white. Nearly all that remained was her eyes and the thin, cryptic line of her mouth.

Now, with his hair gone, Jonah could see all the marks of his father's ninety-four years. The old scars on his face, the terrible, deep grooves on his head from where the mob had attacked him and his mother—the same white woman—during the Draft Riots eighty years before. They beat her with a wagon rim, his father had said, marveling at it still when he told him the story. They beat her with the iron rim of a wagon wheel!

He barely said anything, anymore. He had been nearly silent for over two years now, whether because of a stroke or simply his age, Jonah didn't know. He seemed able to understand things and to move about but he rarely spoke, and then only with the greatest effort. Jonah's talks with him were always one-sided, but still he approached them gingerly. Afraid that his father might want to know something more about Sophia—where she was, what she was doing. Afraid that he might want to know what he was doing.

"We're back from Adam Powell's," he informed the old man now, sitting down across from him on the unbending metal cot.

"Hmm?" his father grunted.

"He wants your endorsement for Congress. That's what it was all about, that's why we were invited," Jonah told him, his voice more sardonic than he had intended it to be.

"He asked after your health."

"Mmm-hmm."

His father nodded, making small, diffident noises, chewing meditatively on one side of his lip.

"How're you making out?" Jonah asked him, a wave of solicitousness suddenly washing over him for the old man, sweeping away all of his self-pity for the moment. He was so old, had lived through so much. Two wives buried. Living here in the back of the church at his own insistence. Sitting at that desk every day, almost as if he were waiting for something. For what?

Jonah got up and walked over to him, standing above him again and stroking the head that he had loved to touch as a child, wondering over the long ruts, and the story of how they had come to be there. The things we have to tell our children. Wagon rims for wagon ruts—until he was six he had it in his head that somehow his father's head had been run over by a wagon. The white woman. Beaten to death in the street, to save his life—

"They treating you all right? Is there anything I can get you? You want me to make you some eggs, maybe?"

He had done that sometimes, coming over to visit his father on restless, late-night rambles. He never seemed to sleep, was awake at almost any hour Jonah went over, in his old-man way, always sitting at that desk. Jonah would make him soft-boiled eggs in the little kitchen, then sit there and watch him eat, slowly sopping up the egg with a piece of toast. It was one of the old man's greatest regrets, he suspected, that he could no longer eat the way he loved. Savoring the codfish cakes Jonah's mother had made him, tossed over and over again in the air to make them light. The crocks of baked beans, cooked all night on the back of the stove, with great, fatty chunks of salt pork, and black molasses on top—

But now he only shook his head, still chewing contemplatively on his lip. Jonah started to back out of the room—

"All right, then—"

—but as he did his father grabbed him tightly around the wrist with one hand, his grip surprisingly sure and firm. Holding him there while he looked up at his son with his large, commanding eyes. Jonah had wavered, inclined at first to gently pry his father's fingers from his wrist and walk back to his home—fighting down the childish desire to cry that welled up inside him now.

Instead, he had sat back down on the cot and told his father all about Oak Bluffs. He had told him everything—about Adam, about Isabel and Hycie, even about crazy, one-armed Wingee, the driver. About how strange and beautiful it all was, and how flattered and yet uneasy, and out of place he and Amanda had felt. Telling him everything, in that rambling, confessatory way that always made him feel good afterward, and that he hated, too. Making him feel, as it did, that he was still a boy. Talking to his father after school in this same room, where he was always willing to sit and give Jonah his undivided attention, interrupting only for a word of advice here, a question there.

Or the way he had when he was still new to the ministry. The diaconate and the elders still wary of him and his father not quite gone yet, his presence hovering over him in the pulpit. Smoothing his way, as fathers did—good fathers—until he should get past all the early snares and coils, and earn their trust.

Except that he never had. He never had made it his congregation—his church, his people. But that was another story, and surely not the fault of this massive, kindly old man sitting at his desk. This man who had always been old to him—

He told him everything—or almost everything, stopping at the incident on the train that morning, which was still too raw for him to talk about, even to his father. When he got to the part where they left the island, he had stopped, and kissed his father good-bye. The old man tried to grab his wrist again but this time he was able to disentangle himself, backing out the door—feeling absurd even as he tried to reassure his father.

"Good night, Pops, that's all for tonight—" all the while thinking, Walk out of the room like a goddamned man. His father's big, drooping eyes mutely accusing him, sensing with his old preacher's intuition that he hadn't gotten it all out of him yet, even as Jonah finally left and shut the door behind him.

The whole way home, he wondered if maybe he shouldn't leave until the old man had died. Thinking, It can't be much longer, what would it matter? At least I would spare him seeing that.

But he had put it off so many times before, his leaving. There was always something. An anniversary, Amanda's birthday. Lost-and-Found Day, the church's most important celebration after only Easter and Christmas, and the central day of his father's life. There was always another reason to stay. If you're going to go, go. Got to be a man about this, at least.

It was dark by the time he started his walk back, the City just now kicking into gear. The streets full of running, laughing sailors and soldiers, radio cars and MP jeeps racing back and forth. Everything wide open now, as it hadn't been for years before the war—all the stores, the movie palaces, the restaurants and dance halls and bars doing a land-office business, their lights glaring through the dimout. The sounds of loud music, laughter, and shouting emanating from every brownstone and tenement. The tense, ominous groups he had noticed before, crouched around their pieces of paper, were gone, at least for the night. Now there were only the silhouettes of young women, standing and smoking in the doorways of darkened department stores as if they were waiting for a bus, which they were not.

They made a carnival, and called it war, he thought, watching all the frantic activity around him. They better make sure it lasts forever.

Ahead of him a Thursday girl was switching her hips, strutting provocatively down the block, and it reminded Jonah that he should go see Sophie tomorrow, though the thought gave him a little chill of both anticipation and foreboding. It had been over a month since the last time, even before they went away, but he knew what it would entail. Going down to her apartment in the Village—

"It's him, it's him!"

There was a sudden arc of light. Jonah tripped, and nearly fell in the blinding, white glare—a letter blowing out in some electric bar sign, or a movie bijou. He blinked rapidly, could just make out a small commotion on the next street corner. More people running across the street to join them, laughing and clapping their hands in wonder.

"It's him! He's come back!"

"Been buried in there for ages!"

"Is it really him?"

Jonah hurried toward them, still half blinded, trying to see what the jubilant little crowd was yelling about. In their midst he could at last make out an elderly-looking white man, with a fringe of wild gray hair, and a drooping gray mustache. He was dressed like someone out of the 1890s—wearing, even in this heat, an antique suit with a gated collar, and a broad, flamboyant bow tie.

"It's the old ghosty man hisself!"

Langley Collyer. His father had first pointed him out to Jonah years ago, hurrying furtively along the street, pulling an old milk crate behind him on the end of a rope. Look, there goes the great white race!

Langley and his blind brother lived in the ramshackle mansion at the corner of Fifth and 128th Street. The yard full of junk, the neighborhood boys amusing themselves by throwing rocks through its few remaining windows. When he was a boy, Jonah and his friends liked to tell each other ghosty stories about how the Collyers spent all their time tunneling under the streets of Harlem, and how they could emerge anywhere they wanted to, in the basement of anybody's building. Sometimes, on a slow day, a reporter from one of the newspapers might come up and sniff around the old mansion, banging on its rotting marble-and-wood doors, staring up at the broken-out windows now stuffed up with piles of newspaper, and Jonah and his friends would gather to watch, jumping up and down with anticipation.

But they were all disappointed, no one ever came to the door. The last time Jonah had seen Langley at all was nearly ten years ago, as best he could place it, in the early hours of the morning. He had been with the brother, Homer—the two of them in their old-fashioned suits, lugging a discarded Christmas tree, with little more than a few strands of tinsel on its branches, back across Fifth Avenue to their home. It had been a strange, disturbing image, the two old white men wobbling under the weight of the tree, Langley gently directing his blind brother.

Yet he strode along now with surprising agility, towing his milk crate along the pavement. His skin an unnatural, chalky white color under the streetlights. The people crowding in around him, trying to touch his sleeve for luck.

"We're with you, Mr. Collyer! We're your friends!" someone called out, and he stopped for a moment, favoring them with a smile that looked harried but not at all displeased.

"I appreciate your kind words," he said in a formal, starchy voice. "It's nice to know that we have some friends. If you could tell the younger element to stop breaking our windows and littering our yard with junk, I would be most appreciative."

The crowd applauded for some reason, the faces all around the old white man grinning broadly. Following him jubilantly on up the street, as he marched on into Schwartz's butcher shop.

"Somethin's gonna happen now! You watch!"

"It's a sign, it's a sign for sure!"

But just then the ebullient atmosphere on the street was broken by a blast of sound. Heads whipped around, drawn involuntarily to the metallic, nerve-grinding noise of racing engines. Jonah knew what it was before he saw them—more of Police Commissioner Valentine's sixty-four-man motorcycle corps. Another precaution sent to keep an eye on Harlem for the duration, supplementing the increased foot patrols, and the mounted officers, and the radio cars, the motorcycle cops went racing down the broad avenues as loud as they pleased, any hour of the day or night.

Six of them came motoring slowly down Lenox now, gunning their engines, the noise unbelievably loud and grating in the humid summer night. Their peaked caps shoved down low over their eyes, wearing huge goggles, and leather hip boots and gloves. They frowned disapprovingly at the sidewalk crowds, looking as alien and sinister as creatures from some science-fiction movie, and as they passed, Jonah watched the lips of all the sidewalk pedestrians, colored and white, curl up automatically.

When he got back to Strivers Row, Amanda was sitting up for him. A smile on her sweet face as she came over to put her arms around him, and kiss him—all too plainly having put aside whatever had bothered her about the train.

"There's a sandwich in the kitchen," she told him, holding on to him, her hands around his waist when he tried to move away. There was a thin trace of perspiration running along the top of her brow, her tightly curled hair swelling in the heat. Once, he knew, they would have already been making love, in need of no further inspiration.

"How was he? How's he been doing?"

"The same—I guess," Jonah told her. "You know with him. It's hard to tell."

"Did he talk at all?"

"No—no, I talked to him," he said, not telling her how much he had confessed.

Like a schoolboy. Like any other of the sad, played-out creatures who walked into his own study every day, to tell him their insolvable woes.

Amanda had left a thick tuna sandwich on toast for him in the kitchen, along with a glass of cold milk from the icebox. The toast still warm, she had figured nearly to the minute how long he was likely to be with his father. Jonah sat down at the kitchen table to eat while she worked quietly around him—putting things away, washing up a couple of dishes. There to talk to, as always, if he so desired. But he ate in silence, feeling both famished and exhausted by the events of the day, and after a few minutes she padded quietly upstairs with another smile—letting him be alone, too, if that was what he wanted.

It would be hardest to leave her, he knew. He would have even considered asking her to come with him, but he knew what her answer would be. And her face was so much darker—

Later, while she slept in their bedroom, he had gone up to his study on the third floor, ostensibly to work on his sermon for Sunday. Fiddling around with yet another variation on how it was that the children of Israel could sing the songs of Zion by the waters of Babylon.

There was always a new variation, a new twist. At the seminary down in Pennsylvania, he had learned all the great sermon forms. There was the Twin Sermon and the Classification Sermon, and the Surprise-Package Sermon and the Three Points in the Palm of a Hand, and the Silent Conclusion. He had learned the Ladder Sermon, in which, like Jacob, the preacher climbed steadily upward, through more and more powerful arguments, and the Skyrocket Sermon, which got out of the blocks quick, with a riveting, human story that burst into a profound if obvious moral—then rained a slew of further, more surprising lessons down over the heads of the congregation. There was the Jewel Sermon, in which the preacher might actually hold up his hand to imitate a jeweler looking over a precious stone from many angles, and the Rabbit in the Bushes, in which the preacher improvised, juking as he went along. Throwing a line out there, and then repeating it. Maybe once, twice, even three times if it seemed to stir something out in the congregation—the very same way that a hunter flushes a rabbit from a bush if he sees it shake.

One had to be fast on his feet to pull off such a sermon, Jonah knew—a master of improvisation, keenly attuned to how his congregation thought and reacted. Picking up in that few seconds just what it was that had made them jump, then clutching it for dear life; worrying it, building on it, never letting it go until you had brought it all the way home.

He had seen his father give such a sermon many times, but he had never had the temerity to try to pull one off himself. He relied on just the opposite, meticulous study and preparation, but the more he wrote this night, the more his words felt strained and spiritless. His hand stayed, as always, by the thought of how any sermon he gave was sure to be compared to his father's. The radiant faces, pumping the old man's hand at the door when he had still been in the pulpit. Exulting, "You preached today!"—or even, from some of the oldest church mothers and deacons, that most venerable of accolades: "He sure can read out of his hand!"

By contrast Jonah would receive, at best, their polite murmurs. Eyes cast down in embarrassment: "Good talk today, Reverend," or "Good lecture!" Or even the ultimate insult, whispered just loud enough for him to hear as they went out the door—"Reverend can't preach!"

He sighed, and put the sermon away in its desk cubbyhole—the Spirit refusing to descend again tonight. He gave it up and pulled another project out of his bottom desk drawer. A thick legal notepad, with a title inked in block letters across the top: A History of the Church of the New Jerusalem.

It was a project he had started years ago, soon after he had assumed his ministry. Intended as a standard, triumphant history of the church's founding and its rise, like the others put out by the leading churches on the tenth or fifteenth anniversaries of their arrival in Harlem. He had hoped to make it both a tribute to his father and an offering to his congregation, one that might serve as a bond between them.

But like everything else, it hadn't worked out as he'd intended. It had never quite congealed into a real history, devolving instead, no matter what Jonah had tried, into no more than a collection of rambling thoughts and speculations about his father's life. By now it was something he picked up only when he was hopelessly stuck on something else. Leafing through the dusty pages, he realized it had been left untouched for a good six months.

They knew the story already. That was the main problem. His father a Moses who had not only made it to the promised land but who had outlived everyone else who had wandered through the Wilderness with him. They all knew it, every member of the congregation, at least as well as they knew the story of the Exodus, and the Crucifixion.

The story of how he had rescued his people from the literal Wilderness, nearly eighty years ago. That dismal wood in northern Virginia, still charred and strewn with moldering bodies from the war that had raged through it twice. Even in Harlem, its pulpits filled with self-made men who had engineered miraculous escapes from the fields and the sharecropper cabins, no one had a story to match it.

Milton had gone down as soon as the war had ended. Gone to find *his* father, Billy Dove—*that proud, scowling black man in the daguerreotype.* Walking all the way down to Virginia, as soon as he could decently take his leave of the neighbor's house where they had been living for almost two years. Ever since the draft riots, when half the City burned and white people ran through the streets like mad dogs, torturing and hanging any Negroes they could find from the lampposts.

They all knew that part, especially—though Jonah had never heard his father put it in a sermon. There was no need to. It was already deep in the marrow of the church. His father had only to refer to the evil he had seen, personally, in the streets of this City, and they knew what he was talking about.

The story of how the mob had come for them, in their home down in the slums of the old Fourth Ward, and how his mother—the white woman, faded away now to just her eyes and that line of mouth in the old daguerreotype on his desk—had gone out into the street to fight for her son's life. How they had already beaten Milton unconscious and stripped him of his clothes, preparing to put him to the rope and the torch just as they had already hanged, and mutilated, and burned alive a dozen other Negroes, men and women and children alike.

She had gone out alone, to fight for her son's life, and the white men had set on her, then, in their blind, hateful fury. Beating her with axe handles and fence staves and those iron wagon rims—but she had clung to her son anyway. Refusing to let go, to give up shielding him with her body, no matter how much they beat her and tried to pull him away.

Afterward—after someone had finally come and put a stop to it, and the men with the axe handles and the wagon rims had fled—they had taken her to the neighbor's house, where she had drifted in and out of a stupor for six weeks. Her terrible gasps for breath filling the house where their whole family was forced to live—where Milton himself still lay, beaten half to death. All the prettiness and the youth beaten out of his face by the mob, preserved still only in that single picture he had. Slowly healing, coming back to life in an upstairs bedroom, even as he listened to his mother's racking gasps for breath.

And Billy Dove, his father, stumping back and forth between them on his broken leg, sustained when he had helped to lead the Colored Orphans to safety—another, only slightly lesser founding story. Hobbling between his only child who was as black as he was and whom he had always been hard on, fearing so much for him, and his dying white wife, whom he had only realized he loved, too late. Until on that Friday in August—as real and as vivid as Good Friday itself—when her terrible breathing had finally given out, and he had risen up at once from her bedside, and gone to pack his bags. Signing on before the day was out with the Twentieth Colored New York, despite his explicit promise to his wife on her deathbed that he would stay and look after their five children. Saying only to the white neighbor woman, Mrs. O'Kane, when she had begged and remonstrated with him that they needed a father, What my children need is to know that their mother cannot be killed in the street like a dog. My children need to know that their lives are worth something.

Not only enlisting, too, but extracting a promise from Milton, Jonah's father, that he would follow him as soon as he should hear that he had fallen. Milton making the oath in good faith, though he could barely sit upright at the time. Actually trying to sign up, too, under the luring, striped enlistment tents along the Battery nine months later, after the battle of Cold Harbor, when he had spotted the tiny line of type in the New York Tribune: "Missing—Sgt. Dove, 20th Colored..."

But Mrs. O'Kane, whom Jonah had met when he was very young at the gloomy old manse up in the Bronx, her hands as dry and brittle as tracing paper on his cheek—Mrs. O'Kane had suspected just such a thing, and had run after him, begging him to come back, and help look after his brothers and sisters. And when Milton had told her, It's not a man's job to look after children, she had not desisted but had hung on to his arm for dear life—for his dear life. Telling him, I'm speaking to you like a man now. Telling him, We have a duty, too, those of us who just abide.

Once the fighting was ended, he had determined to go, no matter what. To find his father, if he was lost, and bring him home, or at least to find his body in the grave where he lay. Packing only a few victuals, an extra shirt, and the twenty dollars he had diligently saved through any work he could find in the City. The details of all he had carried, right down to the twenty dollars, known to every member of the church to this day. Mrs. O'Kane, the white woman— the other white woman—letting him go this time without a protest even though she wished he wouldn't, knowing there would be no stopping him.

He had walked all the way down. Following the spongy, late spring roads through New Jersey and Pennsylvania. Stepping, not without a shadow of trepidation, across the Line into Maryland, and the old slave country. Crossing and recrossing the endless rivers of the war, the Potomac and the Rapidan, and the Rapahannock and the Chickahominy, and finally Topotomoy Creek itself, which ran along the field of Cold Harbor, only a few miles to the east and north of the still smoking rebel capital of Richmond. And there, at the last, he had found—nothing.

Nothing at all but a field full of bodies, half buried and unmarked. Some of them pulled up and looted, still more left where they had fallen, in the trenches and gullies, and wagon ruts by the side of the road. The bodies identifiable only by their remaining scraps of uniform, even most of these faded or missing. All of them reduced to skeletons by the weather and the hogs and the buzzards, so that he could not even distinguish the colored troops from the white.

He hadn't known what to do—so confident had he been that he would retrieve his father in one form or another. His whole journey suddenly senseless, now that there was no possibility of that. He had poked around for a while at this body or that one, out of the thousands. Carefully keeping his distance from the vultures and the other scavengers, the narrow-eyed white people still systematically combing through the corpses for anything they could find. Only after three days had he given up, slipping into his rucksack a skull selected at random—the skull he still kept yellowing on his desk—and started back toward the North.

It was on the way back that he had decided to pass through the Wilderness. Still chary of the local whites, the bitterness and the hatred he had seen in their faces since crossing into Virginia, he had figured that it would be better to go through even the trackless woods than to pass their way again. Once in, though, he had found himself as lost as any army, the woods dark as twilight even at noon. Wandering aimlessly through the tangle of rotted trees and briar and vine; the same ground that had been fought over twice in blind, hopeless battles. Turning up still more bones amidst the scorched oak.

But it was there, lost, that he had found them. It had happened just as he had tripped over a man's shank bone half buried in the dead leaves on the Wilderness floor, still jutting out from the remains of his blue uniform. Milton lying where he had fallen, so exhausted was he by then, while he had a drink of water from his canteen and tried to figure out where he was.

They had emerged from the trees and the stickers around him all at once, as silent and undemanding as ghosts. More than two hundred of them, run off from the ravaged plantations down by the Peninsula, on the move for months, or even longer. Banding together for whatever safety and succor they could provide for each other. Traveling by night, dodging in and out between the raging armies, even more wary of the whites than he was but with no idea of where they were going or what they might do.

He had never seen human beings more utterly wretched, even in the worst slum streets of the City. Half naked, their bellies rubbing up against their backbones. So ignorant of the wider world, he would tell Jonah, They might as well've climbed up out of the earth—

He had taken them in hand at once. Just like that, a sixteen-year-old boy. There was no one else, it was just what had to be done—and he had seen at once where his authority must come from. He was no prodigy boy preacher like the ones that some of the small-fry cults, or the Baptists, like to raise up to their pulpits from time to time. Yet it was there, down in the Wilderness, that he had preached—for the first and only time—the story of his life. Reading from the hand just as the plantation slave preachers did, when books and learning were forbidden them, and as he had seen it done on the sidewalks of his City. Holding up his palm and pretending to read God's word revealed there, reciting half-remembered bits of Gospel, and Bible stories.

But above all, the sermon had been his story. Everything he had witnessed and endured, sparing them nothing of the horrors of the City during the riot, or what he had been through, or how sorely they would be tried themselves. Leavened with just enough redemptive hope in the story of his mother, the white woman, to make the journey worth the chance. It was his conversion and calling and ordination all at once, down in a Virginia thicket—even though he still didn't really believe.

But surely it was a miracle—blasphemous as it was. It had to be. How else could it be that a boy of sixteen should wander all the way down from New York, and find his calling in a bramble patch? What else but divine will could have brought them together, and made them follow him?

They had let him lead them out of the Wilderness. Milton asserting his authority at once, as easily as if he had been born for this purpose alone, leading them all the way up to the City along the now dust-choked summer highways. Past all the gawking farmers, and the suspicious, silent townspeople and sheriffs along the road. Pausing only for a short, solemn ceremony when they ferried themselves across the Potomac, and over the Line. Milton stopping his father's watch to mark the exact time they passed out of the land of their enslavement. All of them kneeling and praying, and singing the old songs—including the very one that had earned Jonah his name:

He deliver Daniel from the lion den,
Jonah from the belly of the whale,
And the Hebrew children from the fiery furnace,
And why not every man?

When they reached the City, it was Milton who had decided
they should live in the wary, shaken, colored neighborhood taking
shape around Minetta Lane in Greenwich Village—the only place
where Negroes had gathered in enough numbers, and with enough
guns, to hold off the whites during the Draft Riots. Taking his own
brothers and sisters back from the O'Kanes, and raising them on
his own there as well. Shielding his new flock as best he could from
all the snares of the City, the gangsters and the two-bit joints, and
the black-and-tan halls over on Bleecker Street. Insisting that they
learn to read, and write, and get whatever education was open to
them, finding them work and food and shelter where he could.

And at the center of it all was the church. Cobbled together from
what Milton could glean poring over the Bible at night or aping
the other churches. A rag-and-bone collection of theology, as he
was aware his brother ministers sniffed at it behind his back. He
didn't mind, Jonah knew—his father never having cared a dime
about matters of doctrine, or even the most basic tenets of the faith.
Building up his congregation instead by the sheer power of his personality, his willfulness and his guile. By turns wily and defiant, his
own relentless ego subsumed into the physical being of his church.

He had been pushed up the Island of Manhattan anyway, along
with all the rest. First to the Tenderloin, then up to Columbus Hill—
soon to be renamed San Juan Hill—but always with a plan, always
with another place to jump to first. Willing, like Adam, to be fully
immersed in the world, using all his connections with the astound-
ingly fecund O'Kanes, now happily rising through Tammany Hall,
to provide for his congregation.

That terrible summer at the very turn of the century, when the
white mobs had come out again—the police themselves leading
them up and down Hell's Kitchen, dragging Negroes right out of
their homes to beat them in the street—it was his father who had
gone to his pulpit in a cold fury one night, and advised his people
to arm themselves. It was his father, too, who had been among the
first to advocate the final exodus up to Harlem, where they might
finally outpace the relentless advance of the white City and the run-

ning battles with the Irish on San Juan Hill, and have some place
to themselves. Milton himself speculating in land up there when
it was still a soggy valley, full of squatters, known as Goatsville.
Beating the white middle and upper classes to the brownstones, and
the vast new apartment houses that had been planned for them, and
even making some money in the process. Plowing most of it back
into his church, and his people, but not hesitating to take some for
himself, too, with the full approval of the church—a small compen-
sation for all the incalculable services rendered over decades. Using
it finally to marry, and to try to start a family, taking as his bride—
just as Jonah himself would—a daughter of one of the poorest,
blackest, least pretentious families of his congregation. And then,
when she died in childbirth along with the baby, marrying another
one—Jonah's mother—just when it was almost too late.

After that it had been a matter of consolidating his gains. Willing his church into being, brick by brick, and penny by penny.
Acquiring the fine house on Strivers Row, with its thirteen-foot
ceilings, and its brass and copper chandeliers, and those French
hardwood floors.

And then, the only thing lacking—an heir. Someone to continue
his dynasty, just as Adam Senior had done for Adam Junior, over at
the Abyssinian, and Hutchens Bishop was doing over at St. Philip's.
And what did he get?

These two white children. Such a departure from Milton's own
color and that of his young second wife's that there was even some
whispering among the more evil-minded members of the congregation—though of course they all remembered the white woman in
the daguerreotype.

Jonah's mother—a lovely, almost preternaturally contented
woman, always smiling and humming hymns as she went about
her duties around the house—had passed untimely, too, more than
seven years ago now. Leaving behind only himself and his older sister, Sophia, who had left the house soon after her death, vanishing
into the world below 110th Street. The truest inheritor of the line,
Jonah thought, vanishing just as her grandfather had, down into the
South, or her father into the church. Her disappearance nonetheless another source of grief to their father in a lifetime full of loss,
and pain—though Jonah knew it was nothing compared to what his
grief would be if he knew what had really happened to her.

Which just leaves me. Jonah scribbled at the bottom of the legal pad—before flipping its leaves over, returning it to the deep, back, false drawer of his desk, where he kept it. For all that our story is known, and repeated, we are still a family of secrets.

He looked at his desk clock, surprised to see how late it was, and padded quietly back down the stairs to the second floor. Running through his tasks for the day ahead as he always did—the home visits he would have to make, the deacons and assistant ministers he would have to see—while he performed his nightly ablutions before the medicine-cabinet mirror.

He went into the bedroom and had begun to undress as quietly as possible in the dark, in a far corner of the room. Amanda lay naked, asleep in the bed, her strong brown body uncovered even by a sheet. An unspoken invitation, he knew, to disturb her.

At times such as this—late at night, coming into the bedroom where his wife lay sleeping and even the roiling, bumptious City was distant and still—he could not imagine leaving. Thinking how nice it would be to wake her, as he so often had when they were first married, aware of how good it would feel to make love on the fresh, crisp sheets she had knowingly put on the bed, the small but telling relief that she could offer from the drenching heat of the City.

Yet he could do nothing anymore without feeling unworthy. He slipped into his pajamas and got into the bed, as far from his wife as he could lie. Certain, now, that he would go.

CHAPTER SEVEN

MALCOLM

When he went back to Small's that morning, Charlie Small looked as if he had been expecting him all along.

"No slicin' yo' chops all the time, no wild antics," he told him as he stumped about the bar, pulling the chairs down off tables.

"Yessir," Malcolm said—hurrying over to help him, running a hand lovingly over the red leather chair backs.

"I don't wanna ever catch you hustlin' no soldiers. You understand me?" he said, looking Malcolm in the eyes. "The blue's tryna put a big damp on me. I got all kinds people comin' in here now'days. The ABC boys. Bulls, dicks, MPs—everybody but the goddamned U.S. Marines. All lookin' for the chance to shut me down."

"That's all right, I can tell a undercover man a mile away. I got a sixth sense for cops!" Malcolm gushed, but Charlie Small shook a finger in his face.

"Listen me now! Most of all—don't you never tell anyone a'tall you can get 'em a woman. You got me, Cholly Hoss?"

"Yessir!"

"All right," Charlie Small nodded. "How you fixed with Uncle?"

"What's that now?"

"The draft, son, the draft! They puttin' the issue on you anytime soon?"

"Nah, I'm Four F," Malcolm told him, with a mixture of embarrassment and pride. "I got the card to prove it."

After that Charlie Small had stopped and looked him up and

down, in his now badly wrinkled and tired-looking drape. A close-mouthed smile moving across his face as quickly and fleetingly as a spark on the subway rail.

"What they say your name was, Malcolm Little? Well, Little an' Small—we should get along all right!"

He flicked a small wad of bills up out of his pocket, pressing it into Malcolm's hand and ordering him to get some proper waiter's clothes—

"Nothin' flash, now! You come back here in somethin' you momma can bury you in."

"You gonna make me a waiter?" Malcolm asked, smiling glee-fully.

"Maybe. If you show me you can clear tables an' bust suds first."

The slave at Small's was the best job Malcolm had ever had. He kept his mouth shut and did everything he was told, and when one of the regular waiters was inducted a week later, Charlie Small kept his word and put him out on the tables. He worked the worst shift in the joint, eight in the morning til four in the afternoon, but with the war on he could still make fifteen to twenty dollars a day in tips alone.

Most of all, though, he just loved to be there. He hated to ever go home, always afraid that he would miss out on something. Working seven days a week when he could; picking up extra shifts when his own were over, or hanging around the Cloverleaf Room to see the cabaret show.

There was always somebody in the bar, with the munitions factories and the shipyards going twenty-four hours a day. Line workers back from the munitions plants in Jersey and the airplane factories in Long Island, still wearing their work boots and dungarees, and smelling of sulphur and cordite, and freshly cut metal. Longshoremen up from Red Hook or the West Side docks, looking to fence whatever they had been able to grab from the night's work, whole crates of whiskey and rum, ten-pound bags of coffee or cocoa beans, and even bunches of mangoes, and coconuts. Sailors from the merchant marine, who brought bottles of cognac, and watches from Switzerland; little balls of opium from Morocco, and thick-rolled joints of ganja and kisca that they claimed came all the way from Persia.

Malcolm loved to watch it all, especially how they showed the merchandise off, and slipped it to each other. All fluid, subtle motions, made on their laps, or under the tables. Letting a bag lie open, unbuttoning a jacket to give a glimpse of a bottle, the glint of a gold watch. The cooks and the bartenders had the regular undercover men picked out by now, identifying them with quick winks and glances to Malcolm, and the customers. Charlie Small walking by to warn him again—

"Remember: I don't want you hustlin' nothin'."

They all knew the plainclothesman from the police, a dour-looking Jamaican called Joe Baker who walked around with his head down and his hands in his pockets, and who they would set up immediately with his usual shot and a beer the moment he came through the door. The undercover MPs who still insisted on going unrecognized they would scrupulously charge for their drinks. They were even easier—usually white men who looked more like police than the police, with set jaws and mean, watchful eyes that brimmed with satisfaction whenever Charlie Small asked them for their money, sure that they had remained undetected.

But Malcolm's favorite time was the late afternoon, usually around four o'clock, after most of the workingmen had gone home and before the tourists and the glamour girls could pack the place. That was the time when the regulars began to drift in. Watchful, quiet men, most of them, blending effortlessly into the bar, speaking softly to each other while their eyes picked over the straight customers. Moving with the deliberate, easy confidence of men who know other men are afraid of them.

There were Black Sammy and Bud Hewlett and King Padmore, who had been strong-arm men for Dutch Schultz, and who each had hands like slabs of ham. There were second-story men like the burglar they called Jumpsteady, who liked to claim that he would work only when he was hopped up, tiptoeing along the window ledges of the wealthiest apartment houses downtown, to steal the jewels from the bedrooms of rich white women.

Then there were the pimps, one called Dollarbill who liked to wave around his Hoboken roll—fifty one-dollar bills with a twenty on the top—and another one called Sammy the Pimp, who always had a manicure and a big diamond ring on his middle finger, and who claimed he could tell if a woman was a whore by the look on her face when she danced. There was Cadillac Drake, a jolly little man with a shiny bald head and a big round belly he liked to call "the chippies' playground," whom they all made fun of for having the skinniest, scrawniest, most worn-looking string of girls anywhere in Harlem. Occasionally one of them would poke her head in the door, looking for him, her face as scarred and wizened as an old man's, weary eyes staring fearfully into the dark interior of the bar, and Malcolm would laugh along with the rest of them.

"Oh, oh, lookit that old settler!" they would point, punching each other's arms. But Cadillac Drake only laughed right back at them.

"Ugly women work harder!" he would insist, his Santa Claus belly shaking with laughter. "You take a chippie that ugly, you got a producer!"

There was an older man, too, with black-blue skin and thick, white wire-brush hair who they called Fewclothes, because he always wore the same clothes—a black felt jacket with frayed collar and sleeves, the lapels shiny with age. He liked to boast that he had been the softest, most undetectable pickpocket in Harlem before the arthritis that had swollen his finger joints into what looked like so many old tree roots. Some of the more skeptical regulars said he had never been a pickpocket at all, and even claimed to remember him as an old middleweight from Natey Ward's gym. But he carried himself with an unassailable dignity, and told stories of Harlem from before the twenties, which to most of the hustlers might have been the Middle Ages.

He picked up on the deference with which they treated him, and whenever Fewclothes came in, Malcolm made a big fuss over him. He would hurry over with a clean napkin and menu, serving him before anyone else—making sure that the others all saw how much attention he paid to the old man.

"Yes, sir! What can I do for you this evening, sir? Right away, sir!" he would boom out, until even the hustlers had stopped their low conversations among themselves and everyone was looking at him. Calling loudly back to the kitchen as soon as Fewclothes had politely put in his order—

"This is for the gentleman here! Only the best!"

And when the food was ready, he would bring it over like a waiter in some fancy hotel restaurant downtown, flourishing the tray high above his head on the tips of the fingers of one hand. Refilling Fewclothes's glass, tucking his napkin carefully up over his worn jacket. Waiting on his every request until he was sure that every one of the regulars and even Charlie Small himself had to look away, blinking or rubbing at their eyes.

On those nights the tips had flowed. All of the hustlers at the bar, he knew, thinking about the day when they would be as old and broken down and unable to make their play as Fewclothes was now. Malcolm satisfied that at least for the moment, he had won their gratitude. He was aware that they still laughed at him behind their hands when he said something foolish, or too loud. Telling each other, Man, that boy's wild as a tenor sideman huntin' a roach!— mocking his clothes, his conk, the way he got excited sometimes and talked and bragged too much despite all that he knew he had promised Charlie Small. Their quiet derision making him feel the way he had back in the white school in Lansing, when all the kids in his class had laughed at him, and called him Chinaman and Snowflake and Eskimo, and he had gone home and told his mother, They don't even know my name.

But he only smiled in their faces, just as he had at the white kids back in Michigan, and eventually they gave him a proud new name. When they asked him what he wanted to be called he had told them simply Red—loath as he was to tell them some tom name like the Sandwich Red he'd been on the train. But there was already a St. Louis Red and a Chicago Red, and a junkie and strong-arm man they called Big Red, so West Indian Archie decided they should call Malcolm after his hometown, too.

"Where you grow up, boy?" he had asked him one evening in his usual low Island growl.

"Michigan," Malcolm had told him—not wanting to admit to coming from any place as obscure, and country, as Lansing.

"Michigan, huh?" Cadillac Drake had sung out. "'Don' mean to boast but you know he's the most / From Kalamazoo-zoo-zoo—'"

"I ain't from Kalamazoo!" Malcolm fairly shouted, surprising them.

"All right, all right then, boy. He's Detroit Red," West Indian Archie had declared, and all the others had nodded.

They always deferred to Archie. He was a big man, with a broad chest and shoulders, and skin nearly the same mariny shade as Malcolm's own. He had a broken hawk nose, and a gold tooth in the front of his mouth, and two long, pink scars on his face—one running down the side of his cheek, stopping just short of the corner of his eye, the other almost tracing the main artery along his throat. Yet he was no bigger, or more scarred, than any of the other old strong-arm men. He dressed better than most of the hustlers, but no flashier. Moving and speaking as quietly as they all did—usually keeping a little distance, sitting down at the far end of the bar, or at one of the small side booths before growling softly for Malcolm to bring him a beer.

There was just something about how quick his hands were, even reaching for a drink or a light, or maybe the particular note of sorrow and exasperation in his voice that made him seem like the sort of man who might be capable of anything. Unlike the other colored numbers runners, he had held on to his own corner of the policy racket, no matter what the Italians or the cops had to say about it. It was an article of faith that he never wrote down a policy slip, keeping all the numbers, even the combinations, in his head; carrying two thousand dollars on him at any time so that he could pay off to his bettors whenever they happened to see him on the street.

Malcolm had seen him pull out the huge billfold many times, ostentatiously peeling off one hickory stick after another. Slipping him a twenty sometimes even when all he'd had on the night was a cup of coffee. Malcolm had been afraid of him at first—afraid as he had been of no other one of the hustlers—shying away like a colt the first time Archie had flashed his sardonic, gold-toothed smile at him. But Archie had only waved him over.

"I seen you hustling," he said, nodding his head approvingly. "I seen how good you treated the old man, letting them see it, too. A young man got to hustle."

"You really carry all those numbers around in your head?" Malcolm had asked him, once he had gotten to know him a little better. Unable to believe all the stories even after he had seen Archie's billfold, sure that it must be just one more hype to run up business. It had taken him days to get up the courage to ask, afraid of how he might react, but Archie had not seemed affronted at all—simply telling Malcolm to put all of his tabs for the night down on the table in front of him.

"All right," he said, passing them each before his eyes just once. "All right, you got your pen? Write these down!"

He had proceeded to rattle off what the sum of each individual tab was, and what the numbers were backward, and every possible three-digit combination of each one.

"You go on back the kitchen an' check out my math, then you see. Go on! Don't take anybody's word on anything in this world, Red!"

Malcolm had done as he said, poring over each of his tabs, at least until the customers were clamoring for attention and Charlie Small ordered him to get himself back out on the floor. And to his delight and amazement, he found that each number Archie had read him—numbers he had to work out torturously with a pencil and eraser—was absolutely correct. Whenever there was any discrepancy, he had gone back over his work—and always found that, sure enough, Archie was right.

"How'd you do that?" he had pressed him. "What's the trick?"

But West Indian Archie had only shaken his head.

"No trick. I just got a head for the numbers, is all. That's why I'm in the numbers business. Man should always be in a business he got ability for. You remember that, Red."

"Yessir."

"But you did good, too, boy. Always question it when somebody tell you somethin'—particularly somethin' 'bout how wonderful they are. Don't take anything on anybody else's say-so."

"Yessir!" Malcolm told him again, and walked away proud to think that he had impressed him. When he went past his table the next evening, Archie had suddenly grabbed hold of his arm, pulling him over again.

"Hold still a minute, Red," he had ordered him—and to Malcolm's astonishment Archie had whipped a measuring tape out of his pocket, and begun carefully measuring every inch of him; legs, waist, neck, and shoulders. Malcolm forcing himself to stand still while the other regulars, and the early sailors and soldiers and their glamour girls at the bar, grinned and tittered.

"Quit your twitchin' now," Archie scolded him—his lilting, stern, Island voice reminding Malcolm of his mother's. "You want a righteous peg, this has got to be right!"

Two days later Frank Parks, the headwaiter in the Cloverleaf Room, had silently handed him a thick package wrapped up in tissue paper. Malcolm had torn away the paper like a child on Christmas morning, and found himself holding the best-made piece of clothing he had ever set eyes on in his life. A beautiful, midnight-blue suit made from summer wool, cut every bit as finely and conservatively as one of West Indian Archie's own suits; along with three fine white cotton shirts, and a gorgeous blue silk tie. Malcolm had laid it all out on the bar and simply stared at it there, until Bing Williams, another waiter on his shift, had asked didn't he know that

West Indian Archie had an in with the legendary Forty Thieves gang.

"The Forty Thieves?"

"Sure. Ain't you heard about them? They a bad bunch a niggers, been boostin' suits all over town," Williams told him confidentially. "They send one their whitest, most respectable-lookin' men into a store just before closin' time. He hides out, then shuts off the burglar alarm, an' calls the rest of the gang. Then they drive a truck right up the back door, boost every suit they got! I hear these days they even usin' a army truck they boosted—"

"Oh, yeah?" Malcolm had grunted, unable to tell if he was being played. But in the days and weeks to follow he loved to think about it, whenever he went home to his rented room and slipped into Archie's suit. A league of thieves—slick black men, melting into the shadows. Slipping like twilight into the best clothing stores in the City. Like some menace the Spectre, or the Blue Beetle might fight, but better than any comic-book villains he had ever read of. Slinking past the guards and the alarms, making off with whole truckloads of suits, jewels and watches and furs—

It affirmed for him what he had already suspected, that there was some greater, secret knowledge hidden all around him, knowledge that would yield up some great treasure if only he could decipher it. He was sure that he saw it everywhere, in every crack and crevice of the City. He saw it in the windows of the Puerto Rican botanicas, with their pictures of Jesus holding open his bleeding heart, and the plaster saints with their eyes turned to God, and their feet placed on a black man's turbaned head. He heard it in the tirades of the street-corner, stepladder orators; or the twang of the subway rails when a train was coming, or the cymbal clash of the mangles when the merchants pulled them down over their storefronts at the end of the day.

He wanted to see everything, to find whatever there was to find. If his shift ended in time, he stepped over to Small's Cloverleaf Room, where everyone ended up eventually because it was the only cabaret in Harlem with an air-conditioning system that actually worked. In the first week alone, he had seen Billie Holiday and Sugar Ray Robinson, come to see Leonard Harper, the Prince of Harlem, and his Chock Full O' Rhythm Revue, featuring the jumpsinger Dell St. John, and the Lucky Sisters, and Bigtime Crip, the greatest of all the one-legged dancers, and Edna Mae Holly, who wore as scanty a two-piece, leopard-skin costume as could be allowed, and did a shake dance on top of a giant African drum that never failed to bring the house down.

When he stepped back outside, it was after midnight, but he felt less than ever like going home. The streets still jumping, all the clubs and the movie palaces still open for the war workers on the swing shift. Instead he might go with some of the other waiters to World Chop Suey, where Princess Shaloo sang every night, or to have yardbirds and strings at Ralph's Spaghetti House, or maybe to the Colonial Tavern just to watch Fannie, the best-looking waitress in all of Harlem.

Or, best of all, they would cross Seventh Avenue to Creole Pete's after-hours club. The club really no more than a couple of "Beale Street" basement apartments, the wall between them knocked down during Prohibition to make another speakeasy. Nobody was sure that this was such a good idea, and every year the ceiling above seemed to sag lower and lower over the customers' heads. But there was always a phonograph playing slow, late-night records, "Mood Indigo," and "Sophisticated Lady," and maybe "Someone to Watch Over Me," and a beautiful young woman called Brown Sugar who served the customers sugary Island drinks in tall glasses. Sometimes, if he had had enough rum to drink, Pete Robertson himself came out—hauling along his huge black pots under his arm, ladling out heaping portions of his gumbo or jambalaya directly on the customers' plates, his head scraping along the dangerously low ceiling. Gesturing proudly with his pot ladle at all the autographed pictures of ballplayers he had tacked up along the walls, the great Negro League stars like Dihigo, and Josh Gibson and Buck Leonard, Judy Johnson and Ray Dandridge, and even a few of the very greatest white stars like DiMaggio and Williams, or Babe Ruth, who Pete swore was really a colored man, and over which he'd oil up your head if you said different.

He wouldn't get home until it was light out—if he did at all. By then he had a room up on Sugar Hill itself, not far from where he had gone to the rent party his first night in town. The building was full of hustlers and prostitutes, and it cost him twenty dollars a month for a single room in a fifth-floor walk-up, where he had to share the bathroom and the kitchen with six other men. But it was a real room, at least, with a real bed, and not something rigged up with a cot and a beaver-board partition. The apartment house was on the corner of West 150th Street, where St. Nicholas Avenue diverged from St. Nicholas Place, and his room was at the very peak end of the building, facing south, so that at night it seemed as if the whole City were coming up to him—the car headlights streaming toward him before they swerved off to one side or the other. Below him, he could see the castle walls of City College, and the lights from all the towering apartment houses of the wealthy along Edgecombe Avenue, and if he walked up to Convent Avenue, he could even see the running lights of the destroyers and the troop ships and the carriers where they lay in the Hudson, wheeling slowly around in the river before they made their way out to sea, and on to Europe and the war.

It was the first time he had ever had a room that was truly his own. One that he paid the rent on, and that wasn't in his half-sister's attic, or some bug-ridden boardinghouse, and that he didn't share with two or three of his brothers. He was so pleased with the idea of it that as soon as the super was out of the room, he had walked all around the it, touching his bed and his chair, the wobbly little dresser in the corner, assuring himself that it was all his.

But it was hard for him to know just what to do, how to go about cleaning up the place, or providing food for himself. He felt that some part of him had been cut off, and glad as he was to be rid of it—to be free—he would wake up in the early morning hours sure that he was suffocating in the little, broiling room. He would sit up with his head spinning, no longer sure of just where he was, or what he was doing.

Those few nights when he did stay home, he would end up just sitting by the window, watching the eternal traffic rushing by, and the bottom would drop out. He would feel numb, and so immobilized with loneliness that he wished he was anywhere else, even back at his sister's house. Sometimes he would even go down to the pay phone in the lobby with all the piles of change he had made from the day's tips, and try to make a long-distance phone call to those of his brothers and sisters who still lived in their old home, back in Lansing. But the phone was usually disconnected, and even when he could get through, there wasn't any answer—Malcolm letting it ring and ring, imagining the sound echoing through the empty little house.

He wasn't sure why he called, since he didn't have much to say to them anyway. The only one he really wanted to talk to was Reginald, and he was away in the Merchant Marine now. Every other week or so, when he was back up in Boston, he would get a cryptic letter from Reginald, telling him he was back in port but unable to even say where, due to reasons of military security. Once, up at Ella's, he had gotten a phone call from him, too—Reginald's cheerful, boyish voice sounding as if it was coming to him through a long tunnel. He hadn't been able to tell him much then, either, about where he was or where he was going, but when Malcolm had confided that he was hoping to go to New York soon, his little brother had told him that he hoped to be there, too. Malcolm thinking about that during his long nights alone, looking at the ships out in the Hudson and wondering if Reginald could be on one of them. But if he was, he didn't know how he would possibly find out, or how Reginald would find him in this vast city, and when he thought about that he would have to plunge back out into the wartime, nighttime streets again, threading his way through the mobs of sailors and soldiers, looking for somebody who knew his name.

By the time he got home in the morning, the whole building felt different—better, more reassuring. The whores would all be out, leaning over the balustrades in their bright dressing gowns, smoking and chattering and laughing, like so many of the songbirds in their cages at Woolworth's. It was only a change of shift, like everything else with the war on. The john-walkers already leading in the morning rush—nearly all white men, obviously making a quick stop on their way to work. Wearing suits and ties, and gold bands on their fingers, their eyes flitting about nervously. The john-walkers speaking to them softly, reassuringly, the way a jockey talks to a skittish horse as he leads him into the starting gate.

Malcolm would have to walk up past the whores himself, and they would tease and fondle him as he went by. Trying their best to embarrass him, rubbing their soft bodies and silky kimonos against him.

"Cheez an' crackers, Jack, look at the double bumpers on this one!"

"Hello, young lane, don't you be no square shuffler. Come cop a squat on my softy—"

"Lookit this hipcat in all his steamed seams. I bet you he's hard as a tonk player's hole card," a big, coal black woman, half a head taller than Malcolm and with muscles like a dockworker's hooted at him, grabbing him by one arm and thrusting a hand down his pants until he had to fight to dislodge it.

"Oh, he is, he is!" She doubled over with laughter, still trying to pull him into her crib. "Oh, c'mon, sweet pea! C'mon in the Jersey side—"

He would pull away and lower his eyes, but he loved their attentions, his head still reeling from the rum and smoke at Creole Pete's. He found everything about them almost unbearably sexy— the smell of their hair and their perfume, the bare shoulders they let slip out of their robes; the glimpse of their breasts when they leaned over the landing. The way they laughed, and laid their soft hands upon him.

There was one girl, in particular, a short, sweet-faced young woman called Bea whose skin was almost white, and who wore her hair in a blond, marceled style. She never taunted him but gave him a sweet, shy smile and brushed against him, as friendly as a cat, when she saw him on the stairs. He had gone straight to her once he'd gotten his first paycheck from Charlie Small—only to find himself suddenly too nervous to do much, once he was inside.

"Ah, that's all right, Mister Man," she had drawled in her high voice, still smiling at him dopily. Drawing his limp self out of her as casually as she might take off an earring and continuing to minister to him by hand.

"Don' worry, honey, I never beat up my gums 'bout the payin' customers. Say, you got a head chick already?"

"Yeah, yeah I do," Malcolm told her, distracted by her hand still pumping at him. Wondering if he could count Miranda.

"'Course I do! What you think?"

"Tha's too bad," Bea told him, rolling her eyes up at him and batting her lashes. "'Cause if'n you didn't, I need somebody to look out for Baby an' me. You know what I'm sayin'? I'd pay ya fifty-fifty, right down the line, valentine—"

"Lemme think about it. I gotta knock a stroll right now—" he said hastily, coming in her hand a moment later with a grunt. He was trying to tuck himself back in and button up his fly when he looked up and saw a white woman standing not three feet away, having watched him come in the middle of the living room.

"Hey, what's the play?" he asked in alarm, backing away as hastily as he could, conscious of his drooping member still hanging out ludicrously. But the white woman didn't react, only staring at him with the same doped-up expression Bea had. She was wearing a blue silk Chinese robe that matched Bea's own, and her arms and legs stuck out of it like a scarecrow's. She had waves of wild, black hair running down over her shoulders, and skin so pale it was translucent, the purple veins clearly visible underneath.

"This here's Baby," Bea said proudly, going over to wrap an arm around her waist. She kissed her on the cheek, then slowly, teasingly pulled down the robe from one of her pale, white shoulders.

"Ain't she got nice skin? Ain't my Baby fine?" she asked, running a hand down her shoulder. "Say hi to Red, honey."

But the white woman only stood where she was. Her eyes so reddened and hollow that she looked as if she had just emerged from a cave, her long hair sticking out like a madwoman's.

"She don' do it with men, but she could watch," Bea said, blithely wiping his jism from her fingers with a tissue, and leading him by the hand back toward the door. The doped-up white woman still staring at him as he left, running up the stairs to his room.

"Thas why we need some protection. You think about it, Mister Man," Bea called up after him. "You need a steady earner, we be here."

As much as they excited him, all of the girls on the stairs seemed ugly and vulgar compared to Miranda. He had never stopped thinking about her after their night together, though he still didn't know how he might find her, or how he would approach her if he did. He had the name of the club, Café Society, where she was supposed to be singing down at Sheridan Square, but anything below 110th Street still seemed distant, and forbidding. He didn't know if he would be welcome there, remembering how it had been one night up in Boston when he and Jarvis had tried to go into a club where coloreds weren't wanted, and he was too embarrassed to ask anyone about it.

Whenever he so much as hinted about having a regular girl of any kind, the regulars at Small's Paradise had scoffed, and made fun of him. Accusing him of wanting a wife, and telling him he wasn't looking out for his opportunities.

"Lookit all the chicks you got around here," Sammy the Pimp told him, pointing them out, and Malcolm had to admit that there were a lot of women of all kinds, from the glamour girls setting up at the bar, to Dollarbill's tired, fearful whores, to the Thursday girls and all the stray women the war washed up at Small's. Some of them obviously brand new to the City, cardboard suitcases even in hand, looking country, and wide-eyed, and confused—the pimps at the bar all but licking their chops over them.

"See all the hens you can get? Fo' a pickup or pay, or anything in between? What you want some head chick for?" Sammy would goad him, and he would have to admit that was the smart play. He would try to follow the example of the older men around the bar, thinking the more women he possessed the better, the more there was to get out of it. Trying to think with his wallet, and not his pecker, as they urged him.

But he still couldn't get over Miranda, sure that it must have meant something to have hooked up with her twice in that night—remembering, as well as the sex, how they had lain together and talked, long into that night, and how she had listened to everything he said. He kept his desire hidden, did not want to make any uncool fuss in front of the regulars, but he kept his eyes open, too. Still hoping that she might walk into the Cloverleaf Room late one night, like everyone else, though he never saw her there.

He went back to the Savoy one Saturday night when Doc Wheeler's Sunset Royals, a hard-hitting road band, was playing, certain she wouldn't be able to resist them. There was a dance contest on, and the gleaming, orange-and-blue ballroom was just as full and lively as it had been the first night he had set foot in it, but it wasn't the same. When they broke into "How 'Bout that Mess?" he couldn't resist pulling a girl out to the floor to compete, trying to swing her about as hard as he had Miranda. But his partner's responses were clumsy, and uncoordinated, compared to hers. When they strayed into Cat's Corner this time, he felt a sudden, stunning pain in his leg, as if his ankle had been broken. Looking down only too late to see Twist Mouth Ganaway's high shoe striking out at him, the man glaring at him until he was able to limp his way shamefacedly off the dance floor.

He had kept going back nonetheless, sure that he would hook up with Miranda sooner or later and dance the King of The Track himself right off the floor. But one evening when he was still hanging around Small's, the story arrived on The Wire that the Savoy had been closed. He had run up to the ballroom at once, unable to believe it—but as soon as he turned the corner and saw the crowd, he knew it was true. The whole block was filled with seething black and brown faces, swimming in the dim light from the streetlamps. The great front doors chained and padlocked, with the same, black-and-white sign pasted on each of them:

"CLOSED—By order of the City of New York and the United States Military Authorities—" he managed to read, before the crowd pushed him on past. A steady river of men and women kept jostling their way slowly up to read the sign, cursing when they read it—then turning back to read it again, still unable to believe what it said.

"It's Jim Crow! It's Jim Crow right here in New York City, that's what it is!"

"You see! You see! We're goin' back to segregation, even here in Harlem!"

"We got to stop this. We got to stop the white man now—"

Even the regulars at Small's had been rattled by it the next day. They talked as if they had expected it all along, but beneath their cynical japes and smirks Malcolm could tell that it had unsettled even them, their words growing more heated the longer they chewed it over.

"Don't make sense! Place never served mor'n ginger ale!"

"Says here the bulls arrested three girls, one pimp, an' one reg'lar employee of the Savoy, for solicitation," Sammy read from his copy of the Mirror.

"Oh, man, that's ole avenue tripe! You get more of a haul Sat'day night down the Wal-dorf-Astoria!"

"You know what it really is. It's the mixin'," West Indian Archie told them with his usual air of authority. "It was just a colored hall, you could fill the place up with 'hos. Fact is, they don't want they boys where black an' white are gettin' together."

"That's who they really fightin'. That's who the goddamn war's really against—it's against us!"

"You hear 'bout that reecheous spade down in Philly?" Sammy the Pimp asked. No one had.

"He was knockin' bones wit' some soldier boys behind a gas station, till some MPs got booted to the play. Mind you, these MPs was chocolate, too, but they broke up the game anyway, an' oiled up his head for him."

"Mothafuckers—"

"That didn't stop him, though. You know what he told them MPs? He told 'em, 'You some crazy niggers wearin' that uniform.

You only fightin' for white trash.' He tol' 'em, 'This be a white man's war, an' a white man's gov'ment, an' neither one is any damned good!'"

The other regulars, even Charlie Small, nodded vigorously in approval, their eyes shining at the story.

"Is that right?"

"Well, well! That's a man for you!"

"That's nothing. You boys hear about what they did down Duck Hill? Down in Mississippi?" West Indian Archie sniffed.

"They got a camp down there with a lot of colored boys, but every time they went into town they got beat up an' run off by the deputy sheriffs. So Fourth July come, they pick up they guns, walk into Duck Hill, an' just shoot the hell outta that little cracker town."

"Damn!"

"Yup. They shot out every window, every light. Until ev'ry white cracker in town is inside his house, lyin' on the floor, coverin' they hindquarters an' prayin' for help from they white Jesus."

"Where'd you hear 'bout this? It weren't in the papers—"

"They won't let 'em put anyt'ing like that in the white snitch-pads."

"You got that right!"

"It was in the People's Voice, Adam Powell's paper. They went down an' asked those colored boys if it happen, but they just said, 'We only havin' a little fun, celebratin' the Fourth July, an' I guess those white folks got worried.' They said, 'Mind you, that could happen, if those white crackers ever try some o' that lynchin' business here.'"

"Damn!"

The regulars were all still for a moment, Malcolm as well.

"You know, we should do somethin' like that here," one of them finally said.

"Give 'em somethin' to think about. Just go down, shoot up the Empire State Building."

"Not so's you kill anybody, nec'ssarily. Just shoot it up some."

"Sure. Shoot up Penn Station. Shoot up Macy's an' Gimbels."

Just then Joe Baker, the undercover man, walked in, and they all fell silent again. Baker going up to the bar for his usual boilermaker, his hands in his pockets and his eyes on the floor as always, giving no indication that he had heard anything. But they stayed quiet nonetheless, until Charlie Small finally cleared his throat.

"Mind you, not that we want those other fellows to win the war," he said.

"Tha's right. We want America to win," Fewclothes added solemnly from the bar.

Malcolm didn't know anybody who really wanted the United States to lose the war. Whenever the newsreels came on up at the RKO Alhambra, or the Regency, everyone clapped when the Americans won, and booed and hissed any pictures of Hitler, or Tojo. But he'd also heard plenty of people say that it was a white man's war. When the cops weren't around, the stepladder orators would declaim about how the war showed that the white man could be beat, sure enough. If those little bandy-legged, four-eyed Japanese fellas could do it, anybody could do it. He would see the listening people in the crowds, even gray-haired old women out doing the shopping, nodding their heads fervently, murmuring, Tha's right, Tha's right, just as if they were in church.

There were things going on below the surface, he was sure of it. He could see, every day, how angry and sullen the faces of the people on the street looked. How when the constant, circling patrols of motorcycle cops came down the avenue—their motors grinding at the nerves—people would curse them openly, and even a beer can or a brick might fly out at them from a tenement rooftop. The words picked up in passing, in the back of barbershops, or on the subway, or in the alleyway outside Creole Pete's, though they were always the same—It ain't our war—

On one of his rare afternoons off, looking for someplace he could get comic books, he had wandered into a strange little storefront on the corner of West 125th Street and Seventh. There was an inscrutable sign over the door that read *"NATIONAL AFRICAN BOOKSTORE*The House of Common Sense and Home of Proper Propaganda, Professer Louis Toussaint, Prop."*, and inside was the most crowded store he had ever seen. It was jammed almost to the ceiling with precariously stacked piles of books and records, and every inch of the walls was covered with posters and paintings and photographs. Malcolm could barely move among them without knocking something loose, at least some dusty old leaflet or broadsheet.

He wandered back through all of these incredible piles of paraphernalia, unable to find any sign of comic books, but not really caring anymore. He reached what he thought was the back of the store, but saw there was actually a small door, leading into yet another room marked BLACK HALL OF FAME. He passed through it, though he had to duck his head to get under the lintel, and found himself in a room little bigger than a closet, where all he could do was stand and gape.

All along the walls of the little room were enormous, larger-than-life portraits of colored men and women. Photographs and paintings, some of them people in old-fashioned clothes, some of them in modern suits and dresses. All of them staring passively back down at him from their pictures, their visages flickering in the light from the large round candles placed in front of each one.

Malcolm looked from face to face, entranced. He didn't know any of them, and wondered what they could have done to be great. All except one. That same face he remembered from his boyhood—round and serious, almost troubled; his eyes looking out from beneath his feathered cockade parade hat into the middle distance, almost as if he could foresee everything that would befall him. It was his Daddy's man. Garvey.

"He's the greatest leader we've had yet. But there will be greater. There has to be," a voice said at his elbow.

Malcolm turned to see a short, grizzled black man with fierce dark eyes and a broad smile standing there.

"You a Garvey man, son?"

"I—don't know. My Daddy was," Malcolm found himself saying.

"Nothin' to be ashamed of. I was—still am. The man may die, the idea lives on."

"I guess."

"Well, don't guess, son. Know," he said, chuckling roughly. Pumping Malcolm's hand and leading him back out to the counter in the front room, under another long banner that read The White Man's Dream of Being Supreme Has Turned to Sour Cream—Back to Africa!

"Professer Louis Toussaint. And I guess you came to be educated."

"I don't know—"

"You don't know much, do you, boy?" Professor Toussaint told him, beginning to pull books out here and there from the tottering piles all around him. "I bet you don't know anybody else in that room, do you? Don't worry, we'll take care of that. First we got to get you religion."

Malcolm peered down at all the books the little man was dropping into his arms. The titles all but unfathomable to him—The
Holy Koran of the Moorish Science Temple of America. The
Onward Movement of America. A Black Man Will Be the Coming
Universal King and The Knowledge of Self and Others and Secrets
of the Lost-Found Nation of Islam and The History of the End of
the World. There was even a final one that had no title or author
at all, just a slim, green volume bound in patent leather, with what
looked like a gold crescent moon embossed on the cover.

"What is all this?" Malcolm asked.

"Why, it's religion, son! The Black Man's natural religion, which
is his real heritage," Prof. Toussaint told him. "I bet you didn't
know that all of human civilization started over in Africa."

"It did?"

"'Course it did! Why, everything that we think of as culture, and
art and science, and literature, and government and democracy
started over in Africa. Practically every week, they're making some
new find from the lost civilizations over there. An elephant can't
stumble without falling on some white man with a shovel over there,
an' what he's digging up. Fossils of the first men! Gold work of
such fine tolerance and workmanship that it has no rival! Ancient
objects, produced and refined by black hands with results that no
human hand today can equal!"

"I never heard about nothin' like that," Malcolm muttered, embarrassed.

"Sure you haven't! And why is that? Why is that? Because everything you've ever been taught has been by a white man, out of a
book written an' published by another white man."

Prof. Toussaint snatched back the top book in Malcolm's arms,
the one entitled Secrets of the Lost-Found Nation of Islam. Flipping it open, and shoving it back under Malcolm's nose.

"You see how it is? All the letters, all the words, they're in black.
All the spaces where there's nothing written, they're white. The
Black Man been whited out of history! You know that's true, don't
you? Don't you feel it in your heart?"

"Yes," Malcolm said slowly, but quietly exultant. Thinking now
that he had found it after all, the key to the secret knowledge that he
already suspected was all around him—that he had always suspected.

"Worst crime in human history was the Atlantic slave trade,"
Prof. Toussaint continued. "White man shipped millions, tens

of millions of Black Men and Women over to build this country for him. Entire foundation of this nation, built on the blood and the bones of the Black Man! But as many Black people as he killed—many as he subjugated, and stole their labor, an' raped their women—the worst thing the white man did was to erase the Black Man's past. To erase his history, so he don't even know his true language, or his religion. Black Man in America today don't even know what his real name is, or what tribe he is descended from, the Mandingo, or the Wolof, the Serer, or the Fula, or the Fanti, or the Ashanti—"

Malcolm's mind reeled at the sound of all those beautiful, strange names—so many questions jamming his throat that he couldn't get a word out. But Prof. Toussaint gave off his talk, and frowned suddenly at Malcolm, as if something had just occurred to him.

"Say, you ain't a Christian, are you, boy?"

"No..." Malcolm said tentatively. Remembering his Daddy's stomping, shouting sermons. How scared they had made him feel, and how he had hated his submission.

"Good!" Prof. Toussaint boomed at him, and chuckled. "That's the whole trouble with the so-called Negro today. He's lost. He don't have a thing to call his own. He speaks the white man's language, worships the white man's God—this man Jesus with the straight hair.

"You see, when a Negro gets the white man's religion, he won't kill so much as a chinch bug. If a chinch bug bites him, he gets up out of bed and prays for that chinch's soul. The white man's religion says, 'Thou shalt not steal'—but what he means is, don't steal from him. He says, 'Thou shalt not kill'—but what he means is, don't kill him. 'Love your enemy.' You see a lot of lovin' of enemies in this big war the white man's havin' just now?"

Malcolm took a step backward, as staggered by the man's words as he was by the pile of books now reaching up nearly to his chin. He had never heard anything explained so clearly and sharply, at least not since he'd been to his Daddy's Garvey meetings. The words like bright, spinning tops inside his head.

"What's this one?" he asked, holding up the last book, the green one with no title at all on it, just that gold sliver of a moon. His curiosity growing rapidly, like a great, sudden thirst.

"Oh, that's the best one of all. You save that one for last," Prof. Toussaint told him, distracted, looking down to ring up all of Malcolm's putative purchases on his cash register.

"That'll be two bucks apiece."

"Two bucks!"

"You know you got it. You know you're just gonna blow it on the numbers anyway," the older man told him.

Malcolm was about to object again, but looking down he noticed the name on the Secrets of the Lost-Found Nation of Islam, as well as several of the others. Elijah Muhammad—one of the same names of the man he had seen, half awake and half asleep, after his night with Miranda.

He paid for them all gladly after that, and took them back at once to the privacy of his room. Not quite ready to go through them yet, laying them all out on his bed so he could simply look at them, just as he had with the suit West Indian Archie had gotten him. Sure that this was the key to something. Thinking over again just who the little man he had seen that night might have been, whether he was real at all or just a dream, a spook from somewhere. He thought that there was something about him that reminded him of his own Daddy, though that frail, light brown man could not have looked any less like his Daddy. Early Little built like a working-man, even if he never liked to work much; tall and black as pitch, and missing one eye.

It was more in the way he talked. That soft Georgia touch to his voice, dripping with all those raw, piney crossroads towns Earl's own father had passed through in his days as an itinerant preacher. Reynolds and Butler, Wenona and Cordele, and Millen and Forsythe and Sandersville, and a dozen more, all but indistinguishable from each other, choking on smoke, and sawdust and bile. Places Malcolm had never been, though his first memories were of his father talking about his people down there.

"Your granddaddy wouldn't let me name you after him."

He was four years old, his Daddy hauling him angrily across a field. His fingers crushed in his father's huge hand, his shoulder feeling as if it were about to be pulled out of its socket. The tall stalks of wild grass scratching his face, and making his eyes water.

"That's right. For all your Momma thinks a you. Your grand-daddy wanted me to name you after him, too—you bein' the seventh child, of a seventh son of a preacher. He was prayin' you'd be a boy, so we could call you John."

Even then, he wasn't sure what his name was supposed to be. Hilda and Philbert called him Chink, and a freak of nature, while the other kids on the street called him Milky, made him want to cry just to hear it.

"But when you was born, an' I wired 'em that you were as white as Gramma, she ashamed. She hates all the white blood in her veins. An' your Grampa John cried when he heard it, an' said he didn't want no al-bino grandson named for him!"

His eyes were blue then. His mother liked to say they were sea blue, the way her own had been, though other people told him they looked green, or gray, or brown. His hair was red-blond, and his mother kept it cut so close to his head that it made his face look as round as a pumpkin. She labored over it for hours, trying to comb the curls out with some of Madam Walker's iron combs that she borrowed from a neighbor, heating them up over the kitchen stove until they glowed red. In the bath she would scrub his face and neck so violently he cried—though afterward she would take him over to show off to Mrs. Stohrer next door, telling her proudly, I can make him look almost white if I bathe him enough.

His mother's hair was straight and shiny black, and sometimes she wore it in a long braid down to her waist. She was slender and tall, and she held herself proudly, and he knew that people were always taking her for white. He had thought it himself one time, when he had looked up from his play in front of the tiny house they rented and wondered who that tall white lady was walking up their street. She liked to tell him that he had been named for her father, who was a prince in Scotland, and who had owned a whole plantation down in Grenada. She told everyone that she had five years of Anglican schooling, and was proud of her accent and her diction, insisting that they call her Louise, instead of Louisa, which had been her name down in the Islands.

She would even make fun of how little learning her husband had, though Earl would beat her for it, raging at her in his frustration. Don't you be putting your smooth words on me. Watching them, Malcolm never understood why she did it—why she couldn't see what was bound to happen when she goaded him like that. Knowing how quick his father was to hit any of them, Wilfred or Philbert or Reginald, or even his sister, Hilda. Whaling away at them with anything, a switch or a belt, or just his big, rough, carpenter's hands.

Except for him. His father almost never beat him—always picking out one of his sisters or brothers unless there was no one else around, or the blind immediacy of his need overcame him.

His mother never hesitated to hit any of them. She would purposely let her anger stoke—sending him out first to cut a good switch for his own beating. He always tried to find one that would break, but when it did she would just send him out for a thicker one, or simply hit him in the back of the head with her hand so hard that it felt as if his skull had been split open.

His only defense was to scream—so much louder and longer than any of the others that she sometimes let him go for fear that the neighbors would hear him. He would run out of the house, shaking his little fist at her. Calling her an old witchy woman and screaming, "I could kill you, I could kill you!"—but she would only laugh, her anger sated by then. Once, when he came home from the Pleasant Cove school to show her his raw, reddened palm from where the teacher had made him hold out his hand and hit him with a ruler as hard as she could, she had just shrugged.

"In Anglican school the teacher used to whip our legs," she told him. "I liked it when he did that. When that teacher lashed me, he woke me up. He made me feel."

He spent as much time as he could with his Daddy, who took him everywhere. During the week he hauled him around to the homes of the Baptist congregations he served as a jackleg preacher, letting them lay out something for them both to eat and drink in every household. Proudly standing him up for his hosts on a kitchen chair—boasting that when he was old, all his children would support him.

"I got it figured," he would say. "Just lookit this little man, you know what he's going to do!"

On Sunday mornings he would take Malcolm with him to meeting. Driving slowly, cautiously through the white neighborhoods in their big old black touring car, peering out the window at the road with his one eye. Sitting Malcolm up in the first pew to listen to his hellfire sermons.

"You better get yourself right with the Lord! That little black train is a-comin', an' you better get your business right!" he thundered at the people in the storefronts and the crude, pine-board churches, and Malcolm would stare, amazed, as his father seemed to become another man right before his eyes—grinning and laughing, jumping and shouting wildly about the pulpit like someone possessed.

"That train take you right to hell, you don't get yourself right! An' there won't be no branch lines, won't be no stops. You can ring an' ring on the bell, but the trolley ain't gonna stop, an' once you dead you ain't gettin' off!"

It unnerved him, seeing his Daddy transform himself right out in public like that. Bringing the whole congregation to its feet, singing and clapping their hands, and shouting in joy until Malcolm trembled in terror, wishing he could get down from his pew and crawl away on his hands and knees while they sang their dreadful, threatening hymns—

Must Jesus bear the cross alone,
And all the world go free?
No, there's a cross for everyone,
And there's a cross for me—

He liked the Garvey meetings better—a room full of somber black men, meeting in somebody's drab back parlor or kitchen. There was an air of secrecy about them, the curtains pulled over the windows while they met, their host staring carefully through the keyhole at any new visitors before he let them in. They would listen to his father preach, too, nodding at his every word, though here he was masterful and intense—in firm command of himself, Malcolm thought, outlining for them all the glorious history of their race—

"Since Ham was a Negro, it follows that all his descendants were. That is, the Cushites—or Ethiopians—and the Egyptians, and Phoenicians, and the Babylonians, and the Assyrians. Even the Hebrew people intermarried with the Cushites, so that Jesus is a descendant of Ham, and therefore a Negro. And so is Adam, and Eve—they all black! Whites is only the spawn of Gehazi, the servant who was cursed by the Prophet Elisha with leprosy, and skin as white as snow!"

Malcolm would listen intently to the names of all those ancient peoples. They reminded him of the illustrations of the pyramids, and ancient temples that he had seen in the Sunday color supplements. Then his father would open up the envelope with photographs of Garvey he had brought to sell, and pass them around. Garvey sitting in an open car, wearing that plumed hat and a uniform full of medals and ribbons. Garvey staring wistfully into the distance—

Malcolm had grasped the big, shiny pictures in his little hands, carefully holding them around the edges like his Daddy had taught him, so he wouldn't get his thumbprints on it. Gazing into the huge, ponderous face of the man, while his father told the others how they were not the only ones. How Garvey had followers everywhere—not only in the United States but in the Islands, and even in England, and of course in Africa, where there were millions of black men, waiting to rise at his command. Waiting to rescue the Lost Negroes of North America, and the Islands, and everywhere else, and bring them back home.

"No one knows when the hour of Africa's redemption cometh," he would always tell them at the end of the meeting. "It is in the wind. It is coming. One day, like a storm, it will be here." Leading them in the closing chant:

> *"Up, you mighty race, you can accomplish what you will!"*
> *"Up, you mighty race, you can accomplish what you will!"*
> *"Up, you mighty race, you can accomplish what you will!"*
> *"Africa for the Africans! Ethiopians, Awake!"*

And afterward, on the car ride back through the dark—his Daddy driving even slower now because of how little he could see at night with his one eye—he would harangue Malcolm about his skin color again, and about how much he hated all white people, and most especially the white blood that flowed in the veins of his wife, and which gave her such airs.

But as he got older, Malcolm noticed that whenever white people were around, his Daddy was friendly to them. Evenings, Early would stand out in front of their house with him—always with him—gripped firmly in one of his huge hands. Greeting their white neighbors like Mr. and Mrs. Stohrer with big smiles, or even going over to knock on their doors and offer them fresh tomatoes and corn and watermelons from their vegetable garden out back—and taking him along again. Only Malcolm noticing how the smiles clenched on their white faces when they opened their doors and saw him.

Once his Daddy had spied one of the white neighbors surreptitiously dumping some of the fresh, yellow corn he had just given him out into his pigsty, and he had raged about the house for hours. Wondering over and over again why the man would throw out his good corn, until finally Malcolm had asked him:

"Daddy, why do you like white folks so much, when we a mighty race?"

The blow surprised him, since his father hit him so rarely, the back of his hand sending him sprawling across the stringy throw rug on their parlor floor. His Daddy standing over him, seething, his hands clenched into two fists. He had propped himself up on his elbows—too scared to get all the way up, but too stunned to cry, just blinking at his father.

"Don't you never say that! Don't you never say anything like that to me again, boy!" he yelled at him.

But later that same night, holding Malcolm on his lap at the kitchen table, he had sipped whiskey and launched into a rambling explanation of himself—a moment that made Malcolm squirm when he remembered it, which he did at least every week.

"Sometimes, you got to deal wit' the devil hisself to get what you need," he'd said, his words coming out slurred and slowed by the whiskey. "Sometimes, you got to play up to the enemy, get what you want, 'fore you can send him back down to hell. I ain't never been a lucky man. I got ten chil'ens, got to dig where I can."

But still Malcolm saw that their white neighbors' aloofness bothered him. He never understood—as Malcolm did—that they had heard all the running fights emanating from their house; the beatings, and the shouting, and the shrieking of women and children. He didn't hear the rumors that he never worked, only faked accidents to collect the insurance money.

It was true that things happened to Earl Little. He had lost his eye when he sideswiped a nail on a construction job, and after that, with his depth perception gone, he was always falling off ladders and roofs, or smashing his fingers. One night he had even turned their old black touring car over in a ditch, with all of them inside. Malcolm had watched it unfold like a nightmare from his place in the backseat, sandwiched between his brothers and sisters. His father driving the car slowly, carefully, right into the ditch—Malcolm wanting to shout out a warning but unable to believe it was happening until the first wheel sank in. The big car toppling over as ponderously as an ocean liner, all of the children screaming and falling onto each other as it slowly went over on its side.

Miraculously, they had all been able to scramble out with just a few cuts and bruises—if only because his Daddy was so blind at night he could not drive any faster. He had pulled them all out, brushing them off, not even yelling at any of them, he was so embarrassed. Unable to so much as look at his wife.

"C'mon, c'mon, you're not hurt," was all he said to them. Lining them up by the side of the road to make sure they were all accounted for. Making them help him right the car, before they all piled back in and motored slowly on through the darkness again.

It was the abiding faith of his Daddy's life that he had never been lucky. He liked to talk about how nobody in his whole family had ever had any luck, how three of his brothers had been shot dead, and how he himself had had a dress shop that made money back in Omaha, until the Klan had run him out of business and burned down their house—though when he did, Louise would always sniff and say it never happened that way.

"You know what really happened in Omaha," she would add meaningfully, and Malcolm always thought they were about to get into it again. But his Daddy would only throw up one hand and mutter in her general direction.

"Women don't want to see any stone what's in a man's way," he said. "It's a man's job to see his way clear."

Despite his bad luck he was always full of plans. He told them that he was going to get a job on the line at the Olds Reo plant, but when he went down to apply he was handed a form for a janitor's job and he had crumpled it up and thrown it on the floor; walking slowly away, daring the white man who had handed it to him to do anything about it. Some days he would say he was going to the employment agency he claimed to run downtown, and leave in the morning whistling, dressed in his business clothes and with an empty briefcase in his hand. But by the time he got back, he was always in a bad mood. The briefcase still empty, Malcolm knew from when he had run down to the curb to carry it for him. Earl waving off his wife when she questioned him about it.

"Money's no problem!" he yelled at her. "Money's no problem for a man like me!"

But one day, soon after his sister Yvonne was born, they had received a letter from the landlord summoning them to court for breaking the white covenant on the block where they lived. When they had rented the house, Earl had sent Louise to see the man— confident that she could pass herself off as white. When the summons came she had looked at it with her mouth open in shock. Holding it up to her husband's face, demanding to know, "Early, what does this mean? What does this mean?"

He had slapped the letter away—"Why don't you tell me, wit' all yo' Anglican schooling?"—then walked down off the porch with his hands in the pockets of his work overalls, scuffing at the dirt.

He had tried fighting it, even going to the trouble of hiring a white lawyer, though that had only succeeded in adding his fee, and the court costs, to their burden. He had promptly ordered the lawyer to appeal—but in those weeks while their appeal was being considered, Malcolm had never seen his father so quiet. Walking around and around their property, staring up at the house as if he expected the structure itself to provide him with the answer to their dilemma.

Malcolm couldn't fathom why any white man would want their house, with its tar-paper shingles already worn from black to red, the paint peeling off it, and the rusted nails bobbing up through the floorboards of their porch. Even as a child he could see it was the worst house in their neighborhood, the most narrow and forlorn.

Yet it was the eviction notice that terrified him, with its salient passage that he read over and over again, trying to decipher its meaning—"This land shall never be rented, leased, sold to, or occupied by persons other than those of the Caucasian race." Unable to believe that it could really mean what he thought it did, until he had his mother confirm it for him, in one of those increasingly rare moments when she could talk about anything instead of just slumping down in a kitchen chair for hours at a time.

What he wanted to ask her then was how it was that the white people in the neighborhood could claim that no one but them could live there forever. What if they were to put a white covenant over everything? What if they put a covenant over the whole face of the earth? Where would they go then?

It was hopeless, as far as he could see, and from his mother's silence he knew that she thought the same. But over the next few days, while the rest of them waited fearfully for the appearance of the sheriff and the eviction men, Earl's spirits seemed to revive. Malcolm actually heard him come down in the morning whistling, and he told Louise that she shouldn't worry, their eviction would be a blessing in disguise.

One Saturday night early in November, when the jagged ridges of hoarfrost had first started to appear on what remnants of grass there were in the yard, Earl had told them all in a loud voice that he was going out to get more kerosene for the kitchen stove. Louise had started to tell him that there was plenty for the night, but he had cut her off sharply, saying that he might as well go get some now since he had to be up early in the morning for church.

They had all sat around the kitchen table, staring at each other while they listened to the sound of the old car rumble into life on the third try and slowly lumber away. His mother hadn't said a thing—but soon after his Daddy had left, she had informed them all that it was too cold to sleep upstairs tonight. She had settled Hilda and herself and the baby Yvonne on pallets on the kitchen chairs, and put Malcolm and his three brothers together under their blankets, on the stringy throw rug in the middle of the parlor floor. There it had felt colder than it ever had upstairs in their bed, but they had enjoyed the adventure. Huddling up close against the wind that sliced its way in through the window jambs, and between the shingles of the aged, ramshackle house. Poking and pushing at each other under the thin blankets, the four boys trying to get comfortable until they achieved a sweaty, drooling equilibrium—legs over each other's legs, arms around each other's necks.

It was a dream-haunted sleep, the wind slapping at the loose corner slats of the house. Malcolm thought he heard something that sounded like a car backfiring, or even a gunshot, and the sound of feet padding rapidly across their little yard outside. Someone was running over to the neighbor's house, where they banged on their back door—then retracing their way across their yard, over to the other next-door neighbors, then running crazily back and forth, all up and down their block until suddenly Malcolm felt a hand on his arm. His mother yanking him up, Wilfred and Philbert and Reginald right after him, from their tent of blankets on the floor.

"Come on," she said—her voice quiet but more urgent than he had ever heard it in his life, even in those moments when he had thought she was mad enough to actually beat him to death. Frantically shoving him and his brothers into pullover shirts and pants, Reginald and Philbert complaining sleepily that she was putting them in the wrong ones.

"It doesn't matter!" she hissed at them. "The house is on fire!"

"I don't smell nothin' burnin'," Wilfred said, sniffing about him.

She slapped him across the face so hard his whole body turned halfway around. Then she grabbed them up by their skinny arms again, two boys to a hand, and began to pull them out toward the front door where Hilda was already waiting, her eyes large with fear and the strain of holding the baby.

"When I tell you somethin', you best believe it!" she hissed, still pulling them forward, until they were tumbling down the front steps.

Malcolm thought Wilfred was right, he didn't smell anything himself save for the usual tang of the kerosene stove, maybe a little stronger than usual. But as soon as they reached the front yard, his Daddy loomed abruptly up in front of them, also shouting that their house was burning down. He looked back toward the house—and as if on command saw a little light spring up, back in the darkness of the house, where the kitchen was. It looked like no more than the flame of a church altar candle at first—then it shot up, and out, already beginning to engulf the whole first floor of their home.

"My house is burning! They set my house on fire!" his father was yelling, stretching out his long arms as far as they would reach. Until it seemed to Malcolm, still half in his dreams, that his Daddy was larger than ever, standing like a great tree before the fire. His endless arms covering the entire width of the little house, and yard—holding, at the very end of his reach, a pistol in one of his enormous hands, and a double-barreled shotgun in the other.

"They set my house afire!"

The neighbors were already pouring out onto their front lawns. Some of them wearing bathrobes and pyjamas, others yanking up pants and wrapping kitchen dresses around themselves. Their visages bleary and slack with sleep still, so that it seemed to Malcolm as if all the white people on the street were somehow wearing their real faces, instead of the clenched, guarded expressions he saw on them all day long. Their confused, wondering cries carrying back and forth across the darkened yards:

"Anybody in there?"

"You call the fire department?"

"Somebody was poundin' on my back door—"

They pulled up short when they reached his Daddy, standing there with his arms stretched wide as a tree's branches. Malcolm could see them grimacing in recognition—the clenched, white faces back in place—but approaching him anyway. Staring past him in amazement at his latest catastrophe.

"Anything we can do, Earl?"

"I'll get my hose—"

"Don't worry! Don't worry!" Earl shouted—his voice surprisingly mild and reassuring to Malcolm's ears, compared to the way he had just been yelling. Pointing to all of them, and his mother, huddled pathetically in their thrown-on clothes and the blankets she had somehow been able to fetch for them.

"Don't nobody worry, I already got my family out!"

All the white faces—and some black ones, too, neighbors who had come over from the next, uncovenanted block—looking up at him uncertainly, obviously unsure of what they should or could do.

Others were already running back to their own homes, dragging out their garden hoses to try and wet down their roofs. Some of them even moving their own possessions out into their front yards, Malcolm staring at all the nice, white people's furniture—the divans and dining room sets, and cabinet radios—looking so strangely exposed out on their frost-covered lawns.

"We can still salvage something—" one of the men in front of their house said. The others, black and white, staring warily at the fast-spreading fire but slowly rolling up their sleeves nevertheless, as if to at least make a demonstration that they were ready and willing to brave the flames.

"No," his father told them adamantly. "I don't want nobody goin' back in there. I can't have that on my soul. Look how far that fire's got, it's almost out on the porch now."

"Maybe we can go 'round the back, through the kitchen," one of the other colored men suggested, but his Daddy turned on him at once, looking as if he might strike him.

"No!" he cried. Then in a softer, bitter voice—

"Let it burn. It's all theirs."

At that moment an explosion ripped out the back of the house. The ground shaking under their feet, a spire of flame shooting twenty feet into the sky from where the kitchen had been. The men stepped back as one, quailing from the heat and the thought of what they had been on the brink of doing.

"Jeez, we woulda been right there!" one of their neighbors explained.

"Yeah, he knew what he was talkin' about—"

"Yes, he sure did. He knew just what was going to happen," one of the colored men from the next block said meaningfully, before they all began to run back toward their own homes.

All that winter and into spring, the arguments had persisted in the neighborhood over whether or not Earl Little had burned his own house down. They went on even after the two insurance policies his Daddy had taken out allowed them to move into their new, bigger house, where they had enough land to grow almost all their own food, plus raise chickens and hutches full of rabbits. Through all the police inquiries concerning such questions as why someone had pounded on the neighbors' back doors just before the fire, or how it was that the two-gallon can of kerosene Earl had bought that evening and that had supposedly caused the kitchen to explode came to be found in the basement, secreted under some old bedsprings.

But his Daddy had patiently told the same story, over and over again, that he had first told to the police when they finally arrived at the fire, long after the house had been reduced to no more than smoking rubble—and on which his wife had backed him up nearly word for word, testifying calmly and unshakeably, sitting up very straight, first in the police station, then on the witness stand, taking care to always smooth her modest flower-print dress carefully over her knees. That it was the Black Legion that had come to burn him out, on account of his being a race man, and a Garveyite, and that he had fired his shotgun at them out the back door, before being forced to retreat and make sure that his family was safe. Sticking to that one explanation—to one word, really—when the assistant district attorney had insisted indignantly that the night riders of the Black Legion had never been active in the area. Replying that, Well, they have now, and that it was probably all on account of trying to preserve their white homeowner's covenant. Letting the single word drip off his lips like an expectoration when he said it, repeating it over and over again from the witness chair:

"Their covenant."

CHAPTER EIGHT

MALCOLM

It was the day after he had discovered the African National Bookstore that Miranda walked into Small's. He heard her laugh, and he knew who it was even though he had his back to the door, leaning over the bar to pick up an order. Turning around immediately, his face split into a helpless grin—only to see West Indian Archie walk in.

He was baffled for a moment. He had been eager to see Archie, too, figuring he was the only one of the regulars he could tell about Prof. Toussaint's store, and all the strange and exciting books he had bought there. But even as he saw him, he knew there was something wrong.

Archie was smiling. That was what Malcolm noticed before he saw anything else. He looked even sharper than he usually did, wearing a brand-new white linen suit, and a new Panama hat. But more than anything else, he was smiling—and not just his usual fleeting, tight-lipped smile, provoked by his own wit, or the foolishness of other people. He was grinning—grinning as no one had ever seen him grin before, his prominent gold tooth glimmering in the soft interior light of the bar. And on his arm, looking up at him adoringly and laughing, was Miranda.

Malcolm went on and picked up his order from the bar, playing it as cool as he could even as the sick feeling spread through his stomach. He walked right past them, lifting his tray over their heads on one hand, even acknowledging Archie with a curt nod—not letting either of them see a thing.

"Hey, De-troit Red!" Archie called out with a gravelly chuckle—pointing him out to her as he went by.

"That there is my boy, De-troit Red—"

Her eyes flickered up at him, giving away nothing. As steady and enigmatic as the first night he had seen her, so that he couldn't even tell if she recognized him.

"C'mon over here, Red, I want you to meet somebody," Archie was still insisting, waving him over to their table with one of his huge arms until Malcolm had finished giving out his drinks. Forcing himself to turn, then walk back toward them, placing one foot in front of another like a movie zombie. Even making himself smile as he came up to their table.

"This here Miranda, she sings down the Village," Archie introduced her, as proud and jubilant as a new parent. "She playin' that big-time Café Society place down at Sheridan Square—"

"How'd you do?" Malcolm mumbled at her, and she gave him her hand, presenting it to him as if she were royalty. He could feel her looking straight at him but he could not meet her gaze.

She was wearing a crisp white sundress with thin red stripes this time, looking as cool and unruffled as a peppermint soda even in the late afternoon heat. He could not keep himself from stealing a look at her long, tanned legs, the high ridge of her breasts—the single trickle of perspiration that ran slowly down the side of her neck from her long, swept-up, white girl's hair. When he took her hand he had all he could do to keep himself from leaning over and kissing her right up that tiny rivulet of sweat.

"Pleased to meet you," she said in that smoky voice he remembered instantly, and he held on to her hand for an extra beat. Her skin just as smooth as he remembered it, too, and still smelling of flowers. He leaned over, inhaling her, about to kiss her hand at least, until he heard the laughter from the bar.

"Lookit Red, the perfect gentleman!" Sammy the Pimp cried.

"He flipped like Mr. Chips!"

Malcolm straightened up, and smiled sheepishly at the other regulars. West Indian Archie was laughing like a schoolboy, and even Miranda was smiling, so that he had to laugh along with them then, shaking his head in his embarrassment.

"Here, Red, you go get us a bottle a black label, keep the change fo' yo'self," Archie told him, tucking a fifty into the chest pocket of his waiter's jacket, and still chuckling out of pure happiness, unable to stop himself. He even called after him:

"I don't blame you, Red—she's truly mad!"

But Malcolm was already moving back toward the kitchen, stop-ping just beyond the swinging doors. There he leaned against the wall, trying to control himself—listening to the other regulars talking about her at the bar.

"She one hard-hitting gray, that's for sure."

"Wish I could get a hen like that fo' my house," Cadillac Drake said, shaking his head then giggling at the idea.

"What makes you think you can't?" Sammy the Pimp asked him, his voice low but serious, in a way that made Malcolm want to go out and climb right over the bar to get at him.

"Any white chick comes up here, you know you can turn her out," he insisted. "You know they lookin' fo' one thing."

"That may be, but I wouldn't mess with it." Cadillac Drake gig-gled again. "Lookit Archie over there. He look— Well, he look—"

"Happy," Sammy the Pimp said glumly. "He looks happy."

When Malcolm went back out to their table, he saw that it was true. West Indian Archie looked happier than he had ever seen him before, his weathered brown face still creased with laughter, as if he found everything in life funny now.

Miranda was not laughing, he saw. But she was smiling at Archie again—one of her delicate hands placed over his big brown paw in the middle of the table. Still looking at him as if she were enthralled by every word he had to say, until by the time he reached their table, Malcolm was gripped by the nearly irresistible desire to grab up the bottle of scotch he had ordered and smash it in Archie's face.

Instead, he carefully set out the two glasses and the bottle of scotch, laying down napkins and a bottle of ice, doing it all pre-cisely, as Charlie Small had shown him.

"There ya are, Red!"

Archie pulled out another five, insisted on shoving that, too, into his jacket pocket—looking like he might just burst out laugh-ing again at the magnanimity of his own gesture. Malcolm opened his mouth to say something then—no longer interested in hurting Archie with the bottle. Realizing that he wouldn't understand some sudden, physical attack anyway, that Archie would think Malcolm was just some crazy nigger, or that he had just been paid off by his rivals in the numbers racket—before he shot him in the head.

Instead, Malcolm was seized by the desire to tell him who she was. Just some cheap white whore, who puts out at cutting parties. Who would even take up with a nigger waiter. With someone like me.

He wanted to tell him that, to just put it out there—wanting to see Archie's face fall in hurt and bewilderment for the moment before it turned to pure wrath. To hear the hustlers' whistles and howls from the bar. Almost unable to bear not saying it, knowing the chaos it would set loose, the attention it would turn upon him. Archie would be sure to cut him up for that, too, maybe even kill him right there on the floor of Small's, but he told himself he did not care anymore—

She stopped him with a look. Almost the same look, he realized in confusion, that the preacher's wife had given him—back on that run a few weeks before, the day he had come to New York for the first time. The same look he had seen countless times before on the faces of colored women passengers, pleading for his help to get out of some situation—to get them away from some white man who was bothering them, or forcing himself on to them or about to explode into the sort of fearsome, unpredictable white people's rage that he and every other colored person he had ever known could spot, often before the man did himself. It was their secret language, he had thought—what he realized now to his confusion must be the same look of all women, seeking help. He just had never seen it from a white girl before—

He thanked West Indian Archie and put the finiff into his pants pocket—grinning blankly, automatically, the way he would on the train. Then he walked back toward the kitchen, stopping this time in a little side pantry by the ladies' room where they kept the extra dishes, a pail and a mop and the piles of crisply folded white tablecloths. She came by less than a minute later and he grabbed her roughly by the arm, pulling her back into the little alcove.

"What you doin' with that old man?" he demanded, holding on tightly to her arm. But she only stared down imperiously at his hand until he released her—an entirely different kind of look now.

"Well?" he said, trying to insist on an answer.

"Who knows? Maybe I love him," she said in her clipped, white-girl's voice—different, too, from the one she had used in the bedroom that night at the rent party.

"I thought you loved me!" he blurted out, unable to keep himself from saying it, knowing how childish it sounded.

She gave a little laugh, and then he was humiliated—but also acutely conscious all over again of how beautiful she looked, how close she was to him. Her face just under his own, her bare legs touching his trousers. Her cheeks looked as full and sensuous as two half peaches, dabbed with a faint sprinkling of powder, he saw. And she smelled of flowers—

"Oh, baby. Why do you think you love me? Because I'm your first white girl?" she asked him, her voice teasing but still sympathetic.

"Well—sure! But also because—because the things you did. An' 'cause you didn't laugh at me none," he said, trying to explain, his voice barely audible. "Then I wake up, you ain't even around—"

"Usually they prefer it that way."

"Goddammit, girl! Why you say things like that—"

"Never mind," she said, and reached out a hand to run it down the side of his cheek, the way she had that first night.

He closed his eyes. No longer caring about where they were now, in the tiny pantry room, with no door or curtain across it so that anybody could come by and see them. Not caring about how dangerous it could be, but turning his face into her hand, just glad to have its touch back against him. When he finally opened his eyes he was surprised to see that hers were brimming with tears.

"Never mind me, Red," she told him, her voice warm and a little sad—the way it had been during their night together. Like that of a white girl trying to imitate a blues singer, he realized now.

"Believe me, I'm not what you want. Go find yourself some nice girl."

"You mean some nice colored girl."

"You don't know what I mean," she said impatiently now—in control of herself again, stepping away from him and toward the ladies' room. "You don't know the slightest thing about me. But you still think you're in love."

"I know you want to be with me, not him—" he tried to tell her, but she had already gone through the door.

"Girl like that come up here, she lookin' for action," Sammy the Pimp told him as he walked him back up toward his apartment that night. "Only question if Archie gonna turn her out hisself, or if it gonna be somebody else."

"She been uptown before."

"Wha's 'at?" Sammy stopped in the middle of the sidewalk, his eyes feral and alert beneath his clean-shaven, bullet-shaped head, and Malcolm immediately regretted that he had opened his mouth.

"What you say?"

"Nothin'!" Malcolm said, and kept walking. "Just I seen her around before. Up at the Savoy, an' like that."

"Well, how 'boot that. So she already been gunnin' her ray here'bouts. That just shows she wants it more."

"You shouldn't go messin' with Archie, 'less you want to end up in the river."

"Whoa, Cholly Hoss! What makes you think Archie shouldn't look out fo' me?" Sammy said, putting a reproving hand on Malcolm's shoulder, stopping him where he was.

"'Sides, it don't have to be like that. All you need is fo' Archie to get word 'bout how she's been knockin' a stroll 'round these parts already. Who she been with, an' where. Sure enough, he'll turn her loose. Then she be lookin' fo' a new daddy—"

"I don't think she needs a daddy," Malcolm said as casually as he could, and tried to walk on. "You heard Archie, she got this gig singin' down the Village—"

"Every womens need a daddy, Nome! Let me tell you how it's done," Sammy said, stopping him again. Smiling voraciously, the dimmed streetlight turning his face and teeth a sickly, jaundiced hue. Malcolm, watching his face, realizing now that he must be at least as old as West Indian Archie, if not older. But Sammy's skin looked as if it had been wrenched back along his skull, stretched into dozens of tight little lines around his eyes and mouth.

"I started out waitin' tables, too," he told him, his hand tightening suddenly on Malcolm's shoulder, until he wanted to squirm under the grip.

"But I looked out for my opportunities. I'd wait till I copped to some hen who was dinin' alone, an' then I'd beat up my chops with her till I found out if she had a man. If she didn't—an' why else would any hard-hittin' chick be eatin' by herself in a restaurant?— then I'd make my play. Not too hard, you understand? Just enough to give her some attention, make her feel wanted."

He could feel Sammy's huge diamond ring as it kept grinding into his shoulder, his large manicured hands squeezing until it felt as if he were strumming his tendons against his collarbone. Malcolm made himself keep smiling.

"Then I ask her out, make sure I get asked back to her pad. But once you up there, here's the trick: You tell her you gonna buy her dinner from some nice restaurant. You insist on it. She don't have to knock herself out cookin' for you, you wanna treat her like a queen.

You borrow the keys, tell her you be right back wit' the food. Then you take her keys 'round to the locksmith an' make a copy."

"What?"

"Oh, you bring back the food, just like you said. Maybe even a candle, or a flower. Have some romantic dinner," Sammy said, chuckling sarcastically as he painted a picture of it.

"Couple days later, sometime when you know she gonna be out, you split the hammer, let yourself in, an' clean out everything. Everything she got—money, jewelry, clothes, everything. Even her pictures, any personal letters she got. Her address book. That part's important. You dig?"

Malcolm kept nodding and smiling as if he understood completely.

"Then—you got her," he said, releasing his hand so suddenly that Malcolm nearly fell over. "Then, she all alone in the world. She ain't got a thing to her name, with all her pictures and her letters gone—even her momma's phone number. She don't even know who she is anymore, all alone in the City. Except for you. An' you let her cry on you shoulder, and tell her ain't that a shame, an' then you give her a little stake to get back on her feet."

"And then?"

"Then she owe you, Red. An' soon she owes you more than she ever gonna be able to repay. An' now she realized she needs you, too—that no woman is ever safe on her own."

"I dunno. It's that simple?"

"Ah, Red, you blind in one eye and deaf in the other."

Sammy had stopped smiling now, his eyes clouded in the light from the streetlamp.

"I don't care who it is, Red, or what she got. You take everything away from a woman, she do whatever you want. They not like you an' me. They weak that way."

He thought about everything that Sammy had said, the next day at Small's. Thinking of how the faceless woman in question would be—how Miranda would be—when she came back and found her apartment completely gutted, right down to her family pictures. *Remembering how it had been during the last months before they had taken his mother away. The house emptying out as they sold off everything, just to have enough to eat, until there was nothing left but bare lightbulbs dangling from the ceiling.*

But then he would think of Miranda with Archie again, and his blood would boil over. Telling himself, I'm just as much a man as he is—

The next afternoon some pitiful young soldier boy had come wandering into Small's by himself. The regulars had all laughed to see him walk through the door, nervously wringing his army cap in his hands, his legs jerking as if he were walking on stilts. Just a big, shy blue black boy from somewhere deep in Georgia, obviously not even out of his teens. He took a seat in the farthest corner of the bar, next to a plastic potted plant, and tried to order corn liquor— his mouth so full of country that Malcolm could barely make out anything he said.

"We don't have none a that, son, this ain't no rent party," Malcolm told him scornfully.

"Well, den," the boy had said, and sat back in his chair as if he had to start thinking all over again.

"Dig the square from Delaware!" Dollarbill was laughing behind his hand by the time Malcolm got back to the bar.

"Fresh from the cotton patch!"

Malcolm had taken him five scotches in a row—the cheapest label they had in the well, watered down with as much ice as he could fit in the glass. He thought for sure the boy would leave once he saw how much they were. But each time he went back over, the young soldier looked up at Malcolm with a pleading, hangdog expression—as if he knew what it was he wanted, but could not bring himself to ask for it.

Finally, on the fifth scotch, Malcolm had leaned in close, pretending to wipe the bare tabletop with his towel. Asking him, in a low voice, when he was just over the soldier's ear:

"Hey, Jack, is it a girl you want?"

The soldier had looked up at him with an expression that was more pitiful than ever. Nodding mutely, his face beaming with gratitude.

"All right, then, young lane," Malcolm said magnanimously, writing down Bea's address at his apartment house, though he had never told her he would take her up, had no idea if she was already on someone else's hook by this time. The idea just coming to him, pleasing him with what he knew, and how far ahead he was of this Georgia country boy. He remembered what Charlie Small had said, but there was before him, also, the sight of Miranda on West Indian Archie's arm, the way she had turned away from him—what Sammy the Pimp had said to him. The wretched, despairing, vengeful thought creasing his brain, Every woman need a daddy. Whether they know it or not.

"You just tell her De-troit Red sent you. You understand? She know exactly who you mean."

"Thank—thank you, suh. Thank you mos' kindly!" the cotton-mouthed soldier said, his face still so doggishly grateful that Malcolm had to turn away.

"You go on now, she be waitin'. You just pay me my commission—" he added, shooing the boy out, but not before snatching up the twenty-dollar bill, and a five-dollar tip the soldier pressed eagerly into his hand.

But almost as soon as he was out the door, Malcolm had a bad feeling about it. There was something about the way that country boy had walked out of Small's—his stride no longer so awkward, but quick and purposeful, not wobbling in the least with the five well scotches he had had. Malcolm had put it down to his eagerness to finally get to the woman—but then he thought of the money he had given him. A twenty and the five. Fewclothes putting it into words first, shaking his head when he looked over the bills Malcolm had shown him so proudly—some extra meaning in his voice:

"Lot a money for a country boy. Livin' on what Uncle pay—"

He rummaged around in his waiter's jacket, pulling out the bills, looking them over closely. Then he saw it, there on both the finiff and the hickory stick. The eyes of the presidents inked in—and a very small but clearly discernible, five-digit number written in the bottom right-hand corner of each bill.

He looked back down at where the country-boy soldier had been seated, searching all around his little table for any hint. The first thing he noticed was the muddy black patch, spreading across the ornamental dirt packed down around the plastic palm. Of course. That was where the scotches had gone—

He ran out into the street, trying to flag down a cab. Starting to walk, then to run when he couldn't find one, too nervous now to wait for the subway, or a streetcar. Panting as he raced the seventeen blocks uphill to his building, mopping sweat with his waiter's towel. He burst through the front door, pounding on up the stairs to Bea's apartment, slapping as hard as he could on the door with the flat of his hand. When she didn't open for him, he hollered her name and banged again, until some of the other whores began to gather sleepily on the landings above, tittering or cursing languidly down at him where he kept slapping at the door.

The door finally opened a crack and Bea's head appeared, her hair turbaned up in a towel, a bottle of nail polish in her hand. Behind her he could see the mad white cavewoman, still staring mutely at him—her wild hair also wrapped up in a towel.

"Hey, Mr. Man," Bea said as dreamily as ever, opening the door a little wider. "We just doin' each other's hair an' nails. 'Course, if you gotta 'mergency—"

"There a soldier up here just now?" he asked, praying he was sequestered somewhere back in the gloom of their apartment, even if they had doped and killed him there.

"No-o—" Bea said carefully, as if she were trying to remember.

"Pitiful young Nome from home? Sayin' I sent him?"

"Why, no, Jack, ain't been nobody since the rush hour," Bea told him, beaming wider at him. "I didn't know you was already lookin' out fo' me an' Baby—"

"I ain't!" he cried violently, backing away from the door and running back down the stairs. "I ain't got nothin' to do wit' you. Anybody come askin' about it, you tell 'em that, you dig? Say you got nothin' to do with me!"

"Oh, Mister Man!"

Before he had reached the door, though, he realized that it was already too late. They were unlikely to even bother sending a man up to check on the girl. What they wanted was him—and the bar. He thought of himself writing down Bea's address—writing down his own address—and he felt sick again. Forcing himself to go over what there was left for him to do. Thinking that he could leave right now. Go up to his rented room, put the few things he had in his train bag, try to cop a free ride on his rail pass out of Penn Station or Grand Central. Or he wouldn't even have to risk going downtown, just go on up to the Port Authority at the George Washington Bridge, take the bus right over to Jersey—

But when he stepped back out into the humming, milling street, he realized that he would have to give it all up. Small's, and Creole Pete's, and all the other clubs and bars. His apartment where he could watch the City streaming toward him, every night. Miranda—

And go back—where? To Ella's back up in Roxbury, popping his rag at the Roseland? To the Pennsy, trying to hump his way up to porter for the next twenty years? Like the other graying, dyspeptic

colored men he saw working the trains. Lording it over their own
and tomming it up for so long with the white passengers they could
no longer tell when it was and wasn't real—

He turned his feet downtown and began to walk grudgingly
back to Small's, knowing what he had to do. Walking as slowly as
he could, the way he had walked back home from school in East
Lansing, after his mother had begun to let everything go. When he
reached the club he went directly to see Charlie Small, working on
the books back in his office.

"I just did somethin', Charlie," he told him. "I don't know why I
done it."

Charlie Small looked at him closely, then nodded—as if he had
somehow been expecting this, too.

"Siddown, Red. An' tell me all about it," he said.

Charlie had heard him out, kicking back in his own chair and
folding his arms behind his head, his paunch jutting up over his
belt. Interrupting Malcolm a few times with questions to clarify
things, but mostly responding with grunts and uh-huhs until he
was through. Not seeming to get angry even when he heard the
worst of it, but leaning forward again when Malcolm had finished,
nodding his head grimly.

"I wish you hadn't done that, Red," Charlie told him. "You was a
good worker, I'm gonna miss you 'round here. But they got you on
impairing morals for sure, an' we can't have that."

Malcolm sat silently before him while the older man lit a cigar
butt in his desk ashtray and thought for a moment.

"Lemme try to head this off before it gets started," he said, and
picked up the phone. "Meantime, you go change and wait for me at
the bar. I'm sorry, Red, but you're done here."

Malcolm nodded and left the room. Doing as he was told, carefully folding up his white waiter's jacket as if in a trance, and leaving it back in the little alcove storeroom where he had stood with
Miranda just the day before. He sat with his back to the bar, staring at the door—wanting to order one last drink but not daring to,
afraid he would not be able to hold it without his hand shaking, not
wanting the regulars to see that. There were a few of them at the
bar, but with their usual hustlers' sixth sense they left him alone,
and he had nothing more to say to them.

After a few more minutes, Charlie Small came out of his office,
and at nearly the same moment Joe Baker, the undercover man from

the Thirty-second Precinct walked in, head down and hands in his pockets as usual. Malcolm looked at Charlie, the fear growing in him, wondering if he had been betrayed.

"This is the only way," Charlie explained, placing a hand gently on his shoulder. "Get you out of here before the MPs. They get you on impairin' the morals of a serviceman, you do time. Joe here'll take care of you."

The detective nodded, pausing at the bar only for his usual shot and beer. Charlie said something in his ear, and Malcolm watched him slip some bills into the detective's hand. Baker finished his boilermaker, then came over and grabbed Malcolm by his arm with surprising delicacy.

"One thing, Red," Charlie called to him just before they left, Joe Baker halting obligingly.

"You can't never come back. You hear me? You can't never come back a'tall, even as a payin' customer. That's the deal."

Malcolm nodded numbly, then hung his head as the plainclothesman led him away. He wanted to say something snappy back at Charlie Small; something, anything to show it really didn't matter to him at all. But he was so choked with sorrow and self-pity that he could not trust himself not to start bawling right there in the barroom.

Instead, he walked out of Small's Paradise without another word and let Detective Baker steer him up Seventh Avenue, then around the corner to the precinct house on 135th Street. He marched Malcolm right in through the scarred, wooden front doors, past all the beefy, leering Irish faces of the uniformed cops. Past the bullpen full of more detectives sitting at scarred wooden desks—jackets off, ties loosened before the ineffectual little electric fans—peevishly pecking away at their reports.

In front of each desk sat a black man, his hands cuffed behind his back. Some of them looking defiant, others frightened or stoical or simply weary, but all of them with their hands cuffed, almost as if someone had cut off their arms. They had trickles of blood on their shirts and jackets, or mouses under their eyes, and swollen lips and cheeks. Answering the interminable questions they were asked without inflection or expression, keeping their faces turned toward the white men who were questioning them, but their eyes staring down at the desks. As they went by, one of the white detectives rolled his form out of the bulky metal typewriter and hoisted his prisoner up by one arm, holding his chair out with the other as if to offer it to Detective Baker. But he only shook his head.

"No, this boy's goin' back in the pen," he said, and the white detective gave him a small, impish grin.

"So's this one," the white detective said.

Malcolm recognized the man whose arm the other detective was gripping, though he couldn't remember his name. A small-time pimp who wandered into the bar sometimes, not one of the regulars. Dressed now in an immaculate, kelly green zoot, the hat lolling off over his shoulder. His face the only one of all the arrested men's in the bullpen that was as yet unmarked—handsome and dark brown, with long eyelashes that even made him look slightly effeminate.

"Doubleheader," the white cop said, and laughed as he pulled the man along—the pimp swallowing hard but his face studiously expressionless, eyes still turned toward the peeling linoleum floor.

"Where we goin'? What you gonna do to me?" Malcolm whispered urgently to Joe Baker, as he frog-marched him along, back toward the holding rooms in the back of the station. Remembering everything he had heard about what went on in the back pens of the precinct house.

"Shut up!" Baker told him loudly—then more quietly, out of the side of his mouth:

"You keep your goddamned mouth shut, you want to get through this. You understand me? Don't you be sayin' a thing to me!"

He nodded his head once—before Baker hit him in the back of his neck, hard, stunning him. The detective hauling him on down the hall to a tiny, high-ceilinged room that held nothing but a tall metal locker, a table, and a couple of wooden-arm chairs. There was a single, closed slit of a window, too small for anyone but a young child to crawl through, and a metal ceiling fan that made occasional, loping rotations, too lazy to dislodge any of the dust that encased it.

"You sit here, an' keep yourself still," the detective warned him, shoving him down into one of the chairs, his dour, Iorian face glowering down at him.

"I didn't really run her. I was just tryna drop some hype on the country boy—" Malcolm pleaded, sure that Baker was about to leave him to the white cops.

"Please—"

"Shut up! I mean it, now. You don't do a thing, you don't sign a

thing, you don't say a thing until I come back for you. Nothing!"
Baker hissed in his face.

"You understand? No matter what they do."

Malcolm nodded glumly, fighting down the impulse to cry out
again as he watched the detective leave the room, and lock the door
behind him. Wondering how long it would take the white cops to
show up—most likely a pair of them from what he had heard. They
would balance a phone book on top of his head, then hit it with the
baseball bat. Roll up three or four oranges in a towel, to work on
the back and kidneys, so the marks wouldn't show—

He sat in the chair, shaking, not wanting the leering white cops
to see him this way but unable to help himself. Feeling his shirt
sticking to his back with his own sweat. The little room redolent
with the stink of fear, and submission; of urine and old vomit. All
of it—the fearful smells, the institutional, pale green paint on the
walls, the wire mesh in the window glass—all of it reminding him
of the last place they had left her.

The state mental hospital at Kalamazoo-zoo-zoo—

He heard a low grunt coming from the next room, then a sound
like air being let out of a tire. Then there was a steady, rhythmic
smacking sound, repeated over and over again—Whop! Whop!
Whop! Whop! The same sound he remembered his mother making
when she beat out their rugs outside on the porch. Whop! Whop!
Whop!—coming from just the other side of the wall behind his
chair. Then the sound of a man's slurred voice, pleading:

"Please! Please don't beat my face, tha's how I make my living—"

Malcolm recognized it at once as the pimp from Small's he had
seen out in the bullpen, the effeminate-looking man whose name he
couldn't remember.

"That face? That how you make yer livin'?"

Now he heard the detective he had seen outside offering Joe
Baker his chair. Then another white man's voice, chuckling along
with him, their laughter as hard as buckshot pellets.

"Please! Please! I'll pay—"

"Bet you will!"

The beating resumed, the sound of hard rubber hitting flesh
repeated over and over, measured and slow. When they stopped
again he could hear the men breathing heavily. Then another plea,
almost a wailing sound this time—a pimp, begging for mercy:

"Please! Not the face—"

"Shut up!"

He heard a sharp crack then, like someone very deliberately breaking a bone. There was another crack, followed by a long moan, and
more laughter, and then Malcolm was trying to pull himself free
from the chair. The handcuffs cutting into his wrists the harder he
pulled, not sure where he could even run to if he got himself free,
but wanting to be out of there, that small, institutional locker room
where he had to listen to a man being beaten. The smells and the
sounds in the next room bringing it all back to him.

The orderlies had been beating someone with a rubber hose
down the hall then, too—the last time he had gone to visit her. The
sound of rubber hitting flesh over and over again, while they tried
to talk to her, and she only repeating, All the people have gone.

I gotta gal
In Kalamazoo—

She had tried to fight it. He would have liked to have told them
that, all the social-worker ladies, and especially Mr. Maynard Allen.
Even after the incident following his Daddy's funeral, when she
had taken the butcher's knife over to the Stohrers next door, telling Mrs. Stohrer how white people had killed her husband and that
she was sorry but that she had to take a white life in return. She
had recovered herself even with the knife in her hand, and prevailed
on Mrs. Stohrer—a kindly, middle-aged woman with no children of
her own—not only not to press charges but even to teach her how
drive their Daddy's old touring car.

His mother had insisted on keeping the car, though the ladies
from the county Poor Commission demanded she give it up. Wanting her to spend her money on a new stove instead, because the one
they had now was an aged flat-topped coal-and-wood burner, and
every night when she made dinner some of the ashes or even a live
coal would come tumbling out before she could pounce on it and
scoop it up with her bare hands, tossing it back into the fire and
slamming the hot grate door shut again.

"That car is our lifeline! As long as my back and my arms are
strong enough, I will drive that automobile!" she railed at them, sure
that the car was the only means she had of finding and keeping a job.

Still, it had not been easy. She had no feel for driving, became easily flustered in heavy traffic, or if anything went wrong. Malcolm was with her the afternoon she had stalled out at an intersection, and could not get it started again. His mother grinding the transmission ineffectually, while the white drivers behind her began to shout and honk their horns. Muttering frantically to herself, Come on, come on, stomping on the gas until the car was obviously flooded and Anna Stohrer put a hand on her arm and told her gently to lay off it, then stepped outside to wave the other cars around them.

Malcolm watching them as they passed. All the livid white faces peering angrily in at them, shaking their heads in disgust before they floored the accelerator and roared away. Louise sitting slumped down in the driver's seat, her head against the wheel, until all the white people's cars had passed and Mrs. Stohrer asked her if she didn't want to try the ignition again.

"You know, if I had been alone, those white people would have run me down," his mother had told her when they were moving again. "They would have killed me right there, I know it."

Yet she had been right about the car. Once she had learned to drive it, she was able to get work with a white family in Lansing, doing their sewing and cleaning before she came home to cook and clean and wash for them, too. Redoubling her usual tireless efforts around the house until she almost seemed possessed, scrubbing and polishing obsessively at the bare floors and furniture. Cleaning their clothes, and the aging drapes she hung over and over again, until they were no more than a yellow scrim the sun poured through in the morning, waking them all at first light.

But after a few months the white family claimed to have discovered that his mother wasn't actually part Indian, as she had told them—the obvious story that she told them, for the benefit of the neighbors. Firing her at the end of a full ten-hour's day cleaning their house, telling her that it was only because they were disappointed in her for having lied, and not because of anything to do with her race, or what the neighbors had found out. She had cried all through dinner that night, unable to stop herself. And soon afterward his Daddy's car had finally broken down once and for all, beyond the ability of Mr. Stohrer or any of the other men on their block to fix.

That was when the real hunger had started. Before another month passed they had exhausted their credit down at the Levandowskis' grocery, the little wooden store run by a grim, skeletal Polish couple from Hamtramck. Taking their meals down at the firehouse soup kitchen, or picking up the sacks of potatoes and cans of meat that were handed out at the relief depot, and always marked with the same stamp, Not To Be Sold, until Malcolm wondered if that was the name of the company that made them—Not To Be Sold Foods.

Still, she had fought them, insisting to the social ladies that she wasn't taking relief at all, but only a loan. Reminding them constantly, "Make sure you're keeping track of how much I owe so I can pay it back." She refused the hand-me-down clothes they brought if they were so much as missing a button. Throwing a whole box of fig newtons one of them had brought for the children out to the chickens, adamant that they were all dried out and full of worm holes.

Twice a week she made Malcolm and his little brother Reginald walk the two miles to the Peter Pan bakery, where for a nickel they could buy as much day-old bread as they could carry home. His Momma would mold it into bread pudding, if they had any milk, or stew it with tomatoes or fry it into bread burgers. If there wasn't any leftover bread, or if some other relief family had gotten to it first, she would send them out to pick dandelions, boiling the greens down into a tasteless limp mass that Malcolm hated, and which made his stomach hurt.

The worst was on Saturday, though, when she made Malcolm go with Philbert to the slaughterhouse to catch lungs. The little knot of boys, gathered on the muddy ground underneath the slaughterhouse windows, down by the railyards. The same faces every week, white and colored—pacing warily back and forth, eyeing each other like stray dogs while the cattle were driven out of the stockyard pens, and into the concrete walls of the slaughterhouse.

He hated it all—the fearful looks on the other boys' faces. The terrified bleating of the cattle, the stench of their frightened pissing and shitting as they were herded up the narrow plankway. The desperate elbowing and wrestling of the boys that started beneath the narrow smoked-glass windows the moment they heard the saw go on inside.

"There it is!"

The first lung came through the window, and there was a wild surge forward. The boys concentrating first on trying to punch and shove each other into the mud. Philbert was good with his fists, and Malcolm was quick. It was his job to go for the lungs while his older brother ran interference, but he hated having to scoop them up from the mud. Grasping the enormous, gray, slimy cattle lungs against his chest like a football. Plowing through the younger, smaller boys with Philbert, while they clutched their meal and ran for home.

Even so, by the time the school week started, there was almost nothing left for their lunches. They would gather wild leeks from the side of the road on their way to the Pleasant Cove School, and stuff them between two stale slices of the Peter Pan bread. Malcolm would try to eat his as quickly and inconspicuously as he could, sitting alone at a table in a far corner of the cafeteria. But the odor was still such that one day the girl who sat next to him in class burst into tears from the smell of it in his desk.

Their teacher had ordered him to have the sandwich burned, and Malcolm had dutifully walked with it outside to where the janitor, a balding, taciturn Italian man, stood raking up the trash from the playground behind the school. There he had thrown his sandwich on the ground in front of the pile, watching curiously as the janitor burned his lunch.

The other kids at Pleasant Cove taunted them for their Daddy being dead, or how they looked, or dressed. He and his brothers and sisters went barefoot in the summer, wore sneakers in the winter that were cracked and busted out around the toes, and jammed with rags and cardboard to keep them warm. They wore nothing but raggedy-ann clothes, and even the other colored kids said they looked like farmers.

Malcolm would only smile or shrug, or even laugh in their faces. He didn't like to fight, afraid that if he did he would start to bleed, and his whole life would slip out of his body, right there. If any boys insisted, he would pick up a bottle or a rock, or a board with a nail in it—anything at hand—and wave it around, shouting crazily until his antagonists backed off. The only exceptions were when he saw the bigger kids picking on someone else, or the time his older brother Philbert was getting whipped by Teddy Simmons, up on the railroad embankment, above the school, that served as their fighting grounds. Malcolm had broken out of the circle of laughing, jeering boys and girls and flung himself onto Simmons's back. Grappling an arm around the older, taller boy's neck, punching and biting at the back of his head, until even Philbert had to intervene and help pull him off.

He preferred to be around the girls. He would pull their pigtails and squirt them with water at the drinking fountains. He would knock them off the swings and kick and pinch them, or snatch away their bikes and try to run them over. Or he would give them piggyback rides over puddles in the road, and wipe the mud off their shoes with a handkerchief, until the other boys howled with laughter, and ragged on him endlessly.

He still didn't care, doing anything he could to be around them—especially Betty Jane Thibodeaux, who brought her lunch to school every day in an old honey can instead of wrapped up in newspapers, and which had convinced them all that she came from money. She was impressed by how fast he could run, and how far he could throw a ball, and Malcolm liked that she wore bright white stockings instead of the tan or black ones that all the other girls wore, and blue denim dungarees with shiny copper rivets at the stretch points.

By the time they were in the fifth grade, they spent nearly every afternoon together after school. They would go down to Eaton Rapids Road and climb a stand of Norwegian maples, and there she showed him how to hang an old purse on a string over the highway, trying to tempt the passing cars into stopping. As soon as they did, she and Malcolm would pull it back, giggling furiously and shinnying higher into the trees as the drivers swore and shook their fists at them. Sometimes he would even play house with her, high up in the maple branches where nobody else could see. Taking on any role she wanted—the child, the little baby; the screaming, helpless mother; the daddy.

He knew better than to ever go to her house, but sometimes he would go into the abandoned lot behind her yard, and wait for her there. Crouching down in the wild broom grass that grew as high as his chest. Pretending that he was a wild animal, a lion or a panther, while he waited for her. When she came out he would jump up and pull her down into the high grass—leaping all about her, over her head and back, and finally landing full on her. Listening to her hurried breathing, the sound of her heart pumping against his own chest. She would lie there giggling helplessly, pushing and grabbing back at him, kicking her white-stockinged legs that he couldn't help staring at, her skirt pushed up high on her thighs.

He would show off for her by leaping across a little creek that ran through their property, but then he would have to go back to help her get across. Standing in the cold, swift-running water in his bare feet. Holding her hand while she maneuvered her way across the rocks, or even taking her up in his arms and carrying her over himself. She would put her arms around his neck, and he was suddenly very aware of how close she was—the starched, fresh smell of her clothing, the heft of her small tomboy's body in his arms; her smiling, freckled face only inches from his own.

When the weather got warm, she showed him how to coon a watermelon, as all the white kids called it. Stealing off with the ripe red melon from a farmer's patch somewhere and smashing it open on a rock. Digging out the sticky, sugary innards with their fingers, spitting the black seeds at each other through the matching gaps they had in their front teeth.

Sometimes it was the only thing he had to eat in a day, and by the end of that year, the ladies from the Poor Commission were back. They were already talking about splitting up the family— sending some of them off to reform school, or to live with neighboring colored families like the Gohannases, who had said they would take them in.

But even then his mother hadn't given up. Instead she had joined the Seventh Day Church of God, which she learned about one day from the pamphlets a couple of evangelists were bringing door-to-door. Becoming more disdainful than ever of the social-worker ladies after that. Refusing to let her children eat any of the canned ham or pork they brought, even turning down the offer of a whole fresh-slaughtered hog from a colored neighbor who kept pigs in a lot down the street.

"My family don't eat any unclean pig meat," she told him on the steps of their porch, her eyes shining with pride, while the rest of them had watched longingly from just inside the door, smelling the almost unbearable, fresh-slaughtered scent of the pig bundled on his shoulders.

She fasted herself on every church holiday now, and always on the Sabbath. Her arms and legs turning into sticks before their eyes, her hair visibly thinning and starting to gray. She talked all the time about what Heaven was like, and the gold crowns they would wear, and of how Jesus would come down out of the sky one day, riding on a real white horse.

Worst of all, she made them go to the Seventh Day Church

every Sunday. Malcolm hated it, just as he had hated all of the Baptist churches he had been to with his Daddy. A squat, sweaty, concrete chapel converted from a truck garage; white aluminum steeple fastened to the roof, the interior still reeking of motor oil and gasoline. Every Sunday morning he would watch the women swaying and fainting in their ecstasy over Jesus, the men booming out Praise the Lord! as they thrust open their arms. Shaking and moaning, writhing about in the pews and aisles, and on the hard concrete floors—their quiet, fathomless dignity abandoned once the services began and the preacher starting shouting. The women's bulky white-and-tan underwear visible to Malcolm under their Sunday dresses as they threw themselves about, the men's eyeballs rolling in their heads. Mouths slack, eyes staring blindly up at the metal industrial fans still embedded in the ceiling, as they gave themselves up to something that he could neither dismiss nor discern.

It embarrassed him, and made him want to run right out the door, just as he had wanted to run from his Daddy's churches. He was frightened by how his mother, especially, looked during services. She had always held herself so rigidly, with so much pride—her mouth yawning open stupidly now, her eyes glazed, waving her sticklike arms in the air. It was then, for the first time, that he thought he saw the look of death on her.

But with the church had come a boarder—Herbert Walker, a member of a Seventh Day congregation in Chicago. A barbershop-supplies salesman who dressed in bright-checkered suits and spats, like some kind of vaudeville comedian, and who always smelled of the products he peddled—congolene and talcum powder, and Caldesene and Cohop and septic.

Malcolm and his brothers and sisters hadn't liked him at first, not least because it meant they had to double up again. All seven of them, boys and girls, living in the same upstairs room now, while Herbert Walker moved into the big front bedroom. He was a tall, loose-jointed man, with reddish skin not unlike Malcolm's own, and Malcolm resented how people would sometimes mistake them for father and son. But he was always friendly, and even-tempered, slipping them nickels, and slices of the green-and-silver-wrapped spearmint gum he chewed incessantly. Bringing home with him all the barbershops he had been to at the end of the day, telling them jokes he had heard, whistling and singing snatches of some new tune from the radio, smelling sharp and fresh and clean.

Malcolm could see how pleased his mother was when he sat down at table with them, or on Sunday mornings when he sat next to her in their pew, singing enthusiastically away at the hymns in a pleasant tenor voice. Soon, he noticed, she had taken to eating with them again, and had even begun to gain back a little weight. She got Mrs. Stohrer to take the gray out of her hair, and started to pay more attention to the condition her dresses were in. At supper she hung on everything he said, Malcolm saw, and quoted him approvingly to the neighbors—

"My boarder, Mr. Walker, he says that this Depression is just about over, and business conditions should be improving shortly..."—never seeming to notice the amused or knowing looks on their faces.

And he started to pay more attention to her in turn, which made Malcolm suspicious. Complimenting her on how nice she looked when she had had her hair done, flattering her cooking and how well she kept the house, and raised seven children.

"Yessir, Louise," he would tell her. "I know you loyal to the memory of your good husband, but you ought to consider marryin' again. A woman with all your talents—you truly are a blessing."

She would tell him not to exaggerate, but Malcolm saw how her face lit up when he said such things. She would even give a little, pleased laugh when he told her that she was a blessing.

Best of all was the five dollars he insisted on paying every week for his room and board, so that they didn't have to eat leeks, or catch lungs at the slaughterhouse anymore. He helped Malcolm get a paper route of his own, too, through one of his barbershop clients, so that now he could buy nickel Hersheys and Three Musketeers and Chicken Dinner bars for Betty Jane Thibodeaux and some of the other girls he liked. He bought a bat and glove, for the ballgames they played continuously, all day on Saturday, down in the schoolyard, and a pair of secondhand skates for the hockey games they played at night, by the light of trash-can fires, on flooded gravel pits and sinkholes at the edge of town.

He was good at sports—so tall by then that the other boys gave him still more new names, jokingly calling him the Mountain, or Little Malcolm. But he hated it when the play began and they ran into him. He could not stand any physical contact with them—their bodies on his when they pulled him down, the stale reek of their breath against his face. He could not forgive himself or anyone else for their shortcomings. From his position out in center field, he would laugh, and rag at them whenever they made an error or struck out, or did anything that looked stupid. He was unable to help himself, although he knew that he should, that it made them mad. Unable to stay off himself, either—reminding the others over and over again of every bad play he had made, until they gave him yet another name, calling him Harpy for how he would harp on everything. He could not help it, he could not shut himself up—always jibing and laughing, trying to come up with something that would make the other boys pay attention.

When the spring came, Mr. Herbert Walker had packed his bags and told them that he had to go pay a call on the barbershops of the camps and the little vacation towns of the Upper Peninsula. Louise had cried when he left, and again for days afterward—suddenly and unnervingly, in the middle of doing the laundry in the afternoon, or while cooking their supper, and at first Malcolm had put it down to her missing him.

Before long, though, he had begun to hear from the other kids on their street that his mother was knocked up again. He refused to believe them—hating the knowing, nasty words "knocked up"—chasing them away with sticks and rocks. But after that he had begun to study her carefully and, soon enough, he was able to make out the bulge in her stomach, standing out prominently in her still skinny body.

It filled him with disgust. Reminding him as it did of how the rail-thin stray cats that lived in the empty lot down the street looked when they were about to breech their litters. Wondering how many children at once his mother might give birth to.

Soon the news about her condition was all over the block, the neighbors who had taken pity on her as a widowed mother shunning her now. She tried to go back to the Seventh Day Church, but that Sunday there was a line of deacons in front of the church door with their arms crossed over their chests, physically barring them from entering the building. Malcolm had stood outside with his brothers and sisters, squinting up through the sun at that line of sober men in their dark suits and jackets, staring back down impassively while their mother railed at them, even beating at their arms with her fists. Screaming at them, "It was you put him there! You put the serpent in my home!"

The church refused nevertheless to take any of the blame for Mr. Herbert Walker, or to so much as give her his forwarding address. Nor would his mother admit to anyone else that the child was his, even when the insurance company cut off her widow's pension because she would not say who the father was. But Malcolm came home one afternoon after school to find her sobbing over an opened envelope, holding two ten-dollar bills in one hand. Moaning over and over again through her sobs, "That's all I am to him. That's all!"

He remembered, now, things that he thought he had dreamed. The creak of footsteps at night on the loose floorboards in the upstairs hall. The sound of adults speaking in whispers. How often he had awakened early in the morning and gone downstairs to find Mr. Walker already seated at the table—his salesman's case by his feet, whistling snatches of the latest radio tunes at his mother while she made breakfast, the two of them casting playful glances at each other. He could never remember any such purely joyful moments between her and his Daddy, which made him hate Herbert Walker all over again.

It was only after he left, he decided later, that she had finally given in. It was after Mr. Walker that she had stopped going outside altogether, keeping the shades drawn all the time and the lights off. She spent all day in her rocking chair in a corner of the kitchen. Swatting suddenly at their heads when they got too close, screaming incoherently about what they had done to her, or how the devil was in them—strange, round, weltlike marks appearing on her arms and legs.

Malcolm was filled with a constant feeling of dread after that. It was a fear that made his stomach knot up, knowing that everything was going to go wrong, but possessing no idea of how to stop it, or what would happen to them all. Watching every day, while the floors and walls grew steadily filthier, and darker. The bedbugs infesting the house in such numbers that no one but their mother could sleep with all the incessant itching and scratching, the youngest children wailing in their misery. They tried soaking all the sheets and the mattresses, and even the floors around the beds in kerosene, until the smell was almost as bad as the itching and Malcolm walked gingerly around the house, sure that the smallest spark would cause him to burst into flames—but even that didn't get rid of them.

In school now he sat in the back, and drew crude pictures of the teachers that made the other kids laugh. He cracked jokes all the time, and squeezed his hand under his arm to make fart sounds—even leapt up and waved his long arms about, scratching at himself and making noises like a monkey when everything else failed.

He no longer stayed around to play baseball, or hockey, or anything else after school, but went straightaway to pick up his papers, roaming the empty streets in the early winter darkness. Peeking through the front-parlor windows when he went to lay the paper up on the porch, or cutting through people's backyards. Staring into house after house at the little yellow squares of light—the families gathered around the kitchen stove, or the fireplace, or the living room radio. He would pull close the oversize, hand-me-down sweater that was all he had to wear against the coldest weather, shivering in the darkness until he couldn't take it any longer. Then he would run on soundlessly to the next house in his sneakers—watching his breath make thin, white traces in the air, pretending that he was invisible, and master over everything he saw.

When he was finished with his route, he would hike the two miles into downtown Lansing. If it was collection day, he would buy something to eat, and if it wasn't, he would lift anything he could—an apple, or some of the crackers that were kept in barrels near the front of the grocery stores. He was quick, but the white storekeepers were quicker. They had their eye on him the moment he came through the door, and when they caught him they would call in the police and the social workers.

There was a new social worker who had begun coming around their home by this time. He was different from the dour, middle-aged women who were always arguing with his mother, and staring balefully at the bare floors and dangling lightbulbs in their home. His name was Maynard Allen, and he was a lanky white man in a rumpled suit, with striking blue eyes and a bald spot beginning to grow in the middle of his disheveled brown hair. He didn't walk around their home staring with obvious disapproval at everything he saw, but was polite and deferential to his mother, and took each of them aside to speak quietly to them, and ask them questions.

Malcolm avoided him for as long as he could, but one day May-nard Allen had cornered him where he was sitting behind the wheel in the broken-down old touring car, pretending he was driving to

Detroit or Chicago or New York. He had come up suddenly and opened the passenger door, sliding into the front seat beside him as if Malcolm had been waiting for him—smelling of stale cigarettes and hair cream, and other, even more mysterious white man smells.

"Where you going to, Malcolm?" he asked.

"I dunno," Malcolm answered him, turning his head away— aware of how silly his child's game must look. "Nowhere, I guess."

"You can go anywhere you want to," Mr. Maynard Allen said, turning his penetrating blue eyes on him then, compelling Malcolm to look back at him. "You know that, don't you?"

Malcolm only shrugged, looked away again.

"Malcolm, I wanted to ask you what you think we can do to help your mother," he began again.

"I dunno."

"But stealing things from stores doesn't help her, does it?"

Malcolm sat silent for a long moment, stunned with guilt and shame by the unexpected question. But Mr. Allen kept looking at him until he replied.

"No," he managed to choke out at last.

"But you know that already. Of course you know, you're a very bright boy. I've seen your test scores at school. You could make something of yourself, if you would just straighten up and try harder. But you know that, too. Don't you?"

Malcolm shrugged again, squirming in the driver's seat of the old car. Feeling uncomfortable yet quietly delighted by the compliment—a compliment unlike anything anyone had paid him before.

"Tell me," Mr. Allen asked him, "what do you think of somebody who burns herself? Or who refuses to take free food?"

"I dunno," Malcolm said again, more slowly this time. Freezing up, trapped where he was on the car seat.

"For a person to do that—to refuse good food for herself and her family when they don't have enough to eat—don't you think that shows someone isn't thinking straight?"

Mr. Allen shook his head, sadly but forthrightly, as if all but daring Malcolm to contradict him.

"I guess," he admitted at last, confused and angry with himself for saying that much. For betraying her.

"Your mother has too much on her mind to always think straight just now. We have to do all we can to make her burden lighter," the white man went on, still speaking gently. His eyes still on Malcolm.

"That's my job as well as yours. In time, it might even mean having to make some big changes. But for right now, no more shoplifting, or misbehaving in school. Okay, pal?"

Malcolm nodded quickly, averting his head from Mr. Maynard Allen's gaze, close to crying where he sat now behind the driver's wheel.

"I brought you a couple things I thought you might find interesting," he said casually then, plunking a package of Lorna Doones, a Hershey bar, then a couple of comic books down on the broad seat between them.

Malcolm picked up the comics before he even realized what he was doing, drawn at once by the bright colors, the frenetic scenes of action on the front covers. Reading the titles in their broad, red, block lettering. Amazing Man, and Sub-Mariner. He had seen such books before, in the same stores where he had shoplifted in Lansing, never daring to take anything so brilliant and beautiful even though he had craved them more than the food.

"You know you're different from the rest of them," Mr. Allen said as he started to get out of the touring car, waving a hand casually in the direction of Malcolm's home, then stopping and ducking his head back in.

"Why do you think that is?" he asked, leveling his bright blue eyes on Malcolm again until once more he felt compelled to say something.

"I don't know," he answered, honestly—unaware until now that he was any different at all.

"Well, think about it. You don't have to go through all this, you know. You can be something else."

The day before Thanksgiving, his mother had given birth to their half-brother, whom she named Butch—just Butch, no matter how much the nurses in the poor ward at the hospital had scolded and tried to bully her. Malcolm had hoped, secretly, that her mood might change again when she finally had the baby, but when she returned home she remained as withdrawn as ever. Retreating at once to her rocking chair in the corner of the kitchen where she spent nearly all of her time dozing and nursing, even the blind rages seemingly spent in her now.

Neither Malcolm nor any of his brothers or sisters bothered going to school much anymore. Instead he spent his days lying around the house. Reading over and over the adventures of Prince Namor, the Sub-Mariner, who was a prince of Atlantis though he looked like a Chinaman, and especially Amazing Man, an orphan who had been raised in the mountains of Tibet by the Council of Seven—mystic lamas who had given him all the qualities of strength, knowledge, and the courage necessary to dominate the world, though he had promised always to be good, and kind, and generous.

He couldn't keep from thinking, too, about how his mother had looked while she was still knocked up, scrawny but fat in the belly, like that stray female cat. When she was asleep he would study his new brother's face. It still looked shapeless, not quite like any of theirs yet, but he could see that the baby's skin was already darker than his own—like that of all his brothers and sisters.

It was then that he had begun to think that maybe his Daddy wasn't really his Daddy after all. That this was what he had been trying to tell him, why he had been so angry with him at times, and dragged him along to his Garvey meetings. It was then that Malcolm had first thought that he might be half white, the issue of some terrible white man who had forced himself on his mother, the way the toms did on the stray cats in the lot. The way Mr. Herbert Walker had. That this was what Mr. Allen had been trying to tell him, too.

That he was half white, superior and cursed. The cause of all the trouble between them, and therefore his Daddy's death—

He had begun to think about it all the time until one night, well after midnight—unable to sleep from his thoughts, and the constant growling in his stomach—he had gone down into the cellar and taken out his Daddy's old hunting rifle from where it still lay buried in a little slit trench, wrapped in rags and forgotten by everyone but Malcolm himself.

No one else had heard him, his mother snoring in her rocker with the new baby. The rest of his brothers and sisters all too exhausted with hunger to be awakened by anything—all save for his younger brother Reginald, who idolized him, and who was as usual attuned to his every footstep. When Malcolm had come back up the cellar stairs with the gun, Reginald was waiting there mutely for him, looking as awkward and comical as ever. His oversize ears sticking out from his head, his stomach extended by the hernia that he'd always had and which made it hard for him to move very easily—but already dressed, ready to follow him anywhere.

At first he had been vexed, not knowing what to do with his little brother, certain he would throw off all his plans. Then deciding that he wanted to have a witness to what he was about to do.

"Well, come on then," Malcolm told him.

They had taken the rifle and a burlap shopping sack from the kitchen, and slipped out the front door. It was a dark night, with no more than a crescent moon in the sky, and they had stumbled and groped their way down the road. The grass was already covered with frost, but though they were wearing only their loose, slowly unraveling sweaters, for once they didn't feel the cold—too intrigued by how different everything seemed in the deep night world to notice.

They walked for nearly a mile, all the way down to Levandowskis' grocery. The square one-story wooden store deserted for the night, its windows dark—Mr. and Mrs. Levandowski, its gaunt, tight-lipped proprietors at their home way over in Hamtramck. Malcolm had insisted on walking all around the building nonetheless, even though the tiny store sat out in the middle of a block full of vacant lots, without another home around for at least a quarter mile. When he was finally satisfied there was nobody else about, he wrapped the burlap bag carefully around his hand, and smashed in one of the side windows.

The old pane had given way easily, the sound of tinkling glass making them both start, and look around. But there was no sign that anyone else had heard it, no other sound that broke the stillness of the night in response. Taking a deep breath, Malcolm had slipped his Daddy's rifle through the broken window, then pulled himself up after it, climbing into the darkened interior.

Inside, the store seemed even more unreal than anything else in the night world. Everything was exactly where he remembered it being from the daytime, but there was no one around—no one to stop him from doing anything. He did a little dance on the broken glass in his excitement, whirling around, his sneakers crunching along the floor as he looked at the food everywhere around him.

The store's furnishings were meager—a splintered wooden floor, a counter consisting of a plank laid over two barrels. But there were bags of flour and sugar stacked nearly to the ceiling, one on top of another. There were shelves and shelves of dusty canned goods, of fruits and vegetables and meat and fish. There were entire crates by the cash register, filled with penny candies and apples, and rice and potatoes, no longer under the watchful eye of Mr. or Mrs. Levandowski there behind the counter.

"Hey, help me up!" Reginald was calling softly from below the window, and Malcolm went over to try to haul him up. But no matter how hard he tugged on his arms, his brother's hernia hurt too much and he could not make it through the low window.

"You keep a lookout," Malcolm told him finally, letting him drop back down to the ground. "I'll be right there."

He unwrapped the burlap bag from his hand, looking over all his choices. Wondering just what it was he should take, what he would be able to explain if his mother or Mr. Maynard Allen, or anyone else questioned him about it. Knowing that he had to act fast, that all it would take was for one radio car to wander by and they would surely stop and ask what a little colored boy was doing, skulking around a store well after midnight.

Yet he could not make up his mind—and the more he looked at the piles of sacks and cans, the more pointless it all seemed. He wanted to take it all back with him, the whole store, even though he knew it was impossible. Wanting to show them, to do something that was more than just what a nigger would do.

Only now that he was inside did he realize that he really couldn't. Understanding that he would have to come back to steal again and again, or it would do them no good—that what few goods he and Reginald might take now would only tantalize them with the illusion of having something, when in fact they had nothing at all.

He thought he heard the sound of a car then, and he picked up his Daddy's rifle, listening, in the middle of the empty store. Everything was quiet, but he pointed it toward the broken window anyway—pointed it at the Levandowskis' old cash register, then at the sacks of flour and potatoes, at the barrels of penny candy. Wanting to do something with it, to fire it at something, at least, if only so that the next day the Levandowskis would return to find the broken window and the bullet hole, and wonder at it.

But all he did was hand the rifle down to Reginald and climb out after it, without taking a thing. Even that—even the idea of a shot fired in the dark store seeming completely, hopelessly futile to him. Reginald surprised by his big brother returning with nothing but knowing better than to ask. Malcolm unable to say anything to him, only clutching his fists, and biting down on his lower lip. The two of them walked home as fast as they could, aware now of how cold it was, out in the night air.

The week before Christmas his class had its holiday party, which he had been fearing. Everybody had chosen a name by lot, and then they were supposed to buy a present for the boy or girl they had selected, and wrap it and put it in the red-and-white papier-mâché chimney that their teacher, Miss Roosenraad, had had them make. Malcolm had told her after class, ashamed, that he could not buy anything for the chimney. But she had explained—speaking very slowly, in very simple words—that it didn't have to be anything fancy, that he could buy anything he wanted, or even make something. Sitting back when she was finished and smiling at him knowingly, as if she had just revealed some great secret.

He had thought about that for a while, about the possibility of trying to make anything in their house, then wrapped three nickel candy bars up together in leftover newspaper, and dropped them into the chimney. But even as he did that he noticed how much bigger all the other kids' presents were. Even those of his poorest classmates were wrapped in real store wrapping paper, with bows and cards and snowmen and Christmas trees on the paper, and Malcolm knew with the sense of foreboding he lived in all the time now that his would not be sufficient.

Sure enough, on the day of the party the other children had all opened up presents from the department stores downtown—toy trucks, and watercolor paint sets and boxes of crayons, and dolls and lead soldiers. He had edged off toward the coat pegs at the back of the room as he watched them, thinking that his might be forgotten, or that he could even sneak out of the school. But Allie Shrewbridge, the girl who got his candy bars, went right over and thanked him, shaking his hand very politely, as if she wasn't really disappointed at all.

"Now it's your turn, Malcolm," the teacher said, although he honestly hadn't thought he was getting anything, due to the paucity of his own gift. The other kids had all known for weeks who their secret partners were, but not one of them had come up to tell him that he or she was his partner.

He had started slowly toward the papier-mâché chimney, still unable to believe he was getting anything—though as he did he noticed that all of his classmates were looking at him, and that even

Miss Roosenraad was beaming broadly now. A little unnerved by all this attention, and the sudden, anticipatory quiet in the room, he looked down the chimney to see the biggest present of all still there, with his name on it. It was wrapped in shiny gold paper, with a huge red bow around it, and a card underneath that said simply, For Malcolm—with no indication of who it might be from. He stared at it, not daring to think what it might be, hoping that it was from one of the girls he liked in class, from Allie, or Betty Jane.

"Go ahead, Malcolm. Open it," Miss Roosenraad urged.

He felt the blood rushing to his head, and desperately wanted to run and hide under a desk somewhere, his desire for attention evaporated now, out in front of them all. He did as he was told, slowly tearing through the nice Christmas wrapping, still intrigued by what it might be, in spite of his embarrassment—and pulled out a coat.

A spontaneous cheer went up around the room as he held it out in front of him, making the floor seem to pitch and sway under him. Miss Roosenraad came up behind him, laying a hand benevolently on top of his head.

"Who—who—" he tried to ask, a lump of agitation forming in his throat.

"Everyone chipped in to buy it," she said throatily, blinking as if she were fighting back tears herself. "Because we knew you needed it so badly—"

The class cheered again, the kids moving in excitedly around him, and Malcolm felt chills of shame and pleasure running up and down his body. He wanted nothing so much at that moment as to run out of the classroom, to go somewhere far away from all their gleeful, smiling faces. Knowing that his went far beyond any of the other presents, and especially beyond his nickel candy bars. Wanting, with one part of him, to take the coat out to the Italian janitor, and put it on the trash pile where he had been made to burn his lunch.

But instead he had stood where he was, still holding the coat before him with a small, uneasy grin on his face. Admiring it desperately despite himself—a gray-green, corduroy winter coat, the nicest coat he had ever owned, and when the party had finally ended and the other kids began to leave, he had carefully slipped it on. His hands lingering along its smooth corduroy ridges, marveling at how bulky and warm it felt.

He had walked back home uncertain as to how his mother would react, fearful that she might make him take it back once she knew that a bunch of white people had bought it for him. He wasn't sure that she wouldn't tear it off his back and throw it into their old stove. When he got home he made sure to walk right into the kitchen, where she could see him—the thought occurring to him that maybe this new piece of charity might indeed spark her old righteous anger.

"Lookit, Momma. Lookit what they give me at school," he told her, filled with trepidation but also a sort of weird hope, standing right in front of where she was bundled up in the kitchen rocking chair with Butch the baby.

But she had only kept rocking slowly back and forth, staring through him, and he was shocked to look at her now. He had not noticed just how old she had become, even in the last few weeks. Her hair was nearly all gray, matted and unwashed, her blouse covered with breast milk and throw-up stains from the baby. Ugly patches and sores ran up and down her once smooth skin, and the flesh hung loosely off her arms.

"Lookit, Momma!"

"Gave you what?" she drawled slowly, her eyes staring blindly— not even aware, he realized, that he was wearing the fine, corduroy coat.

"Gave you what?" she repeated dully, the only other sound she made the constant, dull squeak of the rocker along the kitchen floorboards.

He had moved away, not knowing what else he could possibly say to her, and three days later, on the morning before Christmas, his sister Hilda had come downstairs to start the stove and found her rocking chair empty. There was a heavy snow falling, and Hilda couldn't believe that she would have gone outside, but when she went to look for her mother, she couldn't find her anywhere in the little house. She had awakened the rest of them and they had all run out to look for her, calling and calling her name, even though it meant that the neighbors heard and came out of their houses—all of them milling about, looking and calling for their mother with them in the steadily falling snow.

They didn't see her again until the first Sunday of the new year, only after the patrol car had found her walking along the side of the road, barefoot and talking crazy to herself. Only after the baby, Butch, had been pried from her arms and deposited in the orphanage, and she had been taken to the state hospital in Kalamazoo for observation.

They had stood before her there in the caged, windowless room— so much like the one he was in now in the police station, save for the fact that those walls were also covered with thick gray pads. Wilfred had held out the gift-shop box of chocolates that Mr. Maynard Allen had given them to give to her. The younger children, Yvonne and Wesley, had started to cry, the rest of them not knowing what to say. Malcolm's nose wrinkling up at the overwhelming smells of urine and old vomit, and fear. He could hear the sound of rubber hitting flesh somewhere, over and over again, just down the hall from where they were. Consumed by the one question he did not dare to ask, and did not want to hear the answer to, for he knew he could do nothing about it—

Do they hit her, too? When she does something, do they hit her with that?

She had looked very thin, and clean, at least, almost radiant in her white hospital gown. The sores on her body healing already, her hair washed and tied with a pretty red bow in the back. She had beamed vacantly at them, while the matron told her who they were—giving no sign that she recognized them herself, only repeating Is that so? in a vague, disinterested voice.

They had stood silent in that little room with their mother for nearly the full hour. But as their time came to an end, she began to change. Her face stiffening, the old look of rage creeping back over her again. Malcolm's heart leaped a little bit to see it. She had leaned forward, gesturing angrily at them as she turned to the matron.

"Who are these people?" she asked. "Why are they keeping me here?"

Then she sat back in the chair again, looking neither kindly nor fierce anymore. The fire gone out as suddenly as it had ignited.

"All the people have gone," she said, repeating it sadly. "All the people have gone."

A few minutes later they had heard a cart being wheeled down the hall. It stopped at the door of her room, and an orderly had walked in, carrying a tray full of shiny, silver hypodermic needles— the matron bustling them back out of the room, visiting hours done for the day, but Malcolm's eyes had stayed riveted on those needles, even as he was being ushered out into the hall.

Afterward Mr. Maynard Allen had loaded them all into his big Packard for the long drive back to East Lansing. Malcolm had sat up next to him in the front seat, while the rest of them dozed in the warm car—a real car that could really go somewhere. Still leafing idly through the comics he had given him, while Mr. Allen talked to him the whole way home about what was to become of him, of how he would go live with the Gohannases until they could place him in reform school.

"You know, Malcolm, reform school has the wrong reputation," he told him, speaking in his quiet, compelling voice, as if it were just the two of them alone in the whole world. "Think about what the word 'reform' really means. 'To change and become better.' We all need to reform, all the time."

"Yessir," Malcolm said, staring down at his comic book. There, the yellow Prince Namor of Atlantis was confronting his secret love, comely Officer Betty Dean, of the New York Police Department: You white devils have persecuted and tormented my people for years—

"Reform school is a place where boys like you can see your mistakes, and get a new start on life, and become a person everybody can be proud of. I know, Malcolm. I've seen it happen. And Mr. and Mrs. Swerlin, who run the home out there, are mighty good people—"

"Yessir," he repeated, as Prince Namor began to unleash a tidal wave that threatened to sweep away all of Manhattan.

"Everybody needs to be in the right place," Mr. Allen went on, speaking very softly now so as not to wake any of the others, his brothers and sisters snoring in the backseat. His words barely audible above the hum of the motor.

"Take your mother, for instance. She's in the best place for her now, where they can take good care of her. Soon, all of you will be in the best places for you."

"Yessir."

He turned his eyes from the ferocious, four-color battles in his comic book, looking out at the stark black-and-white Michigan landscape streaming past the windows. The snow and the bare trees, and the broken white line and the asphalt, spooling out endlessly beneath their wheels—

Kalamazoo-zoo-zoo—

He sobbed silently, wanting to moan himself but not daring to out of fear they would hear him. Writhing in the chair he was cuffed to, trying to relieve the ache in his arms and wrists, the sweat dripping freely down his face. The pimp in the next room was crying now, the detectives having worked him over steadily for another half hour—but all he could think about was that room in the state mental institution, and how his mother had looked there. Her eyes, vacant at the end, not even following her children out of the room. Only repeating the last, meaningless thing she had ever said to him:

"All the people have gone."

Why did they have to go? Why did they all have to go, and her especially? They had sent her to that place all alone. She was sick, so she had to go live all alone, all alone, all alone—

A little while later Detective Joe Baker finally returned and uncuffed him, leading him out the back door of the precinct house. Admonishing him sternly as he gave him a last shove, back out onto West 135th Street—"Don't you ever let me catch you doin' nothin' like that again!"

Malcolm barely heard him as he wandered, dazed, along the crowded sidewalk. Blinking in the harsh summer sunlight, rubbing his chafed wrists. Relieved almost beyond reckoning to be free, to have not had to take the humiliating beating he had heard the pimp take. He understood, now, with a combination of gratitude and resentment, what Charlie Small had arranged with the detective—putting the fear of God in him, but making sure that he would evade both the MPs and those white cops' fists on him. And at the same time the knowledge sank in that he really never could go back into Small's Paradise, that he was on his own again.

CHAPTER NINE

JONAH

He swung himself out of bed, already drenched in his own sweat despite the overhead fan sweeping methodically through the heavy air of their bedroom. When it was this hot in the City, no fan was any better than the ones on the subways, doing nothing to dissipate the heat, only pushing it down on everyone's heads.

He looked over for his wife, momentarily disoriented, and alarmed by her absence. Then he heard her—moving around in the kitchen downstairs, softly singing a hymn to herself. He sat back on the edge of the bed, inhaling the primal smell of frying bacon, and eggs, while he listened to her below. Wondering to himself, even as he did, And just how are you going to break away from that?

> *"There is a balm in Gilead,*
> *To make the wounded whole;*
> *There is a balm in Gilead,*
> *To heal the sin-sick soul—"*

On the Vineyard they had risen even earlier, going down to walk along the beach in the first light of day. Both of them wearing white linen trousers and holding hands, the only other people a few men and boys fishing in the surf. They had both felt as if they had recaptured something then, for those few days—as if the clock had been turned back. Amanda smiling at him shyly from time to time and thinking, he knew, about their honeymoon down in Asbury Park.

She had been so loving then—more affectionate and devoted than he could have ever pictured one person being, for all the homilies of Christian love he wrote, and listened to every week. Patient with him in his early, nervous fumblings, and open and willing herself; unembarrassed and never coy, despite her own inexperience. She was always seeking to hold him, to touch him however she could when he was near, as if she knew, instinctively, just what it was he needed then. And afterward, dazed by another day of sun and water, they would go back to their bungalow early, intermittently making love and just lying with each other, while it was still light out.

That was what it would mean, leaving. Giving her up, hurting her. Or would it by now be a relief for her, too?

Down in the kitchen Amanda was smiling and talkative, as usual. Giving no indication of anything that had happened between them on that train back from the Vineyard, or in their three weeks back on Strivers Row since then, moving about each other as warily as cats in their oversized house.

"I got a halfway passable chicken from Oppenheimer's for tonight," she chatted merrily to him while he sipped his coffee. "I'd like to get a good roast for Sunday, but I don't know if we'll have enough ration points left—"

"Uh-huh," he said, sliding into his chair and picking up the Herald-Tribune—happier than he wanted to acknowledge, just being around her in the morning.

She placed a steaming plate of scrambled eggs and bacon, rye toast and fresh orange juice before him. The eggs dusted with red pepper, and minute slices of onion cut so thin they would dissolve on the tongue. She had always been a fine cook, better than his own mother, he had to acknowledge. On Sundays she would make him poached eggs on creamy grits, or ham and sweet-potato biscuits, with red-eye gravy made from the pan juice and a little of her fine breakfast coffee. She was even able to re-create the fantastically light codfish cakes and black molasses beans his father still craved. He shoveled the eggs onto a piece of toast and began to wolf them down.

"I guess I'll go see the chairwomen of my clubs," she said with another rueful smile. "Get all that going again."

"Mmm-hmm. You going to see Mrs. Purvis about the Ladies' Literary Club? Maybe you ought to get some recommendations from Adam, first—"

She hit him lightly on the top of the head with the wooden spatula she had been using to push the eggs around, and he laughed out loud.

"You see? You don't listen to me!"

She cracked him on the head again, harder this time, and went over to the sink, smiling back playfully at him. There she began to clean the counter, sweeping into the garbage the bright orange halves from which she had hand-squeezed the juice, one by one, on the round, horned metal juice squeezer.

She had barely sat still since they had returned from the Vineyard. She had always liked to work through things by taking action, got restless if she wasn't doing two jobs at the same time. It was yet another way she had proved invaluable to his ministry—invaluable to him. Taking care of the church's innumerable clubs, the sewing circle and the cooking club, and the cosmetology class, and of course the literary club. Running the annual women's fund-raisers, the chicken hunts and pot-luck suppers, the candy pulls and fashion shows. Making constant visits to the church mothers and the sick and the old, arranging the annual sheeps-and-goats teas, and the guest speakers for Young People's Day, and Negro History Week. Doing all of the endless, trivial, political things that were necessary to keep a church from fragmenting and falling straight down a hole in the ground through disputation.

There was always a rift, or a potential rift. It was the same for every church. There were rifts over the choir director, or the service, or the hymnals. Rifts over the shade of the choir's robes, or the election of the deacons, or the direction of the missionary society, or that most reliable source of human discord, the collection and disbursal of money.

"But every rift's about the same thing in the end," his Daddy had told him. "Every rift in every church that ever has been, straight back to Peter an' Paul, is about the preacher. Who's with him, and who's ag'in' him."

The rift in their church had begun over skin color, which was not unusual, either. Most of the New Jerusalem's original congregants and their offspring were lighter skinned, ironically enough—a legacy from the men who had enslaved them in Virginia. The later members darker, from their long isolation in New York. His father had been patching over their putative differences for years, but by the time Jonah had returned from the Angel Factory in Pennsylvania, the rift had once again become manifest. Most of the lighter-skinned and the West Indian congregants sitting on the left side of the center aisle; the darker skinned on the right.

Jonah hadn't even noticed the split at first, obvious as it was. Still wallowing then in the trough of his despair, and his final surrender to Jesus. Unaware of anything until he heard the words muttered in the street after services—"That black son of a bitch," "Half-white mothafuckah—"

His father had noticed the split long before, of course, and flayed them mercilessly for it. Mocking all their pretensions of racial pride, or their heritage in the City, from his pulpit. Ridiculing all their discreet little phrases right to their faces:

"Oh, I know how some of you like to say, 'Be black—but not too black!' I know you do now, don't deny it! I see you puttin' on your airs. Don't deny it! But I got some news for ya. To those white people you measure yo'selves by—you all still just a bunch a niggers!"

But his father had known, too, that even his most flagrant, shocking insults wouldn't heal the rift by itself. He had moved on many other fronts at the same time, quietly and clandestinely, as was also his wont. Understanding, as he did, how the rift threatened everything he had built up—and most especially his son's ascension to his throne.

"You ought to get yourself a dark-skinned girl," he had told Jonah bluntly. "Seal up that rift. Someone from an old family."

"But what's it got to do with me?" he had questioned. "What I should do is preach to them the Word of the Lord—"

"They will look to what you do, son," he had informed him. "Words are easy."

His father had pressed upon him not only a dark wife, but also a daughter of one of the very few, very dark Virginia families in the congregation. Covering all his bases in typical fashion, so that Jonah wondered, as he would more than once, what he might have risen to had he ever been allowed to take part in more secular politics. He had docilely agreed to his father's plan, being completely untethered then from everything he thought he had known or believed, and his old egotistical ways. Believing, in his new condition, that he had no right to deny anything that was asked of him, although he had never looked twice at Amanda Robb in his life. She had a plain, pleasant face; strong but thick arms and legs; a ladylike demeanor that fell short of true grace due to a certain startling frankness.

Yet from the first hour he had been with her, he had known that this was somebody he could talk to, somebody with whom he could share his deepest apprehensions about his new vocation. She had a ready intellect, and seemed from the start to grasp what Jonah wanted to say even when he couldn't articulate it himself. She was tenacious to the point of stubbornness, yet was never contentious, or petty. She was the most honestly good-hearted person he had ever known, unimpressed by any nonsense, but moved by real suffering of any kind.

She was, in short, such a perfect preacher's wife that he couldn't help but wonder if this was why his Daddy had thrust them together in the first place, and not another of the New Jerusalem's endless, petty squabbles over color and status. But by then, knowing her, he didn't care. He had already decided that this was someone he could hold to, lest he be swept away by the inadequacies of his own faith and ability, and within a month he was pushing her to marry him, and even to set a date. Surprising and flattering her with his urgency, anxious as he was, then, to get his new life underway.

And throughout their life together, she had never let him down. It was much worse—knowing what he would do to her.

He rose from the table, carrying his plate and cup to the sink.

"All right, then."

"What time should I expect you?"

He shrugged, his eyes sliding away despite himself.

"Can't say, exactly. I'll see who's at the office, then I should make some rounds."

How could she not suspect—something? But she only smiled lovingly at him.

"Whenever it is, won't be soon enough."

She kissed him good-bye at the top of the stoop—being careful to remove her kitchen apron even for the few moments she would show herself outside—and then went back inside to finish cleaning up. Almost perfect, Jonah thought sadly as he went down Strivers Row.

He headed on up to the New Jerusalem—aware with every step he took that he was failing. The word itself running through his head. Repeating over and over again, as inexorably as the Motogram ticker in Times Square. Confirmed by everything he saw, and thought. Failing, failing—

He tried to force the word down, tried to concentrate instead on the sermon he wanted to write, but the words froze and crumbled in his mind. He had not spoken from the pulpit since their return from Oak Bluffs three weeks before, letting one or another of the

assistant ministers fill in for him. The congregation accepting it, so
far. Everything running slower in the summer, though there had
already been solicitous inquiries at the church door after services.
The church mothers asking How you feelin' today, Rev'rend? as
they shook his hand appraisingly. Jonah almost wanting to tell them
his deepest fear, out of sheer exasperation. That there was no voice
left—the words not coming, no matter how much he worked them
over, up in father's old study.

He should have gone, he knew it. Should have been gone three
weeks now. But here he stayed—and why?

There was the sound of a distant explosion a few blocks up
ahead—something more than the usual levitation of a manhole
cover caused by an undulation in the vast pressures coursing constantly beneath the streets of the City. This sounded almost like a
cannon shot, breaking the mid-morning, Harlem stillness, followed
by cheering, and dozens of voices, pitching jubilantly into a hymn,
"We Are Ready for the Battle"—

He could see the people on the sidewalk look up, startled for a
moment—no doubt wondering if they were finally under attack,
but going on about their business, like stoical New Yorkers, once no
ravening Germans or Japs actually appeared. Jonah remembering
that it was only the revival, up under the big tent at 148th Street
and St. Nicholas. The radio preacher, the Reverend Lightfoot Solomon Michaux, as he styled himself, his revival going strong for
over two weeks now, running his ads every Saturday in the Amsterdam Star-News:

> *"WAR! BLITZKRIEG! WAR!*
> *War Declared on the Devil by America's Most Famous Radio Evan-*
> *gelist—And His Wife, Mary, the Soloist—*
> *"The Battle will be fought by heralding gospel, and shouts against*
> *his satanic kingdom. Every devil is welcome. All things preached*
> *will be proved by the Bible. Fighting to Begin At Once—And Will*
> *Continue Until Hell Shakes!!!"*

He had been coming back to Harlem every summer for as long
as Jonah could remember, running his big tent wherever he could
get permission to pitch it. Drawing huge numbers, at least until
a few years before, when there had been a scandal concerning the
funds solicited by his radio ministry. But still he came back, unde-

terred, drawing more penitents than a dozen of the biggest Harlem churches—and endless complaints from the toney residents of Sugar Hill, enraged by all the noise.

His father had always loved the show, attending at least one performance a summer and taking Jonah with him. Unable to stop laughing all the way home, the old man admiring the Elder in his way, although he didn't believe a word—

Jonah had never quite been able to understand his love for such displays. But then Milton had always been a devotee, too, of the storefront churches that sprang up and vanished every season in Harlem, like so many toadstools after a rain. All the small-fry cults, as his brother ministers liked to call them derisively. Jonah kept track of them still, to tell his father—all the jacklegs and the holler preachers, the Spiritualists, and conjurers, and rootworkers, jammed into storefronts, or rooms over billiard halls and chicken restaurants. Boyd's Baptists, and Pentecostals, and the Royal Order of the Ethiopian Hebrews. The African Orthodox Church and the Metaphysical Church of the Divine Investigations, and the Church of the Living God, the Pillar Ground of Truth for All Nations; and The Full-Speed Gospel, and the Weep No More Congregation. Some of their founders sincere, some wanting to be the next Father Divine, or Prophet Costonie, or Mother Horn. Some just trying to make a living. Jonah catching one of the longer-lived signs that always made him smile:

Rev. G. I. Morell:
Funerals and Marriages
Promptly Attended to on Short Notice

But oh, for the faith of a mustard seed! Wondering what it would be like to put up his shingle in a storefront. To just start preaching the Gospel and trust in the Lord to provide the believers. Living on whatever they happened to give him. Living on faith. It was what his father had done, even if he didn't believe—

"Hey, chachem, whatsa matter? You don't come around here anymore?"

He looked up, startled, realizing that he was at the block of the New Jerusalem already, and Jakey Mendelssohn was calling him over from in front of his would-be department store. Sweeping the detritus of another Thursday night into the gutter, smiling wryly at him around the cigarette perpetually balanced in one corner of his mouth.

Too late to make believe he didn't see him, Jonah walked over. Smiling sheepishly back, acknowledging how oblivious he could become whenever he was chewing over something—but keeping one eye out for him, the cousin, just the same.

"All these little mamzers, in from their ships an' their bases," Jakey was complaining, as usual, sweeping up an empty whiskey bottle, a dustpan full of cigar butts and matchbooks, and discarded condoms. Gesturing at his fellow merchants where they swept away at their sidewalks up and down 144th Street.

"I don't care how much business they bring, you spend half the day pickin' up after 'em!"

"How you doin', Jakey?"

"Eh," Mendelssohn said, shrugging his broad shoulders. "Pushin' along, pushin' along. Been a long time—I thought maybe you was drafted."

Jonah smiled at the joke, and at Jakey. The man was a hustler, he knew, running one scheme or another, semi- or illegal, out of the back of his department store. But he was the only white store owner in the neighborhood who didn't charge his customers double what they did downtown—the only one who let them have layaway, and try on dresses and hats before they bought them. Unlike Blumstein's or Koch's or Grant's, any of the other, real department stores on 125th Street, Jakey had always hired colored salesgirls and cashiers, and without being forced into it by Adam's Don't Buy Where You Can't Work campaign. A tall, dark-haired man in his early thirties, with an olive complexion—darker than Jonah was himself—and the face of his Irish father, who had absconded long ago. He had a flattened, boxer's nose, and a bad limp, which Jonah assumed was why he wasn't in the army, though he had never asked. Jakey himself had never volunteered it, always full of jokes and stories, mostly about himself. A sort of sleight of hand, Jonah had recognized, that many whites used to hide their nervousness around colored people, but well-intentioned enough on his part. He liked Jakey—and he had used his services.

It was the cousin who made Jonah dread passing Jakey's store. He spotted him now, behind the glass front door of Mendelssohn's, holding another broom but lingering there, staring anxiously out at the street. His very presence enough to fill Jonah with an irrational sense of revulsion.

He emerged slowly from behind the door now—no more than a

teenager, Jonah guessed. Walking out with the broom and an apron over the blocky, European suit he wore every day, sweeping at the the black-and-white, diamond-shaped floor tiles of the entranceway. Taking small, tentative steps, his flattened, rust-colored hair falling over his forehead.

"Hey, bulvan, you waiting for an invitation? Step on it!" Jakey yelled to him good-naturedly, trying to humor him out of his fearfulness as he always did.

But the boy said nothing. Making a few more hesitant swipes at the tiles, while he looked them over, his eyes fluttering anxiously, sweeping mindlessly back and forth. Jakey clamped his mouth shut around his cigarette.

"Still the same," he told Jonah, and spat out of the side of his mouth onto his newly cleaned sidewalk. "Wait, did I say the same? No—I think he's getting' worse."

Jakey had made him come in to see the boy the first week he had arrived, just over three months ago. Dragging him back through the displays of cheap living room sets, the draperies and bedding, and the bolts of raw cloth piled up nearly to the ceiling. Into the back storeroom, filled with mysterious, empty liquor bottles and tapedup boxes, where he conducted his other businesses, whatever they were. Where Jonah himself had gone, to his incalculable shame, for the extra ration coupons he used for his special purposes—insisting on paying the full price for them even though Jakey had tried to give him a discount. Because I am a man of the cloth—

He had an outsize, electrified orange sign stretched over the front door—a sign slightly wider than the entire storefront, declaring it MENDELSSOHN'S DEPT. STORE. But for all of his pretensions, the store was half the size of Blumstein's, or S. H. Kress. There was an air of desperation about the enterprise—and to Jakey—that was readily more apparent the farther one penetrated into the store. The dresses and suits on the mannequins in his front windows always a little dowdy and out of fashion, even to Jonah's eye. The piled fabrics, the tablecloths and bedsheets and slipcovers in the back so ugly and flimsy they were depressing just to look at.

The boy sat there amidst them, propped up on a stool as if it were his throne. Jakey was right, thought Jonah. Originally, he had seemed less nervous and fearful than he was now. Remarkably cool, in fact, at the end of this five-thousand-mile journey, through God only knew what. Speaking in a matter-of-fact voice and savoring a cigarette, while Jakey alternately translated for him and urged him on. Growling over and over again at him—"Tell him! Tell him what's going on over there!"

The boy had obliged them. Telling them of all the things he had witnessed in Poland. Things that had seemed incredible at the time—not least because of his strangely offhand manner. His family had lived in Berlin up until Kristallnacht, just managing to dodge the rampaging Nazi bullyboys who set fire to their syna-gogue, and turned the streets of the city into rivers of shimmer-ing broken glass. They had managed to flee to relatives in Lodz, in Poland—the wrong way. Trapped there with all the other Jews of Poland. Everyone, without exception, sorted out and pinned with yellow stars.

"Every one of them, the rich and the poor," Lazar's words had come, translated through Jakey's now shaken hustler's mouth— more terrifying in its sudden uncertainty than anything in the boy's own calm voice.

"It didn't matter who you were...or what you did... They took them all together," Jakey interpreted, piece by piece, the horror becoming bitterness with each new word. "They made everybody walk over to the old ghetto...with only what they could carry in their arms...while the goddamned Poles stood by and laughed!"

Incredible, medieval stories. Locked into a walled ghetto. Other, even more unbelievable things, that Lazar, the cousin, had only glimpsed or heard of, while he was making his way out of Poland. Jews shot and beaten, even raped, right out on city streets. The long trains, made up completely of cattle cars, that they loaded up at the ghetto with people every week. Hauling them to factory camps where the smokestacks worked twenty-four hours a day, but where nothing was made, and from which no one ever came back.

"The sons a bitches. You know what they're doing!" Jakey had implored Jonah when they had heard all of it. His eyes welling with tears of helpless rage.

"You gotta do somethin' about it!"

Jonah understood what he was referring to. His political con-nections—his father's political connections, with the O'Kanes, now nicely ensconced in Ed Flynn's machine, up in the Bronx.

But what were they to do about it? Some Irish wardheelers, faced with such profound and incalculable changes in the world?

There had been more of the usual rallies. Led by the fuming little mayor, before full houses at Madison Square Garden, putting the leaders of the fascist countries on trial for crimes against human- ity, in order to raise money for Jewish relief. Jonah had even been to a couple of them. In the dark of the Garden, they bore an uncon- scious, uncanny resemblance to the Nazis' own night rallies, he thought—or one more prizefight, or a hockey game. The spotlights sweeping majestically across the arena, the smoke from thousands of cigarettes and cigars trailing wearily up toward the ceiling, and the disembodied loudspeaker voices shouting out brave sentiments. The usual reformers on hand to speak—La Guardia presiding, and Norman Thomas and Sidney Hillman; the Reverend Holmes and Rabbi Wise—expressing the full measure of their horror and indignation. Adam, recruited by Maurice Rosenblatt at the Amal- gamated, outdoing them all.

"If a black man will give a hundred dollars for freedom," he yelled out, leaping up and holding out a hundred-dollar bill in the spotlight, "what will you Jews do?" The crowd roaring back its approval, carried beyond themselves by his challenge. Men and women rushing into the aisles, holding up their own money, raising record amounts for the refugees—what refugees there were.

But what no one spoke about, Jonah knew, was just what this sort of fund-raising, this outrage-building would do. The Jews were still in Europe, still far away, being hauled off to those mysterious factories every day.

"The murdering chaiserim," Jakey said now, spitting again on the sidewalk. His eyes imploring and accusatory at the same time. "There must be something we can do—"

He had continued to rage against each new atrocity. Raising refugee money, Jonah knew, from the other store owners in the neighborhood, contributing his own meager earnings—even, it was rumored, soliciting from his gangster pals. Searching for any role he could play—

What Jakey didn't understand, Jonah thought, was that this war was something wholly new, just in its scale alone. A rift in the world. The birth of a whole new human existence, perhaps. Ran- domly bombing cities from the air. Trampling out entire peoples, casually burning them up in factory furnaces. Something soulless and faceless and unremitting, beyond the old ideas of human hero- ism, or evil. Ripping away the face of God.

Or was it new at all? Was it waiting there all along, inside the human beast, only now we have the tools to finish the job? The more he thought about it, the less incredible he found it. Of course they would take the opportunity to get rid of everyone they hated. Of course they would, if they thought they could get away with it. Look what they've done to us—

He made his excuses and broke away from Jakey. Reminding himself not to turn into the block from Seventh Avenue again, making sure not to look back at that dull-eyed, frightened boy. Still not sure why he actively loathed him. He was just a boy, after all, another refugee—

Was it for stripping away his own personal immunity? That one description Jakey had told him, lingering in his brain. They were all taken away together. All of them, all of the Jews. And if the Jews, why not us next? Or was it seeing the boy for what he himself would become, if he left? Fleeing, frightened and desperate. Always looking out, always knowing what he had done in order to survive—

He all but ran through the nave of the church. Glad, for once, to finally get back to his office. Settled somewhat by the familiar institutional blue-green walls; the back-church smells of old flowers, and pork-and-bean suppers, and floor cleaner. *Listening for it, as he always did—the rasping inhalations of his father.* The very walls of the church seeming to undulate with his every breath—

Jonah went to check on him first, but the old man was still asleep, as he usually was now in the early morning, after staying awake all night. Lying fully dressed on his metal cot, only the top of his huge, rutted head visible to Jonah. Sleeping just as he always had, flat on his back, snoring away in great, congested chuffs. His mother had always joked about it—Lord, but it's impossible to get any sleep around that man! Between his appetites and his snoring—

He crept back down to his own vestry office, situated directly under his father's apartment. Calling in his secretary, Delphine, to take letters and go over the day's schedule. It was a busier summer Friday than usual, with so much still to catch up on from his vacation—Jonah working briskly, just as happy to take his mind off what he had to do later.

There were the regular weekly meetings with his assistant ministers, and the seminary students doing their summer work at the New Jerusalem; with the head usher, the custodian, the organist.

Meetings on the quarterly budget reports with the directors of youth programs, and the church nursery and the day-care center, and the penny savings bank. Another, blessedly interminable meeting with a representative from the Colored Orphans' Asylum, up in Riverdale, who informed him that the asylum had just decided to accept white orphans for the first time, in light of the pressing need created by the war—Jonah barely able to keep himself from smiling at the irony of the news.

So the war is bringing us closer together as a nation, after all. If only to take care of their orphans—

His burden was nothing, he knew, compared to Adam's over at the Abyssinian, which had over fifty separate clubs, plus its own print shop, and baseball and basketball, and six-man football leagues. The workload not nearly as bad, either, as only a few years before, when it seemed to Jonah as if he and every other minister in Harlem spent all their waking hours at the churches' employment and housing bureaus, and the soup kitchens. Searching the streets, every day and night for years, trying to find anyone who might be hiring. To find members of his congregation he hadn't seen, and whom he was worried were too proud or stubborn to come to him for help even though they might be starving.

Those had been times of constant crisis. A whole Hooverville of unemployed men, living within a stone's throw of the church on abandoned East River barges. People growing potatoes in buckets of earth on their fire escapes, fertilizing them with manure they fought for from the street vendors' horses. More than half the doctors on work relief, college professors driving taxicabs for a living.

And still they kept coming. More and more of them, crowding in every week. Some of them from the Islands, but more from the South. Piling into the tenements just around the corner on 142nd and 143rd Streets, a dozen—two dozen—to an apartment. Arriving without a nickel, without any idea of how to live in the City, just like the original congregation his father had brought north— People so ignorant they seemed like they had just come up from the earth.

There was nothing for them. Men sitting all day in employment-agency waiting rooms just for the warmth and the company, with no hope of a job, cashing monthly relief checks of fourteen dollars. The women up at the Slave Market in the Bronx, or working the presses in some laundry for all of twelve hours a week—even the streetwalkers working The Market on Seventh Avenue, with no takers. People everywhere, just standing around on the street corners waiting, the panic showing in their faces.

It had been better then—at least for himself, he had to admit. There had been no time to think about anything. He had been busy simply helping people, all the time. So bone tired he could have fallen asleep every night as soon as his head hit the pillow. But somehow he had not, always finding the energy, then, to make love with Amanda, or just talk to her for hours. Starting refreshed the next morning no matter how late he had been up, it seemed—buoyed by the knowledge that he had done all that he could to help his hungry, suffering congregation. Oh, how much easier he had lived then, amidst all the misery of his people! No trying to find ways to occupy himself with endless committee meetings.

Our selfishness is unlimited—

By the time he looked up again, it was almost three. His work done for now, at least. All his comfortable boredom falling away, for the growing excitement and anxiety that he always felt on one of *those* days.

He leaned out of his inner office to tell his secretary that he was going out on his rounds, that she should go to lunch—then stepped back inside. Waiting while Delphine, an almost fanatically efficient woman in her fifties, with eyeglasses as thick as the sanctuary's stained glass, quietly gathered up her purse and her typing for home, and limped slowly out of the vestry on her fallen arches.

Only then did he dial up the familiar number in the Village. Almost holding his breath as he did so, unsure if he wanted her to answer or not. After seven rings he was about to hang up when he heard the receiver click, and there was her voice again—languid and smooth, and faintly mocking.

"Yes."

A statement. But he still insisted on talking to her like regular people. Like the regular people they had been.

"So, is it good for today, then?" he said breezily.

"Sure."

The voice sweet and slow as molasses. A stage voice.

"Just as I said. Five o'clock."

"All right, then—"

"That should give you enough time, shouldn't it?"

"What? Whatever you mean—" he started to say, sputtering ineffectually at her clairvoyance.

How does she know? Ultimately, though, he couldn't even bring himself to deny it, simply huffing over the line—

"Five o'clock then!"

"I'll be here—"

—and jamming down the receiver before she could finish the last, drawn-out word. Gathering himself, he shot the cuffs on his light blue linen suit, then looked at his face in the mirror of his office bathroom. He peered at it over and over again, from every angle. Pushing back a particularly curly hair or two, trying to be sure of how it looked in the light. Trying to ignore the first heavy rumbles of his father's footsteps, along the floor just above him.

He always made the change in a place on Third Avenue. One of those little stores tucked away under the el, where they sold cigars and newspapers, and girlie magazines out of the back, and where he could slip in and slip out again without anyone noticing his transformation. It was a ritual by now, and one that made him feel more nervous and excited the closer he got to it. He imagined that this was how other men must feel going to buy dope, or liquor, or dirty postcards.

It was the same routine, every time, beginning when he left the New Jerusalem. Walking down to the train at 125th Street. Going out of his way to say hello to anyone he knew, making sure to wear his clerical collar. Bristling underneath it with the thrill, and the utter degradation, of what he was about to do to himself.

By the time he reached the elevated, he could barely keep from running up the metal stairs to the miniature Swiss chalet that served as a waiting room. There he waited back in the shadows, behind the old potbellied stove and the hurricane lamps still hanging from the ceiling. Emerging only when the ancient electric train, nearly as flimsy as a Christmas toy, came shambling into the station, boarding always on the last of its four cars, sliding quickly onto the woven straw seat by the window.

It was only on the train that he took off the collar. Stealing one more look around to make sure there was no one he knew onboard, no one from his congregation whom he might have missed on the platform. Then he would unbutton it, and slip on the plain, conservative tie he had made sure to stuff into a jacket pocket that morning, as quickly as he could. Yanking down the window and leaning back when he was finished, closing his eyes and letting what faint breezes the train generated blow in his face.

He would take the Third Avenue el down to the 68th Street station, opening his eyes from time to time only to make sure he knew where he was. Staring dully into the reddened faces of the Irish housewives, and the old men who leaned their elbows out on the window ledges of their Lexington Avenue tenements, knocking out their pipes. When he reached his stop, he trotted quickly down the steps, into the dappled, grey half-light beneath the elevated.

It was another world down there, below the trains—a midtown world of dappled light, and blue-winged pigeons nesting in the rusting latticed ironwork. The blocks in its shadow were full of secondhand stores and pawnshops, of foreign-language movie houses and flophouses, and leaning three- and four-story brick tenements. It was a world of the shrugged off, and the neglected, and the faintly shameful. A world to disappear into.

Sometimes he would find a bar. One of the faceless Paddy dives, with perfunctory names like the Blarney Stone or the Jaunting Car. A jar of pickled eggs on the bar and a soaked-in reek of beer, and bad whiskey, and corned beef from the hot plate in the back. There he could easily slip into the squalid booth of a men's room, and emerge a new man. Bars were volatile places, though, and since the start of the war they had been filled with drunken servicemen, many of them angry over having already blown their pay, or been cheated out of it. He had had about enough of that to last him a lifetime—

What he preferred were the newspaper shops. Deep slivers of stores, redolent of cigar smoke, and spilled malt liquor. There he would sidle past the men clustered around the front counter who were buying single cigarettes for a penny, arguing over the Giants or perusing the pink-tinted sheets of PM, or the Mirror and the World-Telegram. He would make his way to the very back of the store, where it was not unusual for men to dawdle among the tied piles of returned newspapers, or the well-thumbed stacks of sunbathing magazines, with their photos of nude young women playing volleyball on the cover, leaping ecstatically in the sun.

There he would wait, pretending to peruse the magazines, or the boxes of five-cent cigars under the counter glass. Gearing himself up, remembering how he was going to walk, and talk, and deport himself. Preparing to think and act, and expect to be received just like one of them. Only when he was sure he was in their mind would he straighten up, and fix his tie in the cigar-display glass. Ready to walk out onto the street a white man.

It was Sophia who had first taught him how to do it, one day out at Coney Island when he was still an adolescent and they were hurrying down the broad ramps from the train amidst the jostling, eager crowds. Drawn on helplessly by their first whiff of the sea, and the smell of frying red hots, and roasting corn.

She had dashed out in front of him. Her white cotton dress twirling in the same dappled half-light under the elevated tracks by Surf Avenue, grinning back at him—whispering into his ear when he caught up:

"Let's be white people today!"

He had thought even then, no more than a boy, that it wasn't right. But he had always been eager to please her.

"All right. But how?" he asked, genuinely curious.

"C'mon!"

She had grabbed his hand, and started to run again, pulling him down the boardwalk. The springy gray boards bouncing under their tennis shoes as she towed him along, instructing him in a close, low voice. Jonah barely able to listen, his head spinning from her nearness to him, the scent of the perfume on her neck.

He had always adored her—was often astonished to think that he might have such an older sister. He mocked her teenage laziness, was hurt sometimes when she casually swatted him away. But she was almost always kind to him—much kinder than the other older sisters he knew, always happy to show him or teach him new things.

And he had been stunned, and not a little embarrassed by how beautiful she had become in the last couple of years. Blushing just to look at the curves of her figure when she came downstairs in the morning, proud of the way her regal face and bearing awed into silence even his blustering school pals, who stood out by the stoop crudely ranking and snickering at every girl who walked by. When his sister Sophie came down, they were tongue-tied, embarrassed by the very fact of their existence there.

By that summer at Coney Island, she had already begun to change in other ways, he realized now. Something, some part of her becoming elusive, even mysterious. He would hear his parents talking about it sometimes when he came upon them in the kitchen, but he was still too young to understand. Sophie had started college by then, one of two colored women in her class up at Vassar. His parents proud as Iorians about it, his father always believing strongly in education for women.

But already she had started coming home less and less. Making excuses for why she couldn't leave her studies, or taking trips with her classmates. At first their parents had been glad—even prouder—to see that she fit in, his sister always a little too aloof and dreamy, even for her Harlem high school. Yet when his father, coming back from an upstate convocation, had stopped in Poughkeepsie one afternoon to see her, he hadn't been able to find her anywhere. He had looked all over the campus, always arriving too late to catch her in her dorm room, or in class, or at the library. Leaving, finally, with the distinct if unsubstantiated feeling, as he had told their mother, that she had been playing some sort of game with him.

Jonah hadn't thought anything of it. He had just assumed, much as he missed her, that she was a grown-up now and would be away more—off on her own, as he sometimes longed to be. When she did come home, he was amazed yet again by her sophistication, by how she dressed and talked and held herself, so much above the other girls and even the older women from the church. She wore evening dresses on occasion now, and jewelry and makeup. Some members of the church swore that they had seen her in downtown hotel bars, alone, smoking cigarettes out of a holder, though this charge had seemed so outrageous that his father hadn't even known how to confront her with it. At home she talked in her droll new college voice about taking up a career singing, or on the stage. Their parents rendered almost speechless by these ambitions, leaving them unchallenged only out of the fervent hope that she would soon understand their impossibility. To Jonah it had only seemed like the natural next step—his sister metamorphosing into something even more marvelous.

That summer, condescending to spend a few weeks at home with them, she had paid attention to him again. Passing most of her days sitting around the front parlor in a pair of sleek white trousers while leafing through copies of Life, or her movie magazines—reading material that made his father so angry when he saw them that his hands actually shook. Going out at night with some of the few friends she still had in the neighborhood to see the pictures at the Alhambra, or the Roosevelt. Or more often, he knew—listening

to her high heels clicking quietly across the upstairs floorboards—
sneaking out after their parents were asleep to go dancing.

But when she did stay in, she would talk to him. Giving him nov-
els of which she knew their father would disapprove. Telling him all
kinds of things about girls who had been expelled from college for
going out to meet their boyfriends at night, or to buy bootleg liquor.
Telling him the things that white college girls said about colored
people when they weren't around, and what they really thought.

"But how do you know these things?" he exclaimed, jumping up
on his mother's fine brocade parlor couch in his excitement.

"Let's just say I'm a good eavesdropper," she had told him, with
the mysterious little chuckle that all the boys liked so much.

That morning at Coney Island they had risen before six to make
the endless subway ride from Harlem. Taking the B train at 135th
Street and St. Nicholas Avenue, then changing to the F at Herald
Square, and riding it through all twenty-nine stops—on into the
Village and through the Lower East Side, then cutting over to
Brooklyn by the Navy Yard, and down through Gowanus, and Fort
Hamilton.

They still hadn't beaten the crowd. The stuffy cars filling up
when they got to Second Avenue, and Delancey Street. Jammed
with Italians and Jews and Ukrainians, whole families toting picnic
baskets filled with coiled bloody-smelling sausages and huge rounds
of bread. Bottles of beer and homemade wine, towels and bicycle
inner tubes, wide hats and umbrellas and jars of cold cream—anything to keep the sun off their wintery, greenish-white skin.

Jonah watching out carefully for any packs of white boys, as he
always did when he went below 110th Street. But their train was
too crowded with people for anybody to do anything but hang on
to the dangling leather straps. When it finally emerged from under-
ground and began to rattle through the flatlands of Brooklyn, he
had gotten up on his knees, like a little boy, on the punctured straw
matting that had been digging into his thighs the whole long trip.
Turning his back on the turbulent, overpacked humanity of the car,
careful not to disturb Sophia, by now dozing beside him in the sti-
fling heat, but staring out his open window at the trim homes and
lawns of Borough Park, and Bensonhurst, sliding by. Amazed as he
always was by the vastness, the interminable expanse and endless
variety of the greater City outside their own dense little ghetto.

As the train clamored on through Brighton Beach, the first whiff of beach and the sea air came through the opened windows, and a murmur of pleasure arose spontaneously, ecstatically, from the throats of every family on the train. Then the doors were open at the Stilwell Avenue stop, and they were out and running, laughing and shouting down the broad ramps along with all the rest, the next tidal wave of people breaking over Surf Avenue—racing toward the boardwalk and the exotic wheels and towers of Luna Park, the great, trellised dome of Steeplechase, Funny Place.

Sophia ran with them, revived on a dime by their arrival at the ocean. She had seemed like a girl again, grinning back at him waif-ishly, as the skirt of her sundress swung up around her knees. Dancing out past the subway change booths, and the big candy stand with its red-and-white-striped peppermint pole. Beckoning to him, grabbing his head with both hands when he came to her, giggling and whispering into his ear:

"Let's be white people today!"

He had done everything that she said—letting her tell him how he should walk and talk, what sort of things he should say, and how to hold himself. They had gone down the boardwalk doing a running parody of the white people all around them. Walking stiffly, holding their arms down carefully at their sides. Speaking in that strange, self-important nasal way white folks had. They had to cover their mouths with their hands to keep from laughing out loud, and Jonah was afraid they would be caught out, but the whites around them remained as oblivious and superior as ever.

"Most of all, it's the attitude," she had told him.

"What?"

"You've got to act like you belong."

Which had always been the key, he thought now, remembering, as he prepared to step out of the twilight world under the train tracks and walk east toward Second Avenue. That had been the hardest part for him to learn, and the most exhilarating. *Still was.* Strolling into any place they wanted to—not glancing furtively at the man at the door, or behind the counter to see if they were not wanted. Taking the hands from their mouths, talking and laughing as brazenly as anyone else, acting as if they had a right to be anywhere at all they pleased, not just at the discretion of someone else.

As he could act now, straightening his tie in the glass of the cigar case one more time as he considered his options. The City his oyster for at least another hour. He might go to a gallery on 57th Street, or buy himself a crisp new shirt at Brooks Brothers, or browse through the jewelry cases at Tiffany's—imagining all of the nice things he would like to buy and take home to Amanda. Then maybe some good restaurant, or a hotel bar where he knew a colored man would not be served.

He had already started to make his way back up the shop, wreathed in his daydreams, when he saw him. On his knees, pawing through the bright carnival colors of a box filled with comic books—the worthless, brightly colored little magazines they sold in every corner drugstore now. He must have slipped in sometime after he did, but Jonah had never noticed him. He stopped dead when he saw him, but there was no way around him, kneeling where he was, directly in front of him in the thin sliver of a store—

The boy on the train from Martha's Vineyard. The one who had rescued them.

He was much changed, but there was no mistaking him. Wearing a sharp new suit instead of his train whites, an outfit far more sophisticated than anything Jonah would have thought him capable of. His ridiculous conk now carefully shaped, with much of the bright red color drained from it. He seemed to have somehow grown immeasurably older just in the weeks since Jonah had seen him, yet he was still going through the box of comic discards with unconscious boyish enthusiasm.

Jonah felt the panic rising in his throat. Wondering, irrationally, if he had been spotted—if somehow the boy had even followed him. Knowing this was impossible, he fought down his apprehension, trying to take advantage of the boy's preoccupation on the floor to leave. Yet just as he had lifted up a leg, trying to step silently over him, the boy had started to rise—trapping Jonah in a desperately embarrassing, awkward position; half-straddling, half actually stepping on the young man where he squatted, having to hurriedly pull his leg back. Making his apologies, even taking his hat off in his confusion.

"Excuse me! Excuse me, I didn't see—"

Stopping then, as he saw the white faces at the front turn toward him. Realizing the mistake he had made, speaking obsequiously to the Negro teenager, squatting underneath him. Thinking he should have just cursed him. He looked back down at the boy, now risen on one knee. Staring right at him but not saying a thing, blinking in

the thin light of the newspaper store, Jonah unable to tell if he recognized him or not.

"Excuse me!" he repeated, unable to help himself.

He hurried out of the tiny store, back into the twilight world
outside. Bumping into one of the older white men at the front as he
did, all of them still staring at him—an outraged, collective sexage-
narian squawk of Hey, watchit! following him as he rushed out onto
the street.

He flagged down a DeSoto cab, its green-and-red back fins
nearly streaking past him. At least able to effect his getaway, as
a white man. Scrambling into its cavernous backseat, and giving the driver his sister's address in the Village—all thoughts of
some intervening trip to a white restaurant gone now. His skin still
crawling with the thought that he had almost been caught.

By that same boy. Not that he knew who he was. Not that he
gave any indication of having recognized him from the train. But
still—there he was. Like some kind of premonition. Catching Jonah
out when no one else ever had, even exposing him to the white
men there, so that he didn't know if he could ever go back to that
store—

He caught a sudden flicker of movement out of the corner of his
eye. Something incredible—a great black beast bounding toward
him at eye level, just outside the open cab window. A steer, of all
things, somehow right out on First Avenue, and looking for all the
world to Jonah as if it were trying to charge his taxi. He sat mesmerized, unable to move while he watched the animal lower its head
and slam a horn into the door right next to him. There was a sound
like someone had hit the side of the cab with a sledgehammer, and
then everything sped up. The driver swerving his taxi away from
the bull adroitly as a matador, Jonah catching just a flash of the
beast's huge black-haired snout, within inches of his own face, its
eyes rolling madly.

Then they were past it—the cabbie calling back to him with
determined nonchalance, "Happens all the time!" Jonah realizing
only then that they were passing the ancient slaughterhouses along
Turtle Bay. Peering out the back window to watch the receding bull
skid on the smooth pavement, a gang of drovers running out across
the street after it, shouting and cursing as they hauled it down. In
his last glimpse of the beast, it was on its knees, the men gesticulat-
ing and yanking at its horns—

.   .   .

The cabbie zizagged down through the Flower District, where restaurant and nightclub managers stood on the curb haggling over
bushels of roses and tiger lilies and wildflowers, then across Fourteenth Street with its drab, dingy, bargain stores, its twin brick cit-
adels of the Armory and the Salvation Army headquarters looming
across the street from each other. When they passed through the
triumphal white arch in Washington Square Park, Jonah got out,
his legs still trembling a little, deciding to walk the rest of the way
to his sister's, in order to calm himself and kill some time.

He felt a little better the moment his shoes hit the pavement,
as he always did when he reached the Village—though here, for
all its bohemian affectations, things were really no different from
anywhere else. Once, just before the war, he had seen a throng of
jeering young workmen besiege a queer Negro couple in a café on
Sullivan Street. The owner had locked the door against them, but
the men outside beat the windows with the palms of their hands,
shaking and spitting on the plate glass and screeching like mon-
keys. Jonah had watched them from across the street, in the safety
of a small crowd that had gathered there. Staring at the two queers,
huddled together deep in the recesses of the café. Their frightened
faces tinted with makeup, fluttering their long, false eyelashes like
women.

He had felt disgust and shame that any colored men could walk
around in public like that—yet he had looked on, fascinated, as they
clung together. One of the fairies with his arm held protectively
over the other's shoulders. Twice damned, black and queer. And
how were they to disguise that, day in and day out?

He strolled south, then cut over through the crooked hump of
Minetta Lane, remembering as he always did the stories his father
used to tell about the old days down here, just after the Civil War.
Fending off not only the whites, but also the franchised colored
Tammany thugs—men with names like No-Toe Charley, and Black
Cat, and Bloodthirsty. Prowling the narrow, crooked streets with
their razors and knives, hired to wring what tribute they could for
the machine out of the all but penniless Negro neighborhoods.

All long gone now, together with the rest of the old neighborhood. Replaced by the Italians, or some of the Village's notorious
bohemian artists—an inviting Italian tavern situated now at the

head of Minetta Lane, where his father's first storefront church had been. His sister lived just across Sixth Avenue, in a yellow-brick apartment building on Cornelia Street, put up only a few years before the present war. Five stories high, sleek and modern, with silver art deco fixtures and fire escapes on the street side, and a white doorman in green-and-gold-buttoned livery at the lobby desk.

"How are you today, sir!" he said, a burst of cheeriness personified as he jumped up to push open the door. A short, bulky, middle-aged man, his gray hair just peeking out of the edge of his green, braided doorman's cap. Looking attentively up at Jonah as he ushered him toward the elevator. A white man, currying his favor.

"She is expecting you, sir, go right ahead!"

He nodded as matter-of-factly as he could, and waited stolidly for the equally sleek art deco elevator, a work of art in itself. Up on the fifth floor her building smelled faintly of polish, and perfume, and the fresh white roses in a vase by the elevator. So unlike the usual hallway smells he was used to in Harlem, of cheap floor cleaner and frying food, hair lye and homemade beer. There were none of the usual tenement sounds of life, either—fighting couples and clanking frying pans; laughter, and children running tirelessly up and down the halls. Instead he felt as if he might have been in a well-ventilated mausoleum, everything cool, and antiseptic, and quiet.

He did catch a hint of life—a recording of "Mood Indigo," sounding soft and slow and mysterious in the stillness.

You ain't been blue
No, no, no
You ain't been blue
Till you've had that mood indigo
That feelin' goes stealin' down to my shoes—

He followed it down the hall to her apartment, knocking on a door that matched the delicate mauve color of the hallway. Standing there while she let him wait, trying to compose himself, to fight down the urge to walk back down the hall, or pound with his fists on the beautiful mauve door.

Finally it opened and she stood there, in a yellow silk dressing gown that he knew she had put on just for the effect. Leaning against the door jamb, one arm over her head, a smirk across her beautiful face.

"You're here early," she said, her voice barely audible above the music. "What's the matter? Run out of real white people?"

"Hello, Sophie," he said.

He balanced on the edge of his sister's day couch, carefully sipping his tall iced tea. Everything in her apartment so soft and luxuriant—the deep carpet on the floor, the stuffed furniture in blended shades of blue and peach—that he was almost afraid to touch it. The music off now. Sophia, leaning back in her chair, across the coffee table, drinking gin on ice with a splash of lemon juice, a teasing smile playing across her lips.

"I brought you something—" he began perfunctorily, pulling a small fold of bills in a money clip from his pants pocket.

"I told you the last two times. I'm set," she said tersely.

"Yeah, you're doing all right," he said, looking deliberately around at the dressed-up apartment, the fine silk dressing gown she was wearing. Vases full of those curious flowers she loved, white on the outside and yellow inside. False jasmine, he knew she called it.

"I got a steady gig at the Café now," she told him, taking a long, deliberate swig from her gin and pausing for effect.

"Archie takes care of the rest."

"Archie!" he nearly spat in frustration. "That gangster!"

"I do what I like, with whom I like," she snapped—then gave him a small, teasing smile. "I was even thinking of making a small donation to the church—"

He waited a moment before replying, trying to control his temper.

"But what's the point of it, Sophie?"

"What?"

"What's the point of living like—like you do, just to take up with somebody like Archie?" he asked, as reasonably as he could.

"Why, because he runs a policy racket? Or because he's colored?"

"Because you're colored, Sophie."

"We're white, Jonah. And we're colored. We're white and colored. White black, black white," she said, as if she were explaining something to a child. "We're as much white as we are colored. You've seen the picture of that white woman."

"But what's the point of it, Sophie? Being kept in a Village apartment by some gangster. No husband, no family. No proper home—"

"No, not like your proper home—"

"Quit that!" he said sharply. "You know what I mean. You have no responsibility to anybody or anything. What's the point of that?"

"The point is to do what I want to do!" she said fiercely, her drink sloshing in her hand. "I want to sing. I want to have fun. But most of all I want to do what I want, all the time. I don't accept any obligation beyond that."

She checked herself then, and sat down next to him on the day couch, squeezing his arm apologetically. So close that he could feel her breath, with its faint sting of gin, upon his cheek.

"I'm not a Christian like you are, Jonah. It's not like third-grade Sunday school anymore," she said, almost gently. "Put my hand up and say I accept the Lord in my heart—"

"And what about the rest of them?" he asked her, more reflectively than anything else. "What are they supposed to do?"

"Who?" she asked. "Who's that? Your congregation? Your wife?"

"You know who. All of them that can't pass."

"We can."

She leaned in close again, but he stood up now. Pulling away from her, irritated, pacing around her seraglio of an apartment.

"And that's enough? We don't have to care about any of the rest of it? We just leave them behind?"

"Maybe it ain't fair," she shrugged. "So what? I heard somewhere it rains on the just an' the unjust, and every sucker in between. But I'm gonna use my color just like I'm gonna use everything else I got. I'm gonna use it just like I use my voice, or my figure. Hell, I know a lot a girls use a lot more!"

She gave a short, rueful laugh, but he had already turned on her.

"Listen to you! Do you even know how you sound?" he asked—trying to hurt her now.

"'Ain't' that, and 'sucker' this. Talkin' like some girl out on the curb," he mimicked. "You're a Vassar girl, baby! You were saying 'whom' just a minute ago."

"So?"

"So where's that comin' from anyway, Soph? Sounds awfully colored to me. Is that Archie's influence? Or is that just for your gigs?"

"I talk the way I want to—"

"Do you? Really? What's your gig at Café Society called again?"

"'Divas in Black and White.' With Hazel Scott," she admitted petulantly.

"Uh-huh. And you're the white. Only not just any white, are you? Not some high-tone, Vassar-girl white? No, no. You a white girl who talks down and dirty. Ain't you?"

"Stop it!"

She jumped up from the couch, starting toward him, as if to shut his mouth, but he stayed where he was.

"No, you a white girl been uptown. A white girl who been with colored men," he kept goading her. "Ain't that it? Ain't it? All that tough street talk. Well, just lookit how exotic you are now!"

She had actually picked up a streamlined art deco ashtray—a beautiful silver piece with a jackal head on it, ears pinned back so realistically it looked as if it might take off running. Holding it up as if she might really hurl it at him. But then she collected herself and put the ashtray back down, the hint of a smile playing around her lips as she faced him again.

"That's right," she said, her voice tight but under control again. "That's right, too. I am just who I wanna be, when I wanna be. Just like any human being. Just like any other white person."

"But why—"

"I don't have to live like other people. I do what I please—and you should, too."

"Ah, hell!"

He waved an arm dismissively—taking in this whole strange place she lived in. All the more annoyed because he was so intrigued by it. Another life, in another part of town. An existence freed from every mooring. Doing whatever one pleased, every day—

"You know you'd like to. You do it now, with your playacting," she told him coldly. "Going around to your restaurants, your bars. Still just like in college—"

"That's enough."

She stared at him now, in the dying light of her apartment. Her face only a little more censorious.

"You got yourself encumbrances," she said frankly—talking like that street girl again. "That ain't my fault. You got to choose. But that's it, you can choose. We both can. That's what that white woman in the picture gave us."

He could not go on listening to her then. Excusing himself and hurrying into her bathroom, his stomach turning over in dismay. Running from her words.

"What's wrong?"

"Nothing, nothing!"

The bathroom even more frilly and posh than the rest of her apartment, all little French soaps, and bunches of potpourri, and hand towels monogrammed with more of her new initials. He felt better, though, alone in there. Standing over the sink, trying to calm his stomach. He splashed some cold water on his face, then mopped at it with one of the matching light blue hand towels. Staring at himself in the medicine-chest mirror, tracing the contours of his cheekbones, then his modest lips and sharp nose, with two fingers.

A still young face, though with lines of worry emerging around the eyes, across his forehead. A face that was not unhandsome, but so serious, and tired. A white face?

Stalling, he pulled the mirror gently open, glancing through his sister's medicine cabinet. His eyes wandered past the same mysterious feminine aids and lotions that he had never deciphered. even after ten years of marriage. They settled on a small jar with a familiar, black-and-white label, tucked away in the upper corner of the cabinet, so that it was barely visible at all. Before he fully realized what he was doing, he had pried it carefully out with the ends of his fingers, was staring more closely at the small print on the label:

"Black and White Bleaching Cream: Plan Today for a Brighter Future!"

He had seen such products many times before, of course. Buried in the pages of the Amsterdam News, along with similar ads for Nix Liquid Bleach and Dr. Fred Palmer's Skin Whitener, and Queen Hair Dressing ("Kinky hair sure comes down!"), and for hair attachments ("Become a glamour girl overnight!"). Their claims always coded in words about "improving complexions" and eliminating pimples. But now he read every line of copy, under the drawing of a smiling white-featured Negro woman:

"Help yourself right out of that skin-torture victim act and let men and women see you in a new light... Blackheads loosen and that dull, darker outer skin seems to actually roll off..."

The next thing he knew he had the cap off and was scooping up the white, buttery lotion in both hands, smearing it vigorously into his cheeks. Looking up into the mirror again to see if it was actually working, the darker outer skin rolling off to reveal the white face just below—

He stopped when he saw himself. His eyes brimming with hope, and fear. His face smeared with large white blotches on both sides, like a clown's makeup, his jaw slack with eagerness.

He stuffed the jar back in its hiding place in the medicine cabinet as well as he could. Running the water again, scrubbing furiously to get the cream off his face even as he heard his sister's worried tap at the bathroom door.

"Jonah? Jonah, you all right in there?"

He took a deep breath, then threw open the bathroom door. Sophia stood before him, frowning with worry. Actually worried about him. He hurried past her, toward the door.

"I got to get going—"

"All right, all right. But you oughta come down an' hear me again sometime, baby brother," she told him. "I got some solid boys behind me for once. Got a six-month gig—"

She gave a little chuckle.

"Funny, ain't it? Your friend Adam's down there all the time, an' he don't even know—"

"I know!"

"You know?"

"Listen, Sophie," he blurted out, "I-I don't know how much I should be comin' down here for a while. I don't know if it's such a good thing."

"All right. Well, you be that way," she said, putting up her hands in disgust. "Let me ask you somethin', though. What're you doin' it for?"

"Huh?"

He paused with his hand on the doorknob, unsure of just what she meant.

"Oh, Jonah-man, Jonah-man. Why do you go around like that— playin' at bein' a white man?"

He stood there by the door, unable to say anything until she came over to him—running a hand along the side of his face where the darker, outer skin still hadn't rolled off.

"Oh, my poor baby brother," she said. "You must be the first colored man in the history of the world didn't want to pass in order to be somebody else. You just want to be invisible."

"I gotta go."

"Fine, fine! Go, then!"

She gave another dry, sad laugh, but he wasn't looking at her by then, only fumbling with the doorknob, then hurrying down the hall. The door closed behind him as soon as he was out, the recording of "Mood Indigo" starting up again.

He stood there in the sunset hallway, waiting for the elevator—alone in this other place, silent except for the faint strains of the music. Looking at the flowers in the vase, the nicely painted walls, staring down at the floors tiled with mosaics of elephant and jackal heads. Thinking how it would be to just stay here, in this in-between place, for hour after hour, as the early evening faded into night.

I'm just a soul who's bluer than blue can be
When I get that mood indigo
I could lay me down and die—

Instead, he took a Fifth Avenue bus back uptown. Walking back to Washington Square Park, and catching the No. 1 where it made its loop around the arch. He rode up in the open top of the red doubledecker Queen Mary, as bulky and unwieldy as a tank.

As the night came on, he gazed up at the passing midtown skyscrapers. The vertical city. Its great buildings rising like ancient ziggurats. Floor after floor, window after window—the same, machine-made, industrial patterns repeated over and over again. They could be duplicated infinitely, he knew, like all the industrial machines of war, the countless tanks and ships he saw in the Alhambra's newsreels. Multiplied endlessly when the screen split, and split again, rows and rows of boots and bayonets and helmets. All identical, too, marching inexorably into battle. This horror of repetition—

He rode the bus all the way up to where Fifth Avenue ended abruptly, at a rusting sign by the Harlem River that read only Dead End. There he stepped down into the gathering darkness, and walked west, past abandoned factories and warehouses, and the 369th Regiment Armory on 142nd Street. The regiment itself gone now, its soldiers dispersed to Georgia and its officers replaced by white Southern officers, according to the letters his congregation kept receiving.

He could remember standing in the mobs that watched the 369th march home, back from France after the first war. The forest of bayonets, with James Reese Europe himself leading the regimental band. Harlem's Hellfighters, they called themselves, coming back covered in medals, and with those proud guns in their hands. When they had passed 110th Street, Europe had them strike up "Here Comes My Daddy Now," and everyone had gone wild.

Well, that was another time, Jonah told himself. The start of a New Age. Harlem still just rising. A time of parades, and great undertakings. Another literary magazine on the table of their Strivers Row foyer every week, it seemed. Poor old Garvey, with his Lords of the Nile and his Knight Commanders of Ethiopia— his whole Negro shadow world, complete with mythical titles and court—leading his resplendent "Back to Africa" marches up Seventh Avenue. The great dance halls along Lenox, the Savoy and the first Cotton Club, not even up yet—even his father's church only a dream still.

And all of that endeavor, for what? Now here it was, another war, and they could not even be trusted to have their own officers. The progress of the race!

But his mind kept going back to Sophie, still a college girl, running out before him that morning on Coney Island. Whispering the magic words to him—

"Let's be white people today!"

They had played that game all day. They had eaten lunch out on the breezeway at Feltman's without going to the neglected, ill-kempt corner that Negroes were unofficially restricted to. They had ridden all the wild, collisive rides in the great glass emporium of Steeplechase Park—the Bounding Billows and the Razzle Dazzle and the Whirlpool—without him having to worry once that the white boy or the white girl he was smashed into, both of them laughing hilariously, would turn and notice the color of his arm, eyes widening in anger or alarm at having been unknowingly forced to touch him. They had skipped freely through the gates of Luna Park, with their huge black-and-white pinwheels, into its tawdry, down-at-the-heels fantasy world of minarets and obelisks and diving pigs. The leering, paper-mâché clown and wolf and pig heads all the more unnerving for how their paint jobs were slowly peeling away.

In the end, they'd gotten lost. They really had forgotten themselves and who they were, black or white. Lulled into complacency by sun and sea, and ice cream and roller coaster rides until, at the end of the afternoon, they had wandered far up the boardwalk, toward Seagate. Trying to find some slightly less crowded stretch of the beach where they might be able to actually lie out full-length on the sand and sleep for a little while before starting the interminable subway ride home.

There they had stumbled out onto a teenager beach, a stretch of the seashore dominated by Italian kids, and Jonah had realized instantly it was trouble. The I-tie boys and girls both smoking cigarettes together in tight, conniving circles. None of them wearing real bathing suits, only canvas pants and old dresses, some of them even sitting out on the sand defiantly naked.

"Sophie, uh, Sophie!" he had tried to warn her, sliding back into his old self at once. But she would have none of it. Lost in her make-believe, stalking gracefully out onto the billowy sand. Holding up the hem of her dress with one hand, and her shoes in the other.

The heads of the white kids began to turn, one by one—looking as feral and ravenous as a pack of dogs, until Jonah finally stood stock-still on the sand, just watching them watch his sister. Then they began to stand up. Rolling cigarettes around in their fingers, homemade beer in bottles dangling from their hands—their faces still undecided, squinting and half-leering into the sun. Jonah began to run toward her.

"Sophie! Sophia!"

She had stopped then, smiling back at him. But one of the Italian boys had already detached himself from the circle. Striding aggressively toward them, a hand shielding his eyes, taking a last, foamy swig from his bottle of beer. He was tall and sinewy, naked except for a pair of cut-off dungarees; black, knotted hair hanging down over his olive, sun-darkened skin.

"Hey!" he called out, his voice ringing along the nearly deserted patch of beach, and off the piled-rock fishing piers.

"Hey, you niggers! This is our beach!"

Jonah at once began to back away, careful to keep his eyes on the boy. But Sophia, to his amazement, stayed where she was—her face angry.

"We ain't no niggers!" she yelled back at him indignantly. Still playacting, trying to imitate some tough street-corner girl from Brooklyn, he had realized to his horror.

"We're Italians!" she had yelled at the boy, even more ludicrously.

For a wild moment, he had thought it might even work, trusting Sophie as he did in all things. Why not—their color even lighter than the wild Italian boys and girls, after a summer not spent on the beach. But the boy only gave them the raspberry, and began to advance on them again. The other white kids running up behind him now, their faces smiling meanly.

"The hell you say! We're Italians! You fuckin' niggers! Get the fuck off our beach, you fuckin' niggers!"

He reached back and let fly with the bottle then, hurling it straight toward Sophia. But Jonah was already by her side, grabbing her hand and pulling her back along the sand, toward the boardwalk. At last she seemed to understand, and she ran with him now—the white kids racing after them, laughing and cursing, showering them with more bottles and rocks and anything else they could find. They fell at their heels as they ran back up the boardwalk steps, a steady jeer echoing behind them now:

"Niggers! Niggers! Niggers!"

Sophia outstripping him down the boardwalk by then. Running like a deer from a fire, from those words.

"Niggers! Niggers! Niggers!"

She had tried to explain it to him then, too, on the subway trip back. Shaking with anger, speaking in furious, whispered hisses in the swaying, stuffed car. Using almost the exact same words she had used this day, down in her Village hideout.

"But we're white! We're as white as any of those I-ties on that beach! We're white and black, our Daddy's momma was white, so why shouldn't we be? Why shouldn't we be whatever the hell we want to be?"

But all he could think of then, and all he could think of now, so many years later, was the lip of that arrogant, half-naked boy on the beach, turning up in scorn and derision after he blew his Bronx cheer at them. Seeing through them as though their color were marked indelibly on something deeper than their skin. Preparing to pelt them with that word until he had run them off the beach with it alone:

"Niggers! Niggers! Niggers!"

CHAPTER TEN

MALCOLM

He kept to his room for a week after he was banished from Small's Paradise. Not even showing his face at Creole Pete's, or the other late-night clubs anymore, he was so ashamed, going out only to buy food and the latest comic books from the corner drugstore, which he would take into the tub with him to read.

He drew himself up to three or four baths a day sometimes, against the worst of the summer heat and the smell of his own body. Always taking them during the middle of the afternoon, when all the other boarders were out at work, or late at night when he could lie back and read the latest adventures of the Comet or Futura, and listen to all the sounds of the City outside: the cars rushing perpetually uptown, or the shuttle and ring of the trolleys, or the New York Central trains, all the way across the City, blowing their air horns as they emerged from the tunnel on Park Avenue.

In those moments he thought sometimes about going back to the railroad, or even shipping out as a merchant seaman on one of the great, gray ships out in the river, just as Reginald had. He had received a letter from his brother—written weeks ago to Ella's house, and somehow forwarded along The Wire to where he was in Harlem. It said almost nothing, as usual, just that Reginald was really hoping to meet up with him soon, now that Malcolm was in Harlem, but he had kept it and read it over and over, until it started to tear away at the creases, thinking of all the great things they might find to do together in the City. Meanwhile, he still tried to call the house back in Lansing, he felt so lonely, willing to talk to any of them there, Wilfred or Philbert or Hilda—but no one ever picked up.

Mostly, though, he dreamed about how he might find a way back into Small's, or how he might get to see Miranda again, and win her away from West Indian Archie. He kept thinking about the feel of her smooth, powdered skin, or how she smelled of flowers. How she had looked when he had told her that he loved her there in Small's—surprised and moved, and interested, too, he was still sure of it. Sorry that he hadn't pressed things then, sorry for all the mean, angry things he had thought about her since.

But he had no real idea of how to get her back. Most of his plans stolen from comic books, he had to admit, involving disguises and miraculous gadgets, or swinging from rooftops and fire escapes. The inescapable conclusion was that he had lost her, and every- thing he had had at Small's, and that knowledge made him almost more lonely than he could bear. Knowing that he was on the outside again, looking in. Smiling while everybody laughed at him, trying to pretend it didn't bother him, just as it always, always had.

He stayed holed up in the bath, nursing the wound that ran all the way through him. Trying to rid himself of himself, to soak the stink of the City and his own sweat off his body. He had been very aware of his own smell since his time with Ma Swerlein, who ran the county juvenile home back in Mason. When he was finished with his bath, he would carefully wash out the ring around the tub, just as Ma Swerlein had taught him. He was always chagrined when someone knocked on the door while he was still in the dirty, cooling water, and any scent of him remained—trying to eradicate any trace of himself in the bath, just as she had taught him.

Mrs. Gold Dust, they had called her, for the soap she used on everything. Cleaning constantly, compulsively around the home, the way his mother had, before she got sick. She smelled different from his mother, though; more like the soap, harsh and clean and antiseptic. And where his mother was straight and thin as a rail, Mrs. Swerlein was a big woman—taller, and at least twice as wide, with gigantic, round breasts that Malcolm always found himself trying to look down when she leaned over him. Feeding all of them, all her boys and her smaller, quiet husband, at the long kitchen table. Doing everything for them, swooping in to give him a big hug whenever he felt lonely— seeming to know it even before he did himself. Talking freely in front of him, too, about the niggers, as if he were not even in the room.

"Those poor niggers, I just can't see how they can be so happy and so poor, living in shacks like they do," she would say, cleaning out the tub with the Gold Dust powder, her great, saucy behind swaying freely back and forth. Malcolm watching it, enraptured. Little Malcolm, she would call him, teasingly. The name so contrary to the near-man he had already become, six feet tall in the eighth grade—and one that never failed to get something fluttering in his stomach, and lower.

"An' all those big, shiny cars they got out front. You'd think they'd sell the cars, buy someplace better to live with 'em. But niggers is just that way, I guess. Little Malcolm, dear, would ya mind passin' me more a the Gold Dust there—"

He would volunteer to help with the chores, following her around the house. Wanting to ask her if by niggers she meant him, too. He was still trying to tell himself, then, that he could be the son of a white man who had forced himself on his mother, but deep down he knew it wasn't so.

He knew it by how he smelled—so different from Mr. and Mrs. Swerlein, and the eight white boys who lived with them there in the rambling, three-storey Victorian that was the county juvenile home. Sure now, every time he sat down at the table with them, or passed them going in and out of the bathroom, that they were as different from him as two different species could be.

He hadn't felt that way at the Gohannases, the neighborhood colored family where Mr. Maynard Allen had taken him to live when his mother had first gone to the state mental hospital in Kalamazoo. There he had shared a room with their nephew, Big Boy, and Mr. Gohannas had taken them both to shoot the rabbits, and go fishing on Saturdays. They were older people, and kindly to him, but he had been restless and bored with their country ways, or how they never seemed to know what he was talking about. He didn't like the Holy Roller church they went to, with all its wild carryings-on, and he hated their friends—many of them the same men he had gone on the rabbit hunt with, and how they came over in their worn, down-home clothes and sat on the porch, speaking slowly and deliberately. Looking at him with those knowing, pitying eyes whenever he came out the porch door; someone tsking and saying something mournful about his mother or his Daddy when he went back inside.

To be pitied—pitied by a bunch of ignorant country Negroes! Before long he started acting up in school and shoplifting again, stealing change from Mrs. Gohannas's bag just to see if he could do it, and Mr. Allen had come and taken him to the juvenile home, just as he had promised. Barely with a word this time, looking down at Malcolm beside him in the big Packard not in anger, but almost preoccupied, as if this was what he had expected all along. And Malcolm, on his side of the huge front seat, suddenly apprehensive, worrying that it was all a plan.

How could some white man know so much, anticipate everything he would do? And what did that mean for him?

And yet for all of it—for all of Ma Swerlein's nigger talk, and the strangers he lived amongst—in many ways the home was the best place Malcolm had ever been. Even he had seen that, and right from the beginning. He was the only boy there Ma Swerlein trusted to come and go as he pleased. She knew everyone in town, and when he said that he wanted to make some money, she had even gotten him a job busting suds and cleaning up at a restaurant downtown, after school. There, while he was sweeping up the sidewalk out front, he would be seized with such irrational fits of joy and relief that he could not stop himself from showing off. Dancing with the broom, doing high-stepping solos for the passersby. They would whistle and grin, and throw him coins, so that by his first payday he had had enough money to go downtown and buy himself an apple green suit that was the most beautiful thing he had ever seen.

He was popular at the Mason junior high, too, thanks to Ma Swerlein. She had invited his whole class over to the juvenile home for a party when he'd first arrived, and introduced all the boys to them—acting as if they were the same as anyone else, and that there was no shame to be had at all from living in such a place. With her encouragement he had joined the debating society, and made the varsity basketball and football teams, even with his job after school. He was still uneasy about playing with other boys, and when they played away games out in the sticks, he would hear calls of nigger or coon or Rastus, drifting down from the bleachers in the dingy little gyms. But his teammates would crowd around him protectively, patting him mutely on the back, glaring back up at the home fans.

The teachers in Mason were different, too. Some of them, like Mr. Grein, the history teacher, even told nigger jokes in class or laughed at Malcolm openly in class when he said something ignorant. But most of them sent notes home with him to Ma Swerlein, expressly to inform her of how polite and well-mannered he was, and how well he was doing in his studies. She made sure in turn to read them aloud to him, her whole face brightening, and exclaiming, "Well, Malcolm, isn't this nice!"

And Malcolm, hearing it, wondered why they should remark so on his being well-behaved and smart, but from then on he had approached teachers whenever he could, basking in their attention. Raising his hand in class, volunteering to wash the blackboards or empty the classroom wastebaskets or do anything else that might be remarked upon favorably. He tried to be as helpful as he could with his fellow classmates, too—always talking to them nicely, offering to treat them whenever he had the money, or to help them with homework; refraining from getting into any fights but always smiling, even when he suspected they might be making fun of him.

By the spring semester he was ranked third in Mr. Kaminska's eighth-grade class. He liked Mr. Kaminska most of all his teachers—a big-chested, former high school linebacker with bristly red hair and a red face, who taught his English classes as if they were a football team, running them relentlessly through one drill after another, and who was always quick to compliment Malcolm when he got an answer right. Near the end of one afternoon, he called them to a special homeroom, to announce that they would have an election for class president, and told them to make nominations, and seconding motions. Malcolm had sat in the back-row seat where he was confined as the tallest boy in the class, saying nothing, not wanting to offend any of his friends in class by offering up one or the other for office.

But to his astonishment, they had nominated and seconded him— and him alone. Mr. Kaminska dutifully chalking up the unanimous vote, student by student, while Malcolm watched incredulously from the back of the room, seeing the tally of little white lines grow under his name. It had all felt like a great, waking daydream, especially in the end, when all the votes were in and the whole class had burst into spontaneous applause. Malcolm had been so close to crying that he had only just been able to stumble to the front of the room at Mr. Kaminska's gruff insistence. Mumbling out his gratitude before the bell rang and he was able to burst out of the school, too embarrassed to stick around any longer—running all the way to his job downtown.

Yet somehow they all knew about it when he got back to the juvenile home after work. Mr. Maynard Allen was there waiting for him, along with Ma and Pa Swerlein, and all the other boys in the home, and most of his classmates, and even Mr. Delmont, who owned the restaurant where he worked. It made him almost dizzy when he saw them standing there, up on the broad front porch under a handmade paper banner reading, CONGRATULATIONS MALCOLM. All these white people, clustering around him as soon as he came up the porch steps, grinning at him and slapping him on the back, while he smiled and twitched at their every touch.

"Oh, Malcolm, we're just so proud of you!" Ma Swerlein gushed, wrapping him up in a tight, bosomy hug that left him anxious and excited at the same time.

She served out homemade strawberry pie, and ice cream just as she did when it was someone's birthday, and all he could do was stand there. The small, sheepish smile still glued to his face while he held the ice cream, melting in his dish. He managed to make his way outside, but Mr. Allen had followed him there, hitching up his pants over his long legs and sitting down beside him on the porch steps. They had sat there together, spooning up at last the soupy remnants of their ice cream without saying anything, while the party went on back in the house.

"I just want to tell you, Malcolm, I've never seen anybody prove better just what the word 'reform' means," Mr. Allen had said at last, in that quiet, confidential voice, fixing him again with that penetrating social-worker look of his. Only this time Malcolm could see that it was not reproving or scolding, but filled with genuine, manly approval, so that once again he almost wanted to cry.

"I mean it. You did a man's job here, Malcolm, between your grades, and how you fit in. We're all very proud of you," he told him. "When I think of what you came from—what kind of upbringing you had…the condition your mother was in, the way that house was when we got you out of there…all I can say is that it gives me hope. You're a living example of how much social progress can really be made, Malcolm."

He stopped then, a smile creasing his face, and held out his hand. And Malcolm had looked at it for a long moment, the mention of his mother still turning over and over in his head. Seized with the crazy desire now to knock the hand away—to run off the porch, and down the street, and all the way back to Lansing.

Instead he had reached out and shaken it. Mr. Maynard Allen still grinning, cocking his rapidly balding head back toward the home.

"C'mon, let's go get some of that pie," he said, and ran a hand through Malcolm's hair. "A stringbean like you could use it."

Later, after Malcolm watched surreptitiously from the window as Mr. Allen went down the steps of the juvenile home to his big Packard with a spring in his steps—after an enthusiastic good-bye to Ma and Pa Swerlein during which they had all gushed over his progress some more—he was sure that the social worker looked more pleased with himself than he had ever seen him before. He was sure that he could almost hear him, like some costumed superhero from the radio or the comic books, announcing it—Well, my work here is done! Another case solved. Boy rescued from his mother!

By the end of the week, he decided that he needed more comic books, his own bad memories leaking in too much to the adventures of Superman, up in his amazing hidden laboratory at the North Pole. He ventured back out on the street, only going as far as the drugstore around the corner at first. But soon they had run out of ones he hadn't read, and he found out that he could get still more of them for next to nothing down in midtown, from a boy with glasses and a scholarly seriousness about him, who carefully compared the numbers on the different books and slipped them delicately into a brown paper bag as soon as he bought them.

Malcolm was still chary about going so far downtown, but he preferred it to being seen on the street by anyone he knew in Harlem, and all the money he had made at Small's Paradise was slowly running out. The address the boy had given him was just a sliver of a stationery store, in an Irish neighborhood under the Third Avenue el. He was nervous when he got off the train there, and more nervous still as he looked for the address, searching through the changeable, murky light under the el. When he found it at last he almost didn't go in, eyeing apprehensively the wizened, sour-faced white men clustered around the newspaper stand up front.

But deep in the back of the narrow store, he found them—whole boxes full of old comic books, selling at a hundred for a nickel. Most of them defunct serials from a year or two before, full of superheroes who had gone out of existence. Some of them he had read and some he had never heard of, but he didn't really care which, delighted with his find, dropping to his knees right there in the store and riffling happily through them.

There was Og, Son of Fire, which was about a caveman, and Don Dixon and the Hidden Empire, and Dr. Hormone, a scientist who parachuted with his granddaughter, Jane, down into a gorge that took them back through time. There they had slept—and when they awoke, Dr. Hormone possessed the ability to turn men into animals, and to give them all kinds of animal attributes and personalities. He battled the evil Assinoff, whom he had given donkey ears, and the Novaslavians and the Nazians, on behalf of the good and pure Urasians.

But his favorite discovery was Phantasmo, who could do almost anything. He had left America and journeyed all the way to Tibet where, just like Amazing Man, he had learned the very powers of creation from the llamas. He wore a bright yellow costume, but the rest of the time he walked around the streets in a hard-hitting trenchcoat. Phantasmo was able to leave his body and fly on the wings of thought. He could pluck up the Empire State Building and put it on his shoulder, or he could shrink himself until he was small enough to slip down a drain. Bullets couldn't hurt him, and the weight of a mountain could not crush him, even if his corporeal body did appear to drop over dead whenever he went out on a thought mission.

Malcolm had rocked back on his haunches, and was fanning through the endless piles of books—when he felt a foot slam into his ribs, a knee hitting his shoulder blade. He had reared up—and seen a man in a good suit and hat tottering over him, staring down at Malcolm in what seemed to be near panic, and muttering repeated apologies.

"Excuse me! Excuse me, I didn't see—," he was saying as he continued to untangle his legs from around Malcolm's body. Malcolm remembering, in that instant, that he had seen the man in the very back of the store when he first came in, looking at himself in the glass of a cigar case. He had barely noticed him then, but he thought now that there was something familiar about him.

"Excuse me!" the man repeated, stumbling on over him and out the shop door, even as it came to Malcolm just where he knew him from.

The preacher on the train. The colored preacher—

He had stumbled to his own feet then, starting after the man. He ran on out the door, trying to keep up with him. The white men at the front staring at him with open suspicion now. Malcolm not sure himself what he wanted from him, but drawn after the man anyway—determined, for some reason, to know who he was and what he was about.

He shot out the door, pursuing him across the old cobblestoned street, under the speckled light of the elevated. Scattering the pigeons before him, dodging the cars that swept by, blaring their horns. Only to lose him anyway—the man ducking into a big DeSoto cab that swept by, not so much as casting a look back at him.

He had stood there for a moment, still in the cooling shadows of the train tracks, then walked back into the sliver of a newspaper store. So intrigued now that he went right up to the white men clustered around the front, still staring at him with undisguised hostility, asking them if they knew who the man was.

"Whazzit to ya?" one of them, the proprietor, had deigned to spit out. The rest of them looking at him belligerently now—and he realized, in the dazzling shock of the moment, that the man was passing. They think he's a white man. Just like those soldiers on the train—

It was after he saw the preacher that he dreamed of the little brown man again. He had been soaking in the tub, working his way slowly through a fifth of bourbon, and some gage he had scored off one of the whores in his building. Blissfully paging through his new comic books, one after the other. Dreaming of all the things he was going to get for himself—a fine car, a mellow pad; a white girl who would put Miranda to shame, more money than anyone he knew had ever heard of—when a low, numbing despair had begun to spread slowly through his whole being. It had wrung the strength out of his limbs, until all he had been able to do was to huddle up in the gray bathwater, wrapping his arms around his legs and rocking slowly back and forth. Whimpering to himself, trying not to listen to the sounds of all the life out on the streets below, the car horns and trains and the people, that usually delighted him so—trying to banish the image of himself alone in this little room, with the vast, oblivious City all around him.

It was then that he had seen him. The same little brown man from the dream he'd had on his first night in Harlem, in his neat dark suit, and the small round hat that was covered with stars, and suns, and crescent moons. He was perched somehow on the edge of the tub, staring at Malcolm with those kind, radiant, knowing eyes, the same gentle smile on his face. Staring at him so intently that Malcolm was certain that he was beckoning to him, just waiting for him to speak so he could answer.

The next thing he knew, he had awakened with his head lolling against the back of the tub, staring dully at the copy of Phantasmo where he had dropped it—the lurid hues of yellow and blue and red leeching out on the soapy skim of the water. He had laid where he was in the tub, letting the water cool around him, until the hazy, summer sunlight had begun to pour through the bathroom window. His head was aching, but to his surprise he found now that the paralysis and the despondency that had coursed through his body like a poison was now entirely vanished.

He mulled over just what he had seen all that day and the next, sure that it was more than just a dream despite all the bourbon, and the tea. Wondering if the little man could really have been there, that he could really have had such a vivid dream. Or, much worse, if it was what he had long dreaded, that what had happened to his mother was now beginning to happen to him.

Movies from heaven, he remembered that she had called them, toward the end, when she had done nothing except rock back and forth with Butch, the baby, in their Lansing kitchen. Her eyes near to closed most of the time but, every once in a while, always in the evening, staring so wide and urgently that Yvonne had dared to ask her about it.

"Momma, what you seein'?"

And the rest of them had held their breath, because by then she would most likely scream or hit out at them whenever they spoke to her, if she acknowledged them at all. But this time she answered, in a slow, wondering voice, "Movies from heaven. I'm seein' movies from heaven"—her eyes closing then, her whole face shutting down.

She had never explained again, or with any greater elaboration, just what she meant, and he dreaded, now, that it might be the same with him if he looked any deeper into his own dreams. But he could not help himself—leafing through the volumes Prof. Toussaint had made him buy down at the bookstore, searching for anything that might help him. He had barely read any real books at all since he had left school, preferring the comics that Mr. Allen had used to win him over, and at first it was difficult for him to get through the long, dense texts, particularly since they were about things that he had never heard of before, in a language that seemed altogether strange and new. He would find his mind wandering, or he would doze off, just as he had over his comics. But soon he began to remember how much he had liked reading, enthralled by all the words; how many there were, and how marvelously they connected and built upon each other. His love for them growing like the sudden revival of something atrophied, some limb or capacity so long neglected he had been unaware that it still existed. He had rushed out to the corner drugstore and bought not another comic book but a dictionary, painstakingly looking up every word he didn't know; even making long lists of other words he came across that he didn't need, but which fascinated him anyhow—studying them until he had them memorized.

Still, for all the words, he knew he did not understand the language. The beliefs and ceremonies and events the books described continued to bewilder him, until he decided to take them back to Prof. Toussaint, even though he knew that meant risking the man's scorn.

"But that's religion," he had told Malcolm, his gray-peppered moustache twitching in amusement. "You got to take it on faith, just like any other religion."

"Faith? You mean believe anything, like a sucker."

"You believe all those things in the white man's Bible?" Prof. Toussaint said, shrugging, and Malcolm thought then how much he reminded him of the little brown man he was sure he had seen, save for the moustache.

"You believe a man rose from the dead after three days? Or parted the sea, or wrestled with a angel? Or got swallowed up by a whale, but then be spit up on the land, an' come out fine as thine?"

The Professer gave a deep, dry chuckle.

"You go down to Coney Island an' try that sometime, provided you can find the whale."

"But it says in these books the white man was invented by a crazy, big-head scientist. Along with all the Chinese, an' the Indians—"

"So?" Prof. Toussaint scoffed. "Where's it say you got to believe every word of it? You think the white man believes every word

that's in his Bible? Hell, white men been killing each other for a
thousand years over whose Bible was right. You think those white
men over there in Germany right now believe the Jews is the chosen people?"

"No—"

"The Bible's all made up of stories—of metaphors, and para-
bles. You think people really started out with Adam an' Eve in the
Garden of Eve? No! First man started out in Africa—even those
big-head white scientists believe that now. So what's that make the
Original Man?"

"A black man?"

"Now you got it! And if the Original Man is a Black Man, then
what did everybody else come from? Who made them—all of those
white folks, and Chinese, and Indians?"

"The black man."

"There you are. You can dress it up in any story you want, it
don't change the truth. White man wants you to believe he's a superior being—that nothing gets done on this earth without him, and
everybody else is a savage. But that ain't the truth. Black men were
building the pyramids of Egypt, and the great city of Zimbabwe,
back when white men in Europe were living in caves, an' wearing
animal skins."

"But why doesn't anybody else know this?" Malcolm asked him
sincerely, and Prof. Toussaint leaned in to talk to him, tapping him
paternally on the back.

"What do you think the truth is, son?" he asked, his voice quiet
and confidential. "You think it just sits out in the sun like a rock,
waitin' for any fool to pick it up? The truth is like a vein of gold,
hidden in a mountainside. You got to dig for it. The truth is like an
old hare, hidin' in the bushes. Sometimes you got to flush it out, and
run it down."

Malcolm had gone back to the books in his room then, approaching them with a feeling of excitement that nearly made him tremble—convinced that here, at last, he had the key to the secrets that
were hidden in every nook of the City, on every corner and under
every street. He had no more nighttime dreams about the little
beige man, but strange, waking visions of his own, all the time now,
just walking down the street. He saw words, and events, and even
flashes of light that made him stagger on the sidewalk, so that the
people around him stared openly, thinking that he must be drunk,

or doped up.

He wondered again if he might be going mad, just like his mother. Yet none of the things he saw made him feel low, or crazy, the way she had been for so long. Instead, they filled him with a restlessness to know more and more. It was the same feeling he had had at his father's Garvey meetings, staring at the pictures of the great man and his followers in their uniforms, with their fantastic titles. Remembering the words of his father's meetings now, as well as the pictures:

Where is the black man's country? His government, his religion?

He had read, by this time, through nearly all of the books that Prof. Toussaint had given him. Turning at last to the small, green, anonymous volume with the gold crescent moon on the cover. The book that he had left for last because it looked much less interesting than the others, without a title or author, and almost unused.

But on closer inspection he saw, now, that it was obviously a book someone had taken great care with, its pages all gilt-edged, the type carefully set, and raised. It was the most expensive-looking book that Malcolm had ever held in his hands, including a Bible. Yet the title page read only:

THE BIOGRAPHY OF ELIJAH MUHAMMAD

As Told By
"X"

Such a strange title and author, such a strange book in every way, that for a moment Malcolm wondered if it really had been the one he'd bought at Prof. Toussaint's shop, or if it had somehow been substituted by Archie or Sammy, or even one of the other men he shared the apartment with, as some sort of a prank. But he opened it up anyway—being very careful, not wanting to crack the binding, or damage any of the stiff, gilt-edged pages in something that seemed so fragile and expensive—and began to read:

He was a frail child, with sleepy black eyes and a stutter. The son of a preacher, and a mother who believed in dreams. Reading the family Bible alone for hours, in a corner of the living room, until by the time he was four years old he knew it well enough to be disputatious with his

father at the supper table. Willie Poole finally throwing up his hands in
exasperation, argued to a standstill at his own table. Telling his mother,
"You know, that boy gets on my nerves."

It was only when he talked about God, and the Bible stories, that
Elijah's stutter left him. By the time he was fourteen, he had started
preaching on his own, bringing grown men and women to Christ,
and reducing entire congregations to tears. But for all that, he still
didn't believe. He doubted the faith of others, even his father. Willie
Poole's sermons drove him to his knees, trembling and shaking in
the pew, wanting to go up to the makeshift wooden altar and throw
himself at his father's feet like all the the others there, begging for
forgiveness and salvation.

But he would not submit, and afterward he would wonder what
he had been so scared about. He would ask his father, and the other
elders and visiting preachers—sitting like Christ and His Disciples
themselves at the long, Sunday supper table, set up on the grass
behind the church after the service—he would ask them, What
does a black man have to fear from hellfire in this world? What has
he done to offend the eye of God?

His father and the visiting churchmen would shout him down—
so incensed they knocked over their chairs as they leapt up to
denounce him, hollering blasphemy, and sacrilege. But nothing they
said could convince him.

The only words from the pulpit that ever spoke to him Elijah
heard one Sunday, when Bishop Henry McNeal Turner was riding
the county circuit, during the Great War. His Daddy had hitched up
the wagon before dawn, and driven them twenty miles, across swollen creeks and down muddy, all but impassable back roads to see the
bishop. Arriving at another small, wooden, whitewashed church,
out in the middle of a field—full of sharecropper families like their
own, some of whom had walked all night to be there.

They were not disappointed. Bishop Turner looking large and
forbidding in his splendid black robes, refusing to be contained by
the pulpit but stalking back and forth in front of the altar. An old
man now, near the end, but still speaking to them in the booming,
country-preacher voice of judgment.

"The black man cannot protect a country if the country doesn't
protect him," he had told them. "If, tomorrow, I were to be called to
this war, I would not so much as raise a musket to defend a country

where my manhood is denied. No, let us ask instead why they want us to fight a war so much. Remember—a people already invisible can be easily made to disappear!"

It was easy enough for Elijah to understand what he meant. Everywhere they moved—working their way back and forth through the same mean piney-woods Georgia towns, Cordele and Reynolds, Butler and Wenona, and Sandersville, the same little cracker towns where the soil was the color of rust on an automobile fender, and there always seemed to be the smell of something burning in the air; his father sharecropping and working as a sawmill hand during the week, his mother cleaning white people's houses only to be paid in chitterlings and pig's feet—everywhere, along the back roads and trails between those same towns were creeks and swamps, and lakes and patches of woods that everyone knew held the bones of black men—and women and children, too—going all the way back to the Civil War.

The only thing that Elijah didn't understand was the white folks' need for secrecy about it. During the lynching season, the bodies would begin to appear again, right out in the open, hanging from trees along the main roads. No one daring to so much as cut them down and bury the dead, waiting until the white men dumped what was left out in the street of nigger town. He had seen the clothing they stripped off the bodies, cut up into piles of neat little squares at the general store, and sold as souvenirs—right beside the pictures, sold as postcards, they took of the charred, pitiful remnants.

It was the summer after the First War that they had started burning the churches. He was already living in Macon by then, with his wife, Clara—a shy, slender, light brown woman from a Holiness family—and their first two children. His lungs were already strained from working in the sawmills and a brick-cleaning factory, but he had worked his way up to tramroad foreman on the Southern Railway. Still hoping vaguely to become a dining room boy, or a Pullman porter someday; still preaching at the humble wood churches out on the road, even though he no longer believed a word he said.

The white men lay in the weeds outside until all the people were inside—until they could hear the singing start. From inside, the people could hear them coming—the heavy clump of their feet beating across the clearing—and they would begin to panic. The white men letting loose with their wild, high-pitched screams as they burst through the doors, and laid about them with baseball bats, and lengths of lead pipe. Punching and kicking anyone they got down on the ground—hanging anyone who could not run from the steeple as the church burned. Their triumphant cries echoing through the field and woods:

"Kill the niggers!"

That whole summer there was smoke in the air, a distant, acrid haze that they would see in the morning no matter where they were, and which would grow only thicker and closer with the dusk. Elijah and his younger brother, Jarmin—who he was as close to as a twin, and had always looked out for—had to move around for their jobs with the railroad, but they tried always to stay as close to the colored parts of town as they could.

One Saturday evening in early September, though, there was no avoiding it, they had had to make their way down from Macon to Cordele. Saturday was always the most dangerous day to travel, after the white sawmill hands had gotten their pay and their liquor, and were looking for fun. But they had had no choice, they had to be in Cordele for their shifts early the next morning, and they had started down a dirt back road Elijah knew, hoping they could slip into the boardinghouse in Cordele's Negro town without drawing any attention.

Before they were within five miles of the town they could see the smoke, already smudging the enormous yellow-red sun that was setting over the trees. Soon black men and women, and whole families, began to appear, carrying all their possessions in bundles on their backs. Telling them only not to go to Cordele, unable or unwilling to say anything else at all about what they were fleeing. Trudging on as fast as they could move with their things, stopping from time to time to peer back at the smoke over the trees, as Elijah thought the people must have looked back as they fled from the Cities of the Plain.

But it was much too late for he and his brother to turn back now, with the night about to come on. They had walked the rest of the way into town single file—Elijah staying out in front, the both of them sticking carefully to the side of the road. Peering deep into the stands of pine, and cottonwood, the thick coils of briar beside the road. The smoke growing thicker as they drew closer to town, until it was nearly choking them, and Elijah had to fight to keep his asthma from overwhelming his weakened lungs. It had an oily scent that mixed uneasily with the smothering odor of the magnolia, and the honeysuckle, in the woods around them.

Gasoline, Elijah recognized—the two of them slowing their steps even more the closer they got to the town.

The back dirt road they were traveling took them directly into the colored part of town, as nearly all back roads tended to do. But when they stepped out of the woods and padded slowly down the first, unpaved street of Cordele, there wasn't a black person to be found. All of the doors, and the shutters, were closed up tight, and when Elijah led Jarmin quickly around a corner—hurrying now to be somewhere, anywhere inside—they stepped out before a crowd of white men, gathered in the town's dirt square.

They tensed to run—Elijah's head reeling with fear and bitterness, certain that they were already caught. But then he realized that the white men were simply leaning on the hitching posts by the watering troughs, or against the closed-up storefronts on the wooden sidewalks. Drinking openly from whiskey bottles, wobbling about the nigger town of Cordele like so many crows that had just been feeding off a dead horse. The ebullient, furious purposefulness that always preceded the worst of their violence vanished now, content to show that they could be here, in the middle of the colored town, and do whatever they wanted.

Elijah led Jarmin along by the hand, his head down, afraid to catch the eye of any of them. Sidling along by the storefronts, hoping they were slight enough to be taken for boys, although he knew that was no real refuge. Afraid to glimpse the poor, tattered bundle that he knew must be there somewhere, amidst one of the little clumps of white men—no doubt still to be kicked and prodded at, and hung back up somewhere as one of their endless warnings. He could smell the gasoline emanating from their clothes and bodies now, stronger even than the whiskey they were drinking, the odor sticking in his throat and making him want to retch.

They were almost through the square when one of the older white men had stepped down from the wooden sidewalk, blocking their way. His jowly, red-baked face smiling at Elijah purposefully in the yellow torchlight. A farmer, he could see—no doubt come into town for the market day, or just for the festivities. His mail-order dungarees still smelling of cow dung, thick white bristles of hair, and his ears, sticking out from under his battered field hat. He had stood there, grinning silently at them, until Elijah wondered if he were stupid with the drink. Trying to calculate how long they should wait before trying to move past him. Holding his hat respectfully down by his side, his other palm pressed so hard into Jarmin's moist hand that he felt it squirm under his nails; both of them knowing enough not to speak until they were spoken to.

Then the white man, still smiling, held out a hand to them. The fingers closed in a fist—but not raised, not menacing in and of itself. Holding it there for another long moment, until he was sure their eyes were on it. Only then had he opened his big hand to them, revealing a brown ear there in his palm.

Elijah had stayed where he was, even as he heard Jarmin beginning to cry behind him—studying the ear, as he knew the white man wanted him to study it. Thinking how beautifully formed it was, in all its complexity. A small ear for a man, if it was a man's—subtly curved, the inner lobes a slightly more delicate, pinker color than the dark brown skin. Severed almost perfectly from the head, only a single dark splotch of blood along the outer lobe. The white man seemingly overjoyed that he could grasp such a thing in his hand, still grinning and staring at them.

Elijah had waited carefully until the white man had closed his fingers over his trophy again, and stepped back from their path, still grinning. Keeping his own face perfectly blank, and making sure that Jarmin saw that he did, with no idea of how the white man possibly expected him to react to such a sight, and unwilling to show him fear no matter what it cost. Only when the man had finally stepped aside did he walk on as quickly as he could without running, holding grimly on to Jarmin's hand to staunch his tears. Not trusting himself to stop or look back until they had found the boardinghouse, far up the street from the sated, meandering white men, and only then losing his composure, the both of them pounding and shouting at the door until they were let in.

After that he had decided that he could not go back into the white man's Christian church again, telling the people to forgive and forget. He had decided instead that night that they should leave. Between the lynchings and the boll weevil running through the cotton, colored people everywhere were trying to get up North that summer. He could see them swarming through the fields, trying to jump the freight trains. The whites—frightened suddenly, somehow by the idea of losing so many of them at once, even after their summer of terror—sending the state police and the local deputies out to stop them. Turning back families from the stations even when they had already bought tickets, throwing them bodily off the trains.

Elijah had had to plan it out, as he would plan everything for his family and his people. Using his railroad job to get them all on a train to Detroit, where he had heard there were jobs, smuggling them all onboard at a lonely country water stop before it was dark. And once they were on, once they were past the Jim Crow line, he had stood in the aisle of the colored car, looking at all of them there before him—his wife and children, and his mother and father, and all of his many brothers and sisters, and their families with them. Suffused with pride to know that it was he who had brought them all up out of Egypt land, and even through the many trials and hardships that lay ahead through their long sojourn in Detroit, and even his own degradation and his betrayal at the hands of those he loved, he would remain proud that it was he who had done this, brought them up North, and the life of a Georgia country Negro.

CHAPTER ELEVEN

MALCOLM

He felt the big hand on his shoulder before he had even realized there
was anybody behind him. He was just walking out of his building,
still not yet synchronized to the pace and clamor of the street after
all his time up in his room. He had turned quickly, afraid it was the
police—and was no less frightened to see the rough, scarred face
that loomed up into his own.

"Whoa there, Detroit Red! I want to talk to you," West Indian
Archie told him, and Malcolm had frozen, afraid that somehow he
knew about him and Miranda. But he saw almost immediately that
the look on the big man's face was benign, even concerned. Grinning, sticking out one ham-sized fist to crush Malcolm's hand.

"How you been keepin' yourself, young lane?"

Malcolm looked down, scuffing his shoe on the sidewalk.

"It's solid. I got my eye on some things."

"That so? 'Cause you know, they all miss you down Small's."

"They do?" Malcolm asked, hating to hear the eagerness in his
own voice, but wanting to know more.

"Uh-huh. Everybody ask about you. Even Miranda want to know
how you doin', says whatever happen to that Detroit Red boy,"
Archie told him, chuckling, and Malcolm felt his heart lift.

"That a fact?" he wondered. But even as he did, he was aware
of how happy Archie still seemed to be, his laugh so inordinately
pleased and self-satisfied. She was still with him—

"Yeah, ole man, she sure do. We all miss you," Archie said—his voice turning more serious, looking him over discerningly now. "You look short as my hair an' ripe for a beg, Red."

"I been comin' up to the tab," Malcolm told him tersely.

"I know you do. I know you do, son," Archie said, trying to placate him. "But I thought maybe you'd like to come work for me anyway."

"Work for you?"

"Yeah, you know. Do some runnin'. Sharpie like you, work you way up in no time. If you got the time, that is—"

"Yeah. Yeah, I guess I could fit that in," Malcolm told him, trying not to sound too eager. Imagining what it would be like, to run numbers for West Indian Archie. To see her again.

"Well, I'm glad I could meet your schedule," Archie chuckled again, sounding more amused and pleased with himself than ever, and Malcolm frowned as he slapped him on the back.

"You come meet me at the Fat Man's Bar, an' we get you fixed up. Who knows? Maybe we even get you back into Small's, Red!"

That was how he had gone to work for West Indian Archie, running numbers from 110th Street to Sugar Hill, up and down the Cannon, and all the main stems. Archie had his regular routes already covered, so he used Malcolm wherever he needed him, putting him into a new area whenever one of his regular runners was picked up, or lost to Uncle.

"You be like my utility man, Red—my Martin Dihigo," he told him, still chuckling that deep, new, jubilant back-of-the-throat laugh that had begun to get on Malcolm's nerves.

"Now listen up—wherever I need you, that's where you go. You get ten percent a all the bets you bring in. You pay off somebody when they hit, they tip you ten percent. You try to cheat me, I shoot you t'rough the ear. That's the rules."

"How you keep track of it all?" Malcolm asked him.

"You can keep the slips—but you be sure an' get rid of 'em if the blue collars you. No slips, no evidence," Archie said, tapping the temple of his huge brown head.

"Runners get picked up a lot?" Malcolm asked, trying to sound casual but thinking back on his stay at the Thirty-second Precinct.

"I already pay the cops their figger. Any a them wanna sweeten the coffee, you tell 'em you work for me. They still want it, you give it to 'em. Then you come squawk to me," Archie instructed him, wrapping one huge arm paternally around his shoulder.

"Main play is, don't get picked up. It cost me more just to come down, bail you out. An' that way the police don't oil up you head for you."

Nevertheless, Malcolm liked to move fast when he was making his rounds. Perusing the lay of every street before he went down it, making sure he didn't see any blue uniforms, any white man in square shoes who didn't look like he belonged there. He had even bought a gun to carry along, though Archie had expressly told him not to. He had purchased it from a small, disappointed-looking man in a gabardine suit and a porkpie hat who lived upstairs from him, and who sold hot cameras, hot bottles of perfume, even hot ice out of his apartment. The gun no more than some lady's pistol, but he liked its shiny silver-plated handle, and how it was light and quick as a knife in his hand.

He kept it tucked carefully away when he was out collecting. Selling his wares just like the fruit and ice and fish vendors, only much more softly, wishing he could make up a song like the ones they sang brazenly to the upper-most stories of the tenements, though he knew that would be too brazen for the police. Quietly repeating, instead, his one word over and over as he walked by groups of men and women in the street, or passed by their first-floor windows yawning open in the heat:

"Policy…policy…policy…"

In Harlem everybody played the numbers. The glamour girls, beckoning him wickedly into their beauty parlors through clouds of steam. Balding men clustered wistfully around their barbershops. Sidemen and hoofers, betting their lucky numbers outside the stage door while they waited to go on, young men in uniform, leaving addresses of sweethearts to give their winnings to if they had to ship out before their number came in. The old ladies wobbling back from church teas on their canes, making him wait while they stopped to catch their breath. Laundrywomen holding out their coins in hands as warm and hard as the ironing boards they worked on, and calkeener broads and maids, handing him their money without breaking stride while they hurried to cook and clean in the homes of white women, and housewives who whistled for him from their apartment windows—expertly shooting the slips of paper wrapped around their nickels and dimes down through the shadowy slats of the fire escape.

The odds were always 999 to 1, the winning numbers in Archie's bank drawn from the last three digits of the Dow Jones index, every day, at the closing bell on the Exchange. Like all the other policy banks, Archie paid off at 600 to 1, skimming his profit off the top, but that still meant a penny would bring in six dollars—a nickel, thirty; a dime, sixty. A veritable fortune, just waiting out there on the sidewalks for anyone lucky or adventurous enough to claim it, and the pockets of Malcolm's suit jacket and pants sagging with coins before he was through with his rounds for the day.

Everyone had their own system. Some stuck with the very same number, every day. Some liked to combinate, betting all six possible combinations of the three numbers they picked, and some kept lists of every number that had hit, going back for years and years, and tried to figure the odds of their reappearance. Some people played the numbers of addresses, or the license plates of the taxicabs that had nearly struck them down in the street, or the numbers of the hymns they had sung in church that Sunday. And some played the numbers they saw on letters, or in box scores; the numbers on telegrams, or on their laundry slips, or of the daily toll of the war dead in the news-papers—all of the endless streams of numbers, great and obscure and terrible, that poured in on them from everywhere, all the time.

Still others went in for supernatural assistance, relying on palm readers or even storefront preachers to divine a number for them. Or, if they had enough money and were frustrated or eager enough, they bought the dream books Malcolm also carried with him, for a dollar apiece. These were shoddy, closely printed little paperbacks, with red or blue or yellow covers, always with drawings of turbaned men, or witches, or gypsy women and men in earrings, or Napoleon himself on the cover—surrounded by stars and crosses, and crescent moons, or staring into crystal balls. They had names like PRINCE ALI LUCKY FIVE-STAR FORTUNE-TELLING DREAM BOOK, or THE THREE WITCHES COMBINATION DREAM DIC-TIONARY—or NAPOLEON MASCOT DREAM BOOK FOR-TUNE-TELLER AND HOROSCOPE WITH COMBINATION NUMBERS. Random, portentous claims on the back—Numbers That Have Made Me Famous and Others Happy! Remember 431! Watch 368 and 327!—with long lists of names, and words for simple objects, and their guaranteed, corresponding three-digit numbers in between.

When he went home at night, Malcolm spent most of his time going through the different dream books—neglecting not only his comics but also the books he had bought at Professor Toussaint's store. He felt slightly embarrassed by them, and even by his visita-tions from Elijah. It all felt like kid stuff to him compared to what he was doing now, moving like a spy along the streets of Harlem with a gun in his pocket. Working for West Indian Archie, picking up some real money, and looked for and welcomed by all kinds of people on the street. He was pleased by their shows of respect, and he spent much of his time thinking about all the things he could get with his money—pearl gray Cadillacs, and suits even finer than the one Archie had bought him—and maybe even Miranda, somehow.

But above all, he was interested in the dream books themselves. The ones that were merely lists of numbers next to objects didn't interest him so much as the more elaborate books, which were as thick as Bibles, and filled with claims to all sorts of knowledge, not just winning policy numbers. They were written in an antique and rural language that was as obscure as anything in the books from Prof. Toussaint. Stuffed with odd little stories, and quotes from Shakespeare, and the Old and the New Testament—looking as if they had just been printed over and over again, from back to the very beginning of when there were books. His favorite had a Negro woman in a kerchief on the cover, grinning and holding up the number 444. A single title page proclaiming it:

OLD AUNT DINAH'S POLICY PLAYERS' SURE GUIDE TO LUCKY DREAMS AND LUCKY NUMBERS

The Analyzation and Interpretation of Dreams
To Which Is Added—
Sibyl's Book of Fate, and the Complete Oraculum
By Means of Which Any Person May Procure
Answers to Questions Touching
Future Events
Containing Also
An Explanation of Human Physiognomy; Or, How to Discern
the Character of a Man By External Appearances, and
Emotive Physiognomy, or Natural Language—Looks, Gestures
and Postures of Different Dispositions
Containing also an Explanation of the Interpretation of Moles,
of Signs, of Predictions, Etc., Etc.,
Also
A Few Good Recipes
And
Addendum

Here he found much more detailed explanations of dreams, and numbers. Not only for names or cars or horses, but also for cities and states and places—Coney Island (171)!—or people—Napoleon (558)!—or mayonnaise (211)! Or states of being—naked (678)!—or the numbers of times you sneezed in a row (seven—879), or anything that one saw, or heard, or felt. When your left eye jumps, 376; Your apartment robbed, 513; When you are in love, 736—

The books instructed a person in how to divinate the future through cards and dice and dominoes, and the lines in your palm, and the grounds in your coffee cup. They told you the significance of the moles on your body, and the color of your pupils, the lines of your forehead and the hair on your head—"Curled hair, and black, denotes heat and drought, like that of the people of the South—"

—and how to see with the eyes closed, and how to communicate in The Silent Language, and what the date and the day of the week they were born on augured for the fate of their children (Friday— He shall be of a strong constitution, yet perhaps remarkably lecherous). And they told of the Nine Keys, and the acorn charm, and how to make a dumb cake, and discover a thief by the sieve and the shears, and how to judge a person by the nails of the toes, and the nails of the fingers, and by the navel, and also by the ribs, and the haunches and hips, and by the hairiness of the parts, and by their coming and going, and their personage and stature.

Malcolm was often unsure if what he was reading made any sense at all, but he kept going during what little time he spent up in his room now. He volunteered for every extra shift he could get with Archie, the job giving him the opportunity to go everywhere, to look into every hidden place as he went on his rounds. No longer dwelling so much on the visitations from the little brown man, or his own visions. The stories of heroes and fabled lands fading now—eclipsed by all the things and the people on the street, right before him, that he hadn't noticed before.

What he saw most of all was how angry people were. Gathered in little clumps, all over the stoops and street corners, jabbing fingers at each other as they talked. He saw it in their eyes when they saw a cop—more than the usual lowered glance full of bitterness and fear, but an active resentment now. Every head on the sidewalk going up when they rode by in their constant, roaring motorcycle patrols; stopping in their tracks, their gaze following them down the block.

But none of that mattered very much to him. Hustling to make his money as he was, betting a dollar a day or more of his own earnings on the numbers, too—hoping to make a big score that he could take to Miranda and show her. Looking out for any other opportunities on the street, which was how he had discovered the ghosty house for himself.

He had heard about the house, and the strange old white men in it, from some of the regulars at Small's. But he had never seen it until well after midnight one night, when he was searching on 128th Street for an address to pay off some musicians who had hit with 888 (smoke!). He had paused at the corner of Fifth Avenue, staring up idly at a high, gloomy brownstone that looked to be abandoned—its yard covered in junk, the windows all either broken or boarded up, stuffed closed with stacks of yellowed newspapers.

But nailed to the front door he made out a crude hand-printed sign reading This is a Ghost House—and as he moved closer he saw a preternaturally white face begin to emerge from the ground, just to the side of the front staircase. He kept watching as he emerged—a very old man, Malcolm thought, dressed in an odd suit, black as an undertaker's, with a high, detachable collar, and towing a wooden box behind him on a rope. He had a drooping gray moustache, with long gray hair and sideburns, and a face that was as white as any ghost's—as white as chalk, or sour cream, or even beyond white itself. It was more the pure absence of the color white, the white of a slug, as if he had been shut away somewhere sunless for many years, and drained of everything—blood, warmth, humor, sustenance.

The man's wooden box scraped gratingly along the sidewalk, echoing down the quiet street and startling Malcolm out of his reverie. He watched as the man climbed up the brownstone steps to the door, where he tugged ineffectually at the sign that had been nailed there. Waving his arms about crazily—then gesturing to him.

"Young man! Young man!" he called out peremptorily, his voice nearly as grating as his box, with its nasal, honking, white man's inflection.

"Young man, will you come here and help me take this sign down? More of your young vandals have put it on my door again!"

Malcolm found himself climbing slowly up the brownstone steps—the stone crumbling like coffee cake beneath his shoes, wondering if it would collapse completely under his weight.

"Come, come, now!" the old man told him, wagging his finger at the offending sign.

Malcolm pulled at the shingle of wood and it tore away easily, leaving the nail in the door. The old white man leaned over, examining it and tsking. Not knowing what else to do with the sign, Malcolm handed it to him, and the man gave him a faint half bow.

"Thank you, sir!" he said politely. "These hooligans think it is amusing, to call us ghosts. But as you can see, we're far from ghosts! We're very much alive!"

The ghosty man rattled on, Malcolm staring at him under the dim light from the streetlamp. The man had keen blue eyes—the only color in his face—and to Malcolm's surprise he smelled of oranges instead of the usual musty old man's scent.

"Well, then. Good day, sir!" he said as abruptly as he had ordered Malcolm up his stoop.

He tucked the sign carefully into the top of his box, as if to preserve it for some future use, then proceeded back down the steps. Disappearing back into the hole Malcolm had seen him emerge from, the sound of an iron gate slamming shut behind him. Belatedly, Malcolm jumped down off the steps himself, and looked to see where the old ghosty man had gone. But all he could discern was the locked gate and a small door beneath the steps—the faint sounds of a box dragging along a wooden floor inside, echoing back to him.

"Langley Collyer. He an' his brother been there forever," Jakey Mendelssohn had told him when Malcolm asked him about the ghosty man.

"He walks around at night like some kinda dybbuk. Always to Hyman Schwartz's butcher shop on 121st Street, to ask for chuck chop an' old bones. He tells Schwartz he got no money. I tell him, 'Hyman, he got plenty, he's just cheap.' But Hyman gives it to him anyway. He just likes to listen to him talk. He used to say he could listen to Langley for hours, even if he couldn't understand the half a what he was sayin'."

"There's a brother?"

"Sure. Nobody ever sees him anymore. Who knows? He coulda killed him in there, nobody'd know the difference. He coulda killed an' ate him, nobody would know. This is the kind of City we live in now."

Malcolm had first met Jakey when he went into his shabby, overstuffed department store on West 144th Street, looking to buy some cheap, conservative suit for his slave waiting tables at Small's. It was the sort of store he and Jarvis never would have been caught dead in, back in Boston—full of bolts of uncut, chintzy-looking cloth, overflowing their shelves. The whole place drowning in dust, with big Sale! One Time Only! signs sticking out of every bin. It smelled of staleness, and roaches, and old food, which reminded him of their house back in Lansing when everything was falling apart, and it had made him want to run out of the store as soon as he set foot inside.

But Jakey Mendelssohn had come bustling right over to him, as if he were a prized customer. Dragging one leg a little behind him, his thick, black, brilliantined hair that was already starting to gray, and deep circles under his eyes. A man still in his thirties, Malcolm realized when he got closer, probably no older than that preacher on the train, though right from the start he talked to him in a confiding, fatherly manner. Within minutes he had told him his name, and shared a joke. Pulling him over to the clothes department—really just a wider niche on the department store's one floor—along with an older colored man who had immediately whipped out a tape to take his measure.

"You see? This is what you want in a suit," he had told Malcolm as his tailor chalked his pants. Holding up a jacket sleeve to show him the lapels and the pants legs, as if they were the finest goods.

"See? This won't ever wear through. I don' care what you do in it, wash windows or scrub floors. Look at that stitching! Button up all the buttons. See how it hangs on you? This is how you tell a real suit."

What he had sold him really wasn't bad for the price, even if it was so boxy and conservative that Malcolm was embarrassed to see himself in it. But he had been intrigued by how much Jakey knew about suits, and the other things that he could teach him as well. Once he had the slave with Archie, Malcolm stopped by his store every day, and Jakey would put a dollar down on a combination, and teach him how to buy and sell food coupons, and other black-market items. He even paid him to help with the bootleg-whiskey business he ran out of the back of his store. He would go all around Harlem, picking up the bonded whiskey bottles that bars had saved illegally, telling the State Liquor Authority they had been broken or stolen. Then, on nights when Malcolm didn't have collections to make, he would have him drive them far out into the Long Island countryside, where Jakey's connections had a still.

"Don' worry, it's foolproof," he would tell Malcolm as they climbed into his tired, prewar truck, with *MENDELSSOHN'S* painted on the side. Piling those musty carpets, so ugly that no one had bought them on layaway, in over the bottles.

"Some cop looks under the carpets, we tell 'em we're just takin' the empties out to the liquor authority on Long Island. The way back, we tell 'em we're just deliverin' real liquor. Here, take this just in case," he added, handing him a snub-nosed .45.

"What?" Malcolm balked.

"It's all right, trust me. I got the gun registered in my name. Here, you just shove it in your pants, like so," he said, demonstrating to Malcolm with his own .45.

"Make sure the safety's on! Anybody stops us, you just let it slide down through your pants, I tell 'em it's my gun. Anyway, the main thing we gotta worry about is highjackers, not cops."

Malcolm would always take the wheel, Jakey never having learned to drive. He liked it just as well that way—liked sitting up in the high cab seats, the truck droning arthritically down the West Side Highway in the moonlight, past all the ships of war anchored out in the Hudson. Then all the way through Brooklyn, past the endless, churning docks and factories still filled with men, and activity, at every hour of the night.

Jakey ate fresh doughnuts, and gulped down coffee he had brought in a gleaming silver thermos. Getting more and more animated as they drove, talking constantly about whatever was on his mind.

"You know what I hate?" he would tell him. "I hate any hebe who changes his name. They say they gotta do it for show business, to get ahead—I don' buy it! For me, it's like colored people who pass. You know what I mean?"

"Sure," Malcolm told him from behind the wheel, unsurprised by his conversation. He had never met a white person yet who could keep himself from talking about race within two minutes of meeting him. He kept his eye on the broken white lines, shining faintly in the dimmed-out highway lights, wondering where this was going. Thinking of that colored minister he had seen. Passing in that store, and what did that mean—

"Take me. I'm only half Jewish. You didn't know that about me, did ya? Not with this punim. Sure, my old man's a Mick. Name a Feeley. Honest to God! Three months after I'm born, he goes out for a pack of cigarettes an' the evening paper an' never comes back. Louse!"

He chuckled humorlessly, and spat out the window.

"So I took her name. What'm I gonna do, take the name a some bastard who don' even have the guts to stay around an' support his family? Point is, I don' even have to be a Jew, but I am. You see what I'm sayin'? I'm proud to be what she brought me up to be. You proud to be what you are, Red?"

"Uh-huh," Malcolm said, still keeping his eyes on the road. Not sure what he should say.

"You know, we're in the same boat, Red. I'm a Jew an' you're colored," Jakey said, clapping him familiarly on the knee. "These goyim don' like either one of us. If the Jew wasn't smarter that the goyim, we'd get treated even worse than your people!"

Malcolm tensed under the feel of his hand, and Jakey stopped then, sensing that he had said something wrong. But at that moment they passed through the last of Brooklyn, the last blocks of workers' rowhouses and tenements. Driving out under the stars now, past little clusters of towns, and through entire forests. Everything else around them pitch-black, so that Malcolm felt as if they might as well be on a boat, making their way out over the water.

They drove on out past open fields of cabbages, and potatoes, until Jakey had him stop at what seemed like an arbitrary clump of trees. Malcolm thought maybe he just wanted to take a leak, but right away a pair of white men emerged from the trees. They were dressed in farmers' overalls and old, soft caps; hauling a large copper vat of sloshing liquid between them, grinning up at them in the truck as if they were in on some grand school prank.

Jakey got down and opened up the back door of the truck, and they all spent the next two hours funneling the gallons of homemade whiskey into the bonded bottles. When they were done Jakey paid them off, and the farmers handed them little tin cups to scoop out the last amber dregs—sharing a little toast to the night's work, though Malcolm had everything he could do to keep from gagging on the harsh liquor.

"Damn! You could get better king kong back in Harlem," he told Jakey, in front of the still grinning farmers.

"Whattaya talk?" Jakey asked him with a wink. "This is scotch, boychik. The goyim can't tell the difference, you put in enough soda, enough ice, serve it late enough in the evening. Just so long's they see it comin' out of their favorite label."

He liked the Jew store owner, despite the things he said sometimes—his attempts to make out that it was he and Malcolm against the rest of the white people of the world. He was always probing, he thought, trying to find out about Malcolm's family, where he was from, but he laid off when he saw that Malcolm wouldn't talk. He would peel off fifty bucks for him after one of their perambulations, stand him to a meal of fresh-killed chicken at Jimmy's, or a steak at the grill at Wells' Restaurant—the two of them nearly dizzy with fatigue, but content with the night's work.

Sometimes he would even take him back to his apartment, over in East Harlem, for a meal with his mother, Sadie. A round, jolly little woman who liked to bring her knitting and sit outside her son's store in a frayed beach chair on days that weren't rainy or too hot. Shrugging her shoulders and replying in her martyred "Pushing along. Pushing along" whenever he asked her how she was. When they'd had a couple glasses of the awful, sweet wine they always served, Jakey would press her to tell the story of how she survived the Triangle Waist fire. The old woman demurring at first, her eyes even filling with tears.

"That was a terrible thing, Jacob. So many girls died in that fire. My best friend, Esse—"

"But she lived!" Jakey would insist, his eyes shining with a strange, fierce pride, hugging her to him. "My mamaleh lived through the whole fire. All these poor girls killed, jumpin' out the windows 'cause the Irish goniffs who run the fire department didn't have ladders to reach. But she goes right down the elevator cable!"

"I had to," she explained, shrugging again. Smiling sadly and patting the head of her son, who still had his arm around her shoulders.

"The elevator went down, an' I knew it wasn't coming back up. It didn't work so good in the best of times. So I thought, all right, I'm not going to die waiting for an elevator. I wrapped my hands up in rags an' slid down."

"Nine stories!" Jakey said triumphantly. "The whole nine stories! It nearly cuts right through her hands, but she made it! That's how they met, it was my old man who found her, passed out on the roof of the elevator car. Nearly drowning in the water from their hoses but alive, goddammit!"

"Jacob!"

The two of them smiled at each other, Jakey hugging her close again, and Malcolm smiled, too. He liked Sadie, she had kind eyes, and spoke to him as she did to anyone else. It was the other person at the table, Jakey's cousin from Europe, who gave Malcolm the willies. The boy almost never spoke. Furtively watching them all when he thought he wasn't being watched, his cow eyes staring fearfully out of his blocky, freckled, pale Germanic face. Jakey talked about him, too, as he talked about everything else on their rides out to the potato fields, but more seriously, as if it were really eating at him.

"You gotta understand, the things he saw over there. Those sons of bitches!"

He would lean over to Malcolm in the cab of the gasping truck, as if he did not quite dare to say it aloud, even here. The aggressive jolliness vanishing from his voice for once. His face angry, but baffled as well—even helpless.

"They're killing them all, you know."

"Who?"

"The Jews, that's who. Don'tch you read the papers? Wherever those scum go, they're killin' any Jew they can get their hands on. Burning the bodies in ovens! It's true! They're trying to wipe out the whole people. As if they never existed!"

He felt uneasy around the boy nonetheless, and even more uneasy when Jakey talked like that, reminding him of the books back in his room. *A people invisible can easily be made to disappear.* He began to stop by Mendelssohn's less often, telling Jakey that he was busy with the policy.

It wasn't altogether untrue. He had been working more, still hoping to see Miranda, almost the one person he hadn't seen since starting his slave for West Indian Archie. He had taken to betting still more of his own earnings, even five and ten dollars a day now. Determined to hit a big score so that he could at least buy a car to take her out in, or maybe even a club of her own where she could sing. Betting always on a combination of the number Aunt Dinah's dream book gave for her name—Miranda: 544.

Before he could hit, though—or buy a car, or a club—he saw her again. It was on a Friday when he went up to pay off to Archie at Fat Man's Bar, which was situated right along Coogan's Bluff, overlooking the Polo Grounds. He had walked in, and there she was, right in front of him. She was sitting alone in a booth at the back, by a window that overlooked the great horseshoe curve of the baseball stadium below. An untouched drink in front of her, wearing a yellow dress that almost seemed to match the color of the woozy evening sunlight pouring through the window.

He knew Archie liked the booth because he could look down the length of the bar and keep an eye on everybody who came in, but she still didn't see him approach. Staring absently at the wall instead, her arms pulled close around herself despite the warm August day, idly kicking one foot, as if she were a schoolgirl. Malcolm had walked up to her before she was aware of him, ignoring all the heads that he could see swiveling around at the bar as he went past.

"I want to see you again," he said to her, even as she started to look up, still not sure of who it was. Trying to keep his voice from rising as he repeated:

"I want to see you again. I know you want to see me—"

"Go away, you child."

"I'm serious—"

"He's here, you know," she told him. "He just stepped around back with the owner, he'll be right here."

Her voice low and conversational, for any ears straining to listen. Smiling a friendly, false smile, extending her hand to him. He took the opportunity to touch her. Holding her hand gently in both of his, not letting it go—marveling at its smallness, the smoothness of her skin. She let him hold on to it, while her eyes slowly rose to meet his again. Malcolm translating everything around him ecstatically into numbers, the way he did compulsively now. The sun coming through the window, 777. The drink on the table before her, 066. Her skin, her eyes, her small hand, Miranda, 544—

"I don't care. I'll tell him right to his face!"

"No, you won't," she said firmly, extricating her hand at last. "You won't do any such foolish thing."

But he had kept after her, relentless, as he always was when he had some idea in his head. Finding excuses to meet Archie nearly every evening after that, at Connie's Inn, or Barron's, or the Golden Grill, up by the George Washington Bridge, whenever he knew she would be with him. Speaking to her whenever he left them alone for so much as a moment to do some business.

"Tell me again—why is it you love me so much?" she asked him at last.

"I tol' you already, baby. You know, sugar, I love you like he could never love you—"

"No," she stopped him. "Look at me, and tell me what you see. Tell me why you love me."

"All right," he said, forced to tell her then. Fumbling over the words, feeling the perspiration coursing down his back, adding to his discomfort.

"All right. You're the most beautiful girl I ever seen," he told her truthfully. "I never met anybody like you. I never met anybody so elegant, so refined. I just like to watch you. I like how you move, an' how you smell all the time…"

His voice trailed off, and he looked away then.

"Yes?" she pressed him. "Look at me!"

"I like—I like how you make me as good as anybody. I like how I don't have to feel bad around you, or act like anybody else. I can trust you to tell you anything, an' I want to look out for you, an' take care of you. I feel like I belong, when I'm with you—"

He stopped abruptly and raised his eyes again to look at her, feeling mortified by how much he had said. But he saw that she was looking at him intently, her large gray eyes glistening.

"Is that what you think of me?" she breathed. "That's what you see when you look at me, someone that good, and kind?"

"That's the way you are—" he started to say, but she stopped him, placing a hand on one of his.

"Listen here," she said, looking quickly toward the back of the bar where Archie had gone to collect his latest payment—then pulling a small pad and an eyebrow pencil out of her purse, scribbling down a number.

"Call me Friday afternoon, and I'll tell you where to meet me."

He nodded dumbly as he took the little slip of white paper, unable to believe he finally had her number in his hand.

"One thing. Tell me one thing," he had managed to get out anyway.

"What?" she asked hurriedly—already cool again, looking past him to the spot where West Indian Archie might appear again at any moment.

"What do you see when you look at me?" he asked, and in answer she raised one hand, and placed it on his lips.

"A beautiful boy," she said. "A beautiful, beautiful boy."

He had found out just what he was during that same spring he was elected president of his eighth-grade year. That year that any lingering misapprehensions cleared up for him, once and for all.

Just the month after he had been elected, Mr. Kaminska announced they would have their evaluations, and career counseling. He had drawn a rocket ship and stars and a moon in one corner of the blackboard, and written the words "Shoot for the Stars!" underneath it. Telling his homeroom class they didn't have to worry, that it wasn't a test. He was just going to go over their grades, and talk with them each privately about what their aspirations were, so they would know what classes to take when they went over to Mason High School in the fall. He warned all of them, though, to think big.

"Think about success in life," he told them over and over. "You're not too young. Think about what it is that you want to be a success at in life—and what you need to do to get it."

Malcolm had been excited when the day came, and his excitement grew as all of them were kept waiting in the school auditorium for what Mr. Kaminska would tell them. He was still in the top three of the class, along with Jimmy Cotton and Audrey Slaugh. He had stared at that drawing of the rocket ship, and the stars and the moon for weeks, and prepared for the best feeling of his life— what Mr. Kaminska would tell him he could be once he looked over his record.

The whole day, other boys and girls from his class had trickled back into the auditorium, looking pleased or thoughtful, or at worst a little puzzled. From what Malcolm could pick up, Mr. Kaminska had asked them all what they wanted to be more than anything else in the world—then told them that they could do it, or better. He had told students who had much lower marks than Malcolm that they could be teachers or veterinarians, nurses or county agents. He told those who had no bigger plans than to go work on their family's farm, or in the store, of the dazzling city careers they might have, and of which they had never so much as thought about before.

They giggled and joked about it, but Malcolm could see the excitement in their eyes, most of them having been told something that they had never really considered before, whole new worlds opening up before them. When it was his turn, he had walked down the hall and into the classroom almost jubilantly—thinking of his high marks, and all the nice notes Mr. Kaminska had sent home to Ma Swerlein. Anticipating already the moment when he would ask Malcolm what he wanted to be, and ready with an answer for him.

He was sitting with Malcolm's school record laid out before him when he came into the room. His thick-chested, football play-

er's body dwarfing the desk—giving Malcolm his brisk, perfunctory coach's smile beneath his moustache as he motioned him into
a chair in front of the desk. He had sat down with a nervous grin,
trying to steal a look at all the papers in front of Mr. Kaminska.
Never having imagined that there would be so much of a file on
him—both fascinated and a little unnerved that anyone would keep
such close track of him.

"Well, Malcolm. Have you thought about a career?" Mr. Kaminska asked him.

Right away, Malcolm was taken aback by the perfunctory tone in
which he asked the question. Of course he had been thinking about
a career. That was the whole point of this, wasn't it? But he had
gone ahead and given the answer he had prepared, confident that
Mr. Kaminska would be impressed once he heard him out.

"Yessir. I been thinkin' I'd like to be a lawyer," he told him, smiling proudly. But when he did, Mr. Kaminska only dropped his eyes
to the desk.

"Malcolm, the first step in finding success in life is for us to be
realistic," he said, looking back up at him sternly. As he spoke he
gathered up all of the papers, the grades and reports spread out on
his desk before him—shoveling them all back into Malcolm's folder
and flipping it closed.

"Don't misunderstand me now," he said. "All of us here like you.
You know that. But a lawyer? That's simply not a realistic goal for
a colored boy. You need to think about something you can be. For
instance, I know you're very good with your hands. Everybody
admires your work in carpentry shop, it says so right here—"

He glanced down at the closed folder, looking quickly up again.

"Why don't you think about carpentry? People around here like
you so much, you'll get all kinds of work. I'm sure of it."

The whole time Mr. Kaminska had been talking, Malcolm had
felt himself sinking. Floundering in the words, wanting to stop up
his mouth as they kept pouring out. Wanting to ask Mr. Kaminska
about what had happened to the rocket ship, and the crescent moon,
and shooting for the stars.

He had gotten up from his chair and gone out of the room in a
daze, without saying another word to Mr. Kaminska—even while
the teacher was still making notations on a chart, saying something
about signing Malcolm up for a vocational curriculum. He walked
back out the door, and down the hall to the auditorium—the teacher's

smooth, authoritative voice still trailing after him, unperturbed—and after that he thought that he hadn't really known anything, that he was seeing everyone and everything around him for the first time.

He could barely stand to be in Mr. Kaminska's homeroom anymore, barely bothered to pay attention in the class. Audrey Slaugh and Jim Cotton, the other smart kids, had tried to encourage him and make him forget what he had been told, but he couldn't stand to have anything to do with them, either. He quit the debating society and the basketball team. He quit his job washing up and dancing at the restaurant downtown, going straight up to his room after school and only coming out for dinner.

"What's wrong, Malcolm? Won't you tell me what it is?" Mrs. Swerlein had asked, noticing the change in him. Putting her fleshy arms around him when he came in the door, in a hug that would once have made him as hard as a log.

But he could no longer bear the touch of her on him. He wanted to ask her if that was what she thought he should do, too—become a local carpenter, a handyman, begging white people for work. But not daring to, he ran up to his room instead, reading again and again the comic books he had read over so many times already. No longer proud of anything he had—being class president, or the one boy in the juvenile home allowed to have the run of the town—but wanting now only to possess a secret, unsuspected identity of his own, so he could sneak off and disappear.

He never went out anymore except to the school dances. For most of them, all they had was the school record player, scratching out Glenn Miller's "Moonlight Serenade," or the Inkspots' "If I Didn't Care." But Malcolm loved seeing the old scarred gym transformed—the bleachers and the backboards covered with Japanese lanterns, and the paper cutouts of palm trees and silver moons they had all made in art class. He liked to stand shyly back by the wall on the boys' side, and watch the other kids shuffle around stolidly on the gym floor, stealing covert glances at the girls he liked. He had finally worked up the nerve to go over and ask one of them to dance—only to have the other boys suddenly surround him, heading him off before he got halfway across the court to the girls' side of the floor. They smiled at him, shoving at him playfully—forcing him gently back to their side, as surely as if they were saving him from some catastrophe. Telling him confidentially, "C'mon, Malcolm. You don't wanna dance with any of those girls. Let's go outside an' steal a smoke—" until he got the point, and spent the rest of that evening and all the others pacing slowly back and forth between the punch bowl and the refreshment table, or working the record player while the rest of them danced.

If I didn't care
Would it be the same?
Would my ev'ry prayer
Begin and end with just your name?

For the last dance of the year, though, they had brought a band in all the way from Lansing. The teacher chaperones nervously hanging back, watching the kids swing out on the floor. Everyone so wrapped up in the music that the other boys didn't look for him until he had made his way over to the girls' side. Wearing the beautiful apple green suit he had bought from the store downtown with his earnings, asking each of the girls, one after another, for the next dance as they came off the floor. They all refused, looking around, as if confused to even be asked such a thing by the likes of him. Malcolm had begun to run through them, trying to dodge the other boys as they began to close in around him, scurrying over beside the band, when he saw the chaperones approach.

Everybody began to dance again, the boys still glancing warily in his direction. Malcolm had watched them, noting their concerned, dedicated expressions—out to preserve something they may not have understood themselves, but which had been drummed into them by mothers and fathers alike—and he had climbed up on top of the upright piano. Leaning over and planting his fingers smack on the keys, pressing them down again and again, until at last the musicians were forced to stop—staring up at him hesitantly, entirely unsure of what they were allowed to do with this boy, this oversize, angry black boy. His classmates had rushed over again, forcing him away from the improvised bandstand. Not smiling this time, forcing him back along the wall, and down the stairs out of the gym, until at last, defeated, he had run off into the night. Retaining enough defiance only to cry back at them, in his shame and his frustration:

"You didn't have a chance to choose your ancestors, either!"

He never set foot in the school again. He had already passed his final exams for the year, but his grades had plunged so precipitously

that Mr. Kaminska had sent home a note to the county home saying there was no point in promoting him to high school. When she
read it, Mrs. Swerlein had tears in her eyes, and she tried to hug him
again. Begging him—

"Please, Malcolm, won't ya tell me what this is all about? What's
happened to you? You know you're better'n this."

He had wanted to scream it in her face then—No, I'm not! I'm
not! He wanted to tell her that it said so in Mr. Kaminska's very
file—a handyman, at best—but instead he had run silently up to
his room again, not wanting to give her even that much.

Soon afterward, Mr. Maynard Allen had been summoned back
to the juvenile home. He had sat at the long dining room table
with Ma Swerlein and Malcolm, and listened to her tell him how
unhappy he had been recently, and watched him read over the folder
from the school. When he was finished, he had taken a long draft
from his coffee cup and looked at Malcolm again—his cool blue eyes
filled with disappointment.

"Well, Malcolm, it looks like from this that you've done considerable backsliding," he said at last. "Mrs. Swerlein doesn't think
you're happy here. Is that so?"

He had only shrugged his shoulders. Meeting Mr. Allen's stare.
Refusing to give him anything more.

"I guess," was all he said.

"You guess? I see. Well, then. Where would you suggest we put
you, Malcolm?"

His voice challenging him, rebuking him, but Malcolm only
looked right back at him. The words bursting from him before he
knew what he was going to say:

"I wanna go live with my own!"

What he never forgot was the look on Mr. Maynard Allen's face
when he said those words. Those big blue eyes startled for once—
even hurt.

"Your own?" he had repeated, slowly. "Who would that be, Malcolm? I thought we were your own. I mean, I thought you were
more—I thought you were mostly—"

He stopped then, in his confusion, and Malcolm let the silence
linger. His arms crossed over his chest, staring steadily at Mr.
Allen, until he looked at his folder again.

"Your brother Wilfred is nineteen now," he said at last. "He's
still living in the family home, with your sister Hilda."

He paused, his eyes appealing to Malcolm once more.

"We could send you back there. To your family. Would that do?"

"Yessir," Malcolm had told him defiantly. "Yessir, that'll do fine."

The next day, Mr. Allen had come with his Packard to take him back to East Lansing. Mrs. Swerlein had made all the other boys come down to say good-bye, and she wiped her eyes with her apron as she saw him off. As he picked up his lone suitcase and walked to the door, she put out her hand—no last, swooping hug.

"I guess I've asked you a hundred times, Malcolm," she had said. "Do you want to tell me now, at least, what's wrong?"

But he only smiled at her. Thinking how dramatic her voice sounded, no doubt to impress Mr. Allen.

"Nothing, Mrs. Swerlein," he said, shaking her hand before he went out the door. "Nothing at all."

Back in Lansing he felt as if he were living in a ghost house. The place so much quieter and emptier than he had remembered it from when they were all there together. Yvonne and Wesley, the younger children, were living in foster homes now, and Butch, the baby by Mr. Walker, was in the orphanage. Hilda, the oldest, was always busy, taking care of Philbert and Reginald, and everything else around the house, and Wilfred was usually out, working any jobs he could find to keep up the mortgage.

Reginald still looked up to him, and did what Malcolm told him, but the rest of them seemed like strangers—nodding when they passed in the hall, or on the way to the bathroom, but with nothing to say. It spooked him to stay around the house too long, and he would take Reginald downtown on the bus, looking to lift something from the five-and-dimes, or just walk around the streets. Sometimes he went down to the Lincoln Community Center, where he bragged to the boys there about how many girls he had had back in Mason, and showed off a set of rubbers he had bought in a bus station men's room. That was usually enough to overawe the others, but there was one white boy, Bo Bigbee, who just grinned and asked him if he knew how to use them when Malcolm showed him the condoms.

"Sure I do!" Malcolm told him, trying to sound as casual as possible, but Bigbee had just kept grinning.

"Yeah? I bet you don't. I bet you never done it with a girl!"

He had an actual girlfriend, named Sally, who went with him everywhere, even down to the community center. She was a scrawny-

looking white girl, with long, straggly brown hair, and bruises on
her face from where her stepfather and mother hit her. She held her
arms tight over her chest all the time, as if she was cold, a cigarette
she had bummed off Bo dangling from her lips. She didn't like to
ever go home, and she would do anything Bo said as long as he let
her hang around with him.

"Let's see if you know what to do—" he had challenged Malcolm.

He had walked with Bo and his girlfriend back behind the old
Nazarene church, where Bo had started to kiss her all over her head
and shoulders. Sally put up a perfunctory struggle to push him
away, telling him, "Quit it! Quit it!"—her cigarette still dangling
out of her mouth. He had started to undress her anyway, right
there in front of Malcolm—pulling off the thin sweater she wore,
then her blouse and skirt, even her bra and panties until she was
wearing nothing but a pair of long, holey socks. Each layer of clothing removed like a revelation to Malcolm—actually seeing the yellowing bra on her, then her white, freckled breasts, then the dark
brown pubic hair—so shocking to him against her pale white skin
that he almost felt he should look away.

Sally had kept exclaiming Quit it! as he began to take off her
clothes, but by now she had stopped. Only continuing to hug her
arms close around her breasts while Bo tugged off the rest of her
clothes, dropping them in the long grass around her. Finally, after
letting her stand naked in front of them for a few minutes, he had
made her lie down next to her clothes. Taking off his own battered
cap and flinging it into the grass, then pulling out his pale pink
dick, now reddened and engorged with excitement—the sight of it
even more shocking to Malcolm than her pussy had been.

"Watch this," he said, grinning back at Malcolm. "You don't need
your rubbers for this—" And slid it into her.

After that it had all been a jumble to Malcolm, a nightmare. Bo
Bigbee's dirty blond head bobbing up and down as he moved on
top of her, the girl still holding her arms over her chest. Malcolm,
almost frantic now, jumping all around them, yelling at them—
"Quit it! Quit it! You'll make her pregnant!"—though he was aware
that he was aroused, and would like nothing better than his own
chance. He watched his friend's head going up and down, the girl
groaning and squirming uncomfortably on the ground beneath him.
Thinking of the pregnant stray cats in the corner lot, their bellies
bulging on their skinny frames—

"Now you try it," Bo said, pulling out of her. His dick still dripping jizz as he zipped up, Malcolm trying hard not to look at it. Bo picked up the strip of rubbers Malcolm had been showing off for so long, hurling them deep into the tangle of woods behind the church.

"Go ahead. See which of us knocks her up!" he told him, still grinning.

"I can't do that," the naked girl said simply, from where she was, propped up on her elbows in the grass. Still stark naked, and stained by the drippings of her boyfriend's effluvium. Malcolm looked down at her dirty face, twisted in shock and repugnance, and her unwashed holey socks.

"Sure you can," Bo said, picking his cap up from the grass and flipping it over to her. "Put this over your face. Make believe it's me."

She stared up at both Malcolm and Bo for a long moment. Then she leaned back in the grass again, holding the cap up over her face—a mask floating above her pale, white, naked body.

"Go on! You know how to do it!" Bo taunted him. But Malcolm was already moving toward her, getting to his knees. Unbuttoning his pants and taking it out—noticing the white boy staring at it keenly, professionally.

He got down in the grass between her legs, looking all over her naked white body, so near to him now. She was so skinny her ribs showed, and her breasts were little more than points. Her hair was unwashed and straight as straw, and her torso spotted with more faded purple and yellow bruises. The soft curls of her pussy matted from where Bo had been—but still holding the cap up over her face with one bony arm. Holding herself so rigidly she reminded him of nothing so much as a department store mannequin.

But still her body smelled sweet, and her skin was smooth under his hands, hovering just above her. He touched her, and she flinched, but she stayed where she was—opening her legs a little more, her arms finally pulling away from her chest, and he had gone ahead and entered her. Despite everything, he had put himself in her. The sensation astonishing to him, even as he looked down and saw Bo's cap, still held over her face—hearing her rapid, frightened breathing through the wool, her face invisible.

"Oh, please. Oh, please, no," he heard her breathe through the cap, and just before he came he had pulled out of her. Letting his jism spurt only then, white on her already white thighs—as white as Bo Bigbee's, who had cackled and jumped about over them.

"Oh, man, oh, man! You didn't do it! You didn't do it to her! Now we'll never know who wins!" he had guffawed. While Malcolm had looked down at the white girl there beneath him, her thin body trembling, the cap still held in place over her face.

CHAPTER TWELVE

JONAH

He walked outside on his Saturday-morning rounds. Certain, still, that he was failing, failing with every step. Noting the large black headlines skittering across the front page of the *Amsterdam Star-News* like so many waterbugs. Not even needing to get close to the groups of people reading them on every stoop, in every barbershop, to know what they said—

WIDESPREAD RACE RIOTS FEARED
OVER ABUSE OF NEGRO TROOPS!

WAR DEPT. SILENT AS MOBS RUN WILD!

ARMED CAMPS IN SOUTH ARE HELL,
IS SOLDIERS' CRY

SECOND FRONT—GEORGIA AND MISSISSIPPI

"Reports from widely separated points in the South, from Georgia, from Mississippi, from Texas, tell of Negro soldiers being shot down in cold blood by civilian police and citizens. Stories of greater measures of discrimination and segregation being heaped upon colored soldiers stationed at the various camps, and of threats of violence and humiliation more searing and painful than actual enemy bullets and bayonets are coming from all sections—"

More of the same awful stories. Two colored troops shot dead, fifteen more wounded when their camp baseball team was ordered out of their truck by a highway patrolman at gunpoint. The troops had knocked the cop's gun away, but a white soldier and the driver of a passing bus jumped to his rescue. Of course. Any white man will jump to the defense of any other white man, anywhere, without even knowing why—

There had been deadly gun battles between black and white troops at Fort Dix, and in Tuskegee, and at Shenango Depot, in Pennsylvania. A strike in Michigan—white workers had shut down the entire Packard plant for a day because three Negroes were put on the assembly line. A riot in Chester, Pennsylvania, because a shipbuilder had tried to start a separate colored plant and whites had attacked it, shooting and wounding five Negro workers. Not even allowed to have our own Jim Crow plant now. A huge riot in Beaumont, Texas, where dozens of Negro businesses and Negro homes had been burned to the ground, and the Texas Defense Guards had been called in, cordoning off the entire town with rolls of barbed wire.

How different was that from Poland? Though none of it affected him as much as the story of James Edwards Persons, caught peeking into farmhouses in Vigo County, Indiana—

He tried to put it all out of his head for the rest of the morning, along with his visit to his sister the day before, and take solace in the day of errands that lay ahead. First he walked up to the church vestry office, where he gave the order of service for Sunday to Delphine so she could have the programs printed up in time. Finalizing the hymn selections with the choir director, slapping an ambiguous name on the sermon he still hadn't written.

He was sure that his father would have disapproved. He had improvised many a sermon in his time, Jonah had seen him do it. Making them up out of whole cloth, around events and observations that had occurred just since the time he had entered the church that morning, as Jonah and the congregation looked on in awe. But he always made sure to coordinate what he said with the hymns.

"The Spirit will not descend without song," he had always tried to impress upon Jonah. "An' that's the whole idea of the sermon, to bring down the Spirit."

"But you don't even believe in the Spirit," Jonah had said to him once, irritated over his own shortcomings. But his father had only laughed at him.

"I don't believe in God! I never said I don't believe in the Spirit."

And his sermons were songs, Jonah knew, beginning and ending with hymns and spirituals. Starting up slowly, while he took the measure of the congregation that morning, or thought up just what it was he was going to say. Slowly building his rhythm—sharing a joke, maybe, or a barely proper story. All the time listening for that rabbit in the bushes, repeating whole lines if they worked. Sometimes even breaking into nonsense words, into mere, alliterative sounds if that would keep the momentum going.

His words actually became song as he neared his climax. The people were swept up into ecstasy before him, jumping up and shouting from the pews. He would finish on a crescendo, or sometimes—in a grand flourish he was famous for in Harlem—sometimes just sitting down abruptly in mid-note. A false stop. The gesture shrewdly hushing the congregation for a moment, allowing for his words to be heard once more. He was up again in an instant, singing and shouting and even stomping his conclusion—throwing open his arms to their approbation. Sitting down for good this time, and letting their shouts and the next hymn sweep over him—but not before he pulled out a white handkerchief, nearly the size of a flag, and in one final, dramatic gesture used it to mop up his sweating, streaming face.

And it was a song, Jonah had realized even before his father told him—a song he sang with the congregation. Aware, but not caring, that some of the more high-hat churches snickered at him for the vociferousness of the responses at the New Jerusalem, calling him a snake-stomping Baptist behind his back.

"Son, the colored folks who say that, they're in white people's churches," he had told Jonah dismissively. "'Course we shout, an' they talk to me. They help me when they do that, 'cause you see we're worshiping the Lord together. And I'll tell you, wherever you see one of our churches, and the Spirit's in that church, then you better believe you gonna hear some noise."

Jonah's own sermon for this week still lay, barely started, on his desk back home. But there was no time for that now. First, he had to make his next round of visits to the sick, and the old. This was the duty he liked best of all. Climbing up endless flights of tenement stairs, walking dingy hallways that smelled perpetually of fried fish and collards, and wet clothes drying on the radiators. Looking into face after face that was strained with sickness, or fatigue, or loss.

Yet at least in this he felt needed. The faces before him brightening visibly just to see him. They were pathetically grateful, even honored, to have the least things he brought them—flowers, a pot of his wife's chicken soup, a little money from the deacon's fund or his own pocket to tide them over. Serving him, in turn, whatever homemade delicacies they could afford—syrupy jarred watermelon rind in the summer, maybe a plate of potato-pone from down home at Christmastime.

He always had to phone at least a day in advance before coming over, of course. He hated to bother them, to announce himself that way, but they would have been humiliated otherwise. Their apartments were always poignantly scrubbed and tidied by the time he arrived. The air still redolent with the putrefyingly sweet stench of Flit or Sure Death; fresh, powdery white lines of boric acid laid down along the baseboard in the endless vain effort to keep the roaches inside the walls. They were almost ecstatically happy just to talk, and grasp his hands and pray, searching for any excuse to prolong his visit. And he, soaking up their gratitude, did not want it to end, either.

What a wretched sinner you truly are, he would tell himself, to draw so much sustenance from their misery—but he did not really try to help himself. Exhilarated by the idea that he was actually doing something, that here his very presence made a difference.

As always, he left the stop he dreaded the most—the stop that belied all of his illusions about making a difference—until the very end. *Harlem Hospital*, though they called it by other names—*The Morgue* or *The Butcher Shop*, or *The One-Way Street*. It still made him flinch to go inside. When he had first started working with his Daddy, as assistant minister, he had been sure that he would catch the TB, or pneumonia there—little understanding that it was what he would *see* that would infect him. Patients lying out on mattresses in the halls, or on the unwashed floors of the maternity wards, next to uncollected bedpans still full of urine and excrement.

What had Christ said? "There is nothing outside a man which by going into him can defile him, but the things which come out of a man are what defile him." Sickness was one thing, depraved indifference another.

There were rumors of even worse things—rumors so persistent that they, too, had made their way into the columns of the Amsterdam Star-News. Stories about the hospital's colored syphilis patients, and how the hospital's colored doctors had to keep constantly "alert against men of an experimental turn of mind." About men who were actually willing to let the disease fester, or even expose other patients to it, for purposes of "scientific" research.

A chill had run down his back when he read that, though Jonah still found such tales to be incredible, certain that no doctors—not even white ones—could be so inhuman. The opening of Sydenham Hospital—and, ironically, the advent of the war—had actually improved conditions somewhat, with all the young men away, and more beds available. Yet as he made his way down the dreary, crowded halls of the hospital, he could easily see how such rumors had started. There were still beds lining the walls, and patients stuffed four and five to a room. He stopped at the sight of one old man, curled up like a boiled shrimp on a bench just inside the emergency-room door. When Jonah bent down over him, he could see that he was shivering with fever, even on such a warm summer's day—just a little old man, with a few white wisps of hair standing up off his head. Hands clutching at the collar of his shirt, eyes closed, with no sign that anyone had even noticed him, much less cared.

Jonah called out angrily for the orderlies, for a doctor, while he hunted around for a blanket to put over the man. And looking at him shriveled up there, the abbreviated story of James Edwards Persons had come floating back up to him, unbidden. The same question recurring again and again to Jonah—

Why? What was the man doing there—a colored man, walking across those white Indiana farms?

Jonah acknowledging guiltily to himself, even as he thought the question, that that was what life in a white man's country did to you. Questioning yourself over where you had every right to be—

But why? Where had he been going? Home to Detroit, or Chicago? Rolled for his bus money or cheated of it in some craps game? A bunch of men on their knees out in back of a Greyhound bus station, maybe passing around a whiskey flask to cloud the sucker's judgment. His money gone in the wink of an eye. Thinking all right then, he could just walk it all the way home. Knowing how it was—that no one was going to pick up a black man on a lonely highway, even one in uniform, with his honorable discharge papers in his pocket.

And had he been, in fact, staring into the windows of farmhouses? Knowing, too, as he must have, what that could cost him. What could he have been looking for? A hot meal, or a warm place to sleep? A few dollars to see him on his way? Surely he knew that this, too, would have been impossible. A black face, glimpsed outside the window on a dark night, scaring the white children and the farm wife. A soldier's face, solemn and cryptic, fading away as suddenly as it had appeared.

Then there would have been the mob, and the dogs. Their cries echoing down the gullies of the lonely country roads behind him. James Edwards Persons, thirty-three, must have known they were coming for him, the only man—the only black man—for as far as the eye could see. Never mind that he had the proper discharge papers in his pocket, was wearing his once sleek tan khakis. A little rumpled now after so many days on the road. Knees still smudged with oil from where he had knelt behind that bus station, to throw the dice with a slick-talking man from Birmingham, or Memphis, or Cairo, Illinois, who even had a pint of Four Roses on hand to ease the transition of your money into his pocket.

(Or maybe nothing like that at all. Maybe only waking up from a dead sleep in the same station—a sleep troubled with worry over the sick momma, or the dying daddy, or the destitute wife and children, which was the reason for the honorable discharge in the first place—to discover that your billfold is gone, picked by the bum or the floozy who had appeared to be snoring drunk in the seat next to you the night before, head lolling on your shoulder, his or her breath stinking so powerfully of bad liquor that you had had to turn your head away and let them do their business. Looking out the window into the dark night, solemn, cryptic soldier's face half-reflected back to you. A black face on a black night—)

But the mob didn't care. Some of them running, more of them tearing up the country dirt roads in their trucks and old Fords. Yelling and laughing as they came, but not out of any deeper despair. The war had been good to them, restored their farms to full solvency for the first time since the last war. Restored them to their full, provincial smugness, wearing the newest overalls and hunting jackets and dresses from the Sears Roebuck catalog—led by the respected leaders of their community, the sheriff and his deputies.

This hunt not some desperate, peasant burst of viciousness and fear and inchoate rage but an outing, a field day, in the brand-new, prosperous Vigo County of the war.

And you know it's for you. You know it's for you, churning up the dirt on the road behind you.

You try to run, to make a fight of it at least. "If we must die let it not be like hogs / Hunted and penned in an inglorious spot..." But there's no place to run, no woods. All the fields cleared for the endless beans and corn and cabbages the government will buy for the latest war effort. Nothing under the sky but flat, plowed land, for as far as the eye can see—and your running only gets their blood up. And you know this but still you run, because what else is there?

The mob still coming for you, James Edwards Persons, age thirty-three—my own age. The mob still coming, just as they came for my family, for my father's own family in this city, so many years ago. Still coming, just as they are in Beaumont, and Mobile, and Newark, and Detroit, and they will never stop—

And so you run, and are caught, and beaten. Break away again, and are caught, and beaten, and still you run. No pretending left anymore, between you, James Edwards Persons, and the mob. Knowing all too well what they have seen, and heard. The half-excited, half-embarrassed accounts from middle-aged farmwives, and apple-cheeked young girls. The only thrill they have had since that two-headed calf was born, since Annie Moore ran off with the tractor salesman. Since the bad days of farm foreclosures and milk dumped out on the highway in pitiful gestures of defiance. Since the last election, complete with torchlight parade.

A black face at the window.

They want you, for a holiday. For showing your face, outside their fearful night windows, the literal boogie man. And still you run, and are caught, and are beaten by men with ax handles. By men with pistol butts, by men with blackjacks and nightsticks and badges on their jackets. And still you run until somehow—a diversion, a thought that maybe you are already dead, an argument over who will hit you next—somehow, you are away. Running free and clear through the fields, while they look on in astonishment after you. Telling each other They can't be human, skin tough enough to take all that and still run. Telling each other Damn, I thought that nigger was dead!

Running and running and running. Until you find—the wreck of a house. The ruined barn beside it. A place where you can lie down inside, amidst the titmouse nests, and the roosting owls. A place where they will never find you, will somehow never even think to look for you. Alone, at last. Feeling your lungs bursting, your ribs and insides and your head hurting like you've never quite felt them before, even when you took that beating from the white sergeant in basic training. Even that time the cop caught you up the side of your head with his billyclub when you didn't move along quite fast enough for him, coming up so quick you didn't see it.

It hurts much more than all those, the normal scrapes and bruises a colored man—though maybe not a colored preacher—can be expected to take. The normal quotient of blows, and broken bones, and degradations. It hurts so much more than that, but still you are exultant. Ecstatic to be alive, to have escaped. To have escaped. The Negro's greatest possible triumph. Letting yourself down to rest there, just for a moment, by the remains of an ancient plow, behind the skeleton of a tractor. You don't even feel the pain so much anymore. Just a nice place to lie, and catch your breath, until nightfall comes and you can move on—

Curled up to die, like a boiled shrimp, on a hospital bench. Like the old man before him now, completely unattended—

Only then did Jonah realize that he was shouting. Shouting in a purposely loud, embarrassing voice—his black man's voice, as Adam liked to call it. Compelling the white orderlies to admit the old man at last. Wrapping a blanket around his shoulders so that he stopped shivering, at least, and walking him slowly on down the corridor and into the ward. Jonah still yelling at them to get a gurney for him, or at least a wheelchair. But the white orderlies ignoring him again now, towing the old man down into the labyrinth of the drab, ill-lighted corridors on his shaky legs.

There is nothing outside a man which can defile him—

He walked slowly home from the hospital, feeling wobbly legged himself. Telling himself that he would not let this moment pass, he would go right up to the study and work on his sermon. But when he got home there was a phone message waiting for him from Charlie O'Kane, requesting his presence up at The Mansion. He was aware of Amanda scrutinizing his face carefully when she told him—suspicious, as she always was, of the O'Kanes and their dealings.

"You know, you don't have to jump lively just 'cause they say," she told him.

"Did he say it was an order? Was he rude to you on the phone?" he asked her with affected patience, nettled by her tone.

Was it true, then? Once you lost a woman's respect, did you ever get it back?

"You know how he is. Butter wouldn't melt in his mouth," Amanda said, imitating the famous O'Kane brogue that waxed and waned according to the occasion, and the number of narrowbacks in any given setting.

"So?" Jonah shrugged. "I might as well go up, then. Sounds important."

"They want to see you so bad, why can't they come here and see you?"

"You know it isn't like that," he told her, frustrated and bollixed by her argument at the same time. "I got a little time. Besides, you know they've done a lot for us."

"And you deliver what they want, every election day."

"It's not like that, you know it—"

"I'm just saying, you don't have to run out to them."

"I'm not running!"

His shout resounded in the empty house. Amanda looking at him closely, her lips twisting.

"Aren't you? Aren't you always running these days?" she told him. "I never seem to see you stay in one place anymore, Jonah. Seems to me you're running around all the time."

"Look, it's just been, uh, a little difficult, trying to get my bearings back. After—after—"

She moved closer to him then, taking his hands in hers. Looking up at him from just under his chin, her face softening in understanding.

"I didn't expect you to die for me, on that train," she said. "I don't expect you to be anything you can't be."

"I know," he said, trying to smile. Thinking that the only thing worse than her scorn was her pity. Wondering again: Do you ever get it back?

"Tell me," she said. "You haven't been with me since—since we were on the island. Not really. Tell me what's the matter. Just like you used to—"

"I will," he promised, giving her a hasty kiss on the cheek and all but running out of the front parlor and down the stairs of their golden house. Rushing off to the subway to answer the call of the

O'Kanes. Making sure not to look at her face, watching him from the high front window.

He took the No. 5 train up to Morris Park, then walked the remaining few blocks to The Mansion, which was on Silver Street. The train rolling slowly past the proud, single-family homes, the massive apartment houses of the Irish and Jewish and Italian middle classes, newly risen from the Lower East Side, and Hell's Kitchen. Knowing the trip by heart, ever since he was a little boy and his father had first taken him up to see Deirdre Dolan O'Kane—the woman who had taken Milton in when the white people had come and smashed their house, and killed his mother.

"So that's him, is it?" she had said, the moment she set eyes on him. "What a darlin' boy—just as handsome as your girl. Come here and let me see ya, child."

Jonah standing before her in the dark, musty room, gawking openly at the incredible tangle of blue and purple veins that showed through her white, translucent skin. His father nudging him, hard, from behind—but she had only laughed and looked up at Milton, her eyes glistening.

"But how good that you have a family, then. Good for you!" she told him. "After all these years!"

She had been a very old woman by then—nearly as old as his father was now. Smelling of old-lady smells, ointments and powder, and dizzyingly sweet perfume. But it hadn't been too bad. At least she hadn't tried to kiss him wetly on the mouth, like the old ladies from church, only hugged him tight and tickled him with her bony, gentle fingers until he laughed and squirmed hysterically in her arms. Placing him carefully back down on his feet then, and slipping him a peppermint while a young man with a funereal aspect served them tea.

"This is my grandnephew, Charlie," she said, introducing him, in a voice that barely contained her distaste. She dismissed him in turn with a curt nod, as soon as he had finished laying out the tea.

She had sat in the middle of the room, in a great, fan-backed chair that looked like a throne. Propped up on pillows, with a fine white-lace quilt clasped up to her neck. All through their visits, Jonah remembered, men would come and go, speaking into her ear in quiet, apologetic tones. She had nodded her head, or shook it adamantly and pursed her lips. Never saying more than "No. No, that's not likely."

His father would pull up a chair, and the two of them would talk like old friends—less guardedly, at least, than he did around any other white person Jonah had ever seen him with. He would stand by his father's elbow, letting the old woman slip him more peppermints with subtle, knowing winks; staring idly at the objects on the parson's table next to her chair. There was always a book or two, usually a collection of Shakespeare, or some Irish poems. A bottle of some reddish medicine, a pair of reading glasses. An ancient, framed picture—a daguerreotype, like the mythic picture his father had—of a tall, broad-shouldered white man in a Civil War uniform, looking so gaunt and hollow-eyed that he seemed about to keel over.

"That was my husband, Tom O'Kane," Mrs. O'Kane told him once. "He fought in the war. On the same side as your grandda."

"Was he killed, too?" Jonah had asked her, and his father nudged him again, but the old woman only smiled and shook her head.

"Oh, no. He was very lucky, God rest his soul. He got to come home an' become an alderman, an' then a state senator."

When Jonah got bored enough by their talk about the old days, or the intricacies of Democratic politics, he would politely excuse himself to go to the bathroom, then go off exploring in the great, gloomy house.

The Mansion had always thrilled and terrified him. It was threaded with long, dark passages that seemed to cross each other repeatedly, or even to lose their way, leading to nothing but locked doors. Most of the windows were made of stained glass, and while some of the scenes they depicted were things he recognized from the life of Jesus, or the saints, the others were strange, even sinister depictions of bats and apes, or jackals with bared teeth. The one that frightened and fascinated him the most was the vast, scaly tail of a sea monster, plunging back into the ocean—the rest of it already submerged, an unimaginable horror beneath the blood-red waves. He would encounter this image at the end of a hall, surrounded by nothing but locked doors, and run breathlessly back the way he had come, calling for his father.

Mrs. O'Kane would only laugh, and chuck his cheek, and hand him a sugar cookie from the tea setting. Serene on her throne there, beaming at the both of them.

"But how nice that you had a boy, then!"

Her papery, old woman's hand running down through Jonah's hair and over his cheek. Looking tenderly at his father.

"How good that you didn't die then, Milton."

The house was a little better lighted now, a little less musty, but no less gloomy. It was more obviously a political clubhouse, overrun with assorted O'Kanes and their myriad cousins, Boyles and McCools, and Quinns and Flynns and Kellys. All these serious-looking Irishmen in new suits, still moving about mysteriously on one errand or another. Both their numbers and their power had increased exponentially with the years, and out in the front hall now there were two long benches filled with supplicants, waiting stoically to see them about some favor or another. Jonah almost turned around and walked out again when he saw them, but an alert young man stationed there took him in hand immediately, ushering him politely inside.

Charlie O'Kane stood up to greet him when he entered the parlor. He sat where the old lady had, in the middle of the large room—a position that now reminded Jonah of pictures he had seen of Mussolini's office. The fan-backed chair long gone, replaced by a sleek new junior-executive's desk, complete with blotter and ink-well desk set, and in and out boxes. Behind it was Charlie, a tall, lean man—the grandnephew. Still funereal and mostly bald, with only a thin laurel of gray hair over his ears, and a clean-shaven, sallow face. He was the head of the family now—the most serious and alert of all the serious, alert men at The Mansion; officially no more than a state assemblyman, but related by marriage to Ed Flynn, who was the boss of the Bronx, and an intimate of FDR himself.

"Jimmy here'll get us some iced tea," he said, coming around his junior executive's desk to offer his hand, his manner with Jonah perfectly cordial, if cool, as always.

"Or would ya be wantin' some coffee? Or perhaps somethin' stronger, Rev'rend?" he asked solicitously.

"Iced tea will be fine, thank you," Jonah said warily.

Like most of the Irish politicos he was acquainted with, he had never known Charlie O'Kane to take a drink. Was he seeking some kind of edge? he wondered, remembering what his father had told him about his grandfather Billy Dove being a drinker. But Charlie only nodded to Jimmy, the young man in a pinstriped suit who had met Jonah at the door, and who went off at once to fetch their tea. He then switched his gaze back to Jonah, staring at him intently across his desk for a long moment, before asking a stream of perfunctory questions about how things were at the New Jerusalem.

"Anyt'ing we can help ya with down there?"

"No, not at the present time—"

"Anyone what needs a draft exemption? A place at a war pr'duction plant? Are there any...necessities we can procure fer ya?"

Jonah twitched involuntarily at the last question, aware that Charlie O'Kane was referring not terribly obliquely to the black market. Wondering if there was any way he could possibly know about his visits to the back of Jakey Mendelssohn's department store—

"No. Thank you for asking," he made himself answer in a level voice. "We're doing all right."

"I'm glad to hear it." Charlie O'Kane nodded gravely, then was silent again. The two of them waiting there without speaking for a few, agonizingly long moments until Jimmy returned with the tea—two tall glasses with a slice of lemon hooked over the lip, served on a silver tray that he held out so primly Jonah almost expected him to be wearing a kitchen apron. Suppressing his smile, he thanked the young man and took the glass and a piled spoonful of sugar. Charlie O'Kane, alert as ever, following his glance and favoring Jimmy with a wintery smile of his own.

"That boy," he said, "should've been a butler in a grand English manor house. He'd a got on famously."

Jonah smiled weakly at the joke, and took a long, thirsty gulp from his tea, realizing how dry his throat was. When he put the glass down again, Charlie O'Kane was fixing him with a look from across the desk—obviously ready to do business.

"Well, then," he said straight out, "I wanted to talk to you about yer friend over at the Abyssinian."

"Adam," Jonah said in astonishment—amazed that anyone would ask him about Adam Powell.

"The skinny is, he's goin' to run for the new House seat next year."

Jonah shrugged, and tried to remain as poker-faced as O'Kane, although he felt like laughing. Adam's ambitions were news to exactly no one—to no one in Harlem, anyway.

"He may."

"Not that we have anyt'ing against it, mind you. It's long past time you had one of yer own in the seat—"

"Yes."

He hesitated again, and Jonah leaned forward avidly, intrigued now to hear just what Charlie O'Kane had in mind.

"There's just somethin' we wanted to clarify."

"Yes?"

"Would you know what his feelin's are concernin' the Metropolitan Life project downtown?"

So that was it. The project had been a growing controversy for the last two months, ever since the insurance company had announced its intention to build a huge complex of apartment buildings just above Fourteenth Street. Already, just from that one announcement and the newspaper coverage, it had become one of the City's leading postwar dreams, Jonah knew. Spacious, middle-class homes, complete with playgrounds, and gardens, and park space, designed specifically for the returning GIs and their families. Affordable and open to anyone—except people of color.

"What do you think his feelings would be?" Jonah asked stonily.

"It's important to us that those projects get built—without any undue delay," Charlie O'Kane said very importantly. "Men'll need work when they get back after the war, an' places for their families to live—"

"Important to us," Jonah repeated.

He tried to think what Adam would say. He was so much better at this, tirelessly leading his crusades to get the bus companies to integrate, then the big department stores down on 125th Street—then Con Edison, and Consolidated Gas, and the New York Telephone Company, and the IRT. Always finding some way to get more attention from the papers, to get people out on the picket lines, day after day. The day a bus driven by a colored driver had started its very first route down Fifth Avenue, Adam had even knelt down before the photographers and kissed the pavement—albeit making sure not to dirty his camel-hair coat.

The only protest Jonah had ever made was when he had prevailed upon Macy's to stop selling "Mugging Sticks"—batons with fashionable silk tassels and a detachable police whistle on the end, that customers were urged to carry with them when passing through "questionable uptown areas" during the dim-out. It had been a farcical experience. He had spent almost two hours across a desk from a store executive, trying to explain how their advertisements—two dark hands, and a menacing Negro face lunging out of the darkness at an oblivious white girl—were offensive. The caption underneath reading, "Don't be caught where it's dark!" The executive still obdurate, finally bleating out—"But it is dark up there—"

"It's important that we have those jobs lined up, that we have the housing," Charlie O'Kane was telling him now, as if he were speaking to an exceptionally slow child.

"So—that means you will do everything you can to see that the project is open to Negroes?"

"Well, now. Some things are beyond our power—"

"Or at least you'll fix it with the unions, then? So that Negro workmen are given a certain number of jobs on the construction crews, in the carpentry and masonry?"

O'Kane said nothing this time. The suggestion that colored men be allowed in the trade unions so obviously outrageous.

"No? I see," Jonah continued. Keeping his voice level, deliberately speaking as slowly as O'Kane had.

"So you've brought me here," he recounted, "to ask if I will talk to a brother minister on your behalf. To give his blessing to a housing project that will keep out all colored people—all of us—and won't even let us help build the place."

Charlie O'Kane sat back in his chair, thumbs tucked in his jacket pockets. His face carefully blank, obviously waiting—looking, for the first time during their interview, much less like an executive and more like the middle-aged wardheeler he was.

"So just what was it?" Jonah asked. "Just what was it that made you think Adam or I would go along with such a project?"

O'Kane sat motionless, still saying nothing, his cadaverous eyes boring meaningfully into Jonah's.

"So it's that way," Jonah concluded. "I'm supposed to tell you what it will take. What personal things you can do for me. Or for Adam, excuse me. With a percentage for me as—what's the word? The procurer—"

"Look, you don't have to talk like that—" O'Kane started to say, grimacing, realizing at last he had made a mistake.

But Jonah was unable to restrain himself any longer, his voice rising bitterly.

"We're supposed to help you get this when our people are paying the highest rents in the City. Three, four families—a dozen people in an apartment! But nothing for us. Not one Negro carpenter allowed to work a union job in the whole City. We're supposed to take what you give us an' lie down. Me, and Adam, and whatever other minister you choose to call up here next and ask to pimp for you—"

"There's no reason we can't build more projects up in Harlem after the war," O'Kane said hastily. "It'll be better like that, anyway. Each with their own."

"Yes," Jonah said drily. "Just like in Mississippi. Or Poland."

"What's that?"

"Nothing."

Jonah got to his feet.

"Don't be such a sorehead," O'Kane said again. Jumping to his feet himself, and trying to wave Jonah back down—looking faintly embarrassed by how he had mishandled their little talk. "Look, our families go back a long ways—"

"Yes, they do," Jonah said dryly. "I will pass your proposal on to Adam, and it won't even cost you a thing. Consider that debt paid."

"Now, just a moment!" O'Kane said, glowering at Jonah as he turned to go. His thick eyebrows pressed together furiously in concentration, actually reaching a hand out over his junior-executive's desk to grab the edge of Jonah's sleeve.

"I'm just tryin' to do yer boy a favor. He ain't sittin' in the Congress yet, ya know. We know certain t'ings about him—t'ings a man a the cloth might not want becomin' public knowledge."

Jonah looked down at the hand on his sleeve, then back at Charlie. Trying not to let any of the shock within him show on his face.

"It's a good thing our families do go so far back," he said slowly. "Otherwise, I suppose you might have started with threats."

"Maybe we should consider this more of a soundin' out, then—" O'Kane tried to recoup again, but Jonah was already heading for the door.

"Well, you do that, then. You sound it out to yourself, and get back to me when you like what you hear."

"Which is it? Which is it yer really offended by, Rev'rend? The offer, or the fact that yer the messenger boy?" he sputtered after him, losing his temper at last—but Jonah never looked back. Striding on out past the benches of supplicants, and all the alert young men, for what he knew would be the last time.

As he walked back to the Morris Park station, his head was filled with turmoil. Questioning whether there was any truth to O'Kane's jibe, whether or not they could really have anything on Adam.

And what would it profit him anyway, all his theatrical defiance? The Metropolitan Life project would surely get built. Even the fierce little mayor had made only the most perfunctory denunciation of its color line, preoccupied by the idea of all that nice middle-class housing, just like everyone else. All of Jonah's indignation would not get one colored family in, or a union card for a single colored carpenter—or one new apartment built in Harlem.

He racked his brain, trying to think if there were some other angle that Adam might have played. Would he have cut some deal? Outfoxed the O'Kanes into giving him something, anything, that people could use? And what would his own Daddy have done? Wouldn't he have used his ancient connection with the O'Kanes somehow—rather than having it thrown back in his face?

Yet try as he might, walking back to the subway, Jonah found to his surprise that he could not second-guess himself. Grinning involuntarily every time he thought of Charlie O'Kane's face again—his smug poker face slipping away into consternation. Relishing the thought that, at least for once, he had surprised somebody.

His rare good mood lasted only until he got home. He had hoped that his visit to The Mansion might sustain him in trying to write his sermon again that night, and he had wanted to tell Amanda all about it, the way he had always told her about everything. But the more he thought about it, the more pathetic it sounded to him— like he was trying to impress her, bragging on himself to make up for his failures in the pulpit, and on that train so many weeks ago. For once she misread his mood and did not try to draw him out, but moved quietly around him, letting him have the room and the quiet that she assumed he needed.

Was this what it would be like with children? he speculated. Always tiptoeing around Daddy? Himself becoming an evermore withdrawn, remote figure, battling with his own demons?

Not that her circumspection did him any good with his sermon, either. He soon found himself bogged down again—distracted, trying to find some way to put a new rhythm to the old words. Working futilely over the old, familiar themes, used again and again until he was sick of even thinking upon them. The Balm in Gilead, and a Song of Zion. A knock at midnight, and the Good Samaritan, and the fiery furnace—and Jonah in the belly of the whale.

He was still unable to understand why his father had named him such a thing in the first place. Milton always insisting it had come from the old slave song, sung by the people he had rescued when they finally crossed the Potomac. After they had knelt and prayed in gratitude, then made their way across the river into the North, singing as they went—

He deliver Daniel from the lion den,
Jonah from the belly of the whale,
And the Hebrew children from the fiery furnace,
And why not every man?

But his father's explanation had never seemed sufficient for the onus he carried around with a name like Jonah. It weighed on him like a millstone, its burden only greater the older he became. He knew that the diaconate had almost denied him his father's pulpit on the basis of it alone and he still heard, sometimes after services, one or another of his congregation insolently whistling that other tune as he went through the door. The one his sister had taunted him with—

My hard luck started when I was born
Least so de old folks say.
Dat same hard luck been my bes' frien'
Up to dis very day...
For I'm a Jonah, I'm a Jonah man...

"Jonah was bad luck only because he wouldn't do God's bidding," his father had tried to explain—as slowly and carefully as he tried to puzzle out all the terrible, vindictive things God kept doing in the Bible.

"He was afraid to!" he had said. "An' the Lord saw to it that Jonah was swallowed by the whale—"

"Yes, yes, I know!"

He understood all that, even as a child. How Jonah had fled the Lord, and the Lord had pursued him. How he had spent three days in the belly of the leviathan before he repented, and bent to the will of God. A sign of the Christ to come, Who would spend three days in the ground before He was risen.

But how did that apply to him? God had always turned His back and swum away from him, no matter how much he had sought to serve Him.

"You will reach them when you preach from your own story," was his father's advice. Vaguely blasphemous, delivered years ago, the day Jonah had first preached from the pulpit. The very day Howard Marsden had come to the New Jerusalem.

Jonah put down the stalled sermon. Lifting the pages of his History of the Church of the New Jerusalem out of its locked drawer, its hiding place. This was yet another passage that had no business in a proper church history, that would never see the light of day. But he had written it down anyway. The whole history spoiled, he might as well put down his own testament, before he left. Let them find it when he was gone, and shock themselves—

It had all started by accident, when he went to the college upstate. Save for that one unsettling afternoon out at Coney Island, when his sister had told him *Let's be white people today!*, he had never even thought to try to be something he wasn't.

The college was simply the best one he had been able to get into, a collection of imitation Gothic towers and dormitories, cloistered up in the Chenango Hills amidst rolling forests of pine and fir and cedar. His parents had been as proud of him as they had been of Sophie, with no qualms about it being a white school. Jonah had felt much the same way, eager to start the rest of his life, barely able to sit still through the trip. Traveling alone by train up to Utica through the brilliant early foliage of western New York, then by cab to the little village that ringed the college. He was giddily hauling his trunks up to his dorm room, everything around him so new and fresh and strange that he could barely keep from laughing out loud, when Howard Marsden had walked in.

"You must be Jonah," he said at once, in the deep, warm voice that was so much a part of his charm. Introducing himself and snapping a hand out—then moving at once to pick up the other strap of the outsize steamer trunk Jonah had been scraping across the floor.

"What do we have here, a geology major?" Marsden had grinned at him—the grin alone, Jonah would always remember, easy and unforced and conspiratorial. Tucking the pipe he'd had in his teeth casually away in a jacket breast pocket, lifting the cumbersome trunk with an easy, one-handed grace—

"You know you don't have to bring your own rocks, old man, they already have plenty. What's the matter? Didn't they tell you?"

He started to chuckle—and Jonah realized how confused he must look, his mouth hanging half open. For the boy at the other end of his trunk was tall and lanky, with blue eyes and freckles, and limp flaxen hair that fell over one side of his forehead—and indisputably white.

"Um, I think there's a mistake," Jonah had mumbled. "I think I must be in the wrong room—"

"No mistakes possible! Not at this institution of higher learning!" Marsden had beamed. "Room 413, right? You're Jonah Dove, aren't you?"

"Yes. Yes, I am," Jonah said, smiling back for the first time.

And for one moment he had thought that it really didn't matter. That he had come all this way into a whole new world—a world of the mind, where anything at all was possible. Where he might actually have a white roommate, and it wouldn't matter in the least, and no one would care what color he was.

How naive he had been, he thought now. As if taking a train up through all those unfamiliar stops, Poughkeepsie and Albany, and Troy and Schenectady and Utica, should land him in a place where the world itself had changed. Having forgotten for the moment about that day at Coney Island, how easy it had been for him to pass with Sophie. Never having given it a thought, how quickly he had been able to hail a cab from Utica—the white hack even tipping his cap obsequiously, and rushing to help with his trunks.

Of course. For almost the first time in his life, he was in a place where no one assumed he was colored. That still didn't mean he wasn't.

His delusion hadn't lasted long. For the rest of that day and night, even for the whole of his first week at the college, he had dared to think it just didn't matter. To this day, he could still remember how heady that week had felt.

Then slowly, little by little, the air had come out of it. There had been nothing very overt—nothing crude, or openly racist. Only the slow realization that came from the very way in which Howie Marsden had taken him so easily under his wing. How he'd introduced Jonah to all his own friends from prep school, or the many he had already made on campus, without the least hint of uneasiness. The way they had all responded to him, without any hesitation or embarrassment, like no encounters with white people he had ever had before. The ready, good-hearted friendship of young men who feel themselves all to be both gods and equals, off on some great adventure together.

The last, incontrovertible piece of evidence was provided one evening when he was hurrying to evening prayers with Howie, and Jack Leonard, and Gilly Mackenzie, and Andy Miller—the other great new friends he had made through Howie Marsden—and they had seen, at a distance, a very tall, broad-shouldered freshman walking ahead of them to chapel.

"Merton Turnbow," Howie had said, pointing him out to Jonah. Then adding, in a purely conversational tone, with absolutely no hidden meaning—

"He's one of about four colored boys we have on campus. They all live down in some rooms in the village."

The boy in question had turned just then, looking behind him, almost as if he heard them. He was too far away for that to be possible, but even so Jonah had had to fight the urge to duck behind his friends. Afraid that somehow Turnbow would see him, noticing how Turnbow's skin was only a shade or two darker than his own—

"Yes, and every one of them a letterman in football," Jack Leonard had added, smiling ruefully. "Real enlightened campus here, huh? The administration's just about out of the antebellum years."

"Well, they're damned good football players," Howie said, with a shrug and a little laugh. And in that moment Jonah knew they had mistaken him. That he was his friend not because he didn't care but because he didn't know.

It was in that moment, too, that Jonah had decided not to disabuse any of them. Wishing, even then, that he had someone to talk to about it, wanting to discuss it at least with his sister. He understood, now, just how it was that Sophie had been able to get so close to the white girls at Vassar, and he would have liked to have known if she, too, had stumbled into it, seduced before she knew it by the promise of a friend.

But Sophie was gone again—off on one of her mysterious vanishings that would get longer and longer, until they finally culminated in her leaving their house, and the rest of the family altogether once their mother died. Jonah had no one to discuss anything with at all—just his new friends—and so he had let the moment pass, and bound himself inescapably to the lie.

Many times he suspected that they knew. There was one night when they had slipped out after curfew to a notorious local roadhouse, and a white co-ed they had brought along would not leave him alone. She had hung on his every word, sliding her arms up around his neck and pulling him close to her when they danced. Just a short, plain-faced white co-ed in a sweater and skirt—so obviously smitten that it had become an subject of amusement to them all, exchanging humorous looks over her head, making little jokes when the rest of their dates couldn't hear them.

Eventually, though, it had come to annoy Jonah, and he had pulled himself away from the girl's embrace on the dance floor. Going out to sit in the open roadster Howard Marsden had parked by the side of the turnpike, and take a breather. Jonah telling himself he was not amused by their jokes—when in fact he had been all but overcome by the idea of seeing how far he could go with the little white girl, just because he could do it.

But when Jack Leonard had trailed him out a little while later, he had made a joke of it again. Shouting to him "You have to get her off me!" Jack had just laughed, and they had sat for a long time, smoking and talking in the roadster. A little tipsy from the crude bootleg whiskey Howie had brought in his flask. Jonah in the front passenger seat with his legs propped up over the door, Jack in the back, both of them staring up at the stars in the open country sky.

Jack had always been the one of Howard's friends Jonah felt the most at ease with, the one he thought he might really have confided in. A stocky, serious sophomore, with black, slicked-down hair, and olive skin that looked darker than Jonah's in certain lights. Glad to get a laugh from him, Jonah had continued to riff on the girl, joking more and more about her until he finally turned around to face Jack where he sat, his head lolling, in the back of the car.

"Will you just tell her I'm black, so she'll back off?" Jonah said, looking straight at him, even if he was grinning.

Jack Leonard had raised his head then, meeting his eye—and for a long moment they had stared at each other in what faint illumination the moon, and the lights from the roadhouse, had afforded. The smile was frozen on Jonah's face, but he was unable to squeeze another word out of his mouth. Waiting there for two, three beats—until Jack had begun to smile crookedly, too.

"That's it! Tell her I'm black!" He had been able to laugh then, the words coming out in a single whoosh of relief.

"You oughn't even to joke like that," Jack had said mildly, still trying to smile at him. "You never know how something like that can go around."

Jonah had laughed again, and then they were both laughing, and he had put his head back down on the top of the front seat. Laughing a little to himself until he had drifted off right there in the car and the others had come out and found him, still smiling up at the moon.

From that time on, he had made no effort to extricate himself. Reasoning that even if it all came to ruin tomorrow, at least he would have this day. He recognized that it was a young man's thinking—but even now, he relished every minute he had had.

He had done everything with them—and above all with Howie Marsden. Despite his gawky, boyish appearance, he was the most sophisticated person his age that Jonah had ever known. He wore tailored suits and brown tweed jackets, and he knew about girls and cars, and smoked a pipe. He made friends easily, and was liked by both professors and other students. Jonah just liked to hear him talk at night, when the lights were off and they were in their narrow, metal-framed beds across the dorm room from each other. Encouraging him to tell him anything he could think of—about his days at Andover, or his summers sailing out on the Finger Lakes or touring Europe, or any other part of the whole, wide world of Howard Marsden.

"But this must be a terrible bore for you, old man," he would say at last, yawning loudly.

"No. No, it isn't," Jonah would say softly, beneath the blankets in his own bed, trying his hardest not to appear too eager. "It's not a bore at all."

"Tell me something about yourself."

"Oh, tomorrow," Jonah would say then, rolling over. "I'm barely awake."

It was easy enough to keep them from pressing him on his own background. He had hinted only that his reluctance was due to an embarrassing lack of money, or social standing—amazed by his own deftness at it. The rest of them had duly left the subject alone. The closest any of them came to the truth was when they teased him for being so naive after having grown up in the City.

"How do you know that?" Jonah had said too quickly, the hackles going up on the back of his neck, and they had all grinned at him.

"Well, there is the way you talk, old boy—"

"You mean my accent?" he had wondered, realizing that he had never even thought about it. But to the rest he sounded hurt, and they were quick to try to cover it over.

"He must be the son of some Episcopal bishop," Gilly Mackenzie had joked—and Jonah had looked down, smiling, and told them,
"Well, something like that—" while they howled, and pounded him
on the back.

"Oh, a minister's son! But it's true, isn't it?"

"He's probably never been kissed, lads!"

"Ne'er swich liqueur had passed his lips—before last Saturday
night!"

It had been the perfect cover, reasoning that at least one of them
was likely to have some impecunious, high-church cleric in the family, a distant uncle or cousin. Jonah had let them kid him, and make
their assumptions—though he should have known, then, that there
were other traces he had left behind. He was too absorbed with the
other world opening up before him, for it was opening up, and so
what if it wasn't exactly as himself that he was experiencing it?

During the week they studied together in the ponderous, gray
library, made of rock deliberately acid-aged to resemble the stones
of Oxford. Reading English literature and American history, and
German philosophy, and Latin and Greek, and the mandatory Bible
courses called things like Old Testament Times and The Mediterranean at the Time of Christ.

On Fridays and Saturdays they would take the roadster, or the
battered, secondhand Dodge that Howard had found and tooled up
for him after advising him to buy it for a song. Hitting the road-
houses and the hidden, illicit taverns with co-eds, or girls from the
village. Driving all the way into Utica or Syracuse when a big band
was playing at the State Theater, or Loew's Bigtime Vaudeville. Dining at a good hotel restaurant, singing and laughing like madmen
and nipping bootleg whiskey that Howie had somehow obtained from
somewhere. The next morning they would smirk at each other, sitting hungover in chapel, then go out to eat stacks of dollar pancakes
in the village diner, and lionize their exploits from the night before.

And all the time, Howard was giving him useful, unobtrusive
tips on how to dress, or what to say to girls, or how to talk to professors. Teaching him lessons so subtle that Jonah barely understood that he hadn't thought of them himself until much later on.
He had even gotten Jonah to go out for the cross-country team with
him and Andy Miller, and Jonah, who had never done anything
more athletic than the occasional game of stickball in the street,
found to his surprise that he loved the sport.

He wasn't fast enough to win a meet but he had endurance, an ability to dog the heels of the front-runner almost to the very end. He loved the longer, harder practice runs most of all. The sound of his own ragged breath, the feel of his heart pounding, all alone in the woods. Putting in ten miles a day, through the winding hill paths in back of the college. Sometimes he would pause there, at the peak of the path. Separated from his teammates, panting for breath but feeling stronger than he ever had before, his whole body galvanized. He would look back down over the gloomy, gray stones of the college on one side of the ridge, the gabled white, and brown, and red houses of the village on the other, and it would seem to him possible then that he really could get away with it forever. That he could even stay here, become a professor or a dean, or something, and never have to go back to any other life.

On Saturday afternoons, after their morning meets, they would go to the football game when the team was playing at home. Another lark—Howard and Gilly Mackenzie smuggling in flasks under their ridiculous, oversize real raccoon coats. Yelling and cheering raucously, stirring up the whole rooting section just for the fun of it. Jonah laughing and cheering along with the rest of them—until the afternoon he caught Merton Turnbow staring up at them from the sideline, his big shoulders twisted around under the gladiatorial pads beneath his uniform jersey. He was not smiling, his brow creased with doubt, as if suspecting that he was being made fun of—

Which he would, Jonah thought even at the time. Which of course he would, listening for the thinly hidden insult, the barbed taunt—

Jonah always paid close attention to the four colored players— all of them far and away the best players on the team, he noticed to his chagrin. The other three were the fastest men on the field, fleet, elusive backs and flankers, playing positions of sheer physicality. Only Merton was different—a tight end on offense, a linebacker on defense. He ran the team, especially on defense, assessing where the play was likely to develop. Roaming about the field from his linebacker position, looking like a Mayan warrior with his leather helmet tucked down tight over his grim face. Taking out the quarterback on one play, knocking down a pass or leveling the fullback on the next. When he played on offense he would lead crushing sweeps, his big, rangy body cutting down the defensive ends and the cornerbacks one by one as they tried to reach the ball carrier. Going out himself once or twice a game on a trick play to catch a pass, and then literally fighting his way down the field—holding off one tackler after another with brutal straight arms, or churning right through them, his knees pounding like pistons into chests and throats.

That was as close as Jonah got to him, those Saturday afternoons in the stands, until the February of their freshman year. By then he had already gone home and come back from Christmas vacation, and was living almost wholly in a world of his own devising. His confidence growing, the overpowering, gut-clenching fear that had overtaken him at night in bed, or just sitting up in the library— the fear that he would inevitably be discovered—fading away now. Looking back on that time later, he thought that he had no longer been fully aware that he was pretending at all.

His main preoccupation by then was getting a date for the college's winter carnival, the corny, gauzy pinnacle of its winter social season. All of his friends had brought in their dates from women's schools down near the City, or over in Massachusetts. They had offered freely to have a friend brought along for him, too, but he didn't dare go quite that far.

Instead, he had taken a village girl named Isabelle Brinckerhoff, the daughter of the white Baptist minister there. Howard Marsden had introduced him to her, supposedly as a joke because he was such a preacher's son but really, Jonah knew, because he thought she'd be perfect for him—a poised, quiet young woman, with long red hair and green eyes, who on their fifth date had allowed Jonah to kiss her on the mouth.

Despite his lust he hadn't tried to go much further than that, sensing that it would be futile. Contenting himself with being welcomed into her house for Sunday dinner. A big meal, of steaming roast beef or chicken served just after services, just as they always had for the deacons and some of the church mothers, back on Strivers Row. Even the grace her minister father said before the meal was the same. It was clear that he liked Jonah, too. Pleased to have heard that he was the son of a minister—another trace that momentarily alarmed Jonah, although her father never did pry too much into his background, not wanting either his daughter or her beau to think he was pressing them.

They had taken their dates to all of the contrived collegiate mer-
riment of the carnival. The toboggan races, and the ice-skating and
ice-sailing competitions, and intramural hockey games played out in
the open night air on Taylor Lake, where they gathered each spring
for graduation. The lake frozen to a deep, purple-black sheen,
rimmed with torches and small bonfires where they stood watching
the skaters stitching deftly back and forth. The domed sky filled
with brittle white stars, infinitely more in number than the three or
four blurred specks he ever saw in the City's firmament. The smiling faces of his friends red-hued in the torchlight, grinning knowingly at each other. And afterward there would be warm mugs of
cocoa laced with butterscotch, and kisses stolen from Isabelle in the
corners of the field house.

The last night of the carnival he had been on his way to meet her,
and Howard, and the others at the grand cotillion. Trudging up the
same steep path from the village he trained on during the cross-country season, the ground covered with a half foot of snow now instead
of pine needles. He was a little short of breath in his hurry, and the
hard going, his fingers and toes already numb with the cold. But he
had paused to look down from the peak of the path again, when he
got there. Gazing contentedly at the village and the college, laid out
before him like matching picture postcards. The sound of the night's
festivities already, faintly audible below. The pines and the stones and
the gabled roofs were laden with snow, the windows glowing with
the red and orange of fireplaces. The bare, black trees of the campus
wrapped in tiny white Christmas tree lights that cut a path directly
to the door of the gymnasium, where the cotillion would be held.

He could already anticipate all the good things that would tran-
spire that night. The dancing, cheek to cheek against Isabelle's
exquisitely soft face. More hurried kisses with her out back of the
gym. Breathing in the faint hint of a scent she had surreptitiously
put on after she left the house, smelling it on her neck and her
breasts when he placed his head against her bosom. And after that—
all the laughs, all the jokes and pranks, all the stolen drinks with
his friends. All the good fellowship, the togetherness that would
wind up with them arm over shoulder, swaying and singing their
way back to the dormitory in their fine, stiff formal wear, a bunch of
swells out on the town—

His reverie had been broken by the sound of someone coming up
the path from the campus. He had started to descend, embarrassed

to think that anyone might have seen him daydreaming there—when he saw that it was Merton Turnbow. Plowing his way up through the snow as if it was some other team's defensive backfield, but with his head lowered pensively, a stack of books cradled in one of his huge, steam-shovel hands. He looked up only when he was almost upon Jonah, standing mesmerized in the middle of the path. He had started to give a perfunctory nod, and push on—when he looked at Jonah again, and stopped right in front of him.

"Hello," Jonah muttered, making as if to get on his way again. But Merton Turnbow stayed where he was, blocking his path. Looking him over frankly, even insultingly, until Jonah was unable to stay silent any longer.

"You're not going down to the dance? I'm sure you'd be welcomed—" he started to babble—but Turnbow cut him off.

"What do you think you're doing?"

"I was just saying—"

"I said, what do you think you're doing?" he only repeated, his voice cracking through the cold air. Making it clear that he was not about to consider moving until he got an answer to his question.

"I don't know what you're talking about," Jonah said, then reached out ludicrously with his hand. "I'm Jonah Dove—"

"I know who you are. 'I'm sure you'd be welcomed.' Jesus jumped-up Christ. I was wondering how much you really believed this. Now I know."

"You don't know anything about me," Jonah said, defiant, though any pretense he had tried to maintain between them was gone now.

He tried to push past him, the big man's body as hard and unyielding as stone against his own. Nonetheless, Turnbow gave way, seemingly about to let him pass. Only at the last moment did he reach out and grab Jonah's arm—squeezing the hand that he had just been offered until the bones rolled. In one quick motion he pulled off the lamb-skin glove Jonah was wearing, then clamped his own enormous hand over his. Jonah looking down at where he held him, Turnbow's bare hand as cold and as hard as an iron vice. The color of his skin all but indistinguishable from Jonah's own.

"You're no different from me," he said, though his voice was softer now—almost wondering for a moment. All Jonah could do was blink at him.

"Whatta you think is gonna happen?" he asked. "Huh? Whatta you think is gonna happen when they find out?"

"Leave me alone, I don't know you!" Jonah had shouted, into the ringing stillness, and Merton Turnbow had let him go without another word. Leaving him to hurry blindly on down the path toward the festivities.

He had gone on down to the dance, and it had been as sweet a night as he had expected, even if he did feel as if the bottom of his stomach had been kicked out, any moment he found himself alone. Half-expecting Merton to appear at any moment and expose him. Waiting to hear that he had been discovered, to see the first dubious glances directed his way all the rest of that week, and into the next.

But there had been nothing. No strange looks, none of the faint murmurings of rumor reaching back to him. Instead, once the snows melted, there had been picnics up in the hills with Isabelle and his friends. It was a warm, early spring and Howard, of course, had found a perfect upper pasture, abandoned with so many of the local farms. There they had hiked on Saturday afternoons and lain out in the early grass, reveling in the new sun. There had been much laughing and drinking, and Howard twirling a loose straw ostentatiously between his teeth, like some local, hayseed farmboy.

One afternoon, shortly before the Easter break, they had gone up to their pasture, as they referred to it now, and had a meal of cheese, and spring apples, and ham sandwiches, washed down with bottles of good Rhine wine that Howie had purloined from his family's cellar. The day was very warm, it was a late Easter that year, and afterward most of them had drifted off to sleep in the grass. Only Jonah and Howard had stayed awake—and Jonah so dizzy with the unaccustomed wine that he had to lie down, his hands folded contentedly under his head.

"Come on now, level with me, Jonah," Howard had said suddenly, and he had found himself instantly on his guard again. Propping himself up on his elbows, his breath slowing. Thinking wildly that this was it—that he knew—and wanting to absorb the very last moment of his new life. He had stared silently at the white boy beside him, and waited for the axe to fall, thinking how normal everything still seemed. Howie sitting there with his same easy self-confidence, arms hooked around his knees. Actual straw and loose grass now threading his limp yellow hair, the tweedy herringbone jacket with the elbow patches he was wearing.

"The truth now, Jonah. Remember, you're with friends, even if it may be difficult for you to admit this."

"Yes, Howard?" he asked at last, determined to keep his voice from quavering. Readying himself for the words.

"You've never been to Europe. Have you?"

"No," Jonah answered, the word seeming to come out of some-one else's detached mouth. His own already full of the excuses and apologies he was set to make. The hillside around them seeming to revolve in his shock and relief, even if he kept talking like a more or less normal person—

"No, I never have."

"I knew it!" Howard said, turning to grin gleefully at him. "I knew you hadn't! That's why you have to! You, especially!"

"Have to go to Europe?"

"You can come with me, and the pater and mater. They're a bore, of course, but once we're over there we can strike off on our own. They'd feel very reassured to know I had somebody along—par-ticularly once they get a load of you, the minister's son!"

"Well, I don't know—"

"C'mon, it'll be the nuts! We always take two weeks in London, then go to the continent. We can see Paris with them, then go off on our own. Germany, Switzerland, down to Italy... Damn, think of the girls we'll meet there!"

Howie whispering excitedly now, so as not to wake the others. And seeing that, Jonah had to ask the question that had already started to form, even so soon after his near deadly shock. Unable to resist it—

"But why me? Especially?"

"What?" Howard laughed out loud. "Why not you?"

"No, you said 'You'—that is, I—especially, should go to Europe," Jonah recounted clumsily. "What did you mean? Why me, especially?"

"Oh! That's easy. Because out of all of us, you're the serious one," Howard said, sweeping a hand back to indicate the others, sleeping in the field.

"The serious one?"

"The serious intellect, the best mind," Howard told him. He was still smiling, but Jonah could see that his face was perfectly sincere.

"You're the real thinker, old man—the one who really has the chance to go places, do great things. Surely you see that? The rest of us are all pretty frivolous—compared to you."

"Aw, scram!" Jonah told him, grinning sheepishly, throwing some torn-up grass at his friend—but so proud that he wanted to get up and shout. He wanted to wake up all the rest of them, Isabelle first, and tell them what Howard had said. Wanted to run back to the dormitory and call up his parents on the hall phone to tell them—if there had only been some way to convey it, some way to get around the fact that this great honor came from his all-white friends, who thought he was one of them.

Instead, he had followed up the tossed grass by giving Howard a shove, and Howard had pushed him back. The two of them laughing and tussling for a little while in the pasture, before their yelps woke up the rest of the party, and they all smiled and shouted in turn to see the two of them going at it.

That had been the last, good day. The last day they had together, before Jonah had had to take the train back through the wet new greenery and the rushing spring streams of upstate. Making his way back down to the City for Holy Week—when he planned to first break it to his parents that he would be going to Europe that summer. Rehearsing how he would tell them so, the whole trip down, without revealing *everything*.

He knew it would not be easy. He had never been very good at withholding anything from his father, and he thought that the simplest plan would be the best—just tell them, straight out, that his roommate had invited him to go with his family to Europe. But maybe he should leave out the family. That was bound to raise questions, he knew. His parents wondering at just who these enlightened white folks would be. Wanting to avoid that, above all. An exchange of happy phone calls, and letters—maybe even an invitation to the church, or to come up to Strivers Row for a meal before they sailed from the West Side docks—

No. Better to mention only his friend. And that he would meet him there, over in France. Bring it all up on Easter Sunday night, just before he left to go back to the college. Say he had this opportunity, that it wasn't even definite yet. Then, as the date got much closer, he could say his friend and his family had already left, that they had booked his passage, left him his steamship ticket. There would be no need even to see him down to the docks, though he didn't suppose he could quite get away with that.

It still had plenty of holes, but he thought it could work. Jonah both pleased and appalled at his newfound ability to deceive. He knew that his parents would want to believe it, which was his main advantage—that they would want to think that he had made plenty of close new white friends. Off to Europe for the summer with his college roommate—that would be just the sort of thing they would love telling the congregation.

By the time the train reached Penn Station he was ebullient, and they had greeted him rapturously. His father, it seemed to him, was especially overjoyed to see him. Lonely for his presence, their daily talks up in the vestry, he had thumped Jonah's back and hugged him impulsively all the way up to Harlem.

From nearly the moment he got off the train, too, his father was after him to deliver his first sermon from the pulpit. It was an ambition for his son that he had first brought up when Jonah was still a junior in high school—and one that he had always resisted. Jonah unsure that he really wanted to follow his father in the pulpit, and not wanting to give the old man any false hope. He was less convinced than ever that it was his destiny when he had stepped down off the train from Utica—but so giddy at the prospect of sailing to Europe in less than two months' time with Howard Marsden (and his family!) that he had finally agreed. Thinking of it as a final gift to the old man, letting him coach him throughout the whole week, suggesting familiar texts and approaches. Going over the very rudiments of the sermon, its rhythm, and the different twists and catches, that would snare the congregation—a better practical education in preaching in one week, he would realize later, than he would receive in two years at the Angel Factory down in Pennsylvania.

For all that Jonah thought of it as a gesture, a propitiary offering to him, he knew that his father dreamed of more. He was already trying to make his debut as auspicious as possible, scheduling it for the ten o'clock service on Easter Sunday itself—the grand culmination of the whole sacred year. Even Jonah recognized a coup when he saw it, the old man obviously hoping to overwhelm any lingering reservations of the diaconate over his successor through the sheer passion and rapture of the event.

Jonah went along with it, nevertheless. Sure as he was that he was through with the whole life they led, a life up in Harlem. That he would be—what? A professor, perhaps. Maybe even at a great European university, in Heidelberg, or at the Sorbonne. Teaching whatever he wished, making a name for himself. Doing whatever the big, serious thing was that Howard Marsden had thought he could do.

So he had gone along with his father. Trying to make it one great, last present to him, to them both. The theme they had agreed upon was a familiar one, working off a text from the Psalms, 68:31: "Princes shall come out of Egypt, and Ethiopia shall hasten to stretch forth her hands unto God"—a verse daring, but direct, in its blatant ambition. His father keeping it short, for his first effort, carefully gauging what he can handle. No more than twenty minutes, at the outside—provided he did as his father asked and built slowly, powerfully to his climax.

For Jonah was the prince—there was to be no doubt about that. It was his claim to the pulpit, made in his own words. Before college, Jonah would have been too unsure to make any such claim, even for a morning. But now, knowing the real destiny that awaited him, he joined in willingly, lovingly, savoring the time alone with his father again.

And when the day came it had been as splendid and sunny an Easter morning as anyone could remember, his father nearly dancing with delight at this augury. The church overflowing with lilies and gladiolas, the windows flung open against the unseasonable warmth. Every seat was taken, with people standing at the back of the balconies. The pews dotted with the church mothers' spectacular new Easter hats of every possible color, and elegance, and jaw-dropping gaudiness. The choir sharp and joyous—their voices, too, seemingly buoyed by the glorious day, the yellow sunlight streaming in through the open windows.

And then, after his father had spoken powerfully and briefly in introduction, Jonah had strode up to the pulpit for the first time. Dressed in his white and purple-trimmed Easter robe, his best black suit underneath, his hair carefully cropped the day before. His father waiting until he got to the very foot of the pulpit—and only then, very slowly and significantly, climbing down and making sure to grasp his son's hand at the bottom of the stairs. A flash-bulb went off at that moment, startling him. Another camera or two clicking—the photographers from the church newsletter, and the Amsterdam Star-News and the New York Age all carefully, brazenly capturing the moment for posterity, his father having let the news of the new prince leak out.

Yet even that had only amused Jonah, as remote as he now was from it all. He had climbed up to the pulpit, to what suddenly seemed like a great height to him, even as often as he had sneaked up into his father's spot as a child. He was aware, now, of all the eyes upon him, the heads and backs leaning forward. Aware of his father watching intently from one side, down by the altar, his mother in the front row in her best purple skirt and vest, and the fine, frilly white blouse, tears already rolling from her eyes. Once ascended, he had dramatically pulled the text of his sermon out of his robe—and dropped it back on the chair behind him. An old trick of his father's, and Jonah had to smile as he pulled it off—for looking down on the pulpit lectern he saw another copy of the sermon, typed up in duplicate by Delphine and carefully planted there, just in case.

The whole church was silent, the short interlude played by the organist dying away. The tension was palpable in the sanctuary, but he had to struggle to suppress a laugh. Determined to do it right, as a final gift for his father and mother—all of their careful planning that he knew he would soon betray.

He had them in his hand, he knew, right from the first word. It was the most confident he had ever felt in a pulpit, even to this day. His timing was perfect, following his father's instructions in every detail. The congregation rising and falling on cue with his every inflection, every change of pace.

He knew they were taken aback, at first, by the sheer audacity of the sermon, the claiming of the throne, he could hear their sharp intakes of breath, and murmured confusion. But as he proceeded their testimony rose steadily. At first only the reliable, repetitive old-lady responses, echoing from the back pews—"Mmm-hmmm." "Well. Welllll." "Make it plain! Make it plain!" Then building steadily, beginning to grow in volume and intensity. "That's right, that's right!" "Praise Jesus! Praise Him!" The rhythm growing, that old Baptist whine of his father's spilling out through his mouth, until Jonah had to hold himself rigid to keep from physically slapping the great Bible in time. His words picking up the beat instead, pounding it out, until there was no difference between the words and the music, the music and the message. The people standing in the pews, swaying and clapping and moaning as he surged to his crescendo, shouting out, almost insensible:

"And the princes shall come out of Egypt! And Ethiopia shall stretch out her hands to God, and God will hear her at last and redeem her!" The organist and the choir bursting in right on cue, one delirious beat after his last word.

Precious Lord, take my hand,
Lead me on, let me stand,
I am tired, I am weak, I am worn;
Through the storm, through the night,
Lead me on to the light—

Then Jonah was walking down the pulpit steps again, through the pure yellow sunlight that poured from the windows. His father embracing him at the foot of the pulpit again, hugging him ecstatically as more flashbulbs popped; his mother sobbing openly. The waves of cheering and stamping of feet washing over him, even over the organ music.

He had stood and sung the hymn with the rest of them, then sat down in his place by the side of the altar. He was unable to keep from smiling there, still overwhelmed by what he had done, and the response he had received. The church still buzzing from the sermon, a sense of jubilation all around him. For all the years since, he had wondered if, in the end, that response would have swayed him—if, in the end, it would have maneuvered him into his father's pulpit, and convinced him to throw over all his other, wild dreams of Europe, and professorships, and big things. The question, forever rendered moot, of course, by the fact that at that moment—at the very end of his first sermon in his father's pulpit—Jonah had looked down the center aisle, and seen his roommate, Howard Marsden, and all his other friends from school standing in the church-house door.

CHAPTER THIRTEEN

MALCOLM

He had barely been able to wait until that Friday, when he would see her again. He had run more quickly than ever through his rounds, raggedly jotting down his betting slips. He even wondered if he should buy her something, though he had no idea what. But when he called her that afternoon, as instructed, she told him to bring her flowers.

"Sure, baby, that's what I was thinkin'," he crooned into the phone, but she interrupted him.

"That's not what I mean," she said sharply. "Go to Cellupica Florists, on Christopher Street, and buy two dozen false jasmine. You got that?"

"What? Baby—"

"Have them put in a box. A long box. With a ribbon on it, and a note," she cut him off. "Have them write on it, 'From your greatest admirer.' Signed, 'Jonah.' You got that?"

"Sure, baby, sure. False jasmine. Who's Jonah?"

"Never mind. Just see that you do it. Exactly that way," she said, telling him the address on Cornelia Street—then warning him again:

"Remember—you don't bring those flowers, you're not getting in."

He did as she told him, going first to the narrow, green-awninged flower shop, in the first floor of a slouching Italian tenement. He walked into the silver-glazed lobby of her apartment house with the box in plain sight, balanced awkwardly over one arm, but he had not taken two steps into the lobby when the uniformed doorman was on him—leaping up from his stool behind the front desk, striding forward. Holding up one big white-gloved hand to stop Malcolm in his tracks.

"Whoe-ho! Where you think you're goin', bub?" he asked, gesturing impatiently at the box. "Who those for?"

"Uh, for Miranda—" he started to say, then stopped abruptly, realizing that he didn't even know her last name.

"Uh-huh," the doorman said, nodding his head knowingly.

"Lemme guess. I bet it's from Jonah again," he smirked. "Yeah, he got it bad for her."

He was a beefy, barrel-chested man, his pungent body odor soaking through the thick green doorman's uniform in the summer heat. He had very pale skin, and bristling red-and-gray hair that stuck out from under his cap, and from his nostrils, and that reminded Malcolm of Mr. Kaminska, back in Michigan.

"All right, it's 5C," the doorman told him, jerking his head toward the equally shiny silver-coated elevators. Scrutinizing him more closely as he did.

"You're a new one, ain't ya? You can go up through here this time, but from now on you come an' go through the service entrance, in the basement. Got it, Mac?"

"Uh-huh."

The doorman stared at him sharply for any sign of suspected insolence. Only then did he move aside, Malcolm having all he could do to keep hold of himself as he proceeded to the elevator, deliberately not looking back.

"Hey, you guys really should wear a uniform," he heard the doorman call after him. "So we'd know."

She greeted him at the door, wearing a long, yellow dressing gown. Letting him stand there while she looked him over, the big white box of flowers crooked in his arm.

"So now you know how it is," she said, her face expressionless.

She pushed the door open wider and he stepped inside, throwing the box down on a chair. Pacing around the room, barely able to speak.

"A delivery boy? That how you make me come up here?" Malcolm said, unable to contain himself any longer.

"Did you bring the false jasmine?" was all she said. Pushing the door open wider so he could step inside, where he hurled the box down on a chair. She picked it up, and slid the bright red ribbon off it, pulling out the long-stemmed, star-shaped flowers—white-budded on the outside, yellow at their heart—while he paced around her living room, sulking.

"Do you know what the rent is here? Do you think they would let somebody like you just come on up in the elevator?" she told him coolly. Her whole demeanor as hard as it had been before she'd agreed to see him—her face as hard as she showed it to the other men who ogled her when she was out with West Indian Archie.

"Someone like me? Goddamn, girl! The way you talk—"

"Yes," she said, cutting him off. Saying the words simply, without any obvious irony or emotion of any kind: "Someone like you. A colored boy."

"If that's the way you feel about it—" he said, taking a step toward the door. But she only scoffed at him.

"Don't play the fool. You know that's not the way I feel about it. And you know it, too. So why do I have to paint you a goddamned picture?"

"Man!" he said, shaking his head. Trying to act as if he were leaving again, but unable to keep from smiling and shaking his head. "You're a killer, you know that?"

"Uh-huh," she said, turning her back on him and attending to her flowers.

Not sure of what to say or do, he walked around her apartment again. Really taking it in for the first time, running his hands over the plush, blue and peach furniture, perusing its tasteful fixtures, the RCA Victor phonograph, and the sleek, wood-covered standalone Emerson radio in the corner; the jackal-headed ashtray that looked as if it were in mid-run. He remembered what Sammy the Pimp had told him about how you could turn a woman out, by just taking all the things she owned.

And what would keep a woman like this from just getting more? he thought. What would ever keep her from having something to fall back on?

He was most impressed with the rows of bookshelves that ran all the way across one wall, from the floor to the ceiling. They made him feel almost giddy, the way he had back in the Pleasant Cove School library, or in Prof. Toussaint's store—like finding a treasure trove. He squinted through the dim light to read the titles, and the names of so many authors he had never heard of: DuBois, Washington, Douglass—His eyes lighting at last upon a shelf full of holy books—a Talmud, the Bible; the Holy Koran. The last title making him feel both excited and guilty, remembering his books about the mysterious brown man, left neglected in his room these weeks since he had been working for Archie. Elijah had called it the greatest book in the world, the Koran, but he had never read it, had never gone back to any of the great things he was going to do since he had been given the chance to see her again—

"What are these?" Miranda asked, frowning, pulling out the violets from where they lay beneath the false jasmine.

"Those are from me, baby," he told her, looking away, embarrassed now to see them in comparison with the graceful, long-boughed white-and-yellow flowers.

"I told them to put 'em in for me, not any Jonah. Who is this Jonah, anyway? What's he got to do wit' you?" he asked, his voice rising defensively.

"He's nobody," she said quickly, picking up the bunch of violets. "It's just a little joke. Who would ever name their child Jonah, anyhow?"

She put her cigarette down in the jackal ashtray, still staring at the violets in her hand. To his surprise, he saw that she was blinking back tears.

"Oh, you boy," she said, shaking her head. "You did this on your own?"

"I could buy you a dozen a those, every day," he told her, his enthusiasm rising as he saw how she looked at them. "I could get you five dozen. I'm makin' good money now. Once I hit the numbers I can get a little stake, set up my own bank, or buy a club. You could come sing in it, too, an—"

He realized he was talking more and more rapidly, but he couldn't help it, swinging his arms around as he told her all the things he was going to do, and acquire.

"I could get us a short, too, so we could go out drivin'. Maybe I could take you out to Hollywood in it, take a screen test. They got lotta singers out there—"

He noticed then that she was walking slowly toward him, across the room. Trying to smile her small, amused smile, but not succeeding, the tears still in her eyes. She went right up to him as he continued to talk—taking hold of his arms, pulling them in around herself.

"Tell me that you love me, Red," she said, her body against his, looking up at him and making herself smile again.

"I told you—"

He was momentarily confused, interrupted in the middle of his splendid dreams spilling out in the middle of her living room.

"You don't have to mean it. Just tell me that you love me, and that you never met anyone like me."

"I never did," he said quickly, then speaking more slowly, his voice strained but serious. Glad that they were alone now, in her cool, dark apartment, where he could speak more freely to her than he had to anyone in his life.

"I told you already," he said. "I never met any girl like you—"

"Any white girl, you mean," she said, her face still smiling and teasing, but her words serious.

"I mean, any girl at all," he said, firmly but not belligerently. Sensing her sudden vulnerability. Feeling headily in charge for the first time since he had met her. Continuing to talk, choosing his words slowly as he gently pulled his arms away and hugged her all the way to him now, caressing her back and thighs and bottom with his hands, swaying back and forth with her as if they were moving to a slow song.

"There's no one like you nowhere," he told her, carefully brushing her hair back from her ear and speaking quietly to her. Following his words with small kisses down her neck that he could feel made her shudder, and lean in closer to him. One part of his mind still unbelieving and ecstatic that he could be moving so smoothly, even as he continued to make her tremble in his arms. And as he did, every moment of his exclusion and his hopelessness came back to him. Smiling as his third-grade class jeered at him, standing on the porch, unseen, as his mother and father flew out the screen door, cursing each other. Looking into other people's homes with the newspaper bag under his arm, watching his breath come up in small white puffs, the only sign he existed; forced back along the gym wall at the dance by that wall of boys—All of those thoughts and images, every one of them banished now, dissolved in her acceptance.

"There's no one like you at all. You're the first person I ever met, made me feel like I wasn't alone—"

"That's good, Red. That's real good," she said at last, and slowly pulled herself away from him.

"It's not hypin' you, baby," he said truthfully, but she had already strode over to the door of her bedroom. Standing there, waiting for him. Looking back at him with another one of those sad half smiles on her face that he never would be able to figure out.

"I'm not—"

"I know you're not, baby. That's why I feel the way I do," she said, and hushed him when he tried to question her again. Still posing at the entrance to her bedroom, needling him, tempting him.

"What do you want, Red? Just tell me what you want."

"Show me," he breathed, looking at her there.

"What?"

"Show me all yourself. Right there."

"All right," she said, and grinned happily now, carefully turning off the lamp next to her first. Malcolm realizing for the first time why it was so dark, the shades in her apartment all half drawn—the world at dusk inside.

But he kept his eyes on her. Still grinning, she had untied the sash of her dressing gown, letting it slide to the floor—and all at once she was naked there before him. She wore nothing at all underneath save for a thin silver chain with a dime on it—a child's charm—hooked around one ankle. Half-turning demurely, teasingly, in the doorway, so he saw her right breast there in profile, the slight, soft swell of her stomach, and her swayed back. Her long, curvy legs, leading up to the surprisingly dark hair of her sex, half-concealed—

He went to her again. Holding her in his arms, feeling the whole smooth sweep of her body against him, somehow more exciting because he was still clothed. Kissing her on the mouth, again and again, moving his hands up and down her—and she let him. Free to roam as he would, over every inch of her, taking his time, until her breath came in short, hurried breaths.

"Let's go inside," she said hurriedly, in between his kisses. She led him into another, dusky room that seemed even plusher, and smelled deeply of her scent. Miranda unbuttoning his shirt as she did, sliding out his belt, and kissing him still, all over his face and head and neck.

"Come here," she said to him, sitting back on the shiny satin bedcover. Beckoning to him, her legs sliding back and forth over each other, reaching out a hand for him when he hesitated. But he waited, just wanting to watch her there for a moment, still happy to be in control, at least a little.

"Why? What you want me to do?" he asked, teasing her, but

knowing that he really did just want to watch her there for a while
more. Still amazed that he could have her, the most beautiful thing
he had ever known, there on the bed before him. He wanted to do
everything he could for her, to chase that sad little smile from her
face—to see through all her mysteriousness, her hidden moods, and
rescue her from Archie and anything else in her life that made her
this way. Before it was too late. To help her before it was too late,
the way it had been with her.

"Come here!"

"Why? What you gonna do to me?" he pretended to tease, savoring that one more moment, looking at her.

"You might call the cops, if the lights turn blue. Come here."

They made love, and dozed on each other, and made love again, all
through the sweltering late afternoon, and early evening. When she
finally turned on the light by her bed, he felt as though he might be
drunk, or at least hungover. His head was groggy, his body weightless, right down to his toes. Miranda was lying with her head on
his chest, her face turned away from him; only the top of her lovely
straight brown hair visible. He stroked her head, and then her body.
Feeling himself readying again, but not rushing it; as eye-opening
as their first time had been, this was so much better.

"But you must've been in love before," she said, her words so
faint that he could barely hear them at first.

"What's that now?"

"I said, you must've been in love before."

"I told you, baby. I never felt like this 'bout anyone before—"

"There must've been somebody. White or black, there must've
been somebody," she said, turning to look up at him again. Her hair
magnificently tousled in the bedclothes, but her face composed and
knowing once more. "I know you too well, you're too kind for there
not to have been somebody."

"No. There never was," he said shortly, so startled by her compliment that he had to keep himself from choking up.

"Maybe not. Maybe nothing like you are now," she conceded,
smiling sweetly at him, looking almost embarrassed herself. "But
somebody you thought you did then."

"No. C'mon!" he shouted, as she thrust her hand out, tickling
him, making him twist away from her on the bed before he could
wrestle her down again.

"C'mon, baby. Tell me! I'll be nice to you!" she said, out of breath beneath him.

"I know you will," he said, but he let his hands slip from her wrists, letting her pull him down on her. Afterward, before they fell back asleep, she had tried to make her tell him again, but even Malcolm knew better than to tell one woman about another. That didn't mean, though, that he hadn't thought on her, even as Miranda slept against him, her head resting peacefully in the crook of his arm. Thinking all about Laura, and Boston, and how green and foolish he had been then—as if it had all been a long time ago instead of a few short months.

He had met her up on the Hill, in Roxbury, a place where nothing was just what it seemed. She had walked into Townsend's Drug-store, where his sister had gotten him a job behind the counter, jerking sodas for eighteen dollars a week. He had noticed her at once, looking so beautiful and poised in her neat gray pleated skirts, her modest sweaters. Laura, with her large brown eyes, and her soft voice, and the proud way she held herself, her bearing reminding him of no one in the world so much as his mother.

He had come to Boston in the first place because of Ella, his half-sister, who didn't look at all like his mother. Malcolm had been struck at once by how much thicker, and darker, and healthier than Louise she looked, when she had come to visit them in Michigan. She was a heavyset woman, solid as a bowling ball, always trundling around the house acting as if she was in charge of something, because she was over thirty and had been married. One day, when she was at the stove boiling water, she had even threatened to scald his brother Philbert if he did not obey her, though he was a grown man by then, and the champion of his boxers' gym. When she actually reached for the pan, Philbert hit her with a right uppercut so quick and hard that it dropped her to her knees—but Malcolm had been impressed by how she quickly got back up, still giving orders.

And Ella had talked to him as no one had since Mr. Maynard Allen, or Mrs. Swerlein. She was always going on about how she owned houses in Boston, and was a businesswoman, and that if she could become rich as white folks, they all could do it, on account of their West Indian blood. Most of his brothers and sisters hadn't been able to abide her, working day and night as it was just to keep the house from crumbling around their heads. But Malcolm had listened, and believed; even let her coax out of him his secret desire to be a lawyer—the first and only time he had confided that to anyone besides Mr. Kaminska, back in Mason.

"You gonna be a lawyer, then you be the best lawyer there is," she had ordered him, in the bellow that was her usual tone of voice. "You could even be president, you set your mind to it!"

The idea that anyone would have such matter-of-fact confidence in what he could be captivated him, much more than the thought of actually becoming a lawyer. He had traveled for two days by Greyhound bus to get to her home on Harrishof Street, arriving rumpled and exhausted, only to have Ella make him stand in the foyer for half an hour while she ripped him apart over his hair and his clothes, and how he spoke and acted, and lectured him on her house rules.

"I don' wanna catch you makin' time wit' any low-life Negroes from down the Town! I hope you be meetin' some of the nice young people your age, from up here on the Hill!"

He had been awed by her house, when he finally got inside it, by the framed pictures on the wall, and whole cabinets full of good china, and glasses. His own room was just a sliver of space under the attic eaves, the roof beams just above his bed. It was freezing in the winter, and suffocating as the spring turned into summer. But it was his own, at least, and Ella was a real Georgia woman in the kitchen, fixing meals of ham hocks and collards, fried fish and sweet potatoes and cornbread that filled even him. And in the weeks and months that followed, he did everything he could to live by her rules. Even duly confessing, scribbling notes to report on own transgressions before he went out:

"I broke three cups. I know I'm going to get killed, but I didn't break anything else."

She talked about the Hill they lived on with a reverence Malcolm had heard other people reserve for God, or their minister. She was always telling him how lucky they were to live among the Four Hundred of Boston colored society—the best-off, oldest, most cultured and well-bred Negroes in the city, whom he came to understand she was not yet part of, but was set on joining. Each morning she would point out to him the stiff-necked, older Negro men who walked by her house on their way to work: "You see him? He's in the law. He's in government. He's in finance..." Dressed like ambassadors in their pinstriped suits and white collars, a newspaper tucked under one arm, their chins lifted high.

Ella had their wives and daughters over as often as she could for dinners, or even teas, openly courting their acceptance. Malcolm could not deny that each of them was possessed of an immense, undeniable dignity, and for a time he had shared in her aspirations. On Sunday mornings he would listen to the slow, stately hymns that issued from the windows of their Unitarian and Congregationalist churches—noting approvingly how little they resembled the shouting and moaning that emanated from his father's old Baptist congregations, or his mother's Seventh Day Church, and he thought that these were Negroes who knew how to behave like human beings.

But before long he had begun to notice the lunch buckets the men carried in their free hands, the rolled-up work clothes carefully hidden under their copies of the Boston Evening Transcript. Discovering as he did that not one of them, for all their airs, was anything grander than a janitor at a downtown bank, a messenger for some bond house. That they were an aristocracy of postmen and Pullman porters, shoeshine men and waiters, and live-in cooks who talked at them in the broad-r'ed, Brahmin accents of their employers, insinuating knowingly, "I'm with an old family."

Their children spurned him, too. That was still before Malcolm had been transformed, and they laughed at how his arms and ankles protruded, scarecrowlike, from the once beautiful apple green suit; at how country his hair looked, all nappy and ungreased. He was embarrassed all over again, just as he had been back in school in Lansing—sticking his chin right into their Hill-boy faces when they laughed a little too close or too near, making the hardest face he could and demanding, "What did you say?"

He had to see them every day, once Ella made him take the job jerking sodas at Townsend's. Working there for a nice old couple named Berlant, who were impressed by his attitude and his energy. Taking the orders of sleep-in maids who told him that they lived on Beacon Hill, and serving women in hospital cafeterias who wore cat-fur stoles around their necks, and called themselves dietitians. The high school girls who turned their faces away when he tried to talk to them, or who coaxed him into singing along with Louis Jourdan on the jukebox before they burst into uncontrollable laughter, then ran out the door screeching.

He spent as much time as he could by himself. As he learned to negotiate the subways, and trolleys, he explored more and more of the greater city around them. Gawking at the big white hotels and restaurants downtown. Hanging around North and South Stations where he watched all the people coming and going from their trains, the families reuniting with each other. Other times, when he had no money at all to spend, he might just wander through the Common. Staring at the monument of the Massachusetts 54th Regiment across from the statehouse, the rows of solemn Negro soldiers, marching determinedly forward with guns on their shoulders; their fierce white commander, Colonel Shaw, riding on his horse, high above them.

Then Laura had come in to the drugstore. She was serene and beautiful, a tall girl who looked taller because of the way she held herself. He saw the resemblance to his mother at once, noted that she even had her long eyelashes, and light skin. She didn't sit and giggle with the other Hill girls, but seemed genuinely unaware of anyone or anything around her—diving avidly, rapturously back into the books she always carried with her as soon as she sat down. The first time he had worked up the courage to say anything to her, he hadn't believed he could think of nothing better than her fountain selection. Yet he had said it anyway—trying to keep his voice down so the snickering girls at the other end of the counter couldn't hear him.

"I'm sorry, what did you say?" she asked softly. Those large brown eyes dancing. The subtle slope of her breasts rising gracefully as she leaned toward him over the counter, until he was almost unable to repeat himself.

"I said, you always get a black-an'-white frappe. Why don't you try somethin' different sometime?" he mumbled, smiling stupidly. "Maybe a banana split."

He thought it was certainly the most foolish thing one human being had ever said to another. But she had laughed and smiled at him, her face guileless and friendly, until he had wanted to lean down and kiss her right there.

"Well, maybe I should let you make me one," she had allowed, in that same soft, quiet voice, and after that he always began to make a banana split the moment she came through the door.

He found better things to say to her, too. He had discovered that her favorite subject was algebra, and that she wanted to be a scientist, and with much trepidation he had told her in turn that he wanted to be a lawyer. But she had only laughed happily, nodding her head.

"Why not, Malcolm? Why not?"

That much about her was different from his mother. How freely and happily she laughed. Her eyes shining—

She had agreed to go out with him, and they had started taking long walks around the neighborhood together after school—Malcolm delighted to see the other Hill boys staring at them together, though she never seemed to notice. She was his first real girlfriend, and she took his breath away whenever he first saw her—coming into the drugstore, or skipping down the steps of her house while he waited for her. He cut his hair, and tried to dress better for her, and sternly reminded himself before every time he was to meet her not to act foolish, but to behave like a gentleman.

He felt good talking to her, and being around her, but he was afraid of her, too—afraid that he might spoil her, or anger her when he so much as touched her. Approaching her like he did all of Ella's fine things, amazed by her but fearful that his clumsiness would just wreck everything. On Saturday afternoons he took her down to see the double feature at the Loews State, sitting next to her in the dark, cavernous theater. It was widely known as a perfect petting spot, but the furthest he had ever gone was to put an arm clumsily around her shoulders, or to hold her exquisite smooth hand for a few minutes, achingly aware of how clammy his own was.

She lived with her grandmother, who insisted that Laura be in by supper. Her face puckered in disapproval whenever she saw Malcolm. She would not even invite him in when he brought Laura home, so he was only able to glimpse a brown, dimly lit parlor from the doorway; the room filled with crucifixes, and pillows embroidered with lines from the Psalms, and pictures of Jesus' suffering white face turned to Heaven. It was just as well by him. He couldn't blame her grandmother, he wanted to protect Laura from everything out there himself, and he rushed to get her home when they were running late.

Nonetheless, they had begun to stray farther from the Hill, and Roxbury, Laura taking him to places he had yet to discover on his explorations. One afternoon they had ridden the T all the way out to Cambridge, and walked through the Harvard Yard, holding hands. Malcolm staring up at the imposing brick buildings as she pointed them out to him—telling him excitedly at one point, "Look, that's the Harvard School of Law!"

"Uh-huh."

"Malcolm, there's no reason you can't pick up where you are and become a lawyer, just like your sister says. Maybe right here," she said, responding to the doubt in his voice, smiling at him with her large, hopeful eyes.

"Yeah, sure. Why not?" he said, and tried to smile at her. Thinking of all it would take for him to become a lawyer, what it would take to please Laura, to live up to what she wanted him to be. He tried to picture them married, him going off to a courtroom every day—gazing down at her pretty, guileless face below him. But before that, he wondered how he could ever do what she expected, going back to some Hill high school, getting his diploma—dressing and acting like all those kids who came in to taunt him in Townsend's?

And if he failed, becoming—what? Another one of those pretend men Ella watched worshipfully on the way out to work, pretending to be a lawyer, a doctor?

"I'm sure your sister would help you," Laura continued in her soft, coaxing voice. "She told me she would. She said she would take in laundry, if it meant helping you become a lawyer!"

"That so?" he said, apprehensive—still trying to smile for Laura, and make her think that he wanted nothing more.

He was flattered that they had discussed his future between them, but not shocked, knowing Ella as he did. When he had brought Laura home, his sister had all but fainted over her. Swooning around, rushing to set tea and cake before her—cooing over each example of Laura's impeccable manners, ecstatic to see him with such a nice Hill girl. And Laura, as was her way, had not been haughty or high hat with his sister, joking and talking with her as if they were old friends. He had sat and watched them, smiling nervously at first, but able to see these two women taking up his whole future in their hands between them.

Yet he couldn't help but wonder what that might mean. By that day at Harvard, he had already seen that Ella, like all her friends on the Hill, was not exactly what she seemed. He had noticed that she still wore her layers and layers of bulky clothing, even in the mildest spring weather, and one day when she hadn't expected him to be at home, he had watched her let herself in through the kitchen door and pull one item after another out of her pockets. A small can of stewed tomatoes, a quarter pound of chuck chop; a few cents' worth of cold cuts, some penny candy, a stick of butter. More and more groceries coming out of one hidden pocket after another like some kind of circus clown act.

Malcolm hadn't known what to say to her, so he had just walked softly away. At first he had thought bitterly that she must be lying to him, that she was like all those pretend men and women on the Hill, and didn't really own anything, not even the house over their heads. But she had shown him the lease many times, bragging on her own business ability, and her bank account to boot. He had gone with her to her other properties, watching her harangue the tenants and extract her rent as only a real landlord could. Men came to the house, to discuss with her lots that she might buy from them, or vice versa, and she was wealthier than any colored woman—or man, for that matter—he had ever known.

He could not fathom why she would steal anything, especially anything so small, right down to penny candy from the grocery store. But one evening soon after he and Laura had made the trip to Harvard, Malcolm had come home to find Ella physically blocking him from coming through the front door of her house. When he tried to go in, she had insisted that he go back out, and not return home until he brought back some food. He had pleaded and joked with her, trying to pretend that he thought she was kidding, frightened by how her whole demeanor had changed. But she remained adamant, and stone-faced, demanding that he go back out on the streets for her.

"But I don't got any money!" he finally wailed, unable to shove past the great bulk of her body.

"You used to lift things back in Lansing, didn't you?" she pointed out. "Least that's what those social workers told me!"

"Yeah. I guess," he admitted—feeling stunned and betrayed by the idea that Mr. Maynard Allen would have said anything about it, to anyone else.

"Then why you got such airs 'bout doin' it in Boston? Ain't I as good as your Momma? Ain't I worth stealin' for?"

"I guess—"

"Then you get out there, don' you come back till you got somet'in' for supper!"

He had wandered through the Hill for hours, grieving over her demand, unable to figure out why she would want such a thing from him. He lingered outside the shops on Humboldt and Waumbeck Avenues, halfheartedly thinking to fulfill her order, but he could not make himself go inside. The stores here so much brighter and sharper than they had been back in Michigan, the cops even bigger and more intimidating.

Finally he had broken away, and run down the Hill into the Town, where all the poor and unruly Negroes that Ella disapproved of lived. Half-blind, the tears filling his eyes, he had been both battered and cosseted by the crowded nighttime streets, all the restless activity eventually soothing him, distracting him from the turmoil inside himself. He wandered around for hours in the Town, peering into its corner groceries and the fish-fry restaurants, the storefront churches and pawnshops. Staring down the narrow, littered alleys, at the little boys there fighting and swearing, shooting craps and pitching pennies with grown-ups. He watched the hipsters pouring into crowded bars, greeting each other with their cool, whispered patter. The other couples, too, going into the dark bars and night-clubs—black men with white women, looking furtive and guilty but holding hands in public.

He had stopped at last in front of a poolroom. There, his cheeks still stained by tears, still bewildered about what he should do, or where he should go, he had stood and gaped at how sharp and bright everything looked inside—the green felt of the tables and the whirring balls; the hustlers' suits and the way their conked hair fell back over their heads as flat and straight as a white man's. He noticed above all another object constantly in motion, a dark, stubby man moving back and forth between the tables. He threw towels at the players and chalked their sticks; fetched drinks and food for them, and filled aluminum cans with the powder they shook into their hands, all without the least indication that his every task was anything but what he chose to do out of his own munificence. And in his confusion, Malcolm knew he wanted nothing more than to be that man. Knowing he wasn't up to being a true hustler or a pool sharp yet, but just wanting to work at their side every day, the same as that stubby little man did.

He had finally been able to lift a beefsteak for Ella that night, taking it right out of a narrow, hole-in-the-wall, colored butcher's shop when the owner had to go in the back for more paper. Looking him in the face before he did so, Malcolm all but daring the man to do anything before he picked up the beefsteak and strolled out.

It had seemed to satisfy Ella, at least for the moment, but afterward he had worried less about all her rules, and all her fine things.

He had gone back down to the Town every night for the next week—knowing how much she would hate it, not even trying to disguise his destination. There, he always stopped at the same pool-room, watching the players inside with his nose shoved up against the glass—until one night the stubby little man with the powder had caught his eye, and grinned, and waved him in. Malcolm had all but fallen over himself to obey. The feeling inside electric the moment he passed through the door, everything louder and flashier. He had just stood there for a long moment, listening to the players calling their shots, taunting and boasting; the smack and clatter of the ivory balls banging off each other. Soaking in the smells of talc and chalk, tobacco and whiskey.

The stubby man had come up to him, wriggling his nose as if he smelled something bad, a grin still creasing his broad face. Malcolm was surprised to see that he wasn't much older than Malcolm was himself.

"Mmm-mmm-mmm! The cat still smells country!" he said, looking him up and down and shaking his head. "That your hair, or you just fall down in a briar patch, son?"

Malcolm didn't know what to say, but the man only chuckled and held out his hand.

"Name's Malcolm, Malcolm Jarvis. What's yours, son? You just get in off the bus from Alabama?"

When Malcolm told him what his name was, and where he was from, the little man's eyes had lit up.

"Homeboy! Gimme some skin! Same name, same town! I come from Lansing ten years ago. What you lookin' for here, son? These hustlers gonna scoff up a square shuffler like you an' spit out the seeds."

But when Malcolm had managed to get out that he wanted a job just like his, Jarvis only shook his head.

"Nah, nah, man. You can do better'n rackin' balls," he insisted.

"But you're doin' it—"

"That's only till I get enough scratch to put my ork together," he said, still smiling at Malcolm. "We gonna put the word out. Then we gonna get you fixed up so you look like you didn't just step out of a cotton field. You stick wit' me, Nome. I'm gonna school you to the happenings."

The slave Jarvis had gotten him was shining shoes down at the Roseland State, the huge ballroom down on Mass Ave. At first he had felt let down that he had just been stuck with Jarvis's leavings. He couldn't believe that this job or anything else could compare to working in the pool hall, although he had long been fascinated by the Roseland. He had passed it many times with Laura on their way back from the Loews, which was right next door, though he had never dared to take her inside—afraid to have her discover how little dancing he had actually done. But all of his disappointment had vanished once Jarvis had taken him down there, and left him with Freddie, the resident shoeshine, who was leaving because he had finally hit it big on the numbers. He was a sinewy brown man, with arms as powerful as streetcar cables, but who moved hunched over at all times like a crab. Malcolm realized that Freddie, too, was at most only a few years older than he was himself, though he seemed to have already picked up a world of knowledge.

"Once they leave that piss stand, you run right up to 'em with a towel," he instructed him. "Lot of 'em don't plan to wash their hands, but you offer the towel an' shame 'em into it. Towels the best hustle you got in here. Cost you a penny apiece to launder 'em, an' you always get at least a nickel tip."

His hands were in constant motion as he talked, Malcolm noticed—filling up the soap basins, checking the toilet paper; piling up the downy white hand towels in the huge, gleaming, tiled bathroom. He held up a whisk broom from his shoeshine kit, like something a baseball umpire would use to sweep home plate—a wry, almost painful smile creasing his face.

"After they take the towel, give 'em a couple licks wit' this. They tip you anything over a dime, you Tom it up some. Make a big fuss, run it all over they suit jacket, the pants. Let 'em feel it. The white cats like to see that. They come back two, three times a night, just for the feel of it.

He led Malcolm over to the shoeshine stand itself then, just outside the bathroom door, and squatted down before it, motioning him to put his right foot up. Malcolm slipped it gingerly into the ornate copper shoe plate, riveted into the stand and worn smooth by thousands of feet. Freddie set upon it at once, his hands moving so fast Malcolm could barely follow them.

"You keep everything in its place. When it gets rushed you never have a wasted motion," he told him, pulling out the drawer of his kit with one hand.

"Keep your shoelaces in this drawer here, an' don't be afraid to tell a cat if he needs a new pair. Buy 'em two for a nickel, charge 'em a quarter. Make sure an' get some rubbers before you go in, too. Cost you two bits each, you charge 'em a dollar.

"You got your rags an' brushes here by the footstand. Polish, paste wax, an' suede brushes here. Brush, polish, brush. Paste wax, shine rag, lacquer. Dig the action? Only you got to go faster than I'm doin' it now. You got to make that rag pop!"

His hands moved even faster, until they were just brown blurs over his black shoes. There was a burst of popping noises that sounded as loud as gunshots and made Malcolm jump. Freddie grinned up at him.

"It's a jive noise. The cats tip if they know you're knockin' yourself out. Remember, Red: Everything in this world is a hustle. Everything."

But Malcolm barely heard him, distracted by the music now floating up from the ballroom. He recognized the tune, of course, and even the band—Benny Goodman's orchestra, slowly building into "Why Don't You Do Right." A woman's reedy voice growling over the bass line:

> *You let other women make a fool of you*
> *Why don't you do right, like some other men do?*
> *Get out of here and get me some money too—*

But only then did it truly dawn on him that they were live, rehearsing right now, just a floor below him. And that he would be working in the midst of such music every night. He turned back only reluctantly, to see Freddie was still smiling at him, already popping the rag over his second shoe.

"Ain't you ever seen a big dance, Country? Ah, but this ain't nothin'. Wait'll you see a colored dance. Our people know how to carry on."

"Really?" Malcolm breathed, leaning toward the stairs.

"Sure. Run on an' watch awhile. You got your whole life to shine shoes," Freddie told him.

Malcolm was halfway down the stairs before Freddie had finished his sentence, racing to see the splendid ballroom, the band playing all alone across it. Playing just for him. Only dimly aware of Freddie calling softly down the stairs:

"Remember what I told you, Red. Everything in this world is a hustle!"

.   .   .

He never forgot the giddy realization of that moment—that here, live and in person, would be all the top musicians and hits he had heard for years, coming from the radio, or some scratched-up record, or out of some local high school band playing bad, slow covers. He had never been that musical himself—for all that he wanted to be a singer, like his half-brother, Jimmy Carlton—but it excited him now, seeing how fast the bands played, and all those people moving to them. He spent as much time as he could at the Roseland watching the dancers, in particular, despite everything Freddie had schooled him in about soliciting tips. He would jump up and down at the edge of the floor, just watching everything, until the house manager had to holler at him to get back up and tend to the customers. Later, he would find how small the dance floor was compared to those of the Savoy, or the Renaissance; the action limited, just as everything was compared to *Harlem.*

But it was so much more than anything he had seen before. When a good band was in, he could barely be bothered with the men who drifted up to his shoeshine stand, unless they were in fact the band leaders themselves, or their sidemen. He sat idolatrously at their feet, hoping they might notice him—Ellington and Hampton, Cootie Williams and Jimmy Lunceford. Lester Young and Dickie Wells, and Johnny Hodges and Sonny Greer who got into such a furious argument over "Day Dream" that they forgot to tip him once, though Malcolm didn't care. He would have gladly shined all their shoes for free, just to listen to them.

The best nights, though, were the colored nights, just as Freddie had told him. His pockets would bulge with tips by the end of the evening, and threaten to rip out. The bathroom trash baskets overflowing with so many fifths of scotch and bourbon that he had to empty them again and again before the dance was over. On those nights, only black bands were good enough to play, too—with the sole exception of Charlie Barnet's ork, which ratcheted up their renditions of "Cherokee" or "Redskin Rhumba" so fast that they made even the best colored dancers swing. The music growing steadily faster and wilder until midnight, when the dancers would start to shout "Showtime! Showtime!" and the band let loose with everything it had left.

On all the other nights, at least half of his customers were white men. They moved about the floor mechanically—doing the same four or five steps, back and forth, as if trying to remember their Arthur Murray dance lessons. They became effusive with bourbon, pumping his hand and pushing a dollar bill into his pocket after he had whisked them with his broom. Others were more secretive, talking furtively among themselves before they approached him. Slim young men with mops of hair and sharp new suits, their faces young yet already wolfish and sardonic in the jaundiced light outside the men's room. Asking him with studied casualness about women, or drugs, while he popped his rag over their shoes.

There was so much, he realized, that he didn't know yet. Only slowly, using his own eyes, had he become hipped to the play— learning who were the hustlers he might be able to score king kong, tea, pills, and powders from, and anything else his customers really wanted. Learning who the plainclothesmen were, and the boys from the narcotics commission, and the play-for-pay girls.

It took up all his time, hanging around the Roseland, even on his nights off, learning what was what. He rarely saw Ella anymore, and he deliberately tried to time his comings and goings so that she wasn't around when he slipped up to his attic room. Lifting her a steak, or some eggs, or cans of soup from time to time, just to ensure that she wouldn't throw him out. He had quit the slave at Townsend's Drugstore as soon as he got his Roseland job, even though it meant that he couldn't see Laura anymore for the time being—and that, to his surprise and embarrassment, the Berlants had nearly wept when he told them he was quitting, and implored him to stay.

He planned to go back, at least to visit. But for now he pressed Jarvis to proceed with his full transformation. He had already taken Malcolm down to the Jew's store to buy him his first zoot. A young man in a yarmulke picking him a robin's egg blue suit off the rack, with Punjab pants thirty inches across at the knee, and twelve at the cuff. The long coat so narrow at his waist that it made him look like something entirely different than what he was—like a comic-book hero, with an immense iron torso and shoulders—and he had loved it. The Jew had even thrown in a blue-feathered hat, with a brim that was wider than his shoulders, and a gold-plated chain that hung down below his coat hem.

All that remained then was the hair. On the big day he had strutted down to the grocery store with the list of ingredients Jarvis had given him for his homemade congolene. Letting the grocer pull

down eggs and potatoes, and a can of Red Devil lye for him. Going
next to the drugstore, where he asked for a big jar of Vaseline and
a bar of soap, a large-toothed comb and a fine-toothed comb and a
hose with a metal spray head, a rubber apron and a pair of rubber
gloves. The colored druggist behind the counter smiling at him—

"Going to lay on that first conk?"

—and Malcolm, unable to hide his pride and excitement, had
grinned right back at the man:

"Right!"

It did burn like the devil—his new hair, burned right into
the scalp. Jarvis had sat him down in a chair in the kitchen of his
cousin's apartment, where both of them peeled and thin-sliced the
potatoes on the table there, and poured them into a Mason jar. Jarvis had pulled on the rubber gloves, looking for all the world like
the mad scientists in the Frankenstein movies, and used a wooden
spoon to stir in the lye.

"Never use a metal spoon for this. The lye will turn it black," he
told Malcolm while he appraised the white, jellied contents of the
Mason jar with a professional air. He cracked in the two eggs last.
Stirring the new mixture furiously at the table, until it turned the
color of a sick dog's eye, boiling and fuming yellow.

"Feel the jar!" he ordered, and when Malcolm did he had to yank
his hand back immediately.

"Damn straight, it's hot!" Jarvis crowed. "That's the lye!"

"That goin' on my head?"

"I ain't lyin' to you, homeboy. You know it's gonna burn bad
when I comb it in. But the longer you can take it, the straighter the
hair."

"I can take it."

"Uh-huh. Now you remember where the sink is, behind you?
Where I told you it is? And where I got the spray hose?"

"I can take it."

"All right, then. Just so's you remember."

He tied the rubber apron tightly around Malcolm's neck—then
slathered the Vaseline on thickly over his ears and neck and forehead, anywhere his hair curled naturally over the skin.

"Here it comes!"

The first, thick handful almost pleasant at first, like warm jelly
on his scalp. Then it had started to work its way into his head.

"Hang on, homie!"

He had writhed, and clutched the table before him. Jarvis raking the comb through his hair, each pass feeling as if it were scraping the flesh from his skull. His eyes filling with water, his nose running freely down into his mouth.

"Hang on, hang on!"

He had reared up then, stumbling blindly toward the sink. Jarvis's hands on him at once, spraying the cold water over his scalp, rubbing the soap in, over and over again.

"There—there—there, homeboy," he cooed to him. "Tell me where it burns, now. Tell me every little spot so it don't burn through the skin—"

Rubbing his hair with a big towel now. Malcolm still writhing, crying and moaning under his touch like one of the converted in his Daddy's church.

"Tell me where it hurts—"

That had been the worst of it—then the pain had slowly subsided into blessed relief. After he had gotten the burning spots out, Jarvis had combed more of the Vaseline in. Using the large-toothed comb, then using the fine-toothed comb, until all of Malcolm's hair hung down in straight, flat tendrils, and then he had taken a straight razor and begun to work carefully around the back of his neck and his sideburns. Shaping it meticulously, refusing to be hurried, until at last he was satisfied enough to let Malcolm stand up and look at himself in the mirror. Jarvis just behind him, his head level with Malcolm's shoulder, grinning proudly at him in the reflection.

"The first time's always the worst. You took it real good, boy— real good."

But Malcolm had barely heard his praise, staring at himself there in the mirror. Still wiping the tears, and the snot and the sweat, from his face, his chest still heaving—but unable to turn away from his own image now. His hair a bright red color, but Vaselined straight back against his grinning skull, just like a white man's.

He knew he had to capture it right away, to make sure it wasn't a mirage, and so he had changed into his new zoot, and gone down to the penny arcade at Scollay Square. He had stepped into one of the automatic photo booths there, and had a strip of four full-length photographs taken of himself for a quarter. Profiling for the camera the way he had seen the hustlers do it around the poolroom. Dangling his hat in one hand, knees together, feet apart, both hands in his belt, with his index fingers pointed toward the floor. When the pictures came out, they were everything he had hoped they would be. He stared at them for hours afterward, amazed by how tough he looked, his face pulled up into a hard, leering smile. Like the devil himself—

"It's me," he whispered in wonder. "It is me."

He had cut them apart and autographed each photo. Mailing one home to his brothers and sisters in Lansing. Giving one to Ella, who had only screamed and bellowed that he had become no better than some cheap Town nigger hustler. She had even sneaked into his room at night, and tried to cut a swath out of his new conk— before suddenly shrugging in acquiescence the following day, Well, I guess it had to happen sooner or later, another of her own unfathomable transformations.

He had given the third picture to Jarvis, who Malcolm was pleased to see looked truly touched by the gesture, averting his eyes and tucking the photo away in his pocket.

"Thanks, homeboy," he had said. "But who you gonna give the last one?"

He had waited for Laura outside Townsend's. Leaning against a lamppost, twirling the long gold chain of his zoot in one hand. Hardly able to contain himself while he waited to see the look on her face, wanting her to see him like this instead of her Harvard-lawyer-to-be. But she hadn't seemed surprised at all, only breaking into her usual warm grin—his first disappointment. She had dropped her books and put her arms around him, right there in the street.

"Malcolm! You're back!"

"Hey, baby."

Trying to sound as cool as he could—though she was already walking around him, gawking appreciatively.

"Look at you! You're gorgeous!"

She picked up the chain where he had let it fall, holding it teasingly in one hand until he pulled it away from her.

"Yeah, well. This is how I am, now," he told her roughly. "I got me a slave at the Roseland. I go beat my hoof riffs there most every night, matter-of-fact."

"Really? You mean lindy-hopping?"

"Uh, yeah, that's what it is—"

"I just love to lindy," she told him.

"You do? Where'd you learn that?" he asked, his voice betraying the depth of his surprise.

"Oh, some friends of mine have lindy parties all the time, over their houses," she laughed, then looked at him daringly. "But I've never been to anyplace like the Roseland. Do you think you could take me sometime?"

"But what about your gramma—"

"That's okay. I can just tell her I'm staying over my cousin's. She'll cover for me, and I'll meet you at your sister's. All right?"

"All right. All right, then," he had told her, grinning, but staring back at her over his shoulder as he walked away.

The night of the dance she had come running up the steps of Ella's house to him. Her eyes larger than ever when she saw the huge pearl gray Cadillac he had arranged to borrow through Jarvis. Smiling shamelessly as she told him how she had gotten away from her grandmother's:

"That's the first time I ever lied to her!"

She had kept her arms entwined through his the whole way to Roseland, nuzzling her head against his shoulder. And when they arrived she had peeled back her long spring coat, to reveal—not the modest pink sweater and pleated gray school skirt that was practically all he ever saw her in, but a shiny red silk blouse, and a short matching lindy skirt. Even holding up a pair of sneakers she had secreted in her overnight bag. Squealing out loud when she saw the golden, waxed dance floor, and all the dancers—all the hustlers and fancy men, the b-girls and painted women, already throwing themselves around it.

"Oh, Malcolm! It's just like I pictured it!" she told him, laughing as happily as a child.

"It is?"

"Come on!"

She was already scampering out on the dance floor, pulling him out with her—and right away he knew he was in trouble. He tried to take control, pushing her around before him. Trying to remember everything he had learned from his lessons, and all the nights watching the dancers after he had run down from his shoeshine post.

But each time he did, she floated effortlessly away from him. Moving much faster than he possibly could have, breaking out one move after another, until he realized with a growing sense of astonishment and panic that he was simply not in her league. He had tried to shrug it off, tried to dig in and keep up then. But she kept moving ahead of him, her face gleaming with sweat. Smiling back fiercely at him, as if she was having the time of her life—as if this was no great effort at all for her. He went after her again, but the faster and harder he tried to move the heavier his feet got, until he knew he was clomping about ridiculously on the floor, his pointy orange zoot shoes feeling like big clown feet. He reached for her waist again—but his hands slipped off, leaving him flailing foolishly. Then she was gone, lost in the crowd for the rest of the number, while Malcolm slunk back off the floor.

Only later, when the final encore had finished, had she come running back to him. Still wiping the sweat and hair off her face, her big eyes shining.

"Where did you go? I'm sorry I lost you! Oh, that was the best time I ever had!" she babbled happily at him, putting her arm through his again, as if it belonged there.

"Thank you, thank you so much for taking me, Malcolm," she told him, in her soft, gentle, earnest voice, her hand stroking his arm. "It's the best thing anyone's ever done for me. I can't thank you enough—"

"Sure, baby."

"If there's anything I can do for you. Anything at all—"

He had driven her back up to the Hill in silence, maneuvering Jarvis's car carefully through the streets, his mind a jumble of humiliation and undirected anger. When he reached Waumbeck Street he had driven slowly, right by her house, as if daring her to say something. But she hadn't—she had just looked over at him from the passenger seat, her big eyes glistening in the dark.

He went right on by, then turned the corner, headed over to Dale Street where he knew there was a little cul de sac at the end of the block, a dead end next to a couple of empty buildings and under a streetlight that was always broken. There he had pulled up the car and cut the engine, dousing the lights so they were submerged immediately in the dark. All he could see by the ambient light was the vague silhouette of her body, sitting very still on the seat next to him. The whites of her eyes gradually emerging as she stared at him silently.

He had grabbed her roughly, then, on purpose. Pulling her over to him with one arm in his anxiety, pressing his lips crudely up against her face. He had done almost no kissing before with any girl, had only had sex the one time behind the church in Lansing, with Bo Bigbee's girl holding his hat over her face. He wasn't even sure what to do, kissing Laura wetly all over, trying to seek out her lips, to hold her head in his hands.

"Wait, wait—" she tried to tell him, but thinking she was putting him off, he had pressed against her all the harder, pushing his body across the seat and into hers.

She had elbowed her way free—but not to get away, just to make him slow down. Putting her soft hands on his, pulling them down. Still speaking to him in that infinitely soft, tender voice, even as she found his lips and kissed him, opening her mouth to him.

"There—there, baby—like that now. Do you like that now, baby?"

Her voice was not quite like anything he had heard from her before, suddenly knowing and adult and passionate. She had kept kissing him, and letting him kiss her. Letting him explore her mouth with his lips and tongue, even encouraging him to kiss her down along the soft indentation of her neck.

At first it had been wonderful. The best sensation he had ever felt, obscuring for the first time he could remember every other thought he had in his head, every fear. He had kissed her even more urgently then, leaning back over her, pressing her down along the leather seat of Jarvis's big borrowed Caddy. Scrambling up over her, his hands groping along her body. Pulling at the buttons on her blouse until she made a little wincing sound, sucking in her breath—and he realized that he was being just as clumsy as he had been out on the dance floor, pressing in just as blindly and stupidly when he didn't know what he was doing.

He had sat back up—pulling himself away from her now. Mortified by the very heft of his body, the sweaty, groping ignorance of his hands. She had tried to pull him back down again. Leaning back against the door of the Caddy, and looking at him through the fading darkness, her face very serious now. Beckoning to him, then reaching down and lifting her blouse lightly over her arms and head, just like that. Reaching back and undoing her bra, sliding it just as effortlessly over her arms, so that she was half naked before him. Those fine, gentle brown slopes of her breasts bared to him now, in the distant lights from the city.

"C'mon," she told him, her soft voice more sincere, even demanding, than ever now to his ears. "C'mon, baby. I want you to. I do, baby—"

Malcolm was shocked, though no more shocked than he had been at the Roseland. All he could think about was how beautiful and above him she had seemed when he first saw her—in her little pleated skirts, spooning up her ice cream, her back straight and proud. Nothing like what she was now, her face and hair dripping with sweat after dancing him off the floor, her shirt off and her breasts exposed, all but begging him for it. She was nothing like what he had expected, and he was unable to move to her again, to risk any further humiliation. Not willing to even look at her while she pleaded softly with him some more, until she had finally given up and slipped her brassiere and her blouse back on and let him drive her home through the sedate empty streets of the Hill. Not even able to look at her when he dropped her off at her grandmother's, back on Waumbeck Street, and she had given him a kiss on the cheek—her face warm against his—and told him that she had had a very nice time, and that she would call him the next day.

Even then he had only nodded, and let her get out of the car and go back into her grandmother's home alone. Driving the gorgeous pearl gray Caddy carefully back down into the Town and to Jarvis's where, by the time he arrived, he had recovered sufficiently from his mortification to make up a whole series of winks and struts and stories.

She had called the next day, and every day after that for a week, until Ella had demanded that he call her back. But he never had, not through all the rest of that month, or the month after.

By then the war was on, and Jarvis had set him up this time through some friends with a slave building minesweepers, at the Casco Bay Shipyard in Portland. But it had been cold as hell there by the water, and lonely, and Malcolm had only had a glimpse of two or three other colored men in the whole town. He was leery of the tall, thin wooden poles that held the ships up in the dry dock, certain they would snap at any moment and send the gray steel hulls crashing down on their heads. At night, he had to watch out all the time for the white welders and joiners roaming Commercial Street, drunk and mean, and just looking for a black boy to beat up.

But it had gotten him off the Hill for a few crucial weeks, at least, and when he went back down to Boston, there were jobs everywhere. He found work bussing tables at the Parker House, and then on the Yankee Clipper, making the long runs all the way down to Washington. He had gone back to see Ella at Christmas, before flopping at a colored trainmen's boardinghouse, but he never went back to Townsend's Drugs. And as much as he would fantasize and plot about what he would say and do, what pose he would strike and how indifferent he would seem if he ever ran into her, he never saw Laura again.

The memory of it still stinging, even now, as he drifted off into another pleasant, light doze before Miranda had to be up for her show. Just as all of his humiliations still hurt, no matter how long ago or otherwise forgotten they were—but all of them at last made good, he thought. All of them redeemed by his having everything he needed and wanted sleeping right next to him now.

CHAPTER FOURTEEN

MALCOLM

He had left Miranda's apartment building out the back way. Slipping down the six flights of stairs to the basement as quietly as he could, pausing at each landing to listen for any of her neighbors out in the hall—letting the officious doorman think he had left long ago through the delivery entrance. He had wanted to stride right back through the lobby, as big and arrogant as a waterbug, but he didn't want to get Miranda in any trouble.

He had pleaded with her to let him go with her, to her gig at Café Society that night, but she had told him she was expecting West Indian Archie to drop in, and that it was too dangerous. Instead, he had lain on her bed and watched her shower and dress, reveling in the sight of her naked white body again. She had acted modest, and pulled the shower curtain closed against him, but giggled at him from behind it, pleased and blushing like a girl at his attention.

He had left then, just as she wanted him to, lest they get started again. Though on his way out the basement delivery entrance he had carefully stuffed two chewed sticks of gum into the door jamb, so the door wouldn't quite close all the way—leaving a secret entrance for himself, whenever he wanted.

After that he had strolled back through the Village and taken the A train up to Sugar Hill. It was a mild evening, the heavy heat of the last few days having broken, as it suddenly would in the City, and he had whistled to himself all the way up to Harlem—confident as he was, now, that she was his for good. That it was just a matter of time and strategy, working out their mutual escape from West Indian Archie, but that she would be with him from now on. So certain of it was he that Malcolm was wondering only about how hard it would be to let Archie down—when he spotted the man himself, standing in front of his apartment building.

His first inclination had been to run—to turn around and simply dash back down onto the subway platform, or flag down a cab. But there were no cabs in sight, and anyway, Archie had already seen him, was raising a huge hand in greeting and coming down the sidewalk toward him. Malcolm made himself walk on steadily toward him, made himself smile. Resisting the impulse to reach for the small silver pistol in his jacket pocket, telling himself that Archie's greeting meant that nothing was wrong, that it wasn't some kind of ambush.

"Red! Detroit Red!" he called out, opening his mouth, and with a burst of relief Malcolm realized that he could see the man's prominent gold teeth, smiling at him in the streetlight. He grabbed up Malcolm as if he were a child, pressing his skinny body to him until he was almost out of breath.

"What you layin' down, Archie?"

"Where you be, boy?" Archie bellowed, chuckling, the smell of rum and cigar smoke heavy on his breath. "I got to talk to my utility man!"

"Anything you want, Archie."

"Lookit you, Red," he went on, sniffing ostentatiously all around him. "I think you been layin' up somewhere, son. I think you been doin' some tomcattin'!"

Malcolm was immediately on edge again, but Archie only punched him lightly in the shoulder, obviously delighted about something.

"What you need me for, Archie? You got to pay off?"

"Nah, nah, Red, it's this," he said, and flashed some papers out of his jacket at Malcolm, something he couldn't quite make out in the evening gloom. "A trip for two. I'm takin' Miranda down to Asbury Park for a couple weeks. Got the best hotel rooms there is down there, we're gonna have us a fine time!"

"That so?" Malcolm said, trying to sound as disinterested as he was able. The rushing in his head so bad that he almost blew it right then and there, and asked Archie what about her job down at the Café Society.

"Yah, I got her a break from her gig an' everything. All-paid vacation! It's gonna be fine—but I need you to cover for me, Red. I need you to do extra routes every day, an' make all the payoffs. Huh? How 'bout it? An' don't worry 'bout a little more work—you be makin' more scratch for that girl you got!"

He had gone on chuckling to Malcolm, and pounding his back and shoulder as he laid out his extra duties. And Malcolm accepting it, pretending to listen carefully, all the while trying to fight down the roaring voice in his head telling him that he was a fool—that nothing was truly his at all, and that it never would be.

The very next day, after Archie and Miranda had left on their vacation, Sammy the Pimp had come by to see him. Malcolm had been up most of the night, sleepless with misery to think of them together—unable to see her, or talk to her, or hold her for all that time, wondering if he would ever really have her back. He had been still logy with sleeplessness when Sammy the Pimp stopped by, which he told himself later was why he had ever listened to Sammy's proposition to double the money he made from Archie.

"Kisca. Tea, from Africa. You dig? I got a merchant marine, bring it back," Sammy told him. "I know enough sailor boys to keep it comin', too."

"So?" Malcolm shrugged.

"So you already knockin' your trilly all over town, runnin' numbers for Archie. He's already got it all squared with the blue, too. Don't you see it, Red? I'm just askin' you to take the opportunity, move a few sticks f'me along the way."

"I don't know," Malcolm said thoughtfully, smoothing a hand back over his conk. But Sammy wasn't wrong, thinking how easy it would be, with the police already paid off, and believing him to be just another one of Archie's runners.

"Archie oil up my head for me, he know I was runnin' gage with his numbers."

"But Archie ain't here, is he?" Sammy countered. "An' he don't ever have to find out."

"I don't know."

"What don't you know?" Sammy scoffed. "It's all cozy, groovy, an' nice. You already ruggin' wit' half my customers anyways."

"I don't got the money for a stake," Malcolm said, still hedging. Thinking now of everything he had heard at Small's about what the cops did to drug runners. Thinking of that little room at the Thirty-second Precinct. Listening to the pimp next door, begging them not to mark up his face—

"Hey, I ain't playin' you Fourteenth Street here," Sammy said slowly, as if he thought Malcolm didn't understand. "You got a position I need, I stake you to the stake. You just take ten percent the first week. After that, we all even, split everything down the middle."

He plucked a folded-over paper bag out of his inside jacket pocket, and tossed it over to Malcolm.

"That meet wit' your approval, Nome?"

Malcolm could smell the deep, sweet scent even before he opened the bag—the best weed he had ever sniffed. But when he peered inside, he was surprised by how little there seemed to be.

"We can make enough from this?"

"Sure we can, Red! You just got to roll the sticks tight enough. Here, lemme show you," Sammy said, taking the bag back from him and producing a pack of rolling papers from the corner drugstore.

They spent the rest of the morning rolling sticks on the kitchen table, Malcolm's roommates having departed for their defense jobs. Sammy showing him how to clean the tea and roll it tight, so as to maximize their profit out of each bag. The finished joints each about as large as a wooden matchstick.

"But then you give 'em just a little pinch, there, so they look like they fatter for the squares. You dig?"

When they had rolled a hundred sticks between them, Sammy had shown him how to hide them in a half-empty pack of Lucky Strikes, and how to stick the pack high up in his armpit, close to his body.

"That way, someone comes up on ya, you just go 'round the corner or into a doorway an' let your arm drop," he told Malcolm—demonstrating it, the cigarette pack falling soundlessly out of his wide jacket sleeve.

"You see? You just let it go. Let the pack fall right out, while you keep walkin'. Nobody will even see it. Then, if you can, you go back an' collect it."

He made Malcolm practice it a few times, walking back and forth across the kitchen floor until he had it down cold. Complimenting him on how cool, and natural, he looked, Sammy the Pimp's taut bald head grinning merrily.

"You see, Red? They can't touch us!"

·   ·   ·

It was only when he began selling drugs that Malcolm knew he was truly free. It seemed to him as if time itself had expanded, and he lived his life exactly as he pleased, and just as he had always dreamed that he might before he came to Harlem. For the first time, he had all the time in the world to himself, to do whatever he wanted to throughout the vast City.

He liked to kill his morning with a movie. There was no action before the afternoon anyway, and movies played twenty-four hours a day in the City now, serving the defense workers as they went off their shifts. On a slow day he might see five in a row. Taking his pick of all the neighborhood theatres in Harlem, the airy, blue-and-white Moorish villa at 126th Street and Seventh Avenue that was the Alhambra, or the Washington or the Roosevelt, or the Regent.

When it got too hot he went down to the new, air-conditioned newsreel theatre in Grand Central Station, or the vast palaces at Radio City, and around Times Square. Excited, now, to spread out through Manhattan. Nervous as it still made him to go anywhere below 110th Street, he would steel himself to the pleasure, loving just to sit in the downtown theatres, even before the movie came on. Staring up into the vast, golden bowl that was the Roxy, or the Paramount, with its gold and glittering chandeliers, and huge marble columns. There was a promenade around the top of its lofty, vaulted ceiling, where people could walk, and look down on the entire theatre below. Sitting in his seat, he could hear their whispers drifting down to him, slipping in through the movie dialogue, not quite comprehensible—more secret communications from the City.

He saw everything that came out, no matter what it was—gangster flicks and war movies, musicals and comedies and domestic dramas. His favorites he saw over and over again, moving with them as they traveled around the City—Casablanca and Johnny Eager; Cabin in the Sky, and Stormy Weather, which was always playing at the Roxy. Sometimes slipping in near the end, just to watch Cab Calloway sing "Old Geechy Joe," and "The Jumpin' Jive," or the Nicholas Brothers do their seven—seven—consecutive splits over each other—one after another, leaping hand to toe, with no pauses and no cuts, all while descending a staircase for their big finish. When he had finally had enough, he would stagger out into the dizzying afternoon sunlight. Trying to imitate Bogart's walk, or his grimace, or the way John Sublett pulled his hand along his grinning, bare skull—so much like Sammy the Pimp's—as he sang "Shine"—

Just because my color's shady,
That's the difference, maybe, why they call me
Shine, sway your blues'ies.
Why don't you shine?

Sometime about mid-afternoon he finally made his way back to his room, or over to Sammy's apartment on W. 144th Street to roll the sticks. To his surprise, Sammy seemed to live there with only a single woman, named Hortense, a very tall, very beautiful Spanish girl, with mocha-colored skin, and jet black hair that was held loosely in a single red ribbon before plunging halfway down her back. From everything that Sammy had told him about how to get a woman, he had expected someone fearful and unsure, but Hortense strutted imperiously through the kitchen when she chose to, leaning down to pinch Sammy's cheek roughly between two of her long, bright red fingernails. When Sammy demanded that she make them something to eat, she only stared at him disdainfully, and when he cursed her she laughed.

"Did you know chico used to be a waiter? In Paducah, Kentucky!" she said to Malcolm, her dark face flashing with mirth. "But then he knocked up a girl an' had to get outta town. That's how he become a pimp. Careful you don't end up back in Pa-du-cah, chico."

Sammy cursed her again, but she only strode out of the room, still laughing, and he turned back to cleaning and rolling the gage with Malcolm.

"See? That's the kinda woman you get when you know how to operate," he said when she had left—nodding his head sagely, as if he had been trying to teach Malcolm something all along.

"I see, all right."

"None a my other girls could get away wit' that, I'd beat 'em silly for it. But you don't want no mousy, useless types around when you got work to do. You want someone can watch your back!"

When they had rolled a few hundred sticks, Malcolm would start out on his rounds. He tried to figure out the best routes beforehand, to cover Archie's customers as well as Sammy's, and to bring in new clientele. He made most of his own connections in the bar of the Braddock Hotel, on West 126th Street.

The bar itself wasn't much—tattered and musty, and crowded with working girls, including transvestites who made Malcolm squirm when they winked and made eyes at him. But he could listen to Walter Brown and Jay McShann's band playing "Hooty Tooty Blues" at the Apollo, just across the alley, and between their sets the musicians would step out through the open stage door, and buy his sticks. He charged them five dollars for ten sticks, and threw in two more free for the regulars—excited to see that many of them were the same singers, and sidemen, and bandleaders whose shoes he had shined up in Boston. They called him Red, and let him hang around on the back stairs, smoking the skinny, matchstick joints that went up in a flash, one after another. The musicians sticking the roaches in their mouthpieces, or even in a dried-out, hollowed-out chicken-thigh bone, trying to preserve a last, faint contact high for later.

When he finally got home in the early morning, Malcolm would lie in bed and smoke a few more sticks by himself, running through the list of all the stars who were now his friends. There was Sonny Greer, who played the drums for Ellington, and Cootie Williams, and Ray "Blip-blip-de-blop-de-blam-blam" Nance, the scat singer. Eddie "Cleanhead" Vinson, who did "Hey, Pretty Mama, Chunk Me in Your Big Brass Bed," and Sy Oliver, who wrote "Yes, Indeed!" for Tommy Dorsey, and who lived up on Sugar Hill with a red-com-plected girl who never seemed to smile. Even Billie Holiday would step over occasionally and buy a pack of Luckies off him, a large-armed, brazen woman who lovingly called everyone motherfucker and told obscene jokes that cracked up the others.

Malcolm would have imaginary conversations with her, with all of them, back in his room. He would tell them how they should try certain standards, or give them tips on their playing—though out on the back steps of the Braddock, he rarely dared to talk to them at all. He just laughed and smiled when they teased him about his red conk, or asked him for more sticks, basking in their attention.

He did so well with the kisca that before long Sammy was press-ing him to push Nembutal and Seconal, Benzedrine tablets and opium—whatever else he could get from the sailors and the mer-chant seamen down at Small's, or his gangster connections. Between the drugs and Archie's numbers, he had begun to clear up to fifty, even sixty dollars a day now, which was enough for him to get into a card game, or play craps in the back room of one bar or another every night. He handed over bread to anyone who put the touch on him, and was playing five dollars on the numbers himself now, every day—sure, now, that he couldn't miss, that he would hit big, and buy the car and maybe even the club that he needed for Miranda.

He liked to tell himself, though, that he didn't really need even her. Not now—not with all the stars he knew, and the money he could make. The first few days she was away he had not really been able to believe that she was gone, thinking, especially when he busted down, that it must be some sort of trick, or ploy, by Archie. He had even gone back to her apartment house one afternoon, not showing his face to the burly white doorman, but sneaking in through the entrance he had made for himself, down at the basement delivery door. He had slipped back up the steps to the fifth floor, and stood in the still hallway outside her door, listening for any sound of activity. Thinking, with a pang of infinite regret, of how good he had felt that evening—not so many hours ago—when he had skipped out her basement back door, sure that she would be his before much longer.

But it was as silent as death in the apartment now, even when he listened for half an hour, and finally even dared to ring the doorbell—the electric buzzer echoing uselessly inside her place. He had slipped back out into the City then, where time had gotten away from him. He worked whenever he wanted to, with both her and Archie away, did whatever he felt like. Coming out of his movies in the middle of the day he felt weightless, as if he were floating above everyone else in the ceaselessly milling, hustling City all around him. The crowds of people rushing down the subway holes to get to their work, hurrying into the bars and restaurants, scrambling up on the crosstown streetcars with their big "X" up front.

He felt at such moments that he was infinitely superior to all of them, especially if he'd already been able to smoke a quick stick or two in the Palace men's room. That he was living as if he were indeed some sort of invisible superhero—as if he had finally obtained that secret knowledge that he was always sure was there in the City for the taking, and it had taken him beyond the need for Miranda, or Mr. Maynard Allen, or his mother and his brothers and his sisters, or anyone at all.

Later, though, he would come down hard—there by the window in his single room, watching the beetlelike cars rushing toward him, their headlights feeling their way blindly into the darkness like so many antennae. He would panic and fear that he had indeed become invisible, without anyone in the world to care if he lived or died. He would try smoking still more of Sammy's sticks, but they just made him all the more antsy, and he would flee down into the streets. Feeling the same way he had when Ella had first sent him out on the streets of the Hill—or when he had run across the yards of all those oblivious white homes back in Lansing—and wanting nothing more than to go down and see Miranda; seriously considering even taking the train down to Asbury Park to search her out, though he knew that would be suicide.

Even his work had begun to make him edgy, and nervous. Wherever he went now, he noticed, cops had started to follow him—something that had never happened when he was merely running numbers for Archie. Why this should be he couldn't fathom, but soon plainclothesmen and even uniformed cops had begun to flash the badge on him, every day. He really had become good at spotting them by now, and whenever he did he would lift his arm and let his stash drop, just as Sammy had shown him.

When the cop caught up and started patting him down, he would shout out that he didn't have anything on him, and that he didn't want anything planted. That never failed to bring the crowd—the people pouring off the steps, and out of the bars and stores, and beauty shops. It was the same phenomenon he had noticed before, the crowd truly angry, pushing in around the police in a way he had never seen colored people do before. The men grumbling, the old women wondering loudly, What's he done? A fine-lookin' boy like that—what they stoppin' him for? until the cops would let him go right there and walk quickly away, not even bothering to take him down for the usual precinct-house workover.

But before long Malcolm came to realize it was not only the cops who were following him. One evening when he had spotted a plainclothesman and dropped his stash by the curb on West 127th Street, he saw a seedy little man who couldn't possibly be a detective dart out of a doorway and grab up his crumpled cigarette pack, dodging across the street before the cop could see him, or Malcolm could figure out what to do next.

From then on he became increasingly aware of the others. Disheveled, dirty people, men and women both, who seemed to spend all their time in the streets and alleys. Dogging his every step, just waiting for an opening, their very presence a flag to any cops who hadn't spotted him yet. Other nights he could see them trailing the police, who were trailing him—all of them on one long chase together.

"Yeah, well, that the trouble with junkies," Sammy had said, shrugging, rolling more sticks with Malcolm up in his apartment. "They can't keep they mouths shut. They get copped, they squeal first thing. It was prob'ly one your musician friends, turned the police on to you in the first place."

"My musician friends?"

"Yeah, well, whoever. But even if they don't talk to the police, they tell each other. They generous creatures, junkies. Give up most anything—'cept junk," Sammy said, and grinned—then drew a big black .45 out of his pocket, brandishing it under Malcolm's nose.

"Just make sure you don' stumble an' fall, you hear me, Red? An' if you do, don't be slicin' your gums about nothin'."

Malcolm tried utilizing his own gun when he went out—the little .25 automatic he had bought from the disappointed-looking man in his building, and which Sammy taught him to keep shoved down the small of his back, just under his belt, which was the one place where the cops supposedly never laid hands on when they frisked you. But even that only helped him so much. One evening Malcolm had heard footsteps keeping pace with his again—he had grown such rabbit ears that he was sure he could hear even a solitary follow through all the crowds along Lenox Avenue by now—and he veered suddenly, expertly around the corner and into the doorway of an abandoned shop.

There he had hung back under the tattered awning for a moment, waiting to see who the follow was. When another, dirty little man came around the corner, reaching down for the cigarette pack, Malcolm stepped out and grabbed his wrist, and made sure he could see the automatic in his other hand. But the man only flicked a knife out of his own pocket—even grinning at him, and clutching the Lucky Strike pack.

"Whassat gonna do?" he hissed, nodding toward Malcolm's gun. "You gon' blow a hole in me right here, with everybody goin' by? You go right ahead, Jack, see how far you get. But if you ain't gonna try it, let go my wrist an' lemme have that gage fo' I cut you fo' yo' troubles. Ain't nobody ever heard a knife yet."

He had let the man run off, what else could he do, and after that he had considered getting a knife of his own, but he wasn't sure where he could hide it, or even if he could use it. He tried changing his routines, and his routes, instead. He would leave the packs of Luckies in the top of ashcans, or behind lampposts, or even in the empty Red Cross bandage boxes that you found on the curb every-where—then tell his connections where they could find them. But his musician friends didn't take to having to search through gar-bage for their sticks, and it didn't fool the followers anyway.

He even tried going out later at night, when the City was dark-est with the dimout. Yet somehow, they still spotted him, his fol-lowers—and then his rounds became a blind, frightening chase through the half-lit streets. The footsteps growing louder and nearer, then stopping when he turned around. Men bumping into him around corners, their fingers prying stealthily into the pockets of his jacket and pants before they stumbled back into the shadows.

By the time he got to the Braddock, most of his connections had already found their connections somewhere else, and they were cool to him now. Malcolm stood around by the bar, feeling helpless, while the capons and butterflies there mooned and giggled at him, making little kissing noises until he stomped out.

He walked hurriedly down 126th Street, toward the east. Not sure where he was going, thinking vaguely of trying to sell off his remaining sticks at Creole Pete's. Before he'd gone half a block, though, he heard the footsteps behind him again. Glaring back through the gloom of the half-light, he could make out only a vague silhouette, though one he thought was probably too short and too dark to be a cop. Another follow.

He quickened his steps, pushing the light to hurry across Sev-enth Avenue—some drunken white sailors and their colored glam-our girl joyfully screaming curses at him as he ran in front of their Checker cab. He kept going east, sure he had lost the follow now— but to his consternation the footsteps only seemed to multiply, and grow closer.

There's more than one of them, he thought, as he hustled across Lenox Avenue. Still moving east, thinking he would surely lose them, whoever they were, as he approached the Italian and Jew blocks of East Harlem. Instead, the number of people behind him only seemed to grow. He knew it wasn't a smart idea but he had to look back then, thinking that he must be mistaken, that they couldn't all be following him. But to his horror, now, he saw there were at least six or seven of them, shadowy figures, moving quickly.

He squeezed the little automatic in his pocket, but he was sure they would be armed, too, and with real cannons.

He heard them calling to him then—sounds that made the hairs on the back of his neck stand on end. Most of them not even words, just high-pitched whistles and mocking, clucking noises. He broke into what was nearly a run, and cut suddenly behind a small knot of people coming toward him. Hoping to lose his followers behind their screen, turning the corner when he got to Fifth Avenue and heading uptown now.

But as soon as he got around the corner, he knew they were still after him. He began to run in earnest then—hearing the feet behind him do the same. Their small, muted cries to each other, "Get him! Don't let him get too far!" He dropped his arm, swearing bitterly as he let still another stash that he would have to owe Sammy fall to the ground. Letting it go openly, right in the middle of the sidewalk, hoping at least that that would appease them. When he looked back over his shoulder, he saw two of the wraith-like shadows dive for it, lashing out furiously at each other. But the rest still came on—no doubt figuring that he had more, or that he had money from his stop at the Braddock on him.

He was running as fast as he could now, cursing how deserted Fifth Avenue was this night, cursing even that there were no cops. He kept moving, his breath coming shorter now, hearing the steps gaining behind him. Thinking, They're more desperate than I am. They need it more—

He ran across 128th Street, right through the traffic, a half dozen horns blaring at him. One of them was another cab, and for a moment he considered pulling his gun and throwing out its passenger, making the hack take him out of the neighborhood. But he could see there were at least three figures in the backseat, large men in uniforms—their hands already on the door locks.

He ran on, toward a lone, dilapidated brownstone, looming by the street corner—and he realized to his surprise that he knew it. The yard filled with junk around its sole forlorn elm tree. What looked like the same taunting sign that he had ripped down, nailed back up on the front door—This is a Ghost House—

"Let me in! Let me in!" he shouted out in his desperation. His cry breathless and garbled, knowing how senseless it was as he stared at the blocked-up windows, the iron-gated doors—still not sure he hadn't just dreamed up the strange slug-white man inside.

But as if on command, the white ghosty face emerged from the ground again, right in front of him. The same old man, in his same old-fashioned black suit with its detachable collar, pulling his same wooden box along on a string. To Malcolm's astonishment he seemed to be signaling to him, waving his arm for him to come on.

"Come on, come on! They are gaining on you!" he cried, unmistakably referring to Malcolm, then jabbing his finger agitatedly at his box.

"Take the box! Take the box, while I secure our entry!"

Malcolm glanced back over his shoulder—the figures pursuing him now less than half a block away, derisively hooting something at him. They would eat my bones, he thought—then scooped up the box, which was surprisingly heavy, piled high with fruit that came tumbling out.

"Mind the oranges!" the white ghosty man snapped at him, even as he waved him onward, through a gap in the iron fence, and down a half flight of stairs to a basement door. There, with a key, he pried open a rusted iron gate, then a rotting wooden-and-marble door. Pulling it open to reveal—a transom stuffed to the top with moldy old newspapers, with a descending tunnel burrowed through the middle of it. A terrible smell emanated from it, some combination of dust and cockroaches, of wet paper and wet plaster, and cat piss, and all the other most awful smells of the City, mixed together.

"Quickly, quickly! They are almost upon us!" the white man's voice sounded behind him, his tone more annoyed than frightened.

Malcolm hesitated for another moment, the box in his hands still, looking back at the followers racing toward him. Then he took the plunge—sticking the box under his arm like a football and diving face-first, into the hole in the newspapers. He slid down into the darkness, yelping with terror as he did, until he had tumbled all the way down to the floor. Going abruptly silent then as he tried to get his bearings in the nearly total darkness—listening to the sound of a thousand, tiny, constant rustlings all around him.

"Well, that was rather melodramatic," the ghosty man said behind him, walking hunched over, down the hole Malcolm had dived through. Somehow keeping his balance in his high, gaitered shoes even along the slick newspapers. As he did, Malcolm could make out at least a dozen cockroaches the size of his thumb and what looked like several mice scuttling out of the piled papers, and he understood what the sound of all that rustling was.

"Like something out of a blood-and-thunder down at Hurtig and Seamon's. Still, at least you got the point in time," the ghosty man continued, lighting what looked like a miner's lamp near Malcolm's feet as he spoke.

He held it up, and for the first time Malcolm could see the extent of the vast, yellowed cave he was in. In its moldy airlessness, it felt like the drawings of King Tut's tomb that had once fascinated him in the Sunday supplements. The stacks of newspapers all around him were as dense and symmetrical as stonework. They reached to the ceiling, armies of roaches and silverfish crawling lackadaisically over them until Malcolm felt his skin crawl. And just beyond them was—everything.

There were piles of boxes and egg crates, and scraps of old wood. There were empty baby carriages, and twisted old bicycles with flattened tires and crumbling leather seats. There were heaps of shoelaces, and balls of string, and blown-out umbrellas, and broken sawhorses. There was a crib, and boxes of shiny toy trains, still unopened, and a wooden school desk with the initials "H.C." carved in it over and over again. There was a towering grandfather clock, and an old-fashioned phonograph with a horn, and a sewing machine. And an X-ray machine, and a Magneto-Electric machine, and a monstrous, glass-and-metal cabinet full of balls and cranks and bells that the man called a static machine. And there was a small rowboat, with oars, and an entire, neatly disassembled car—all of its parts laid out as if they were about to be lifted onto an assembly line and wrenched together.

"My father's Model T," the man told Malcolm apologetically. "I keep meaning to put it together."

"Why?" Malcolm asked.

The man looked taken aback.

"So we could generate our own electricity, of course."

"You could do that?"

"Certainly! I have degrees in chemistry and mechanical engineering from Columbia University!"

"What about the boat?" Malcolm asked.

"My father used to carry it on his head every day to the Harlem River, then row it down to Bellevue Hospital, where he had his practice. He was the finest gynecologist in New York in his day!"

He bowed slightly to Malcolm, though he kept his hands at his sides.

"I am Mr. Langley Collyer," he said formally.

"I know," Malcolm told him, and the ghosty man looked surprised at first, then slyly pleased.

"My celebrity precedes me!" he proclaimed—and began to chatter at Malcolm in a long string of words, nearly as overwhelming as all the junk. Picking up the miner's lamp and starting off through the dense maze of the ghost house as he spoke, gesturing at Malcolm to take up the box and follow.

"Our family is one of the oldest and most distinguished in New York, you know. The first Collyer came over from England on the Speedwell, which was really better than the Mayflower. My mother and father were cousins of the Livingstons. Mother used to read us Greek in the original. As a matter of fact, I have a smattering of that language myself—"

"What all's in the box?" Malcolm asked, in part just to stop the dizzying flow of words. Holding it up close to his nose to try to block out the awful, tomblike stench, breathing in the same citrus tang that he had noticed before emanating from Langley Collyer.

"Oranges, and meat for my brother. Milk, wine. Fresh-baked, whole wheat bread I walked over to Williamsburg to buy today—"

"Williamsburg—in Brooklyn?" Malcolm asked, still hazy about the geography of the vast City.

"Certainly! An invigorating walk! Keeps the system circulating. As a matter of fact, I had just returned when I saw you—"

"Why did you help me?" Malcolm asked him.

"Oh, I know what they can do," he said. "I have seen people held up right under that old elm tree out there. I've peered out at night through the shutters, and seen them stabbed and robbed."

He shook his head bitterly as he led them onto a flight of stairs.

"These terrible people. They break my windows, and pour rubbish in my yard. They make my life miserable. They call me Spook, and say I drag dead bodies into the house after dark—"

He interrupted himself with an emphatic "Stop!," pressing a hand back against Malcolm's chest. Malcolm obliged, though he couldn't see any reason why they should. But then Langley pointed down at the stairs, toward a thin line of metal wire that Malcolm could make out only when he stared at it intently. He pointed back up at the stairway ceiling above them, then—where Malcolm could discern a jumble of pots and pans and enormous cannery jars, packed full of what looked, incredibly, like urine and feces, hovering precariously on a shelf just above him.

"You see? I've booby-trapped the place against these people," Langley said gleefully, leading Malcolm carefully over the tripwire, the pans and jars of excrement jangling faintly against each other in the stillness.

"Maybe they can still get in—but they won't get out!"

They traveled on up to the higher floors, which were just as dark and gloomy, and infernally hot in the summer night. Here, too, every window blocked up with more towering piles of newspapers, the rooms piled chockablock with junk. As they proceeded, a gentle snow of papers drifted continuously down on them. Malcolm simply brushed them away at first, only half aware of what they even were, just wanting them off him. But after a while he began to examine them in the flickering light from Langley's lantern, staring at each of them in turn, trying to decipher just what they were, and why anyone would want to keep them.

There were yellowed photographs of women in old-fashioned bathing suits, smiling boldly into the camera, and an advertisement for cognac from Flegenheimer Brothers in the Bronx. There was a program for The Magic Flute at the Metropolitan Opera from February 27, 1914; and a certificate of merit for punctuality and good conduct, awarded to Langley Collyer at Public School 69, on April 19, 1895; and a handful of tickets to the annual excursion of the Trinity Church Sunday School for Saturday, July 8, 1905. There were even sheets that had no writing on them at all that Malcolm could make out, only tiny bumps that moved like goose flesh under his touch.

"Braille sheets, for when Homer was going blind," Langley explained without being asked, glancing back over his shoulder. "Of course, he could have learned it. But then, with the rheumatism, we decided I should just read to him instead."

As they climbed up through the building, Malcolm slowly realized that many of the rooms were organized by objects. One was filled completely with grounded gas chandeliers; another with framed weapons—pistols, shotguns, rifles, a bayonet, a sword. In one room he counted thirteen different mantel clocks, including one that was a metal bust of a maiden, with coins still dropping mechanically from her ears and chest—the metallic, ticking sound unnerving in the otherwise still room. In another there were piles of musical instruments, pipe organs, and a trombone; a cornet, and an accordion, and a clavichord, and five violins piled on top of each other, the whole edifice wheezing and sighing as they went past.

The eeriest room of all was one crowded with old Christmas trees—half of them still strewn with strips of tinsel and balls, their brittle, dried-out needles raining down on the floor as Malcolm walked through. But everywhere, in every room, there were pianos—pianos of every conceivable kind, grands and baby grands, and boxes and uprights.

"We own fourteen of them, including one that Queen Victoria herself gave my mother," Langley said proudly, running his fingers over the keys of a baby grand, but too lightly to make any sound.

"A lovely tone, that one!"

"You play piano?" Malcolm asked him.

"Oh, I haven't touched any of them in a long, long time. When I did play, though, I won ten grand prizes. I could play twenty-five hundred different pieces from memory! None of this modern nonsense, mind you—"

"Why don't you play anymore?"

Langley stared bleakly back at him.

"My last concert was at Carnegie Hall. Paderewski followed me. He got better notices than I did. What was the use of going on?"

He led Malcolm into what seemed like a large front room, although he was too disoriented by now to have any very good idea of where he was. When Langley Collyer held up the lantern, he could see that this room, alone, had some swaths of empty floor space. Yet every inch of the walls was filled with great, fat books, covered in mats of dust. The dust was so thick that it fell away intact in the molds of the book spines when Malcolm swiped at a few shelves nearest him. Revealing the rich, brown and blue and red leather covers underneath, the gold-stamped titles all Roman numerals and the word LAW—LAW—LAW, repeated over and over again in the dust.

"Don't touch those!" Langley thundered at him. "Those belong to my brother, Homer, and he will want to use them again when he gets his sight back and renews his practice. It is the finest library on admiralty law in existence! My family have always had an interest in the water, you know. My great-grandfather, William Collyer, owned the largest shipyard on the East River waterfront. Our people built the finest steamboats on the Hudson—"

He went on and on, talking about the greatest this and the best that, while he led Malcolm deeper through the tunnels catacombing the house. Malcolm had begun to wonder if his brother Homer really existed at all, despite the fact that he had heard Jakey Mendelssohn say there were two of them. Has anyone really seen him? he thought. But just then they came out into a kitchen, with a kerosene lamp burning in one corner. Sitting there on a cot in front of them, with his knees doubled up to his chin, was the oldest, most tortured-looking human being Malcolm had ever seen.

He was dressed in a frayed gray nightshirt that reached down to his ankles, a burlap bag and an old great coat the only covering on his cot. His body was emaciated, his skin was the same larval white color as Langley's, though his hair and beard were much longer, and matted and tangled in knots. He sat so still on the cot that Malcolm wondered if he was actually dead—until his jaw dropped down, and he cried out in a mournful, wailing voice.

"Langley! Langley, is that you? Who is that with you? Another one of those intrusive police officers? I am Homer L. Collyer, the lawyer. I want your name and shield number!"

"Why your knees up at your chin like that?" Malcolm asked.

"My legs are doubled up with rheumatism. I can never lie down again," Homer Collyer told him more matter-of-factly then. "Langley, who have you brought home?"

"They were after him—outside," Langley explained, going over to his brother. He tucked the coat up over his shoulders, then set to work piling the oranges on the kitchen table, where he peeled and quartered them.

"Oh, those terrible people," Homer tsked. "When our father bought this house, Harlem was a wonderful neighborhood. The millionaires of the City used to pace their trotters up and down Lenox Avenue. They played the finest music at Pabst's Restaurant on 125th Street! Ladies went calling in their Victorias! Look at what's happened to it now."

"When's the last time you went out?" Malcolm asked.

"My brother lost his sight nine years ago," Langley said, bringing the oranges over to Homer, who began to pick at them with surprising delicacy. "We decided that Homer will rest his eyes, and eat one hundred oranges a week, until his sight returns."

Homer seemed to smile—his mouth a tangled, orange maw—and popped in another section.

"I believe it's already improving!"

Langley went over and lit a small kerosene stove that rested on top of the huge black iron stove bolted to the wall. He put a small piece of skirt steak into a frying pan and began cooking it up, the smell of frying meat temporarily dousing the overpowering stench of body odor, and mildew and dust that pervaded the kitchen—even if there was an alarming new rush of unseen roach scuttlings that made Malcolm's stomach turn over.

"I cook all his meals for him, and he's never had indigestion!"

"Why don't you use the real stove?" Malcolm asked.

"Oh, we had the gas and electricity turned off years ago," Langley told him as he pushed the meat around in its pan. "Homer can't see, so he doesn't need light. And as for me, well, I prefer it a trifle shady."

He took the finished meat, now cooked down to a small, burnt strip, and put it on a plate along with a knife and fork, and a large spoon. Then he took it over to his brother—carefully tucking a threadbare monogrammed napkin into Homer's nightshirt first, and turning on an ancient crystal radio, by the side of the cot, that Malcolm saw was hooked into a storage battery. A long, beautiful burst of classical music flowed out, then trailed off to an end—followed by a piping, irritated voice.

"This is your mayor, Fiorello H. La Guardia! You are listening to the people's radio, WNYC—"

Langley shut off the radio at once.

"Who is that irritating man?" he groused. "He's ruining the most wonderful classical music station!"

He commenced to feed his brother the tiny cubes of the meat with the spoon as he spoke. Homer dropped open his mushy orange mouth like a baby bird—his eyes closed, trusting Langley to place the less-than-bite-size pieces right on his tongue, from where he seemed to swallow them whole.

"I used to read to Homer at night," he told Malcolm as he chopped the blackened strip of meat into smaller and smaller pieces. "We have all the classics in our library, of course. I would read to him from Shakespeare, or Dickens. But then my eyes went bad, too, and I stopped. Now we just talk and listen to the radio. The music is wonderful, save for that annoying Italian fellow who keeps claiming to be the mayor."

"Why you have all these newspapers, then?" Malcolm asked.

"Oh, for when Homer regains his sight, of course! Then he can catch up on everything that's been going on."

He finished spooning the bits of charred meat into his brother, then dabbed at his face carefully with the napkin before removing it. Homer actually looked contented, his mouth closed in a small child-like smile.

"You know, when Homer first lost his sight, he used to have visions of beautiful buildings—always in red. He would describe them to me, and I would try to paint them just as he directed. Here, let me show you—"

Langley led Malcolm over to the recesses of the kitchen, where he held up his lamp again to reveal row after row of stacked canvasses—each and every one of them filled with fantastic buildings, and all slashed with blood red paint. There was painting after painting of mansions and brownstones, skyscrapers and single houses—all of them smeared in thick, coagulated gobs of the red paint.

"Did he dream all these?"

"Not really dream," Langley said in a whisper, sidling up close to him, glancing back at where his brother sat, stock-still again.

"He never really sleeps. I have to bathe him and tend to all his wants. He sits there all the time with his eyes closed, but he never really sleeps! I have lost fifty pounds in that time because I never sleep, either, but I'm not complaining! I have a way of relaxing without sleeping so I can write down whatever he says in the middle of the night. It's most worthwhile. Not only the pictures, I mean, he has invented the most marvelous telescope in his head—"

Malcolm reached for one of the blood red canvasses, and noticed a large wooden baby crib behind it. He squinted down into it—and found himself peering at a tiny, two-headed baby, floating in a jar of formaldehyde. Next to it were a pair of yellowed human skulls, along with the bones of a spine, a rib cage, hands and feet. Malcolm dropped the painting and jumped back, the grub-white face of Langley looming up right next to his.

"I gotta go," he said hurriedly, wondering now if he might have to kill the old man to get out. And how would he ever find his way?

"Hmm? Oh, those are old medical specimens that belonged to my father," Langley said with a dismissive wave of his hand. "Did I tell you he was the finest gynecologist in New York? But let me see you out."

They moved out of the kitchen and back into the labyrinth of tunnels—Malcolm glancing back at Homer, who looked now like nothing so much as an effigy from a waxworks show down on 42nd Street. One of the world's great murderers or scoundrels—sitting there doubled up on his cot, unnaturally still and white, with his eyes closed.

"Don't worry. He'll be all right until we get back," Langley assured him.

But what worried Malcolm more were the traces of a woman he kept noticing everywhere as they started back down the tunnels. There were bottles of violet perfume scattered around on different pianos, and tabletops. They passed a glass-fronted dresser, full of strange, perfectly preserved dresses, embroidered with silk and glittering jewels. There was even a long skein of knitting, encased in dust, with two wooden knitting needles still embedded in the loops of wool.

"Whose that?" Malcolm asked at last, holding it up by one end, trying to see what the color was.

"That was our mother's," Langley said, taking the knitting carefully out of Malcolm's hands. "She was a world-famous opera singer, before she married my father. And a great beauty, in her day."

"Oh, yeah? Where she at?"

"Cypress Hills Cemetery. She passed on fourteen years ago," Langley said, folding the knitting over twice, oblivious to the small explosions of dust that erupted from it.

"Oh. Sorry."

Malcolm looked away, and in the narrow swath of light from the miner's lamp, he could see that they had reached the end of the tunnel. A great, wooden-and-marble door stood before them, piles of unopened envelopes choking its letter drop, and spilling down into the foyer. Malcolm noticed that many of them were stamped with the return addresses of banks, and utility companies. Langley evinced no interest in them, sweeping the dead letters away with his feet, unbolting the huge door and straining at its rusty frame.

"I will let you out here, if I can. That will surprise anyone who's watching," he said, pulling the door away with startling ease.

"You really think somebody's watching you?" Malcolm asked him.

"Our life here has been forty years of being harassed by hoodlums! Those people out there have broken over two hundred of our windows," he began to rant again. "I never carry more than seventy-five cents in my pocket at any time, out of fear of being mugged!"

The door finally cracked open, swinging slowly, diffidently through the mounds of mail like a battleship moving through a choppy sea.

They had emerged on the 128th Street side of the building, Malcolm saw. Directly above them was a dimmed streetlamp, but it shone on them like a spotlight after the greater darkness inside the house—Langley's perfectly white face looking yellow now, as if reflected on a movie screen.

"Why'd you bring me in here?" Malcolm said abruptly, interrupting Langley's long spiel about how they had been besieged by those people.

"You know what I am. What made you bring me in here?" he repeated, staying where he was in the doorway.

"There was a girl, once," Langley said after a long pause, staring out into the street. "She came here for music lessons. I was training her on the piano, she had great potential! Then, one day, she stopped coming. I don't know if it was something I said—something I did.

"I wrote to her. I even went to her home, I offered to continue her lessons for free. But her mother only said that she had gone away. That was all! Nothing else—no address where I might reach her, no further excuse.

"She shut the door in my face, but I went back to her street every evening for months, trying to spy a glimpse of her. I would even sit on the stoop across from her house all night and into the morning, to see if she was there—just to know she was still there!"

He was looking at Malcolm now, his dusty pale white face very close to his. The skin oddly unwrinkled and fresh, like a much younger man's, he could see now.

"But she never came back, wherever she was. I never saw her again. I saw you—well, you know how beautiful you look. I didn't want to fail, to act again—"

Malcolm didn't wait to hear the rest of what he had to say, reaching out and pushing him away. The ghosty man falling back into the house, against the stacks of his newspapers, like an empty sack, while Malcolm ran up to the sidewalk, and down 128th Street toward Lenox Avenue.

CHAPTER FIFTEEN

JONAH

It started to rain before dawn that Sunday, hard little pellets that raked their bedroom window, so that Jonah knew he would have to be up early. By the time he eased the big green Lincoln out of its back-alley garage, the rain had begun to taper off, but between the weather and the gas rationing, he was sure the buses would be out again. After he dropped Amanda off at the church, he trolled up and down Lenox, and Eighth Avenue, in the big car, looking for any members of his congregation who might still be waiting at a bus stop.

All along the way he saw the ministers from every other church in Harlem, doing the same. Exchanging friendly waves and honks with them—at least all those who still had a car, and the ration points to fuel it. Picking up entire families still huddled under the bus shelters—more women than men, as was always the case, but especially so now with the war on. The older church mothers in their proud hats, undaunted by the rain. The children with their hair and clothes immaculately combed and pressed. The boys in blazers that were too big or too small, showing inches of white cuff, and the plastic tabs on their neckties; little girls in dresses that spread out above their knees like umbrellas, and shiny black patent shoes—

Jonah would fill the Lincoln with as many as he could, then move on to the next family, rolling down the window to tell them the buses were out. The mother or father would lean in, nodding— the news nothing they hadn't expected to hear. They would thank him solemnly and begin to walk slowly up toward the church, moving as fast as the youngest or the oldest among them could manage.

.   .   .

By late morning it had settled into a blustery, turbulent day; the dark gray clouds skittering across the sky, and the fleeting water rainbows forming and dissolving on the sidewalk. A day of illusions, and second glances. Passing "Beale Street," at 133rd and Seventh, Jonah glimpsed the working girls there already staggering along the curb—soaked to the skin, disappearing into doorways. Men in uniform climbing up from the after-hours bars below the street, ducking back down behind the stoops when they spotted the armbands of approaching MPs. *Harlem never did shut down anymore. Not even on Sunday—*

At 132nd Street, idling at a light, he noticed a crowd drawn to a pair of women evangelists. He had seen them on the corner before. The one tall and slender as a reed, reading out Bible passages in a commanding voice, the other short and pudgy. The short one held the umbrella, stretching to raise it up over her partner, and the Bible—while at the same time she interpreted each verse in a shrill, raucous shout, and according to her own vehement theology.

"I'm ain't talkin' 'bout no Pharaoh an' the Israelites, I'm talkin' 'bout the he-in' and she-in' a you Harlemites, right here an' right now!" she ranted, while the crowd around her laughed and clapped.

"I'm talkin' 'bout how mothers and fathers teach their chillen one thing in the South but they do another thing in the North, and they will surely pay the penalty. God will not be mocked!"

The people gathered there laughed some more. The Harlem of the simmering anger, of all the strange curbside congregations of angry men and women he had noticed gone for the moment, between Sunday, and the rain. Just in front of him, at the perimeter of the crowd, Jonah watched a young man, still wearing the sports shirt and slacks he had no doubt put on the night before, smiling sheepishly. Telling the woman with him, "Man, that old lady is sure steppin' on my toes! Gosh, that one hit my pet corn awful hard!"

After a little while he had become almost mesmerized by the drizzle and the steady beat of his windshield wipers, the ever changing street scene before him. Making wider and wider loops around the neighborhood, swinging down past the Harlem Defense Center, where he watched the happy, smiling young men on leave, walking out with pretty, slim brown women on their arms. Driving past a group of sailor messmen, who stood and squatted on their haunches outside Jock's

Place—pulling on cigarette butts, their faces blank and desolate, while they listened to the jukebox blasting "Don't Stop Now" through the open door. Still more families, still plodding their way toward church—his, or someone else's. Walking with immense, careful dignity, trying to avoid stepping into puddles or being splattered by the passing cars, waiting every few yards for the children to catch up.

And watching them, Jonah was filled with a surpassing love. For the churchgoing families—but also for the high-stepping soldiers and the blue sailors, and the Mutt-and-Jeff evangelists, and the insecure young man. Even for the working girls, soaked to the skin out on the pavement. He was almost dizzy with it, in that moment. Feeling his love encompass all of it, here where he lived in Harlem, this little enclave of so much sin, and despair, and hopelessness, but also of such immeasurable beauty. At 125th Street, he noticed the Checker cabs already taking the more optimistic fans up for the doubleheader scheduled that afternoon at the Polo Grounds—each of them with enough empty seats to carry an entire family to church. The white faces in the back windows staring out alertly, awash in apprehension and distaste. Jonah was in turn filled with nothing but pity for them, to be passing through this wondrous place but to know it so little. Thinking of the verse from Lamentations—"Is it nothing to you, all ye who pass by?"

"Good morning, Rev'rend Minister!"

The booming voice was familiar but impossible here. He swung his head around to see Adam Clayton Powell, large as life—larger!—and grinning playfully at him. Pipe clenched firmly in teeth, seated behind the wheel of his jaunty Cadillac.

"And a beautiful morning it is!" Adam sang out.

Beside him, in the passenger seat, sat the cryptic, one-armed Wingee. Four of the most elderly church mothers from the Abyssinian were seated comfortably in the back of the Caddy, which was about as wide as Adam's boat up at Oak Bluffs. Jonah rolled his own passenger window hurriedly down, thinking that he should warn Adam about his encounter up at The Mansion, but not sure how or if he should do it here and now, stuck at a public street corner.

"I thought you were still on the Vineyard—," he began, stupidly.

"Oh, I just thought I'd drop in for a little Harlem! I got lonesome for it, up on that fancy island!" he shouted gaily, smiling at the old women in his backseat, who smiled back at him as if he were their own son, home from Harvard.

"Listen, I, uh, had a talk with the O'Kanes yesterday," Jonah said haltingly. "They want you to lay low on those Stuyvesant Town houses—"

"'Course they do!" Adam thundered, laughing even as he did. Pulling the pipe out of his teeth at last and stabbing at Jonah with it. "They'll do anything not to have to live next to black people, Brother Minister! Anything! What you tell 'em?"

"I told them—" Jonah said slowly, trying not to sound too proud, "I told them that they would have to find themselves another bag man."

"Good for you, Rev'rend! Don't worry, we'll hold their feet to the fire. The Communists, the Democrats, the Republicans—we'll play 'em all against each other, till in the end they'll be asking to integrate!" Adam barked, banging a fist off the steering wheel for emphasis. Grinning and turning to his backseat choir again:

"Ain't that right, ladies?"

"That's right!" they cried out as the light changed and Adam sped off in his Caddy. Waving gaily back at Jonah.

"Good-bye, Rev'rend! See you in church!"

Jonah drove on more slowly, shaking his head and smiling despite himself, feeling the pride coursing through him at Adam's compliment, even though he knew it was foolish. He tried to keep his head level, at this unfamiliar surge of confidence, and even happiness—trying to concentrate on the task at hand. At the corner of 126th and Eighth he spotted an unlikely trio, just emerging from The Clean Spot, the little diner on the street level of the Braddock Hotel. There were two women, modestly dressed for the Braddock; one of them young, the other grey haired. Both of them walking arm in arm, with a tall, broad-shouldered young man in army dress khakis, a broad, black-and-white "MP" band around his upper-right arm. All three looked a little lost, and although they were not his parishioners and he could not remember having seen them before, Jonah pulled up to the curb in his ebullience.

"Excuse me, Rev'rend, but we was just looking to find a church," the MP said, grinning at Jonah so ingenuously that he could not help smiling back.

"You're welcome to come to mine, son. If you'd like to get on in, I'll take you all right up there."

"Why, that's full service now!" the MP beamed at him again, opening the back door for the two women. "Thank you, sir! Thank you very much, it would be an honor!"

Jonah thought he looked little older than a teenager—just a big overgrown boy in his army khakis—and he wondered at his being an MP. The young man bundled the two women gently but enthusiastically into the Lincoln's backseat before him. The younger lady looking even younger than he was—the other clearly a relative, wearing an older, womanly version of the boy's credulous, young face.

"This is my Mama, Mrs. Florine Roberts. And my fiancée, Miss Susan Torbohn," he said proudly, extending a hand up to shake Jonah's in the front seat. "My name's Robert Bandy. With the 730th MPs, over in Jersey City—"

"Good to know you, Robert," Jonah said, shaking the young man's hand while he watched him in the rearview mirror. Trying hard not to smile too much at his overflowing enthusiasm.

"You know, you ought to be careful around the Braddock," he told them as sternly as he could manage. "It used to be a classy place, for show people. But since the Depression... Well, I'm sure it's on your off-limits list, Robert—"

"I know, I know," the MP said, as earnestly as ever. The easy smile dropping from his face at once, looking like a chastised puppy.

"Mama was just stayin' there 'cause it's the only place she could find, comin' down from Middletown to see me," he said, a note of pride rising again in his voice. "It's hard to find anywhere now, with the war—"

"I been worse. I can take care myself," the older woman interrupted. Her accent from somewhere in the Deep South, Jonah thought, probably Mississippi—speaking with her son's same pridefulness, and a dose of motherly self-pity. "It's best I can do, workin's a maid up there in Middletown."

Jonah could really see the resemblance now—the MP's proud, hopeful face wrung through a lifetime of cleaning other people's toilets, and kitchen floors. She was a large, dark, bulky woman who looked as if she could indeed handle herself, wearing a respectable if aging burgundy dress, a white hat with plastic yellow flowers. Despite the heat she even had a secondhand imitation fur of some kind, fake fox or fake mink; rubbed down to a motley bit of fluff around her neck but still worn with indomitable self-esteem. Next to her, the future daughter-in-law looked all but overwhelmed. Pretty and slender, modestly dressed; sitting as demurely as possible in the middle seat, over the hump, with her thin shoulders hunched up and her eyes lowered.

"It's not so bad," the old woman insisted. "I seen cleaner places. But the wors' thing is the police comin' in all night. Throwin' colored an' white people out just for bein' together, they say. Excuse me, Rev'rend!"

"That's all right."

"But I seen worse. Just hard gettin' any sleep there, is all! But I wanted to come down, see my boy 'fore they ship him out."

"Oh, Mama, I don't know if they even will ship us out," he told her in a consoling voice. "Besides, it's not so bad for MPs—"

"Huh!" Mrs. Roberts snorted. "Tha's what you say! You should see where they keepin' 'em out in Jersey City, Rev'rend, all the colored boys. Got 'em stacked up on ships, half the time, while the white boys get the barracks. Ship holds, all full a rats an' like that. Now I ask you, Rev'rend, is that fair?"

"Mama! That's classified information!"

Robert Bandy put a hand on her knee, obviously embarrassed. But his mother only leaned forward, appealing directly to Jonah, who kept his eyes firmly on the road.

"I'm askin' you—ain't there somethin' you can do?"

"Mama, he ain't even our minister!"

"Well, seems like there must be somethin' a minister in this big city could do," she concluded, letting her son pull her back into the cavernous seat of the Lincoln, but with more than a hint of reproach in her voice.

"I apologize for my Mama, Rev'rend," Bandy said quickly. "She just worries about me too much. I don't want to trouble you with anything. I'll be fine. We all be fine."

By the time he got back to the New Jerusalem, Jonah only had time to splash some water on his face, and throw on his white ministerial robe in the vestry. The service starting late as it was, something that had become necessary since the war, and the periodic and unannounced disappearance of the buses. *No time even to visit his father, as he always liked to do on Sundays before services.* The old man rarely came out for them anymore—which Jonah worried in his heart might be a reflection on him, too. Attendance had been falling off again, more empty spots appearing in the pews than there had ever been in Milton's day. Jonah tried to tell himself it was due to the war, and the breakdown of the buses, but he knew better.

He breezed through all the usual preliminaries—what his father liked to call the rigamarole. Moving by rote through the opening greeting and prayer, the benevolent offering, and the church announcements. Two hymns and a spiritual from the choir, along with a solo by Miss Stella Jones, a young woman who was training down at the Institute of Musical Art. More prayers, for the sick and the dying, and the sons of the congregation who were off at war—

Unlike his father, Jonah always enjoyed these rituals, liked hearing of all the births and the weddings, connecting the familiar names with the faces of the people they were praying for. Yet this morning he had begun to anguish over the fact that he wouldn't be delivering a sermon for Mrs. Roberts and her boy. He had introduced them to Amanda just before the service began, and they were seated next to her now, up in the first pew before the altar. The traditional seat for the preacher's wife, out there in front of everybody, where he could remember his mother sitting so proudly, and which he knew his wife hated. Nevertheless, she was there every Sunday, regal yet reposed, setting the perfect tone. Always willing to do her duty. Even from where he was, seated up by the side of the pulpit, he could see how attentive she was being now to Sergeant Robert Bandy, his mother, and his fiancée.

His father had been right, it had been the perfect marriage. He couldn't help but notice, though, how the church had divided itself again. All of his good feeling from earlier this morning already snuffed out. The half circle before him split almost laughably into light skin, and dark. How little he had done, in his ten years. Even after all his daddy's scheming, his best efforts to prop Jonah up having failed—

Up above my head I see
Trouble in the air,
Up above my head I see
Trouble in the air,
Up above my head I see
Trouble in the air,
There must be a God somewhere—

The choir reached the end of the old spiritual that his assistant minister had ordered up, after Jonah had called him late the night before and asked him to fill in. He introduced the man briefly, then sat down—trying to pretend that he hadn't heard the rustle of speculation that went through the congregation, the murmured agitation

over why Jonah wasn't preaching again. The assistant minister—a
large, well-fed man named Morgan whose ambition was all but palpable—stood silent in the pulpit, pretending to arrange his notes
until the muttering had run its course. Letting the rising discontent
in the church register clearly, Jonah couldn't help thinking.

"There must be a God, somewhere," Assistant Minister Morgan
began at last, repeating the last line of the spiritual. Carrying the
hymn on into his sermon, the song on into his words. A common
enough beginning. Down at the Angel Factory, in Pennsylvania,
they had joked about the minister who started his sermon "A-men,
a-men. But what do we mean when we say A-men?…"

Outside, the rain had stopped completely but the wind was still
blowing, mild and warm, though with a force that was uncharacter-
istic of the season. Sending the clouds skittering across the stained-
glass windows of the sanctuary. Turning the sweet Bible scenes
there as sinister as the bats, and the scaly tail of the sea serpent, in
the stained glass up at the O'Kanes' Mansion—

Jonah forced himself to turn his eyes and his attention back to
his assistant minister, who was still working his way through the
boilerplate.

"Brothers and sisters, I come to you today filled with fear," he
intoned, trying to sound weary, though he looked as if he were
capable of plowing the north forty before breakfast.

"I am afraid that I do not have it within me to speak to you with
strength, and power—"

The standard device—a way of lowering expectations. The
preacher claiming that he was too heavy laden, or under the
weather, to truly speak well on his own. Relying on the Holy Spirit
to lift him up, offering up to God any success his sermon might
have. Shucking the blame off on Him, too, if it don't go so well,
Jonah remembered his father saying.

"—and then the Hebrew people asked themselves, 'How shall we
sing? How shall we sing the Lord's song, in a foreign land?'"

Brother Morgan declared himself at last. Using the very same
staple Jonah had tried to fall back on, the 137th Psalm, and the Bab-
ylonian captivity.

"'By the waters of Babylon, where we sat down and wept, when
we remembered Zion. On the willows there we hung up our lyres.
For our captors there required of us songs, and our tormentors,
mirth. Saying, 'Sing us one of the songs of Zion—''"

Jonah knew all the standard forms of it—he just hadn't been able to shape an answer that might convince himself. How were the Israelites to sing a song for their tormentors? The people who had murdered their brothers and sisters, and torn down the great temple of Solomon, and stolen them away from their land—the people who had enslaved them. How were the Jews of today to sing such a song? Shot down like dogs in the ghettos of Poland, exterminated like cockroaches in the camps Jakey's cousin had seen? How are we to sing?

"Perhaps it is as Paul wrote in the Corinthians: 'I glory in my infirmity, I have a thorn in my flesh.' Paul thought he had been given a thorn in his flesh on purpose, to keep him from being too elated by the abundance of his revelations, and he asked God to remove it but God told him, 'My grace is sufficient for you, for My power is made perfect in weakness—' "

But what did that mean? Just quoting other, random pieces of Scripture to answer the unanswerable. "Be content with your weakness, because God gave it to you." But why? "Sing your songs to God, even though he has allowed your enemies to enslave and slaughter you." And why? Because He says so?

It was the same old question, it seemed to Jonah, repeated over and over throughout the Bible, yet never really answered: What kind of loving God would let His chosen people suffer so?

The other ministers he knew, the theologians he had studied under down at the Angel Factory, had all sought to respond to it in two, or three, basic ways. It was a punishment, for even the most righteous had sinned. Like those little Jewish children, marched out of their Polish ghetto at gunpoint? Yes, they must have committed terrible sins—

Or the answer was that this world was all a test of faith, or—at the most modern, liberal congregations—part of the Grand Design. The world as a sort of great, literary metaphor. But it amounted to the same thing: Job, suffering the death of his children to test his faith. The Apostles, butchered all over the Mediterranean. The endless slaughter of the innocents, everywhere—for what? A metaphor? A great, cosmic work of art? Or God as a concentration camp capo, putting everyone through sadistic little tests to show they had enough faith to march on through this world to death—

No. In the end it was unknowable. The best ministers tried saying that, too—what they used to laughingly call the Confessatory Confession down at the Angel Factory, or Hands-Up! Theology. I confess it, I don't know! But you know God got to have a reason, He says He do—

It was enough, almost, to push him to his father's brand of benevolent atheism. But then there was the Christ. That sacrifice, His words—striking too deep a chord for Jonah to simply dismiss it all, to say it was all a lie. That irrational, spontaneous love, resonating a thousand million times, every day. Just the way he felt watching the people make their way through Harlem this morning—watching his wife, sitting so proudly in her pew now. Proud for him—

But what did it all mean, then? Even if it were true, there was still only faith. And God was still so far away—farther away than ever, it seemed to him now. Leaving them only these few, all but indecipherable traces of His Will—

The assistant minister was wrapping up now, concluding with another, lame exhortation to blind faith. Wiping his forehead busily with his handkerchief, to remind the less-than-moved congregation that he had been weak today, after all, and had relied on the Spirit to help him. One more failure to lay at God's feet, Jonah thought, stepping up to smile and shake his hand, and sing along with the choir the sermon-closing hymn—

There is a balm in Gilead,
To make the wounded whole—

As Jonah sang he glanced down again at his wife, her face perfectly composed, staring up lovingly at him. Their guests looking up at him with nearly equal reverence as they sang—Mrs. Roberts, and her daughter-in-law-to-be, and Private Bandy. Jonah scrutinizing his open, credulous face, wondering if he was as trusting and obedient in the belly of that great beast, the army. We all be fine—

It occurred to him that they were probably all of the congregation that believed in him now. Remembering what it had been like that morning when he had first ascended to the pulpit. The Easter Sunday when he had looked down and seen not the broad, trusting face of Private Bandy but that of Howard Marsden, coming through the doors of the New Jerusalem.

From the moment he spotted them, he knew it was over. Unable to forget, even now, fifteen years later, the looks of horrified, rueful recognition on their faces. He hadn't tried to call out, or to signal them in any way. Sometimes wondering what might have happened if he *had* chased after them—if he had strode openly down that aisle, hand extended, broad Stepin' Fetchit grin on his face before they had time to back on out. Booming out, *"My friends, my friends, do come in!"* Pulling them on back up the aisle to the altar with him and announcing them to the whole awed, adoring church— *"My friends from college!"* Imagining them carried along by a forest of black hands—like heroes hoisted off the football field—to his father's house for the celebratory dinner to follow. Feigning incredulity there, if any of them still dared to ask him. *"But—didn't you know I was colored?"*

It would have put the finishing touch on the day—and it was his suspicion that they would have remained his friends for life, or at least until graduation. Jack Leonard, the only one he ever confided his speculation to, the only one of them who would still have anything to do with him afterward, had chuckled painfully over it with him one night.

"I think you're right. They would all have been too damned polite to tell you off if they thought it was really their mistake," he had told Jonah. Adding:

"But they never would have forgiven you anyway."

He remembered hearing his friends planning to meet up in the City over the spring break—Howard Marsden the instigator, as usual. Jonah had begged off—but he had forgotten about the freshman directory, the guide the college published, complete with the pictures, and names and addresses, of all the new undergraduates. Howard had said what a great prank it would be to go over and surprise Jonah, the pastor's son, on Easter Sunday, and they had looked him up.

Even then they hadn't figured it out immediately, none of them being that familiar with the City. Simply assuming, once they saw the uptown address, that it must be one of those crumbling white neighborhoods still fringing Harlem—some stranded, low-church parish, squeezed between the blacks, and the Jews and the Italians. Getting dressed up in their finest clothes, chortling to themselves over how much fun it would be to embarrass him. Thinking they would just slip into the back pews, maybe try to catch his attention during the service. Hoping to catch him in nothing more mortifying than giving a particularly unctuous prayer—

It was only when the Checker cab had dropped them off that it had finally begun to dawn on them what was what. The hack insisting that this was the place, and offering to wait for them. Listening to the soaring, unmistakable Negro hymns pouring through the open windows, staring at the black stained-glass Jesus his father had always loved, in the window just above the front doors. Howie Marsden himself, Jack remembered, saying as he stepped down from the cab running board—

"This has gotta be a mistake. Or the old son of a gun's having us on—"

And then, pushing open the heavy wooden doors, tumbling in past the startled ushers, they had walked right into the sanctuary and seen—him. Jonah at the moment of his greatest triumph, sitting like a prince before a sea of colored faces.

He hadn't pursued them. He had even delayed his departure back to school, taking the night train in order to give Howard Marsden more time for what he knew he would do. His parents delighted, thinking he was staying on to savor his triumph. Seeing him off at the train, along with a coterie of loyal members of the diaconate and the board of elders. A little tipsy at Penn Station from the couple of glasses of bootleg wine they had each had to celebrate— still deliriously happy. His Daddy squeezing him in a bearhug, his mother still tearful. And Jonah only glad the whole, long way back to school that he had said nothing to them about a boat.

He hadn't been surprised by what he'd found when he got back to their room—only, perhaps, by the thoroughness of it. Howie had moved out everything, absolutely everything he owned, in just the few extra hours Jonah had given him. There was not a trace of him remaining—none of his exquisitely tailored clothes in the closet, or in the chest of drawers they shared. None of the wonderful implements on his desk that Jonah had secretly coveted, the beautiful set of Waterman fountain pens, the blotter and the circular typewriter erasers that looked like little medals; the gorgeous, streamlined Smith-Corona portable on which he insisted on pecking out his own papers, a matter of constant amusement among them all. None of the books on his shelves; the fine old beat-up first editions of the classics, with their cut pages, and their cracked bindings and covers that his father—the father Jonah would never meet, now—had given Howard as a going-away-to-school present, and that he just loved to smell for their scent of musty libraries, and ancient knowledge.

The shelves, the closets, the drawers, all conspicuously empty now—with none of his own things reordered yet to take over some of the space. Entirely empty of that style that Jonah had so envied, that ease and self-confidence that had permeated even his possessions. Howie—that stupid prep school boy's name; how could he have ever loved anyone named Howie—had simply disappeared. Out of his room, his life, his closets. Leaving behind, above all, no note, no words of any kind—his silent removal of himself more eloquent a rebuke than anything else he could offer.

For the rest of that Easter night, Jonah had simply sat on his roommate's immaculately made bed and stared at the half-emptied room around him. Not bothering to get undressed, barely summoning the energy to take off his overcoat, only staring at the room around him while a dozen thoughts ran back and forth through his head. He never did move his own possessions into the empty spaces he had been left. Instead, the next morning he had packed up his own things, informing the college that he was moving into the house the four other colored students shared down in the town— the one place, it had been subtly understood between town and school authorities alike, where they would be tolerated.

The harder part had been figuring out how he should try to approach the rest of them, Jack Leonard, and Gilly Mackenzie, and Andy Miller. He had thought about going over to knock on their doors directly, take whatever names they wanted to call him, and face them with his presence. He had even thought about confronting, or at least writing, Howard Marsden. But in the end he had not been able to make up his mind to do anything, and save for Jack, none of them had spoken to him, or had anything to do with him again, turning their faces away distastefully when he happened to see them in a classroom, or along the walks of the small campus.

He had worried even longer over what to say, or write, to Isabelle Brinckerhoff, the blond minister's daughter he had dated. Sitting down in the evening every night for weeks with pen in hand, yet never able to come up with anything. Somehow, he suspected that it wouldn't be necessary, and he was proved right in this, too, when a letter finally arrived from her Baptist-minister father, threatening to have him killed—"or worse!"—if he should ever approach her again.

He took all these affronts with the same, stolid numbness. Moving on down into the house the colored students shared after humbly asking to live with them. Telling them frankly—"I think I made a mistake."

They had accepted him immediately, and he had lived there for the rest of his time at the college, welcoming in turn the other few colored students the college accepted over the rest of his years there. He had helped them all with their studies whenever he could, and unlike every other college athlete he ever encountered, they were attentive students—eager to seize the opportunity they had, devoid of any illusion that they could make their living after college on a football field. And in their turn they had never thrown his earlier denial of them in his face, leaving the subject as blessedly mute as his old white friends.

Except for Merton Turnbow. He had given his permission for Jonah to move in when the others were for it, brusquely dismissing the question with a wave of one huge hand—"He's gotta live somewhere, I suppose." But he never forgave him. Saying no more than a few perfunctory words to Jonah for the remaining year they spent living in the same house together—even refusing his aid when he was on the verge of failing out of the school altogether. It was only then, exasperated, that Jonah had gathered enough courage to ask why he continued to hate him so.

"It's too easy for you," Merton had told him coldly. "You can just go back, do it again whenever you want."

"I said I made a mistake. What else can I do, besides ask for forgiveness?"

But Turnbow had only snorted at him.

"Don't you see?" he had said, waving a hand at him—at his whole light-skinned body. "It's too easy for you. You can go on repenting, an' being sorry your whole life! You can just repent, an' go right back to where you were, an' there's no consequences for you."

"That's not so—" Jonah had tried to say in his defense, but Merton shook his head.

"Ah, man, I almost feel sorry for you. You got no idea where you even are," he said, and walked away then. Having nothing more to do with Jonah for the few remaining weeks before he did flunk out, and left the college as quietly and proudly as he had always walked around it.

Some years later, after Jonah had graduated, and had gone through the Angel Factory down in Pennsylvania and come back to his father's church, he had heard that Merton Turnbow was playing for a semipro team in Harlem that called themselves the Spiders—a team made up of former Negro college stars who were considered too good for the best white pro teams to play. Jonah had snuck over one Sunday to see them playing in Mount Morris Park, under the shadow of its high bell tower, the Spiders pounding away at another colored team from Philadelphia. The crowd meager—probably not enough to pay their expenses. But there was Merton Turnbow, Jonah saw in a shock of recognition, slashing away through the defensive backfield, legs churning right through the other players, homing in unswervingly on the ball carrier, just as he had in college. Jonah made no attempt to talk to him after the game was over, sure that he would be just as unyielding now. He had only watched him wander off with the other players, jersey covered in mud, limping stoically toward the subway. Sometime later Jonah heard that he was working in Harlem as a short-order cook. Then there had been a picture he had seen by chance in the Pittsburgh Courier, a few months after Pearl Harbor. Merton in an army uniform—his face staring back accusingly at Jonah.

He had remained friends over the years with the other young men he'd met in the colored house, corresponding with them at Christmas—some of them even becoming members of his congregation, if they moved to the City. But the only one of his old white friends Jonah had kept in any touch with was Jack Leonard. He alone had trudged down to the little house where he lived now, and had coffee with Jonah. The two of them so unsure of what to say to each other about the real issue between them that they had remained silent on it that afternoon, and for a long time to come. For the rest of their years at the college, he would see Jack sporadically—the two of them even going out sometimes to their old haunts again, as wary as they were of running into certain people on those occasions. He also saw him walking around campus with his other friends, with Howie and the rest of them. But Jack never brought them over—and Jonah was relieved that he didn't.

"It's not that he hates you," Jack Leonard had finally tried to explain to him, after they had been referring to it elliptically all night. Another night out at a roadhouse—only this had not been under the stars in a convertible, but in the middle of winter, shivering inside the clunker Howard Marsden had helped him buy, passing the last of a flask of bourbon back and forth.

"He just feels betrayed, that's all."

"He feels betrayed."

"Well, you gotta admit, it wasn't like you were exactly honest with him—"

"If I were white, you think he'd've cleaned out his things without so much as a word? Even if I had told him some other lie? Even if I had stolen something from him? You think he would've moved all his things out in the middle of the night, never given me a chance to explain?" Jonah asked him straight out.

"It's not that, exactly," Jack Leonard said, grimacing, squirming a little in the passenger's seat. "It's more—it's just the shock of it, is all. You think somebody's white, they turn out to be Negro. That's all. It's just a matter of—expectations, I guess."

"Uh-huh," Jonah said bitterly. "And what're my expectations supposed to be? And how come you weren't shocked when I disappointed your expectations?"

"Well, you know, it's different for me, Jonah," Leonard said, taking a hurried nip from the flask, passing the rotten bootleg bourbon back over to him. It roiled his stomach and had already given him a headache, even while he was still drunk, but Jonah took another long swig nonetheless.

"Whatta you mean, it's different for you?" he asked Jack. "What's so different about it?"

"Nah—you know, Jonah," Jack said, smiling wanly at him. "I mean, I'm a Jew. Well, you knew that, didn't you?"

"Jewish. Sure, sure," Jonah said. His voice to him sounding like it was coming from a long way away. Wondering to himself, Is everything hidden to me? How foolish can I be?

"I know what it's like, passing. My grandfather was doin' it soon's he got off the boat," Jack was saying, beginning to slur his words. "I don't know as he ever really converted. Next thing he knew, my old man said we're all Episcopalians."

"Howard knew that, though—didn't he?" Jonah asked slowly. "He and all the rest of the guys? Gilly and Andy? He knew you were Jewish right off, didn't he?"

"Well, sure, yeah," Leonard said. "He made some joke about it—"

"But you never told him about it. Did you?"

"No. No, I guess not," Leonard said, sitting up again, beginning to realize what he was getting at. "I guess he just assumed it. It never made any difference—"

"And there it is," Jonah said, cutting him off.

"Yeah, I guess there it is," Jack sighed.

Jonah had stuck it through the rest of the semester, and the remaining three years at the college. He had stuck it through even though he had wanted to get on the next train and go back home immediately, the moment he saw that Howard Marsden had cleared out of their dorm room.

Secretly hoping that he wouldn't. Secretly hoping he had decided, somehow, to stay, after that Easter Sunday in Harlem. Still wanting to sit down across from him at his desk, when he was at his most serious—when they would have their best talks about literature and theology and philosophy, and the whole idea of what a man could know, and not know. The whole happy, silly range of undergraduate thought. And he had wanted to sit there, and talk to him seriously about what had happened, and how much he had gotten from it, and what would happen now.

Picturing that whole lovely scenario just in the time he sat on Howard Marsden's bed that night, looking at his cleaned-out room. Picturing, even, some kind of grand rapprochement in which they talked all night, and ended up shaking hands, then going down to the college cafeteria, arm in arm, for breakfast. Picturing Howie Marsden telling him he could still come along on his family vacation to Europe—

But not surprised when it didn't happen. Thinking, too, during his long night sitting on his roommate's bed: This is our dominant trait: the singular ability to anticipate disappointment. Bred in the bone from so many years of living so close to white people. Thinking that sitting there on his roommate's bed like a dog, like a goddamned, pining dog—

He didn't go. He stuck it until graduation without even a hint to his parents—then—about all that had transpired. Sticking it out in good part because he couldn't conceive of a plausible explanation as to why he should drop out and come home.

He didn't go to Europe in the summer, of course. Instead he went back to his Daddy's church in Harlem, and worked in the soup kitchen, and learned the ins and outs of the preaching business. All the little professional secrets his father had to tell him—for it was a business, like any other, he realized, though for the moment he had lost all his previous desire for it. All of it seeming more and more hollow the more he knew it, despite what he had thought had been his conversion, so many years before.

That was his first crisis of faith—what he had thought was so firm, crumbling away beneath him. Nor was there anything he could cling to up at school anymore, no ambition he retained, nothing he got out of the various lectures or professors. Only going back every semester for his parents, to do the penance he had inflicted upon himself.

The only person he had told, finally, had been his father. Not even Amanda, after all these years—just him. Unable to keep anything from him since his first days of school, when he would go talk to him in his vestry office. Confessing it to him in the same way, during the Easter recess of his senior year, weeks before he graduated. More afraid than of anything else in his life of what his father might say, but feeling too broken by then to keep it in.

"I made a mistake—" he told his father, standing before him where he sat at that big rolltop desk. The old man listening gravely to him the whole time, looking over the top of his reading spectacles, not interrupting him once until he was finished.

"Never let that happen again," was all he had said when Jonah had finished—then turned back to the Easter sermon on his desk.

He had been stunned that that was all the old man had to say to him. Leaving Jonah with nothing for it but to back slowly out of his vestry. The one time he could ever remember his father letting him down. Hoping for something more, even in the form of a rebuke, a scolding. Something to make him feel it. Speculating endlessly to himself, in the days and years that followed, whether his father had simply been too rattled over how close he had come to losing him. Or whether, with almost supernatural foresight, he had deliberately left it to Jonah to figure out. Left it to him to find the bottom himself, and thereby to raise himself up again.

But either way, it hadn't mattered at the time. A few days after their circumscribed conversation, Jonah had journeyed back upstate to the college for the last time, to take his final exams. He had worked hard, finishing seventh in his class, despite feeling the entire time as if he had been kicked in the stomach. The graduation was held on an unusually warm, muggy spring day, and that morning Jack Leonard had come down to the colored house in town, and shaken his hand, and wished him well.

"I hope we stay in touch," he told him—and, "I'm sorry."

"Me, too," Jonah had said in turn, squeezing his shoulder, and then he had gone to the train station to meet his ecstatic parents.

That afternoon they had sat out in the temporary bleachers set up on the great lawn of the college, along with all the other parents. Jonah had paraded past them in his cap and gown with the rest of his class, ordered only by academic rank. All of them were given another handshake from the dean, and handed a small maroon leather book with a graduation program and diploma inside. Then they had lined up around Taylor Lake. Each of them holding the small leather book in one hand and an unlit torch in the other—waiting while the class valedictorian circled the entire lake, lighting their torches, one by one, with his own.

Jonah's had been lit near the beginning—and while he waited he stared down at the smooth dark surface of the lake, watching all their reflections as the fire seemed to spread and surge up through the water. The same lake where they had stood with their dates, watching the ice-hockey players at the winter carnival that first year; all the laughing red faces glowing in the light of the bonfires. In the dark water now he could not distinguish Jack Leonard, or Howard Marsden, or any of his other old friends, with their identical black caps and gowns.

The valedictorian finished lighting the torches, and there was nothing left then, save for the grandson of the college's founder to say a few words. He was a tall, severe-looking man—a little stooped with age, with a white mustache and beard cut into a sharp V, and dead blue eyes. The country was already well into the Depression, and his talk was exceptionally bleak. There was little promise of hope, or joy extended, the founder's grandson only lecturing them severely on what little they had to look forward to.

"Do not fool yourselves," he told them. "Life has stricter rules, harsher judgments, and more cruel limitations than any of you have known here. It is a hard game, and its rules are inexorable."

When he had finished, all of them knelt down carefully together, as they had been rehearsed, and doused their flames in the lake at the exact same moment.

His college days were ended.

CHAPTER SIXTEEN

MALCOLM

After he was saved by the ghosty men, he took to staying in both night and day—too rattled to go anywhere anymore. He hit Sammy up for more of his weed in advance, saying he would pay him back but smoking it up himself. He went through as many as twenty of the little matchstick joints in a night, then popped himself back up with some of Sammy's Benzedrine tablets. He felt too jittery now even to pay much attention to his comics, or his dream books, his mind just clicking restlessly through the endless numbers for anything and everything. *Apparel, 016. Arrows, 371. Automobile, 213. Affliction, 590.*

He started sleeping whenever he felt like it, keeping the window shades drawn now, against all the blank yellow window squares of the endless City, numbing and meaningless in their endless repetition. He knew that he should get back out there, and at least make Archie's collections for him, but after the Collyer house he was no longer sure he even knew what was real anymore.

Wondering, now, if he really was going the way she had. Thinking on something he had been told or read once, that nobody ever knows they are going crazy. Wondering if it had been that way for her, then—slipping into madness without knowing the difference.

He almost never went outside at all, anymore. He paid his roommates, out of his dwindling money, to bring him back what little food he needed. By then he had lost nearly all track of time, no longer sure if it was even morning or night, save for the pinholes of sunlight that pierced the tattered shades. He had received another letter from his brother Reginald, postmarked from Newport News, and hinting that he would be up in New York in just a few days' time. But Malcolm couldn't even bring himself to do anything about that, to plan where he might go with Reginald, and how he could convince him to jump ship and stay with him, as he had hoped to do before.

He felt as if he were borne down under an unbearable lassitude now, scarcely able to drag himself off the bed. All he was able to do was to tune in the radio, and thumb through the mysterious books from Prof. Toussaint's African National Memorial Bookstore. Turning again, as he had known he would, to the small, mysterious volume without any words, any title or author on the cover, only that gold, crescent moon. Opening it once again to the title page, wondering over the words there, which were no less mysterious:

THE BIOGRAPHY OF ELIJAH MUHAMMAD

as told by

"X"

But inside, everything seemed to make more sense now. He wondered if this, too, was a sign that he was going the way of his mother, if before long he wouldn't be seeing movies from heaven himself. But he kept reading, more and more avidly as he went on, so enthralled by what was before him on the page that he forgot where he was, the room around him and all of his nameless misery. The words tumbling out as if they had been written just for him—as if it was the story he would have told, the life he would have lived:

He was living in the Black Bottom when he first saw the face of God.

He had been hearing the stories for weeks—all about a small elegant man who was going door-to-door in a red Chevy coupe, selling bolts of cloth and silk, and talking about the true religion of the Black Man. A man who no one could quite say was black, or white, but who had large black eyes that never blinked, and could see into the depths of your soul. Who could pluck a hair from his head, and dip it into a glass of water and make ten thousand more hairs sprout from it—and who said that he could destroy the white man's America just as easily.

Elijah had only put it down to more spook stories. He had been wandering through the mills and yards of Detroit for ten years by then. Living down near John R. Street, on the western edge of the Black Bottom, with Clara and the children, and his parents. All of them together in a little house so close to the railroad tracks the coal trains would take your head off if you looked out the window at the wrong time. The floorboards shaking all the time from the hammering of the metal-stamping machines just down the street, the constant rumble of the trucks and trains, and even the planes swooping down from above.

When they had first arrived in the city, he had taken any jobs he could find, at American Motors, and American Wire and Brass, then finally the American Nut Company, where he worked separating by hand steel shavings from the nuts and bolts. All the American companies, anything American, thinking it was a good sign, that maybe he would finally find the real America he had heard so much about. But at the nut company the little metal shards cut into his fingers until they were swollen and bloody, and he had to quit. He had gotten work as a forge helper over at the Chevy plant, but the white heat of the forge scalded his already weak lungs, and made him cough up black phlegm for hours every night, until he had to quit that, too.

They had been forced to live mostly on Clara's jobs as a maid after that, while he got day work where he could. Stuck down by the train tracks, buffeted all day and night by the reverberation of the ceaseless white man's industry all around him. Dodging the drunken Polack workingmen, who were at least as big and angry as any cracker in Georgia, and who didn't even speak the language. The taste of ash in his mouth all the time, no matter how many bars he took himself to.

It was when he was still a forge helper that he had first started going up into Paradise Valley, the sporting section of the Black Bottom, to try and ease his thirst. Seeking out the cheapest, barest blind pigs along St. Aubin Street or Gratiot, joints that were no more than wood-and-tin shanties with a couple of tabletops propped up on barrels, serving homemade gin and corn liquor to men who couldn't look each other in the face. The booze so bad that, when he woke up the next morning, he was afraid to open his eyes lest he find that he was blind.

He had tried to stop the drinking. He had started going to

Garvey meetings, and joined the Ancient Egyptian Order of the Nobles of the Mystic Shrine of North and South America, and the Moorish Science Temple—looking for something, anything he could find that would fill up the hole in him where preaching had been; that could tell him he was something besides one more out-of-work Georgia Negro, supported by his wife.

But none of it worked, and before long he had stopped even try-ing to look for work. He was too ashamed to go home with noth-ing, even to eat—scrounging instead for food out in back of chili parlors, and fish restaurants. Letting Clara and their five-year-old, Emmanuel, search him out in the bars around their neighborhood. They would always find him and drag him home—a little brown woman and a little boy, propping up a little man on their shoulders. One night near Christmas they had even found him passed out cold on the railroad tracks, and somehow managed to pull and lift him off before the next one of the coal freights that came hurtling down the track every twelve minutes.

Even after that, he would not stop drinking, until one spring afternoon he had staggered out of another blind pig over in the Eastern Market, just behind Joe Muer's fish restaurant—so drunk that he had fallen down right there, and lain where he was in the muddy back alley. He had awakened around dusk. It was a chilly Michigan night, but he had lain there inured in his inebriation to the cold, content to watch a small colored boy working his way up and down the alley. He was a slight boy, dressed in a raggedy sweater and torn pants and sneakers, hauling a rusted, red toy wagon behind him, and in his drunkenness, Elijah had been trans-fixed by the sight. He watched as the boy searched systematically through all the alley trash cans—pulling out squares of card-board, and empty milk bottles, and anything metal that looked as if it might be brass or copper, and piling them all into the wagon. He watched, too, as he went through the cans behind Joe Muer's as expertly as any hungry bum, pulling out the remains of pick-erel, and trout, and fried perch, calmly eating each and every scrap of food he found, right off the waxed paper or the used napkins they were wrapped in. He had stared at that boy for nearly half an hour—but only when the boy had turned toward him, running his tongue over a scrap of butcher's paper that held some last, red, raw trail of meat, did he realize that it was his own son, and that he was waiting for him.

And yet, even then he did not give up the drinking. It was not until the Fourth of July that he had first heard the name of his savior. He remembered it because the Polack kids had decided to celebrate the birth of the nation by bombarding the Black Bottom with bottle rockets and Roman candles that came shrieking down amidst their yards, scattering the women and children, and making them scream. It had all been too hard on his nerves, and he had been inside, drinking beer with his father at the kitchen table, the sweat running freely down his face and back in the little house. Too hungover from corn liquor to even sit up without the support of the table, thinking seriously of sticking his head out that back window when he heard the whistle of the next freight train blow.

"I been speakin' to Brother Abdul Muhammad—" his father had started to tell him.

"Who's that?"

"You know—the brother call himself Brown Eel when he was with the Moors—"

"Why's he call hisself—what? Abdul Muhammad?"

"Well, this man give him a new name—"

"What man?"

"He calls hisself Far-rod, or Ford, or somethin'. Says he's here on a mission to the black man," his father said guardedly; still reluctant to talk to his son about anything that touched too much upon theology.

"A mission? Like a missionary?"

"Best I heard it, he sayin' the black man is the Original People. He sayin' the white man is the devil."

The moment he heard those words Elijah had felt his heart leap, and he had lifted up his head.

"I like to hear that man! That is good what Brown Eel said to you!" he exclaimed.

Yet so far had he sunk, so heavy was the weight that the white man had laid upon him, that even then he had not gone down to the Moorish Temple to hear this man speak. He had wanted him to come to his door, but he never did, and Elijah kept drinking, even though he knew that he would be ashamed if the man were to come and find him in such a state.

Then one day his wife had come home from the Moorish Temple and told him that she had met the man there, and that Elijah had to come and listen to him. But he was still too drunk, and his lungs were wheezing too badly that day even to let him stand up, and Clara had had to walk all the way back to the temple, just to invite Mr. Fard to come to dinner that night. Elijah had been sitting in his living room, still trying to catch his breath, when there was a single light tap on his door. The bells of the far-off Polack church had just rung six o'clock when he heard the tapping—just that, a sound no greater than what a bird might have made—and he had gone to answer it.

To his astonishment, he saw there was a white man standing in his doorway.

"Invite me in, Elijah," the white man said. "I am the one you've been waiting for."

So great had been the aura about him, so strange and otherworldly that Elijah had simply stood back and opened the door wide. Welcoming him into his home, though he wasn't able to get a word out even to ask the man who he was.

"I know you think that I am white, but I'm not," he told Elijah gently, as if he were reading his mind already. "What I am is an Asiatic black man. You've never seen anything like me. Have you?"

And it was true, he never had. He was a slight man, only a few inches taller than Elijah was himself, with waves of jet black hair oiled up high on his head. When he came into the light, Elijah could see that his skin didn't look quite like the hue of any colored man or any white man he had ever known; it was a sort of light olive color that seemed to change every time he looked at him. He had on an immaculate dark blue pinstriped suit, and a maroon fez that he wore with such dignity and poise that Elijah thought at once he must be some sort of ambassador.

"No, I'm not a diplomat. Unless by that you mean an ambassador from your true past."

The man had smiled at him suddenly then, showing his rows of gleaming-white perfect teeth. But what had really captivated Elijah were his eyes. The pupils like two black moons, vast and unblinking—

"My name is the Honorable Wallace D. Fard, and I have come here to save my uncle, who has been lost in the wilderness of North America for the last four hundred years. And I have come to save you, as well, for you have been just as lost."

"What do you mean?" Elijah asked him, even though he already had the uneasy feeling that he knew exactly what the strange man meant. But Master Fard merely sat down on Elijah's lumpy old living room couch, the one he had found on the street with the boy, and smiled back up at him from there.

"But you have seen it," he said easily. "By now you have seen all that the white man's great civilization has to offer. You with all of your white man's dreams. Now you have seen all that they amount to. You once were lost, but now you are ready to be found."

And when he heard those words, Elijah felt as if an electric shock had run down his spine. He stood rooted to the spot, transfixed in the gaze of those warm, luminous eyes until Master Fard had come over and taken him by the hand, and led him over to the couch.

They had sat there in Elijah's house, and talked until dawn, and the Master had given him his very first lesson in The Knowledge of Self and Others. He had taught him how time had begun with a spinning atom, seventy-six million years before, and how that atom had evolved into a Black Man, who was the Original Man. How he was that self-made Man who came to call Himself Allah, or God, and who created all things in the universe—and not some spook god who dead souls flew up to on angel wings, like the white man believed in. He taught him how it was Allah who had molded the Original People in His image, and how for many millions of years they had lived on the single continent of Asia, in peace and contentment. There they had raised up the pyramids of Giza, and all the mountains of the Earth, and even caused the deportation of the Moon, through all their great knowledge of the sciences that remained unrivaled, even unto the present day.

And Master Fard had told him the story of Dr. Yakob, the Big Head Scientist, who was the greatest, and most arrogant, of all the great scientists among the Original People, and who had learned how to draw the black germ out of babies through the secret of magnetism. It was Dr. Yakob and his followers who had bred the white man, and all the other races, over thousands of years of horrible experiments in their laboratories on the Isle of Patmos.

Now the black gene Dr. Yakob had drawn out of them was the most dominant gene, being the darkest, and so these white, bleached men had still been little more than animals who lived in caves, and whose women fornicated with dogs. They had not one-third the strength, or the intellect, of the Original People, and they were unclean, and the source of all diseases in the world today. Yet they had come to rule over the Black Man anyway, through their evil new science of Tricknology. They had taken away even the names of the Original People, and called them Negro, which means something dead, and lifeless, and neither this nor that.

They had committed the greatest crime in history, murdering six hundred million of the Original People in the slave trade, and they had wrecked and robbed and spoiled many more, until they were truly no more than white people—Yakob's People—in black skin. Eating swine and other unclean food, and fornicating like beasts, and drinking alcohol. Blaspheming, and fighting their brethren over nonsense, and living on credit, and handouts from the white man's government, and forsaking Allah and loving the devil who was their master.

Now when Master Fard had finally finished telling him all that he had to tell him that first night, Elijah was silent. For he knew that every word was true—knew that he had always known it, somewhere deep in his heart—but he was amazed to hear it from the lips of any man. It explained everything. It explained how it was that God was human, and not some indifferent, faraway sky God who had willed it that Black People should be slaughtered, and enslaved, and carried away from their homes into bondage, just so they could hear His word. It explained how the depraved and ignorant white people he had trembled before all his life in Georgia, and here, too, in Detroit, could so much as dare to consider themselves the master race, and impose themselves over all others.

It was all right there, so clear and so simple that Elijah didn't know why he hadn't seen it himself—the answer to everything that had stilled his voice in the pulpit, and rotted out his faith, and made him see the world as nothing more than a cruel accident. Yet still so burdened down by his life in the white man's country was he that when Master Fard had finished speaking, all he could blurt out was the question—

"But how do you know all this?"

"Because I am an Original Man."

"But you don't look black."

"The Original People don't look the way the so-called Negroes look today," Master Fard had told him, the gentle, knowing smile never leaving his lips. "They have straight hair, and fine features. It was only in the jungles of East Asia—what you call Africa—where they went to harden themselves for the ordeal to come that the

Black Man became coarse of feature, and his nose became wide, and his lips swelled up. It was only there that his hair became kinky and curly, and that he allowed himself to be ruled by his weaker parts."

"So where you from?" Elijah had blurted out, and was immediately embarrassed by his challenge. But Fard had not seemed bothered by it in the least, as if he were expecting this very question.

"I am the son of Alphonso, from the Koresh tribe, and of Baby Gee, my mother," he told Elijah. "I was born in Mecca, which is the holiest of cities, and I lived there until I went abroad to study, and received a degree from the university at Oxford, in England, and another degree from the University of Southern California. I have studied history, and mathematics, and astronomy, and the Bible and the Koran. I have traveled for twenty years all around the world, studying the educational system of every civilized nation, and I can speak sixteen different languages, and write in ten. And when I arrived here in North America, I was received with honor as a diplomat at the White House, as a distinguished guest of the your president, Theodore Roosevelt."

He stopped for a moment, then smiled almost shyly.

"Do you want me to show you?" he asked.

"Yes, please!" Elijah cried, and he was embarrassed again, afraid that his faith was not sufficient.

But Master Fard had only smiled his same knowing smile, then opened up his mouth and spoken in one language after another. The words going on and on, as easily as if he was just continuing their conversation, and Elijah knew then that it was all true. He felt as if he were basking in the words, all the strange, beautiful sounds that he did not know, but that came tumbling out of the man's mouth like a golden stream. He closed his eyes—and he realized then that his lungs no longer hurt, and that he was able to breathe easily, and was not even thinking of the three beers still left in the kitchen icebox.

Only when Master Fard finally paused had he opened his eyes again, and looked straight at his guest.

"Who are you?" he asked him then, for the first time.

Fard had looked right back at him. His smile gone now.

"My name is not important just yet," he said. "You may call me Master Wallace D. Fard. But soon, should you prove worthy, I will reveal my real name, and I will give you a new name, as well. For you will be a great prophet, too."

"I will?" Elijah asked weakly, stunned by Master Fard's words—but realizing at the same time that he had known it all along, that it was something which had always been inside of him.

"Do not think yourself unworthy. I, too, was once like you, wallowing in wickedness, and depravity, a slave to the white man. You have to reach bottom before you can know—before you can lead the people."

"Let me ask you one thing more," Elijah had entreated him, though the grimy Black Bottom dawn had already broken through the windows, and Master Fard was standing up to go. Pausing at the doorway to hear Elijah's question, his face as gentle and open as ever.

"Why have you come? Why here, and now, and to me?"

"Haven't you figured it out by now?" Master Fard asked. His smile almost playful now, teasing him as he walked out the door.

"I have come to destroy the world."

From that night on, Elijah had never felt the need of a drink again. He had smashed his remaining bottles of homemade beer out on the sidewalk that very morning, and gone out again to look for work. It wasn't easy, with the Depression weighing heavily on the great city now, the plants and factories of the white man shutting down. Even the metal-stamping machine down the street finally fell silent, and the coal trains no longer whistled by their window.

But somehow, he was able to find enough work to feed his family and get them off the welfare. It was always hard work, but it felt as nothing to him now. He could work all day without being tired, his hands and his lungs no long hurting. Clara was quietly proud of him again, he could tell, and at the end of the day he would come back and sit in what was now the blessed peace and stillness of his kitchen. Drinking a cool glass of water, or buttermilk there, and thinking on Master Fard and how much he had already changed his life.

In the evenings and on weekends, he went out with the Master and some of his other disciples in his red Chevy coupe, preaching The Knowledge of Self and Others. And every Sunday afternoon, he went to hear the Master speak at the Moorish Science Temple on Hancock Avenue, which was renamed the Allah Temple of Islam. More and more people pushed in to hear the Master speak every week, even following Master Fard down the street to ask him questions, or just to touch his sleeve. The people coming in such multitudes now that Elijah thought this was how it must have been in the olden days of the Bible, when Jesus had walked through the Holy Land.

Above all, Elijah was overjoyed to see that the Master's power had spread to him, and that at last he was able to preach again. When he first spoke in the Allah Temple, he had stumbled over words, and mispronounced them, where back in Georgia he had always spoken easily, even glibly, when preaching in the little piney-woods churches. He was mortified, and glanced over uneasily at Master Fard. But the Master was still smiling serenely at him, and he had recovered himself then, and delivered the most powerful sermon he had ever given.

"Do not be surprised. The truth is harder to speak than lies," the Master told him afterward, when he had confessed his shame and bewilderment over his stumbling. "People like to think it's hard to lie, but in fact it's easy. That's why so many people do it."

Soon Elijah was speaking at the Allah Temple every Wednesday and Friday night, and on Sundays when Fard was away on one of his mysterious errands. Every time he spoke, he gained more and more confidence. He had converted all of his close friends, and his family, to followers of the Honorable Master Fard, so that they looked up to him again, and did as he said. They even looked healthier, and better—their skin shinier and better complected from following Master Fard's dietary rules, which included forsaking the pig, an animal that Fard had told him was part dog, part cat, part rat, and the carrier of 999 poisonous germs.

But it was not only his family who looked up to him now. He could see all the people in the temple nodding at his words—their congregation of bellboys and factory hands, waitresses and laundry workers; reformed drunks and gamblers, thieves and adulterers. All the humbled and the pure of heart, now willing to follow him just as they did Master Fard, and Elijah felt exalted, and glad to be alive for the first time in many years.

One winter evening after services he was alone in the temple with Fard, putting away the prayer books, when he caught a whiff of the distinct, musty smell of churches that he had always loved. Some combination of candle wax, and dust, and onionskin paper that overwhelmed him, and filled him with love for this man who had raised him up from his drunkenness and despair, who had allowed him to preach again in these places he loved so much. He had turned to Fard then, with tears in his eyes. The Master turning to meet his gaze, as he always did, as if he had been anticipating it. Smiling at him in that infinitely gentle way of his, the black pools of his eyes deeper and more compassionate than ever. Elijah asking him directly, at last, the question he had held in abeyance for months—since their very first meeting—but had never dared to broach before:

"Are you the God that's supposed to separate the righteous, and destroy the wicked?"

To his surprise, Fard's gentle demeanor had melted away instantly then, his face turning a deep red color in the candlelight. Elijah amazed again to see just how white he really was, how red his skin could turn when he was angered.

"Now, who would believe that but you?" he had cried, thrusting a warning finger into Elijah's face.

But then the redness and the anger had vanished from Master Fard's face as quickly as it had appeared. The slight, well-dressed man smiling warmly at him again. Touching Elijah affectionately on one cheek, and winking at him.

"When I'm gone, you can say whatever you want about me."

But after that Elijah had not been able to restrain himself. Asking him again, a few weeks later, when the Master had deigned to visit his home once more:

"You are that one we read in the Bible? That he would come in the Last Day, under the name of Jesus? You are that one?"

The smile had faded from Master Fard's face again, just as it had in the Allah Temple—but this time he had not looked so much angry as very serious, the way the apostles and the saints looked in the Bible pictures. Staring deep into Elijah's eyes for several long minutes, until his pupils seemed to swell, and spin like pinwheels.

"You are ready now," he had told Elijah finally. "Yes, I am the One, but who knows that but yourself, and be quiet."

And Fard had given him a new name then, which was Ghulam Bogans, and which he told him meant Slave of God. He had told Elijah that from then on he would be his closest servant, over all others. But he had instructed him not to tell anyone at all, not even in his family, so that Elijah had had to lock himself in the clothes closet at home to keep from blurting out the truth in his ecstasy. Prostrating himself there amidst the family's shoes, and the coats smelling of mothballs, praying to Fard where no one else could hear him. Asking only that he might see the day when he brought forth the kingdom of God on earth, and punished all the white devils.

Then, one Sunday, just before he was about to introduce Master Fard to the temple faithful, Master Fard had turned to face him, as if he could read his mind, and said:

"You want to know something. Go ahead and ask."

And then Elijah had looked at him very seriously—more seriously than he had ever looked at anyone or anything in his life—and asked him for the third time:

"Who are you, and what is your real name?"

"I am the one the world has been expecting for the past two thousand years."

"What is your name?"

"My name is Mahdi. I am God. I came to guide you into the right path, that you may be successful and see the hereafter."

And when he said those words, Elijah felt as if he had been struck blind. He had to close his eyes, and hold his arm over them in order to keep out all of the glorious golden light that flowed in on his brain. The next thing he knew he was on his knees, and then Fard was lifting him up again, and smiling at him, laying a hand paternally along his cheek.

"You may go ahead and tell them, and I will acknowledge you as my prophet," he told Elijah.

And Elijah had walked out onto the speakers' platform, pausing to look over the crowd of janitors and day laborers, maids and short-order cooks. The long unemployed and the half-starved, with their eyes glazed and their cheeks caving in, who had nonetheless given their last two bits to come in out of the cold and hear him preach. He had straightened his suit, and adjusted his bow tie and the maroon fez with the crescent moon, and the star on it—not nervously, just making sure he had everything perfect for the big moment—and then he had said it out loud, for the very first time in public:

"Fard is Allah, who came to save the dark people."

He could hear them stamping on the floorboards in their approval. All of the disinherited, the poor and the bound over, pounding on the old wooden floor with their tattered boots, and shoes, and anything else at hand, until the whole temple was shaking. Malcolm realizing only belatedly that the pounding was actually coming from the front door of the apartment—the banging so hard that it was the front door that was bouncing on its hinges.

He froze where he was—afraid that some of the people who waited in the shadows had followed him home now. Afraid that it might be the cops, though he had never known them to ask for entry, anywhere in Harlem. Hurriedly, he stuffed his notebook, and the books from Prof. Toussaint, back between the bedsprings and the mattress, and pulled on a pair of pants. Then he padded down the hall and through the kitchen as quietly as he could in his bare feet, wondering if he could sneak over to the front-door peephole and peer out without whoever it was noticing the telltale shadow eclipsing the light—

Before he could get there, the door came flying open, just missing his head. Malcolm throwing himself back, falling over a kitchen chair and landing on the yellowed linoleum floor—where he found himself staring up at the ferocious-looking figure above him, more massive than ever from Malcolm's new perspective on the floor.

"Why don't you open yo' door in a timely manner, son?" West Indian Archie growled down at him.

He lifted up one of his huge feet then, and stepped over Malcolm. Limping over to another kitchen chair, where he rubbed gingerly at his ankle.

"Makin' me kick it in like that! Man, I'm gettin' too old for that kind a nonsense!"

Malcolm stayed where he was on the linoleum, limp with relief. He had been terrified when Archie first came through his door. But already, even from his position on the floor, Malcolm could tell that he was only annoyed with him and not truly angry. Archie gesturing at him from the chair, where he had removed his shoe now and was working on his foot through an argyle sock that was the size of a grocery bag. When he was satisfied, he stood up and went over to Malcolm, offering him one ham slab of a hand.

"Get on up, son!" he said, looking him over critically as he pulled him back to his feet—Malcolm's arms still clutched over his chest. "You don't look so good. What you been gettin' you self into, young lane? Here, lemme look at your eyes!"

He lifted Malcolm halfway up off the chair. Malcolm flipped his head back, and tried to pull away, but Archie turned him back with one hand behind the neck, using the other to force up his lids, one at a time.

"Uh-huh. Yah, I see it now. You been ballin' day an' night, ain't you?"

"I'm fine as thine," Malcolm said quickly.

"Don't you be drivin' me some nail, Red. You know you ain't been workin' for a whole week now. Not makin' any a my payoffs, or my connections. Don't hype me now, Red. I checked up."

"Yeah, well, I been workin' up some new hustles," he said, looking Archie in the face as sincerely as he dared.

"Yah, you been up to somethin', that's for damned sure," Archie said skeptically, squinting at him closely then. "You sure you feelin' all right, Red?"

"Sure, Archie—"

"You lookin' a little skinny. Siddown, I'm gonna make you a real breakfast."

He took his jacket off and hung it very carefully on the back of some mission-furniture chair, then rolled up his sleeves and pulled three eggs out of the icebox. He lit the stove and mixed them up in a pan on the stove top, with a little milk and some butter.

"They ain't mine," Malcolm protested mildly. "They the other boarders—"

"Shut up, Red," Archie said calmly, "an' go get some clothes on. This'll be ready in a minute."

He did as he was told, and went back into his bedroom. Hastily stuffing away his remaining matchsticks, and Benzedrine tablets, along with his books on the secret knowledge of the Lost-Found Nation of Islam—hiding them all as well as he could hide anything in his single, sparse room. By the time he came out, West Indian Archie had the omelet plus two pieces of margarine-smeared toast, a slice of tomato, and a fresh cup of coffee waiting for him—all set primly at his place at the table, complete with a napkin and a knife, a fork and a spoon.

"I hadda learn this when I come up from Trinidad," Archie told him as he began to eat. "I had to learn to take care a myself."

Hovering over him paternally, his voice almost fond as he reminisced.

"I was just like you. Runnin' policy fo' Alex Pompez, then Big Joe Ison's mob. Out all the time, eatin' anything off the street. It run a body down."

He squeezed down on Malcolm's shoulders—the huge hamhock hands suddenly feeling a little ominous to Malcolm, though he kept eating anyway. It was the first full meal he had had in days, and he was suddenly ravenous, the eggs and toast more delicious than anything he could remember.

"That's it. Dig in, Red. You got to take care yo'self, you want to last. How you think I steered clear a Dutch Schultz's boys, all those years? Or the I-ties, even worse. You got to be alert, so you keep yo' eyes open all the time on the street. You hear what I say?"

Malcolm nodded enthusiastically, and kept eating, averting his eyes. Archie's hands moved roughly. Rubbing gruffly around the back of Malcolm's neck as he ate, as if trying to help move the food down his throat.

"That's solid, huh? I had a slave as a short-order cook, back in those days. Hadda learn to cook on the job," he chuckled proudly. "It weren't pretty at first, but I did."

"An' the numbers, Archie," Malcolm asked him, honestly curious. All of his jealousy over Miranda slipping away under the effects of the food, forgetting for the moment all his scenarios of killing him.

"How'd you learn how to do the numbers? Figure all of 'em in your head like that?"

"Ah, Red, I just did," West Indian Archie told him, shrugging. "When I come up, the cops catch you with any slips, they take you down the precinct basement, work you over bad. Schultz had 'em all paid off, do his work for him—"

"But don't you ever think how it could be different, Archie?" Malcolm persisted, speaking quickly, everything he had read in his books from the night before still lingering in his head. "Don't you ever think about how if it wasn't for the white man, we wouldn't have to live like this? Why, you could be a engineer, or a scientist. Maybe a college professor in mathematics!"

Archie came out from behind him and sat down in a chair, looking at Malcolm closely.

"We're hustlers, Red," he said, his face more somber than Malcolm had ever seen it before. "We be hustlers if the white man never existed. That's just the way things are."

"But don't you see, Archie? The white man is the devil!"

"I don't doubt it," Archie shrugged. "Somebody gotta be."

"But you ain't hipped to what I'm layin' down—"

"No, Red. You listen up, now," he said firmly. "Where I come from, I had nothin'. I get up here, people callin' me monkey chaser. People callin' me coconut. Everything I made, I had to earn out on the street. You see this?"

He lifted up his chin, and Malcolm could see a thick scar, running nearly all the way around his jaw. Malcolm stared at it, fascinated, wondering why he had never noticed it before, until Archie pulled his head back and it receded into the loose, leathery folds of his middle-aged jowls.

"Three I-talian boys jumped me, up on 147th Street, when they was makin' a move on Dutch Schultz's territory. I was lucky the streetlight was out, an' they aim wasn't too good. I paid 'em for that, though, you can bet on it."

He stood up, laying his hands on Malcolm's shoulders again, although this time Malcolm felt a chill go through his body and he stopped eating.

"You say the white man's the devil? All right," Archie repeated softly. "But I do what I got to do to make my way. Out on the street, man gotta have eyes in the back of his head to live. And I do."

He leaned suddenly forward, his head next to Malcolm's, his heavy, rum-sweet breath on Malcolm's cheek.

"I see everything that goes on, Red. Everything. Don't you be messin' wit' me."

"I won't, Archie," Malcolm said, his blood still. Forcing himself to pick up another forkful of the eggs.

"That so?" he asked, in a mournful voice—his hands clamping suddenly around Malcolm's neck. "That so? 'Cause I know you been shortin' me, Red."

Malcolm froze, his fork clattering back on the plate. He tried to say something, to reassure him, but it was as if Archie had already choked any further words out of his head.

"I ought to shoot you through the ear."

West Indian Archie bent his head down again until it was right next to Malcolm's. His voice soft, almost crooning to him. One hand left his throat, and Malcolm could feel something hard prodding into his kidneys now, just under the chair backing. Then Archie sighed softly.

"But I like you, Red, so I'm only gonna scare you a tiff. But I got to tell you, boy—I am disappointed."

The huge hands released his neck, the rod pulled back out of his kidneys—and Malcolm fell off his chair, to the floor. Sobs wracking his body as he turned to Archie on his knees, grasping at his pants legs.

"I hadda do it, Archie," he confessed between sobs. "I couldn't go out there anymore. They was waitin' for me, everywhere I went. They was just waitin' in the dark for the money, I couldn't do it anymore."

"People holdin' up one a my runners? Where the hell was all those cops I pay for?" Archie frowned, mystified—pulling his .45 back out. "You tell me who they was, son, I'll go take care a them!"

"No, Archie, please! I just can't do that no more! Please, Archie! Just give me some other slave!"

"All right. All right, now, Red," Archie said uneasily, still frowning down at him. He gave Malcolm a light pat on the side of his head. "You take it easy now. What's goin' on with you, son? You sure you all right?"

"Please!"

"All right, I got another job for you, son. C'mon now, boy."

He lifted Malcolm bodily back into his chair.

"You comin' all to pieces on me. Well, that's okay, son," he said solicitously, though obviously still puzzled. "Some boys just ain't meant fo' the street. You eat some more now, you got to take care a yourself."

Malcolm nodded, picking at his eggs again, his tears subsiding. Trying to think, now, how he would ever get to see Miranda again, much less take her away from Archie. Telling himself, even as he felt Archie's huge hand still patting his shoulder in concern, I'll just have to kill him, then. I'll just have to kill him, before he kills me.

CHAPTER SEVENTEEN

JONAH

The day that had begun with such quiet, rainswept promise began to slowly unravel after the service. Jonah had wanted to invite Private Bandy and his family back to the early Sunday dinner they had on Strivers Row, but he was due back on his transport ship, and his mother had to get her train to Connecticut. Jonah had bid the three of them good-bye at the door of the New Jerusalem, Private Bandy pumping his hand vigorously, a big, ingenuous smile on his face.

"That was real fine, Rev'rend, real fine! Thank you for havin' us!"

"Please do come back anytime—"

"Maybe sometime we can hear you preach," Bandy's mother said pointedly, but the tall MP had quickly smoothed over her remark.

"That was a wonderful service, wasn't it, Mama? Can't ask for a better service 'n that!"

Instead it had only been the usual deacons and church mothers at their table. Amanda serving up a whole roast beef that she had somehow managed to finagle from Schwartz's butcher shop. It was a heavy meal for the summer, but when the clouds returned and a steady rain began to beat on the skylight, they had all dug in. These Sunday dinners were always the height of affected gentility, a ritual so polite that it nearly reduced Jonah to tears of boredom. But this afternoon all of them found themselves eating with unusual, silent vigor, as if hunkering in against the storm outside. Only peering speculatively over their food at Jonah when they thought he wasn't looking—as if they might spot what was wrong with him.

As if it were a physical ailment—

He was just as glad to let them think what they would. Once he had seen the last of them to the door, he just sat around the living room, nursing a rare glass of scotch, while Amanda cleaned up. They gave the cleaning woman the day off on Sunday, and usually he helped Amanda with the dishes. It gave them a chance to talk over the service, the endless politics, and gossip, of the church. It was another way they worked together, and often they would go upstairs and make love when they were done. Napping together— spending the rest of the day and evening up there, when he had an assistant minister working the evening service for him.

Today, though, on this blustery, rainy afternoon he had not approached her. Preferring to stay down in the gloomy front parlor with the lamps off, the light through the blue, eye-of-God skylight dwindled to a weak gray funnel. Thumbing moodily through the Sunday papers while he listened to the classical music programs on WNYC. He worked his way through the war news; on through to the last, smallest police items in the back pages. Where the Negroes were.

There had been another gang stabbing on West 147th Street. A pastor's son, knifed coming back from a church meeting. Jonah made a mental note to call the boy's father. A doctor the papers were calling "The White Angel," for treating Harlem residents free of charge, had been lured into a tenement on 117th Street, and robbed and beaten by four youths. An eighteen-year-old girl taken to a rooftop, where she was robbed and stripped of her clothes— another young woman used as a human shield, in a shootout at a tavern in Brooklyn. The brother of one of the few colored police lieutenants in the City, stabbed to death after a drunken brawl with his female companion on West 154th Street.

"Maybe I killed him and maybe I didn't," the woman had reportedly told police. "I don't know much because I was asleep when you fellows came in here."

Jonah read through each item with as much interest and even more loathing than he had the stories of racial assaults throughout the country in the Amsterdam Star-News. Asking himself, with the grim satisfaction of one who had long become convinced that the world was falling apart, What are we becoming? Even though the answer was readily apparent: Exactly what they want us to be—

Those had been the parts of Lazar Mendelssohn's narrative that he had found the most chilling—back when Jakey's cousin was still talking. Worse even than his accounts of the cattle-car trains, and the human factories, were his stories of what life was like in the Polish ghettos. People reduced to acting like animals, just to survive.

It was the same here. Making us into what they want us to be. So they don't have to feel guilty about what they do to us. So that we will do it for them.

"What are you doing to yourself?"

Her voice broke through his reverie, compassionate but stern. He hadn't noticed that Amanda had come into the room, was squatting now by the foot of his chair, a hand on his paper.

"What are you doing to yourself, reading all that bad news all the time?" she asked softly.

"They're my people—" he stammered at her, but she only shook her head.

"Your people! Like you're responsible for everyone in the world."

"I'm not saying that," he snapped. "I'm just saying I have a duty—"

"No, honestly, Jonah. It's blasphemous, is what it is," she said, cutting him off. "I see you. Reading about every bad thing everyone's ever done. All the crimes, all the war news. All the lynchings. People are people, you taking on all their sins isn't going to change that."

"But don't you see what's happening?"

"No, Jonah, I don't," she told him bluntly, and he saw to his surprise that she was genuinely angry now. "I don't see it at all, because you're never here anymore. Always worrying about somebody's troubles, somewhere. Why don't you tell me what's happening to you?"

He put down the paper and was about to say something to her. Just what, he wasn't sure himself. Maybe confess it all, everything, the very worst thoughts about what he had been planning, with no idea of how she would take it. Trusting her, his wife.

"Amanda, I—"

But it was then that they both noticed the music had stopped. The radio was blurting out a news story now, all bulletins and flashes. For a moment he assumed it was something about the war, another new advance, or a landing on a Pacific island he had never heard of. But no: the story was coming from Detroit—another race riot. It had started with an automobile accident, or a fistfight at a picnic grounds, no one was sure, but already there were stories of rapes, and drownings, and murders. White mobs attacking a housing project that a few colored defense-worker families had been allowed to move into. Colored men and women attacked in public, pulled off streetcars and beaten right in front of city hall. The police doing nothing to interfere. Pouring into some colored neighborhood called Paradise Valley, joining in against any Negroes they found, using nightsticks and riot guns, machine guns and even deer rifles—

The radio report went to a siege of something called the Vernor Hotel. Police were firing tear gas at what were said to be fifty armed Negroes holed up inside—at least one of them with a machine gun of his own. As they listened, stupefied, they could hear the crack of what the reporter breathlessly assured them were police sniper rifles.

"We are informed they told the police, 'Come and get us!'"

After a few minutes Amanda had stood up and walked wordlessly out of the room. Jonah kept listening through the rest of the afternoon and evening, even as the long summer evening faded into final blackness through the skylight above. Getting up to twist the dial around for more news from time to time, going from one station to another, until at last he cut it back to WNYC just in time to hear a blast of martial music.

"…we are proud to claim the ti-tle of United States Marine!"

"Patience and fortitude!" a shrill but pompous voice followed immediately, just as it did every Sunday night.

Mayor La Guardia had been speaking directly to the City every Sunday night since Pearl Harbor—a half-hour torrent of threats, advice, and imprecations. Telling housewives to buy snap beans or wear their galoshes, giving out his wife's recipes. Reeling off phone numbers of gambling joints in Passaic that local bookies had been calling, in order to put the local cops over there on the spot. Menacing loan sharks and war profiteers by name.

"Cut it out. Cut it out right now, you no-good, thieving, chiseling tinhorns!" he railed into the microphone like some comic-book hero. "That sort of business don't go in New York. Not while I'm mayor. Get me?"

Tonight, though, the little mayor sounded surprisingly calm, his voice somber and level after his usual salutation.

"We must not forget that in New York City we still have the aftermath of prejudice, racial hatred, and exploitation that has existed in

many parts of the country," he said slowly, sounding almost unnaturally controlled—and it occurred to Jonah then that La Guardia, too,
was scared.

"Let nothing happen in our city that will disturb our tranquil-
lity! Let no snake agitator come here in New York seeking to start
racial trouble. I want to assure the people of this city that with just
a bit of cooperation and understanding on the part of the people
themselves, we will be able to cope with any situation. I am depending on the people of this city to keep our record clean."

Jonah leaned over and snapped off the radio, unable to listen to
any more. He liked the frenetic little mayor well enough. It was
impossible not to. Until the year before he had still lived in a walk-
up tenement, over on 109th Street in East Harlem. He had fired or
transferred the most brutal and corrupt Harlem cops, built new
public housing, opened Sydenham Hospital to finally take some of
the pressure off The Morgue.

Yet Jonah thought that the man often acted and sounded as if
he had just discovered that race existed. "The aftermath of racial
hatred!" What did that even mean? As if there were no more bigots
left in New York—only his mysterious snake agitators. For all the
time he spent racing to fires or dumping slot machines in the river,
the mayor seemed oblivious to what went on all around him, all the
time, in his City. How routinely members of Jonah's church ended
up with broken heads, and under arrest—even when they went to
the precinct houses to report a burglary or a mugging that had
been perpetrated against themselves.

Nor was it only Harlem. He had heard other stories from rab-
bis, told in hushed tones at interfaith dinners, about Irish cops who
stood by and laughed while Christian Front youths up in Washington Heights and the South Bronx attacked elderly Jews with baseball bats. The young thugs bursting into synagogues while services
were being held and screaming, "Kill the kikes!"

The Jews, again. Their other obsession. And now, with modern
science at their disposal, it was going to become...a process. The
Jews first, Negroes next. It would be such a simple thing—We are
already in our ghettos. The Nazis were doing it now. Even if they
were defeated, once they showed it could be done—

Why not us? Isn't it the natural course of such unslakable
hatred? They always wanted to get rid of us, now they have the
means. They even have the blueprint.

He knew then, for the first time, that he truly would go. Pass once and for all into that monstrous white world—not for fame or money or some sense of freedom like his sister sought, but just so he wouldn't have to watch from close up anymore. He was not the man to protect them—his church, his people—from this terrible new day. He could not even speak from the pulpit anymore. He could not even protect his own wife on a public train.

Jonah jumped up from the chair where he had been moldering all day. He jumped up and ran out right then, pausing only to snatch his raincoat, and the umbrella from the hall stand, then running on out into the night. He hurried to the avenue, where he was stunned for a moment by a blare of horns, somewhere in the darkness before him. Elder Lightfoot Michaux's revival, he realized only belatedly. Still going strong even in the rain, annoying the good people up on Sugar Hill, their chanted hymns and rhythmic clapping sounding like a call to war.

We are ready for the battle—

He turned his collar up against the rain, and began to jog in the general direction of the noise, hurrying toward what was supposed to be his church.

He found the old man where he usually did, sitting up behind his desk. His big black scarred head bent down, its crown facing Jonah as he came in. Jonah feared for a moment that he might be dead or in some sort of state, but he looked up when Jonah called his name—a look that might have passed for concern crossing his stonelike face.

"Daddy. Daddy, I got to go," Jonah told him right away, sitting down in the little chair next to the desk, holding his father's hands in his. Speaking in only a barely raised whisper, not wanting to awaken or alarm the Spottswoods, keeping guard in the next room, but hoping that he could make himself understood to the old man.

"I'm going, Daddy, do you understand? I have to."

To his horror, the old man had started to pull himself to his feet then. Grabbing on to the edge of his desk, lifting himself slowly upward.

"Daddy!" he hissed, astonished.

But his father kept going. Lifting himself on up until he was standing on his own two feet, unaided. He was still half bent over at the waist, but Jonah was surprised again to see how big he really was. Not only bulky and solid as granite, but tall—certainly taller than Jonah was, had he been able to straighten himself out.

"Son," he began to breathe—the word little more than the breath itself, one long inhalation, but unmistakable.

"Son. Son, son, son," he kept saying, in a sort of rasping sing-song, until Jonah could not stand it any longer. He jumped up in turn, and wrapped his arms around his father's vast bulk—slowly, carefully lowering him into his chair again.

"You're going to hurt yourself!"

His father's words, the first he had spoken of any kind in months, wound down to long, openmouthed gasps for air. He seemed so winded that Jonah considered rousing the Spottswoods—but when he started to go, his father locked one of his big still strong hands around his wrist, holding him close. Jonah stared down at the tracks of that wheel rim, still creasing the top of his father's head. Thinking again how hard his life had been. All alone at thirteen. His mother killed in front of him, his Daddy gone off to the war. The loss of both his wives, Sophia run off. Jonah's eyes brimmed with tears at the thought of what a cruel thing he was about to do.

But it will be better if I don't stay. It will be better for everyone.

"You got to—stick," his father breathed, stunning him. The old man seemingly exhausted from the effort, flinging himself back into his desk chair so he could stare up at Jonah. Letting his wrist go, the immense, ancient head lolling back, but his eyes still holding him.

"No, Daddy. You're their preacher. I never was," Jonah said, meeting his gaze. "I can't do anything for 'em, Daddy. I can't help anybody."

"Stick in their craw!"

The words coming a little easier now, as if he were just getting worked up. Jonah still not sure what he was talking about—the church, he assumed. His father's eyes still boring into him, as much like some great, wounded beast's as a man's, he thought. As much like the bull that had rammed his taxicab by the East River stock-yards. Still furious. Still willing to fight it out, against what anyone had to offer. Fighting the gangsters, and the police, and the white politicians, all through the long exodus up the West Side. Fighting to put up his church. Fighting against even the diffidence of his own children.

"I tried to tell it to you once, but you didn't want to hear any more," Jonah told him. The words tumbling out unplanned, but he was determined to deflect his father's gaze.

"Sure, you can look at me now! You couldn't look at me then, back when I tried to tell you what I was! You didn't want to see it, then! But take a good look. What do you see now?"

His father's eyes blinked, slow as a lizard's, then looked back up. Jonah advancing on him in his chair, half out of his head, he knew, but determined to get some sort of answer—to at least make him look away.

"Huh? Come on, old man! Tell me! Can you stand to look at me, to know what I am? Tell me—what do you see?"

His father blinked again. Jonah hovering right over him now—dimly aware that he had been shouting, aware that the Spottswoods must surely be getting up, but not caring. Needing only to see what his reaction would be—

To his surprise, his father's eyes seemed to soften. His voice croaking out a single word—his throat so rusty that it came out more as a bark than anything else, having to repeat it two or three times more before it became intelligible.

"Ruth," he said. "Ruth—"

Jonah still not understanding right away. He had so rarely thought of her by her given name—remembering it now only by dint of the affection filling his father's eyes. The name of that white woman in the ancient picture. Her face largely lost to the rest of her family, its memory abiding solely in Milton's mind.

Ruth. His mother.

Then Jonah was walking swiftly back down the vestry hall, running down the stairs into the church. The sound of people waking behind him—voices calling, lights being turned on.

"Who there? Who there, now? Rev'rend Minister?"

He ignored the Spottswoods, kept running on through the church, out a side door into an alley. Fervently hoping, even as he did, that that would be the last time he ever had to endure anyone calling by that appellation. Reverend Minister. He was nobody's minister, even less someone to be revered.

He ran out onto West 144th Street, then started to walk west. Swinging his umbrella wildly around him as he walked—wanting something to hack at. The rain had stopped, but the street was still unnaturally quiet, devoid for the moment of its usual wartime revelers, and he could hear his own rapid breathing. He heard a motor behind

him, and a ponderous, long-snouted Packard came rumbling down
the street, pulling up fast by the corner of Seventh Avenue, throwing a sheet of water up over the curb and making him jump back.

A jowly, middle-aged white man opened the passenger door
of the big sedan and stepped out on the sidewalk, waiting. Jonah
could see that he looked obviously ill at ease. There was another,
colored man who remained where he was behind the wheel—and
Jonah understood in that instant that he was not the white man's
chauffeur. Sure enough, a third man came around the corner, moving toward the uneasy white man with an easy self-assurance, as if
he had been expecting him.

Jonah gripped the umbrella harder, squeezing it until he nearly
broke the spokes. He had seen such men here before. John-walkers,
he knew they were called—colored men who escorted whites from
downtown to the "specialty" prostitutes they preferred. The wheel-
man had met the nervous white john at some hotel downtown, and
driven him up here, passing him along to the man who had just
turned the corner, the john-walker. Jonah had tried to get the trade
at least pushed off this corner before, falling back on the influence
of the O'Kanes after many appeals to the local precinct. But they
always came back—another indication of his failure. His father, or
Adam, would have moved them off once and for all—

Jonah was almost upon them now, staring right at the john and
his new guide. The white man turned his face away, but the john-
walker hadn't spotted him yet. Jonah studied the colored man
closely—his face creased with an easy smile, hand reaching out for
the white man's arm. Dressed like any other experienced hustler in
a sharp suit and tie, hair combed back in a flamboyant conk under
his wide-brimmed hat. His face leering in the dim streetlight, but
oddly boyish and innocent at the same time—

Then Jonah recognized him—unable ever to forget that face.
The boy from the train. It was impossible, but it had to be him,
no longer buying comic books, but here to walk a white man to a
colored whore. The boy—now a man, he supposed, in his sharp
new suit and his professional conk—staring back at him. His face
equally astounded. Breaking into an even wider, incredulous grin at
the sight of Jonah, who in turn started to run toward him, umbrella
clenched tightly in one hand.

"What you doin' here?" the boy asked, still smiling. "What you
lookin' for?"

"Damn you!" Jonah cried out, running straight at him. "Damn you for living!"

The boy's sleepy eyes widened when he saw Jonah wasn't going to stop. He turned back around the corner, deserting his confederates. The driver put the Packard into gear immediately and made a long, looping U-turn, squealing off down Seventh Avenue. The middle-aged white man making a futile grab at the rear-door handle, then bolting off himself into the Harlem night.

Jonah ignored them, chasing the boy around the corner, even when he saw how much faster he was. Already a block away, the soles of his shoes flying from the sidewalk. Glancing back to see if he was still being followed, his face looking more baffled than angry. While Jonah continued to chase after him, long after he knew there was no hope of catching him and he had vanished from sight altogether. Still holding his umbrella up over his head, shouting like a madman even as it began to pour again. The furious rattle of the rain along a deserted street swallowing up his words, which now merely echoed the boy's own:

"What are you doing here? What are you doing here?"

CHAPTER EIGHTEEN

MALCOLM

The new slave Archie had for him was transporting the numbers slips from the Bronx across to New Jersey. Every day he would take the Third Avenue el up to the Mott Haven railyards, where a short dark woman who called herself Mrs. James handed him a large bag full of betting slips. He would take it back down to the George Washington Bridge, where he would catch any bus on the Red & Tan line over to Fort Lee, the first stop on the other side of the river. There he would hand the bag over to a white man who was waiting for him as soon as he got off, then cross the highway overpass and take the next bus back.

He never knew why numbers from the Bronx had to go over to New Jersey, or what Archie had to do with it. He only knew what they were, from looking in the bag one day. Both hoping and dreading to discover it was filled with cash, but finding only the scribbled numbers of the Irish factory hands and Italian piano makers of Mott Haven.

It was as simple as that. When he described the work to Sammy the Pimp, he told him his full capabilities were being wasted, and sometimes he thought so himself, but after his tearful confession he couldn't very well protest. The job was a relief, he had to admit, though he still felt ashamed to be reduced to it, hoping above all that Archie hadn't told her anything about his failures. But there were no more followers, at least, and it gave him time to read all the paperbacks he had recently discovered in the drugstore, where they sat in the racks next to his comic books—detective stories, and

Max Brand westerns, and the Edgar Rice Burroughs stories about Mars. Leafing through a Life magazine if he was still too stoned or hungover from the night before—studying every page, the huge photographs and even the elaborate hand-drawn ads that were whole stories unto themselves.

Some days, when the weather was a little cooler, he liked to go up on the upper deck of the bus station and just stare out at the great gray-and-silver bridge, glinting in the sunlight like a gigantic snake at rest. Letting a bus or two go by, content to watch the cars passing through the gaping mouths of the bridge towers; the great coiled tentacles of cable, reaching all the way across to the flinty gray-brown cliffs of the Palisades. He always sat on the right-hand side of the bus, where he could watch the river bulge out luxuri-antly above the bridge before it disappeared into the mist. Wonder-ing perversely, sometimes, what it would feel like to just open the bag and let all those prayerful scraps of paper go flying right out the window behind them.

When he got to the other side, he would feel obliged to apolo-gize for his bad conscience. The men waiting there varied, but it was always the same one—dressed in a sharp, pinstriped suit; lean-ing against the metal frame of the bus stop, smoking or working a toothpick over in his mouth.

"The el was runnin' slow today," he tried to tell them. The bag-men never evincing the least interest in this or anything else about him, save for the time his connection stomped out his cigarette and snorted as he strode away, without so much as looking at him:

"Like I give a shit, shine."

Then they separated, into the echoing, shadowed, concrete-and-metal world around the highway bus stop—two bodies with nothing to do with each other save for the transaction they had just concluded. The mob bagman disappearing instantly. Malcolm making his way across the overpass, above the constant traffic that whooshed and surged below him like the ocean. Trying not to think about the name the man had tossed at him, lost forever in the whoosh of the concrete underpass, though he couldn't help but feel hurt anyway.

With the new job he could no longer pretend he was his own man, either. He had to be certain places at certain hours, and he had lost the sense of the secret, superhero preeminence he had felt over everyone he passed on the street. His money was less, too, with no tips, and almost no chance to sell his sticks anymore, which was the worst thing. He could no longer bet much of anything on the numbers, and without that dream he couldn't see how he would ever be able to afford a club, or a Cadillac, and wrest her away from Archie.

He had seen Miranda only a couple of times since their return from Asbury Park, when he had gone to report to West Indian Archie, once at the Fat Man's Bar, the other time at Jimmy's Chicken Shack. Both times she had given him the high sign when he'd stolen a glance in her direction. At first he couldn't understand her attitude, but then he was sure she was simply afraid. Looking more beautiful than ever, he thought—a little darker, from their time at the shore, even more slender and elegant, her face pensive when she thought there was nobody watching her. He was sure that she missed him, but with his new job he had few chances to get down to her apartment at a time when he knew that Archie wouldn't be there, and she would. He had even thought of writing her, but he was ashamed of his spelling and his grammar, afraid they would only make her laugh, and think of him all the more as a boy.

The answer to everything, he was sure, was more money. Ever since his visit to the ghosty men's house, an idea had been slowly percolating in his brain as to how to get it. He had taken it first to Jakey Mendelssohn, thinking that he would be necessary to any scheme—that as a white man, and a Jew, he would know what all the junk they had in there would be worth, and how to turn it over. But ever since their last bootlegging trip to the Island, Jakey had seemed gloomy and preoccupied when he went to see him, and refused to show him any new hustles.

"You want to be like me? Lookit what a schlemiel I am—a bum!" was all he said when Malcolm came around.

"Better you shouldn't learn these things. Lookit me. Boys I went to school with, they had no more money or brains than I did. Now they're lawyers. They're doctors, and scholars. They're fighting for their country against the Nazi chaiserim. I gotta bum hip, from a bullet some gangster put there," he said.

"It's my play all the way 'round," Malcolm prodded him, uncomfortable with all the other distractions he talked. "All you gotta do is lemme know what's solid an' what ain't."

But Jakey only shook his head—looking over at the nephew of his who always gave Malcolm the willies. His big cow eyes even now gazing fearfully, stupidly, at them above his broom.

"I'm a businessman," he said, his voice grimmer than Malcolm had ever heard it before, all the usual bluster gone. "I do what I gotta do to make a living. That's why I know all these cheap, goyishe hustles. But I can't help anybody."

He patted Malcolm's face affectionately, his voice softening.

"Leave the crazy old gentiles alone," he told him. "Don' always try so hard to be a businessman."

Edging close to him then, as if to confide in him. Tapping a finger into the palm of his hand.

"We got to find some way. Some way to do something!"

"What?" Malcolm asked—but Jakey was already walking back into his department store, waving him away.

Sammy the Pimp had a solution to his problems. He had listened to his troubles with his usual attentiveness when Malcolm had broken down and laid his spiel on him. He walked him through his neighborhood around West 144th Street, pointing out different establishments of one kind or another that he had cased, and telling Malcolm how easy they would be to knock over.

"You just go in there an' show 'em your gat, an' they hand it right over," Sammy told him when they got back to the apartment he shared with Hortense. "Most of 'em just owned by some ofays anyway."

He laid another of his pistols, a .32-20, out on the table before him, and pushed it toward Malcolm.

"'Course, you be needin' a bigger piece for all that. Not like that .25 peashooter you got now—"

Malcolm had stared at it, tempted. The .32-20 not as intimidating as Sammy's favorite army .45 but much bigger and more formidable than the little silver pistol that was still all he had for himself. For a moment he thought he might take Sammy up on it. But then he remembered the sawed-off shotgun Jakey Mendelssohn kept at his store—just under the counter, within easy reach, the safety off—and he thought better of trying to pull off any stickups with Sammy the Pimp.

Instead Malcolm had convinced Sammy to give him another job in his racket: steering the johns up to the women he kept in a crib up on West 144th Street. It was nearly as good a hustle as running numbers and sticks—the product guaranteed, the tips good. Best of all, it allowed him to dress up in the nice suits that Sammy fronted him, and go down to the best midtown hotels. There he would stand on the pavement just outside, knowing the house dick or the cops would be run if he set foot in the lobby; a fresh white carnation in the lapel of his suit jacket or his raincoat, waiting for the car full of nervous white faces to pull up beside him.

If it was a private car, Malcolm would get in the driver's side and take the wheel himself. If it was a cab, he would politely direct the driver, "The Apollo Theatre in Harlem, please," like any other tourist, just in case the cabbie was a plainclothesman. Once they got up to the theater, Malcolm would have them switch cabs, getting a colored hack to take them the rest of the way.

He liked the whole espionage feeling to the job. He liked to watch the faces of the johns as they drove up, trying to figure out just who they were, and what they did. They were mostly older men, whether because of the war or what Sammy charged, he wasn't sure, but what they wanted usually was expensive. A few of them he recognized as singers or actors from the movies, no matter how much they had tried to change their hair or pull their hats down. Some of the johns were politicians, also trying hard not to be recognized, or men with the belligerent, edgy haste of gangsters.

Usually they were businessmen, salesmen in town for the day or the week to make a deal. Chattering nervously most of the way up, trying hard to make some small talk. But with all of them, Malcolm noticed how they began to relax the farther they got into Harlem. He laughed at their jokes, doing his best to make them feel at ease—but once they crossed 110th Street, it really wasn't necessary. Their faces seemed to physically loosen the farther they got uptown. Mouths slackening into sickly, guilty smiles, backs slumping comfortably into the mold of the worn backseat. He would have guessed they would get more nervous the farther uptown they went, but it was just the opposite. They stopped talking so much, paid him less mind—looking about themselves as freely as if they were planning to buy the place.

That was when he understood it: This is a white man's heaven. This was their paradise, their reward, where they knew they could do anything. Relaxing into their slumped, smaller selves even as he watched. Knowing that here they could indulge.

Sometimes Malcolm would be the one to meet the steer up at the corner of West 144th Street. Walking the john the rest of the way into the apartment, where he was supposed to stay out in an anteroom and keep watch. But it was the customers he watched, curious to see what they could need so much. They didn't seem to care, didn't seem even to remember his presence by then, exposed completely as they were. Their soft, pale guts drooping down over their groins, pubic and chest hair whiter than the hair on their head. Some of them even keeping on their socks, and the thin black sock garters that held them up.

They liked different things, but all of them liked the women to be as dark as possible. Some of them liked to have their flaccid, old men's cocks sucked. Holding the waiting brown face close to their loins to dribble the thin remnants of their spunk over it, seeming to delight in the contrast. Some of them liked to be powdered all over with talcum, and diapered like a baby. Some of them liked to be spanked, taken over the knee or tucked up on all fours in the cor- ner, like a dog. One of Sammy's most popular girls was a strapping, coal black amazon, taller than Malcolm was by a head and bigger in the shoulders, with the rippling arm muscles of a steel riveter. She dressed in leather, and greased over her whole body and her face to look even shinier and blacker. Lashing her customers fiercely but expertly with a cat-o'-nine-tails, drawing just the finest, diamond- shaped nicks of blood up and down their withered, quivering but- tocks.

The one thing he never saw was a white woman with a white man. Sammy had some white girls on his string, he knew. One of them was Baby, that mad cavewoman dope fiend he had known back in his first apartment house, working for Sammy now, along with her lover, Bea. They did a number with a tall black man who had the longest dick Malcolm had ever seen. Some of the white men just liked to watch—sitting up in an armchair, where Malcolm watched them watching. The tall Negro taking Baby, usually from behind, often over a kitchen chair with one leg up, so they could see as much of the man's cock go in as possible. Bea leading her to him by the hand, Baby looking almost as if she were in a trance. Bea helping to put it in, holding her Baby's hand and wiping her forehead. Whispering words of comfort to her as she twisted and groaned, and cried, stuck there, until even Malcolm felt sorry for her—trying not to look at the white man ecstatically jerking off in the chair before him.

Sometimes Malcolm would even bring a white woman up. Always accompanied by her husband, or her lover. Usually late at night, both of them dressed for a formal party, or the theater. The woman always stayed nervous—her mouth dry, shifting about constantly in the car. The man trying to calm her, patting her thigh or holding her hand, smiling at her in the false, reassuring manner of a parent taking a child to the dentist. Most times she wouldn't look at Malcolm, and he tried to address everything to the man. Helping pretend that she wasn't really there, while he watched her, through the rearview mirror, bite her lip or try to smoke a cigarette, her hand trembling. Once they were up in the room, they would usually stay standing, the man's arm wrapped protectively around her shoulders. Watching the Negro with the great big dick plow into Baby, or maybe Baby and Bea having sex together as well. The white man whispering to his woman the whole time, "See, honey? That's not so bad. See how it's done? It's natural, baby. See how natural it is—"

There was even a fairy, old enough to be his father, who he had to steer up to West 144th Street sometimes. Sammy had a friend from the Braddock who said he wasn't that way normally, but would do him for the money. The aging fairy would take off his clothes and get on a table, and Sammy's friend would massage him all over with oil, then pull on his cock until he came. Malcolm had watched it a couple times even though he was ashamed of himself for it, making sure to hang far back behind the anteroom curtain. Nonetheless, the next time the fairy had beckoned to Sammy's friend to lean down, and whispered something in his ear. The masseur had grinned, and nodded—and then to Malcolm's horror had come walking straight toward where he was hidden behind the curtain.

"He says he wants you to join us," Sammy's friend told him, grinning from ear to ear, his gold teeth shining in his mouth.

"He say he give you double. Just between you 'n him, Sammy don't gotta know."

"Tell him to go fuck hisself. Tell him I'll oil up his head for the mothafuckah, that's what I'll do!" Malcolm had sworn, then dashed back out the front door, the masseur's laughter trailing after him.

"What's wrong with that? Make you some good money fo' not much work," Sammy had teased him when he heard about it.

"You can go to hell, too."

"Ah, now don't be like that! Seriously, I got some he-shes down the Braddock, they pay serious money just to give some soldier a suck job. It's just you sittin' back an' enjoyin' it—"

"Don't even talk that shit!"

Sometimes, in the beginning, Malcolm had needed to take a Nembutal or a Seconal to calm himself down, prepare himself for his assignments in the downtown hotels. Never spending more than five minutes even on the sidewalk outside, acutely aware as he was of the doormen and the house detectives sizing him up. But before long he had had to switch to Benzedrine tablets just to get himself going. He would pop a couple bennies in the morning, after he had awakened in another new room, trying to remember where he was—then another bennie in the late afternoon, and still another if it looked like it was going to be a long night. When he finally got home he would smoke a few sticks, or some opium or hashish, in order to get to sleep.

Sometimes Sammy would pay him partly in cocaine, and Malcolm would take a snort or two of that to get himself going in the mornings. Sammy tried to get him to shoot some heroin as well, but he wouldn't have anything to do with needles.

Remembering that afternoon when they had left her in Kalamazoo. A nurse bustling past them with an array of silver hypodermics on a tray, headed for his mother's room—

He found himself thinking more and more of his mother, and he was filled with a greater sense of foreboding than he had had at any time since those last weeks before she was taken away to Kalamazoo, when she only sat rocking in her chair with Butch, not talking to anyone. His sleep was different now, too, deeper, but bothered by dreams he could not remember. He often didn't know just when he had fallen asleep—waking up sometimes to find himself propped up in bed, a lit cigarette still burning in the ashtray on his lap. He didn't even think about Miranda all the time now.

He did dream still of making enough money to buy her a car, or a nightclub, and cutting her free from West Indian Archie. If he finished early enough with the johns he would root up a card game— tonk or blackjack or poker, or maybe a game of craps. Betting freely, winning or losing forty, even fifty dollars a night. Shrugging it off and acting as if it were no big thing if he lost; taking himself home carefully if he won. He would circle the block at least twice, when he left the game, switching from the trolley to the subway, or vice versa, if he thought any other face around the table looked bitter or angry, or hungry enough, when he walked out the door. And when he finally made it home, before he got into bed, he crumpled pages

of newspapers or magazines all around his room, which was a trick
he remembered from The Maltese Falcon.

Then one night he came home to find that his room had been
turned over while he was gone. The signs were subtle, whoever had
done it hadn't meant to be caught at it, but Sammy the Pimp had
taught him how to tell if his room had been searched, and he was
sure that someone had been there. None of his few belongings had
been taken; even his bankroll was still tucked away in his sweet-
potato shoes. But he could still tell—how the bedspread was a little
less tight around his pillow, the way his suits had been reordered
and the piles of comic books under his bed had been reshuffled and
put back out of order.

"What you gotta look out for is what is there, not what isn't,"
Sammy the Pimp instructed him again when he had run up to his
apartment to ask him what this might mean.

"What's that mean?"

"Them vice cops, lotta times, they don' find what they need, they
plant it anyhow. Then they come back an' find it when you there."

Malcolm had not wanted to return to his room at all, after
that—finally slipping back in only after he had watched his apartment house for hours, walking back and forth across the street. He
had bundled up everything he had as quickly as he could then, stuffing it into a couple of cheap suitcases and running back down the
stairs, going out again through the back, boiler-room door.

By the time he put his head on his pillow that night, he had
moved into another rented room in another building. The next
day he kept moving. Staying in no one place for more than a couple
days, a week at most. Taking furnished rooms and suites of rooms,
depending on how much money he had. Staying in the same neighborhood around the foot of Sugar Hill that he had always liked since
that first night at the rent party, though usually now in basement
rooms that Sammy the Pimp told him was where all the biggest
drug dealers lived.

"It's perfect if the cops come," he explained to him. "You got bars
on all your windows, an' anybody comes down to see you they gotta
walk right past 'em. You can be out through the janitor's door, or
up to the lobby 'fo' they even done knockin'."

Malcolm himself would walk right past the door of his latest
apartment once, twice—then bolt suddenly down the outside stairs,
just as it looked as if he might walk past again. Pulling out his little

.25 as he did, whipping the door open but not going inside just yet, straining to hear any sound from inside the darkened rooms. He would rifle hurriedly through all his things to see if anything had been messed with, checking to see if his telltale traces—a hair wrapped around a book that only he would know about, a sheet folded in a certain way—had been disturbed. Checking it all over again sometimes, unable to remember just where and how his traces had been. Only when he was satisfied that nothing had been removed, or planted, would he be able to relax, and pull out his stash.

But sometimes, too, late at night, or after he had shared some gage or too much whiskey at the card game, he would forget where he had moved that day and go back to his previous basement room, where a careless super had not bothered to change the lock. Then he would burst in to find every single trace of himself vanished, even the walls stripped bare and splotched with a white undercoat of paint—looking around, terrified, until it slowly dawned on him where he lived now.

On top of it all, he still wasn't making any money. The rooms cost more than he had ever expected—more than he had ever even heard of an apartment costing before, outside of New York City. He hung on to his slave with Archie, mostly because he didn't dare give it up and risk his wrath, but also because he needed the extra cash. Squeezing in his trips up to Mrs. James up at the Mott Haven yards around his work for Sammy. Making, sometimes, as many as two and even three trips a day across the great, humming grey bridge, as the war-production plants boomed, and the betting slips multiplied.

It was all he could do to get down to the Main Stem from time to time to buy himself a few sticks—Sammy having cut off his supply of kisca for the time being, until Malcolm paid up what he owed. He didn't mind so much, just as glad to see less of Sammy, who he didn't trust for reasons that he couldn't quite put his mind on, but that he felt in his gut. He preferred strolling along with the crowds on 125th Street, anyway, looking for his connection. Picking up whatever hype was coming over The Wire, just seeing all the sights, the gaggles of glamour girls, and the smirking soldiers and sailors.

He always liked to walk by the lounge at the Braddock Hotel, on the off chance that he might see some of the stars he had sold to, although he was too embarrassed to go into the lounge and say hello. Eating a quick lunch in the window of the Clean Spot diner, hoping that some of them might walk by and see him there, though they never did.

Whenever he did, he stopped by Prof. Toussaint's National African Bookstore and House of Common Sense, too, and sometimes he ached to go in and see the Black Hall of Fame, and its grizzled little proprietor again, and ask him all about the books he had given him. But he always balked at the last moment, too ashamed of what he was doing, knowing how Prof. Toussaint would look when he told him.

Instead, he would linger outside, gazing in the dusty windows. Taking in the sidewalk speaker who had set up his stepladder and flag on the curb just outside. The last time he'd gone by, he'd noticed the speaker was different from any he had seen before—taller, without any fez or skullcap, but wearing what looked to be some sort of homemade uniform, with a row of medals on the front, including one of an orange and yellow rising sun, just like the one he had seen in the newsreels. When he looked at the man's face, he saw that he didn't look like any regular colored man, either, but like some sort of mix between a Negro and an Oriental, his skin a light brown but his eyes narrow, and Japanese.

"My friends, I am Commander Robert Leonard Jordan, and I am here to tell you that a new epoch in world history is upon us!" he began to shout once he had climbed to the top steps of his ladder. "I can tell you that I was there for the historic Japanese victories at Bataan, and Corregidor, and that this is only the beginning! Don't believe what you read in the white man's papers 'bout the war! Even as we speak, the masses of Asia are rising, and following the lead of our Japanese brothers, half a billion strong!"

He had attracted an immediate crowd, as he could hardly avoid doing, set up on a busy corner of 125th Street. Malcolm noticed that some people pushed angrily by, swearing, but that more seemed genuinely interested in stopping and listening. A few of them whistled and heckled him from the back, but more laughed, and nodded their heads fiercely.

"That's right, that's right! They gave the white man the boot down there," he heard someone say.

"Those ofay got the surprise a their lives—"

"Believe me, brothers and sisters, when I tell you I'm gonna have President Roosevelt hisself pickin' cotton after Japan crushes this country!" the man on the stepladder went on. "Secretary Knox an'

Secretary Stimson gonna be ridin' me around in rickshaws! Support the Onward Movement of America! No one should be afraid to join this movement! We are protected by big people—"

By now, a bunch of white servicemen had joined the crowd, jeering Robert Leonard Jordan more angrily. The colored men and women laughing at the whole spectacle at first, but then beginning to shove angrily at the white sailors and soldiers.

"Let the man speak!"

"He's a goddamned traitor—"

"Let him have his say! You don't come up Harlem, tell us who can speak an' who can't!"

The shoving turned into a fistfight, and then there was the sound of a siren from a few blocks away, and the roar of the ceaseless motorcycle patrols coming down Seventh Avenue. Malcolm watched as the white servicemen ran off, and when he looked back at the stepladder, he saw that Robert Leonard Jordan was gone, too, as quickly as if he had disappeared into thin air. But most of the rest of the crowd stood its ground, a couple of bottles even smashing at the tall black boots of the motorcycle patrolmen as they pulled over to the curb.

"All right, all right! Move it on!" one of them called out, though Malcolm noticed that he stayed where he was, straddling his bike in the street. "Nothin' to see here!"

"Nothin' for you here!" a woman's indignant voice called out from the crowd. "You go on your business, go pick up your money from those white gangsters. Nothin' here but people talkin'!"

"Damned straight!"

Other voices took up the refrain, the colored faces all around Malcolm seething. The cops stayed where they were, as if still debating with themselves over whether to wade into the crowd. Malcolm took a quick step or two backward himself, remembering the sticks he had just purchased, in his pocket, the gun he carried all the time now in the back of his pants.

He felt a hand on his arm, and spun around. His right hand feeling for the gun in the small of his back, even as he realized what a foolish move that would be if it was a cop's hand he had felt. But just then he recognized the grizzled little man from the bookstore, Prof. Toussaint, grinning at him beneath his gray-specked moustache—wearing a small round cap that was just like the one he had seen on Elijah, only without any of the planets, or other insignia.

"Hello, young man! How's that education comin' along?"

"All right," Malcolm said uncertainly, wanting to tell and ask him so much more, but unsure of just what he could actually say, afraid that he might sound too foolish.

"Man can learn a lot for himself, just sitting in his room an' reading," Prof. Toussaint said meaningfully. "Not so much he can learn watchin' a pack of fools on a street corner."

"I know it," Malcolm said, starting to turn away. Knowing that he had to get up to the George Washington, but afraid to tell Prof. Toussaint what he was doing.

"I got to get back to work now—," be began to tell Prof. Toussaint, but the man's grip on his elbow was like steel now, his other hand poking into Malcolm's side like a shiv, as he steered him over toward his store.

"That's fine! Glad to hear you're gainfully employed. Where you workin' now?" he asked deliberately, and Malcolm, wanting to change the subject, asked him a question of his own that he had not even realized was on his mind.

"Who's 'X'?" he said.

"Pardon?" Prof. Toussaint said, although Malcolm could see his eyes were already shining merrily.

"Who's 'X'? The front a that little green book you give me, it say, The Biography of Elijah Muhammad. By X. What's that?"

"Why, people who write books use 'X' when they wanna be anonymous," Prof. Toussaint told him, a grin looking up at the sides of his mouth. Malcolm thought at that moment how much he seemed like the little brown man of his dreams, and he wondered wildly if Prof. Toussaint could have written the book himself.

"But then, 'X' could be every Black Man in America," he went on. "We're *all* anonymous. We all been stripped of our real names, our real history. It could be any one of us, just waitin' for you to read it, an' give him a real name."

"Me?" Malcolm asked, confused.

"Sure. You the one readin' it, ain't you?" Prof. Toussaint chuckled. "That 'X' could stand for anything you make it. That 'X' stands for everything you been, an' everything you can become. Ex-drinker. Ex-doper. Ex-gambler, ex-hustler. Ex-slave."

"I gotta go," Malcolm said, noticing now that the crowd was beginning to break up, the police looking around. But to his surprise, Prof. Toussaint let go of him easily now.

"Go on, then," he told Malcolm, as cheerily as ever. "Man can run from the truth for a long time. That don't mean it ain't still the truth!"

But by then, Malcolm was already yards away from him, moving rapidly down 125th Street. He was so intent on being away that it was only when he was about to walk down into the A train that he noticed the bulge in his jacket pocket, right below where Prof. Toussaint had poked him so hard in the ribs. He reached down, felt a familiar smooth, rectangular object there, and realized to his amazement that the little bookstore owner had planted something on him. He pulled it out at once—knowing all the same, as he did, just what it would be: another copy of that strange book. What looked to be exactly the same copy, in fact, right down to the green patent-leather cover, and the gold crescent moon—the same mysterious words on the title page: THE BIOGRAPHY OF ELIJAH MUHAMMAD. By "X". The very same edition of the same book— only this one was marked, with a long, black sliver of paper at the start of a chapter about halfway through the manuscript.

Malcolm put off opening it until he got all the way up to the bus station. He stood out on the platform there, watching the constant hum and buzz of traffic through the gaping mouths of the bridge arches; the ships in the wide, lazy summer river. Letting two, three buses go by, allowing the steady flow of the traffic to lull him into a near-sleep. Pacing back and forth on the bus platform, the book burning a hole in his jacket pocket, wondering if he should crack it open here or not.

It seemed to him a sacrilege, somehow, to open it up in such a public place, when it should be taken home, read by him in the intimacy of his room. Already, he could imagine all the things that could go wrong if he took it out—picturing a sudden gust of wind pulling it out the open bus window, dropping it down a sewer drain. But he could not help thinking about the bookmark, wondering if it was there just by chance, or to point out some specific passage Prof. Toussaint wanted him to read. Wondering, until he could stand it no longer, just what that might be.

He ran back down the narrow staircase from the platform, holding the book in his hand—still in his jacket pocket—as he did so. He went down the main terminal level, then down another flight, where the long-distance buses left from. He went into the men's room there, forcing himself not to look around, not to look too conspicuous—trying at the same time to scope out which of the flabby, down-at-the-heels men circling around the shoeshine stand at the entrance might be a vice-squad man.

He continued on inside, and went into a stall, sitting on top of a toilet seat there but not undoing his pants—not wanting to get caught unprepared by anyone. Then, when he was sure that the stall door was latched, and he could no longer see the brogans of any more men shifting around on the sea green floor tiles outside, he pulled out a pack of Sammy's marijuana sticks—the one he had retrieved once the crowd had rescued him from the cops. He smoked his way through one, then another, then two more after that, trying to pull himself together. Only then was he finally calm enough to open the book, and begin to read.

Elijah had known the little Chinaman meant trouble from the moment he first laid eyes on him, slipping into a side door of the Allah Temple near the end of services. The Fruit of Islam were supposed to be guarding all the doors, but a fight had broken out among the faithful, and when they moved off to stop it he had slipped right in, as if he had been waiting for that very moment. Even worse, he had gone right up to the Master at the end of the service, greeting him like an old friend—pumping his hand and slapping his back, something Elijah had never seen Master Fard do with anyone before, black or white.

Elijah had slipped out after the Chinaman when he left, afraid he was a police informer, or maybe some kind of devil. But the man had stopped in the alley beside the temple and faced Elijah head-on, as if he had been expecting him, a hand slipping into his side pocket.

"You must be George's new partner," he said, a smile slowly pulling up his mouth. He had big ears that stood out from his head, a sharp, hawklike nose, and the hardest eyes and mouth Elijah had ever seen on a man.

"Why you call him George? It's Master Fard—," Elijah started to say, indignant, but the Chinaman only cut him off with a harsh little laugh.

"Whatever you say, chief. He always did like to give out the names. Mine's Donaldson. Eddie Donaldson. Maybe he mentioned me."

"I don't believe he did, sir," Elijah said formally. "And Master Fard is the Mahdi—the revealed incarnation of God—"

"He always loved his religion," the man said, and spat in the alleyway. "All that Azusa Street shit. But I gotta hand it to him, it's a better play than morphine. Less trouble from the bulls."

"What do you mean by that?!" Elijah had exploded, moving toward the man before he quite knew what he was doing. "You take back your blasphemy!"

But Donaldson had sidestepped him as adroitly as a boxer, moving up the alley, away from him—still grinning his sardonic, unnatural grin.

"Don't worry, I won't get in your way! Just tell him to remember: You can't trust a Jap. Remind him how much trouble he got in to in 'Frisco—and Seattle!" he called back to Elijah—words that filled him with a deep uneasiness.

When Master Fard had first raised him up over all the others and made him Supreme Minister, everything had been perfect. He had been at Elijah's humble little house night and day, for nine months, instructing him in all there was to know about the Knowledge of Self and Others. Talking on and on, well past midnight, until Elijah's head flopped down on his chest, and he wished that sometimes the Master did not favor him quite so much.

But sometimes, too, Master Fard had Elijah over to the suite of rooms he kept in the Fraymore Hotel, where he let him listen in on his special receiver, to the radio communications he claimed that he received from the people on Mars. Elijah had to admit that he had doubted even the Master's ability to do this at first, but he had to admit that the words he heard coming through the radio were in a language that he had never heard anything remotely like before— high and whispery, almost like a song. The radio, too, was unlike anything he had ever seen, with odd silver dials and levers, and strange markings on it that he could not decipher.

After Master Fard had let him listen and wonder over their communications, he would take him out driving in his red Chevy coupe. They would drive all the way up through the Polack neighborhoods in Hamtramck. Elijah was apprehensive about them being spotted there, two black men in a flashy red car, but he saw that Fard remained as serene about it as ever. Driving on through Hamtramck, and up a low ridge where they could look down on the industrial morass below them. The stunted houses, and the shuttered plants, hunkered below like a man bracing to take a blow. The only lights the flickering red campfires and ash-can fires from over in the hobo jungles—the greater fires from the forges and the smokestacks all banked now.

"You can see it, can't you?" Fard asked him in his soft voice, as mildly as if he were talking about the weather. "The day of the white man is coming to an end. His factories are shutting down. His great cities are falling apart. Out in the country, his farms are drying up and blowing away. All his tricks won't save him now."

"Yes," Elijah answered, and in that moment, watching the darkened city, he really believed it to be true, and that Master Fard was the greatest prophet of all.

Soon afterward, though, the Master had begun to hold other meetings, at night in his rooms, with all the curtains drawn—meetings that were open only to the innermost circle of the Fruit of Islam. These meetings were always fraught with tension for Elijah, for he knew that Master Fard had angered the others when he had raised up Elijah over them, especially Othman Ali, and Abdul Muhammad, the brother who used to call himself Brown Eel, and who had been with Fard the longest. He could see from the looks they shot him, whenever they thought he wasn't looking, that they would just as soon see him dead, and he never left or went to their meetings by the same way, and carried himself as warily as he had around the white men back in Georgia.

It was at these gatherings that Master Fard instructed them in secret things—things that he had never mentioned down at the temple on Hancock Avenue. It was here that he had first told them about the Mother Plane, which was misnamed Ezekiel's Wheel in the white man's Poison Book Bible. He told them how he had built the Mother Plane himself, in Japan, and how it was one-half mile by one-half mile in size, and how its belly was filled with fifteen hundred baby planes. Each one of these was piloted by a Black scientist who had been trained from the age of six for his mission, and who had never laughed, and never cried, and had never known a woman.

On the Day of Destruction, at his command, the Mother Plane would let go of her burden. The baby planes would drop their bombs from twelve miles above the Earth, and they would turn all of white America into a great lake of fire that wo uld burn and not stop burning for the next three hundred and ninety years. Only the Original People would be spared. They would emerge from where they had been hiding, and purified, and given their inheritance. And then Allah would finally explain to them why He had ever allowed white people to be created in the first place.

By the time Master Fard had finished, Elijah's eyes were closed. He wanted to concentrate only on the beautiful words, without seeing anything that might disturb them. Not the dumbfounded faces of the other Fruit of Islam around him—not even the image of Fard himself.

Of course that was how it had to be. The reason for why God had left the black people to suffer so long in this land. There was a reason for it after all.

They had remained silent, and then Master Fard had stood up and walked into the other room. When he returned, he was accompanied by an elderly, round, Japanese gentleman. There was no mistaking him. He was wearing Coke-bottle glasses, a dark suit, and a bowler hat, and the rest of them could have been no less surprised if he had come back in with an actual demon.

"This is the Honorable Satohata Takahashi, of the Kokuryukai, the Black Dragon Society, and the Onward Movement of America," Master Fard had introduced him.

"But he's not—," somebody had started to object.

"The Asiatic race is made up of all dark-skinned people, including the Japanese, and the Asiatic Black man," Fard had cut him off sternly. "Our brothers in the East did not know that you were even here until sixty years ago. Now that they know where their lost Uncle is, they are only waiting upon my word to slaughter the white man!"

Mr. Takahashi bowed again, and came forward then—a little uncertainly, putting a hand out before him to touch the edge of the table.

"Negroes! You are too easy to be fooled by anybody, and especially white people!" he said, in a high, singsong voice that was in English—but which in its timbre and its rhythm reminded Elijah of nothing so much as the voices of the Martians he had heard on Fard's radio.

"The white man pushes you ahead as cattle in any war, and will use you as a shield! But when the spoils of war are to be divided, the white man is in front and if any Negro raises only a finger of disapproval of the white man's action, the white man cuts off not only the Negro's finger but his whole hand! Why should you respect the white man when he has nothing for you but a bloody whip?"

There was an angry stirring among the Fruit of Islam at such words, but the Master had come before them and quieted them again. He had laid out copies of a small book on the table before them then, and told them each to take one. Elijah thought that they looked rather like dream books. On the cover were mystical symbols of crescent moons and stars, and the words: Secret Rituals of the Lost-Found Nation of Islam.

"Here, each of you take these, and read them carefully," Fard had commanded them. "There are precise instructions in them—at least there are for those among you who have ears to hear, and eyes to see."

Elijah noticed that even Mr. Takahashi was looking distinctly ill at ease at this, speaking in an urgent whisper to Master Fard.

"You must urge them to be careful. We do not want what happened in Seattle to reoccur prematurely—"

But Fard had only held up a hand to silence him, and turned back to his men around the table.

"Take these, and read them for yourselves, and watch for the signs of the times. You will find instructions on how to deal not only with the white devils in the days ahead, but also those imps from our own race who have been so brainwashed they prefer to help the white man."

But by the time Elijah got back to his house, he found that he was wheezing again, his lungs bothering him again for the first time in months. There were things in the little book that he had never heard Fard preach on so directly before—instructions that alarmed him, and that he was sure would bring down trouble on all their heads. And he noticed that, on the title page—unlike the dream books—there was no indication of who had written it, or even where it had been printed.

It was Master Fard, as usual, who saw how the little books troubled Elijah before Elijah himself had worked up the courage to ask him about them. Turning to Elijah suddenly, one evening when they were alone again in the Allah Temple, and asking him as gently and with as much concern as ever:

"What is troubling you, my most faithful one?"

"This book—there are dangerous things here," Elijah tried to tell him, but the Master remained undisturbed.

"Those things you mean, they are necessary to take the fear of the white man out of the hearts of the followers," he told him.

"But what about those who are ignorant, or do not wish us well?"

"Never mind that," Master Fard said, making a dismissive gesture. "Don't I always know where there are unbelievers amongst us? You have seen it."

It was true, too. The Master was always able to sniff out the spies the police sent, no matter how carefully they tried to disguise themselves at services as regular Negro workingmen. There was always something too reticent and nervous about them, as one might expect from any colored man who had offered up his services to the Detroit police department. Yet for Elijah, the very presence of the police spies confirmed that they had already drawn the attention of the white man, and that they had to be all the more careful.

"I don't like this Japanese fellow," he said. "I don't like how some of the others are runnin' their mouths about the book, an' what's in it."

It was as frankly and as critically as he had ever spoken to Master Fard, and when he was finished, it was all he could do to keep from cringing, out of fear that the Master would strike him down on the spot, in all his wrath. But he had only smiled all the more gently at Elijah, and taken his hands in his own.

"Have faith a little while longer, my son," he said, his face so radiant that for the moment Elijah forgot all of his worries. "The white man's day is done. Have faith in me when I tell you this."

But all of their troubles had come home to roost on the Sunday of that Thanksgiving weekend, just a few weeks later. Elijah and his family no longer celebrated the holiday, following Master Fard's strict rules for dieting and fasting that had restored their health to all of them, and not seeing in any case what the Black Man could possibly be thankful about for having been brought to America as a slave, and worked for four hundred years against his will. But that Sunday, Robert Karriem, who was one of Master Fard's chosen Fruit of Islam, had announced he was holding an induction for a new member, and Elijah had agreed to go over to the rooms Karriem rented in a rowhouse on Dubois Street and witness it.

He had been apprehensive from the moment he arrived at Karriem's home. Elijah had always thought he was one of the more excitable, and naive, of the men around the Master, and he had never heard of any temple induction ritual. Yet when Elijah reached Karriem's home, he saw that someone had set up twelve chairs in his apartment living room, along with a makeshift altar—and another chair just in front of it. The seats filled with Karriem's wife, his two young children, and other members of the temple—all of them looking every bit as nervous and jumpy as Elijah felt.

Then Karriem had entered, and called out the name of one James Smith. Mr. Smith had gone up and sat in the chair facing them—a small, fastidious man, dressed in a gray suit and bow tie, and swinging his feet a little nervously while Karriem said a prayer over his head. When he had finished praying, Karriem pulled out an eight-inch butcher's knife from somewhere under the altar, holding it just over Smith's neck.

"James Smith, are you willing to give your life for Islam?" he intoned, the knife moving slowly closer to the man's neck.

"Yes," Smith had answered in a wavering voice.

"Go, then, and lie upon the altar!"

Smith had done as he was told, moving rubber-legged and slowly, but climbing up on the white sheet of the altar as if hypnotized. Elijah was already standing by then, starting for the door. Stumbling over the legs of the other, uncomprehending witnesses, who remained riveted to their chairs.

"In the name of Allah, then—"

He only glimpsed the big knife coming down, the arc of blood spouting up from Smith's chest. The room dissolved into panic behind him, Karriem's children screaming, Smith screaming and trying to get to his feet. People were trying to get to Robert Karriem, to restrain him even as he pushed Smith back down and pulled a car axle up from under the altar—slamming it into Smith's skull with an awful, mushy sound.

Elijah was already down the hall to the stairs by then, pushing past the neighbors pouring out of their rooms. More of the witnesses fighting their way down out after him, knocking each other aside, all of them tumbling down the stairs together in a blind, writhing knot. Spilling out into the chilly, wan, late Sunday afternoon sunlight, where Elijah could still hear the awful screams behind him, Karriem wailing at the top of his voice:

"I had to kill somebody! I could not forsake my gods!"

Elijah had run on down the street then, waving for the streetcar—nearly falling underneath the iron wheels as he grabbed hold and scrambled onboard. Jumping off after a few blocks and running on toward the Fraymore even though his lungs felt as if they were on fire. Bursting into Master Fard's rooms at last—managing just to blurt out the one question he had before his lungs bent him in half, his hands on his knees and his head down.

"What was he?" he asked, between gulps of breath.

Fard was standing in his front room, along with the brother once known as Brown Eel, and Elijah's own brother, Jarmin, whom the Master had renamed Kallatt. And that Chinaman again. Eddie Donaldson. For a moment, Elijah was filled with apprehension at the very sight of them all together, fearing that he had stumbled into a trap. But Fard only smiled his same, reassuring smile at him.

"What was he? A police spy? An imp? A white man?" he asked more urgently, into the uncomprehending silence, when he was finally able to raise his head.

"Who's that?" Master Fard asked, and though his face looked as serene as ever, Elijah could tell—with a rising sense of fear—that he really didn't know, that it wasn't a test, or an ambush, and that Master Fard was as ignorant about what had transpired as any of them.

"What are you talking about, my most faithful servant?"

"He did it," Elijah said, telling him all about Robert Karriem's ritual sacrifice. Pleading with the Master, once again, when he was finished:

"Why. Just tell me why."

But to his chagrin, Master Fard's face looked troubled, and he went immediately into his bedroom and began throwing his fine silken clothes into a suitcase—Brown Eel and Kallatt hastening to help him, though the Chinaman called Eddie Donaldson just stood around watching them, an amused expression on his face.

"It may be time for us to relocate for a while," Fard told him, his voice still calm as he packed. "The white devils will try to use this against us—"

But despite his haste the police were already there by the time they got to the lobby. Two thick-faced Irish cops, with their guns already drawn. Pausing for a moment, despite the desk clerk's frantic pointing, when they actually saw the Master.

"Jesus, buddy, you're Fard?" one of them asked. "You're as white as I am!"

"Hey, you all right in there? Everything all right in there, buddy?"

Malcolm jerked his head up at the sound of the gruff white voice, just outside the stall door. Trying to shake off the daze of the reefers, and all of the incredible, glowing words before him, and figure out what he should do.

"Hey, chief, you been in there awhile. Everything okay?"

Malcolm snapped the book closed and secreted it back in his jacket. Glancing down under the bottom of the stall door, he could see a pair of thick, heavily rubbered shoes. Cop's shoes? He thought desperately about what he could do, cornered in a bathroom stall with a pack of marijuana sticks—sure now that he had been followed all the way from 125th Street. For a moment, he even considered trying to sling himself under the side wall, come out the next stall, and catch the cop by surprise. He was sure he would get a running start of at least ten feet on him, and after that the cop would never catch him—

But then he looked again at the usual layers of men's-room filth ground into the stall tiles. Thinking that he would ruin his suit for sure, and how ignominious it would be for him to be caught there, trying to crawl out along a bathroom floor. It occurred to him, too, that the cop might have his vice-squad partner with him, stationed at the door and waiting for him no matter how fast he ran. And maybe they wanted him to run—

"Hey, buddy, you dead in there?!"

He slipped the little .25 into his hand, then slowly slid the stall latch back. Thinking with a thrill that rippled through even his marijuana daze that this might be it—that he could be dead within moments. He waited for the fat white cop's hand to yank the door open, and reach for him. Slipping the safety off his .25, thinking, with the bravado of the gage, that that was all right then—that no matter what, he wasn't going back to the precinct house, to that little, caged green room, so like the one that they had her in—

Nothing happened. He inched forward on the toilet seat, pushed the door open a little more with one foot—hand still wrapped firmly around the .25 in his pocket. The door swinging open to reveal more of those thick, rubber-soled cop's shoes…and then a mop, and a bucket. The gray-uniformed attendant of the men's room stood before him, an old man with a permanent crick in his back, a pair of Coke-bottle glasses, and a permanent grimace on his face.

"There you are! Whatta you been doin' in there—," he started to exclaim, but Malcolm was already out, pushing past him, heading back up the two flights to the bus platform again.

Once he was out there again, in the breeze from the river, away
from the dizzying, combined antiseptic and piss smell of the men's
room, he felt able to breathe again. Hopping the first Red & Tan
bus over to the other side. Settling into a seat near the back with
his Life magazine open now—not daring to risk further sacrilege
by bringing the book out again. His eyes flickering fitfully over
an elaborate half-page illustrated ad, featuring a GI grinning and
toasting with a bedouin on a camel—

"Have a Coca-Cola=Sa-LAM-oo a-Lay-koom (Peace Be Unto
You)...or how Americans make pals in Palestine. Peace be unto
you, says the hospitable Moslem when he greets a stranger. Have a
"Coke" says the American soldier in return, and in three words he
has made a new friend. It's a phrase that works as well in Haifa as
in Harrisburg—"

He looked up from his ad, yawning, and glanced idly around the
bus. The few scattered midday passengers were all either dozing or
gazing out the window, except for one, a man sitting bolt upright in
the very front seat of the vehicle. Malcolm could make out only the
back of his head, but somehow he thought he knew him. Then it
struck him—the same rounded hat the man was wearing, complete
with its familiar golden symbols. He couldn't think why he hadn't
noticed it before. Elijah.

"Hey!" he called out, getting up from his seat and starting to
stagger up the aisle of the rattling, shaking bus. Not wanting to
offer any disrespect, but at a loss for what he should call him.

"Hey! Hey, you! Sir!"

Somehow, the little man still didn't turn around, or give any sign
that he had heard him, though Malcolm did not see how that could
be so. For that matter, none of the dozing passengers awakened,
either, and when he got up toward the front, Malcolm could see
that the bus driver himself was asleep, his arms cosseting his head
against the wheel. He realized vaguely that he should be alarmed
by this, but the bus seemed to be lurching steadily forward, and he
stayed focused on where Elijah was sitting, just in front of him. He
kept going until at last he was able to grasp the metal handle on the
back of his seat, pulling himself the last couple of feet toward him.
Even daring, then, to reach out his hand and tap the man lightly on
his shoulder, barely breathing his name.

"Elijah?"

The little man turned around in his seat then, looking Malcolm straight in the face, his eyes boring into Malcolm's so intensely that he took a step backward, grasping the seat across the aisle for support. Elijah's jaw dropped open then, sounds pouring suddenly out in a strangely loud, abrasive, white voice.

"Fort Lee! Fort Lee!"

Malcolm whipped his head up from his lap, realizing he was still sitting in his original seat. He stumbled on up the aisle, his eyes fixed on the front seat—but there was no sign of the little man, or anyone else there now. He hurried on out of the bus, thinking that maybe he had already gotten off, so sure was he that Elijah had been on the bus.

He tripped on off the bus, locating the usual I-tie bagman in the usual place, right by the shelter. Only this time, to his shock, when he handed over his slips, the I-tie handed him a bag in return.

"What's this?" Malcolm asked, confused. There had never been a return package for him before, and this one felt much heavier than the airy bag of policy player hopes he had just handed over.

"For your boss," the bagman told him. He was the same man who had deigned to speak to him before, Malcolm thought—his voice equally contemptuous now. He turned and walked back up the stairs that led up to the highway overpass without another word— leaving Malcolm to weigh the bag in his hand.

He stood there for a moment, dumbfounded, then the bennies kicked in and he began to walk quickly away. Wondering if he had been set up for something, half-expecting a patrol-car siren to come blaring down on him at any moment. Ready to ditch the bag by the curb at a moment's notice, feeling safe enough to look in it only when he was safely situated deep in the back of the bus. He unfolded it gingerly even then—keeping his head up, facing the Manhattan skyline, as if the bag held nothing more important than his lunch. Only when he had it all the way opened did he take a deep breath, force an expression of casual boredom onto his face, and look down into the bag. Nodding when he did, despite the way his heart was jumping, confirming that it was filled with what he had dreaded and suspected all along: money.

He crumpled the top of the bag closed, and looked hastily back up. Half-expecting to see a plainclothesman or a couple of uniforms stepping toward him even now from their places of concealment somewhere on the bus. Telling himself that he wouldn't even open the bag again, would just leave it on his seat when the bus got back to Manhattan, as if it had nothing to do with him.

But looking around him, he saw that there was nobody on the bus, as usual, except for the same few stragglers—a defense-plant worker or two, back from his shift; a couple of older cleaning ladies, coming back from their Jersey jobs. Slowly, his hands trembling, he lowered the paper bag to his lap, and opened it up again. But there was no mistaking it. The bag was filled with money—fat bricks of money, wrapped with rubber bands; money that looked as if it had been handled and folded and turned over a thousand times. Most of the bills smaller denominations, tens and finiffs and ones, but so many wads of it that he knew there must be hundreds, maybe even several thousand dollars, right there.

He closed it once more as the bus trundled back into its bay at the 175th Street station. Telling himself that Archie must have set him up, that somehow he must have found out about him and Miranda, and that as soon as he stepped foot off the bus, a couple of big, white cops would be right behind him.

But when he did get off, there was nothing more than a few pigeons in sight, bobbing about in the shadows of the bus station, making their endless genuflections in pursuit of pretzel scraps, and old hot-dog rolls. The bus driver only yawning at him—slouched in his seat, his face revealing none of the added tension or excitement to be expected from an impending bust. Malcolm took a deep breath and ran down the steps of the bus, ready for whatever was to come. But there was still nothing. The driver shutting the doors impatiently behind him with a whoosh of air, pulling his bus around for the next meandering loop through the suburban villages of Bergen County. Malcolm even took the added precaution of descending a different, distant flight of stairs from where all the other passengers had gotten off. Padding as quietly as possible down onto the main concourse of the bus station—where there was only the usual midday quiet; a few GIs lugging their bags, the same Jersey matrons coming or going from a day of shopping in the City.

He hurried down from the station, walking as fast as he could without running to the apartment he had lit on for the moment— three basement rooms on West 147th Street, between St. Nicholas and Convent Avenues. Taking even more precautions than usual when he went in, checking under the bed and listening for any sound of trouble. Everything was quiet, even silent—a sultry Harlem Friday afternoon in the summer—but he couldn't take any chances, did not even dare to pull the money out of the bag long enough to count it.

Instead, he looked around the rooms for someplace to hide the stash, but he knew that this wouldn't do, either. Sammy had told him the tenant in the back basement apartment, just behind his wall, was one of the biggest dealers in Harlem. He had been proud to be living in such proximity, even if he had never seen the man. But he had already noticed a steady trickle of junkies coming down the stairs to his apartment, past Malcolm's own windows, and he knew he couldn't possibly leave so much money here.

Instead he pulled out a money belt he had bought from Sammy, shoving the wads of money into it as quickly as he could. Forcing it closed around his waist, under the band of his trousers—hoping the bulges of money wouldn't mess up the line of his suit too badly. Only then did he feel it was safe enough to go out again, carting nearly every cent he had around on his person. Now all he had to worry about was West Indian Archie.

For the next two days he had stayed in motion. Driving constantly back and forth between Sammy's apartment and midtown. Volunteering for one job after another, asking Sammy if there wasn't something else he could do until Sammy began to notice something was up.

"You all right, Mr. High Pockets?" he asked, eyeing Malcolm carefully.

"I'm cool, I'm cool!" Malcolm tried to assure him.

"Yeah? 'Cause you flippin' an' you ain't floppin'. You flappin' an' you ain't flyin' at all."

"I'm solid!" he cried—not daring to tell Sammy what was up, afraid he would just as soon turn him into Archie on speculation.

"Yeah? Well then, come in here, young lane. You might as well have a snort," he said, ushering him into his kitchen.

He brought out some cocaine and cut it on a mirror on the kitchen table—his own stash, Malcolm noticed, uncut with the regular heavy dosage of talcum powder for the square shufflers. He invited Malcolm to do a line, then two more. Looking him over thoughtfully the whole time, gently prodding him to talk some more. Ushering him out of his apartment only after offering up a final snort, and letting Malcolm score a new bottle of bennies on credit.

"Member, Nome. I'se you friend. You got anyt'ing troublin' you, you come to ol' Sammy," he said as he let him out the front door, tapping his back affectionately.

"You know I will. You a good friend," Malcolm said, as sincerely as he was able—thinking now that somehow Sammy knew, that he must have noticed the money belt bulging beneath his pants. Sure now that he would put the word out on The Wire.

He had not dared to go back to his rented rooms at all after that. He made sure to always keep himself out in public, meeting his steers in front of the Astor Hotel, on the busiest corner in Times Square, or sitting in a crowded barroom when he wasn't working for the moment. Going down to visit a white actor on the East Side he had sold sticks to, when he could not bear to go without a bath any longer. Meanwhile, he kept his ear glued to The Wire, too—much as he dreaded what he might hear. Trying to discover as discreetly as possible if Archie was after him, if he even knew his money was gone yet. Having to do it subtly—noticing how the faces of old friends and connections grew quietly interested the more he talked.

Above all now, he wanted go down to the Village and see Miranda again. Soon he could think about nothing else but how it would feel to simply caress her, to rest with her. He wanted to go, he knew that she would never give him up—but was too afraid that he might run right into Archie there. He thought about trying to see her at her work, down at the Café Society, but he couldn't seem to figure out when she would be there. Time was beginning to slip away from him now, the hours passing in the space of a thought, seconds lingering on interminably. Even the air was beginning to change around him, he thought, the pressure dropping steadily. The sky lowering darkly, visibly—the day becoming steadily hotter and more oppressive.

When it began to rain, at last, he felt relief. Coming back to himself a little. Standing out on the pavement and lifting his head up to receive the tepid water. Hearing a good-hearted laugh or two from all around him, and not minding it in the least—glad to discover that he was back in Harlem, at least, and not downtown.

He tramped up and down through the rain for a while, trying to clear his head. Stamping puddles, shaking his head, not even caring that he was messing up his conk as he tried to get the cobwebs out. Wondering what he was going to do with this money strapped to him—if he could parlay it into some really big score, hit the horses or the numbers, or break a poker game. He would have more than enough to pay West Indian Archie back, with interest, he figured,

and soon he was picturing how even Archie would be impressed
when Malcolm walked in, telling him coolly how he had doubled
his money—

He made his way blindly back up to Sammy's, not quite sure if
he had missed some job, or was due for another. He swung by Sugar
Hill on his way, circling warily around his last crib to see if there
was anything suspicious. He didn't see anyone—but then, he was
no longer sure what he could or could not see. That noisy evange-
list revival still going on up the street, distracting him, making him
think he couldn't hear something vital.

He had stopped outside the big white tent for a few minutes.
Scowling at the sight of all the excitable Negroes thinking they
were saved. Kneeling and praying with some whooper preacher
with a saddle brown suit that perfectly matched the color of his
skin, and a mouthful of gleaming-gold teeth. A hustler who would
have been spotted for exactly what he was in a New York minute in
Small's Paradise. All the sinners praying with their heads bowed,
with their hands lifted up to God.

Just as he had watched people praying all his life, for nothing.
Just as he had watched her pray, at the Seventh Day Church of God.
Sneaking loving looks out the corner of her eye at Mr. Walker, that
barber salesman, that congolene dealer standing next to her—

He turned away, angrily now. Trying to calm himself—trying
not to miss anything. Trying to keep from opening the bottle of
bennies, now only half full, in his inside jacket pocket. Fearing as he
did that just one more might be enough to push him over the edge.
Making himself think instead on what Archie had told him: I am a
hustler, boy, that's what I do—

At Sammy's he tried to put a big front on it. Slipping in as coolly
as if he had just left, asking casually if Sammy had anything more
for him. And Sammy still looking him up and down with interest,
nodding his head. Telling him, yeah, sure, and instructing him to
meet another steer from downtown, out at the corner, and walk the
john in. Malcolm nodded, trying to get a read on Sammy but not
quite able to, what with his head pounding again. The heat already
rising again. Funny how it happened in this City. Not even the rain
dispelling it.

He made an effort to concentrate. Trying to picture the white
john he was to meet from the familiar nickname Sammy told him.
Doughface. A picture of a soft, skittery white man in his fifties, with

large, moist eyes came to mind—someone who would present no problem. He nodded and smiled at Sammy as normally as he could, then walked out to the corner. The rain slacking off now to passing spits and drizzles, the money belt pressing hotter and heavier than ever against his thighs. Trying to hold it all together. Seeing the car coming up already, the sad, paunchy Doughface climbing out. Malcolm mumbled something, some nonsense at him; grinning at him, trying to make him feel safe. And then there he was.

He heard him before he saw him, coming at him from down the sidewalk. Yelling something unintelligible—feeling him before he quite saw him, and freezing there. Leaving the soft, sad-eyed white man in the lurch, his friendly, well-intentioned hand hanging out in the air. Car tires squealed, and Mr. Doughface ran off into the night. Only Malcolm was left standing there, smiling in stupefaction to see who it was. Ready to shake his hand, even calling out to him in his relief and recognition that it wasn't Archie, or someone Archie had sent, but only that preacher again, come out of nowhere—

"What you doin' here?"

—and jumping back only when the man kept coming on. His face contorted in fury, that umbrella brandished above his head like a spear, or a cross. Surprising Malcolm so much that he ran, too. Easily outdistancing the preacher up Seventh Avenue, yelling back at him in his bewilderment. Afraid that he might do the preacher bodily harm if he stayed, though he would have liked to ask him what the hell he meant bringing down that awful curse on him, worse than anything his father or his mother ever said to him, combined:

"Damn you for living!"

CHAPTER NINETEEN

JONAH

That Monday morning he had walked out of Harlem for the last time. Trying to take careful note of everything around him, for he knew he would not come back here again. Walking the length of both blocks of Strivers Row, up and down, committing to memory each of the exquisite sand- and rust-colored houses, the slender, gracious trees. Staring for the last time at the gateposts from a forgotten era with their admonishment, *Walk Your Horses!*—even staring down the back alleys, with their garages and servants' rooms, and the neat rows of ashcans.

He made his escape easily enough. The logistics of it had come readily to him, Jonah realizing that he had been thinking about this day for years. He had packed a briefcase with a few of his immediate needs. A couple of clean shirts, enough socks and underwear for a few days. Some more of the ration coupons he had stockpiled from Jakey. A Bible. Doing it all late at night, once he had said good-bye to his father, and Amanda had finally given up waiting for him and gone to sleep. After chasing off that crazy boy who seemed to dog his every footstep, he had walked around aimlessly for hours, deliberately waiting out his own wife. He had set the alarm clock on his bedside table but it hadn't been necessary, he hadn't slept at all. He had been up as soon as the sun came through their bedroom window, showering and shaving with the awful sulfuric shaving powder he needed to cut through the tough stubble of his beard—dreadful-smelling stuff that she had often teased him about. Dressing as quickly and quietly as he could in the bright early light.

She had still been asleep by the time he was ready to go, just as he had hoped. Lying facedown, sprawled diagonally across the bed-clothes. That had been one of their little jokes together, too, how once she was asleep she would spread out and take up as much of the bed as she could get away with. He leaned over her now, kissing her once along the backs of her supple shoulders, just above the simple cotton shift she was wearing. Letting one hand linger along the marvelous smoothness of her skin, thinking how much he would miss that.

She stirred slightly, muttering something into the pillows, but she did not open her eyes. He lifted his hand immediately and padded quietly toward the door, whispering to her only Good-bye, baby. Just as glad that she hadn't gotten up, afraid that he couldn't take a breakfast of lying to her face while she made him bacon and eggs, and squeezed his orange juice for him. Thinking that it was better this way, that he would write her from wherever he was going and try to explain the whole thing. Thinking it was better that she hate him a little, at least right away.

He had flown on down the stairs then, not taking so much as a last look at the immaculate, child-free adjoining parlors. Not even glancing up at the blue eye of God, now pouring through in the sky-light. He had opened the beautiful wooden door with its etched glass as he had done thousands of times before, ever since he was a boy—a privileged prince of the church—and trotted on down the stoop and out into the street. Just like that, leaving the house he had lived in for some twenty years. His legs quivering beneath him as he walked away but still managing a genteel hello to the few other residents who were awake at this hour, and not away at Oak Bluffs, or Asbury Park. The writer who wrote bitter polemics on race for the People's Voice, and merry satires of the colored upper crust he lived amongst for the Pittsburgh Courier. The lawyer who was employed by the NAACP's legal-defense fund, still working on his twenty-year strategy to integrate the state university in Texas. The Reverend Earl Ward, a young assistant minister to Adam over at the Abyssinian who was walking his bicycle over to Riverside Park for his vigorous morning ride. A health faddist who was always walking something over there, a bike or even a canoe—giving Jonah an entirely too hardy wave and Hello! for this time of the morning.

People they had had at their dinner table. People he had stood with at a hundred cocktail parties and receptions, trying to make small talk. Politely discussing DuBois and Walter White, and A. Philip Randolph and Franklin Roosevelt. The relative merits of psycho-analysis, and the NAACP, and vigorous bicycle rides. All that trivia, to pass the days. Were those the sorts of things the Jews had talked about, too? In Warsaw, and Cracow and Lodz, before the war?

Out on Seventh Avenue, it was a beautiful summer's day. The sun was shining brightly, but it was cooler than it had been in weeks. The first, teasing harbinger of fall, the blessed season in the City. Everything looking cleaner and tidier, the rain having chased much of the usual debris off the street, and the mattresses and bedding off the fire escapes.

The angry little knots of people he had seen together on the stoops and the streetcorners all summer were gone, too, at least for the moment. Everyone sleeping in, or moving around a little more, taking advantage of their temporary respite from the heat. The supers and landladies already wedging open their front doors. Keeping them closed later most mornings to try and hold in the cooler night air but throwing them open to the elements now, trying to flush out their heat-fouled apartment houses. The windows above them filled with stars and little American flags, each one denoting a young man off serving his country.

The streets were already cluttered with children not wanting to miss a moment of their summer time off. Playing paddle Hi-Li, or chalking out hopscotch courts. Jonah maneuvered around stickball players, and pig-tailed little girls, obliviously chanting their usual jump-rope ditties—Oh, I won't go to Macy's anymore-more-more / There's a big, mean policeman at the door-door-door—

When he reached the Fabian toy store on 128th Street, he saw that it was Yo-Yo Day, the monthly visit of the traveling yo-yo salesman. An arc of boys and girls, and not a few adults, stood on the sidewalk out front, watching a silver-haired white man with a splotchy, soft, drinker's face impassively working two yo-yos to a hand. He walked the dog, and went around the world, rocked the cradle and reached for the moon. The brilliantly striped and spiraled wooden circles whirling far out into the air and just over their heads, before being yanked adroitly back in. The kids flinching and oohing and watching solemnly, the grown-ups grinning like kids despite themselves, lowering their heads and laughing in embarrassment.

He walked all the way over to his usual elevated stop on 125th Street, making sure that he saw it all one more time. Making sure to pass the knife grinders coaxing the old nags towing their wagons down the streets for one more morning, the I-Cash-Clothes men staggering along under their many colored coats and layers of hats. Past all the fish vendors and the fruit vendors and the greens sellers, the iceman and the ices men, and the rag man and the crab men, singing their jubilant songs to the open windows above—

"Got blackberries today, folks!
Blackberries for the baby,
Blackberries for the ol' lady,
Blackberries for the ol' man—

And then the inevitable, teasing pause—

"If you ain't got no ol' man, take me!"

Sung not with the usual wry weariness or calculation of the salesman but with real exuberance, as if, for just this once, to be out walking the streets of Harlem for hours trying to sell fish or berries or fifty-pound blocks of ice was reward enough in itself. And Jonah—his briefcase crammed with shirts and underwear, and that Bible—was filled even then with the doubt that he could actually go.

But then he bought a paper, putting down three cents for a Herald-Tribune with the boy at the bottom of the steep metal staircase leading up to the miniature chalet of the station platform. Scanning the headlines of the usual daily affronts—whites walking off the job because a handful of colored workers were promoted to machine jobs at a naval arsenal in New York, or an engine-parts plant in Indiana; hired to run streetcars in Philadelphia; to work in a defense plant in Newark—but skipping over them for the most part.

He turned instead to the accounts of the riot in Detroit, the pictures of colored men lying dead and wounded in the street. There they were, sure enough, just as he had heard on the radio. It wasn't a hallucination. There were the men being pulled off a streetcar, in a northern city, by whites gripping lengths of lead pipe, and beer bottles by the neck. Lined up against a wall by the police. Hands folded behind their heads, like prisoners of war—or like men being lined up for a firing squad.

Just like in Poland—

The rickety little elevated train finally arrived, and Jonah stepped on. Thinking as he did that this was the last contact he would ever have with Harlem—his feet technically off the ground already. Not having bothered to wear his clerical collar this time, just his best light blue summer suit; the same hue as the eye of God in the skylight. Not hiding anything. Welcoming the idea that some member of his congregation might see him—some church mother able to tell her story to the police, and over and over again to her friends at her beauty parlor, or in her mah-jongg club—"I seen him that morning. That must've been him, settin' off as easy as you please! He even nodded, an' smiled at me!"

But as it actually happened, no one he knew stepped onboard, and Jonah took the train to his usual midtown stop. Descending the long metal stairs again, down into that cool, dappled middle world where he shucked his old self, the world of whirring pigeons and gloomy bars, and novelty shops. It wasn't really his stop, but he wanted to do it right, this last trip, holding to the ritual—yet not venturing into the little smoke and news shop this time. His encounter there with that crazy boy from the train still too fresh in his mind.

The memory of that man-boy continued to plague him as he walked on downtown. Wondering how he kept popping up, like a bad penny. Like God with his namesake, the o-riginal Jonah. Plaguing his every attempt to get away, to fit into what surely must be the anonymous muddle of His creatures even to Him at times. But how had he come to be there? Jonah had scarcely believed it was him at first, transformed in such a short time from that wild devil boy on the train to the slick, self-assured john-walker—the pimp's assistant—he had spied on that streetcorner last night.

How could that have happened so fast—even in this City, in this time? And would he ever know what that gesture on the train had meant—jumping into Buzzards Bay like that, in front of the whole car?

He cut east, heading for a place he had had in mind all along—for at least several weeks—to spend the first, few nights of his new existence. Someplace not too far from his gloomy midtown world under the elevated, but a world away. The exclusive Roanoke Hotel, an all-white establishment—what would be the site of his last, secret triumph. And what will you do for fun now? he could picture

Sophie sneering at him. Drop in on the colored folks for a change of pace?

He strode right into the lush, carpeted lobby of the hotel. Not worrying in the least that he would be spotted now, only afraid that it might be full up with the usual wartime crush of salesmen and dealmakers, politicians and brass. But he was in luck, there was a room open, No. 1555. He took it at once, trying not to look too eager, paying with cash in advance. Upstairs, he had sat on a bone white bedspread, the briefcase balanced on his knees, after the bellman had closed the door with a conniving smile. Wondering why it was he had come back to this place. Knowing only that he had conceived of it as a halfway point, some neutral, secret place from which he could move after a couple of days, into his new life.

He had gone to the Roanoke for the first time just this spring, after two women from the church had been turned away from the hotel restaurant outright, told bluntly to their faces that it did not serve colored people. He had gone back with them the next Saturday afternoon at lunchtime, even though he had no idea what he could actually do, and his stomach had churned at the very idea of such a confrontation.

Instead, a gentleman who was obviously the maitre d' had appeared, a tall, insolent, tired-looking man in a tuxedo, with the thin mustache and brilliantined black hair of a movie gigolo—who had insisted that he was what he obviously was not.

"I asked to speak to the manager, sir," Jonah had told him, trying to make his voice as icy as possible.

"I'm the manager," the man said in a heavy Brooklyn accent, not so much as bothering with a salutation. "What can I do for ya?"

"These two ladies were told that you do not serve colored people—"

"That's impossible we serve everyone."

The voice a monotone now, not even bothering to affect surprise.

"Do you? Well, then, we'd like to get a table for three. Right now!"

"I'm sorry but that's impossible all our tables are booked."

"I want to see the manager!"

"I am the manager."

Jonah had peered pointedly over the man's shoulder, into the nearly empty dining room, but the maitre d' had not even bothered to follow his gaze. He shifted his weight uneasily from foot to foot, thrown a little by such open impertinence. Trying to decide just what he should do—

"All right, then. We'll have a table out here, at the bar."

Jonah had moved swiftly to one of a set of small tables just off the bar, ushering the women into the other two chairs. Aware even as he did so of how jerky and undignified his movement had seemed.

The maitre d' had simply shrugged.

"Certainly let me get you some menus."

They had sat and waited then. The two church ladies older women, in their sixties, willing to follow their minister in whatever he did but clearly mortified to find themselves seated in a bar. They stayed still as mice, not so much as removing their coats. Jonah hadn't removed his, either, not sure of just what was happening, or what he should do—finally deciding, even more absurdly, he realized afterward, to remove his hat. Putting it down prominently in the middle of the small table.

There it had remained, a fedora in the middle of the table, for the next hour while they tried to get any kind of service. After the maître d' had walked past them twice, Jonah had signaled to him, raising his hand like a child in a schoolroom—knowing even as he did it how stupid and ineffectual it looked. The maitre d' had ignored it, of course. Finally, on his next pass—increasingly desperate, beginning to sweat in his good camel's-hair coat, the two ladies looking down at their hands on their laps, to save him any further embarrassment—Jonah had reached out and grasped the man's wrist, the maitre d' peering down at him through his half-closed lids as if he had been suddenly seized by a lizard.

"Yes?"

"We would like those menus, please—"

"Oh, yes."

He had released his wrist, smiling stupidly across at the ladies, who smiled back, hoping that something, anything might finally happen then—and the maitre d' vanished behind the curtains leading to the dining room. They never saw him again. From time to time a waiter went by, each one ignoring them as completely as the maitre d' had. Jonah had finally been able to procure some menus by going over and asking the barman directly for them—but this had led to nothing more, no one coming over to take their order. Even the slow trickle of waiters drying up, the bartender disappearing from his post once the last white customer had drunk up and left.

Jonah had sat where he was, fuming. Wondering if he should have appealed to the white customers at the bar, or to the diners as they were leaving the dining room. But when he had stared pointedly at them, trying to make some sort of appeal with his eyes, they had only looked away. Just like the people on the train would do. The two ladies across the table visibly shriveled up into themselves, into the best Sunday coats and the feathered hats they had put on deliberately for this occasion. Both of them doctors' wives, who had no doubt read about this place in Diana Vreeland's column in Vogue, or heard about it at their last meeting of Smart Set, or Girl-friends. Proud women, with some money and position in their own community, who now sat across from him in sadness and confusion, humiliated twice over.

After an hour of sitting there, with his hat on the table in front of him like some mockery of a meal, Jonah had decided that he had to do something. Determined to go and find the missing maitre d' and manager even if he was forcibly ejected. He had raised himself to his feet—soaked in sweat now beneath the warm coat—and put his hat back on, nodding to the women from church.

"Ladies—just give me a moment—"

He had walked over and flung open the thick drapes veiling the dining room, ready to confront anyone. But all he had seen, far across the restaurant, were a couple more waiters laying out the cloths on the bare tables for the dinner service. They had ignored him, too, staring right through him when they happened to catch his eye. Only unfolding another cloth, flinging it up into the air above their heads before allowing it to flutter down to the table like a great white dove.

And now, here he was, upstairs sitting on this white bedspread, in a white room. He stood up, and paced around the room, trying to keep his mind on the practicalities. A day or two here at the Roanoke, while he got his bearings, and decided just where he was headed. California, he thought. That was where he had always assumed he would go whenever he thought at any length about leaving. It was as far as he could go, and to him it had always seemed the closest possible place to Heaven, or at least non-being—someplace where the climate was always the same, and there were lots of fruit trees.

He still thought of joining the army, somehow. Envisioning himself in the front lines, cut down recklessly charging Germans so that at least he could say he gave his life for something. But he was aware of how weak his eyes had grown through all the years of writing out sermons, and pawing through books of theology. How old and easily winded his body had become, compared to all these teenagers he saw shipping out every day. He would be just as likely to spend the duration as some clerical orderly, pecking out reports and camp regulations.

No, better to just accept that he could do nothing for anybody, really—nothing to stop this whole new world from coming into being. California it would be. But to do what? Work in a defense plant, maybe, and serve as one more cog in this bright new machine of a world? To preach on the street corner, then, like all those whose faith he so envied?

He walked into the bathroom and ran some cold water into the porcelain basin by the sink. Taking off his reading spectacles, he splashed it over his face, then looked into the cabinet mirror above the sink as he dried himself with a cloth. He pulled out his comb next, and started to experiment, brushing his hair forward and back. Putting his glasses on and off. Trying to make his face go as blank as possible, so that it seemed to him his entire personality slipped away. Leaving him as anonymous as possible, a wholly different person, facing himself there in the mirror—

It scared him, losing himself there, and he turned away. Thinking that he might go mad if he stared any longer—wondering how his sister kept from doing it, all these years on her own. He went back to walking around the room, noticing how bone white it was, reminding him of something. White, pearled bedspread, painted white furniture and furnishings and drapes—even a white ceiling fan over the bed. All designed, he knew, to make the room look as light and airy and jim-clean as possible against the season's moldering humidity outside. That is what they love about their color, it is the color of germlessness, of sterility. Of blissful blankness—

Today, though, was a beautiful, light day, and he raised the shade of the nearest window. The window itself was already open, but he pulled the screen up as well, telling himself it would let the newly cleansed air in as quickly as possible. He stood in front of the open window for a long moment, breathing it in. Staring down at the slow procession of traffic at the intersection below, at the heads of people crossing the street. He leaned far out over the windowsill, closing his eyes, trying to concentrate on just what it was he was going to do in his new, independent life—

It occurred to him, then, just what the room reminded him of. He pulled himself back in from the window to look at it again, the honks and shouts from far below receding dizzily behind him. Yes, it was true. The all-white room was just like the room he'd had at the seminary, in the Angel Factory down in Pennsylvania. A little better appointed, a carpet on the floor instead of an aging throw rug. A double bed instead of two singles, and his mischevious room-mate Johnny Kirk smirking over some volume of Rauschenbusch, across the room—but otherwise very much the same in its blinding whiteness.

All the rooms were white, all the maids were white, all the fac-ulty were white. All white tombs, filled with corruption, they used to joke.

It had felt almost like a monastery when he got there. No locks on any of the doors, strict attendance required in chapel and at meals. Constant personal inspections by the head dean they called Creeping Jesus for his relentless, soundless creeping around the dorm rooms, sniffing for trouble. Jonah had welcomed it. Sure that he deserved it, after his deception. After all his years sticking it out at the college upstate, his shame had ground him down to a nub. His father had objected—relieved that he was going into the ministry, but urging him to try for one of the better, integrated seminaries in Boston or New York. The Angel Factory even then something of a running joke between the students at its affiliated liberal arts college, its faculty and students both varying wildly in ability and dedication. His fellow seminarians themselves had joked about it—If you can't do anything else, then preach.

Jonah hadn't cared. By the summer after his graduation, he had been walking around in a daze, as if everything he had known and accepted was no longer true. His entire earlier conversion, his sure acceptance of Jesus Christ now worn away like a morning mist. By then Sophia was already gone most of the time, or he might have tried turning to her for some direction. The fissure he hadn't even recognized, meanwhile, had opened up between him and his father. It had begun from the moment he had poured out his confession of passing at the school upstate, and the old man had said simply Don't do that again and looked away from him—unable to set his eyes on what his son had become. There had been no one left to talk to, then.

The seminary had been the perfect place for him, as something—Jesus? A blind desire to disappoint and disappear from his father's sight again? His own crushed ego?—had told him it would be. He had studied beside the sons of ministers of the most prominent Negro congregations in Philadelphia and Pittsburgh and Baltimore—and with the sons of jackleg circuit preachers from down in the Florida pine barrens. Taking classes with high Baptists, and snake-stomping Baptists, and those Baptists so starchy and full of themselves that Johnny Kirk liked to call them Episcopalians. The professors ranging from toothless old Bible thumpers, washed up on the haven of the seminary, who taught them the many kinds of sermons, and The Three Ps—proving, painting, persuasion, to actual theologians and vigorous Christian intellectuals—"the kind who have to think up an excuse for Jesus," as Kirk had sneered.

It was, Jonah considered later, the best education a minister could have. He had learned the rudiments of how to speak from the pulpit (hoping the heart would come later, even if it never did), and he took his classes seriously. Reading Augustine and Spinoza, Nietzche and Tolstoy and Marx, anything he could get his hands on. Truly studying the history of the Bible for the first time, how it was written, and how even its most blasphemous interpreters had construed it. Reading right through the night sometimes, genuinely wanting to know everything he could. Reading the sermons and the writings of the great colored ministers for the first time, Francis Grimke, and Bishop Henry McNeal Turner, whose words at the depth of the Georgia race riots and lynchings, three decades before, he had always remembered: "Remember—a people already invisible can be easily made to disappear!"

The Angel Factory was perfectly located for his purposes too, in a small, picked-over industrial city outside Philadelphia—a place full of sullen white people, most of whom spent their lives in factories, stamping out tin cans. The seminary cut off from almost everything, leaving him all the time he needed to read and study. Johnny Kirk mocked him for how seriously he took it all—his relentless studying, and how he kept his clothes neatly cleaned and pressed. Making his bed so tightly, even before the maids got there, that he could bounce a nickel off it. Determined not to be one of those Negroes—messy and always late, laughing too much in their embarrassment. He chided Johnny in turn for how sloppily he kept his half of the room, his irreverence. How he eyeballed the younger white maids when they came to pick up the room—asking Jonah after they'd left if he ever thought about seeing how far they might go.

"Don't talk like that," Jonah had told him grimly.

"Why not?" Johnny had grinned back at him. "These little Irish an' bohunk girls—they're probably dying to know what it would be like. What with all the stories in their heads about jungles, and wild beasts. It'd be the one time they could look back on with pride an' say they'd really sinned!"

"I don't care about them," Jonah told him.

"Well, that ain't very Christian of you—"

"I care about us—about lowering ourselves to that sort of talk!"

"Why? We're just animals, too. Even in our most divine form."

"We have to stand for something. We have the burdens of the Negro race on our shoulders—" Jonah had started to tell him, but Johnny waved him off.

"So what?" he laughed. "So we have the burdens of the whole race. So what? We didn't ask for 'em. And we can't possibly carry 'em!"

Johnny's father was the minister of one of the biggest colored congregations in Philadelphia, and he had insisted on taking Jonah into the city on the weekends, saying that he would show him the burdens of the Negro race. Towing him on Saturday nights through the lowest bars and pool halls he knew—getting him to drink beer, and play pool, even though Jonah had sworn he would never again partake of these pleasures—and many more—as part of the penance he had decided on for himself. But after a time he found that he was able to laugh and joke, taking real pleasure in things amidst the laughing, bleary, accepting faces all around him. Finding, to his surprise, that small, irreducible kernel of faith still within him.

But it was she who had really nurtured it, who had built him back up. By the time he had graduated from the Angel Factory and returned to his Daddy's church, he was still wary, and desperately lonely. Not trusting himself, not knowing what he could possibly do for anyone else. He was clumsy in the pulpit, on those Sundays when his father prodded him to speak, uncertain and stumbling, the magic of his effortless debut long forgotten. He had taken some solace in the ministerial work, the visits to tenement apartments and railroad flats, the hallways stinking from the trash moldering down in the dumbwaiter. The visits to The Morgue, once he managed to overcome his fear and revulsion. All the long, hard, useful work— setting up labor bureaus, besieging welfare offices, wangling stays of eviction, and medical leaves—

But he had only been able to do it with her help, every step of his way back. That marriage so adroitly arranged by his Daddy— Jonah secretly resenting that this, too, was his doing, but not feeling he had any right to resist in his demolished state. Still flattened by Christ, and only just lifting himself back up. Amanda had found what was best in him from the start, forgiving him his fearfulness, forgiving him his every fault and weakness as automatically as she might have done a child's. Accepting everything in him, even his deepest, ugliest confessions as only human. She was cheerful and silly with him when he was exhausted, listened earnestly when he wanted to talk about the endless circumvolutions of church politics. She did more than her share both at home and at the New Jerusalem—running her clubs, appeasing the church mothers, keeping a fine house, and making a good appearance. Always demure but intelligent, informed at the endless receptions, the dinners and receptions on Strivers Row, and Sugar Hill. Shy and inexperienced in bed, as he had been, but always eager and unabashed. Seeking always to please him—

It was best that he leave her, he had assured himself. Best for her, for the church—for everyone. A sacrifice that he would make, was how he had thought of it. A final penance for all of his failures. For his cowardice, his ineffectuality, his inability to face the coming Poland. The time of the Jews, here and now, and for us—

And yet, he realized now as he walked once more around the room and came back to sit on the bed, he had always thought of it as akin to disappearing. That he would cease to be conscious. That he would be gone out of his own life, as well as theirs—a positive good. The disturbing notion only just beginning to overtake him that this halfway point, this way station he had planned, might be all there was. Sitting for the rest of his life on a white bed, in a white hotel room. Not good, not bad, only gone. And meanwhile, his brain ticking on and on. Thinking of his Daddy, dying up there. Thinking of the smoothness of her back and arms. The fierceness in her face when she was determined, all the continual moments of kindness, flowing from her as involuntarily as water.

He stood up, feeling almost as if he were choking. Looking back over at the window now, he saw to his bewilderment that it was already starting to get dark. Realizing that he had been sitting and pacing here in this white room for hours already, without any idea how much time had gone by. *His first day, already squandered.*

He had hurried on down to the restaurant dining room then, ready to fulfill the main reason he had come back to this place. It was what he usually ended up doing, when he was passing—going to some smart restaurant, or hotel bar, where a colored man would not be served. It made him all the more ashamed, thinking of the money, and the black-market ration coupons he had dropped over the past few months in such silly, pretentious places. But he could not help himself.

Down in the restaurant, the very same maitre d' had been on duty. Fawning over Jonah immediately, informing him in some sort of vaguely foreign accent that they would have a table for him right away. Jonah had waited half a beat—as much time as he dared pause in a sermon—then let his eyes fix on the man's. Daring him to take this moment to question him, to remember who he was.

He waited—but the maitre d's eyes only slid submissively away. Producing a single menu from the coat-check stand—so that's where they were!—after quickly ascertaining that Jonah was alone.

"Right this way, sir—"

Leading him halfway across the dining room, to a prominent table where anyone entering the restaurant would see him immediately.

"Is this all right for you, sir?" the maitre d' murmured.

Jonah could only nod, and sit down in the proffered chair, opening up his menu. The words swam before him, and he was relieved, yet oddly disappointed, too, at how easily it had gone, at how very little had changed. He had sat down gamely, ordering the pork chops as soon as the waiter came. Leaning back, then, knowing from experience that this was the loneliest part of it. Sitting by himself at a table, or at the end of a bar—afraid to strike up a conversation with anyone, to have to make up too much about where he lived, or what he did, or why he wasn't in the war.

This is how it would have to be, he knew. Living wholly in isolation, or at least until he could come up with another family, another job, another city. And then living a lie, with his past erased, in constant fear of being found out. Dress white. Talk white. Tell everyone that you are the only child of only children who both died long ago, and that you are Greek, Italian, South American. Don't tell anyone your secret, save maybe your children, and thereby weight them with the same terrible burden after all—

His pork chops arrived, delivered promptly and steaming hot from the kitchen, just as he had been promised. Jonah cut into them at once, stabbing furiously at the meat. But after a mouthful or two he almost wanted to laugh. The chops were thick, and tender, and completely bland—more flavorless, Jonah thought, than anything he could have ordered in the greasiest hash house north of 110th Street. There were some watery green beans and applesauce on the side, a small mountain of mashed potatoes whipped to an equivalent tastelessness.

He stole a glance over at the other diners, curious to see if they found the food as insipid as he did. But all of them seemed to be eating and talking enthusiastically. Honking away at each other in their strange, nasal voices, spitting out sentences in endless staccato reams. He thought of something Amanda had told him once, and nearly choked with laughter on his pork chop.

White people, she had said, sound like geese with typewriters.

After a few more pointless bites, he gave up on the chops and ordered an iced coffee. Looking around him and wondering, as he drank it, what it would be like. To be surrounded always by these honking, oblivious, self-righteous people—

He finished his coffee, and asked for the check. The waiter moving discreetly away while he fished out cash and the extra meat coupons Jakey had gotten him for just this purpose, no questions asked. One sin always summons another. Flourishing it triumphantly as he handed it over, along with a big tip. The waiter gave him an open grin, a grateful nod before scurrying off. Jonah hesitating at getting up from the table, dreading already what he would find to do for the rest of the night. Wondering what there was, once his little charade of passing was over, and now there was no normal life to go back to—nothing to do but stay here with the geese.

What will it be like to be one of them? Or never really one of them?

He thought of Sophia, then, wondering, How did she do it? How did she just cut herself off from everything she loved, even everything she hated? How does she stand the loneliness?

A thought came to him, and he grabbed at it. Shrugging on his suit jacket again, and all but bolting out of the dining room. Wondering what time she would be going on tonight, and if he could catch her at her apartment still, but not breaking stride. Needing to speak to his sister now, face-to-face, so he could ask her just how the hell he was supposed to do this.

CHAPTER TWENTY

MALCOLM

The white women made their way through the sugarcane fields in the moonlight. One of them, in a nurse's uniform, leading the other—a tall, thin blond woman who walked as if she were in a trance, with a trace of a smile on her face. The high, papery husks of cane rustled eerily above their heads as they moved through the fields, and there was the sound of beating drums, growing steadily louder from all around them.

They came out of the cane at a crossroads—where a skeletal, half-naked black man loomed up suddenly in front of them, wraith-like and bug-eyed. A zombie. The first white woman bit her fist in surprise, a look of ecstatic fear spreading across her face. But the zombie didn't interfere with them—letting them pass on to the voodoo circle even though one of the women lost the protective badge pinned to her dress, the little piece of white cloth fluttering helplessly on a long spear of cane.

Malcolm edged to the lip of his seat in the nearly empty balcony of the Alhambra. Hugging himself tightly at the shoulders, trying to get himself dry after his long run through the rain. He had doubled back downtown to here, at West 126th and Seventh, as soon as he had finally lost the minister, looking for someplace where he could get out of the rain, and think for a minute. He had ducked into the Alhambra as soon as he spotted its light blue, Moorish facade, looming like a fairy-tale castle in front of him; the glistening, electrified marquee that read OPEN ALL DAY ALL NIGHT TWO NEW FEATURES W/ NEWSREEL/ CARTOON *I

Walked with a Zombie Plus They Came to Blow Up America with George Sanders.

He had made his way up to the balcony, where the only other people were a few bored defense workers just off the nightshift, and some muscatel drunks, most of them sleeping and snoring loudly. Malcolm had been just as glad, moving all the way up to the highest row, where his back was to the wall and he had the whole theater out before him. There he could smoke a few more of Sammy's sticks, and figure out what to do without having to worry about anybody else surprising him.

But he found himself being increasingly drawn into the movie, which delved into so many of his fantasies, right down to the woman in the nurse's uniform, and the smiling blonde, who had also been turned into a zombie. They entered the secret voodoo conclave together, walking past rows of black-skinned drummers, in all their savage markings and trinkets, beating out a furious tattoo on their primitive drums. Moving inexorably toward the closed, forbidding shack of the voodoo priestess, the white nurse steeling herself, leading her companion on. They reached the shack—and a black hand shot out, yanking them both inside.

But there was no priestess there. Only the older white matriarch who owned the plantation, and who it turned out was using the natives' own superstitions to trick them into taking the medicines they really needed—

Malcolm sat back, exhaling, bitterly disappointed for so many reasons. Not sure of what he had wanted to happen to the white women, the nurse and the serene, smiling blonde, but wanting something. All just another hustle.

The movie wound down to its predictable ending after that. Malcolm went on working his way through the cigarette pack of Sammy's sticks, offsetting them with another Benzedrine tablet from time to time, to make sure he stayed awake. The only scene that engaged him again was right at the end, when there was a close-up of a masthead, from the ship that was supposed to have first brought the black slaves to the island the zombies were on, centuries before. He stared at it in fascination as the closing credits rolled. It was a blackened, wooden sculpture of St. Sebastian from the waist up; the figure's mouth opened in agony, real arrows sticking out of the wood—so lifelike that Malcolm thought he could almost hear the wooden man screaming—

"Lies! Lies! White man lies!"

Malcolm blinked, and saw that the movie screen before him was filled with a cartoon now. The title unfurled over the usual jolly cartoon music: Coal Black and the Seven Dwarfs. A fat, sassy, kerchief-headed colored woman sashayed across the screen with a bag of sugar she was hoarding—followed by seven tiny black soldiers. There were more shouts from the now awakened patrons in the Alhambra orchestra, then a growing chorus of whistles and boos. A barrage of popcorn bags and paper cups of Coke splattered against the screen, and the cartoon ground to a halt, then flickered out altogether. There were more whistles, then clapping and derisive laughter echoing through the darkened movie theater.

Malcolm pulled himself to his feet, and slipped out the balcony exit. Running down the separate back staircase, left over from when the Alhambra had still been segregated twenty years before, and all its black patrons confined to the nigger heaven in the balcony—the back entrance where all the hustlers he knew preferred to come and go now.

But that's what I am. A hustler.

When his feet touched the sidewalk, he saw that the rain had stopped, and for a moment he just stood there, genuinely confused about where it was he should go now. Back up to Sammy's, for another assignment, more sticks? But the cops were just as likely to be around now, with that preacher going on. Where, then? To his latest rented room? But he could not even remember where that was just now, with his mind clouded by so many sticks, so many pills back in the movie theater.

Where?

Before he could think it out any further, he simply started to move, heading downtown. As soon as he could, he got off the streets, the fear rising in him as he went that somebody, somehow, was still following him. Making his way through Morningside, and Central Parks, as far as he could, sprinting the few blocks in between them only when he was sure there was hardly anyone around. Running and walking all the way to midtown, through the teeming night world of the parks. Interrupting the transactions of sailors and their girls, or their boys, in the bushes along the walls. Drawing the curses of winos bunked down under the trees; the stares and titters of children out on their own adventure, entire families lying out on the grass for a respite from the infernal heat of their apartments. Dodging the strolling cops swinging their clubs, the horses of the mounted patrols clopping their way down the paved pathways. Swearing that he even heard the call of owls in the deep darkness, could see the swoop of hawks against the Great Lawn in Central Park. Listening all the time for the sound of any footsteps coming up behind him.

By the time he reached the end of Central Park, he decided that it was all right to risk showing himself. He ran out from behind a huge boulder, to catch his breath, and down into the subway, under the familiar sign that warned Hold Your Hat! against the sudden vacuum suction the trains created. Hanging back against the tiled walls even when he was down on the dim, filthy, concrete platform, his head down. Grateful, for once, to feel the rush of dirty air the A train drew in with it from all over the City—the warm, disgusting subterranean belch of discarded hot-dog nubs, and sewer water, and sticky-sweet fruit drinks, washing over him.

He rode the train the rest of the way into the Village, where he walked the block over from Sixth Avenue and slipped into the alley behind Miranda's building. Vaulting a couple of low brick walls, ignoring the wear and tear on his suit, and the barking dogs, until he had made his way to her apartment house. There he pried open the basement door he had so carefully prepared, and took the stairs up to her place—pausing to listen on every landing for any foot-steps that might be coming back down. Listening carefully again at her door, even though it was nearly dawn by then. Unable to hear anything, but still jumping back by the elevators when he rang her bell. The little .25 in his hand, ready to flee or to shoot, although he couldn't make up his mind which.

"That you?"

The door opened, and Miranda came out in her dressing gown, shielding her half-closed eyes against the sudden hall light.

"Is that you?" she asked again, hands on her hips this time, and somehow Malcolm knew she meant him. The sound gratifyingly personal, despite how impatient her tone was. The way nobody had called him since she had.

"They anybody in there?" he whispered.

"Who would be in here with me, after three shows tonight?" she demanded crossly, spotting him now by the elevator. She shook her head impatiently, but Malcolm thought she looked concerned just the same.

"Get on in here now, before you wake up the neighbors."

She sat him down in the kitchen and made him some toast and eggs. Forbidding him to have any coffee or any scotch, either, once she had looked closely into his eyes. Undressing him like a little boy and carefully hanging up his suit. Feeding him a Nembutal, and letting him bust down on a nice, fat mezzroll with her once they were in bed together. And after they finished she let him hold her, and put his face in the warm, smooth crook between her neck and her shoulder—still high, still jabbering on about anything that came into his head, while Miranda slowly rubbed his back.

He tried to tell her, then, about everything that he had planned for them, and everything he had been doing. He tried to ask her why she wouldn't see him, and if she was afraid of Archie, or if she loved him, but she wouldn't answer any of his questions.

"It's all right now," she murmured. "You just rest and get better. We'll talk all you want in the morning."

After what seemed like a long time he finally fell asleep, not waking up again until light was streaming through the dark blinds. They made love then because he insisted—still half asleep, simply and primally pushing away at her, clutching her, until they were both satisfied. He wanted to talk to her then, but he dozed off again before he could say a word. Dimly aware of the lights in the room going on and off—of her moving around him, trying to get him to eat something. Falling deeper into sleep—

He awakened into darkness. Groping around himself, panicked for a moment when he couldn't remember where he was, or what this place could possibly be. Only after a few minutes of scrambling about the room, searching frantically for his clothes, his money, his stash, did it come back to him what he was doing here. The apartment silent now, Miranda no doubt gone out to her gig—how long ago he wasn't sure. He didn't even know if it was still light outside, behind the close-pulled blinds all over the apartment.

Instead of checking, though, he went over to his suit jacket, where Miranda had hung it neatly in her closet. Pawing through it until he was able to recover a new cigarette pack of marijuana sticks, a little vial of pills—and a book. He frowned for a moment when he felt it out, then remembered: the book from the bus station, that Prof. Toussaint had given him.

He pulled it out again, looking at it in the thin light from Miranda's bedside table. The green cover still wet and streaked from the rain now, he saw with regret, the gilt-edged leaves pocked and warped. The print, too, he saw, was less expensive than it had looked, and it had run badly on several pages, making them all but unreadable now. Even the title page that had fascinated him so was partly obliterated, the only legible part reading "Elijah Muhammad By "X". Still, the pages of the book that he had yet to read seemed to be intact, and once he had perused them, he gave over any other thoughts of what he might be doing, getting dressed and leaving, or making himself something to eat. Instead, he leaned back in Miranda's bed, where he lit himself another one of the matchstick-thin joints, and began to read again.

When Elijah saw Master Fard again, he was in a straitjacket, in the psychopathic ward of the Detroit Receiving Hospital. The jacket was swaddled all the way up to his chin, so it looked as if the Master were drowning in its thick, white folds, and Elijah had all he could do not to ask him why he didn't break out, why he didn't throw off these shackles and walk out to freedom.

"Patience, my faithful one," Master Fard told him, as if he were still reading his mind.

"Don't you know, if I wanted to, I could throw off these bonds at once and walk out?" he asked Elijah, smiling his radiant smile at him—the smile that Elijah had missed so much during the days he had been away. "But the white man has a little more time. Allah has willed it."

"I thought you were Allah," Elijah blurted out.

"Then why do you need to ask any questions?" the Master told him. "Just make sure you talk to my lawyer."

He had turned to leave then, but before he could go, Master Fard had called him—had drawn him back, actually, he was sure, with the strength of his will alone. His face still gentle but so serious and sorrowful now that Elijah felt that he might easily fall at his feet and beg his forgiveness, just as he had been tempted to do the same at the feet of his own Daddy after one of his sermons, so many years before.

"One thing. You must be a leader now, at least so long as I am in here," Master Fard told him.

"Yes," Elijah answered, feeling something stir in him at the words.

"You must lead the people," Master Fard repeated. "And above all, trust no one."

"No one?"

"No one. No matter what they tell you. Not even if they bring you the greatest truth that ever was. And above all else, there is one thing you must know—"

"Yes?"

"Never trust a white man."

Elijah had taken up his charge to lead with renewed enthusiasm—unsettled though he had been by his last exchange with the Master. He had been there every day during the trial, commanding all the members from the Detroit temples when they went downtown to protest at the trial. And he had done it all himself, now that Brown Eel, and Mr. Takahashi, and all of his other rivals had disappeared, with the police combing all through Paradise Valley to question the Fruit of Islam.

It was Elijah who brought the faithful out every morning. Forming them up in the street—rows and rows of the Fruit of Islam, all the men in the temple, including his brothers and his father. Each one of them dressed alike in dark suits and maroon fezzes, and standing at perfect attention. All of the women, including his wife, and his sisters and mother, dressed in their white headscarves and long, white dresses that flowed down over their shoes.

Elijah had never been prouder than when he saw them marching, straightbacked and solemn, to the courthouse every day. Lining up in perfect rows out in the street, all around the courthouse, trooping in to fill up all the seats in the courtroom. Unnerving the white cops and judges by their very presence there. It was, at last, an army of their own, just like the one Marcus Garvey had envisioned. One willing to follow him as well as anyone, even the Master himself.

My people, he had thought for the first time, watching them. *Look at my people!*

They had stayed with him throughout the trial. Robert Karriem's testimony had unnerved them a little, Elijah knew, with all his craziness. Refusing even to remove his fez in court—putting it back on again and again, every time the bailiff took it off, until Karriem and the bailiff stood up there by the witness stand doing a Charlie Chaplin routine that made every white person in the courtroom shake with laughter.

"It was crucifixion time, and I killed this man with the crucifixion. I said, 'Ali-kerslump,' and he fell dead!" Karriem had shouted from the stand, then sprung to his feet again.

"Well, I got to go now," he said matter-of-factly, and started to walk off the witness stand. Looking genuinely surprised when the bailiffs had grabbed him, shouting at the top of his lungs, "Let me go! I'm the king here, and everywhere!" His wife and children sobbing and wailing, and trying to cling to him, the officers dragging him out of the courtroom.

Behind him the room was hushed. The faithful were looking down at their shoes, embarrassed in front of the white man, Elijah could tell. He had done his best to buck them up. Reminding them back at the Allah Temple that Master Fard had yet to testify, that when he did he would surely set everything right, and present the true side of their faith to the world—and they had believed him. Some of them even breaking into spontaneous chants of "Fard is Allah! Fard is Allah!"—and then, "Elijah the Prophet! Elijah the Prophet!"

They had barely been able to sit still when Master Fard finally took the witness stand the next day, Elijah included. He was gratified to see that the Master looked nothing like the pitiful, helpless creature he had seen strapped into his straitjacket in the psychopathic ward just a few weeks before. Instead, he walked into the courtroom in his best blue suit, and silk tie, looking as calm and confident and immaculate as ever. Elijah had leaned forward on his bench seat, along with all of his brothers and sisters from the temple, so eager were they to hear what they had been waiting a lifetime for—to hear someone put the white man in his place.

"Is it true that you are the author of the book in question, the—," the assistant district attorney began, pausing for a moment to read from his legal pad.

"—The Secret Rituals of the Lost-Found Nation of Islam?"

Elijah had held his breath then, and shut his eyes. Nearly unable to bear the anticipation of what the Master would say—waiting for the same exquisite flow of words to usher forth from his mouth, just as it had that first night in his living room. But when he heard nothing, he opened his eyes again, only to see Master Fard smiling that small, secret smile of his, and shaking his head slightly. The fez no longer crowning his head, either, Elijah noticed for the first time—only his waves of straight, oiled, white man's hair.

"No, no. That is simply a holy book in our religion. Some of the brethren"— and here Fard made a small, condescending gesture with his hand—"some of the brothers and sisters think too much of me."

"Doesn't this book in fact condone just the sort of ritualistic human sacrifice the defendant is accused of making?" the white lawyer demanded—and the first small tendrils of fear began to slip through Elijah's mind. Thinking he must have somehow misunderstood the rules of the trial, wondering why it was that the government's lawyer was questioning Master Fard first—

"Oh, no. No, there are many things in this book—just as there are in the Koran, just as there are in the Bible—which the uninitiated do not begin to understand."

"But did you in any way, through word or deed, or promise, authorize or sanction the murder of Mr. Smith or others?"

"Oh, no, certainly not!"

"Didn't you promise any true believers that they would be rewarded with a button with a picture of Muhammad on it, and a free trip to Mecca, if they brought you the head of four white devils?"

"Oh, no, no, no," Fard said on the stand. He looked genuinely shocked, the words puttering out of his mouth like a motor running down. Then he smiled again.

"Didn't you tell colored schoolchildren that the American flag means nothing to them, and that they would get a material award for the murder of white people?"

"They have misunderstood my teachings," Fard went on, his voice sounding a little embarrassed, now—drawing the sympathy of even the bailiffs and the attorneys and the court reporter, Elijah could see. Everyone in the courtroom leaning unconsciously toward him.

"The tenets of Islam certainly do not call for murder," he told them sadly.

"It is true that your followers think that you are God, is it not, and obey you as such?"

"Well, our new converts are very enthusiastic," Fard replied, in a knowing tone that made Elijah's breath stop. "Sometimes their enthusiasm exceeds the bounds of their knowledge, when it comes to certain theological concepts. They mean well. They simply take some things too far."

Elijah could see the bailiff and the judge both beginning to smile. The thoughts running through their minds so obvious to him that they might as well have shouted them aloud. You know those Negroes. Those fools, and dupes. Always getting carried away.

He thought that he should do something—try to rescue Master Fard, cause a disruption in the courtroom, anything—for surely the Master was being coerced into speaking and acting like this. Surely they had drugged him, or altered his mind in the mental hospital, or were holding something over him. But all Elijah could do was sit where he was, paralyzed, listening to the assistant district attorney go on and on.

"Would you characterize your organization, the Allah Temple of Islam, as a racket? Designed to get all the money you could for yourself, through the selling of clothes and even names to your followers?"

"Well, I guess you could call it that," Fard said, still smiling slightly.

"And if this court were, in its wisdom, to see fit to let you go free, would you continue to run said racket in Paradise Valley?"

"I now understand the danger of my teachings," Fard told the white attorney gravely, "and I promise that if I am spared incarceration, I will use my influence to disband the Allah Temple of Islam, and leave the city of Detroit and vicinity as soon as possible."

He was dismissed then, and Elijah watched as he made his way down from the witness stand and out of the courtroom, accompanied by two of the jail guards. Smiling again, a little man walking slightly hunched over, as he made his way past the benches filled with black men and women who believed him to be God—not so much as turning his head to look at them. All of them sitting in stunned incomprehension as they watched him go. The silence broken at last by a single loud guffaw—a scornful white man's laugh that made all their heads whip about resentfully. Only Elijah hadn't bother to turn, knowing already who it must be. Knowing that, no matter how white the laugh sounded, it came from a Chinaman.

Once he was released, Fard had told the remaining faithful at the Allah Temple that it had all been a trick to fool the white man. He had them put out that nobody could really tell what was said in that courtroom—that he had released a silent, invisible mist to cloud men's minds, so that in the confusion Robert Karriem could be whisked off to the Island of Nippon, instead of the Ionia State Hospital for the Criminally Insane, where the government said that it had sent him. He said that he had done it all for them, his people, and hadn't it worked? After all, he had walked out of the white man's courtroom free, and wasn't that a miracle no one in the Black Bottom had expected when the trial began?

The Master had even changed all their names again, and made them stop wearing the red fezzes that distinguished them from the unbelievers on the streets of Detroit. He had even changed the name of the Allah Temple of Islam, to the Nation of Islam, and named a whole new guard of the Fruit of Islam, headed by Elijah, to take charge of it. But by then the white newspapers were all running wild headlines about voodoo cults, and human sacrifices. The names of all known Muslims were stricken from the welfare rolls, and their children were taunted, and beaten up in school. Before long, they no longer had enough people to hold services in the Hancock Avenue temple, and were reduced to a storefront on Hastings Street, along with all of the other small-fry churches.

Worst of all, Master Fard had been ordered to leave the city and never return, under threat of having to do hard time. He had left on a warm late spring day, after a final Sunday afternoon service. Elijah, of course, had been chosen to drive him down to Chicago, in a black Ford Model A—the conspicuous red Chevy coupe gone now. It had been a day of tears and remonstrations from the few, remaining faithful—Elijah making sure that they had all turned out to bring the Master gifts, and place garlands of flowers on his Model A, while Master Fard stood on the running board and addressed them one last time.

"Don't worry! Don't worry, I am with you!" he had cried, raising his arms toward the heavens. "I am with you, I will be back to you in the near future to lead you out of this hell!"

He had climbed on into the backseat then, with the crowd still calling out his name, and when he looked in on him, Elijah saw to his surprise that the Master was crying. The tears filling his eyes and flowing down his cheeks as he turned away from the window, and his weeping people.

"I love the black people. Tell them I love them, Ghulam, my faithful one," he pleaded with Elijah. "Tell them I will destroy the Nations of the Earth to save them, and then die myself!"

At that moment the whole scene shifted, as it would in a dream—as Malcolm knew it would in a dream. Yet he still could not seem to shake it off, and wake himself. Instead, there was only the image of Elijah standing before *him* now, pointing his finger at him as he repeated the Master's words.

"Remember—don't trust anyone. No matter what he tells you. And don't trust the white man."

"But I do trust her," Malcolm heard himself saying.

"Do you, son?"

"But I love her!"

"Do you? I don't even think you know what you are anymore. I don't even think you know if you a man or a woman!" Elijah told him—then reached out with his long index finger and jabbed him hard in the chest.

"Do you?"

He felt a sharp, stabbing pain at the spot where Elijah had touched him, a pain much worse than anything a finger could cause—and when he looked down, he saw that an arrow had sprouted there, just like the ones in the figure of St. Sebastian, in the movie. He reached a hand up, to try to pull it out—and brought his fingers back covered in a white gelatinous liquid. Even as he watched, more of it continued to flow freely from his nipples—obviously and indisputably milk.

"Jesus God!"

He screamed and jumped up out of the bed, running into Miranda's bathroom. Ripping open the bathroom cabinet, where he tore through all her neatly stacked medicaments and beauty aids, searching for something, anything, that might help him. Half-reading the names on the labels of the boxes and bottles as they tumbled into the sink below—endless cold creams and hair dyes, little jars of Hydrox, and Nix Liquid Bleach, and Dr. Fred Palmer's Skin Whitener. Thinking distractedly that all those ads in the Amsterdam Star-News must be on the level about improving complexion if even a white woman like her bought them. Unable to find anything, though, that would stop the milk from pouring out of his breasts, coagulating now on the bathroom floor.

Desperately, he tried to stick two Band-Aids over his nipples, though they were quickly made limp and useless by the continuing flow. He struck at his chest then, squeezing his breasts, trying anything that might shut them off or squeeze them out. None of it working—the milk finally just petering out as he sat shaking on top of the toilet seat, breathing in long, dry sobs. Remembering how his mother had looked when his half-brother, Buster—the son of the barber salesman—had been born.

The milk bubbling up, darkening the inside of her shirt at any moment. She who had always been so careful about her appearance. Not bothering to change it even after days, when her whole blouse had become soured and stiffened with milk—

Malcolm jumped up again, not wanting to spend another minute in the apartment. He ran back into the bedroom, where the little green book was still where he had fallen asleep on the bed. He scooped it up, then threw his clothes on—glad at least he had been naked when it all started. Grabbing the sheets up off the bed and hurling them into the bathroom hamper, cleaning his mess as best he could but then bolting back down the stairs, and out the basement door. Running his hand constantly along his chest even as he ran—afraid that he might start lactating again at any minute, right out in public.

When he got to the street, he saw that it was already dusk again. The crooked, humpbacked Village streets as crowded as Harlem's, filled with sailors and soldiers and their girls trying to crowd into the little Italian restaurants, and coffeehouses, and music clubs. The dream of Elijah still disturbingly vivid, more lasting than any tea dream he had ever had before. His warnings still lingered in Malcolm's mind, but he didn't know where else he could go. He pulled his suit jacket tighter around him, and ran the couple of blocks over to Sheridan Square and down the stairs to her club. Sniffing out the back door and prying it open, sliding into her dressing room before she even knew he was there.

"Miranda!" he whispered at her, startling her where she was sitting, head bent down in front of her vanity.

"Red! Goddammit, don't scare me like that!"

"Miranda, we got to get out of here. You got to come with me—"

"You all right yet, Red?" she asked, frowning, standing and reaching up to place a hand on his forehead. "I thought some sleep might do you good, but I don't know. You still look off the beam from those bennies."

"I know how I can get some money, get a short. We can go out to Hollywood, you can get into the movies. Miranda, I got—"

—the words sticking in his throat, unable to tell her what had happened, back in her bed.

"Somethin's happenin' to me, Miranda. I got to get out of here."

"You look terrible, Red. You got to go lie down—"

There was a knock on the dressing room door and Malcolm jumped back to one side, fumbling his gun out of his pocket.

"Put that away!" Miranda hissed, waving his hand back into his pocket. "You think he'd knock? Besides, there's going to be none of that anyway—"

She opened the door and a chubby little white man stepped in, looking warily at Malcolm before he turned back to her.

"I'm sorry, Miss Dolan. But there's another gentleman to see you. Says his name's Jonah—"

"Jonah!"

Malcolm started toward the manager, but she ushered the little white man quickly back into the hall.

"Yes, thank you, I'll see him. Just give me a minute—"

"Jonah! So there is a Jonah. You said it was a joke!"

"It is," she sighed. "Look, I can explain—"

But he was already yanking the door back open, his other hand still clutching the gun in his pocket. Stepping out and looking down the hall only to see—him, again. That crazy preacher from the night before, still coming after him. Having somehow, some way tracked him all the way down here, even through the parks at night.

He stood where he was, too startled to move—and the preacher coming down the hall stopped, too, as if Malcolm were watching him in a funhouse mirror. Looking as if he were just as startled. The incredible possibility swimming through Malcolm's head. Could it be that he was Jonah? That same high-hat preacher from the train?

But then the man was moving toward him again, beginning to run, and Malcolm took off running, too, as if released from a spell. Hearing Miranda cry out something, but not stopping, the heavy fall of the preacher's shoes hard behind him. He raced on up the back stairs, back up to the street, looking all around him in the crowded bustle of Sheridan Square. Trying to figure out his options, whether or not to run back down into the subway—even as he wasn't quite sure just what it was he was running from.

He ducked around a newsstand, and the truck delivering the thickly bundled copies of the evening editions. Spotting an open green and red taxicab just pulling up to the curb, grasping at the door, pulling it open and standing back to let out—his brother.

He just stood there for a moment, unable to believe what he was seeing. His brother Reginald, standing right there in front of him—looking impossibly big and strong. Wearing some kind of blue uniform, a seaman's bag slung over his shoulder. Only the face remaining on this big man, the same face of that small, worshipful boy, dragging around his hernia—

"Malcolm!"

Beaming wider, and more boyish than ever now, throwing his arms around him. Malcolm dazedly hugging him back, unsure of what to say or how he could possibly be here, now, in the middle of Greenwich Village.

"They told me to try down here—"

"Who did?" Malcolm asked, alarmed again at once—wondering who else might know where he was.

"That bald guy. Sam, I think he said his name was."

His little brother shrugged happily.

"I been chasin' you around for three days now. Damn, but you move a lot!"

"You don't know the half of it, baby brother," Malcolm chuckled. Pushing Reginald back in the still open cab door just as the hack began to pull his cigar out of his mouth to complain. Following him in and directing the cabbie back uptown, without so much as another look around—even the crazy preacher forgotten now.

"You don't know the half of it!"

CHAPTER TWENTY-ONE

JONAH

He ran down into the ambiguous yellow light of the club. The basement room already booming with noise—with all the separate noises of laughter and conversation, of glasses and plates and live music that made up the one distinctive noise of a club full of people. Someone was playing jazz piano beautifully, the sound something he recognized, though he couldn't place where he knew it from. The serious students of jazz were packed in around the bar, trying to listen to it. Severe-looking co-eds and assistant professors, nervous high school students from Brooklyn and the Bronx in their fathers' ties and jackets. A smattering of local artists and hipsters, and musicians on their breaks from El Chico, or The Nineteenth Hole over on Barrow Street.

All of them were united in glaring at the celebrities who were heedlessly talking and whooping it up at the little tables around the floor—movie actors and show people, and newspaper columnists. Joking ostentatiously with the flippant waiters, as if they were trying to live up to the antic, clever murals on the walls above them, the caricatures of playboys and heiresses, ascot-wearing polo stars and Latin millionaires, jumping on tables and dancing with musicians and waiters. The resolutely jolly slogan of the club winding all around them: Café Society: The Right Place for the Wrong People!

Jonah wedged his way in at the bar, ordering the wildly overpriced beer the bartender urged on him, and listening to more of the music. Out on the small club floor was a stunningly poised, beautiful young woman, playing piano in a gold lamé gown. Her cocoa brown Island skin was nearly flawless, her hair tucked up in a glittery snood. She sat straight as a rod, her face very serious, even somber, her eyes locked on the keyboard, ignoring all the noisy talk and laughter that threatened to drown out her music.

He recognized it then, even above the din—what sounded like classical piano, transformed into long, elegant jazz riffs. Hazel Scott. The same music pouring out of Adam's phonograph that last night on Martha's Vineyard, waking up the boy, Preston. Jonah blinked against the fog of smoke filling the room, then closed his eyes for a moment to concentrate on it. Remembering that last night on Martha's Vineyard, all of their easy, friendly talk.

There was a commotion on the stairs behind him. The jazz aficionados at the bar swiveled their necks about angrily, only to see a clump of army officers tumble loudly into the club. Their hats cocked at jaunty angles, obviously drunk. Staring bemusedly at the scene in front of them until one of them, a captain, called out in his slurry, incredulous drunk's voice: "What is this, a nigger joint? What are all these jigs doing here?"

A phalanx of waiters and bartenders rushed the drunken officers at once, pushing and wrestling them on back up the stairs and out of the club almost as suddenly as they had appeared. The serious young woman at the piano playing on, unperturbed, as if she might play right through the end of the world. But everyone else had gone quiet. The club was integrated, the only completely integrated club in the City, below 110th Street, which was its claim to fame. But the few Negro patrons who were there—the musicians, the celebrities sitting with otherwise all-white parties, the scattered others who had just dropped down to see for themselves if it was real and who were already standing around uneasily—seemed to Jonah to be limned now by a steely bright spotlight. The white aficionados at the bar and the beautiful people at the tables unable to look at them—suddenly, miserably, united in their righteousness and their embarrassment. Until both were dispelled just as abruptly by a great, mocking belly laugh that boomed out over the music and their pretensions and everything else, the source of which Jonah could identify at once.

It was Adam—his laugh unmistakable. Jonah saw him now, sitting up at a front table, just to the side of Hazel Scott's piano. Mostly hidden by the crowd, but so close that he could have reached out and touched her hand. Holding court there with three other men, all of whom Jonah recognized as longtime Negro ward-heelers around Harlem—his table the only all-colored party in the joint.

Jonah craned his neck forward, looking for some other way past the floor and back to his sister's dressing room, but he could see none. He almost had to laugh at the ludicrousness of the situation. The first day of his new life, and here was already a whole table full of people who knew him.

It occurred to him, then: No one knew he had vanished yet. He had just left to do his rounds this morning. No note, no luggage gone—even his briefcase back at the hotel. For all anyone could tell, he was still himself—the Reverend Jonah Dove, Minister, the Church of the New Jerusalem. It was still even possible for him to go back—if he wanted to.

Hazel Scott finished her last number as perfectly as ever and stood at her piano. Bowing once with typical gravity, a brief, pleased smile crossing her face as a wave of applause washed over her from the now attentive crowd. In the commotion that followed the end of her set, Jonah tried to slip down past Adam's table and into the hall that led to the dressing rooms—but just as he had reached the edge of the floor, the whole party stood up as if on cue, suddenly hemming him in.

"Brother Minister!" Adam cried, pulling him over. Introducing him around to the politicians, who stood scrutinizing him with the smiles of extremely well-mannered foxes. "You know the fellows. Ray, from Carver Democratic—"

Jonah duly shook their hands, feeling foolish. Wondering how long it would take him to make his escape backstage, before Sophia came on. But Adam was already pressing him into the seat next to him, his big hand so forceful on his shoulder that Jonah feared he might break the delicate little cabaret chair.

"Sit down, sit down!"

He saw, though, that the politicians were not sitting back down, obviously on their way out, and he began to wonder with a rising sense of panic just what would happen when his sister came out to sing. Mortified by the idea that Adam would recognize her, watching her sing with her brother sitting right there in front of him—

"So how is your father?" Adam was asking.

"Oh, he's getting by—"

"Fine, fine! You know, I hope he can see his way to giving us his support next year. I'm looking for all the help I can get!" he exclaimed.

Jonah was sure that the opposite was true, that he had his congressional seat all but wrapped up by now. At first he speculated that Adam had already picked up the politician's ability to say the exact opposite of what he meant, but then Jonah realized he was only being kind—making him an offer to get on the bandwagon, now that victory was assured.

"I'm sure he will do everything he can. I'd be happy to help, myself," Jonah told him. Trying to think just what the endorsement of the founder and the heir of the New Jerusalem would be worth once he had disappeared.

"Well, that's fine, fine now!"

The emcee returned to the stage, a mountainous white man who called himself Zero. He seemed able to all but metamorphose into another species at will—a bull, a bear, a gigantic dog. Moving about the stage with alarming speed and menace. Mugging and growling, his eyes bulging wildly, titillating the crowd with his daring, foul-mouthed act.

"Zero's not my real name. Who the hell would name their boy Zero?" he barked. "My name is Sam! The commie who runs this joint wanted to call me Zero. I said call me shit if you want, I just want to work."

Adam howled with the rest of the crowd and rocked back in his chair, looking positively ecstatic, Jonah thought. A glass of scotch in one hand, using his opposite thumb to tamp down his pipe.

"I wanted to tell you, I thought you handled those fellows in the Bronx just right," he said, turning effortlessly to Jonah again.

"What?" Jonah asked, surprised.

"On that Met Life project," he said. "Trying to build a Jim Crow housing project in New York in this day and age! We're going to beat them on this."

"We are?" Jonah asked.

"Sure," Adam nodded. "They're finished, all of them. Fred Ecker, Bob Moses. All the clubhouse boys, and that little fraud La Guardia. It may take some time yet, but we'll do it."

He lit his pipe, puffing it quickly to life, then tossed the match away dismissively. Jonah thought he had never seen a more confident man in his life than Adam Powell.

"That's the politics of the past. I've been talking to the unions.

The Amalgamated, the Ladies' Garment Workers. Marcantonio and his Renters' League. This is where the power is now. This is the people's century."

"Don't you think that—"

"There's a different kind of Negro here now," Adam cut him off, sweeping away the possibility of any doubts with the wave of a hand. His jaw clenched tightly around his pipe. "They can't frighten us anymore. Can't buy us off with a new hospital wing here, a few new apartments there. Sending up MPs, and shutting down the Savoy! Whites and Negroes are going to mix, and there's nothing anybody can do about it."

On the floor the mountainous emcee sang a short, surprisingly sentimental ditty, then capered off the floor to another storm of applause. Adam stood up, grinning again. Reaching down to shake Jonah's hand, and at the same time letting bills fall on the table like loose napkins.

"Sorry to get on my soapbox," he said. "Listen, I got to get going, got to get up early tomorrow and back to Oak Bluffs. Feel free to order anything else you want, put it on my tab. And say hello to that lovely wife of yours!"

No sooner had he left than the emcee returned to introduce his sister. Jonah inutterably relieved that Adam had left, but feeling newly uncomfortable—knowing that he would have to sit out in front now, all alone at his table.

He thought that she looked more beautiful than ever when she came out—even better than when she was in high school and college, and he had thought then that she was the most beautiful woman he had ever seen. She wore a low-cut, sleeveless white gown, a large matching jasmine of some kind pinned in her hair. Her face a little thinner now with the first turn of age, but her cheeks and lips still slightly swollen and sensual. Showing the crowd a soft smile before launching right into a slow, melancholy rendition of "I'm Yours"—

When you went away
You left a glowing spark
Trying to be gay as
Whistling in the dark
I am only what you make me
Come take me
I'm yours—

She sang well, he thought. Her voice was better now than when she was starting out and he had snuck off to see her in little Village clubs like this—better than when she had sung her choir solos of "Love Lifted Me" and "Come Ye That Love the Lord" before the whole rapt church of the New Jerusalem. It was more interesting now, and more mature; husky and knowing and expressive. Yet the set she sang included nothing original—mostly covers of the same numbers that Billie Holiday had been doing around town for the last few seasons. Songs about heartache and broken romance, all sung slow and torchy. "I'll Get By" and "Travelin' Alone"; "I Didn't Know What Time It Was" and "I Love My Man," and "More Than You Know"—

More than you know
More than you know
Man of my heart, I love you so
Lately I've found you on my mind
More than you know—

He knew she had seen him from almost the moment she walked out on the floor—looking straight at him, her eyes widening just perceptibly, then taking no notice of him again. But he kept his gaze on her throughout her set, determined not to look away. Seeing everything about her clearly now—for the first time, he thought. Noticing the calculated throb in her voice, the way she sang almost everything the same way—marking her whole presentation of herself as a slimmer, sexier, whiter Billie Holiday. Try as he might, he was unable to shake the feeling of how imitative, how artificial she seemed, even as she finished with a perfectly emotional, nearly whispered version of "In the Still of the Night." Seeing clearly for the first time how very unoriginal his sister really was—

...will this dream of mine
Fade out of sight
Like the moon growing dim
On the rim of the hill
In the chill still of the night...

There was more heartfelt applause, nearly as enthusiastic as it had been for Hazel Scott, and looking around the room, Jonah saw to his great surprise that even the aficionados around the bar were clapping and whistling. Understanding, in that moment, why she lived the life that she did—

As soon as she had taken her bow and stepped off the floor, he set off after her. He gave his name to a manager standing guard backstage, was waiting for him to come back from her dressing room at the far end of the hall—when he heard that familiar irresistible laugh for the second time in the evening, coming from just a few feet away. Sure that he must be mistaken, he looked into the first open dressing room on the hall—and saw Adam Powell and the young woman who had played such wonderful piano in each others' arms.

The position they were in was unmistakable—Adam kissing fondly at her nose, her mouth, even as Jonah watched. She was aware of Jonah's presence first, directing Adam's attention to him only then with a discreet nod of her head. Pulling back modestly, adjusting her gold lamé gown, while Adam strode toward him. For a crazy moment Jonah thought he was about to punch him, or slam the door in his face—but instead he just stepped out into the hallway, closing it gently behind him.

"Well. Brother Minister," he said dryly, looking as confident as ever.

"What are you doing?"

"I'm sorry you had to see it this way," Adam said, as if he were talking to a child.

"What is she? Your back-door woman?" Jonah asked, trying to keep the shock and outrage out of his voice, but not succeeding. Not sure just why he should be so surprised, having heard the same rumors on The Wire about Adam Clayton Powell that everyone else had heard for years, but stunned nevertheless.

"It's nothing like that," Powell was saying impatiently, as if he had been somehow affronted. "As soon as it's viable, we're going to be married."

"Married? What about Isabel?"

Adam shook his head sadly, sticking his hands in his pockets.

"Yeah, well. You know, Jonah, one day I just caught up with her. And then I passed her. That's how it happens sometimes."

"Oh, I see. And now your speed is a jazz piano player," Jonah said sarcastically, but Adam only shrugged.

"Hazel is an artist. A true artist."

"I see. And what about Preston?"

"That is a shame," he sighed lightly. "I'm going to miss that boy."

"What about—what about all of it, Adam? I don't understand. What about running for Congress, and your church—"

"They'll understand," he said. His voice more than a little patronizing again, as if explaining things that Jonah had no knowledge of. "They'll understand. I won't give Isabel the word until after the election, just for the sake of propriety. But don't think they wouldn't back me anyway. They never much approved of her. Some hoofer from Connie's Inn—in too close with the light-skinned folks—"

"How can you say that, Adam?" Jonah asked. Stunned most of all by his friend's calculation—his certainty that he would get what he wanted, no matter what.

"I'm not saying I agree. I'm just saying how it is," Adam said, shrugging again, patting Jonah on the shoulder and reaching for the door to the dressing room.

"Don't you see, Jonah? What they want is me."

He half-turned as he went back in, looking at Jonah where he stood in the hall, still blinking at him in shock.

"You'll see. It won't make any difference, Brother Minister," he told him, completely earnest, as if afraid he had neglected Jonah's real concern. "Don't you worry. We're still gonna beat 'em on that project!"

The door shut in Jonah's face then, and he turned automatically back down the hall. Starting toward his sister's dressing room— only to be confronted by the manager, who stopped him, his jowly white face reddening in embarrassment.

"Mmm, if you'd be good enough to wait a little longer, sir? Miss Dolan will see you. It's just—"

Even before he could get the words out, Jonah had glimpsed a tall, dark figure emerging from a door at the far end of the hall. Unable to fathom that he could be here—even as Jonah recognized immediately the way he moved, the shape that had come to shadow him everywhere. He started to run after him, just as he had the night before. Wordlessly now, more curious than tormented. Just needing to know what he was doing, that boy from the train, following him everywhere. If he was real at all, anymore—

The boy saw him at the same time and began to run just as Jonah did. Moving silently, flying out a door and up the back bolt hole to the street. Jonah heard his sister call out something as he ran by, but he ignored her. Chasing the boy right on out and up the iron steps, into the sudden, blaring swelter of Sheridan Square at night.

A hot wind of exhaust blasted his neck—the Village streets just as filled as Harlem's were with traffic, with soldiers and sailors drunkenly romping about with their girls. A newsstand right in front of him, a couple of grunting men in gloves and overalls throwing bundles of newspapers from a truck to the sidewalk. He ducked around them, looking past the truck, but Jonah still didn't see him until the last possible moment. There, on the other side of Sheridan Park—just climbing into a cab with another tall colored man in a uniform who looked remarkably like him. Jonah wondering if his hallucinations could be multiplying as he watched, but there was no mistaking him—grinning back with that same sweet man-boy grin before he ducked down into the taxi, and was gone.

"What was that all about? You lost what's left of your mind?" Sophia asked him when he stepped back into her dressing room.

"Have I lost my mind? Do you know who that boy is?"

"I dunno. They just call him Red," she murmured, looking down, arms crossed over her chest.

"Sophie, he's a pimp. A john-walker. I saw him with my own eyes."

"Ah, he just gets himself in trouble," she said, shrugging defiantly. "How do you think people make a living, Jonah?"

"What're you talking about, Sophie? Are you seeing him? Are you really involved with this boy?"

"I wouldn't call it involved," she muttered, waving a hand at him and sinking back down in the chair before her vanity.

"A pimp now? West Indian Archie wasn't enough? Or are you seein' him, too?"

Her whole body seemed to sag into itself, as if she didn't have the strength to hold herself up anymore, and she looked away from him. He took a step toward her, then stopped—the truth just beginning to occur to him. Looking at the marquee card tucked into a corner of her vanity mirror. Her smiling face above the stage name she'd made up for herself: "Miranda Dolan." The photograph just slightly overexposed, in order to make her look more white than ever.

"Or doesn't he know? That's it, isn't it? That poor child thinks Miranda Dolan is white. Doesn't he?"

"What's it your business, anyway?" she snapped back at him, but her voice was more weary than angry. "What you come up here for? Just to harangue me about my life? You know, when I first saw you sitting out there, I thought maybe Daddy had died."

"And that would still matter to you?" Jonah asked tentatively, his anger and astonishment seeping away. Sophie sitting on her little chair looking to him now as vulnerable as she had back in high school, when she was mooning over some boy, or a sentimental record.

"But he didn't, did he?" she said. "He ain't never gonna die, is he?"

"Sophie," he said, squatting down by her and taking her arm. Saying her name as he couldn't remember saying it.

"Sophie, I see what you are here—"

"Jonah, you heard me. I can sing!" she flared up, pulling away from him.

"Yeah, you can sing. You can sing all right. Is this what you want to be?" he asked her bluntly then. "The white Billie Holiday? Or maybe the white Ella, or the white something else next year—"

"I do what it takes. What they want—"

"—dating boys like that? 'Cause they think you're a white lady, too?"

"Goddammit, I told you! I live the way I want to. I don't have to be what anyone says I am!"

"Yes, you do," he told her, standing up then. "You have to do it, we all have to do it. You can't be what you want any more than those Jews in Germany can go on saying they're Germans. We have to be what we are, we can't hide in some little place like this, nice and generous though it is."

"Don't preach to me, Jonah! Goddammit, don't you dare stand there and try to make me feel guilty, preaching at me like he would."

She turned away from him again, her neck bent over, straightened hair flowing down over her face. Jonah wondering to himself, even as she did, if it was something like what their father would say.

"Come back with me," he urged her gently. "Right now. Or anytime you want to. You can live with me and Amanda if you want. Have a home with us for as long as you like. Anytime you like. There's plenty of room. That's all I'll say, but you'll always be welcome."

She said nothing, head still bent away from him, and he wanted to lean down and kiss her cheek. He walked quietly out of the room instead, not wishing to intrude on her anymore.

He walked back up into Sheridan Square again, and caught a cab. Stopping off at the Roanoke Hotel only long enough to check out and retrieve his briefcase with its two changes of clothes, and his counterfeit ration coupons, and his Bible. Standing for one last moment in the neat white room, taking in its pleasantness, and its silence and its vacancy.

He had the cab take him directly to Strivers Row then. Getting out at the corner on Seventh Avenue where he stood for another long moment, and marveled at the same clamorous nighttime scene he had never expected to see again. In the distance he could hear the thunder of Elder Michaux's revival still going strong, the steady thump of his tent band, the choir roaring through a rendition of "I Been 'Buked and I Been Scorned." Yet even as he listened, the words were drowned out by another phalanx of Commissioner Valentine's motorcycle patrol, cruising down the avenue—the cops wearing their high caps pulled down hard over their eyes. The mobs of servicemen on the sidewalk stopping to stare and grin. The unlikely clumps of people half hidden behind them, gathered together again—staring out from the shadows of the stoops with eyes that showed nothing but hatred.

But he turned away from them now. Springing up the steps of the house that he thought he had left for the last time this morning, and bursting in the front door. Wanting to shout out the news to Amanda that he was back, although he had already decided in the cab that he would say nothing about it. He had told himself he would not burden her with it, even though he knew that it meant his own shame was buried without a trace. That he was absolved, once again, just as Merton Turnbow had predicted back in college. Sure that no one need ever know what he had done, what he had been about to do—until he saw the suitcases stacked neatly in the graceful marble foyer and he stopped in his tracks.

He thought, in that moment, that he was wrong, and that somehow she had found out. That with her usual empathy for him she had all but read his mind and packed up all of his things to ship them out with him.

Yet when he saw her, he realized that was impossible. Catching sight of her first where she sat on the edge of a chair in the front parlor. Pocketbook in hand, a light shawl wrapped around her shoulders despite the heat of the day. Standing up as he came into the room, her red eyes and the dried trails of tears down her cheeks visible, even in the muddled light of the single parlor lamp she had turned on.

"Why're you sitting here in the dark?" was all he could think of to ask. Knowing the answer already, but not daring to ask another, more pertinent question, such as, Why are you ready to go out in the middle of the night?

"I was waiting for you. I wanted to wait for you, even though I got worried you weren't ever coming back," she told him. Her eyes on him so sad, so pitying that he wanted to turn away but he could not. Stupefied, the full realization of what was going on falling on him like a ton of bricks.

"But I didn't go! Look, I'm back!" he cried, even as he understood how nonsensical and desperate he sounded.

"It doesn't really matter, Jonah. You've been gone for a long time now," she said, her voice steady no matter how much she might have been crying "Gone from me, anyhow. Brooding on all your secret things. Running around, never talking to me anymore—"

"We talk!"

"Not like we did," she said, her voice so sad and certain that he wanted to sob. "Not like we used to, and you know it. You won't let me close to you anymore, Jonah, and I'm done trying to get through."

She stepped forward, touching his face affectionately.

"Don't worry, I'll make it easy on you with the church. I'm just going to my mother's. You can put it out that she's not feeling well these days. I'll just ease on out—least until we decide what we want to do for sure."

"You're leaving me," he said, still unbelieving. And right then he wanted to tell her everything he had been through that whole day and night, everything he had been thinking and hurting about for so long. But the words, the shame, stuck in his throat.

"It's that train, isn't it?" he said bitterly, instead. "It's that boy on the train, those drunken bums. Isn't it?"

"It isn't that at all," she said, shaking her head. "Is that what you've been thinking about, all this time? You see, that's what I mean. Was a time you could've told me that."

"But I have! Now, anyway—"

"You think that'll do? Jonah, you've been away for so long now. Maybe you never were all here, all the years we've been married. And I thought about that and I started to cry for myself, but I really feel worse for you."

"That's why you're leaving me," he said, bitterly. "Because you feel worse for me."

"You have to decide where you're going to be, Jonah. You have to be here, or somewhere, and I'd still like it to be with me. But you have to decide."

She walked back into the kitchen, and he sat down in the parlor chair she had just vacated. Sitting there for hours even after she had called for the taxi, and come back in to kiss him on the cheek, and tell him that she would call him. After she told him they would talk about it more, and carried her bags down the stairs with the help of the hack—always a strong, able, competent woman. Sitting there long after he had heard her cab drive away, and the darkness burned away on Strivers Row, and he could finally say to himself, in the earliest gray dawn, that his wife had left him.

CHAPTER TWENTY-TWO

MALCOLM

He took Reginald back up to the latest basement room he had been renting, as soon as he could remember where it was. Telling the cabbie to just keep driving north, while he tried to recall the address.

"This just a temporary crib I got. For purposes of business, you understand," Malcolm told him, but Reginald had just nodded, as trustingly as he had whenever Malcolm had told him anything when they were both boys.

When they'd gotten to his place, he had gone into the bathroom to pull the cash he'd taken from Archie out of his money belt—not wanting Reginald to think that he was scared of anything. Rolling it up into seven big impressive wads, and stashing them in all his different coat and pants pockets. Then he had gathered his few belongings and taken Reginald up to the St. Nicholas Hotel, where he flashed a roll around like Dollarbill's down at Small's, and demanded the best suite they had. The clerk had still looked doubtful, but Malcolm threatened to make a big scene, pointing to his brother and telling him about how nothing was too good for our boys in uniform. They got the suite he had asked for, and soon he and Reginald were sitting back deep on the high plump-mattressed bed in his room. Smiling shyly at each other and swinging their feet above the floor like kids, while they talked over how the rest of their brothers and sisters were doing.

"Yeah, Wilfred still teachin' at Wilberforce," Reginald told him. "Hilda an' Philbert both still up in Lansing. They both thinkin' a gettin' married, last they wrote—"

"Both of 'em?"

"Yeah, that's right. Philbert got religion now, too. Wear one a those little round straw hats all the time—"

"That right?" Malcolm slapped his knee with exaggerated laughter. "What about Yvonne? An' Wesley an' Robert?"

"Oh, they still in school there."

"You, uh, see anything a Butch?" Malcolm asked cautiously—his brother's eyes shifting downward the moment he heard the name.

"No, man. He still in the orphanage, I guess," Reginald told him, then hesitated. Both of them understanding what any mention of Butch, son of the barbershop salesman, would lead to.

"You know, I went to see Mama, 'fore I shipped out."

"Oh, yeah?" Malcolm asked, his voice studiedly casual. "So how she doin'?"

"Oh, all right. Sometimes she knows me. Sometimes…"

His brother's voice trailed off, both of them silent in the big white hotel suite. Malcolm had tried going back to Michigan for a few days, soon after Jarvis had fixed him up with his new look, but nothing had gone as expected. He had anticipated the trip as a chance to strut in front of the folks, and show them all that he had picked up. Dropping in at the homes of his old classmates with his brand-new conk and zoot and asking gleefully, "Do you remember me?" But when he tried to pull the latest steps he had learned at the Roseland, they had only grinned stupidly in embarrassment—the women giggling and refusing to talk to him.

He had stopped by to visit the Gohannases, and even Mrs. Swerlein at the county home in Mason. She had let him in, but sat facing him in the parlor with her head down, as if able to do no more than glance fleetingly at his new clothes for a few moments at a time, flinching whenever he forgot and used some dirty word. After that he hadn't even tried to look up Mr. Maynard Allen—or to stop by the state home in Kalamazoo. Afraid that she wouldn't know him, but even more afraid of what he might hear and could do nothing about, the sound of that rubber hose hitting flesh.

"So—how long you been in the navy? Why'n't ya tell me you was signin' up before you did, Nome?" Malcolm teased his brother, trying to push the thought of home away, and plucking at Reginald's sharp blue and white dress uniform with a mixture of envy and wonder.

He had received his own draft notice when he was living back in Roxbury, after quitting the shipyard up in Portland. The day of his examination he had brushed his conk until it stood almost straight up, into a bright red hedge of fuzz, and worn his flashiest, loudest zoot. He had walked into the induction center talking about how he couldn't wait to get hold of a gun so he could kill himself some crackers down South—calling everyone Baby and Daddy-o. All of the white boys at their physical had laughed and smirked knowingly at him, while the other colored inductees had stared at him as if they would just as soon cut his throat, and the pretty, young colored nurse looked disgusted. But the whole act had gotten him sent to the psychiatrist, all right. The next week, when his draft card had come to Ella's—classifying him 4F with the taut explanation: Psychopathic personality—he had stared at that for a long time, knowing it was all part of his hustle, but wondering about it anyway.

"Ah, Malcolm, this ain't the navy. It's the merchant marine," Reginald said, smiling.

"Oh yeah? What's the difference, exactly?"

"Well, we take supplies an' things. Did a convoy all the way through to Murmansk, up in Russia," his brother told him proudly, then laughed. "Man, you thought Michigan was cold!"

Malcolm recalled hazy images from a newsreel about the fighting on the Russian front. It had seemed incomprehensibly vast— rows and rows of tanks moving across a landscape of endless fields. Soldiers fighting their way through razed cities, commentators talking about the war at the very gates of Asia. There had been film, too, of the American convoys steaming through the North Sea, and the Arctic Ocean. Destroyers dumping depth charges over into the churning gray-and-white seas; torpedo wakes streaking through the water. Even the silhouette of a distant, stricken ship, rising up and plunging down into the water—tiny figures still jumping hopelessly off it, no larger or more significant than maggots off a bone.

"I don't know as you should be doin' that," he told Reginald seriously—an idea starting to form in his mind.

"Ah, it ain't so bad, Malcolm. They got lots a ships to protect us. They say they got the U-boats on the run, now."

"Yeah? Well, they say a lot things."

For the rest of his brother's leave, Malcolm had taken him all around Harlem, trying to talk him into jumping ship. He took him to Jimmy's Chicken Shack, and to Dickie Wells's. He took him to the

Renaissance Ballroom, and up to the buzzard's roost at the Apollo for amateur night, where they fell all over themselves watching Moms Mabley, and a big Puerto Rican man in a tutu chasing the acts off the stage at gunpoint after they had sung their hearts out.

But he spent the whole time, wherever they went, trying to drum into Reginald all the different hustles there were to make a fortune from in Harlem. How they could live together and share expenses in some apartment, or even at the big suite at the St. Nicholas still. Assuring him that the MPs would never catch up to him, not up here in Harlem—that Malcolm would never let them.

He made a point of paying for everything with the thick rolls of money he had gotten from West Indian Archie's bagman. Slapping down big tips everywhere, giving out to any acquaintance he saw who hit him up for a loan. It was true, he kept one eye over his shoulder at all times, afraid that word would make it back to Archie over The Wire about his spending—but he wanted so much more for Reginald to see what he had. Watching the rolls steadily diminishing, too, reminding him every time he flashed them of what he owed.

By the end of Reginald's week in town, he was reduced to taking him back to the Braddock Hotel with him. He had hoped to run into some of his old musician connections, so he could impress his brother—afraid at the same time that they would ignore him if he did. They sat up at the bar, working on the Braddock's watered-down brandy together, Malcolm still trying to convince him of how much money he could make.

"I got the perfect hustle," he told Reginald. "Learned it from some old Jew. It's solid, an' jim-clean. All you got to do is get yourself a peddler's license, an' a case full a cheap seconds—"

" 'Seconds'?"

"Watches, rings. Shirts, dresses. Anything what's got a defect in it. They sell it to you for a beg. Then you take 'em around to barbershops, beauty parlors, an' come on like it's real hot—like you can't wait to get rid of it. Those niggers give you twice what you paid for it, easy. An' there's no risk, baby brother. That's the beauty part! You get clipped by the blue, all you do is show 'em your peddler's license, an' the bill of sale for what you paid for those seconds—"

"I dunno," Reginald said, shaking his head and looking down at his drink. Smiling shyly, the way Malcolm remembered him doing when he had been embarrassed as a little kid.

"C'mon, Mr. High Pockets! What don't you know?"

"I don't know if I can do that sorta thing, Malcolm. 'Sides, we shippin' out tomorrow night."

"Don't you worry. I'll set it all up by then. You can do one with me 'fore your ship goes, an' see how you like it."

"I dunno," Reginald said again, still looking embarrassed. "I got some other interests, you know?"

"Other interests? What you talkin' 'bout, ol' man?"

"You, uh—you know any girls we can meet, Malcolm?"

"Why'n't you say so?" Malcolm proclaimed, slapping Reginald hard on his shoulders. "'Course I know girls! I know any girl you want. Big or small, tight or white."

He was unable to hold back from telling him about Miranda then. He hadn't mentioned her before, out of fear that they might somehow run into her, out with West Indian Archie. But now he couldn't resist bragging on her—trying anything to impress his little brother.

"I got a white woman myself, you know. She's beautiful, too."

"Yeah?" Reginald asked, looking up. "She your girlfriend?"

"Sure she is! She's more 'n that, though. Sings in a club, too. I'm managin' her career, least till I decide to start my own, just like Jimmy Carlton—"

"You think I can meet her? I mean, you think she got any friends?"

"Sure," Malcolm said, thinking. Tapping his long fingers on the edge of the bar.

"Yeah?"

"Sure, sure. She the most beautiful white girl you ever seen," he repeated, thinking of Miranda with West Indian Archie. Thinking of the rolls in his pocket, quickly diminishing.

He peeled off another bill of West Indian Archie's money, throwing it down on the bar for their drinks. Deciding.

"Come on," he told Reginald, pulling him off his bar stool.

"We goin' to meet her?"

"Yeah. I gotta get somethin' first, that's all."

He took Reginald with him up to the apartment on West 144th Street. Sammy opening the door a crack, looking him over from behind the chain—his eyes rimmed with redness.

"Who you with, Red?" he asked suspiciously.

"This is my brother—"

"Well, come in, come in! Lookit him, Cholly Hoss! Even bigger'n you are!" Sammy exclaimed, unlatching the chain.

Inside, the apartment seemed changed to Malcolm from the last time he had seen it. It looked dingier and messier, and there was a funny smell, like old food. Sammy himself seemed different, besides his red eyes. There was a little bristle of hair growing up around the sides of his usually smooth-shaven head, and he was still in one of his silk Japanese bathrobes, walking around in his surprisingly small, childlike bare feet.

"You all right, Hoss?" Malcolm asked him.

"I'm fine as thine, Red," Sammy assured him quickly, moving all about the apartment, in one room and out the other, as if he were looking for something. "I just been takin' a little vacation from work, tha's all. You wanna do some more john-walkin', I let all the girls have a couple days—"

"That's all right, Sammy," Malcolm cut him off quickly. "I just need to borrow somethin' you offered before."

"I'm short, old man—"

"I don't mean scratch," he said directly. "I need that .32-20."

Sammy stopped his padding around, and looked both him and Reginald up and down again.

"You an' your brother wouldn't be plannin' to knock over those scores I showed you, would you, Red? 'Cause that would be a solemn drag."

"Nothin' like that! It's a score a my own. Truth, I'll cut you in. I need somebody to fence it, on the level—"

"You better be, it's my piece you usin'," Sammy told him, retrieving the .32-20 from a notch in the wall behind the icebox. Watching Reginald's eyes widen as he brought out the gun, spinning the cylinder.

"This a big score?" Sammy asked, looking at Malcolm more curiously than ever.

"Biggest I ever knew. But you can see fo' yo'self, soon as I pull it."

"All right, Red," Sammy said slowly. "Let's drink on it."

He had gone into the back bedroom—but instead of bringing out a bottle he returned with a small wooden box full of blow. Cutting the lines out on a mirror on the kitchen table, insisting that they join him. Malcolm could tell that Reginald wanted to leave, but he wanted the surge the coke would give him—that feeling of being keyed up but in control of everything, which Sammy swore was necessary to get nerved up for any stick-up job. They had each done three lines—Reginald dutifully snorting up his powder, too, while they had smiled and cackled at him. And after they had done the coke, Sammy brought out some sticks, just to take the edge off. Then, when they were done with the tea, he had brought out more coke, treating them to a few more lines, afraid that they might have gotten too low.

By the time Sammy returned with a bottle of good scotch, Malcolm had almost forgotten his plans—forgotten even about Miranda, and Archie. His body longing for nothing more than to sink down and go to sleep right on the floor of Sammy's kitchen. But Reginald was pulling at his sleeve. Looking at him through glazed eyes that still reminded Malcolm of how he had been as a little boy—beseeching him as he had that night when he was the only one to hear him get up to go and break into the Levandowskis' grocery.

"You said somethin' about girls—"

"Yes, I did," Malcolm sighed.

He did think of Miranda then—of the money he needed to take to settle everything with Archie, and take her away. Money he could get only one place. He pushed himself up from the table, pulling Reginald along with him. Waving off Sammy, who sat half-slumped over the table, still urging them to have another scotch, and only just remembering to take up the .32-20, which had been laying right out in plain sight. Handing Reginald his own .25, and showing him how to hide it.

"Right down the center of your back—like this."

"That's right! You learn good, boy!" Sammy the Pimp called encouragement from where he was crawling up to lie across the table.

Reginald solemnly hid the gun as Malcolm showed him—and then the two of them were walking out on the street. The bustling night world looking distorted and incandescent from the coke, and the gage they had blown. It was a dark night, cloudy, with no more than a crescent moon in the sky, which Malcolm took as a good sign for their job. He walked slowly, carefully, making a concerted effort to walk straight with his spaghetti, drunk legs. He winked at his brother, and turned toward downtown, starting for the ghosty men's house—only to see Reginald keep walking the other way, back in the direction of their hotel.

"Hey, bro', you got turned around!" he called after him, grinning, hooking onto his brother's arm and attempting to turn him back around. "The score I got in mind is this way—"

But to his amazement, Reginald simply shrugged off his arm, and kept going, walking rapidly back toward the St. Nicholas, Malcolm scrambling after him.

"Hey! You ain't lost your nerve already, have you, Cholly Hoss?"

"I ain't doin' any stick-up job, Malcolm," Reginald said, his voice trembling but plowing on ahead.

"But you just said you would!"

"I only said it so I could get you outta there," Reginald told him, stopping, finally, to confront him on the sidewalk. "Malcolm, I ain't no hold-up man, an' I ain't gonna jump ship. That's desertion, they could put my ass away for the rest of the war. An' I don't trust that Sammy's far's I can spit him."

Malcolm remonstrated with him all the way back to the St. Nicholas, and even as Reginald stalked grimly around their suite there, collecting his things and piling them into his seaman's bag. Telling him again about how much money they could make, and how many girls they would get, and how safe he would keep him from the MPs, and the cops. But even as he spoke, Malcolm could hear how weak, and unconvincing, his voice sounded. Maybe it was all the blow and the liquor they had ingested at Sammy's that made him keep losing his train of thought, but there was also the voice he heard in the back of his head now that kept asking, *But when have you ever kept anybody safe? When did you ever keep even her safe?*

At last, when Reginald was all packed up, he pulled the .25 from the small of his back and handed it back to him.

"Malcolm, I ain't doin' this," he said, his eyes glistening. "This ain't like when we was kids. I don't think you should do it, either."

"Just think about it. Another minute! That's all I'm sayin'—"

"No, man—"

"You think this ain't safe? They gonna *kill* you on that boat a yours!" Malcolm burst out, regretting it as soon as he saw how startled Reginald looked. Then Reginald slowly shook his head, looking him determinedly in the face.

"I gotta get to my ship. I'll let you know, next time we're in port."

He shook his hand, then pulled Malcolm to him in an awkward, tentative hug.

"All right, then. All right. But I'll still be here, waitin', if you change your mind on your way to the navy."

"Good-bye, Malcolm," Reginald said softly as he went out the door—looking back at him with the very same expression of alarm and concern he had had on his face that night outside the Levandowskis', years ago. "You go easy, now."

"I'll be here! I'll still be here!" Malcolm called after him.

And when he was gone, when Malcolm finally heard his shoes echo down the hallway, and the elevator arrive, he had felt even emptier, and more lonely than he had any of those other nights, alone in his room these past few months. He went in to sit on his brother's bed, hoping that somehow Reginald might feel as bad as he did, separated from the last of his family again, and was even now hurrying back along the Harlem sidewalks.

But there was nothing—no bing of the elevator, or sound of footsteps headed back up the hallway. Malcolm bounced himself idly up and down on the bed to stay awake. Noticing how tight and firm the bedspread was, Reginald insisting on making up his own bed every morning, just as he had learned in the merchant marine, and before the maid could even get in.

He pulled out Sammy's .32-20, and laid it on the bed next to him, then. The .25 Reginald had handed back to him, too, the safeties off both guns—telling himself he had to be ready if Archie came by. Then he popped a couple more bennies out of his stash, and started on another pack of sticks. Next he pulled out the little green book Prof. Toussaint had given him—thoroughly battered now, only the "X" remaining on the title page—and sat back down on the bed. It was almost dawn now, and he stopped and waited to watch the sun come up as it had on his first morning in Harlem, after his night with Miranda. Waiting until it turned the sky blue, then a dirty yellow through the grime-streaked window. Then he opened the little green book, and began to read the end of the story.

The day that Master Fard left, Elijah had driven him on down to Chicago through the spring sunshine. Motoring along roads splayed with apple and lilac blossoms, the fields freshly turned for planting. They had kept mostly to the main highways nonetheless, never sure what they might encounter if they wandered too far down the back roads amongst the scenic farms and pretty, white country towns. Only after they had passed through Indiana did they stop for food, pulling off into a little grove by a watering hole. It was a pleasant spot, full of singing birds, where the car could be concealed behind the surrounding trees. There they had eaten the lunch that Clara had packed for them, made as always from the best food they had in their house, then dozed and talked for a while in the shade.

"You will be in charge until it is safe for me to return," Fard told him sleepily, lying out on the ground beneath a high oak tree in his open vest and shirtsleeves, the jacket of his immaculate suit left back in the car for once.

"Yes," Elijah said, but his voice sounded distracted, and Fard, alert as ever, looked over at him sharply.

"You know that you are the last of the prophets, do you not?" Fard told him very seriously, sitting up and trying to fix him with his eyes again.

"Elijah of Cordele," he mused. "At least two-thirds of the true Bible—not the white man's Poison Book—is written about you, and it is you who will be judged first of all on the Judgment Day. Did you know that?"

"Thank you," Elijah said automatically.

He knew that he should have been more attentive, but he was preoccupied at the moment. Thinking about the familiar slender figure he had noticed, on the far edge of the weeping crowd that had seen off Master Fard that morning. He had picked him out at once: the Chinaman, Eddie Donaldson—in a hat and suit, and his usual sardonic smile, a slim cardboard suitcase dangling from one hand.

"You know, I think that I will give you a better name than Ghulam," Fard said, standing up and walking over to the car, where he took a towel that Clara had provided out of the backseat, and started toward the watering hole.

"I think that you will be called 'Abdul' from now on—"

"Respectfully, I decline, Master," Elijah said, and Fard stopped where he was on his way to the water, squinting slightly at Elijah through the dappled sunshine.

"That was the name that you gave Brown Eel," Elijah said calmly, "who was my blood enemy. And besides, he was not faithful to you."

"What do you mean by that?" Fard asked him sharply, but Elijah only looked calmly at him for a moment before replying.

"Where is he now?" he said, and Fard stared at him for another long moment.

"True enough, my most humble servant," he said then, and smiled—that dear, warm smile that Elijah had always loved so much.

"I was only testing you, and as always you have passed the test. I will give you a better name yet. I will give you your own name back. And with it, you will take my original name. Muhammad."

"Yes," said Elijah, sounding it out in his mind. Elijah Muhammad.

"Yes, thank you," he said, satisfied.

Fard looked at him again, then proceeded to the water, while Elijah got up and went back to the car. He had noticed that one of the rear tires was dangerously low, portending a blowout, and who knew what might happen to them then—two slender, well-dressed men of color, caught out alone on the shoulder of a public highway. He got the axle and tire jack and the spare out of the trunk, and was preparing to change it when he saw Fard kneel down by the watering hole and begin to pray.

Fascinated, Elijah began to walk quietly toward him, the tire-jack crucifix still in his hand. He had never heard the Master pray by himself before—but before he could hear what he was saying, Fard had finished and leaned down, splashing his face with water and then mopping it with Clara's towel. Elijah was left to stare at the back of his olive-skinned neck, the pompadour of white man's hair oiled high on his head.

"What will you do in Chicago?" Elijah asked him, and Fard started, as if somehow he had not been aware of his presence so close to him.

"Oh, I don't know," he said distractedly, still looking down into the water. Producing a rubber comb and beginning to work it stiffly through his hair, still staring into the water.

"It has been a long time since I saw my people. Maybe it is time I made a trip back to Mecca, the Holy City."

"Yes," Elijah said, listening now, and walking a couple feet closer. He thought he could hear something rustling in the bushes—a bigger sound than could be made by any rabbit, or badger.

"I don't know when I'll be back, actually," Fard said, seemingly oblivious to the noise, though Elijah didn't know how he could be. His voice sounded strangely light and animated, Elijah thought, as if he had left off some great burden.

"There are many places I should visit, to bring wisdom and enlightenment before the Last Days. You will have to be strong in my stead."

"I will be."

"You know, you must be careful how you judge others, my faithful one," Fard went on. "You will find that within every man there are many different men, just waiting to get out. One of them can even be God, but that doesn't mean the other men aren't there."

"Yes."

"You will find this is true even within yourself," Fard said, straightening up on his knees now, but looking straight ahead over the water. "It is true even with those you love, and trust the most, and you must think on this, and have mercy."

That rustling again. The Chinaman?

"Yes," Elijah said, peering into the underbrush. "I understand."

"Good," Fard said, dropping his face to the water again. "I knew you would, my son."

He weighed the heft of the tire jack in his hand, listening intently but hearing only the sound of the birds singing, the quiet splash of the water on the Master's face as he drew closer.

CHAPTER TWENTY-THREE

JONAH

He had waited until the very last moment to bring him in. Until the processional had entered, singing the old hymn "What a Beautiful City," and marched all the way up to take their place around the altar. The choir waiting for him there, standing, along with the assistant ministers, and the choir director. The congregation still standing, too—looking around at each other, wondering what the delay was about.

Only then had he entered the New Jerusalem, with his father on his arm. Walking down the aisle only as fast as the old man could totter forward, bent half over to the ground, clutching Jonah's elbow, but still refusing to use a cane. The congregation, still on its feet, watching them creep forward in awe. His father sneaking Jonah a ghost of a smile across his broad, rigid face, as if to show his appreciation of a dramatic flourish worthy of his own.

He reached the front pew, and settled his father very slowly there, in the seat next to the aisle. The head deacon scooting hastily over—right next to where Amanda always sat. Jonah still half-hoping that she would be there, though she had said that she would not be. He had snuck a look out at the crowd through the vestry door before the service, telling himself that maybe she had decided to come after all—but there was still no sign of her. They had spoken on the phone every day since she had left, with Jonah mostly listening. Trying to think of something that would convince her to come back but able to come up with almost nothing. Listening to all she had to say, her heartache and her worry, and her loneliness—after these ten years, living with him—and all he could find to say was, Come see. I'll show you, just come see.

He looked out over the entire congregation again before he stepped on up to the pulpit—taking one last look for her. Taking the opportunity to look at all of them, the great, half circle of the faithful, gathered 'round. Still subtly and not so subtly separated by skin color, darker on his right, light-almost-white on his left. The church mothers with their grand, feathered hats. The gravely self-important deacons in the front pews, hands on their chins, nodding sagely over nothing at all. The ushers trying to stand at full attention, white-gloved hands behind their backs, no matter how old they were. The balconies fuller than ever before with young, truly serious-looking men in uniform—their mothers and girlfriends clutching their arms even now, as if they were afraid to let go of them for a second. He even spotted Private Bandy and his mother and fiancée, sitting up dead center in the balcony, and gave them a wink—the private grinning happily back at him.

He looked out over all the church—his church—and he wanted to laugh for the love of all of them. Seated there uncomfortably before him. Sweating in the heavy heat, fanning themselves with their programs, or rounded little rattan fans. No doubt thinking more of the ballgame later that afternoon, or the policy number they had bet, or how hungover they were from the night before. Thinking on who they would marry, or what murderous corner of the Pacific or Africa they were about to be shipped out to. Thinking of sex and liquor, and the good book, and kindness and generosity, and how to hustle their neighbors, and the kind heart of Jesus, and how hot they were at just that very moment. All the good-bad things that human beings think of, a million times a minute. All mixed up together so that what sort of prayer could ever possibly go out to God, save for the entire chaotic outcry of all his creation, all at once?

He felt the way he had that rainy Sunday, just the week before— only with much less of the melancholy now. Feeling that weight-lessness, that just-after-the-fever has broken relief that the worst had happened, and things could not possibly get worse. And that, even if they did, there was not a thing he could do about it. Thinking that God was a fever, leaving us in cycles fearful and despairing, senselessly ecstatic and burned down to a crisp of helpless tranquility. He stepped past the altar, up to his pulpit, listening calmly while the assistant ministers hurried through the announcements and the prayers, and the choir led them in another hymn. Pulling out the thin, folded sheaf of paper that he had read to his father the night before, wanting him to hear it first. Ready to take back his church.

"I want to talk to you today about the sign of Jonah," he began straight out, speaking in a calm, quiet voice. Pretending to look down at his text, but not even seeing the words, knowing everything that he was going to say by heart.

"You all know it—I would hope. Know it from the Sunday school story, how Jonah was swallowed by the whale. But maybe you've forgotten just how it was Jonah got there, swimming in that raging sea. Maybe you've forgotten that Jonah was commanded by the Lord to go to the mighty city of Nineveh—a city the Bible tells us it took three days just to pass through—to go to that mighty capital of the heathen Assyrians, and to tell them that they had been found wicked in the sight of the Lord! Yes, he had been ordered by God Himself to tell the people of Nineveh that they were evil, and that the Lord would destroy them in forty days' time!

"Not a pleasant task," he said quickly, drawing a light chuckle of relief from the crowd. Stopping to mop his sweating face with his handkerchief—looking up specifically at Private Bandy in his uniform then.

"Not a very pleasant mission, as we have so many of us been given unpleasant missions these days. Almost as unpleasant and as dangerous a mission as going to war—to tell a great people that they are wicked and that they are doomed, 'less they foreswear their wicked ways. In fact, it was so unpleasant to Jonah that he refused to do the Lord's bidding, and he rose and tried to flee to the ends of the earth, thinking that God would not find him there. He bought a ticket on a heathen boat, to sail him so far away that he would be out of the presence of the Lord."

He paused again, taking a long drink of water from the glass on the podium before him—wanting to get the timing just right for what was coming next.

"But there's no place you can go that is beyond the presence of the Lord. No place beyond the will of He Who maketh all things, of He Who causeth the wind to blow, and the sun to rise. You can't sail out of the presence of the Lord. You can't row out of the presence of the Lord, though Jonah and his heathen sailors tried. You can't even take a modern steamship, or a car, or a train. You can't take the fastest plane there is—and escape from the presence of the Lord.

"The Lord found Jonah, all right. And He made a mighty tempest to rise up in the sea, so that Jonah's boat was in peril of capsizing and drowning all aboard. Jonah knew it was the Lord, too. He knew it the same way we all know it when we commit some sin— when we know we've done wrong. Jonah knew that he was the one responsible for making the sea churn and the boat flounder. Just as, to this day, we call someone we think is responsible for all our bad luck and misfortune 'a Jonah.' Just as many of you in this church today have thought me to be the cause of all our troubles—the one who is responsible for the shrinking of our spirit, and for our failure to love one another as we know we should."

A stunned murmur rose up through the church then—not the usual call and response of approval or encouragement, but a babble of exclamations and pure shock. Jonah letting them have that moment, to voice their consternation over all the surprises of the day, the presence of his father and the absence of Amanda, and his own audaciousness in preaching a sermon on himself. Putting up his hand against it, but letting the sound run its course before he tried to speak again.

"You are not wrong to have thought so. I have to confess to you that there have been times when my spirit has been weak. There have been times, too, when like Jonah I wished I was many miles away from here, even at the ends of the earth. When I did not feel worthy of taking up the mission that the Lord gave me—that you gave me to minister unto you.

"Now the heathen sailors tried to have compassion on Jonah— just as you have had compassion on me. They weren't about to throw another human being overboard, into a raging sea—just as you have been good enough not to throw me out. They tried hard to row the ship back to land, but the Lord would not have it. It did no good for them to sail. Did no good for them to row. They didn't have a motor, didn't have a boiler—and if they had, they would have done them no good either, for there is no power that can stand against the power of the Lord! Finally Jonah had to beg them to throw him over the side. As I would have liked to beg you, many times when I felt unworthy, to throw me over."

He spoke the last sentence in a suddenly hushed, soft voice, so that the whole church went quiet with him. All but hanging on his words now.

"Well, I guess you know what happened next. Once Jonah was in the water, the Lord sent a whale—a leviathan—to swallow him up. And though it might seem impossible—though it might be unlikely—the Bible tells us that Jonah lived for three days in the belly of the beast. It tells us, too, that Jonah prayed to the Lord then. But that he did not pray for help, as you or I would surely have done. He didn't pray to be delivered, as almost anyone would have done in his circumstances. He didn't pray, 'Lord, please help me' in the present tense. Didn't pray as a bargain, 'Please help me, Lord, and I will be good, I will do your will!'

"No, instead he prayed a prayer of thanksgiving. He prayed as if he already had been delivered, for so great was Jonah's faith that he had no doubt but that God would preserve him. He prayed, 'I called—called!—to the Lord, out of my distress, and He answered me.' He prayed, 'I called from the belly of Hell, and the Lord did hear my voice.' He prayed, 'I went down to the land whose bars were closed upon me forever, yet thou didst bring up my life from the Pit, O Lord my God. When my soul fainted within me, I remembered the Lord, and my prayer came to thee, into thy holy temple.' That is what he prayed. And the Lord heard his prayer, and He caused the leviathan to vomit him up on the shore.

"Now I know that many of you—that many of us—have felt that same way. Ever since the great beast vomited us up on the shores of this land, we have felt that way. We have called out to the Lord from the belly of the beast, and the depths of hell. We have called out from where the prison bars shut upon us, and where doors shut in our faces, for the Lord to hear our prayer!"

He paused abruptly for another drink of water. Weighing the response of the church before him, the rising, increasingly excited cries of That's right! That's right! and Tell it! Tell it plain! Hearing, he thought, the first rustle of the rabbit in the bushes.

"The Lord heard Jonah, and delivered him, and that is a great sign unto us all. Christ Himself tells us in the Book of Matthew, and again in Luke, that Jonah is the sign of that generation. 'For as Jonah was three days and three nights in the belly of the beast, so will the Son of man be three days and three nights in the heart of the earth.' Before rising. Before rising out of hell.

"So, too, is Jonah a sign unto this generation. But oh, my brothers and sisters, so are we all a sign to this nation, to this sick world. For like Jonah, we are stuck in the craw of this mighty nation, this great beast. And like Jonah, we are not going away.

"We are the indigestible truth. We are the leavening in the bread—

and the nation cannot rise without us. We are God's hidden church in the Wilderness, which He has preserved for Himself as a witness, and we will be a light unto the world!"

Men and women alike were coming out of their seats now, laughing and shouting. Waving their handkerchiefs, and pointing toward him. Telling him, Say it true! Say it true! The rabbit, running at last.

"Right now we are engaged in a great, global war. It's a war that started mostly because some people over in Germany thought they could just expunge a great and ancient people from human history. But they will not succeed, for we will stop them. There are some people—not over in Germany, but right here in the United States of America—who would like to use the war to do the same thing to all of us. But they will not succeed, for we will stop them, too. Though it may seem impossible—though it may seem incredible—we have already labored in this country for over three hundred years, through slavery and Jim Crow, and we are not going anywhere. America is talking about making a new world now, but its conscience is still filled with guilt. It is not making anything—it is not going anywhere—until all Americans can sing a prayer of thanksgiving for our deliverance!"

The whole congregation was up on its feet now, repeating his words after him. The men punching the air, the women waving their handkerchiefs and calling out Yes, yes, glory! Jonah pausing to mop his face again, feeling the literal reverberation of their excitement swelling up through the floorboards of his pulpit. Staring down then, deliberately, to the first pew, where tears were running down his father's face—and where his wife's seat was still empty.

"One more thing!" he said, holding up a hand—stilling them, even at the moment of their greatest ecstacy. Stilling them, then slowly building back up again, banging his hand on the pulpit to mark the beat as he moved to the end.

"One more thing—when Jonah finally got to Nineveh—when he finally fulfilled his mission, the people of that mighty city were so overwhelmed by his preaching that they fell on their knees, and they covered themselves with sackcloth and ashes, and begged God for forgiveness! And being a merciful God, the Lord forgave them, and spared their city. But this only made Jonah angry. Jonah told God that he was afraid He would do such a thing, all along. He couldn't understand, after all he had gone through, and all the risks he had taken, why it was that God did not go ahead and strike down the evil city, just as he had said—and just as it deserved. He got so angry that he actually asked God to take his life, and he went and sat outside the city and waited to die.

"And the Lord God came to him, and He asked Jonah, 'Do you do well to be angry?' He asked Jonah why shouldn't He pity even Nineveh, that great city, if its people truly and earnestly repented. So I say to you today—do you do well to sit, and be angry? For I have seen you. I have seen you out on the stoops, sitting in the barbershops and the bars, and the beauty parlors, just making yourselves more and more angry. I have seen you sit and brood on the injustices done to you and I have to admit I have done the same thing, and I say to you again, 'Do you do well to sit and be angry?'

"I say to you, don't be so angry that when the day comes that this great and evil city repents, you won't take any joy in it. Don't be that angry! Don't be so angry that you despair of your own precious life. Don't be so angry that you won't take the hand of friendship any man, of any kind, offers you in sincere equality and friendship, don't you be that angry! Don't be so angry that you will come here, to the very house of God, and refuse to sit too close to your brother and your sister because their skin is too dark or too light! God doesn't want you to sit and be angry like Jonah did at all, but to stand up against injustice, so that we can all rise up from the belly of the beast, and truly make a new world out of this terrible war! Thank you, Jesus, thank you, Lord!"

He bounded down from the pulpit then, letting the shouts and the praise sweep over him. The choir and the congregation all standing and booming out "Precious Lord Take My Hand" even as he stepped down and took his father's arm again. Leading him slowly back down the aisle with every eye in the congregation on him, even as they sang. Looking down and seeing through the tears—through the big crooked grin on his ancient face—his father give him a quick, secret wink, before he led him out into the hazy sunshine of a Harlem summer Sunday.

CHAPTER TWENTY-FOUR

MALCOLM

By the time he raised his head from his brother's bed, the sun was already setting again. He pulled himself up and into the bathroom, where he popped a couple more bennies to get himself going. There was no sign of Reginald, no sign that anything from the night before had happened, save for the guns laid out on his brother's taut bedspread. He picked them both up and pocketed the .25. Holding the .32-20 in his hand, turning it slowly over and over, while he tried to decide just what to do next. Slowly, gingerly, he put it, too, back into his jacket pocket and set out for Sammy the Pimp's apartment—still unable to think of anywhere else he could go.

"What happened to that big score you gonna make, Red?" Sammy asked, eyeing him suspiciously from behind the chain of his door.

"We had a little stumble on that," Malcolm tried to explain. "I'm still gonna do it, you'll see. I just came to bring your piece back."

"Uh-huh."

Sammy regarded him for another long moment, then closed the door and pulled the chain back. He led him on down to the kitchen, still wearing the silk bathrobe he had had on the night before, his eyes looking redder and blearier than ever—the bottle of scotch sitting empty on the table.

"Let's have it then," he said, holding out his hand, and Malcolm hesitated for just a moment before he drew the gun out. Wanting to hold on to it for some reason, wanting to do something, anything with it. But finally he handed it over, a great sense of relief flooding through his chest as he did so.

"Fine, fine!" Sammy said, taking the .32-20 back and checking the cylinder. Rolling it once and clicking it back in place—before pointing it squarely at Malcolm's chest from across the table.

"Whatta you doin'?" Malcolm asked him, standing very still.

"It's all over The Wire, Red. West Indian Archie is lookin' everywhere for you. Say you got his money."

"That's a lie!"

"You can tell him that yo'self, Red. I'm gonna take you right to him," Sammy said, shrugging, waving the gun blearily at him. "First, I want you to gimme what you got left—an' whatever it is you got from that score—"

But Malcolm was already diving across the table for him by then, going for his gun hand before Sammy could even finish his spiel. Sammy pulled the gun up instinctively, squeezing the trigger as both of Malcolm's hands clamped around his wrist, and it fired upward, the bullet creasing Sammy's own slick bald head—the detonation deafening them both as they fell to the floor.

The next thing Malcolm knew there was the sound of wild screaming that seemed to be coming from a long way away, and the feeling of claws tearing at the back of his neck and his face. He wrested the gun from Sammy where he lay, still stunned, on the floor. Trying to push himself up and away from Hortense, who had come out of a back room somewhere in the apartment, and was intent on twisting his neck around to someplace it couldn't go.

"It just grazed him! It just grazed him!" he shouted at her over the ringing in his ears. But she only screamed more curse words in Spanish and went for him again, her long red nails reaching out for his face.

"What? What?"

He stumbled a few steps backward and bumped up against a wall, backhanding her with the gun when she kept coming on. The blow sending her sprawling back across Sammy, blood running out of one side of her mouth—still cursing and spitting at him.

"He's the one pulled the gun on me!" Malcolm exclaimed, in a tone of sincerely injured innocence.

"Fuck you!"

She cradled Sammy's head protectively in her arms, cooing endearments to him. Sammy tried to stand up, but he couldn't arrange it—his limbs surprisingly spindly sticking out of the folds of his bathrobe, looking like a big cockroach tipped over on its back.

There was a long, even groove from the bullet that ran the length of his smooth bald head, but the blood was already dissipating.

"I think you better run, Red," he managed to say.

"Yeah? I think you finished tellin' me what I better do."

He trained the gun on Sammy, holding a hand to his own throbbing, wounded face where Hortense had clawed it.

"Get out! Get the hell out, you cocksucker! Look what you done!" Hortense screamed, starting to get up again, and he turned and ran out the door. Slamming it behind him, leaping down the stairs—not even remembering that he still had the gun out in his hand until he was almost through the front door.

He was stumbling back down along the nighttime streets then, his head still reverberating from the gunshot. His face and neck aching from Hortense's nails, hoping no cop would pay too much attention to the blood dripping slowly down his cheek and onto his shirt collar. He clutched desperately to the .32-20, telling himself he would shoot it out if he had to, just like the gunfighters in the movies. He could feel his breath coming raggedly, his heart beating so hard and loud he thought it would tear through his chest.

After a few more blocks, when he felt he was far enough from Sammy's and no one was coming, he ducked into a broad alleyway with a whole series of single-car garages running up and down it. He was dimly aware that he must be in back of one of the blocks that made up Strivers Row, and normally he would have walked on, afraid that these were the only colored folks in the City who might actually be able to summon a cop.

But now he didn't care, he had to rest for a moment. Trying to think what to do—his slave with Sammy done, Archie out looking for him. And his brother gone. Not even having stayed to do the big job with him, the one that might make all the difference.

He tried to swallow, and fought down the fear, and the bitterness. He popped a couple more bennies, then smoked three sticks in quick succession, feeling the smoke spread through his head, calming him. He adjusted his tie and smoothed down the tails of his suit jacket, dabbing at his face and the blood on his collar with a handkerchief. Telling himself that it didn't matter, that he would do it anyway—go through with it all just as he had planned. It was simple now. Just two things, nobody else involved. Go to the house of the ghosty men, then go find Miranda—and Archie. That was all there was to it.

.   .   .

He moved unseen down Fifth Avenue, toward 128th Street. He had waited deliberately until the hours after midnight, killing time by smoking a few more of Sammy's sticks, then having a couple of bourbons in a dive he knew that Archie would never set foot in—just to calm his nerves, and make sure that his hand was steady. There it was—the lifeless, ramshackle house, stuffed to the rafters with the white men's junk, the single forlorn tree outside in a sea of trash. He stepped down to the door beneath the stairs where he had first seen the old ghosty man emerge. *Imagining—wishing—that his little brother was here with him, standing lookout just as he had that night back in Michigan—*

He pulled tentatively at the door's ancient iron grate, prepared to jimmy it open with a length of metal pipe he had found in the street. But when he did, the door gave way immediately even to his cautious tug, swinging open so easily that he dropped the length of pipe in his surprise. It made a hugely loud, clanging noise on the sidewalk of the silent street and he froze in the shadows of the doorway, waiting for some reaction.

But there was nothing, no shouts or sirens, and he went back to business. Softly kicking in the rotted front door, the moldy wood giving way like so much cardboard. The repulsive wet splintering sound made his lips curl back, until he felt as if he were smashing in some infinitely foul, decayed old hive. His foot went through once more—and the whole spongy door fell away as if by magic, leaving only the passageway before him, even more dark and bottomless than he had remembered it.

Gathering all of his remaining courage and concentration, he started to make his way down, into the house. An odor of unspeakable corruption, also much worse than anything he remembered, wafted back out at him. He reached for the lighter he had in his jacket and took it out—hesitating before he lit it, though, knowing what he was about to see and hear, all the scuttlings of countless roaches and mice all around him. He pulled out another stick and lit it, letting the smoke of the gage at least for a few moments. Then he turned the lighter back down the tunnel—and saw why it had indeed seemed even darker and fouler than he had remembered.

There, a few feet before him, he could see the body of a man in an antique suit, lying facedown in the middle of the tunnel. Malcolm recognized immediately the old-fashioned shoes and suit, one of the slug-white hands—a body too thin to possibly block up more than half of even this narrow passageway. The trouble was that the rest of his torso and head were covered by what looked to be half a ton of debris—buried under pressing irons and dumbbells, a rusted engine and several thick volumes of admiralty law; an old Christmas tree, and a tricycle, and several broken canning jars, filled with excrement.

Malcolm stood staring at it all, feeling just as he had that night in the Levandowskis' store, so many years before. Peering down into all that junk, the house full of junk, and knowing that if Langley Collyer had broken his neck in one of his own booby traps, there were doubtless more traps throughout the dark house. Knowing that even if there hadn't been—or even if he had been able to spot and evade them all—he would never be able to extricate what was worthwhile from what was merely junk. That none of it would have made any difference at all.

He had taken another long toke from his stick, and turned back toward the street, when he saw him. Sitting right by the entrance to the tunnel, perched atop a high pile of the ghosty men's accumulated newspapers as if they were a throne. Staring right at him, instantly recognizable in his neat brown suit and that rounded little cap—the gentle, knowing smile on his face. Elijah.

"And you still say you don't love the devil," he said softly. His presence so much more real to Malcolm now than the other times in his dreams when he had seen him, or thought that he had seen him. More real even than on that first night, when he had spoken to him.

"Oh, yes, I have rolled away the stone, and opened up the tomb," he said now, as if answering his thoughts. "For that's what it is, a tomb, full of corruption. But here you are, still craving the white man's cave. Still willing to climb through all of his foulness, if you can get at his things."

"An' why not? Why—not?" Malcolm shouted, the words revolving in his mind, as if he were talking to himself. Feeling the tunnel reverberate with the noise, and worrying that it might bring down the whole rest of the house, all about him, but unable to help himself.

"Why shouldn't I have them?"

"Yeah, you almost at the bottom now," Elijah told him, as calmly as ever. "Livin' in the sewer like some criminal. White man got you almost all the way down—just like he done with me."

"You mean how you was drinkin'—"

"No, I don't just mean the drinkin'," Elijah corrected him. "That wasn't all what I was talkin' about, though it was the bottom of my ignorant self-degradation. No, I mean even lower. Take a look!"

Malcolm peered harder at him, a little brown man, sitting way up at the end of a tunnel—and suddenly the pile of newspapers he was sitting on melted away, and a whole room began to rise up around him.

"Look!" Elijah shouted suddenly, raising his hands above his head—and the room began to grow, and envelop both of them now. The house of the ghosty men, the street, the whole Harlem night all fading into the walls now. Until Malcolm saw, to his fear and amazement, that they were both surrounded by the high stone walls. Elijah sitting on the side of a metal cot now, in a jail cell. All of it around them as clear as day—as clear as a movie set—the bare sink and seatless toilet next to his bunk, the endless rows of bars, and cells beyond them.

"That's right. It's a prison, son. In Milan, Michigan. That's where the white man has me."

"A prison," Malcolm repeated, uncomprehending. Staring at the stark pale green walls, the bars and the locked steel doors. So much like where she was.

"That's right," Elijah told him, the words flowing out of him relentlessly. "After I got back from Chicago, the hypocrites turned on me, Brown Eel, an' all the others. They asked, 'Where is Master Fard? Why has no one heard from him?' until they even turned my own brother, Kallatt, against me.

"They wouldn't listen when I told 'em I had last seen Master Fard in the airport terminal, in Chicago, or that he had appointed me, Elijah Muhammad, the sole messenger of Allah in his stead before he raised up his arms and ascended into the sky. They wouldn't listen, they turned all the people against me, until one night a shotgun was fired through the window of my house, and I knew that I had to flee to save my life.

"I went all over the white man's country then, living like a hunted animal. But even then, the hypocrites an' the white devils pursued me. Birds have trees, and foxes have their holes, but there was no place for me to lay my head. J. Edgar Herrod put me in jail for refusin' to sign up for the draft, an' fight the white man's war. His agents hauled me out of my mother's house, wrapped up in a carpet. Like some criminal—like a dog!"

"But—you come an' go as you please!" Malcolm said, unable to understand it. The little man was still wearing his skullcap embroidered with all the marvelous suns and stars and moons. But his neat black suit and tie and handkerchief were gone now, replaced by a blue prison work shirt, with a number on the pocket.

"That's right, son. I go where I want because they can't hold me in here. Because I grow greater in The Knowledge of Self an' Others every day, while my enemies, the hypocrites, diminish. But don't worry, son. Your day is coming, too. Soon they will have you in they prison, too, an' then you will learn. Then you will grow as you never did before—"

"No!"

"—grow in knowledge, in wisdom. In the words of W. D. Fard, an' Elijah Muhammad, which is me—which is my last, an' final, name. So you shall be my prophet, and my herald!"

"No!" Malcolm shouted, stumbling backward. The prison walls looming up gigantically now, yet wobbling, threatening to come crashing down and threatening to entomb him just as the ghosty men's house had done to Langley Collyer. Elijah had risen up off his prison cot and stood above him now, his hands still lifted high in the air, as if he were commanding the walls to stay up, trapping him.

"You will, son, you will! You will become the greatest prophet of all, even greater than W. D. Fard—even greater than me! An' when you do, son—when you do—all I ask is that you remember the man I am here, and now, even after you find out all the other men who are inside me. All I ask is that you remember me as I am in prison, and have mercy on me, even as I crush your bones!"

But Malcolm had already stopped listening. Trying to push his way past the little man, feeling for the sidewalk.

"No! No, I don't want to go to no prison like she did! I want Miranda!" he cried out.

"Miranda!" the risen Elijah cried, and threw back his head and laughed long and loud. "Miranda! Oh, son! That's the biggest joke of all!"

"I love her!"

He could see the streetlights of Fifth Avenue flaring up dimly again, the outlines of the prison beginning to shrink and fade—Elijah fading with it, as if he were walking off down a long tunnel.

"I love her!" he cried out one more time, and Elijah turned and smiled his radiant smile at him one more time.

"Oh, son!" he called back faintly. "And you say you don't love the devil!"

CHAPTER TWENTY-FIVE

MALCOLM

He heard the motorcycle engines coming from a long way away, as they throttled down Fifth Avenue. Their sound rising from a low growl to an unbearable, high-pitched screech. He cried out—and saw that he was lying facedown on the slabs of moldy newspapers that lined the tunnel down into the ghosty house. He scrambled to his feet at once, brushing desperately at himself and his suit with his hands, trying to sweep off all of the vermin he knew were crawling all around him.

It was daylight out now, the sun high in the sky, and, running his hands over himself again he shivered to think how long he had been lying in the entrance to the old house. He waited under the shadow of the old stairs until the motorcycle patrol had passed, peering out at the police riders who looked like so many gigantic, arrogant beetles in their dark glasses, and high, peaked caps. When they had passed he skipped quickly on up to the street, putting distance between himself and the ghosty house as quick as he could manage without running. When he was a block away he slowed to a somewhat more deliberate pace, inspecting more of the damage to his suit, and face—checking to make sure that he still had both guns in his pockets.

He knew what he was after now, even if he didn't know just where he was headed yet. The visitation from Elijah Muhammad still lingered in his brain, more vivid than any dream, but even so he felt clearer in his own head than he had in a long time. Sure, now, that there was just one more thing for him to do—find West Indian Archie before he found him.

He went methodically from one bar and club to another, doing everything he could to put it on The Wire. Making his way down to the Braddock, then back up to Chick's, and the New Thrill, and the Fat Man's Bar. Letting himself be seen, calling out in a loud, clear voice everywhere he went to ask if Archie had been in. He made sure to stop and talk to everyone he knew on the street, including the worst squealers in Harlem, telling them straight out that he was looking for Archie. He had even walked into Small's Paradise, where he stood just inside the door for a few minutes, his arms crossed over his chest, saying nothing but taking care that everyone got a good look at him. Jumpsteady, and Dollarbill, and a few of the other regulars at the bar staring at him as if they had seen a ghost—and not even Charlie Small, standing behind the bar, had dared to say anything to him before he went out again.

The day had started out hot and wet, and it got steadily hotter and more humid as it went along. The waves of heat wafting visibly off the sidewalks before him, wilting the collars of his shirt and coat. He didn't bother to stop for a meal, but kept drinking dime beers as he went along, to relieve his thirst, and to try to get the ringing in his head to stop. Popping bennies to stoke himself back up afterward, scoring a snort in the men's room at the Braddock, another at Bowman's, and one in the Rhythm Café.

He pushed on up through the throngs of Sunday promenaders on Seventh Avenue and Lenox, the churchgoers turning out in their sharpest new dresses and suits, and good shoes. Bumping hard into anyone who got in his way, stopping if they stopped and looking back at them, smiling to himself to watch the men swallow their curses and move on. He slid his hands down to both his guns, in his front jacket pockets. No longer worried about being picked up with them, telling himself that he would kill any cop who tried to run him in. Thinking of himself as Gary Cooper in The Westerner, stepping out into the street with his guns on.

At some point when he stepped out of yet another bar, he noticed that it was coming on dusk. The heat still not letting up, the night air promising to hang just as heavy as it had all day. He stopped down a little alley along Beale Street, snorting, over some trashcans, the last of the blow he had scored. The streets seeming to tilt and tremble as he walked back uptown, his shirt sticking to his jacket.

He was nearly back to the hotel, his clarity from earlier in the day, so simple and confident, all but melted away under the unremitting sun by now. Unsure of just what he would do if he still couldn't find West Indian Archie, leave town or spend another night there; go down to Miranda's or try to force his way into the ghosty men's house again, or just put the gun up against his own head—when he looked in the window of the La Mar-Cheri at 147th and St. Nicholas, and saw that there they were, together.

The La Mar-Cheri not much more than a storefront, a run-down little bar with barely a space for a combo to play in back, out on the very edge of Archie's territory. But they were there, all right, sitting up in one of the two window booths. Leaning over the table toward each other, their heads almost touching—Archie's huge, rough brown hands encasing one of hers. Malcolm thought that he could take him right there through the glass, less than three feet away. But she was there, too—laughing and smiling at him, her face glowing and carefree. Looking more beautiful than ever in a white, flowered sundress. Her hair pinned up with one of those flowers she loved so much—false jasmine—so that he could see the full, graceful curve of her neck and shoulders.

He yanked open the door, the blast of voices and jukebox music making his head vibrate. Slide-stepping immediately to their booth, pulling out his .32-20 as he did—only to see Archie's .45 already trained directly on his gut, even as his other hand still held on to hers.

"Hello, Red," he said evenly. "You got my money?"

"I heard you been lookin' for me. Well, here I am!" Malcolm told him—trying to sound just as calm as Archie had, but aware that his voice was quavering wildly. Trying not to look down at Archie's .45, two feet away from his stomach, its barrel as big as a cannon's. The only noise in the bar now the sound of bar stools scraping the floor as the customers scrambled out of the line of fire, or to get a better view.

"Stop this right now. The both of you!" Miranda hissed at them. She had looked shocked when he first appeared, her mouth falling open, but she had recovered herself quickly, Malcolm saw.

"I ain't got yo' money!"

"I see. So you thinkin' you gonna kill me, then," Archie said, his voice still level and patient—and Malcolm slowly nodded his head.

"Then lemme give you somet'in' to think about, Red," Archie continued, his voice low, and weary, and a little bit sad. "One a two things is gonna happen here. You gonna kill me like you say, or I'm gonna kill you. Either way, I'm a old man. I'm sixty years old. I been to Sing Sing, I can do it again. My life is over anyway. But you kill me, you lost just the same. You gonna spend all the rest of your young years in prison."

"She don't love you!" Malcolm blurted out then. "She loves me!"

"Red, stop this foolishness. Right now!"

"So that's what this is about," Archie said, a look of pained understanding crossing his face, and making him look suddenly so much older that Malcolm almost felt a pang of pity for him.

"So that's it?" he asked, turning his eyes away from Malcolm completely, and looking at Miranda now. She avoided his gaze, looking down at the table, and he let her hand go. Uncocking his .45 then, and placing it quietly on the table between them. Still ignoring Malcolm, turned all the way toward Miranda now, who kept looking down at the table, her hands clutching her arms.

"How long has it been?" Archie asked, in a voice that sounded far away, like that of a man coming upon the scene of an accident. And when Miranda still said nothing, Malcolm could not help but answer for her, going on uncontrollably.

"Since the first night I seen her. Before you took up with her, so it's not really like we been steppin' out on you. But I'm gonna make it plain now—"

Unable to help himself, an adrenaline surge of relief swelling up from the deepest pit of his stomach. Stopping only when he noticed that the two older people in the booth were paying no attention to him whatsoever.

"Oh, Daddy," Miranda said, in a small, wistful voice. Reaching out her hands to Archie, running one palm along the side of his rugged brown face. "Daddy, Daddy, Daddy."

"That's right. An' I can give her what she wants," Malcolm started up, still unable to control his mouth. "I'm gonna take her to Hollywood, so she can be a real star. Big man like you, Archie, always get yo'self some other white girl—"

"Shut up, Red!"

"A white girl?"

Archie looked back and forth between Malcolm and Miranda, his face now filled with an incredulous, bitter mirth.

"A white girl. So that's it. And you let him think so, didn't you, baby?"

He gripped Miranda's hand in his again, kissing it along the line of her knuckles, then carefully let it go. Retrieving his .45 from the table and placing it carefully in an inner pocket of his jacket before he hauled himself up out of the booth. Moving right at Malcolm, who retreated a couple steps before him, still holding up his pistol.

"Don't make me shoot you!"

"Red, Red," he said, shaking his head. "She as colored as you or me. I thought you knew that. Her brother even got a church up here in Harlem."

"That's a lie!" Malcolm shouted then—thinking even as he did on all those skin creams and complexion whiteners in her bathroom cabinet. Remembering, now, who her face reminded him of the very first night he met her. That same, nearly white minister from the train—

"But that's what you wanted, wasn't it? Someone thinkin' you were a great white lady. Worshipin' you for it. Wasn't that it?" Archie said, looking back at her now.

"You were the last thing I'll ever love in my life," he said, and Miranda turned her head abruptly down toward the table again, as if she were dodging a slap.

"You're just tryna trick me!"

"Go ahead an' ask her," Archie said, shrugging. "She ain't a white girl. Her name ain't even Miranda."

Archie came toward him—and Malcolm was shocked to see that there were tears flowing freely down his cheeks. He pushed Malcolm's gun casually out of the way, and pulled him into a bear-hug, squeezing him until he thought his ribs might crack. Then he kissed him forcefully on the forehead, and pushed him away.

"I don't care about the money, Red," he whispered to him. "I just wanted to make sure you was all right. That's the only reason I put it out on The Wire."

He patted him once on the shoulder, then turned to pick up his hat and walked on out the door. Malcolm standing there with the gun still in his hand, the bar coming alive behind him again.

"Son, you wanna put that away—," the bartender called out—Malcolm ignoring him.

"That ain't true. Is it?" he asked Miranda instead, the words still bubbling out of him. "He just sayin' that to throw me, ain't he—"

But she only looked at him, letting him babble on some more. Her beautiful face nearly hidden in darkness now, silhouetted as it was in the setting sun through the window.

"Goddammit, Red," she said at last, her voice more sorrowful than angry. "Goddammit, Red. How much of a child can you be?"

"But you said—"

"You said it didn't matter. At least you acted like that. You said you never met anybody like me, never loved anybody like me, black or white!"

"I know," Malcolm said, his mouth dry as cotton against his tongue now. Barely able to look at her there in the booth—tears running down her cheeks now. So everybody can cry but me.

"I know I said that. But you didn't love me, did you? Ain't that the whole story? You liked bein' the big white lady to me, didn't you?"

"Ah, Red," she wept, and raged at him. "Ah, you were so god-damned innocent!"

"But you was just playin' with me, wasn't you? And with Archie, too, I suppose. Weren't you?"

She looked down at the table again, unable to say anything else through her tears, and he dropped the gun in his pocket, and followed Archie on out the door of the La Mar-Cheri. Walking slowly, without any real idea of where he was going. Barely noticing the men starting to run past him on the sidewalk, their excited shouts, or the wail of sirens in the distance.

CHAPTER TWENTY-SIX

JONAH

He had just settled his father into bed at the church when he heard the shouting—the shouting and the sound of running feet, rushing over them like a great wind. Their strange, wild chant, nearly incomprehensible, but telling him all that he needed to know, once he was sure that he had heard it correctly.

He was worried that he had overtaxed the old man, having had him out for so long on such a humid day. But his father had only seemed to grow stronger, even loquacious, the more that people came over to greet them. Basking in the rain-forest heat, the mobs of promenaders strolling down Seventh Avenue and on up Lenox. The women in their best chiffon dresses and flowered hats, their pocketbooks and shoes dyed to match. The men in their white linen suits, coming out to chat and ogle even if they hadn't been in church.

And everyone coming over to Milton, even the worst hustlers and sharpies and glamour girls. Looking so genuinely happy to see him alive that tears came to Jonah's eyes. And all of them shaking his own hand, as well. The word already out about his sermon, some of his congregation even exclaiming exultantly behind him, for the first time he could remember, *"Rev'rend* preached *today!"*— so that he had to smile, though he told himself he was just pleased to be out with his father on his arm.

The Sunday like so many he remembered from growing up in Harlem and even before, down on Columbus Hill—before all the years of separation and doubt, all the worst years of the Depression. A warm, slow day. Everyone out in their best clothes, and looking well enough, happy enough—even if there weren't so many young men around. Even if he could still see the little groups of angry men and women, gathered on their stoops, reading their newspapers and letters to each other. Fighting to ignore the hole inside himself as well—the fact that his wife had still not returned.

He thought, of course, that he should have done this years before, even though he pushed the idea down as completely unhelpful. Certainly, it had sparked his father. Milton still hadn't wanted to go home, even as the afternoon began to dwindle and Jonah insisted on starting him back to the church. There the Spottswoods had made them a light summer meal, but the two of them, father and son, had remained both too exhilarated and too anxious to eat much of anything. The absence of Amanda still hanging heavily between them. Milton talking more than he had in months to cover it, reminiscing at random about his brothers and sisters, and his father.

"I never could find him," Milton told him, after Jonah had finally prevailed on his father to leave the chair at his desk, and actually lie down on the stiff metal cot.

"That's what always ate at me. Couldn't find him down there. All those bodies laid out like that. Just brought back that skull. But nobody could tell me it was him. Nobody could tell me it was even a black man's, for all their talk about the races."

"You found the church, instead."

"I know. But he was a proud man, my Daddy. Wouldn't want his bones lyin' down in a slave state like Virginie, all these years."

Milton chewed at his lip for a little while more, frowning contemplatively, until a mischievous look unexpectedly crept across his massive face—the ghost of a laugh wheezing up from his chest.

"But—he sure as hell be glad he got outta South Carolina!"

Jonah stayed with him until he nodded off. Watching him there in the late summer light, unaccustomed to seeing his father's big head in repose. He was still there with him, just happy to watch him sleep, when he heard the shouting and the running feet like a rush of wind—like a wave rolling over them. It surprised him, he had to admit that, not having suspected the day and the hour—but he couldn't say he was really shocked. Watching the excited people, men and women of all kinds, running past the front door of the church. Listening for some minutes to their wild, garbled yells before he could finally discern what they were saying—the words so at odds with the gleeful, carnival expressions on their faces.

"White man kill black soldier! Get the white man! Get the white man! He's to blame!"

By the time Jonah got back to his office, the phone was already ringing. He took and made half a dozen calls to other ministers, trying to piece together what had happened.

"Word is some white cop killed a colored soldier at the Braddock," Earl Ward, Adam's vigorous assistant minister from down the block, finally told him.

"Oh, no. Is it true?"

"We don't know. But it's just like '35 already," Ward said. The situation they had been dreading ever since then, when a rumor had spread that a store dick had killed a colored boy for shoplifting at Kress's, and the looting and burning, and the rage had spread all through Harlem before anyone could quite understand what was happening.

"Where's Adam?" Jonah asked automatically, wanting to bite his tongue even as he did.

"He's up in Oak Bluffs. There's no way he can get back tonight. The mayor wants any ministers who can make it down at the Twenty-eighth Precinct."

"All right."

Brother Peter Moore and most of the other deacons had already begun to gather in the nave of the church, asking Jonah what they could do. He gave them, and the Spottswoods, directions, telling them to keep the doors locked and fill anything they could with water, in case of fire. His orders sounding unreal to him even as he gave them, certain that no harm would fall to the New Jerusalem. The Spottswoods wanted to know about moving his father, but the old man was still sleeping through all the commotion, and Jonah instructed them to move him only in an emergency.

"I'll be back as soon as I can," he told them, and went out on the street, following the crowds.

Everyone was still moving downtown, no one doing anything more than shouting, but all the stores and bars he passed were already shutting their doors. The sheet-metal mangles slamming down onto the sidewalk like rolling thunder, one after another. *The big circus closing down for a night.*

At the end of the block he saw Jakey Mendelssohn and his cousin, standing grimly outside their department store. The store was shut up tight behind them, but both of them were holding baseball bats—the cousin's big cow eyes staring out at the world more fear-fully than ever.

"You should take him inside," Jonah told him, gesturing at the people running down the street like madmen. "You should go, too."

"This is my store. I'm not letting anything happen to it—not so long's I can help it," Jakey said truculently, looking through Jonah to the excited crowds hurrying down the sidewalk.

"I'm going down to the Twenty-eighth Precinct now, I'll do what I can about getting some protection up here. Don't be fool-ish!"

"It's my store!" Jakey repeated, flinging up his arm contemptu-ously in its direction.

"Get him inside!" Jonah told him again, backing down the street, hurrying as the mob was hurrying now.

He had thought about stopping back at Strivers Row first and getting the big green Lincoln, figuring it would be quicker to maneuver around Harlem. But as he went on he saw that the crowd was still swelling, overflowing the sidewalks and blocking traffic. At 135th Street they had clotted around Harlem Hospital. Hun-dreds, maybe thousands of men and women, simply milling around in the dark, talking excitedly to each other.

"This where they took him! They inside right now!"

"This where the white cops took him!"

Every time the door to the emergency ward opened, a shout would go up, and the crowd surged in a little closer. A sea of dark faces pressing toward the entrance, shouting out questions at any-one they saw in a white coat—"*Is he alive? Is he still alive?*" Groaning in disappointment until a man boosted himself up on a corner mail-box—teetering on its rounded sides there, waving his arms wildly to get their attention.

"He prob'ly dead already!" he shouted out. "You think they wouldn't say if he was still alive? He dead already! What you waitin' for?"

The crowd roared, surging forward and then back, the man on top of the mailbox toppling into their midst. A bottle smashed against the wall of the hospital, then another, and then people started to break away, running along the side streets, and on down-town.

Jonah heard a steady *pop-pop-pop* sound, and turned to see a group of teenage boys racing along Seventh Avenue, knocking out every streetlight as they ran by. Hitting them with lengths of pipe, table legs, even tree limbs they had pulled down. The block went instantly dark, and he heard the sound repeated again and again in the distance—*pop-pop-pop*—echoed by a heavier, more ragged series of reports that sounded very much like gunshots. The people around him still whooping and laughing giddily, raising the same strange cry he had heard before—

"White man kill black soldier! Get the white man! Get him!"

He plunged on down toward the precinct house, and 125th Street—and as he did, he heard the heavier, crushing sound of whole plate-glass windows falling. All along the avenue now, people were smashing at things. The front display windows of all the big stores, Blumstein's and Orkin's, Koch's and Lerner's and McGrory's, were already cleaned out. The denuded white store mannequins, headless or missing limbs, lying strewn out along the sidewalk. A pretty young woman stepped over one of the dummy corpses, and kicked daintily at a remaining section of window glass. A man chivalrously held her hand while the people around her egged her on—*"Tha's it! Tha's it, girl!"* She smiled shyly at the attention, and pushed away the remaining shards of glass with her toe, her companion helping her on up into the window where she posed for a moment, just like the displaced mannequins, before dissolving into giggles. As she did, three teenage girls passed her on the way out—their faces dreamy, holding yards of puffy party dresses bundled up in their arms.

But it was not just the big stores that were being cleaned out, Jonah saw. People were smashing their way into pawnshops and grocery stores, bars and liquor stores, furniture and clothing and jewelry shops. Twisting the protective mangles and metal gates right off their hinges with terrible metallic squeals. Smashing the glass with bricks or ashcans, or the things they had taken from other stores.

They jumped inside, grabbing for whatever they could in the darkness. Howling and cursing as they cut themselves on the jagged remains of the plate glass, but most of them still laughing—the carnival feel of the wartime City at night still prevailing. The poorest, shabbiest-looking people in the crowd leading the way, some of the men not even wearing shirts. Jonah was sure that he could recognize many of them from the little aggregations he had been seeing all summer out on the stoops and curbs, stoking and nurturing their anger. Their faces now distorted with excitement, with amazement, with sheer wonder at what they had done.

He could see the better-dressed men and women on the street, too, in their hats and suspenders and Sunday show-off shoes, only watching at first, their faces animated with a mixture of suspicion and disbelief. But then they plunged in, as well—visibly shrugging and jumping in to take what they could from stores that were already wrecked beyond salvation anyway, hauling away whole armfuls of merchandise. Not just the things of obvious value—fancy dresses and suits, slabs of beef and bottles of liquor, jewelry and coats and radios from the pawnshops—but anything and everything they could use, every little necessity, or not. They took milk and bread, and cans of beans and peas, and sardines and dog food. Boxes of cornflakes and laundry detergent, towels and bedsheets and mattresses, pots and pans and dishes. Tubes of toothpaste and single shoes, and shoehorns; eyeglass samples, and pawned mandolins and flutes and accordions. Boxes of baking soda and bandages and cans of Flit; bottles of vinegar, and hot-water bottles and pairs of socks, and of course jars and jars of all those cold creams guaranteed to erase that outer, darker layer of skin.

Jonah tried to stop them at first. He shooed one group away from a grocery, pulled others out of a Florsheim's window—those particular looters shamed by his clerical collar. But more just slapped his hands away, or casually shouted curses at him, only moving on to another store when he could move them at all.

He gave it up finally, wandering down 125th Street and just watching the mob going about its business—amazed to see how many *things* there were. It was as if all of Harlem had been turned inside out before him, like the stuffing of a pillow. The sidewalks carpeted with loose clothing and bedding. Groups of looters staggering down the street together, trying to haul away dressers, vanities, entire kitchen and bedroom sets. Others had already set up shop on the curb, where they were eagerly reselling things they didn't want or didn't need at cut-rate prices. The big things they couldn't do anything with—emptied cash registers, industrial scales, refrigerators and iceboxes from the backs of stores—lying smashed out in the street like so many flattened waterbugs.

All this stuff, Jonah thought, staring at it. *And all this wanting. Who could have suspected there were so many things, hidden away behind store windows, and guards? What could have been done with it all?*

Some store owners had been quick-witted enough to post signs announcing their color, but mostly the mob either didn't believe them, or it didn't care. At C. D. King's shoe store there was a gaping hole in the glass, just below where someone had chalked the plea, *COLORED STORE—NEGRO*—the shelves and trees all stripped of their shoes. Jonah watched as a bunch of men lined up a clothing dummy at the window of the bar at the Hotel Theresa, only to be stopped by another man who ran over, telling them, erroneously—*"Don't break out that window, ol' man. That's Joe Louis's hotel!"* They acquiesced—moving the dummy a few windows on down, to bash in the front of A. Philip Randolph's National March on Washington headquarters.

A lone bus intervened in their revels just then, somehow not having been warned off. It tried to nudge its way through the crowd, stopping momentarily in the middle of the 125th Street intersection as if it were stalled, or the driver couldn't make up his mind whether to try to continue. A barrage of bricks instantly smashed in its windows, and for a moment Jonah could see the faces of the passengers inside. Almost all of them colored, fearful, and stunned—one woman's face already covered in blood, her mouth gaping open.

The bus accelerated again, plowing determinedly uptown now. The mob scrambled out of its way, but there was a new, more voracious edge to their shouts and screams. Men began to knock over the wooden pushcarts that were parked all along the street, the stands of the hot-dog and fruit and ices vendors, who had already fled. They set them on fire where they lay—more small fires flickering up inside the emptied stores now as well.

Jonah watched, and cursed to himself, hurrying the rest of the way down to the Twenty-eighth. The precinct house was surrounded with patrol cars, civil-defense and army trucks, fire engines, and lines of MPs and cops ringed the block, their batons and nightsticks in hand. They stared at him stonily when he approached, but a police sergeant spotted his collar and led him on into the station. Taking him down into a large, airless basement room where hundreds of people were streaming in and out, most of them cops and MPs—but also dozens of colored men and even women.

Jonah realized that he recognized most of them—could even call them by name. They were his fellow ministers and pastors, church deacons and deaconesses, ushers and air wardens and auxiliary police, volunteers and activists of every stripe. *All the respectable Negroes, come to save the reputation of the race,* he couldn't help thinking—all except the ones who had been caught out of town at some summer resort. They were solemnly accepting armbands and whistles, nightsticks and steel civil-defense helmets—all these kindly, sociable, thinking, meddling, responsible people, transformed by the oversize, faintly ludicrous steel helmets. Blinking at each other as if confused themselves over who they were.

Jonah was nudged along to where the mayor himself stood. The wide little man immersed in sweat, but uncharacteristically composed and civil in the sweltering, chaotic room. Working a bank of phones and police radios with his police commissioner, sending a bevy of cops and assistants scurrying to carry out orders. He wrung Jonah's hand at once when he was presented, pulling him along with him, back out of the room and up the stairs.

"We got a report they're tryna take out the New York Central station, at 125th an' Park. Will you come with me?" he asked him very earnestly.

"Certainly—" Jonah started to say, having no idea what he could possibly do to keep a mob from taking over an elevated train station. But before he could say anything else he was pushed into the backseat of an open car, next to Walter White of the NAACP—La Guardia insisting on riding on the side closest to the sidewalk himself.

"No offense, gentlemen, but they know my face better 'n yours!"

They sped off toward the elevated train tracks—Jonah realizing belatedly it was just the three of them alone, without any accompanying police or MPs. Stopping almost immediately on La Guardia's orders—the mayor rearing up to his full five feet, cupping his hands and yelling at a group of teenage boys pawing through the innards of a butcher's shop.

"Put—that—stuff—down!"

The youths looked up, saw the mayor standing there just above the door of the car—and turned and ran. The car sped on to the rail station, only to find the whole area peaceful, the train and track unmolested, La Guardia swearing under his breath.

"We need better information!" he barked. "Let's get back!"

They wheeled around and headed back toward the Twenty-eighth Precinct house again, the trip long and dizzying, like some funhouse ride, Jonah felt La Guardia ordered his driver to stop half a dozen times more on the way, so that he could yell at looters. But now most of them only stared at him, and at White and Jonah, when they tried to appeal to them to stop. A milk bottle was even hurled in their direction—barely missing the mayor's head, smashing on the street behind them. Others freely cursing and taunting them, once they saw they had no police with them.

"Go back downtown!"

"We don't need *you!* We don't need yo' goddamned white man's war!"

Their faces twisted in bottomless, vindictive anger, beyond anything Jonah could ever remember seeing. Even La Guardia finally ceased ordering the car to stop, all three of them only staring glumly out at the rioters as they passed. The looters indifferent in turn to their presence. Jonah saw an old man, gorging himself directly from a fountain-parlor vat of vanilla ice cream. A group of teenage boys grinned and postured, cavorting about with silk top hats and blond wigs on their heads, necklaces and dress coats hung over their shoulders. A lean, toothless old woman hauled along a teenage boy by the arm—his eyes still half hooded with sleep, her other hand clutching a pair of pillowcases. She found an opening in the broken window of a grocery store and climbed in with surprising agility, pulling the boy in along with her. They filled the pillowcases with cans, and boxes of cereal, and stepped out again, all in the time it took their car to pass. The boy still looking half asleep, the old woman's toothless mouth smiling sublimely.

Jonah turned away, ashamed to bear witness to such sights in front of a white man—and as he did he noticed that Walter White had had to look away, too. La Guardia tapping White's knee as if trying to console him, his face somber and not unkind.

"It's just some bad apples," the mayor kept repeating stubbornly. "Just some bad apples, we got 'em in every neighborhood!"

They pulled back into the station house, lit up now like an aircraft carrier, with portable klieg lights and headlights, and the constant whirring sirens from a dozen vehicles. In the brilliant, flickering yellow-red-and-blue illumination, Jonah could see two long lines of colored people, moving past each other. One was that of the volunteers he had seen before, with their nightsticks and helmets, moving out to the streets. Passing them was an almost equally long line of looters, under arrest—most of them still carrying the merchandise they had been picked up with. Jonah noticed the teen-age girls he had seen before at Blumstein's, their bouffant dresses still clutched to their chests, their faces somber and teary-eyed now.

As soon as he was out of the car, Captain Harding, the com-mander of the Twenty-eighth Precinct rushed up to him, a large bruise and a bandage plastered just over his left eye.

"That wounded soldier is askin' for you. You wanna go see him? He's at Harlem Hospital."

"He's asking for *me?*" Jonah asked, bewildered.

"He says he don't know nobody else in Harlem! I can send you up there with the sound truck."

"All right," Jonah assented, more perplexed than ever.

Minutes later, he was slowly making his way back up Seventh Avenue in a sound truck from WNYC, the city-owned radio sta-tion. Roy Wilkins from the NAACP, and the Reverend John John-ston from St. Martin's, and Bishop Jones from Methodist Episcopal beside him in the close, suffocating interior. Taking turns blaring messages to the crowds along the street. Each of them turning back to the rest and looking slightly embarrassed, slightly guilty after they did—confronted with the full extent of both their impotence, and their responsibility.

"The rumor that a Negro soldier was killed at the Braddock Hotel tonight is *false!* He is only slightly wounded and is in *no* dan-ger. Go back to your homes! *Don't* form mobs or break the law! *Don't* destroy in one night the reputation as good citizens you have taken a lifetime to build!"

—Jonah cringing at the unintentional suggestions—*Negro sol-dier killed... Don't mob, don't destroy, don't take a lifetime! And what reputation, what law?*

Their appeals were greeted with more raucous shouts and obscenities. A steady hail of bricks and bottles began to strike the roof, falling from such a height their impressions dented the ceil-ing, making them all duck. Out the back window, Jonah could see more bottles and cans and bricks falling steadily on the patrol cars accompanying them. Even as he watched, a man rushed out to one of Commissioner Valentine's patrolling motorcyclists, breaking a bottle over his wrist. A small gush of blood spurted up, the man running off—the motorized cop wobbling and crashing his cycle up against the curb.

. . .

The emergency ward at Harlem Hospital was awash in blood. Thick red rivulets ran freely down the floor, the orderlies mopping at it continually, until their heavy mops were saturated with it and Jonah was sure that dozens had perished. He was relieved to see no bodies, but the whole room was filled with bleeding people, cops and MPs and passersby cut by bottles, and sometimes knives. More looters under arrest—these, too, still made to carry their loot— slashed by nightsticks, or shards of broken window glass. Everyone holding on to bleeding arms, legs, faces, the blood oozing through their fingers. The surgical gowns and even the masks of the doctors and nurses covered in it.

Jonah was taken upstairs to a secluded ward. It was guarded by an outer perimeter of cops, and at the door by two big MPs, one white and one colored, both holding their nightsticks out. And inside, on the edge of his bed—sat Robert Bandy. His dark brown, almond-shaped face looking younger and more bewildered than ever. His left arm in a sling, the right one still manacled to the iron bed frame.

"Oh, Robert," Jonah said, exhaling softly. "Tell me it's not you."

"I'm sorry, Rev'rend," the private said, ducking his head involuntarily, as if taking his words as a blow. "I'm so sorry, Rev'rend, I didn't mean to get you into this. I just don' know nobody else, an' I'm worried about Mama."

"I'm already in this, Robert," Jonah assured him, pulling a chair up next to him. "You didn't do anything to me. How are you feeling?"

"I'm all right," Bandy said softly, trying to smile—the effort flickering out just as it passed his lips. "A little nervous, I guess. I don't feel so bad, though. Guess I ain't, if I can sit up here an' shake your hand."

"How'd you get into all this?"

"Ah, there was this woman in the hotel," he tried to explain, his eyes looking more and more hurt and desperate as he did.

"A woman?"

"Yeah, just some woman. She didn't have nothin' to do with me, neither, that's the darnedest thing. You warned us 'bout that hotel, Rev'rend. It's just it was so cheap for Mama—"

"What happened, Robert? With the woman?"

"She got in some argument with this cop. Next thing I knowed he was tryna arrest her—beatin' on her with his stick. She yelled out. She said, 'Somebody save me from this white man!' so I went over with my Mama to see what the trouble was. He try to hit me then, too, so I took the stick away from him an' give him a swat with it. I didn't mean to, Rev'rend—I just got carried away, I guess, when he try to hit me. When I saw him fall down, guess I panicked, tried to run out. That's when he shot me in the shoulder."

Bandy tried to flex his arm in the sling, grimacing slightly as he did.

"It don't hurt so bad, though. I could go back to my unit tomorrow, forget all this mess—"

"That's all right. What we need to do is to get you a lawyer."

"Don' worry about me," he said, glancing nervously toward the window, through which they could clearly hear the sounds of the riot. "I just want 'em to stop this carryin' on over me. I wouldn't agree to it—won't do me no good. I want you to see about Mama, an' let Susan know about it."

"Where is your Mama now, Robert?"

"They arrested her with me, took her down to the precinct. She helped take that cop's stick away. I don't want nothin' to happen to her."

"All right, son. I'll do what I can."

He stood to go, and Private Bandy looked up at him—his desolate eyes belying his lack of concern about himself.

"Whatta you think they gonna do to me, Rev'rend? I'm in some trouble now, ain't I?"

Jonah had a quick talk with the police and the MPs out in the hospital corridor, trying to do what he could. But all he could find out was that Bandy was under military detention, awaiting court-martial charges, and that his mother had been taken to the Women's House of Detention. Concluding there was nothing more he could do before morning, he decided to head back to his church, and went out on the street again.

Outside, the wail of fire engine sirens was almost continuous now. Jonah could see more yellow threads of flame flicking up all along Seventh Avenue, and in the middle of the street a car was tipped over on its back, black smoke billowing up from it. The 135th Street trolley came clanging its way across the intersection, making a mad dash for who knew where—and as it did, a group of youths in gang jackets lunged at it, breaking the windows and try-ing to strike at any white faces inside.

"Get the hell out! White man kill black soldier! Get the hell out!"

"We won't fight your cracker war!"

Jonah moved past more wild scenes of people dancing and laugh-ing, and just staggering about in the street. The whole City seem-ingly engulfed in darkness now, with the streetlights smashed and most of the lights in people's windows out, lest they attract some unwanted attention. The street brought to sudden, shimmering life only when a patrol car or a fire engine swept by and all the broken glass was suddenly illuminated, like a wave receding along the sand at night. The darkness folding quickly over it again, bringing only the sound of feet crunching over the broken shards, the pop of more gunshots somewhere in the distance.

All of Harlem seemed transformed to Jonah now, from the gen-tle, even faintly optimistic place it had been just this afternoon. Changed over into something dark and violent, lit only by bril-liant flashes. He knew it was an illusion, of course. He knew that the other, daytime Harlem was still there, had been there all along. But tonight he could not find it. Tonight, he felt blinded by all the seething, random hatred around him, and he ran back to his church, his legs and his lungs pumping slowly in the heavy night air—knowing that there was something to protect.

Malcolm strolled slowly up the avenue, watching all the frantic car-ryings-on around him. Feeling as if he were moving in slow motion, too—the way a projection reel slowed before it started to flap, and give out. Watching passively as the mobs looted stores all around him. Smiling sometimes, such as when he saw some boys carry-ing away an entire stripped carcass of a calf from a butcher's shop, a wino turning around and around in a liquor store as he tried to make up his mind—but never bothering to join in himself.

He followed the crowds when they headed toward some new commotion, ran with them when a detail of police or MPs swept through. He saw one mob of young men surround a couple of white British sailors, knocking them down, kicking them and stabbing one of them in the chest. The man managed to run away, holding his chest and screaming as he did. Malcolm watched him—then walked on up to the curb, where he helped some more men rock a car over onto its top and set it on fire, the choking black smoke rising through the night air.

But then he walked away, still moving uptown. Not sure exactly where he was going or what he was doing. Possessing a vague idea of going back to the St. Nicholas Hotel, where he still had his room, or maybe going to settle things with Sammy the Pimp. Mostly just wanting the hurting inside him to stop, the miserable emptiness to go away.

He looked into each of the gaping, looted storefronts as he passed them, though he was never tempted to venture inside. Sure that he saw a dark figure lying still, just inside the entrance of a ransacked bar. Spotting another body in a vacant lot, a couple blocks later, though no one else seemed to notice or to care.

He heard the sound of another crowd and turned around a corner that seemed familiar, but also strange in the near total darkness. There he saw a dozen men or so, trying to force their way into a small, shabby department store. Thinking that it looked familiar he started toward them, curious to see what they were getting at. So dazed and preoccupied that he didn't hear the police whistle behind him, the shouts of alarm, until the other men who had been trying to batter their way in had turned and begun to run. They ran into him, almost knocking him down. Dislodging his hat in their panic, so that when he stopped and turned to pick it up it was too late to avoid the policeman's hand that reached out for him and him alone. Grabbing him by the collar and pulling him up so hard that he choked, his windpipe cut off. Malcolm certain that he was about to pass out even as he grappled for the gun in his pocket—sure that he was dying, and that that was the only reason he saw that minister who kept dogging him moving toward him once more.

Jonah witnessed the whole scene before him as he came back onto the block. The mob smashing its way into Mendelssohn's. The metal mangle already ripped away, and two men with grim, businesslike expressions on their faces smashing away at the front windows with a couple of ashcans. Jakey Mendelssohn stood off to one side, one arm around that cousin of his. The baseball bat still clutched in his free hand but not interfering, only looking bleakly at Jonah, appealing to him with his eyes, as they began to bash in his storefront.

"Nice. Real nice!" he called out, all of his rage choking in his throat. "Couldn't be any better if I was in Poland!"

But it was the cousin Jonah was looking at. The boy staring out at the shouting, gesturing mob, with his dazed eyes as big as pin-wheels. Jonah suffused with pity for him now, wondering how many times he had seen such a scene before. Striding purposefully toward the looters.

"Stop that!" he shouted at them. The men pausing, but only staring at him sullenly, as if undecided as to who he was.

"Stop that right now!" he yelled again, on them now, seizing the ashcan from one of them, and wresting it out of his hands. Other faces coming up around him now—Jonah exhilarated and relieved to see that they were members of his congregation.

"Get off this block!" he shouted at the looters once more. They hesitated a moment longer, as if still undecided—then began to scatter from the police whistle screeching behind them. Jonah feeling his chest loosen with relief, starting to turn back to Jakey and his cousin, when he saw the cop coming charging into them.

Just a single cop, thick-shouldered and hermetically white, as only the Irish can be. *Just like the cop he had passed for so many years, winking at him at the corner of Strivers Row.* Charging into the crowd of looters, striking randomly at shins and backs. Jonah watching as he grabbed hold of one man who hadn't done anything, was only reaching down for his hat, and yanked him back up by the collar of his shirt. *Not a whole mob, like his father had gone out to face—but a single white cop. Surely he could stand up to that—*

The cop was already frog-marching his collar back down the block. The innocent man grasping desperately at his neck, one hand thrust into his pocket. The members of his congregation stirring behind him, but Jonah paying no attention to them. His eyes on the collar instead, not quite believing who it was even as he approached him.

That boy again. Pursuing him even here.

He ran up to them, laying a hand gently on the cop's shoulder. Trying to talk to him as he stared at the boy's unmistakable face, the hand wriggling in his pocket. *What was he trying to get to? A knife? Worse?*

"Excuse me, Officer, this man wasn't involved—"

The nightstick caught him by surprise. Flashing at him, just above eye level, leaving a scorching line of pain where it met flesh and bone across the top of his forehead. The blood flowed down immediately, like a red shade pulled down over his eyes—but Jonah managed to reach out and catch hold of the cop's arm nevertheless.

Hanging on desperately with both hands, keeping him from yanking the stick back and hitting him again.

"Leggo a me, you black son of a bitch!"

Through the blood, Jonah saw him toss the boy in the street, his hustler's slick shoes slipping and giving way on the broken glass. Jonah still clutching on to the cop's nightstick even as he saw the officer's freed hand slipping down to unbuckle his holster. Reaching for the gun barrel there—Jonah trying to find the words that had been addled in his brain even as the cop kept yelling at him.

"Leggo right now, you son of a bitch or I'll kill ya right here in the goddamned street!"

Then their hands were all over him. Holding him up, wiping away the curtain of blood that kept dropping down over his eyes. Folding something over the cut on his head that stung like crazy, then numbed him—even as he watched more hands lift the cop's nightstick right out of his grasp, and take the gun away from him. The man's arms pinned back behind him until he was totally immobilized. His pasty, absurdly white Irish face only inches from Jonah's own, looking both outraged and terrified.

"He hit Preacher!"

"Shoot his white ass! Think he can come up an' hit a preacher like that!"

"Hit him with that stick, see how *he* likes it!"

"*No!*"

More hands were trying to lead him away, and Jonah reeled, racked with nausea, wanting nothing more than to sit down right on the curb. But he pushed them away—knowing that time mattered now. Knowing that he had to say something, *now*, before it got out of hand.

"Nobody's hitting anyone!" he cried, looking at the worried faces of the men and women from his congregation, standing all around him. Looking at the panicked white face of the cop. Feeling as if he were about to pass out, but knowing that he had to find the words, *now*.

"Give me the gun!" he ordered.

The policeman's .38 special delivered to his outstretched hand—Jonah surprised by the heft and the solid metallic feel of the gun. *No wonder you think you can do anything, carrying this around.* He broke open the cylinder, knocked the bullets into his palm and thrust them into his jacket pocket, then shut it again.

"Give it back to the man! His stick, too! All right, let go of him!"

They did as he told them, although their faces remained wary and cynical—some of them grumbling their dissent. Jonah knowing he had to make this work.

"He just gonna make trouble!"

"He'll have the whole force up here in no time—"

"No one's doing anything!" Jonah snapped, looking the policeman in the eyes where he stood, surrounded by black faces—gun and nightstick back in his belt, exposed as next to useless now. The man still petrified.

"Listen up!" Jonah called out, as much to the surrounding crowd as to the scared Irish cop, but looking him in the eyes. "I'm saying you fired all your bullets in the air, fending off looters and protecting the block. Isn't that right, Officer—?"

"Murphy," the cop said, nodding dumbly. Jonah continuing to look him in the eyes as he talked.

"Officer Murphy. Then you continued to stand on the corner and saw to it that the church and the block were defended all night long. For which I will go to the precinct tomorrow and commend you. 'Less you want me to tell a different story to the mayor, who I was just riding with."

"Yeah, sure. All right," the cop said slowly, looking at the barely mollified faces all around him.

"All right, then! Go back to your post on the corner!" Jonah said.

The circle of people around him grudgingly gave way, and the cop looked all about him. His face still a muddle of fear, rage, hurt, and relief—but he walked slowly off to the corner, doing as he was told. The faces of his congregation still angry, but filled with a newfound respect—looking to Jonah for what to do next.

He quickly doled out more tasks and orders—assigning people to stand guard outside Mendelssohn's, and the church, to watch for fires, and gather water, and keep any outsiders off the block. More people crowding up around him now, touching his face in concern, helping him back toward the church—Jonah letting them carry him along. Feeling nauseous again and barely able to stand, but still searching for one face among them. Finally spotting it—the face of that boy again, moving along warily on the outskirts of the crowd. Jonah stumbled toward him, still wanting to ask him one thing— the boy backing away in alarm even as he did, watching him guardedly from a few feet away.

"What did you do that for?" Jonah called to him, still puzzled by that first time he had seen him, that incident on the train, more than anything else.

"What? Whatta you talkin' 'bout?" the boy called back—no more than a boy, really, Jonah could see that again, despite the grown-up clothes he wore, the gun he undoubtedly carried in his jacket pocket and had been about to use on that cop. *Just a boy*—his face alternately sweet and Satanic, even here and now. Looking as if he wasn't sure whether to be grateful or resentful.

"On the train!" Jonah called to him. "On that train, after you—after you helped us—"

"Yeah? What about it?"

The boy bouncing back and forth on the balls of his feet, as if he were still about to flee—as if worried that any admission might catch him up here.

"What did you jump in the water for?" Jonah asked, at last. "By that whistle-stop—what did you do that for, go and jump in the water in front of all those white people?"

"Oh, that!" the boy shouted back, grinning and shrugging then. His voice barely carrying from across the street, over the wail of the fire engine sirens and the continuous pop of breaking glass.

"I just wanted their attention!" he called over. "Ain't you ever felt like that? I just wanted to make sure they all saw me."

"But *why?*" Jonah called again, unsatisfied, knowing that the boy was about to run off.

"Because they should see me. 'Cause they should get a real good look!" he yelled over, grinning, and then was gone, running into the contentious night.

Jonah tried to get up and go after him—but then he was aware of her hands, her smell around him. Amanda helped him to sit down on the church steps again, and he, grasping at her arm, kissed her as he did.

"Go easy, now. We need to get you a doctor."

Her voice cool and practical as always—but proud of him, too, he could tell. That sound in her voice like a cool drink of water.

"I really preached today. You should've been there!" he babbled.

"I know, baby. I heard."

"Don't ever go away again."

"I won't, baby," she said, smiling and leaning in to gently kiss his mouth. "Not so long as you're here."

EPILOGUE

Because the building inspector insisted that they start from the top, it took them eighteen days to get to the bodies of the Collyer brothers. First they had to clear away the room full of gas chandeliers, and the room full of weapons; the room full of ancient musical instruments, and the one full of used Christmas trees, and the room full of mantel clocks, including the one that was a metal bust of a maiden, with coins still dropping mechanically from her ears. They had to take away the fourteen grand pianos, including the one that was given to their mother as a gift from Queen Victoria, and the ten grand prizes for piano playing, and the certificate of merit for punctuality and good conduct, and the finest library on admiralty law in existence.

They had to dig down through the twenty-seven paintings of buildings painted in blood red paint, and the specimen of a two-headed baby preserved in formaldehyde, and the grandfather clock that played "The Campbells Are Coming." Past the sewing machine and the X-ray machine, and the Magneto-Electric machine and the static machine, and the entire, neatly disassembled Model T, and the estimated 136 tons of accumulated newspapers, saved for the day that Homer Collyer regained his sight and could catch up on everything that had occurred during his fourteen long years of blindness. They had to pull out their mother's silk dresses and her unfinished knitting, and their baby carriages, and their school desks and model trains and bicycles and opera tickets, and Sunday school report cards, and designs for the perfect telescope, and the canning jars of their own excrement that had crashed down upon their heads, before they were able to find and remove the lifeless, half-starved, rat-gnawed, perfectly slug-white bodies of the ghosty men.

As the work crew dug their way down through the house, a brisk wind—the first of the fall—blew through the windows. Dispelling some of the foul vapors emerging steadily from the bowels of the house. Sailing the thousands of loose sheets of paper—the personal letters, and the old bills, and the sheets and sheets of the Braille alphabet for the blind—like old leaves into the streets below, where they were grabbed up and scrutinized by all the people of the neighborhood as they picked idly through the mounds of trash piling steadily up around the house.

Jakey Mendelssohn opened a dusty cardboard box his cousin handed him from the pile. Staring at the pristine white shirt, and the bright red tie perfectly preserved inside. A price tag from Macy's for ninety-seven cents still attached, along with a card dated October 3, 1918: *"To Langley, with many happy returns this day, Pop."*

"To get such a present from a father, and never open it!" he sighed, handing the box back to his cousin, who went on poking and digging through the enormous piles. His eyes more alert now, Jakey thought approvingly. Some of the old blind terror fading—the boy taking more of an interest in things. Jakey had thought of starting him in a high school next month, if his English proved good enough. Not sure just where that might be, now that he was considering giving up on his own stunted department store at last, while he might still get something for it. Dreaming at night of the open potato fields he had driven past, far out on Long Island.

Jonah strolled along the sidewalk with Amanda, taking in the incessant, hivelike activity before them. Watching the old mansion hollow out before their eyes. Their progress slowed by everyone who stopped to talk with them, and shake his hand—men and women from their own congregation, and from many others.

His reputation had spread since the night of the riot. He could see the respect and admiration in people's eyes when they spoke to him now. They had heard the famous story of his bargain with the cop, the whole tale already inflated into some classic story of folk wisdom, of outwitting the white man at his own game. He was now supposed to have converted his forbearance in sparing the white cop's life into great riches, and political power—for his church, his people, himself.

The story fast becoming its own reality. He was here today looking over the deconstructed ghosty men's house at the behest of both

Adam Powell and his old O'Kane patrons. Already appointed to half a dozen official, and quasi-official, and ad hoc boards on the reconstruction of Harlem by the mayor; the Council of Churchmen, the local Democratic clubs—anyone and everyone interested in staking their claim. Adam's wolfish political associates from Café Society, Mr. Jones and Mr. Jack, looking him over with newfound interest.

It wasn't just the story of the cop, he knew, or his finding his voice. He had come into his inheritance, at last. A week ago he had stood at the altar of the New Jerusalem and presided over the funeral of his father, Milton Dove, who had passed in his sleep a few nights before. The old man's chair draped in black, sitting empty behind the altar. His massive face looking as pleased and tranquil in death as it had when Jonah had put him to bed that night. And why not? Having lived to see his church secured, and passed on to his son; his daughter-in-law returned. Jonah had given his eulogy, reciting again the sacred legends of the church. The story of how Milton had gone out into the street to face the mob, and how he had been saved by his mother, that white woman. How he had descended into the South to bring back his father, and had found his church wandering in the Wilderness.

It had been a necessary ritual. By the end of his eulogy everyone in the church was weeping, and the New Jerusalem was his. Amanda sitting up straight and tall in her usual seat, looking lovely and exquisitely dignified in her black dress and veil. The crowd spilling out onto the sidewalk and down the block, like one of Adam's congregations. Adam there, too, in one of the front pews, along with his politico friends. All of them leaping up to shake his hand when the funeral service was done—to affirm his succession before all the rest of Harlem, as if there could be any remaining doubt about it.

He wondered, on the long drive out to Brooklyn to lay his father's body in the ground, if the prize would be worth as much as they thought. The tires of the hearse and the limousines crunching over the nuggets of broken glass that still lay in the street. So much glass shattered during the riot that it could not be replaced; with the war now they simply weren't making enough for civilian use, so that many of the reopened stores still had planks nailed over their windows. Others would never open again, their owners wiped out, without any insurance. Even the Elder Lightfoot Michaux's revival had finally packed its tents and moved on, leaving a small heap of debris and a whirlpool of evangelical pamphlets, blowing all over the neighborhood as a final, insolent salute to the good people of Sugar Hill. For days afterward there had not even been enough milk to go around, and Jonah and the other ministers had had to organize runs over to New Jersey and up to the Bronx, so the babies and children would have enough to drink.

There had been a great show of unity in the immediate wake of the riot. By common consensus it had all been blamed on hoodlums, and a bad element, and on unattended youths. Everyone—even Adam—was talking about how it had not been nearly as bad as Detroit, and praising Mayor La Guardia and the police for their restraint. The mayor had announced that he would do all he could to see to it that the new Metropolitan Life housing project would be integrated. There was much talk of all the grand new things that would be done once the war was over, and the city council had appointed an investigative committee of prominent citizens to root out the underlying causes of the riot, and ensure that such a thing could never happen again—exactly as they had done after the last riot, eight years before.

Jonah had read the editorial in the Amsterdam Star-News, decreeing that "Harlem has sung and danced, when it should have been working and praying"—but in fact the one thing that had mollified people the most was the military agreeing that the Savoy Ballroom could be opened for business again. Already, the servicemen had begun to return, the nightly carnival starting up again. The soldiers and their glamour girls walking the streets, laughing louder and drinking more than ever. But somehow even this felt different—as if they, too, sensed that something had changed, and were trying a little too hard to make up for it. The neighborhood looking inescapably more tawdry, and run-down, with all of those boarded-up windows. As if maybe something had finally and irretrievably been yanked out of Harlem, the old Harlem that Jonah knew, and that—after the years of war and the years of the Depression, after all the years and decades before that of suffering and frustration and hatred, tracing back so far in the life of the City and the life of the Nation, to before Harlem even was Harlem—it could never be put back right again, no matter what miracles of harmony and prosperity were guaranteed for the world when this war was finally ended.

It didn't matter, at least not to his future. Jonah had dutifully signed his name to all the statements of civic unity, and accepted his role on the commissions and committees. Knowing that he was here to stay now, come whatever may—that this was what it meant to give himself over to a place, a church, a people. His people. He wished for it nothing but the best, would give his all to bring about nothing but good, but whether it happened or not—he would be here. Even if the very worst happened, he would be here. And if it was instead, as usual, the big something in between—the in between men's best visions and the very worst, that God had seen to it for whatever mysterious reason was how we were to almost always live—he would be here for that, too. The big empty house on Strivers Row to be filled up first of all with the running of children's feet—with other voices besides those of himself and his wife, that they could love and cherish, and pass it on to.

Even with his sister's voice, maybe. He stopped to pick up an old-fashioned picture postcard the wind had blown down on the sidewalk in front of him from the ghosty men's house. It was a hand-tinted photograph from Coney Island, a picture of a spectacular, illuminated amusement park that had not existed for at least thirty years—the ink on the back long ago rubbed away.

He had been receiving blank postcards himself for the past two weeks now. Arriving from points moving inexorably west, across the country, from Chicago, and Kansas City—then most recently an idyllic shot of a little cottage somewhere in Southern California, next to a grove of orange trees. There was never anything on the back of them, not even a signature, but he had no trouble guessing who they were from.

A few days after the riot, as soon as he had had a moment to himself, he had gone downtown to check on Sophia. Surprised but not surprised to discover that she had thrown up her contract at Café Society. The elegant new apartment on Cornelia Street abandoned just as abruptly, no forwarding address of any kind left behind with the oafish doorman.

His sister, disappearing into the broader, white world. He wondered if he would look up at a movie screen someday and see her face there. Or if she would vanish even more completely, subsumed into marriage, in-laws, a whole new set of ways and customs. Disappearing so thoroughly that one day she would not even be able to remember herself what she had been, and where she had come from. Jonah drawing consolation only from the fact that the postcards had been sent at all, hoping that someday one might include a forwarding address. Wishing only that he could convey again that there would always be a room for her, no matter how long she was gone, if one evening they should hear her uncertain tap on the back door of their home.

He smiled at his wife, and patted her hand where it lay along his arm. Amanda smiling back, reaching up and tracing her finger along the groove that the white cop had put into his forehead, just below the line of his hair. The cut healing up well now along its stitches, though it had stung like hell when the doctor had first put them in, down at Harlem Hospital. Smiling with pride, even as he winced, wondering if it would be as prominent a mark as the one across his Daddy's head.

The wind blew a new shower of paper into the street, and they picked up their stride. Trying not to fall too far behind Adam, who was walking along in front with his politico pals, and a whole phalanx of O'Kanes and Murphys and Quinns, sent down from Ed Flynn in the Bronx. Pacing back and forth, all around the corner lot of the Collyer property, moving ostentatiously through the curious, sightseeing crowds drawn from all the surrounding neighborhoods. The streams of colored people who lived on the block, and the battalions of Irish cops and City workers, and the Jews and Italians and Puerto Ricans who came from just over in East Harlem, all to see to the demolition and disposal of the ghosty men's house.

Charlie O'Kane was gesturing munificently at the property before them, trying his very best to appease Adam. Explaining once again just how many brand-new, public-housing apartments might be squeezed into a project on such a grand corner lot. Explaining how one or two of the skilled men working on the site might even be Negroes—in exchange, of course, for letting the all-white Metropolitan Life project go through as planned.

And Adam Powell, walking along with him, had grinned around the pipe clenched in his mouth. Nodding his head vigorously, as if he understood and agreed with all that the O'Kanes were saying even as Jonah, watching from a distance, could tell how much they were deceiving themselves. Ready for it when Adam swung his great head back, exploding in that infinitely gleeful, infectious laugh of his.

"Oh, no!" he exclaimed, so loud that heads turned all up and down along the site of the ghosty men's old place.

"Oh, no! It's going to take so much more than that!"

Malcolm made his way back to the observation car at the rear of the train. Knowing that the conductors weren't fond of free riders, especially young colored men coming back here amidst the white passengers, but not really caring. Just as glad, actually, to see the white mothers and children there eyeing him warily, even picking up to go. The older white men rattling their newspapers and settling them in front of their faces—their open conversations ruined, but damned if they were going to move for any black boy.

He ignored them, standing in the very back of the car with its glassed-in open roof and three-quarter walls. Watching the sun go down over the top of the woods, and the marshes and bogs of the South Shore of Massachusetts. Watching the birds roosting by the hundreds in the slowly darkening summer trees, knowing that they would be cawing away raucously to each other until the last light of the day.

There was another indignant rustle of paper behind him, a stomp of feet and the scent of a cheap cigar leaving, and Malcolm settled himself down in the last seat of the car. Breathing deeply and contentedly, as if he could actually inhale the rapidly cooling, late summer evening air through the train glass. His body still feeling limp and exhausted, but at peace for the first time in days now.

After his narrow escape from the cop on the night of the riot, he had gone back to the St. Nicholas Hotel, and slept almost nonstop for the next two days. Then he had gone down to Pennsylvania Station and used his free trainman's pass to get on the first train he could out of town. Taking a taxi all the way down, keeping his head low just in case anyone was still looking for him. Deciding to head back up to Boston for a little while, at least until he could sort everything out. Sure that Jarvis or even Ella would let him stay with them until he got himself situated again. Feeling the first, awakened desires of new hope, new ambitions, the wish to see old friends and even his stepsister, Ella, again.

In the meantime he sat in the last seat of the observation car, heading north, and watched the land slide gently into darkness behind him. The last evening light making him think about Michigan, and how it looked and felt when he was outside with night coming on, delivering his newspapers, or making his way back home. He thought about his brothers and sisters, then, and his father, and even his mother, in the hospital in Kalamazoo. Seeing all of their faces in the brilliant gold and purple rays of the sun setting behind the tree line to the west. And emblazoned there above them all, he could see the kindly face of the Prophet, Elijah Muhammad, who had first told him that he was certain to fall.

He shielded his eyes from the image, from the last, piercing rays of the setting sun. Still not certain how much he wanted to see of it—still thinking more of what hustles he could pull with Jarvis up in Boston, of girls and cars, and big money, and doing what he liked. Yet knowing with certainty now, as he peered into the fading summer sunlight, that he was surely moving toward his own glorious destiny.

A GLOSSARY OF NAMES, WORDS, AND EXPRESSIONS

Many of the expressions defined here came from the Harlem jive of the day, and for them I am indebted to the *Amsterdam News's* tireless Dan Burley. Burley must have worked without ceasing in the 1940s, turning out not only weekly columns on entertainment, society, and sports, but also serious pieces of reporting on racial injustices, and the mistreatment of black workers and soldiers around the country…and ongoing, joyous accounts of the latest developments in Harlem's ever-evolving, hep argot.

It should be remembered that jive was not, of course, the regular, everyday language of Harlem. It was, instead, the selective language of self-styled hipsters—club denizens and jazz musicians, gangsters and glamour girls, and all the wannabes—and even then, it seems to have been spoken at most times with considerable irony and playfulness. Nonetheless, it is astonishing to see how long jive's legacy has been; how many of its expressions and turns of phrase have lasted, influencing what was thought to be the fresh patter of both the 1960s and hip-hop nation.

Not all of the expressions below are from jive, of course. Others have roots even further back in African-American, Caribbean, and African history, or are the professional verbiage of trainmen, musicians, cops, robbers, and others; or they are simply general, New York slang of the 1940s. I have included as well the names of a few individuals who have passed from the public consciousness—often with good reason. Readers should keep in mind that some expressions had different meanings in different places.

ABC BOYS: Inspectors from the state liquor board, or "Alcoholic Beverages Commission (or Control)"

BEALE STREET: In Harlem, an area of cheap, often after-hours bars and music joints along West 133rd Street. After the famous Memphis street.

BEAT UP MY GUMS: Talk all about.

BILBO: Theodore Bilbo, a noxious, aggressively racist, populist senator from Mississippi.

BLUE: Police.

BOOTED TO THE PLAY: To be hip, understand what's going on.

BUFFET FLAT: A whorehouse.

BULLS: Police.

BULVAN: Yiddish, for oaf.

BUNKER HILL APPLE: Boston, in jazz vernacular, just as New York was the Big Apple, Chicago the Windy Apple, etc.

BUST DOWN: Get high.

BUST SUDS: Wash dishes

BUTTERFLIES: Homosexuals, transvestites.

CALKEENER BROADS: Live-in domestics.

CANNON: Broadway.

CAPONS: Homosexuals.

CHACHEM: Yiddish, for wise guy.

CHAISERIM: Yiddish, for swine.

CHALK CHICKS: White women.

CHEESE AN' CRACKERS, JACK!: An exclamation, as in "Good grief!"

CHIPPIES: Women, usually loose.

CHOLLY HOSS: For "Charlie Horse," a way of saying "buddy," or "homeboy."

COLLAR SOME WINKS: Go to sleep.

COLUMBUS HILL: The area near the current site of Lincoln Center, from 57th to 64th streets on Manhattan's Upper West Side. Soon after large numbers of African Americans settled there in the late nineteenth century, it was popularly called "San Juan Hill," for the constant assaults on are blacks by local Irish Americans and other whites.

COMING ON THAT TAB: Falling for something, or going along with something.

CONK YOU UP: In this context, not the agonizing hair-straightening process, but a threat to knock one silly.

COP A SQUAT: Take a seat.

COP A TROT: Take walk.

DEAD-BEAT FOR SHUT-EYE: Wanting to sleep.

DICTY NIGGERS: Blacks who try to imitate white people, or act as if they're above other blacks.

DOPE: In this context, and capitalized, trainman lingo for the B&O Railroad.

DOUBLE BUMPERS: Bottom. Or breasts.

DRACULA: A fine-looking woman.

DRAPE: A suit.

FAUST: A beautiful woman.

FIGGER: Percentage; the payoff a cop would get in protection money.

FINE AS AN OCEAN GULL: A fine-looking white woman.

FINE AS THINE: Doing well.

FINE CARSTAIRS: Fine stuff, often used for a good-looking woman.

FINIFF: A five-dollar bill.

FOUR HORSEMEN: Four notoriously tough, no-nonsense black cops in Harlem, as per *The Autobiography of Malcolm X*.

FRAILS: Women.

GAGE: Marijuana.

GATE: In this context, a friend. Can also be a gun.

GLAMOR GIRLS: Good-time, party girls, particularly during World War II.

GONIFFS: Yiddish, for thieves.

GOYIM: Yiddish, for gentiles.

GRAYS: Whites.

GUNNING HER RAY: Looking over.

GUNNING THE HENS: Checking out the women.

HARD-HITTING GRAY: Good-looking white woman.

"HE SURE CAN READ OUT OF HIS HAND": An expression used to express admiration for an inspiring sermon in a black church. It has its origins in slave days, when the first black ministers—not officially allowed to read, or own a book—would hold up their hand to symbolize a Bible, and give a sermon based on what they had heard and memorized from white services, and/ or their own thoughts.

HEAVY ON ALL FRONTS: A lot of trouble.

HEN: Woman.

HICKORY STICK: A twenty-dollar bill, for Andrew Jackson, or "Old Hickory."

HIPPED TO THE PLAY: Aware of what's going on.

HOME FROM ROME: A variation on "homeboy."

HOOF RIFFS: Dancing.

HOT ICE: Stolen jewelry.

'HOW 'BOOT THAT?': How about that?

HURRICANE BLIZZARD: Something extraordinary, usually a beautiful woman.

HURTIG & SEAMON'S: An old name of the Apollo Theater in the days before there was a large black community in Harlem—and when blacks were still not allowed inside.

IORIANS: Trinidadians. Like most Harlem blacks who hailed from the West Indies, they were considered to be overly proud and obnoxious by other African Americans. Islanders, on the other hand, traditionally considered themselves to be harder working and more ambitious than American blacks, and were proud of having been out of slavery for a longer period of time.

ISSUE: A uniform, or "government issue."

JERSEY SIDE: Rhyming slang for "inside."

JUMPING SALTY: Fly off the handle.

KILLER DILLER: A very sharp suit, usually a zoot suit.

KING KONG: Corn liquor.

KISCA: Marijuana.

KITCHEN: The back of a black woman's hair.

KITCHEN MECHANIC: Euphemism for a cook, or dishwasher.

KNOCKING BONES: Playing dice.

KNOCKING HIS GUMS: Spouting off.

KNOCK A STROLL: Take a walk.

KNOCK ME A SHORTIE: Pour me a drink.

KNOCKING YOUR TRILLY: Walking yourself.

LID: Hat, or head.

LIGHT AND BRIGHT AND DAMN NEAR WHITE: In good with someone.

MAIN STEM: 125th Street, or any main drag.

MAKING A FLASH: Making a splash.

MAMMY DODGERS: Men.

MANGLES: The metal storefront guards, pulled down at night (or in moments of danger) over shop windows and doors in New York, and many other cities.

MELLOW AS A CELLO, RIPPIN' AN' ROMPIN', TRIPPIN' AN' STOMPIN': Doing all right.

MEZZROLL: A particularly long, thick joint, after the jazz musician Mezz Mezzrow.

MR. HIGH POCKETS: "Mr. Big Stuff," or a hotshot.

MR. SAMUEL D. HOME: A variation on "homeboy."

NARROWBACK: An Irishman, and usually a workingman.

OFAY: A derogatory term for white people. Commonly thought to come from Pig Latin for "foe," its origin probably goes back to Africa, possibly to the Ibibio word "afia," for "white or light-colored," or the Yoruba "ofe," said to protect one from danger.

OIL UP YOUR HEAD FOR YOU: Hit you upside the head.

OLD SETTLER: An old woman; usually a derisive expression.

OLE AVENUE TRIPE: Nonsense.

ORK: Short for orchestra.

PENNSY: The Pennsylvania Railroad.

PLAYING YOU 14TH STREET: Playing you cheap, 14th Street being known for its cheap and second-rate stores.

PONIES: In this context, the railroad.

PUNIM: Yiddish, for face.

PUT THE TWISTERS TO THE HAMMERS: Turn the knobs and open the doors.

RANKIN: John Rankin, a notoriously racist congressman from Mississippi.

REECHEOUS: Variation on righteous.

REET: Variation on right, or righteous.

RENT PARTY: A longtime Harlem device to raise the rent money, by throwing a party to which all comers would be charged a small admission. By the 1940s, such house parties sometimes turned into venues where perhaps the greatest jazz in the world was played, with top musicians coming up after their gigs to join in ruthless competitions against each other.

RIGHTEOUS PEG: Good-looking suit.

RUGGIN': Flipping out.

SALTY: Mean, grouchy.

SAN JUAN HILL: The area on Manhattan's Upper West Side between 57th and 64th streets, near where Lincoln Center stands now. It was the next stop on the long black march uptown after the Tenderloin, and the one just before Harlem. See "Columbus Hill."

SCHOOL: Teach.

SHORTIE: A small drink.

SHORT: In this context, a car, which "shortens" the time between any two points.

SLAVE: A job.

SLICING YOUR CHOPS: Running your mouth.

SLICING YOUR GUMS: Ditto.

SNITCHPADS: Newspapers.

SOFTY: Pillow, or bed.

SOLID: Great, fine.

SPLIT THE HAMMER: Open the door.

SQUARE SHUFFLER: An honest person, but more likely someone with a dreary, workaday job and a humdrum existence.

STEAMED SEAMS: Nice clothes.

STUMBLE AND FALL: Screw up; get caught by the police, and/ or sent to jail.

TEA: Marijuana.

TENDERLOIN: The old name for the area of Manhattan from Fifth Avenue to Seventh Avenue, and 24th Street to 42nd Street. The City's most raucous entertainment district soon after the Civil War, it was crowded with bars, brothels, clip joints, dance halls, and gambling dens, and thus fat, easy pickings, or "tenderloin," for corrupt police officers seeking protection money. The Tenderloin was another stop on the long, black exodus up Manhattan, between their sojourn in the West Village and that at San Juan, or Columbus Hill.

THE TRACK: The Savoy Ballroom.

THURSDAY GIRLS: Domestics, who usually had their one day off on Friday, and thus would go out dancing and partying on Thursday night.

TOGGED TO THE BRICKS: All dressed up.

TRULY THERE: Really beautiful, or stylish.

UNCLE: In general Harlem parlance, Uncle Sam. In W.D. Fard's terminology, the Lost-Found Shabazz tribe of Original People, in the United States.

'WHAT YOU LAYIN' DOWN': "What are you saying?" or "What are you trying to pull?"

WHISTLE: A brand of soda.

WILD AS A TENOR SIDEMAN HUNTING A ROACH: The marijuana kind, that is. Out of control.

"YOU MIGHT CALL THE COPS, IF THE LIGHTS TURN BLUE": A come on.

YOUNG LANE: Young man.

ACKNOWLEDGMENTS, AND A NOTE ON SOURCES

The first questions on most readers' minds will no doubt concern those parts of *Strivers Row* that involve Malcolm X, Elijah Muhammad, Wallace D. Fard, and the history of the Nation of Islam. There is now and probably always will be a great deal of room for speculation on these matters, but what I have written is based closely upon the actual, documentary evidence.

My starting point for the remarkable story of the man who was born Malcolm Little was, unsurprisingly, *The Autobiography of Malcolm X*. This is, of course, a great American document, a story of transformation and redemption that was—like Malcolm himself, and as much as he would resent the identification—inextricably American.

There can also be no doubt that parts of the *Autobiography* are not strictly factual, or even wholesale inventions. I do not mean this as a criticism. No autobiography can be relied upon for the full truth. Malcolm X's was published after his death, and it was written with a collaborator, Alex Haley, whose adherence to the factual record has been challenged on other occasions. Moreover, the *Autobiography* is not simply Malcolm's life story, but also a political document, a book intended to rally support for a cause that Malcolm himself had not yet fully formulated, and was refining even as he dictated his words to Haley.

The most minimal research quickly reveals that Malcolm X was intent not only on recounting the wrongs done to him by a white supremacist America, which are manifest and undeniable, but also that he was making a case for himself as the leader of a new, as yet inchoate movement for black empowerment. Thus, he has exaggerated the extent of his youthful criminality and bad conduct in some instances, and excised it altogether in others. He makes the classic convert's argument, the claim that by having been the greatest sinner, he has also found the greatest redemption. He has known the depths of black existence in America, thus he can know its pain as well as any other.

Other episodes, which he may have considered too shameful or tawdry, or that otherwise strayed from the image he wanted to present of himself, apparently never made it into Malcolm's *Autobiography* at all. Such is every man's right. Suffice it to say that nearly every incident from Malcolm's life as a child in Michigan, in Boston, on the train, and in Harlem, has been drawn either from the *Autobiography*, or from other, reputable sources. Nothing that Malcolm's character does in this novel is inconsistent with the tenor of his thoughts or actions, even as he presented them himself. These scenes have, furthermore, been drawn with great sympathy for their subject, a man who really did pull himself up from the abyss, whose views on race in America, while sometimes ugly, were always candid; who, ultimately, always proved willing to face the truth, and who was in the midst of transforming himself yet again when he was tragically murdered, before his fortieth birthday.

Once I had read over the *Autobiography* several times, I turned to Bruce Perry's superb biography, *Malcolm, The Life of a Man Who Changed Black America*. This is an assiduously researched, remarkably honest, and revealing book, one that sheds a great deal of light particularly on Malcolm's childhood. It actually bedeviled me with a surfeit of material. Peter Goldman's *The Death and Life of Malcolm X* was also an invaluable source. First published in 1973 by a journalist who interviewed Malcolm extensively, it is a groundbreaking meditation not only on Malcolm's life, but also its broader meaning both for African Americans and for America in general.

Many readers will have found the most outlandish passages of *Strivers Row* to be those concerning Malcolm's encounters with Wallace D. Fard, Elijah Muhammad, and the Nation of Islam. Could Malcolm X have seen visions of Elijah Muhammad before they met? *He* claimed that he did, in the *Autobiography*. Or rather, Malcolm claimed that one night in his cell, in the Norfolk Prison Colony in Massachusetts, he was visited by a "light-brown-skinned" man with "an Asiatic cast of countenance" and "oily black hair," who was suddenly "sitting beside me in my chair."

Malcolm would imply for years that this spectral visitor was Elijah Muhammad. Later, after his break with Elijah, he would claim his visitor was really Fard, the founder of the Nation of Islam, who appeared in a "pre-visit." Malcolm would never meet Fard, and how does one have a "pre-visit" when there is no visit? In the same vein, Bruce Perry notes that Malcolm described the man in his visitation as brown-skinned, while Fard "looked white," according to all surviving descriptions and photographs of the man. Malcolm was also corresponding with Elijah on a regular basis while in prison. Whatever the case, I have only moved his claimed vision up by a few years, and had it occur in a context that augurs his coming conversion, rather than following it.

The whole remarkable story of Fard, Elijah Muhammad, and the Nation of Islam would take up a book in itself. Fortunately, two splendid ones have already been written. Karl Evanzz's *The Messenger, The Rise and Fall of Elijah Muhammad* is a first-rate work of biography, including a meticulous investigation of Fard's cloudy and incredible past, and the stranger-than-fiction efforts of a couple of Japanese agents to turn American blacks into a pro-Japanese fifth column. Claude Andrew Clegg III's *An Original Man, The Life and Times of Elijah Muhammad,* is an equally outstanding work, one that concentrates more on Elijah's early struggles and on the theology of the Nation of Islam.

Doubtless, many will find this theology to be a collection of crackpot theories and mystical nonsense. Yet it is actually no more difficult to swallow than any number of other religious texts; as James Baldwin points out in *The Fire Next Time*, the Biblical curse on Ham was long used in this country to justify slavery and white supremacy. The appeal of the Nation of Islam's creed, like that of almost any religion's, is its metaphorical truth; its story of a people robbed of their homeland, their ancient heritage, their language, culture, and self-respect, by the brutality of the Atlantic slave trade.

The Nation of Islam's history obviously lends itself to other unresolved controversies. To address the primary one head on: I make no claim that W.D. Fard was in fact done away with by Elijah Muhammad. I am only echoing here the accusations made by Elijah's enemies within the Nation at the time—accusations that forced him to flee Detroit in fear for his life. No one actually seems to know what happened to Fard. Karl Evanzz makes a strong case that he returned to California, and perhaps his native New Zealand, and as late as the 1970s, Elijah Muhammad and his son both claimed that he was still alive, and in touch with them. Here again, it is unlikely that we will ever know the whole truth.

Strivers Row is the third and final book of my New York, *City of Fire* trilogy, and faithful readers will remember the introduction of the Dove family in the previous installation, *Paradise Alley*. Jonah Dove, the protagonist here, is an amalgam of Harlem ministers, past and present, but certain parts of his past, including his proclivity (and that of his sister) to "pass" as white, were based on actual incidents in the life of Harlem's most famous minister, Adam Clayton Powell, Jr. For these—as well as for my depiction of the historical Powell in the novel—I am indebted to two more fine biographies, Wil Haygood's *King of the Cats, The Life and Times of Adam Clayton Powell, Jr.*, and *Adam Clayton Powell, Jr.: The Political Biography of an American Dilemma*, by my old seminar professor at Columbia, Charles V. Hamilton. Professor Hamilton will be astonished, I am sure, to discover that I was actually listening.

For descriptions of the glory, and the agony, that was Harlem, I have relied on many sources, most of which were gathered at one of the unsung treasures of New York, the Schomburg Center for Research in Black Culture, a research center of the New York Public Library, located at W. 135th Street and Malcolm X Boulevard, a.k.a., Lenox Avenue. Begun by the black Puerto Rican bibliophile Arturo Schomburg, the center was an invaluable resource, and I recommend it highly to anyone interested in researching anything about Harlem, or the African-American experience.

While on the subject of libraries, I must also express my profound gratitude here for the help provided by the New York Public Library's main research library, at 42nd Street; its branch facilities, especially in my neighborhood, the Bloomingdale branch on West 100th Street; and the Columbia University and Barnard libraries. Many is the happy hour that I have spent at all these facilities—so much so that it is a wonder I ever completed these books.

To name just some of the volumes that were of the most use to me on *Strivers Row*, I will start with the collection, *A Renaissance in Harlem, Lost Voices of an American Community*, edited by Lionel C. Bascom, which extends beyond the chronological years of the renaissance, and which includes everything from essays by Dorothy West to descriptions of a Garvey rally to the wonderful street songs that Harlem vendors used to improvise. Another collection, *Visual Journal: Harlem and Washington, D.C. in the Thirties and Forties*, edited by Deborah Wills and Jane Lusaka, put a photographic "face" on the place and time.

Just as valuable to me in getting a sense of the now-vanished Harlem before the war, was Cheryl Lynn Greenberg's *Or Does It Explode? Black Harlem in the Great Depression;* Nat Brandt's *Harlem At War: The Black Experience in World War II;* Jervis Anderson's *This Was Harlem;* Gilbert Osofsky's *Harlem: The Making of a Ghetto, Negro New York, 1890–1930;* and Jim Haskins's *The Cotton Club.* The Roi Ottley and William J. Weatherby collection, *The Negro in New York, An Informal Social History,* remains even now an unrivaled guide to the entire history of the black experience in Manhattan.

Of course, no research into Harlem of the 1940s would be complete without consulting the writings of James Baldwin. His still-dazzling novel, *Go Tell It On the Mountain;* and the Toni Morrison-edited, *James Baldwin: Collected Essays,* as well as the above-mentioned *The Fire Next Time,* were all a great help. I owe a large debt as well to the many other great African-American fiction writers and journalists to emerge in Harlem and elsewhere during the tremendous intellectual ferment between the wars. These would include first and foremost, but are hardly limited to, Ralph Ellison, Richard Wright, Langston Hughes, Dorothy West, and Zora Neale Hurston. Informing all my understanding of the African-American experience is the work of that formidable intellect and spirit, W. E.B. Du Bois.

Finally, nothing was as valuable to me in uncovering Harlem's past as the morgue of its now-venerable weekly newspaper, the *Amsterdam News* (then the *Amsterdam Star-News*). I spend hours combing through its wartime editions at the Schomburg, and was always enthralled. The *News* provided vital guides to Harlem's political battles, bars and cabarets, street life, cultural activities, church programs, and lingo, and was a courageous voice in protesting atrocities and injustices perpetrated against African-Americans around the country.

Lawrence Otis Graham's candid study, *Our Kind of People, Inside America's Black Upper Class,* was very helpful to me in learning some of the grim rituals of passing, the history of black fraternal organizations, and some of the social life at Oak Bluffs.

The first volume of Taylor Branch's incomparable history of the modern civil rights movement / biography of Martin Luther King, Jr., provided me with the popular names of African-American sermons, and a few tricks of the trade. The Schomburg also contains an almost inexhaustible collection of books on black church doctrines, denominations, rituals, sermons, hymns, and the like. Some of the ones I found most informative included: Professor Hamilton's *The Black Preacher in America; Images of the Black Preacher: The Man Nobody Knows,* by H. Beecher Hicks, Jr.; *The Soul of the Black Preacher,* by Joseph A. Johnson, Jr.; *Flames of Fire, Black Religious Leadership From the Slave Community to the Million Man March,* edited by Felton O. Best; *African American Religion: Varieties of Protest and Accommodation,* by Hans A. Baer and Merrill Singer; *Best Black Sermons,* edited by William M. Philpot; *A Fire in the Bones: Reflections on African-American Religious History,* by Albert J. Raboteau; and *The Black Church in the African-American Experience,* by C. Eric Lincoln and Lawrence H. Mamiya. Deborah Burns was kind enough, at my request, to send me her work *Mothers of Pearls, Mothers of Zion,* which gave me much insight into the role of the church mother.

More general descriptions of New York in this period were informed in good part by two lyrically descriptive, impressionistic books. One of them was Jan Morris's valentine to the vanished city, *Manhattan '45;* the other, my old friend Jeff Kisseloff's *You Must Remember This: An Oral History of Manhattan from the 1890s to World War II*—from whence came, among things, important information on Café Society. Jeff, I finally got to use your work. Stuart Nicholson's biography, *Billie Holiday,* was also very informative about both the singer and the cabarets and halls she played in New York. Kenneth T. Jackson's *The Encyclopedia of New York City* was once again my boon companion on this book, as it has been on the whole *City of Fire* trilogy, and numerous shorter pieces. My copy is so battered by now that I will soon have the happy obligation of updating to the latest edition.

Franz Lidz's *Ghosty Men, The Strange but True Story of the Collyer Brothers, New York's Greatest Hoarders,* is a lovely, poignant history-cum-family memoir, that tells New York's ultimate cautionary story. I have relied upon his research (and upon a chance picture and mention of the Collyers in the *Amsterdam News*), and told their story just as it was recorded. My only embellishments have been their encounter with Malcolm, and the pushing of their grisly deaths back by some four years, from 1947 to 1943.

.   .   .

My meager knowledge of jazz and of the great dance halls of
Harlem was exponentially enhanced by Geoffrey Ward and Ken
Burns's marvelous *Jazz, The History of America's Music,* companion
volume to the magnificent 2001 Burns documentary series, which
I watched avidly. Also very helpful was Gary Giddins's *Visions of
Jazz, The First Century.* These books—along with much earnest
listening to the many, dazzling stars who played Harlem halls and
clubs in the era of *Strivers Row*—gave me some rough foundation in
the medium. Any and all gaffes are my own.

My descriptions of the old dream books were drawn from the
fantastic collection still beautifully preserved at the New York Public Library's main research branch, at 42nd Street—and by their
emaciated descendants, still available at the counters of many newspaper stands in New York to this day.

The Ephemera Press's map and self-guided walking tour, "Harlem
Renaissance, One Hundred Years of History, Art, and Culture," text
by Marc H. Miller, illustrations by Tony Millionaire, design by Kevin
Hein, proved very helpful in quickly pinpointing historic locations.

The background information for Malcolm's very real comic-
book jones came from *Ron Goulart's Great History of Comic Books,
The Definitive Illustrated History From the 1890s to the 1980s;* Richard
A. Lupoff and Don Thompson's *All in Color for a Dime;* and Coulton
Waugh's *The Comics.*

General information about Detroit, I gleaned mostly from Elaine
Latzman's *Untold Tales, Unsung Heroes, An Oral History of Detroit's
African American Community, 1918–1967,* and Arthur M. Woodford's
This Is Detroit 1701–2001.

All of the movies mentioned were actually playing in Harlem
or other Manhattan theaters at the time. I have watched the ones
that were Malcolm's favorites, and I also learned a great deal about
I Walked with a Zombie from Martin Scorsese's documentary com-
mentary on the film.

I would very much like to thank Steve Fabian for the day he spent
taking me around the haunts of his old Harlem childhood. I came to
know Steve through the good offices of Bonnie Claeson and Joseph
Guglielmelli, the delightful owners of one of Manhattan's best independent bookstores, *The Black Orchid,* where I have spent many a
convivial evening.

I would also like to thank my good friends, Dr. Mana Lumumba-Kasongo, and Milton Allimadi, for getting my lazy old self up to the Abyssinian Baptist Church on Sunday morning; my friend, and my brother-in-law's longtime legal colleague, Earl Ward, for showing me around his Strivers Row home; Melissa Jones, for filling me in on typical barber supplies of the 1930s; my wonderful German translator—also a great writer and a cracker-jack gardener in her own right—Ingrid Krane-Mueschen, and Randy and all the guys down at Embassy Florist, on Broadway and 91st Street, for all their help concerning "false jasmine" and altar flowers; the teachers of the Sunday school at The Presbyterian Church at Tenafly, for giving me my first Revised Standard Version Bible, which they will be happy to know is still in use; and my old friend, Melanie Thernstrom, for lending me her very helpful New Oxford Annotated Bible, which I swear I will return to her one of these days.

My wife, Ellen Abrams, has been unstinting in her support and encouragement, as always, through the often-trying times of this project. I love her, and thank her once more for her confidence, her faith, her love, and her boundless affection.

My mother, Claire S. Baker, originally told me about the Collyer brothers, years ago, as an admonitory talk, intended to get me to clean up my room. Didn't work. She also gave me the love, and the care, attention, and security to accomplish all that I have in this life. I only hope that I can give some of it back in the days ahead. My sister, Pamela Baker, and her husband, Mark Kapsch, have been absolute rocks, during what has been a difficult time for our family. They have all my love and respect.

My friend and agent, Henry Dunow, has been as always a steady source of comfort and assistance, even calling from New Zealand to tell me how much he liked this book. At the same time, he did not waver in pointing out what needed to be improved, and I hope that I can always count on his frank advice and intelligence. I would also like to thank everyone else at his thriving, steadily expanding DCL Agency, a growing force of nature.

At HarperCollins, my friend and longtime editor, Dan Conaway, rose above and beyond the call of duty—as usual!—by insisting on finishing the first edit of *Strivers Row*, even though he had already taken another position elsewhere. It was a typically classy gesture. Dan's place was taken by the remarkable Jill Schwartzman, who soon proved herself to be the Mariano Rivera of relief editors, and a terrific friend, as well. I would like to thank everyone at HarperCollins for all their help during what has been a very rewarding and enjoyable relationship during the publication of this whole trilogy of books, and particularly Jonathan Burnham; my publicist, Marie-Elena Martinez, and Josh Marwell. You guys are the best.

In previous acknowledgments, I have thanked all of my extended family, and the many good friends and professional colleagues I have been lucky enough to have in my life. That goes double for all of you! Some of those I neglected to mention before, or that I have only gotten to know over the past four years, include Heather "Smart Bomb" Chaplin and Aaron Ruby; Darin "Rot" Strauss and Susannah "I Wouldn't Read It" Meadows; Pamela Talese and Michael Sandlin; David Lipsky, and Grace; Gillian Mackenzie and Andrew Miller (despite their taste in ballteams); Nicholas Dawidoff and Rebecca "T.L.S." Carmen; Lili Schwartz and Ben Agronick; the rediscovered Angela Bonavoglia and Andrea Pedolsky; Dani Shapiro and Michael Maren; Heather Juergensen, Kevin Hench, and the rest of the valiant Ice House gang; the e-mailers, Peter Moore, Mary "Tee" Nelson, Bob "Big Unit" Altman, and John Armstrong; Douglas "Sky Pilot" Kelley; the newlyweds, Josh and Laura; Richard Snow and Fred Allen, at American Heritage; Frank and Malachi McCourt; Thomas Fleming; Jonathan Mahler and Danielle Mattoon; Constance Rosenblum and Frank Flaherty, at the City section; and all of the next generation—Zoe, Julian, and Griffin; my redoubtable goddaughter, Ann Elizabeth Tarpley Hitt, and Steve's redoubtable goddaughter, Clara Pringle Yancey Hitt; my godson, Teddy Spelman; his long-suffering older brother, Gus; Sadie Ray; Samuel Ellis; Jacob, Gus Mahler, Miles, and of course, the great Niky Bear, with love from your Uncle Shaggy.